The Twentieth Century

Treasury
of
Sports

The Twentieth Century

Treasury of Sports

Edited by

Al Silverman
and
Brian Silverman

VIKING

VIKING
Published by the Penguin Group
Viking Penguin, a division of Penguin Books USA Inc.,
375 Hudson Street, New York, New York 10014, U.S.A.
Penguin Books Ltd, 27 Wrights Lane,
London W8 5TZ, England
Penguin Books Australia Ltd, Ringwood,
Victoria, Australia
Penguin Books Canada Ltd, 10 Alcorn Avenue, Suite 300,
Toronto, Ontario, Canada M4V 3B2
Penguin Books (N.Z.) Ltd, 182–190 Wairau Road,
Auckland 10, New Zealand

Penguin Books Ltd, Registered Offices:
Harmondsworth, Middlesex, England

First published in 1992 by Viking Penguin,
a division of Penguin Books USA Inc.

10   9   8   7   6   5   4   3   2   1

PUBLISHER'S NOTE
Some of the selections in this book are works of fiction. Names, characters,
places, and incidents either are the product of the author's imagination or are
used fictitiously, and any resemblance to actual persons, living or dead, events,
or locales is entirely coincidental.

LIBRARY OF CONGRESS CATALOGING IN PUBLICATION DATA
The twentieth century treasury of sports / edited by Al Silverman and Brian
Silverman.
p.   cm.
ISBN 0-670-84662-7
1. Sports — Literary collections.   2. American literature — 20th
century.   I. Silverman, Al.   II. Silverman, Brian.   III. Title:
Twentieth century treasury of sports.
PS509.S65A615   1992
810.8'0355 — dc20   92-53516

Printed in the United States of America
Set in Cheltenham Book
Designed by Cheryl L. Cipriani

Acknowledgments

Never would we have been able to put together this collection without the advice and wisdom of numerous friends and informal advisers. One of those is an absent friend, Jack Newcombe, who, early on, found surprises for us. We remember him warmly.

Others who helped immeasurably include John Walsh, who did a marvelous job in the eighties editing a fine magazine, *Inside Sports,* and directed us toward gems from his era; and Diane Osen, an authority on the literature of sports who suggested some stories that might easily have escaped our attention. So did Berry Stainback, the one-time editor of *Sport* Magazine, and we are grateful for his input. Special thanks to Larry Ritter for his graciousness, especially in personally rating his all-time favorite baseball works. Thanks for the help given us by Charlie Butler, Richie O'Connor, and Steve Robinson of *Sports Illustrated,* and, most especially, to Steve's old man, Ray Robinson, who allowed us to pillage his overflowing sports library of rare and wonderful books and offered us the fruits of his overflowing sports wisdom.

We never would have been able to bring this volume to a proper conclusion without the help of our Viking colleagues, the editor of this book, Michael Jacobs, and the indomitable watch dog *and* editor, Caroline White. We are beholden to Alice Van Straalen of the Book-of-the-Month Club, and her colleague, Stephanie Ricks. And our gratitude to the original coordinator and conscience of the book, Maron Waxman.

Finally, our profound appreciation to the wisest man we know, Clifton Fadiman, for reading *everything* within and gracefully showing us our missteps, and for being a mentor and inspiration all these years.

Contents

Contents xi

Contents

Introduction

When I left *Sport* Magazine in 1972, after having been its editor for a dozen years, I wrote a farewell address that I labeled, with inflated pretension, "The Future of Sports." I reread the piece recently with a distinct sense of unease. Turned out, however, that I wasn't as deficient in prophetic gifts as I feared. But neither was I as prescient. I did have one ringing prediction: "You will see in the years ahead increased bitterness between the athlete and his paymaster." Not bad. But a lot of my other future shocks were mostly low-decibel, high-minded generalities rather than deep and dirty specifics.

I talked, for instance, about how the excitement of sports on television would continue to grow, "making us all battlefield reporters, giving an undreamed of intimacy with the grand events, an intimacy that can only flower in the years ahead if sports on television is used wisely." I should have realized even then that sports would come under the *control* of television, with wisdom not entering into the equation.

I also talked about the future in terms of the athlete himself (one thing I didn't do in all those days was refer to the athlete as *herself,* but more on that later). I saw the athlete of the future becoming not only more amazing than ever physically, but also more multifaceted, more independent, more complex, and thus more interesting as a person. But that was an easy one: the trend had begun in the 1960s, a corollary to all the other upheavals of that pivotal decade in American life.

It wasn't like that in the Eisenhower era. I remember the time in the mid-fifties when I went to Las Vegas to do a magazine story on a reigning golfer of the day. We had agreed to meet in the lobby of the opulent Desert Inn. The golfer didn't know me from a caddie, but I recognized him right away. I went up to him and introduced myself. Smiling, I said, "How're you doing?"

He looked at me with flat, cold eyes. "What do you mean by that?" he snarled.

In the sixties cold distrust began its transformation to disarming candor. In 1964 I helped Paul Hornung, the Golden Boy of Notre Dame and the Green Bay Packers, write his autobiography. The title we chose was *Football and the Single Man.* Some critics fell on the book—"kiss and tell," they sneered. Well, yes, Hornung did have the temerity to celebrate his life as a bachelor, never mind that he did so in the most decorous way. I like to think that Hornung and I were at the cutting edge of the new morality. For shortly thereafter, a flood of sports books, some of them out-and-out confessionals, washed through the streets of our popular culture.

Surely one of the most representative of those, and most conspicuous, was Joe Namath's autobiography, modestly titled *I Can't Wait Until Tomorrow . . . 'Cause I Get Better Looking Every Day.* At the 1969 Super Bowl we at *Sport* Magazine gave Namath a sleek Corvette automobile for being the most valuable player in the New York Jets' Cinderella victory over the heavily favored Baltimore Colts. Immediately after the game I went down to the locker room to tell him of his honor. In the midst of his beatification, surrounded by a horde of reporters, he caught my message enough to look me in the eye like that golfer in Las Vegas and say, "Is that one of those cars you have to give back after a year?" Namath, wise in the ways of the world, knew well enough that some awards of automobiles to athletes *were* leases for a specific period of time, not outright ownership, as this was.

We presented him with the car—to keep forever or as long as he so chose—at a luncheon at Mama Leone's restaurant in midtown New York City. Before the event I escorted Namath out to the restaurant's parking lot to take pictures of him beside his Corvette. We had to push our way through a mass of adoring and distinctly unfeminist bobby-soxers, one of whom groped to caress Namath but managed instead to rake my face with her long fingernails. I found myself standing by the Corvette, holding a handkerchief to my cheek lest a drop of red blood spill on the gleaming white of Namath's car.

A different work from Namath's—a truly ground-breaking book of the era—was Jim Bouton's *Ball Four,* published in 1970 and written with the considerable help of sportswriter Leonard Shecter. For the first time an active major-leaguer was telling all about the inner game of baseball, about how ballplayers were treated in those days by management, how ballplayers misbehaved on the road—and everywhere else. *Ball Four* was not only revelatory in the extreme, it was also hilarious, and it became the biggest-selling sports book up to that time.

Ironically, part of the impetus for the book's large sale came from the publicity provided by the scandalized Lords of Baseball, mainly Himself, baseball Commissioner Bowie Kuhn. Kuhn, another one frozen in the fifties, called Bouton in and said to him, "You've done the game a great disservice. Saying players kissed on the Seattle team bus— incredible! Or that some of our greatest stars were drunk on the field. What can you be thinking of?" After the meeting the commissioner commented more soberly to the press: "I advised Mr. Bouton of my displeasure with these writings and have warned him against future writings of this character."

But Bouton carried on, lecturing widely on college campuses and finding himself something of a Holden Caulfield of his time. "What they got from the book," Bouton writes in the piece you will read beginning on page 66 "was moral support for a point of view. They claim that *Ball Four* gave them the strength to be the underdog and made them feel less lonely as an outsider in their own lives." One reviewer, praising the book, said, "It's about failure, success, defeat, loneliness, courage and human frailty. It's also about nonconformity vs. conformity, an issue confronting every aspect of American society in 1969."

The 1960s saw not only the loosening of the Puritan ethos, but also the beginning of a new "golden age" of sports: new, that is, as compared to the original in the twenties, what Westbrook Pegler, a leading chronicler of those times, called "the era of wonderful nonsense." Well, there is much to be said for the twenties. It was the time of Babe Ruth, Jack Dempsey, Bill Tilden, Helen Wills, Bobby Jones, Sonja Henie, Red Grange, Knute Rockne, Babe Didrikson, Earl Sande, Johnny Weissmuller (later to become "Me, Tarzan!"). They were a compelling group, this first wave of American sports superstars, many of whom continued their exploits into the thirties.

The superstars of the sixties came out of a different culture, with modern technology offering them exposure never dreamed of in earlier generations. And there were more of them vying for the affection of that widened audience. Listen: Mickey Mantle, Willie Mays, Sandy Koufax, and Hank Aaron; Jim Brown, Johnny Unitas, and Vince Lombardi; Wilt Chamberlain, Oscar Robertson, Bob Cousy, and Bill Russell; Gordie Howe, Maurice Richard, and Bobby Hull; Arnold Palmer and Jack Nicklaus; Wilma Rudolph and Billie Jean King, who set off a different sort of liberation movement in sports; and the magnificent and ultimate symbol of the times—Cassius Clay/Muhammad Ali.

One reason that it's so much easier to rate this golden age over the golden oldies of the twenties was that we could all *see* these gods in action. Dos Passos's "camera eye" had become literal: television. And so there is one other working symbol of the sixties, a perfect complement to Ali: Howard Cosell. He was an original, this gut fighter whose pennon was emblazoned with the words, "Tell it like it is," and who more or less did just that throughout his career. In 1962, the first spring-training season of the New York Mets, I chanced upon that prowling aardvark one afternoon at the Mets' camp in Florida. I asked Cosell, who had been covering the team from their first coming together under the palm trees, how this new franchise looked.

Cosell pulled the large cigar from his mouth, his eyes sad as always but maybe a little more so as he prepared to pass sentence. "Al," he answered gravely, "it's enough to strain the credulity of a rational man."

A few years later, in 1971 when I was down in Miami with my family for Super Bowl V, I came upon Cosell holding court in the lobby of our hotel. The coeditor of this volume, then fourteen, was with me.

"Howard," I said, "this is my son Brian."

Cosell, a quick study, noted that Brian was wearing a New York Giants sweatshirt, this at a time when the Giants were in decline. He looked owlishly at the boy and said, "Ah, I see you subscribe to mediocrity and failure." Brian was never quite the same after that, although it must be said in his favor that he has remained a Giants fan to this day, patience that has paid off for him in recent times.

Cosell was the preeminent television sports guru who helped nurture the new golden age. His finest hours came in his close relationship with Muhammad Ali and his steadfast defense of Ali's decision to resist the military draft, a decision that caused the establishment to strip the fighter of his heavyweight title, and thus of his livelihood.

But the print people were in there, too. A new breed of sportswriters was bringing to fun and games advanced professional skills, advanced sensibilities, and a born-again lust for the "truth." This was a pronounced contrast to the journalists of the first golden age.

The superstars of the twenties were sanctified and sheltered by a group of influential sportswriters such as Pegler, Damon Runyon, Grantland Rice, Bill Corum, Bugs Baer, John Kieran, W. O. McGeehan, Ed Sullivan, Ring Lardner, and Paul Gallico. It's interesting to observe (if one sees parallels, as the editors of this volume tend to, between the life of sports and the game of life) how many of these writers moved from sports to, uh, higher pursuits: Pegler became Hearst's flaming right-wing political columnist; Runyon used sports as a vehicle to carry his guys and dolls to international fame; Kieran was a renaissance figure who continued as a sports columnist while becoming a naturalist of high repute, as well as a pundit on the most intellectual show ever on radio, "Information Please"; Sullivan went on to become the wildly popular great stone face of, yes, "The Ed Sullivan Show"; Lardner and Gallico wrote fiction that captured large audiences. It was Gallico who once described his then sportswriting fraternity as "the gee whizzers . . . suckers for the theology of the good guys and bad guys." It was the code of the time to cosset these gilded athletes both for the sake of the public morality and for public illusion—myths and fables were to be protected—and maybe to make their own journalistic lives more peaceable.

Babe Ruth was the classic example of the superathlete and renowned public idol whose private affairs were always shielded by his Boswells. In the spring training season of 1925, Ruth engaged in a series of drinking and sexual debaucheries that went even beyond normal Ruthian excesses. And the true story never got out. Ruth finally had to be operated on for what was described in the press as "an intestinal abscess." The colorful phrase accepted by the public was the one coined by McGeehan—"the bellyache heard 'round the world." In private some writers used other medical terms, such as gonorrhea and syphilis.

A true exception to the Gee Whizzers was Ring Lardner. As a sportswriter in Chicago before the twenties, Lardner mostly conformed to the mores of his colleagues. Later, as a writer of serious fiction, he transformed his observations of athletes at work and play into such classic stories as "Alibi Ike," "You Know Me, Al," "The Busher," and "Champion" (see page 387), Lardner's most ironic boxing tale. Lardner, wrote British journalist Brian Glanville (represented in this volume with an excerpt from his novel, *The Olympian*), "was perhaps the first writer to exploit the possibilities of working class speech and idiom in sports fiction . . . who can be read by intellectuals without shame and by working men without labor."

The influence of the Gee Whizzers, which dates back to the beginning of the century but didn't intensify until sports became big-time in the twenties, lasted for years in an innocent America until after World War II. This volume, incidentally, purports to represent the entire twentieth century, and it does. The truth is, however, that fine writing about sports—nonfiction and fiction—didn't begin to flower until the end of World War II. Something happened—it came to be called "the new journalism." The trailbreaking postwar event occurred in 1947 when *The New Yorker* devoted an entire issue to John Hersey's *Hiroshima.* "In writing *Hiroshima,"* said Norman Cousins, then the editor of *The Saturday Review of Literature,* Hersey was showing, first, "convictions that human values, human feelings, and human experience are the basic building blocks of good writing." Second, said Cousins, "was Hersey's sense that history-in-the-making calls for the most painstaking care and research, the ability to devote oneself to the task at hand, however time-and-energy consuming that may be." It is instructive to note that Hersey put those same principles into the writing of his next book, *The Wall,* which was a novel about the Jewish resistance in the Warsaw ghetto at the time of the Holocaust.

Thus the line between nonfiction and fiction began to blur, and powerfully elevated the craft of nonfiction toward something different and better.

Some critics date the beginnings of the new journalism in newspapers to the late 1950s, and to one paper in particular, the *New York Herald-Tribune,* "the writer's newspaper in America," as one of its staffers called it. The *"Trib"* was then in its last years (it expired in 1966), but before its demise it did play a pivotal role in the rise of the new journalism. A regular writer for the *Herald-Tribune*'s magazine was a young Southerner named Tom Wolfe, who became the *persona* of the new journalism. And the sports department of the *Herald-Tribune* was full of budding new journalists, many of them hired by its legendary sports editor, Stanley Woodward.

All his newspaper life, Woodward had new-journalism instincts. In his first period as sports editor of the *Herald-Tribune,* beginning in 1938, The Coach, as he was called, developed the finest sports staff in the country. After the war he completed his master building by hiring Joe H. Palmer, a gifted writer as well as horse-racing authority, then lured Red Smith away from the *Philadelphia Bulletin.* "Get me the smell of cabbage cooking in the halls," he told his number-one columnist. Smith did just that, all his life, for his credo was, "The English language, if handled with respect, scarcely ever poisons the user."

In 1948 Woodward was told by the owners of the *Tribune* to cut staff, so he cut himself. He returned to the paper in 1959, just in time to light firecrackers under the new journalists. In those last years he had youngsters like Jimmy Breslin, Roger Kahn, and Dick Schaap cutting their teeth in the columns of the sports section. It wasn't so much that Woodward was an advocate of the new journalism—he may never even have heard the term. What he wanted from his staff were writers who would present his department in a manner, he said, that would be intelligible to the nonsports reader should one happen to fold back the paper in the wrong place.

At about the same time other newspapers around the country were also hiring young journalists with an instinct for writing narrative, for reporting the facts in the John Hersey manner, as if they were writing fiction. One of them was Gay Talese, then with *The New York Times.* Talese always denied he was part of a movement. "I resent particularly the new journalism," he told an audience gathered in Albany, New York, in the spring of 1991 to hear a group of nonfiction masters argue about their craft. Talese said he grew up loving fiction. F. Scott Fitzgerald's story "Winter Dreams," which he read at age fourteen, "carried me forever," he said. It also influenced his craft to the point where, at times, he wasn't sure whether he was writing fiction or nonfiction. The line seemed to blur so much, so rapidly, that Tom Wolfe once exclaimed about people like Talese and Breslin, "The bastards are making it up." He could have said the same thing about himself.

The truth is there were practitioners well before the new journalism got its name. In 1952, W. C. Heinz, who had been a sports columnist and war reporter for the *New York Sun,* wrote a story for *Sport* Magazine on Rocky Graziano. In an essay in the *Dutton Review* some years later, Jack Newfield, one of the most politically conscious journalists of our time, cited the Heinz story as representing the new journalism, "advocacy, complex detail, personal feelings," at its best. Not so different from Norman Cousins's definition of John Hersey's *Hiroshima.* It is amusing to note that the Heinz story in our collection, "A Fighter's Wife," deals with the emotions of Norma Graziano on an evening when she was at home and Graziano was on the job, battling a hitter named Charlie Fusari. This story certainly follows the Newfield definition of this new form of writing nonfiction.

All right, while we're on W. C. Heinz, we'd better come clean here. As we started to compile our stories for this anthology we established one unshakable rule besides excellence—sports as literature—and that rule is one story per writer. A century's worth of sports stories encompasses riches of all sorts, from all manner of writers, so we knew we had to resist the temptation to include multiple stories under the bylines of such masters as Heinz, and Gay Talese, and Frank Deford, and Ring Lardner, and his eldest son, John Lardner, writers whose output included numerous sports stories of star quality. The problem, of course, was trying to pick from each writer his or her most appropriate story; that is, the one that reflected the taste and evoked the emotions in the editors of this volume, and that also fit best with everything else we picked. You'll have your favorites among the writers that you know but, once the guidelines were set, the contributions in this volume, we assure you, came out of our own visceral reactions. This means that while you'll find a good number of old favorites here, you'll also find surprises and, among them, we hope, discoveries.

Whatever the origin of the new journalism there is no doubt that it came of age during the tumult of the sixties; race, sexual permissiveness, flower children, women's lib, the Vietnam War, assassinations were all flashpoints that raised the telling of the truth, in some areas at least, to an art form. Think of Truman Capote's *In Cold Blood,* Tom Wolfe's dazzling fandangos celebrating the fads and follies of the period. Read Norman Mailer's nonfiction triumph, "Ego," in this volume. It staggers if not kayos William Hazlitt, the nineteenth-century essayist who once held the title with his essay called "The Fight."

Throughout his career Mailer has always been ambivalent about fiction vs. nonfiction. His 1960 Pulitzer Prize–winning *Armies of the Night* was subtitled, *History As a Novel, The Novel As History;* and *The Executioner's Song,* which won the Pulitzer Prize for fiction in 1980, was originally published as nonfiction. Another Pulitzer Prize winner, J. Anthony Lukas (for *Common Ground*) remembered Mailer on the witness stand in 1969 at the trial of the Chicago Seven. And he tells of this colloquy:

"I was in a moral quandary," Mailer said to Judge Julius Hoffman, who was presiding over the fate of Abbie Hoffman, David Dellinger, and five others.

"Stick to the facts," said Judge Hoffman.

"Facts," Mailer told the judge stiffly, "are nothing without their nuances, sir-r."

Facts discovered, interpreted through nuance, and piercing through their surfaces to revelation: that was the marching order of the new journalists, and their ranks began to swell. Its early sports pioneers, at least in the eastern half of the United States, came to be known as "chipmunks." The nickname is of uncertain derivation except that one of the original new journalists had two elongated front teeth. Whatever. Chipmunks burrowing away at the nuggets they found was an image that fitted the breed. These young sportswriters began to probe beyond sports as just fun and games, attempting to use John Hersey's building blocks while opening up the athlete. The most representative chipmunk repartee from daily beat reporters that I can recall came the day the New York Yankees were celebrating their 1962 seventh-game World Series victory over the San Francisco Giants. I was in the Yankee locker room listening to the writers interviewing Ralph Terry, who had pitched the decisive victory. I was there because *Sport* Magazine's custom each year was to award a new Corvette to the Most Valuable Player of the World Series (as we did in pro football, à la Joe Namath). Terry was it in '62 and the happy pitcher was conversing graciously with the press when, suddenly, he was called to the phone. It was his wife, he told the writers when he returned. She wanted to tell him how happy she was for him and also that their new baby was coming along fine.

"What was your wife doing?" asked a reporter, possibly a chipmunk.

"Feeding the baby."

"Breast or bottle?"

The writer's question certified his membership in the chipmunk society of the sixties.

So the literature of sports also made room for the new journalists—a number of whom are represented in this volume—but the clubhouse today holds a diverse band of angels. The truth is that the best writers about sports, from the dawn of this century and before, are those who resist classification. For poets and storytellers there never have been and never will be any ideological demarcations. The best fiction in this volume comes from writers who use sports to elaborate on their own visions of the human comedy.

Here's the way Frank Deford, a sportswriter first and a fine novelist maybe second, once put it: "I'm a writer who happens to write sports, not a sportswriter. It's not like we're all some kind of monolithic phalanx marching along with our typewriters." You'll see what Deford means when you read his story on a basketball coach named Al McGuire.

One of the best contemporary writers about sports is the *Wash-*

ington Post's Tom Boswell. He had this to say about his job: "The fun of writing a column about sports is that much of the time you aren't writing about sports at all, you're writing about what might be called the commonsense tales of everyday living." You'll see what Boswell means when you read his piece on the uncommon Jack Nicklaus (page 56).

John Lardner is a prime example of a writer who belongs to no sect. Lardner started on the *New York Herald-Tribune* (where else?) in 1931. In 1939 he began writing a column in *Newsweek* magazine, mostly on sports. They found the perfect person in Lardner: an individualist who was the best answer to the group journalism the newsmagazines practiced then, and still mostly do today. In World War II he became a war correspondent of some daring; the fact that he wore thick glasses never bothered him a bit. As A. J. Liebling said of Lardner, "He walked toward the bomb flashes in order to see better."

After the war Lardner resumed his career at *Newsweek* and also wrote memorable profiles for various magazines. Lardner's craft, as one of his admirers Roger Kahn has written, "was purely writing: writing the English language, fusing sound and meaning, matching the precision of the word with the rhythm of the phrase." Lardner used the language to a purpose, combining irony and satire and gentle mockery in a way that formed wit, unassumingly. In this way he was different from his harder-edged father. He treated sports gently, while always probing its soft underbelly for weaknesses that could be transformed into laughter, or at least a satisfying chuckle. I am unable to resist this small sampling of Lardner at work, the opening paragraph of his contribution to this volume:

> It develops that there are certain parts of the country in which the thing called the Roller Derby is still unknown. The people in such places live in the same state of uneasy innocence as the Indians did before the white man came among them, bringing civilization, uncut whisky, glass beads for all hands, and two or three other variations of hoof-and-mouth disease.

In sports literature, which as we have implied is what this book is about, humor cuts its way into even the most somber of tales. You will read, for instance, of the anxieties of the novelist of the inner city, Richard Price, as he departs his safe normal venue and travels to Alabama to do a nonfiction story on that personification of southern rectitude, Paul

"Bear" Bryant. Alighting at the Birmingham airport the uneasy Mr. Price wonders "why the hell I am keying so much on the hairdos I see all around me. The Dolly Parton pompadours, the rockabilly duck asses, the military knuckleheads. Then I look in the mirror. With the possible exception of a photo of Duane Allman, I have the longest hair of anybody I've seen all day. I start getting visions of rusty scissors in a sheriff's office. Ah, that's all Hollywood horseshit, I tell myself. But I go into a men's room and remove my earring."

The New Yorker, once a glorious hangout for humorists, invented a writer who also became a worthy opponent of Hazlitt's, A. J. Liebling. Liebling once explained his gifts as being able to write faster than anyone who could write better, and write better than anyone who could write faster. Indeed, he is not only a comic genius but also one of the most stylish journalists America has ever produced. Liebling's reputation is something of an irritant to the young humorists at *The New Yorker.* Mark Singer, one of the best of them, said, "I was taught to read Liebling to find the use of humor in a column." Respectful pause. "I had this image of Liebling moving paper off the typewriter and smiling."

Never mind. Read about Liebling's accidental meeting with a fellow journalist from Wales by the name of Tommy Farr who, in another life, survived fifteen rounds with Joe Louis. About his second career Farr told Liebling, "I'm a write-ter. I love write-ting. I give it to them straight. No split affinitives, you know, other Oxfer stoof. Oh, of course I split an affinitive now and then, to show I know how, but I don't believe in it."

The new generation of sportswriters, as we have said, didn't just generate spontaneously. Currents were rising in postwar America and journalists, and some articulate athletes, were actually developing social consciences. In 1970, before an Ivy League bacchanal known as "the Heptagonal Indoor Track and Field Championships," the Heptagonalists issued a manifesto decrying the "unending war in Southeast Asia," the killing of the Kent State students, the repression of "political and racial minorities." It went on, "As athletes and trackmen we understand that our sport is not, and must never become, a hideout from our basic responsibilities as human beings."

That expression of shared concern by students and athletes, to want to do things differently, certainly mirrored the times. But well before 1970, an individual changed the whole face of sports in America. Jackie Robinson. With his quicksilver presence at bat, in the field, on the bases, Robinson set off a revolution that was to have a profound effect on sports and on a changing America, a country in John Lardner's phrase, "of uneasy innocence." His presence, followed by the fuller presence of a generation of black major-league baseball players, not only made spectator sports more exciting and fulfilling but also transformed sports into one of the most democratic institutions in American life. (We're talking here about sports *on* the field; off-the-field employment in sports for African-Americans and Hispanics and other minorities, including women, is still light years away from parity.)

We've spoken about the emancipation of one athlete, Muhammad Ali, who contributed to the creative mayhem of the sixties by flaunting convention and sticking to his principles. Against the hostility of a majority of Americans, including the boxing establishment (that meant much of the press, too), Cassius Clay changed his name for religious reasons to Muhammad Ali and refused to take part in the Vietnam War. He was by that time a Muslim minister and besides, he said, "I don't have nothin' against them Viet Congs." For that he was unable to make a living at his chosen profession for forty-three months, and it was four years before he could fight once more to regain his title. But in that period Ali retained his dignity, and after his thrilling return to the ring and his epic championship fight with Joe Frazier (read all about it in Norman Mailer's "Ego"), his popularity with the American public soared.

The ordeal of Muhammad Ali in those troubled years of American life followed the pattern as it had been for black athletes throughout our history, and, in perhaps a less traumatic way, for other minorities. In the newly industrialized post–Civil War America, spectator sports began its phenomenal rise; this allowed gifted athletes among the wave of immigrants pouring into the country to use sports to spring into the mainstream of American blue-collar life. But not without pain. It seemed that all of these minorities—Germans, Poles, Irish, Italians, Jews—had to fight their way through a thicket of ethnic distrust, even hatred. In the early 1900s these "new" Americans who made it to the major leagues were the target of raging epithets from opposition players, spectators, and sometimes their own teammates. Italian athletes were routinely referred to on the playing field, and in the press, as wops or dagos. As late as 1936 a Boston newspaper in an editorial complimented Joe DiMaggio on being a credit to his "race." It went on: "Our citizens of Italian descent whom we used to consider a grade or two weaker than the descendants of English, Irish, Scotch and German are really of tough fibre." Hank Greenberg, who suffered such indignities throughout his baseball career, had the taunts burned into his memory—"Hey, Heeb," or "Jewboy," or "Sheeny Jew." For Jewish boxers in the early years of the century it was so bad that many of them had to adopt Irish names to get fights.

But none of the torments suffered by these minorities paralleled the black experience. Two years after the Civil War, a committee of a major baseball league of the time issued this recommendation:

> It is not presumed by your Committee that any club who have applied are composed of persons of color, or any portion of them; and the recommendations of your Committee in this respect are based upon this view, and they unanimously report against the admission of any club which may be composed of one or more colored persons.
>
> —Nominating Committee,
> National Association of Base Ball Players, 1867

Occasionally, a black ballplayer was able to slip through, but not for long. In 1887 the Newark team of the then International League had a black catcher named Fleet Walker and a black pitcher, George Stovey; indeed, they became known as "the Mulatto Battery." But when the game's biggest star of the age, Cap Anson, then the manager and first baseman of the Chicago White Stockings, balked at playing against them in an exhibition game, the two players left the team. And the color line was drawn.

Black players had formed their own teams soon after the Civil War, but now they began to start their own leagues. In the golden age of the twenties, and the not-so-golden thirties, the Negro American League and the Negro National League took firm root in the East and West. And they drew huge, enthusiastic crowds. They also barnstormed extensively, playing exhibition games against white teams, again to big crowds. I remember a night in the early forties when the Kansas City Monarchs, led by Satchel Paige, came to my hometown of Lynn, Massachusetts, to play a game against a powerful team of at least high minor-league caliber, the Lynn Frasers. I was selling hot dogs at the stadium that night to a near sellout crowd but business was light while Paige was on the mound. He pitched three innings. In that third inning he gave his outfielders the inning off. Nonchalantly, he struck out the side.

Some years later, in the early seventies, I was asked to do a television piece with Satchel Paige that would be shown on a new show on public television called "The Great American Dream Machine." It was shot in Cooperstown, New York, home of The Baseball Hall of Fame. The producers had gone country on Satch. They dressed him in coveralls and high boots, and let him carry a shotgun (Satch loved hunting, so the legend went) and the two of us strolled around a local reservoir while cameras atop a truck followed our every move. It was a little disconcerting for me—I had never done anything like this before—but Paige was a good talker and soon I forgot about the cameras and listened to what he had to say.

One of the things I asked him was what it was like for his team to go barnstorming around the country.

"For one," he said, "we'd stay with people in a kind of way we could stay with 'em, six in a room—sometimes the whole club'd be in one room as far as that's concerned."

The whole club? In one room? I was struck dumb by this colossal image. Meekly, I asked Paige, "So, did some of you sleep on the floor?"

"Some of us slept on the floor," he went on shamelessly, "or we slept across the bed. You could sleep five or six across a bed." Not a glimmer of a smile touched his stern, weatherbeaten face (he was after all giving white folks what they always wanted to hear about his culture) and I noticed he had tightened his grip on the gun. We walked along silently for a minute. Then Paige, an instinctive master of the medium, stopped and looked directly into the camera.

He said: "The world is something else, and they'll keep you guessing."

They did keep you guessing. In the early years of the century boxing was the only sport in which blacks could gain a foothold. And when they managed to get a fight with a white opponent, more often than not they had to agree to lose.

The first black heavyweight champion of the world was Jack Johnson, but he didn't have an easy time getting there. In 1905 Johnson began chasing the then heavyweight champion, Tommy Burns, all over the world, trying to get Burns to fight him. The match was finally made in 1908, in Sydney, Australia, and Johnson easily took the title from Burns. This alarmed many citizens, who felt uneasy that this "uppity Nigger" now held what had always been a white championship. And the call went out for Jim Jeffries, who had retired as heavyweight champion in '05, to return and restore white supremacy to the throne. Before that championship battle, which was held on Independence Day, July 5, 1910, a reporter wrote of Jeffries, "Let's hope he kills the coon."

Here's how Jack London began his newspaper story of the fight itself:

> Once again has Johnson sent down to defeat the chosen representative of the white race and this time the greatest of them. And as of old it was play for Johnson. . . . And he played and fought a white man, in the white man's country, before a white man's audience.

Twenty-five years later, when a black heavyweight hero had emerged, one who was the exact opposite of Johnson, not "uppity" at all, it still hadn't changed much. At the beginning of the Joe Louis reign, the Gee Whizzers simply couldn't cope with this sports artist. In 1935, after Louis knocked out Primo Carnera (himself reviled for being a dumb "wop") a major wire service started its story this way: "Something sly and sinister and not quite human came out of the African jungle last night. . . ." Some months later, on the eve of Louis's fight with Max Baer, the normally cultivated Paul Gallico wrote a piece referring to Louis as "the magnificent animal. He lives like an animal, untouched by externals. He eats, he sleeps, he fights. He is as tawny as an animal and he has an animal's concentration on his prey."

Sportswriters began to come out of their own jungle late in Louis's career when institutional racism in sports coverage became somewhat more tempered. Now some of these same writers began to judge Louis as a human being, not an animal, and to admit their admiration. But the jungle mentality of the time has never been completely erased. I remember the evening in 1963 that a group of us went to a movie theater in White Plains, New York, to watch the closed-circuit fight between Sonny Liston and Floyd Patterson. The man on my left was a renowned writer, a person of liberal bent, a humanist. But in the ferocious first round he lost his bearings and hollered, "Come on, Floyd, kill the nigger." Alas, the fight ended in that round, a Liston victory by a kayo.

Having been somewhat in the hot center of the sixties as it applied to sports, all I can say about the magazine I edited is that we tried to keep in step with the new openness, the new thinking of the times; all right, maybe a half-step ahead of our readers. But we weren't revolutionaries. We sought the writers who used the language well and who we felt understood the era enough to sing the ballads of the day, and make up some of their own. And there were no quotas. We never counted black and white faces while assembling an issue. In 1971 I did receive a complaint from one of the owners of the magazine, who chided me, with a nervous smile, for putting too many blacks on the covers of the magazine. He used black dialect to loosen me up while making his point. I laughed it off and kept on doing what I'd always done.

Of course, we would receive occasional complaints about our excursions into what some readers saw as a realm of sport that had nothing to do with fun and games. There was one letter from a gentleman who said he had been reading *Sport* Magazine for twenty years and, "I much preferred your Frank Merriwell–type articles to the type of drivel that appears in your magazine these days."

All of us of a certain age remember Frank Merriwell, and maybe boys still read him. For those of you who have never made Frank Merriwell's acquaintance, he was the creation of a man named Gilbert Patten, who adopted the pseudonym Burt L. Standish because of his love for Longfellow's poem, "The Courtship of Miles Standish." Merriwell was a saintly being and superb athlete for Yale, whose hairbreadth triumphs inspired the Gee Whizzers to insert a new phrase into the lexicon when describing the bang-bang climax to a sporting event—"a Frank Merriwell finish." It was those finishes, as well as Merriwell's good deeds and homespun philosophy, that endeared him to millions of young readers.

After receiving that letter I looked up a novel called *Frank Merriwell's Alarm.* I came across this passage:

> "Now, Master Frank," cried the darky, appealingly, "don't go fo' to be too hard on a po' nigger! De trubble wif me is dat I'm jus' a nacherl bo'on coward, an' I can't get over hit nohow. Dat's what meks' mah heart turn flip-flops ebry time dar's any danger, sar.'"

A clear majority of *Sport* readers, it would seem, since the magazine's circulation increased significantly in the sixties, accepted the issues of the time as we reflected them. As another reader wrote: "We believe that no real sportsman gives a second-class damn whether an athlete is Negro, Italian, Protestant, Jewish or Arabian. The real sportsman loves to watch the best and will pay to watch the best."

Still, a nervousness about race exists in sports; after almost a half century of ascendancy for the black athlete in almost every sport, the nervousness is perhaps even heightened today. Indeed, the battle goes on in sports as it does in the country at large: sometimes a dialogue,

more often an evasion of the central issue, every now and then a confrontation. It is a struggle for America's soul that may endure through
time without solution.

The novels of John R. Tunis were almost as wildly popular in their
time as were those Merriwell stories. Tunis is the writer's real name and
he was a far finer writer than Burt L. Standish, and I believe his sports
stories for boys are still being read today. We have an adult story from
Tunis about a woman tennis player and the Svengali-like influence of
her mother. And if that doesn't make connections with reality in tennis
today, then reality is dead. Tunis's story brings up another inequity in
sports that issues from a larger inequity; that is, the discrimination
against women in sports, whether athletes or writers.

Confession: in my time at *Sport* Magazine we never had a single
female editor. (This situation, I have to say, was corrected almost immediately after I left the magazine when Dick Schaap, a fine all-around
writer and television sports personality, took over.) And we never had
more than a handful of stories written by women. What we did have in
those days was something called a "Campus Queen" contest. Almost
every month we would run a photo of an attractive collegian, not an
athlete, just a "cute" coed, from those sent into us by various colleges
and universities. From these leading candidates we would pick *the* Campus Queen of the year. I suppose this was our answer to the magazine
success-story of the day, *Playboy.* We finally got rid of the feature in
1972, the decision announced in a ringing editorial. "We believe," I wrote
with unconvincing piety, "there are better ways to portray women in
our magazine than as mere sex objects."

It was Billie Jean King, the Mother Courage of the women's movement in sports, who finally showed the way. "Write about us," she urged,
"but write about us as athletes, not as symbols of women's lib."

With this woman, it was not so easy to separate the athlete from
the symbol. Billie Jean was the first of her sex to feel this surge of pride
from other women coming out of the still new movement. In 1973, after
the Associated Press had named her Sportswoman of the Year, one
woman came up to her, grabbed her by the shoulders and told how she
had been forced to give up sports when she was a teenager because of
family pressure. Emotionally, she told Billie Jean how happy she was
that women finally had somebody of their own sex to look up to. In her
autobiography, Billie Jean mused, "I sometimes forget how tough it is

for women to even have the opportunity to succeed. I really feel sorry for all the women who never had the chance to develop their careers, athletic or otherwise, because they were taught to believe it was the wrong thing to do."

It is better today for women who want to play big-time sports; parental repression of their daughters' athletic desires has given way to understanding, and organized athletics have come into their own in the last decade or so. For women who want to make a career as sportswriters the opportunities are there now, although pockets of resistance remain from the male supremacist element in sports. So this collection, alas, is not represented by enough women authors. But watch the nineties explode with writers who happen to be women and who also happen to write about sports as well and as true as their male counterparts.

2.

If this collection of sports memorabilia has a unity to it, it is a unity based on the intimate relationship between sports and life. Sports as a barometer of life harbors all of life's symptoms. And the literature of the pastime, while it entertains, explores those symptoms, seeking revelations. The abiding urge of the serious writer springs from what John Updike has called "the mad notion of the writer that your society needs to know only what you can tell—needs the truth that only you can deliver." And with the truth comes an illumination of the age in which we live, a most informing and useful weapon for a writer in this improbable twentieth century, this "monstrous bouillabaisse of life," as the Canadian novelist Robertson Davies so vividly put it.

The bouillabaisse was maybe a little less monstrous in Hazlitt's time, in the early 1800s when he wrote his brilliant discourse on boxing and everything else that struck his fancy. For at least the survival of the planet was not a towering issue of the day. In our century we have witnessed the awesome advance of technology that has left in its wake reeling institutions when, as Tom Boswell says, "almost all our compasses have become demagnetized." And sports, suffering at least sympathy pains with humanity, has run alongside, holding up a mirror to reflect our times, while also trying to offer release from the bewildering uncertainties and complexities of modern life. With its order, its prescribed boundaries, its rock-ribbed rules, its nourishing distractions, sports has become an oasis for those who still seek, and can no longer find in real life, a sense of community. The great drummer Art Blakey

once defined jazz as "the music to wash away the dust of everyday life."
You can say the same of sports.

Think of this: What was the most enduring image seen on television
during the 1991 Super Bowl game between the New York Giants and
Buffalo Bills? It was those live shots of American GIs—sweaty and fatigued men and women—watching the game at three in the morning,
Persian Gulf time, awake and cheering and finding their own sense of
community in a region of the world that has never in all its history been
anything but fragmented.

We are of course talking about spectator sports because in the
twentieth century the United States has become a nation of spectators;
it is the same throughout the industrialized world. So this book deals
with men against men, women against women, team against team—
what that letter-writer meant when he talked about *loving to watch the
best.* Pure participant sports that have a proud literature of their own
—hunting, fishing, mountain climbing, and the like—are not part of this
volume. Spectator sports concern not the self so much as the self reacting to the heroism of other selves, those athletes we have loved to
watch, and marvel at, and read about, and understand.

Heroism. A character in Bernard Malamud's *The Natural* says: "Without heroes we are all plain people and don't know how far we can go."

A definition of the hero in sports was movingly expressed by Robert
W. Creamer in his book *Baseball in '41,* about Joe DiMaggio's fifty-six-
game hitting streak that summer (Creamer is present in this volume
with an account of the turning point in young Babe Ruth's life):

> It was a wonderful feat, maintained over a long period. Whenever
> anyone does something marvelous, something truly admirable and
> endearing, other human beings feel a sense of pride and exaltation.
> We are pleased that someone human, someone who eats and
> breathes like us, who has arms and legs and ears and eyes like
> us, has done this splendid thing. It gives us a vicarious sense of
> accomplishment and even self-satisfaction. We did that. When we
> were applauding DiMaggio we were applauding ourselves.

I must confess a certain tilt in this book toward heroes and acts of
heroism that almost certainly comes out of my own upbringing. When
I was a kid growing up around Boston, my heroes—saints—were Frankie
Brimsek, the Boston Bruins' goaltender; a football player named Boley
Dancewicz, who lived in my hometown of Lynn and then became a Notre

Dame quarterback; and Wally Berger. That's right, Wally Berger. In 1935 Berger played for my all-time favorite sports team, the Boston Braves (I remained a fan even when the Braves moved to Milwaukee, but abandoned them when they carpetbagged to Atlanta). In 1935 the Braves won 38 games and lost 115 (all right, I was a bit of a masochist), and Wally Berger led the National League in home runs and runs batted in. Of course he was traded away a couple of years later and that was the end of that love affair. Later on my hero was Warren Spahn, and not just because he was lefthanded like me, but because of his eminent grace as a pitcher and his endurance; he was the Nolan Ryan of his time, winning twenty games a year in thirteen different years, winning twenty-three games when he was forty-two years old, pitching a no-hitter at forty, hitting more home runs than any National League pitcher ever, striking out at least one hundred batters for seventeen straight years.

There was one other who came into my life when I was a boy, came and left in a flash, an ordinary moment it seemed at the time; but as the years wore on that moment assumed cosmic significance for me; to this day I remember it as though it has just happened.

I believe I was either a sophomore or junior in high school, sometime in the early forties. On a cold winter morning we were in a gym class, working the parallel bars, climbing the ropes, doing other gymnastic gyrations, when our teacher Tom Whelan (he had gotten into the majors for one game, in 1920, with my beloved Braves) suddenly appeared with a stranger. The man was wearing a black, nondescript overcoat and he held a brown felt hat in his hand. Whelan blew the whistle that dangled from his neck.

"Come over here for a minute, fellas," he said. "I want you to meet someone."

We moved in and took a closer look at the stranger. He didn't seem very tall and because of the coat we couldn't tell about his body, but he looked heavy. He also looked ill. His face had a pasty, yellow-brown pallor. His hair was thick and flecked with gray. The other features of his face gave a feeling of raw, cruel, but used-up power—the close, slit eyes, the broad, bashed-in nose, the thick twisted lips, and protruding jaw. But his face was softened by a shy, sheepish smile that seemed to say: sorry to take up your fun, boys, but it's not my doing.

"Fellas," Tom Whelan was saying, "I want you to meet a good friend of mine. But more than that, I want you to meet the man I think is the greatest athlete this world has ever known. Jim Thorpe."

Jim Thorpe? The name was maybe faintly familiar. Tom Whelan went on to tell a little about his friend, about the Jim Thorpe who had won the decathlon and the pentathlon in the 1912 Olympics, about the Jim Thorpe who was a smashing fullback for the Carlisle Indians, then the Canton Bulldogs, about the Jim Thorpe who played seven years of major league baseball. But all of that had been twenty or more years back and Jim Thorpe had faded from fame, and so, at best, his name was a remote one in our young heads.

Tom Whelan finished talking and Jim Thorpe, that sad, sweet smile still on his face, waved goodbye and moved out of the gym without saying a word. The whole thing could not have lasted longer than five minutes and then we went back to our chores—and Jim Thorpe went back into limbo.

What Whelan didn't tell us that day was how Thorpe was stripped of his Olympic medals because, in 1909, he had accepted money to play semipro baseball; of how Thorpe had spent his postathletic years drifting over the country, forgotten. He would find work as a house painter or a laborer, or he would appear with carnivals, or play bit parts in Hollywood. This Sac-Fox Native American, who was named Bright Path by his mother, didn't have the price of admission to the 1932 Olympics in Los Angeles.

Then, in 1950, the memory of that morning burst back into my consciousness when, in an Associated Press poll, Thorpe was named the greatest football player of the half century, the second greatest track-and-field star of the half century, and, finally, the greatest athlete of the half century. Tom Whelan hadn't exaggerated.

Three years later, in 1953, this Jim Thorpe, in many ways the quintessential American hero, was found dead of a heart attack in his last home, in a trailer camp. Years after his death, the ruling body of international Olympics reinstated Jim Thorpe in the Pantheon, returning his medals to his family.

My addiction to heroes continued up to 1951. That was the year I first became a full-time wage-earner, having secured a job with *Sport* Magazine! Never in my wildest dreams as a child did it ever occur to me that I might someday be able to earn a living from the passion of my youth. That rookie year for me was also the rookie year of two promising ballplayers, Mickey Mantle and Willie Mays. But my attachment to heroes had begun to subside as sports became not a pastime but a profession.

Baseball, as you will see, occupies a lot of territory in this volume. If the twentieth century belongs to America, as it has been commonly said, then American sports dominate, too. Virginia Woolf tried to explain it this way: she believed that Ring Lardner used baseball where an English writer would use society, as a "clue, a center, a meeting place for the divers activities of people whom a vast continent isolates, whom no tradition controls." That is as good an explanation as I've seen for why baseball is called "The National Pastime."

Baseball is of course much more than a national pastime now. In Latin America and the Caribbean it resonates slightly larger than life. And the influx of Latin players into United States professional baseball has added elements of imagination, grace, and artistry to the game. And soon, I'm sure, Japanese players will be breaking into the major leagues of America.

Beyond the internationalization of baseball (which, of course, is going on in other sports, too, as we speak) there is another reason for the inordinate richness of the literature. That is because it is still the one sport that seems to enter into the bloodstream of American children and stay there until they grow up to be writers. Well, not all of them, maybe; but, for instance, one can make a pretty good case for Jewish writers of past generations (and modern generations, too) being particularly attuned to this sport. Somehow, it was understood at an early age that baseball was a way for the Jew to assimilate without unpleasantness, or guilt, into the mainstream of the country. Thus Bernard Malamud's first novel was *The Natural*. And Philip Roth has continually used baseball as one weapon with which to come to terms with America. He did it in *The Great American Novel*, a greatly underrated Roth work, by the way; in his memoir of his father, *Patrimony*; and, as you will read in this volume, in the novel that awoke the world to his gifts, *Portnoy's Complaint*. And Chaim Potok's first novel, *The Chosen*, opens with an account of a softball game between two Yeshiva schools. As the narrator remarks, "To the students of most of the parochial schools an inter-league baseball victory had come to take on only a shade less significance than a top grade in Talmud, for it was an unquestioned mark of one's Americanism."

But you don't have to be Jewish to grow up loving baseball. David Lamb, who wrote two books about Africa and the Middle East (he was a foreign correspondent in both areas), was compelled to write a third book, *Stolen Season*, about baseball. As he said, "When I was fourteen I had mastered most of life's mysteries, and understood that baseball more than politics, religion, or other national institutions was what the rhythms of our days was all about."

This is a shared experience. I can, if I put my mind to it, still smell the essence of my boyhood when, on a lazy summer afternoon, I would wander down the playground alongside Lynn Beach and chase after soaring fly balls hit to me by a friend, one at a time, hundreds of them through the day. Loping after the ball, looking up to a beckoning sky, the smell of freshly mown grass and crushed dandelions underfoot, the salt airborne on an east wind blowing into my nose and mouth, it was like a cleansing of the soul, leaving in its wake a comfort and happiness and purity, and I felt I could keep chasing after fly balls forever.

> *The sound of the crowd.*
> *The clear colors of the sky.*
> *The warmth of the sun.*
> *The light of winter coming.*

This is one man's reaction to baseball, too, an ode composed by Sadaharu Oh, the Babe Ruth of Japanese baseball, taken from *A Zen Way of Baseball,* the book he wrote with the help of David Falkner. Oh tells of his two heroes, Lou Gehrig and a legendary samurai, Miyamato Musashi. Gehrig was his hero because he had played in 2,130 consecutive games, what Oh calls "an event of the spirit." And Musashi beat his arch rival Kojiro using strength and technique, and something much more— *ki,* spirit power.

In this volume you will read of spirit power and events of the spirit. You will read of individual victories and shared victories, of acts of heroism and of failed heroism, of glory, tragedy, conflict, and joy—all cemented, as much as possible, through the power of the language.

In sports the expression of tragedy is most easily established through the art of bullfighting. You will taste it in one of Lorca's greatest poems, "Lament for Ignacio Sánchez Mejías." And also in Barnaby Conrad's *The Death of Manolete.* The ultimate lesson of Manolete's end came from an aged *banderillero* as he gazed at the corpse of the fallen matador: "They kept demanding more and more of him, and more was his life, so he gave it to them."

Throughout this volume a debate of sorts forms between those who believe sports ennobles the human soul and those who feel exactly the opposite. The most aroused dissenter, a person whose life and writings ennobled the word *dissent,* is George Orwell. In 1945 after watching the Moscow Dynamics soccer club play British teams in a series of exhibitions, the outraged Orwell proclaimed, "Sports is an unfailing cause of ill will." Orwell allowed that it hadn't always been that way but that beginning in the late nineteenth century and rampaging through the twentieth century, "the cult of the games" became bound up with the rise of nationalism. International soccer of course is a story unto itself with its series of stadium riots and stampedes among spectators, a recurring Orwellian condition.

The twentieth-century Olympic games have almost always been bound up in conflict behind the scenes—from the fascist dictates of Adolf Hitler in Berlin in 1936, to the revolt of some black American athletes in 1968, to the massacre of Israeli athletes at Munich in 1972. It ends up, almost always, with the athlete suffering not from an opponent on the playing field, but from the consequences of irrational acts coming from the outside. As the Soviet decathloner Vasily Kuznetsov put it, "If everyone in the world were an athlete, we would break records—not each other's heads."

Not likely, but the games arouse such sentiments. I remember standing in the hot sun with my wife at the Rome Olympics of 1960 watching the opening-day ceremonies. And here came the United States team, with Rafer Johnson, a decathloner, out front carrying the American flag. It was, even for this now jaded sports watcher, an inspiring sight. A German woman sitting beside me said in perfect English, "This is the way the world should live together."

For the last word on the subject, we offer you the wisdom of one of our gladiator-contributors, Bill Russell: "I used to joke that if you could bottle all the emotions let loose in a basketball game you'd have enough hate to fight a war and enough joy to prevent one."

3.

Hate comes to the surface now and then in sports, among the spectators *and* the participants, but hate surfaces far more often in life. Joy, however, is a life-affirming element in sports, the stuff of sports, while joy in life is rationed. No sportswriter has better expressed the joy of sports than Arnold Hano, who is represented in this volume with his classic and joyful story of sitting in the centerfield bleachers of the Polo Grounds during the 1954 World Series, thereby becoming the only professional to witness Willie Mays flying right at him in desperate pursuit of the long, soaring ball hit by Cleveland's Vic Wertz. At another time, in a magazine story, Hano wrote about other problem-solving moments in sports:

Hit a pitched ball that arrives a half second after it leaves the pitcher's hand, and is moving towards you on a horizontal plane and down and away from you on a vertical plane at much the same time. Loft a golf ball over a tree and onto a green where it must bounce once and spin back toward a cup you can't even see from the spot you make your shot. Problems. Solved by mind and muscle in mysterious concert under punishing psychological stress. When the concert is synchronized and perfect, it sings in your ear and in your heart.

In the years that I was editing *Sport* the athlete who sang in my ear and heart, who gave me the most esthetic pleasure, was Jim Brown. I'll never forget those games in the sixties the "Jim Brown" Cleveland Browns played with the New York Giants. I don't remember the scores. I don't even remember who won, but I do remember Jim Brown in action. I can see him now, taking a pitchout from the quarterback, Frank Ryan, and gliding like a Balanchine dancer along the line—his feet, I swear, were off the ground—then punching through the tackle or driving outside the hole, meeting a wall of blue uniforms, cutting sharply to his right, pirouetting maybe 180 degrees in a flash of balletic beauty, then uncoiling all the speed and power combined on his 6'2", 230-pound frame and diving into the end zone. He would drop the ball and move slowly, painfully to the sidelines, as if he would prefer crawling back to the bench. In the next series of offensive plays he would drag his body into the huddle the same way—oh, how he seemed to be hurting—and then slash his way through defenders once again.

Sometime around this period I was asked to testify at the trial of a famous professional athlete who was being sued by the Internal Revenue Service for not declaring certain gifts given to him as awards during the course of a season. The contention of the athlete, and his lawyer, was that the prizes were earned by extraordinary performance; indeed, one of the athlete's baubles was that Corvette automobile from our magazine for his performance in a championship event. At that time there was an exemption in the Internal Revenue Code for artists and writers who received material honors because of their work; the Nobel Prize was such an example. The judge asked me if I regarded such sports as baseball, football, basketball, and boxing as artistic endeavors. I said they could qualify.

"If you had to name one person in sports today who typifies the artist-athlete, could you name one?"

"Yes, your honor," I said.

"Who would that be?"

"Jim Brown."

The judge had also asked me to define the artist in sports. That caught me off guard but I mumbled something to the effect that it was "a person who creates, who does wonderful things that the ordinary person cannot do, who does them through instinct, through sheer natural instinct backed by years of training and experience."

Sounds a little feeble as I read this transcript now. I wish I had had in my head then what I have in my head now, the words of the wise Robertson Davies who explained the essence of his own profession this way: "In the end, imagination is at the heart of any novel that may claim to be considered a work of art."

Some athletes, through performance, have defined their art in exactly that way. But as the century winds down it becomes more and more difficult to think of sports so purely, for in the progress of the century, some purity has been lost, along with innocence. It is true of sports as of all other institutions. Our athletes today, in *every* sport, are bigger and stronger and faster, and certainly richer than the athletes of any other time. But athletes' lives are complicated, too, by the stresses of the age in which we live. They are beset by the same ills of society that plague nonathletes, a whole population. Drugs, including the consequences of steroid injection, have ruined lives in sports, and the worst is probably yet to come. Heavy drinking, always a problem in sports, prevails still, with alarming consequences. And because audiences are increasingly dissatisfied with their own lives, animosities between players and spectators are rising.

There are "fans" who resent the hard-won independence of the professional. The athlete's demanding and finally gaining a say in his personal destiny is a recent phenomenon, but growing in every sport. But that's what the world is about. And why should athletes be any different? Today, more athletes have better minds, more athletes have sophisticated outlooks, more athletes are unafraid to reveal to the public their inner nature.

The fact that some athletes today earn multimillion dollar salaries, and sometimes cannot match performance to the money, rankles people. In corporate America business executives do the same thing, pulling in huge bonuses awarded by their boards, even when the corporation has had an "off year." But CEOs don't play in a public arena. Athletes, who have maybe a six- or seven-year big-earnings lifetime, do; they have no place to hide.

For all the reservations people have about today's athletes vs. yesterday's, or the big-money taint on sports, consistency of performance still sets the great athlete apart from the ordinary athlete. And consistency of performance, *excellence* of performance, probably exists in our history now as it never has before. And, always, athletes continue to rise above mere consistency. The creed of the great pianist, Arthur Schnabel, was "safety last." It is their creed, too—that of the men and women who entertain us by going flat out, all out on some court, in some arena, in the grass and dirt, the memory of their performances echoing in the playgrounds of our minds.

In Brian Glanville's novel *The Olympian* the protagonist of the novel, a runner, hears his coach, who is at least partly a mystic, offer a definition of sports as performed at its highest level: "It all lies in the conception. Once these things have been conceived as possible, they are achieved. And that is why athletics are important. Because they demonstrate the scope of human possibility; which is unlimited. The inconceivable is conceived, and then it is accomplished."

Our intention in this collection has been to convey the diverse excellence of sports, even with its problems, as much as possible through the diverse excellence of writing. Conrad once wrote that his task was to use "the power of the written word to make you hear, to make you feel, above all, to make you see." The best in the literature of sports does that, too, even as it entertains. So do not dismiss easily the games that offer laughter, virtue, hope, and joy, and lighten hearts. This is sports at its cleanest and truest, enriching for us that landscape which bears more than a close resemblance to the life we all live.

Al Silverman
White Plains, New York

The Twentieth Century

Treasury
of
Sports

Roger Angell

Agincourt and After

Since 1962, when Roger Angell published his first collection of base-
ball essays from The New Yorker, *he has become widely acknowl-*
edged as "the most astute and graceful chronicler the sport has
known." Grace and astuteness indeed shine in this account of game
six of the 1975 World Series, the Boston Red Sox vs. the Cincinnati
Reds. Was it, as many wise observers of the sport have proclaimed,
"the greatest game ever played"? Leave it to Angell to put it in
perspective.

Game Six, Game Six . . . what can we say of it without seeming to diminish it by recapitulation or dull it with detail? Those of us who were there will remember it, surely, as long as we have any baseball memory, and those who wanted to be there and were not will be sorry always. Crispin Crispian: for Red Sox fans, this was Agincourt. The game also went out to sixty-two million television viewers, a good many millions of whom missed their bedtime. Three days of heavy rains had postponed things; the outfield grass was a lush, Amazon green, but there was a clear sky at last and a welcoming moon—a giant autumn squash that rose above the right-field Fenway bleachers during batting practice.

In silhouette, the game suggests a well-packed but dangerously overloaded canoe—with the high bulge of the Red Sox' three first-inning runs in the bow, then the much bulkier hump of six Cincinnati runs amidships, then the counterbalancing three Boston runs astern, and then, *way* aft, one more shape. But this picture needs colors: Fred Lynn clapping his hands once, quickly and happily, as his three-run opening shot flies over the Boston bullpen and into the bleachers . . . Luis Tiant fanning Perez with a curve and the Low-Flying Plane, then dispatching Foster with a Fall Off the Fence. Luis does not have his fastball, however. . . .

Pete Rose singles in the third. Perez singles in the fourth—his first real contact off Tiant in three games. Rose, up again in the fifth, with a man on base, fights off Tiant for seven pitches, then singles hard to center. Ken Griffey triples off the wall, exactly at the seam of the left-field and center-field angles; Fred Lynn, leaping up for the ball and missing it, falls backward into the wall and comes down heavily. He lies there, inert, in a terrible, awkwardly twisted position, and for an instant all of us think that he has been killed. He is up at last, though, and even stays in the lineup, but the noise and joy are gone out of the crowd, and the game is turned around. Tiant, tired and old and, in the end, bereft even of mannerisms, is rocked again and again—eight hits in three innings—and Johnson removes him, far too late, after Geronimo's first-pitch home run in the eighth has run the score to 6–3 for the visitors.

By now, I had begun to think sadly of distant friends of mine— faithful lifelong Red Sox fans all over New England, all over the East, whom I could almost see sitting silently at home and slowly shaking their heads as winter began to fall on them out of their sets. I scarcely noticed when Lynn led off the eighth with a single and Petrocelli walked. Sparky Anderson, flicking levers like a master back-hoe operator, now called in Eastwick, his sixth pitcher of the night, who fanned Evans and retired Burleson on a fly. Bernie Carbo, pinch-hitting, looked wholly overmatched against Eastwick, flailing at one inside fastball like someone fighting off a wasp with a croquet mallet. One more fastball arrived, high and over the middle of the plate, and Carbo smashed it in a gigantic, flattened parabola into the center-field bleachers, tying the game. Everyone out there—and everyone in the stands, too, I suppose—leaped to his feet and waved both arms exultantly, and the bleachers looked like the dark surface of a lake lashed with a sudden night squall.

The Sox, it will be recalled, nearly won it right away, when they loaded the bases in the ninth with none out, but an ill-advised dash home by Denny Doyle after a fly, and a cool, perfect peg to the plate by George Foster, snipped the chance. The balance of the game now swung back, as it so often does when opportunities are wasted. Drago pitched out of a jam in the tenth, but he flicked Pete Rose's uniform with a pitch to start the eleventh. Griffey bunted, and Fisk snatched up the ball and, risking all, fired to second for the force on Rose. Morgan was next, and

I had very little hope left. He struck a drive on a quick, deadly rising line—you could still hear the loud *whock!* in the stands as the white blur went out over the infield—and for a moment I thought the ball would land ten or fifteen rows back in the right-field bleachers. But it wasn't hit quite that hard—it was traveling too fast, and there was no sail to it—and Dwight Evans, sprinting backward and watching the flight of it over his shoulder, made a last-second, half-staggering turn to his left, almost facing away from the plate at the end, and pulled the ball in over his head at the fence. The great catch made for two outs in the end, for Griffey had never stopped running and was easily doubled off first.

And so the swing of things was won back again. Carlton Fisk, leading off the bottom of the twelfth against Pat Darcy, the eighth Reds pitcher of the night—it was well into morning now, in fact—socked the second pitch up and out, farther and farther into the darkness above the lights, and when it came down at last, reilluminated, it struck the topmost, innermost edge of the screen inside the yellow left-field foul pole and glanced sharply down and bounced on the grass: a fair ball, fair all the way. I was watching the ball, of course, so I missed what everyone on television saw—Fisk waving wildly, weaving and writhing and gyrating along the first-base line, as he wished the ball fair, *forced* it fair with his entire body. He circled the bases in triumph, in sudden company with several hundred fans, and jumped on home plate with both feet, and John Kiley, the Fenway Park organist, played Handel's "Hallelujah Chorus," *fortissimo,* and then followed with other appropriately exuberant classical selections, and for the second time that evening I suddenly remembered all my old absent and distant Sox-afflicted friends (and all the other Red Sox fans, all over New England), and I thought of them— in Brookline, Mass., and Brooklin, Maine; in Beverly Farms and Mashpee and Presque Isle and North Conway and Damariscotta; in Pomfret, Connecticut, and Pomfret, Vermont; in Wayland and Providence and Revere and Nashua, and in both the Concords and all five Manchesters; and in Raymond, New Hampshire (where Carlton Fisk lives), and Bellows Falls, Vermont (where Carlton Fisk was *born*), and I saw all of them dancing and shouting and kissing and leaping about like the fans at Fenway— jumping up and down in their bedrooms and kitchens and living rooms, and in bars and trailers, and even in some boats here and there, I suppose, and on back-country roads (a lone driver getting the news over the radio and blowing his horn over and over, and finally pulling up and getting out and leaping up and down on the cold macadam, yelling into the night), and all of them, for once at least, utterly joyful and believing in that joy—alight with it.

It should be added, of course, that very much the same sort of celebration probably took place the following night in the midlands towns and vicinities of the Reds' supporters—in Otterbein and Scioto; in Frankfort, Sardinia, and Summer Shade; in Zanesville and Louisville and Akron and French Lick and Loveland. I am not enough of a social geographer to know if the faith of the Red Sox fan is deeper or hardier than that of a Reds rooter (although I secretly believe that it may be, because of his longer and more bitter disappointments down the years). What I do know is that this belonging and caring is what our games are all about; this is what we come for. It is foolish and childish, on the face of it, to affiliate ourselves with anything so insignificant and patently contrived and commercially exploitative as a professional sports team, and the amused superiority and icy scorn that the non-fan directs at the sports nut (I know this look—I know it by heart) is understandable and almost unanswerable. Almost. What is left out of this calculation, it seems to me, is the business of caring—caring deeply and passion-ately, really *caring*—which is a capacity or an emotion that has almost gone out of our lives. And so it seems possible that we have come to a time when it no longer matters so much what the caring is about, how frail or foolish is the object of that concern, as long as the feeling itself can be saved. Naïveté—the infantile and ignoble joy that sends a grown man or woman to dancing and shouting with joy in the middle of the night over the haphazardous flight of a distant ball—seems a small price to pay for such a gift.

Eliot Asinof

The Rookie

"I could have been a real good minor-league ballplayer," Eliot Asinof once told a friend, "but I didn't have the power." Asinof did play three years for the Philadelphia Phillies' farm teams; then, at the age of thirty, he decided to become a writer. Asinof wrote the acclaimed book on the Black Sox, Eight Men Out. *But before that work, in 1955, Asinof wrote* Man on Spikes, *a novel encapsulating some of his experiences as a minor-leaguer, but turning those memories into art. In this excerpt, Mike Kutner, thirty-five years old, a minor-leaguer all his life, has just been called up to play his first game in the majors. And comes to the moment of his life.*

The rookie walked into the batter's circle behind home plate and listened to the noise of the largest crowd he'd ever seen. He swung two bats over his head, stretching the muscles in his powerful arms and remembering the deafening crowd-sounds of his past. Dropping to one knee, he stroked his favorite piece of shiny ash and wiped the dirt from the tapered white barrel. He could not resist looking up at the towering stadium around him. For the fourth time today, he waited there for his turn at bat; each time he had tingled at the exultation that ran through him, repeating under his breath for his senses to enjoy, "You're in the big time, Mike; you're in the big time!" And he reveled in the excitement that beat against his insides and almost made him laugh.

But now a wave of savage noise rose from the stands and brought him back to the sticky afternoon of this crucial September ball game. He turned to watch Red Schalk fidgeting in the batter's box and then the pitch twisting at half speed to the plate. He saw the hitter's badly timed stride and watched the ball curve elusively by him, the bat remaining ineptly on his shoulder. He heard the umpire's elongated cry:

"Stee-rike one!"

Mike braced himself for the new roar of the crowd, multiplying the tension in this ninth-inning climax, and considered the game situation. There were two men out, and the tying and winning runs danced helplessly off second and first, itching to head for the plate. The game was going down to the wire; it was clearly up to Red Schalk.

The rookie joined the bellowing mob behind him, calling aloud his desperate hopes.

"Keep alive, Red. Keep alive!"

But within him, he knew he meant something else: keep alive for me . . . for *me.* Get on base and leave those runners sitting out there. Mike felt himself begging for the hero's job—a chance to hit that big blow and bust up the game. He transferred his body, his power, his timing, his coordination, and most of all, his will into Red's. This day was a personal climax, far more important to him than the game. It had to be his day; he knew damn well he had it coming to him.

"Mike!" he heard. "The rosin. Gimme the goddamn rosin!"

He looked up to see Red walking toward him from the plate. He picked up the rosin bag and went to meet him.

"Sonofabitch." Red was muttering under his breath.

"Take it easy, Red." Mike tried to steady him. The young outfielder, a veteran now, was taking it hard. "Get loose."

Red rubbed the rosin over his sweaty hands.

"Can't get 'em dry enough. . . ."

Scare-sweat, the rookie thought. The guy is scared up there. A chance to be a hero and the guy is scared.

"Take your time, Red."

"Sonofabitch, Mike, can't get loose."

"Take it easy." He noticed now the guy was shaking.

Mike went back to the batter's circle and spat his contempt. He'd give half his pay to be in this spot right now, but the redhead was blind with fear, frozen solid up there. And this was a bonus baby. Red Schalk, the new-type ballplayer. They had handed him sixty thousand dollars for being a high-school hero, for hitting .400 against seventeen-year-old pitchers. Sixty Gs for merely signing his name! Mike thought back to the brick wall black with coal dust and to Durkin Fain, and the two hundred and fifty dollars he ended up swallowing. He'd been born in the wrong decade.

He grunted his disgust. "Com' on, Red." Then his tone became one of demand. "Get on that sack!"

Mike watched the pitcher lean into the shadows to pick up the catcher's sign, his intense concentration hidden under the lowered peak. The pitch spun in, an exact facsimile of the previous strike, and it tied the redhead in the same knot. Mike groaned helplessly, and bit harshly into the back of his hand.

Fooled him twice. The lousy redhead. Fooled the big-time major leaguer, overanxious in the clutch like an overgrown high-school kid. Red had never even waved his stick. Christ, you'd think a guy three years in this league would know how to get set.

He shivered as if an icy wind had passed through him, frantic now that everything vital to him seemed so far beyond his control. The batter was out of the box again, playing with the rosin bag.

"Mike. . . ." The voice was low and charged with fear. "I've got a pain in my gut. Can't work it out."

Mike looked up into the quivering face, amazed at its pallor, and he knew that the kid had given up on himself.

"I don't feel good, Mike," Red was saying. "I can't stand up there. . . ."

Mike thought of the drunks he had sobered up; this looked like the toughest job of all.

"Don't tell that to the skipper, Red," he said. "I got a feeling old Tracy wouldn't appreciate it."

So now the bottom was really falling out. This was supposed to be the hitter who would give Mike Kutner a crack at the big one. Mike felt himself sinking helplessly into the quicksand of the other man's fear. The towering double tiers that enclosed them seemed to loom higher, much higher.

"Com' on, Schalk," the umpire growled. "Let's get the game movin'."

Mike grabbed the hitter by the arm. What the hell could he say? "Get back in there and hit or you'll never hit again. Not in this league, anyway." His voice was harsh and charged with anger. "Be tough, Red. Be tough up there!" And he turned away, spitting out the taste of his words. Maybe the jerk oughta pray too.

Oh you bum, you cruddy bum! He muttered the words under his breath, and let his memory take him back four years to a Florida spring-training camp. There he had first come across Red Schalk, a pink-cheeked, nineteen-year-old kid out of Georgia. He remembered how they had babied him, trying to justify the ridiculous sixty-grand investment.

He was Jim Mellon's fair-haired boy, the big prospect. He had heard later how they coddled Red all season, letting him nurse his Texas League .302 batting average to make it look like something. A year later, they had moved Schalk up to Chicago.

Mike had burned up at the move. He'd outhit Red by two dozen points, and in a tougher league. He was a dozen times the better glove-man. What about the promises they had made? Why not him? He had demanded an answer.

He remembered the present of a box of cigars and the soft, ingratiating smile of Clark Mellon. "Sure, Mike, you're a better ballplayer at the moment. But we're after the younger kids. By all rights you should be up there, and if it hadn't been for the war and those years you lost, I'm sure you would be. Sorry as hell, Mike, but that's the way she goes. A kid of nineteen has a much longer ride ahead of him."

Sure, the wrong damn decade. Now he was thirty-five, an old man of thirty-five, a rookie of thirty-five playing his first game in the majors. It did not escape him that he was here by a fluke. Chicago had been riddled with injuries driving down the stretch, and they'd decided to use Mike in this crucial September series rather than some green youngster. At the last moment, Mellon had called him in Minneapolis.

It was weird, the way it happened. He was just about to go for a walk with Laura, a simple little morning walk that would take them away for a lingering breakfast in a pleasant family restaurant they enjoyed. He was sitting on the bed, watching her finish dressing. She was putting on a fall suit for the first time, and it crossed his mind that she was doing it to remind him that the summer was ending, and another winter coming on. The thought set off a depressing chain of emotions. It was then that the phone rang and he listened to the peremptory orders from Chicago. They came so suddenly that he became dizzy. Afterwards he had to lie back on the bed to ease the shock.

He had to hurry with Laura to catch the plane. Now he thought sourly, Two minutes later and I wouldn't have been there to receive the call.

They flew down to Chicago a few hours before game time and taxied directly to the ball park, with hardly time to catch a bite to eat. Sixteen years he had plugged away for this chance. When they finally found they needed him, they threw it in his face like an insult.

In the locker room before the game, he knew the others were watching him dress, but he didn't care. A thirty-five-year-old rookie was something of a freak. Those who knew him saw his determination and understood. To the others it was simply a matter of winning a pennant and the pile of dough that goes with it. But to Mike it was more, much more. He looked at them quickly, responding to their greetings. He knew that some must be thinking he was good, as good as almost any of them, and if the ball had bounced differently, it might have been Kutner up there all these years instead of them. But now he was thirty-five, and he could be called old. He saw those who did not know him look curiously across the room at the partially bald head, the dark leathery skin of his neck, the heavy, uneven walk; and he thought they'd be wondering how many years they had left for themselves. Respectfully, they had left him alone while he dressed.

Mike had waited to finish until they were all out. His uniform was clean and he liked its fresh, sterile smell. He laced his shoes tightly and put on his new cap. With pride he didn't bother to conceal, he walked over to the big mirror by the shower room and stood solidly before it. He looked at himself for a long moment, allowing the glow to penetrate. The excitement of it tickled the back of his neck, bringing goose pimples to his skin. He had never felt so wonderful.

"You're here, Mike . . . ," he said out loud. "You finally made it!" Then he clenched his fists as the emotion welled up within him. "You're here, goddammit, and you're not going back!"

Behind him, he heard the scuffle of heels on the concrete floor. He shifted his focus briefly to see an old man coming down the aisle. Finally, he turned from the mirror to get his glove, suddenly conscious that the man had stopped and was watching him for a longer time than Mike felt natural. But this was not the time to wonder and he closed his locker and got ready to leave for the diamond.

Then he heard him, and at once it began to make sense.

"Hello, Kutner."

Mike spun around to face him, drawn by a quality in the voice he somehow recognized. He saw the old man, older-looking than anyone he thought he knew, wrinkled and squint-eyed, yet erect and alert. He saw the smile as he moved toward the outstretched hand, and at once his memory bridged the gap.

"Hello, Mr. Fain," he said.

They shook hands warmly, and Mike met his piercing eyes.

"I was in Chicago for this Philly series, Kutner. I heard you were here. Just thought I'd drop back to say hello."

The words sounded trivial as he said them, too trivial for the importance of the moment. But their hands remained clasped for a long moment, covering the silence between them, and he saw in Durkin Fain's searching look that he felt deeply about Mike Kutner's finally making it.

What do you see, old man? Don't compare me with the kid you went out on a limb for. You're looking at an aging athlete, tired, almost bald, as old in his profession as you are in yours. Remember what you said, Mr. Fain: "I'm gonna make you a major leaguer." That's what you told me.

Sure. Here I am.

But this ain't what you meant, Mr. Fain. This ain't the way you meant it to be. I shouldn't be a rookie, Mr. Fain. I sure as hell don't look like one.

He looked hard at the old scout again, suddenly tired of this feeble self-examination. He could see the other man now and the brutal thing that the years had done to him.

"I heard you've been coaching the college boys, Mr. Fain."

The old man smiled. "No more, son. Too old to do that well. I haven't been up to it the last year or two."

Mike didn't know what to say to him. He turned back to his locker and grabbed the fifty-cent cigar he'd bought at the terminal. He had planned to smoke it later, as a kind of celebration for himself.

"Here, Mr. Fain," he said. "Have a cigar for old time's sake."

Fain took it, and put it in his pocket.

"Thanks," he said briefly.

"Don't you smoke 'em any more?"

Durkin Fain nodded.

"This one . . . after the game."

Mike nodded. He tightened his belt and started to the door, stopped and looked back. It was all so brief, so incomplete. There was nothing said. After all these years, there was nothing to say. It seemed strange, for he had thought of the scout a thousand times.

Fain smiled at him.

"Have a good day, son," he said, and then he nodded. "It ain't never too late."

The umpire's voice brought him out of his reverie.

"Play ball!" he hollered.

Mike raised his eyes to Schalk at the plate and watched him feebly waving his bat through the air as if he were flagging a train. Red was now an empty shell, a skeleton of bones in a big-league uniform, faking through the motions of being a hitter. Look at him, Mike thought. Look at what they picked instead of me!

The years of resentment boiled up inside him at this sickening symbol of his frustration. His disgust rose to his throat, almost choking him, and he exploded with angry violence.

"Stand up there like a pro, you punk!" he hollered. "Get on that goddamn base!"

He looked out to the pitcher's mound, thinking how much he'd like to be the chucker for this one pitch. If that mug knew the insides of Schalk's guts he'd be laughing out loud. But the pitcher was fingering his own rosin bag, and Mike smiled in spite of himself; that one was probably scared too. The rookie felt like the only veteran in the ball park.

The pitcher looked for a sign, a studied smile on his face. He'll curve him again, Mike thought. Any decent curve will get him. Red can't see any more, just little colored spots in front of his eyes. Count him out, ump. Red Schalk, K.O.

The curve spun rapidly in. Red went through the motions, stepping like he knew what he was doing, as if to take his cut. The ball curved sharply away from the corner too far inside, but it never reached the catcher. It bounded off Red's leg.

"Take yer base!"

Red lay moaning in the dust, rubbing his thigh.

Well, kiss my butt, Mike thought as he went to him. That was a sharp-breaking pitch but Schalk could have stepped back.

"You O.K., Red?" Maybe the guy did pray at that.

"Yeah . . . yeah. I'm O.K.," he mumbled. "It's funny, Mike. I never even saw it." And he got up, loosening his leg on the way to first. There was applause from the stands.

Mike grinned. It's good you didn't. It's goddamn good you didn't. Then he turned back to the plate, his concentration quickly on the job at hand.

Behind him, the crowd's excitement rose at the bases-loaded climax. He swung the two bats like a windmill and listened to the wild stampede.

It's all yours now, there's nothing left to the day but you. Go back, Mike, go back ten thousand turns at bat. None of them matter, none of them. Just this one, Mike. Just this one, big, beautiful moment.

He heard the manager, Al Tracy, from the bench, an anticlimax to his own thoughts.

"It's up to you, Kutner. Show me something!"

I'll show you something, Tracy, you dumb bastard. He tossed away the extra stick and started to dig a foothold in the batter's box. This is the turn that counts. The other three meant little. The neat sacrifice bunt, the base on balls, and that long well-tagged fly ball the left fielder dragged down. They were all routine. This is the spot, Mike. Blast one. Bust up the game.

They were really down to the wire now. All around him a tremendous din, wild, persistent, racked his ears. He looked up through the tight joy in his heart to face the pitcher. He saw the three runners dance anxiously off their bases. From the bench they were hollering at him:

"Com' on, Mike. . . . Clobber one!"

The pitcher was getting his sign, this time without a smile.

Here we go, rookie. Tag one and you're a major leaguer for the rest of your natural-born life. This is judgment day, the final one.

For Mike, there were no doubts. As sure as he was standing in the batter's box, he knew he was going to come through. He could hardly keep the smile off his face. This is the spot he'd waited sixteen years for.

He watched the pitcher take a full, slow-swinging wind-up. He cocked his bat high over his shoulder and waited for the throw. It came at half speed, spinning toward the outside corner. He stepped toward the pitch and lashed viciously at the ball with full power. As he finished his pivot, he knew he had gotten only a slice of it. The ball skidded off into the upper grandstand behind him.

"Stee-rike one!"

He leaned over to pick up dirt, muttering profanities at himself. He was set. He saw it all the way. Yet he hadn't met it squarely. Was it because he was tired? Or too eager? Then he realized it had happened to him too many times over the past year. His memory flashed him pictures of powerful drives off just such a pitch, years ago. But now he didn't always get around in time. There was something missing; the thin edge of timing and coordination had dulled over the years. He kicked viciously at the dirt at his feet and sprayed it over the ground. He remembered the words as they came from Clark Mellon: Thirty-five and past your prime.

He heard the cries from the other bench now, beamed directly at him over the crowd noises.

"Hey, pop, how'd you break in here?"

He took a moment to adjust his cap, and looked squarely into their dugout. They were all on the front step, nervously bellowing at him. He knew most of them from the minors, from training camps in March, from exhibition games year after year. Christ, who's been around more than Mike Kutner! Look at them: Black, Donnelly, Simpson, Caulfield. Yeah, Charlie Caulfield, the clown. Lost-in-the-sun Caulfield, the club's fifth outfielder.

His voice was as sharp as ever.

"Well, well. If it ain't the great lover! I thought you'd been pensioned off, Kutner."

Mike hitched up his pants. Very funny, he thought. What the hell does he do on that ball club—floor shows on washed-out nights? The guy who laughed his way to the top. Seven years in the majors, the only full-fledged clown on spikes.

Goddamn.

"Hey, baldy, where's your cane?"

He stepped back in the box and dug in again. Frig 'em all, big and small. He would talk with his bat. He thought now he would like that same pitch once more, just to prove he could still ride it. But he knew damn well he wouldn't get it again.

"Hey, rookie. Let's see that fine head of skin."

Be set, Mike, and stay loose. This punk has nothing he can throw by you. The ducks are on the pond, Mike, yours to knock in. It's a picnic, man. A picnic!

He watched the arm swing up and around, the big stride toward the plate, and the little white ball spun bullet-speed toward him. It came in shoulder high but too tight, and Mike fell carefully away from it.

"Stee-rike two!"

No . . . no, dammit . . . *no!* He turned fiercely on the umpire, ready to begin his protest. Then he backed away, knowing that rage would serve only to defeat him. Swallow it, Mike. Eat it!

No anger, Mike. You can't hit in a rage; not in this league, anyway. Let the crowd do the bellowing. Not you. There's no way to measure the pitch any more; it went by too long ago. The pitch is dead, long live the goddamn ump!

He slid his hand down the length of the smooth barrel of the bat and began thinking two-strike thoughts. You gotta stay loose, Mike. It's just another human arm throwing baseballs at you. You hit guys faster than this down in Texas twelve years ago when you were a kid. Just protect that plate, and cut away. You'll put a dent in this new stick and hang it over the fireplace like it had antlers. "This is the bat, sonny. Ten years ago your daddy blasted one they'll never forget!"

Easy, Mike. No anger, no anger.

"Play ball!"

Mike stood a few feet from the plate, still trying to collect himself. It had been a terrible call, that strike, at a terrible time. It put him behind the pitcher, making it tough for him to cut loose. He had to guard the plate now, instead of making the guy come in there with it. He couldn't pick out the throw he liked. He thought it was the kind of call umps would never make on a star. But on a rookie. . . .

Mike turned, still feeling the drumming in his gut.

"Take it easy, ump. I got something riding on this pitch, so take it slow."

The ump lifted his mask and leaned toward him.

"You're pretty sassy for a rookie, buddy."

Sure, Mike thought. There it was.

"Yeah," he said, as sour as he could make it.

"Get up there and hit, buddy."

Behind him he heard the skipper again, yelling to him as if his words were worth a million.

"To hell with him, Kutner. You got the big one left!"

Mike cleared his throat and nodded. Sure, Tracy. Nothing to it.

And Tracy would say: Sorry you had to swallow a call like that, Kutner, but you still gotta produce. That's what you'll get paid for, and nothing else matters. The umpire could call another zombie against you and you're out, just as if you whiffed one; and the game is gone. An hour later, it don't matter that it wasn't your fault. You didn't produce. That's what mattered. It's just a big round zero in the papers tomorrow.

Then he heard the jockeys again.

"Hey, grampa, who does yer grandson play for?"

"Get out the rockin' chair. Here comes ole Kutner!"

Mike reached down to finger some dirt. He rubbed his hands dry and gripped tightly the narrow handle of his bat. Back in the batter's box, he dug his spikes in position. He faced the pitcher and started thinking baseball again.

Get set, he told himself. Be ready for anything. It's still up to you. He can't get it by you, he can't get it by you. . . .

"Baldy! Hey! B-a-l-d-e-e-e-e-e!"

The arm swung around, and Mike's eyes followed the movement of the pitcher's hand, picking up the small quirk in the pitcher's delivery that indicated a curve ball. He set himself and moved his body toward the pitch. The ball spun down the inside and started curving too soon.

He pivoted with all his power and met the pitch out front with the fat part of the bat. A sharp crack rang out, beautiful and clear, and everyone in the park knew the ball had been really tagged.

Mike took off for first, watching it sail up and up into the sky, way above the stadium roof, soaring deep toward the left-field bleachers. He heard the tremendous ear-splitting roar of the fifty thousand; and his feet left the ground and he was floating on air. It was the big one! You've done it, Mike! You blasted one in the clutch, with the sacks loaded!

He rounded first base with tears in his eyes and a single all-embracing thought in his head: you've done it!

As he made his turn, he looked up again to follow the end flight of the ball, wanting to feast on the sight of it disappearing into the seats out there. Suddenly, his throat constricted. The ball . . . it wasn't falling right. The wind above the roof had caught it and was pulling it toward the foul line. He followed it down now, sinking deep into the bleachers, but at an angle he could not guess. He saw the foul pole, the tall white shaft, and he froze as the ball fell out of sight into a wild scramble of spectators.

He never heard the umpire's call. Short of second base, he stopped and turned slowly back toward home plate. From some place deep within him, his instincts had called it a foul ball.

He was right.

It took him a long time to walk back to the plate. He needed all the time he could get now. A sense of failure swept over him and he couldn't shake it off. For a moment, he thought he'd been feeling it all day. Luck was down on him just like always; the *real* luck, luck when you needed it. Then he realized what he was doing to himself, and he cursed his weakness. He looked toward his dugout as he walked and nodded toward the players shouting encouragement from the steps.

But the thought of trying again depressed him, as if he were suddenly very tired. He wondered how much drive he had left in him. For too long, he had pushed his body and his spirit. Now, it seemed to him ridiculously unfair that his entire effort was to be packed into one brief moment of time. One more pitch, maybe. It must be now. There's no more time. No more.

Maybe it was too much to ask of a man.

What do you say, Mike? Time is a string running out. You can't wind it back. How long is the string for you? There's a beautiful woman named Laura sitting back there, choking on her fears and probably crying her heart out right this minute. She'll sit this one out, loaded down with all your jockeys and umpires and foul balls. She's sitting out time. For her the string unravels under a box seat at a ball park, day after day, year after year. And all she can do is sit and watch.

Maybe it was too much to ask of a woman.

He felt the knocking of his heart against his ribs. He tried to breathe deeply again. He moved in toward the plate where the bat boy was holding his bat, waiting for him.

"Straighten it out, Mike," the kid said.

Sure, sure. Stop the wind and straighten it out.

He ran his hand along the end of the bat, subconsciously feeling for the dent. He wished he had more time.

"All right, Kutner," the umpire called to him. "Batter up!"

Mike played with his belt, trying to stall. His mind was cluttered with doubts and he had to shake them loose. Hitting is a state of mind, as important to coordination, timing, and power as a good pair of eyes. He was thinking of too many things now to be a hitter.

"You're through, baldy. Too bad. You shot yer wad on a foul ball!"

"Back to the mines, old-timer!"

He was about to step in and the yell backed him away. Back to the mines. The words rattled around in his head like loose marbles. Can you hear that, Pop? Wherever you are, can you hear that? Is that what you meant way back when you threw my glove in the furnace? Is that what you meant? Back to the mines?

"Com' on, Kutner. Get in there before they dig you under."

"Wrap him up and send him home. He's through!"

"This is it, four-eyes. Three strikes is dead!"

He seemed to feel their hot breath on his neck and the overloud voices blasting in his ear. The ump was at his side, impatiently fingering the ball-and-strike tabulator.

"Let's go, Kutner. Two strikes." The blue suit was insistent. "Play ball!"

Come on, Mike. You gotta get up there. You gotta get up there and hit.

("It ain't never too late, son.")

Christ, Mr. Fain . . . yes it is. I can feel it now. For the first time I can feel it. It doesn't really matter any more, does it? You must know this, Mr. Fain. What's in this pitch for you? It's only your pride that's at stake now and nothing more. There'll be no apologies to you, no rewards. It's too late for that. You're a has-been with a record of improper decisions. Your string has run out long ago.

They've beaten you, Mr. Fain. You did what was right but they threw you away. But I won't let them do it to me, goddammit. Not to me.

Suddenly, Mike leaned over and picked up a tiny pebble. He told himself that unless he put it in his pocket he wouldn't hit. For a moment he stood there, studying the pebble, debating what to do with it. It was the kind of foolish superstition he had always rejected. If you let yourself go, a million little things distracted you, threatened you, stripped you of your will to hit. He had seen guys who became slaves to their petty superstitions. Like Herman Cruller. This stopped him again; he hadn't thought of the guy in years. Herman the weak, Herman the softhearted. ("Never be like me, Mike. Be tough. And then learn to be tougher.")

He threw away the pebble and stepped up to the plate.

They were ready for him again.

"Yo, daddy. I heard you were in the war. Which one?"

He moved his bat around, trying to loosen the clothing on his shoulders. It didn't seem to set properly. He dug and redug his back foot into the corner of the box. He felt that something about his position was different, some minute arrangement of his feet or the balance of his body as he set himself. He watched the pitcher get his sign and his mind began an agonizing conjecture. Would he curve him again, half speed? Would he waste one, or make him cut at something bad? Would he try to throw one by him, a hard one under his chin, or low outside? It was hard not to guess. Don't guess, he told himself. That's suicide. You're still the hitter. Just be ready.

He cocked his bat over his shoulder and was conscious of the wet pull of his shirt against him. He made a quick movement of his body to release it. He thought of stepping out of the box again. Then he remembered the pebble and he wondered about his scorn of superstitions. He regretted not saving it.

Mike watched the pitcher nod to the man crouched behind him. The wind-up was calm and kept him waiting. It seemed endless.

O.K., Mike, guard that dish. No fear. Guard that dish. The ball spun lightly off the pitcher's fingers and fluttered toward the plate. He saw it start to break, a slow curve breaking toward the outside corner. It didn't look good to him, but it might be. In a split second he had to decide, his judgment shaken by his fear of the umpire. The delicate instrument of timing was shattered and the balance of his power upset. He stepped toward the pitch and started his swing, lashing at the ball with half a will, half a prayer.

He didn't come near it.

The game was over.

For a moment, he just stood there, wondering how sick he must have looked. He even tried to guess how far outside the plate the ball had passed. Then, the roar of the crowd rose from the stands like a wave, blasting into his ears the full consequence of his failure. It was too much for him.

No. It couldn't be. No!

"No!" he screamed. *"Goddammit!"* And he beat the plate brutally with his bat, refusing to accept it. He turned to face the pitcher's mound, swinging his bat as if ready to hit again, demanding that the game go on.

"Throw the goddamn ball!" he hollered savagely. *"Throw the goddamn ball!"*

But their entire team had gathered around the pitcher-hero, slapping at his back, clutching and tearing at his triumph. They lifted him to their shoulders to cart him off the field. Mike could only watch them, letting their spirited laughter bite into him, as if it were aimed at him. He hated them now—the lucky sonofabitchin' pitcher, the lousy jockeys. He stared at them furiously, trying to smear them with his hatred, hoping to provoke one more derisive catcall that might unleash his rage and goad him to attack them all. But they never saw him. Finally, he turned away from the plate for the long walk in.

He moved toward the bedlam of the stands now, and the screaming faces. A moment ago they were all yours, Mike. They were yelling for you. He looked into the dejection of his dugout and his naked failure came home to him. In a rage, he pulled his bat back, ready to fling it into the crowd, to scatter them and shut them up. But somehow he knew better. He held on.

In the stands behind the dugout, they were waiting for him, the harsh faces of the two-bit punks who wallow in the luxury of a last kick at the guy who is down.

"Kutner . . . you stink!"

"You're a bum."

"Ooh . . . what a bum!"

He bristled at their hoots and sneering laughter and wondered how he could get through that gantlet. He gripped his bat tightly as he approached them, trying not to hurry his walk.

"What a star! Where'd they pick you up?"

"Back to the minors, Kutner."

Their stale-beer spittle sprayed into his hot face. A rough hand reached over and stole his cap from his head.

"You won't need this no more."

"Naah. Back to the bush leagues!"

He stopped on the bottom step and looked up at them. They taunted him, waving his cap just out of reach. Inside him, suddenly, the dam burst—the dam of repression and control and patience. He flung himself toward the cap, over the dugout and into the stands. In a second he caught the terrified heckler and wrenched the cap from him. With his other hand, he started smashing at him in a wild silent fury.

At once the crowd dispersed, scrambling over each other and the seats like scared chickens. Out of danger themselves, they watched in terror. The ushers and cops came for him, four of them pulling him off, trying to hold him still, for his rage was only partly spent.

They carried him down the steps again, into the dim corridors below the stands, and stood him hard against the wall, just outside the locker room.

"Take it easy, rookie," a cop said, his hands tight on Mike's wrist.

Mike breathed heavily, and looked through the door at the ball-players inside. He saw them, glum and silent on their stools, unlacing their shoes, quietly passing around smokes and beer. As he felt the heavy restraint of the cops, he saw Red Schalk amongst them, close to the door, and their eyes met. His arms were pinned to his side and he tried to wriggle loose.

"Shut the door!" he hollered suddenly. *"Shut the friggen door!"*

"Easy, rookie, easy," he heard again. "That ain't the way for a major leaguer to act."

The words knifed into him, twisting into his thoughts, and he lowered his eyes from the redhead's. He stared blankly at the floor, wanting to cry. There was a pain in his chest as though a ton of rocks were pressing on him.

It was time to stop struggling.

He heard the door of the locker room close, and looked up to see Durkin Fain standing in front of it. The old man turned to one of the guards and nodded.

"That's all right," he said. "He'll be O.K. now."

One at a time they released him, furtively, anticipating some renewed outburst. But Mike just stood there, without even moving his arms, oblivious to his freedom. Gradually, as he subsided, he began to cry. As the tears came, the muscles in his face did not move or alter his expression. It was as if he did not believe he was crying at all.

It's all right to cry. Nothing much matters. Go ahead and cry. The whole damn day is unreal anyway—a crazy, wild, sweating dream. The dream you never remember. What's happened? Why is everything so different?

You're all washed up, that's why. You're empty. There's nothing left in your guts to drive you.

Cry, Mike. You've finally blown off the lid. Cry. No one cares if you cry.

He stood against the wall, letting the tears come, a flood of anguish and bitterness and despair. When it was spent, he took off his glasses and brushed his uniform sleeve across his face. His chest was heaving, he was weak and tired. But somehow, in a way he did not understand, he felt very much relieved. He nodded at Durkin Fain and opened the door to the locker room. Together, they went in.

The players looked up from their quiet dressing and nodded at him. They had stripped and showered and for the most part, he knew, cleansed themselves of the transient pain of defeat. There would be another crucial game tomorrow. He sat in front of his locker, staring at his feet. The late afternoon sun pouring in the window glistened off the metal of his spikes. Like a jewel, he thought. He flexed the muscles of his feet, enjoying the snugness of his shoes. No other shoes could be so comfortable. Whenever he put on spikes, he wanted to run. His whole body was tired now, but not his feet. They never grew tired in spikes.

Behind him, he heard the door open and shut. By the sudden stillness around him, he could guess who it was, but he chose not to turn. He felt as if he might have been waiting for this.

"Where's Tracy? Where is he?"

Mike listened to the coarse, old voice, and he repeated the words to himself with imitated inflections. He couldn't answer the question. Tracy was probably taking his shower.

No one bothered to answer. The voice defied their silence and bellowed on.

"Tell him to use Hahn tomorrow! Tell him to shove his goddamn logic up his butt!"

And the door slammed shut again.

Tell him to use Hahn! Not Kutner. Hahn. Kutner was a mistake. He folds up like a scared kid. Strictly minor league stuff. Like I always said, goddammit; just like I've said for years.

Yeah. You're Jim Mellon. You're always right.

He leaned over now, ready to unlace his shoes, depressed by the fullness of his failure. Suddenly, he stopped and rose to his feet, to stand again on spikes, trying to recapture, if just for a moment, the joy of his love for baseball. Then he sat and took them off.

He heard his name called from behind and turned toward it. Durkin Fain laid his hand on Mike's shoulder.

His tone was almost apologetic. "I'm sorry, son."

Mike shrugged. "Don't be, Mr. Fain. A man makes his choice. He has to take his chances." And he remembered the words of his wife. "There are no guarantees, none that I know of."

Fain nodded. "By God, that's true." He shook his head. "But, still. . . ."

Mike began to strip. He did not want to talk about it now. "Right now," he said, trying to smile, "I'm gonna take me the goddamn longest shower in history."

He let the hot water soak into him. He was too exhausted to think, to take stock of what this afternoon had meant to him. He was dimly aware that at some point he would have to make a decision. But he let himself alone, simply showering for a while, holding his humiliation at a distance. He had never admitted he was capable of such complete failure. He had never imagined facing its sickening consequences.

Instinctively, he felt that he was different now, a different man. He had been slapped down hard, and it didn't matter any more that he had succeeded year after year all the way up to the end. What mattered was that the assumption of his inevitable final triumph had been shattered. He could not keep on pushing knowing this to be true.

He turned his face to the hot, stinging spray, wanting to wash away irrevocably the marks of his grief. He thought quickly of that crying jag, the almost childish breakdown, and felt shame. Deep within him, he guessed, he had been pitying himself with those tears. Perhaps he'd been saving them up, actually suspecting he would lose this bitter struggle in the end.

Now it was all over. He was through. The gate had slammed shut in front of him, and he himself decided it was for the last time. It was final. Complete. To add substance to his thought, he said the words out loud: "It's all over! It's all over!" And he smiled, for he could feel himself coming up, off the bottom.

Gradually he eased the temperature of the water to cold, and he stood for a moment, stoically, under the fierce needles of icy water.

By the time he had finished dressing, the locker room had cleared out. He stood in front of his locker, reluctant to close it. He picked up his spikes and clapped them together, trying to remove the last cakes of dirt. Then, gingerly, he tied the laces together, and just to see how it felt, he hung them up on a hook.

Behind him he heard the old man, and he turned to see the look of apprehension on Durkin Fain's face.

Mike smiled and extended his hand. "I guess I'll say so long, Mr. Fain."

Durkin Fain grabbed his hand. He nodded, a smile forming on his lips.

"I think I'll have that cigar now, Mike."

Mike watched him light up, enjoying the way Fain handled a cigar. In all his life, he had never seen any smoker caress a cigar with the appreciation that lent such style and quality to smoking. This is Durkin Fain, Mike realized, the number one baseball scout of his time. A time long past. Fain, for whom scouting was an art. Fain, whose only rule of judgment was pure talent, whose only conformity was to his own set of high standards.

Mike said finally, "I'm proud that it was you, Mr. Fain. . . ."

The old man interrupted him with a smile.

"Thank you, son. You got a right to be proud for more than that. You ain't a failure, no matter what they say. I can tell you that. You ain't a failure."

Mike swallowed heavily.

"Goodbye, Mr. Fain. And thanks for the sixteen years."

From the locker-room door he turned again to look back. He saw the old scout on the bench by a pile of dirty towels, lost in a cloud of smoke. Mike shut the door and turned into the shadowy corridors for the winding passage to the street.

The musty smell changed the direction of his thinking. Yes. Laura. Laura would be there by the players' entrance, he knew. Laura the beautiful. Laura the loyal. Laura the wife. "I love you, darling," he said out loud, just to hear the sound of it. Oh, I love you for everything that's happened to us. For all the lousy years. For sharing them as if there was something special in it for you.

And suddenly, he couldn't wait to see her.

He hurried up the last ramp, feeling a quickening anticipation, as though he'd been away for a long, long time. He wanted to take her in his arms, to tell her what had happened to him, to make her know, at last, that he was her husband and life was for the both of them.

Mr. Fain had said it. "It ain't too late, son. It ain't never too late."

He pushed through the big door and into the street, reaching for her with his eyes as he blinked in the sudden light. But she wasn't there. There was no one there.

He waited for a moment, scanning the streets for her, feeling a sudden panic. Then his eye picked out the neon-lit bar on the far corner, and he knew for sure that he would find her there.

He realized then how long she must have been waiting, how crushed she must have been by the game and what had followed. For Laura, he knew, this would be old hat . . . failure piled upon tired, never-ending failure. She would have prepared herself, as usual, for the wreck of a stubborn man chasing the rainbow with a tin can tied to his tail, over and over, round and round. The man who never gets dizzy, at least not in public.

No, Laura, no more. No more. I'm through with it. I'm free of it! I want *you* only, and we'll begin together this time. Just like you've wanted it for years, darling.

He tore across the street and into the cluttered haze of the bar. She was there, sitting in a lonely corner booth with her hands on a tall glass. He went to her with his gathering tears, bursting with the love and gratitude in his heart.

Everything is all right! Laura, darling, it's all right! Look at me, darling. It's all over. Look at the way I feel.

He saw her look up dejectedly as he came to her, ready to cry out of habit, out of the layer upon layer of frustration that had made up their lives. She almost began, but he pulled her up with his smile, and she found her way into his eager arms.

For a while, they were unable to control the wonderful laughter that poured out of them.

Russell Baker

Love Me, Love My Bear

In 1991, Yale University gave Russell Baker, the New York Times *columnist and peerless humorist, an honorary degree for employing "a subtle mind, and an elegant style, and a piercing wit" in his writings. All of these weapons are gainfully employed by Baker in this mock-interview with the czar of czars of the New York Yankees, George Steinbrenner, on a subject that was always close to Steinbrenner's heart—the art of firing.*

have never been able to fire anybody and, as a result, promotions have always passed me by. This is why I sought out George Steinbrenner, the owner of the New York Yankees and probably the most successful firer in the annals of unemployment.

Naturally, I had expected to meet an ogre, and, so, was delighted by the charm with which he received my proposal. I began by confessing that it was unusual. "Mr. Steinbrenner," I explained, "I want to study firing and I want to study under the best man in the field. Will you help me learn?"

Instead of the tirade I anticipated, these words produced a strange silence during which his eyes moistened and he struggled to hold back emotion. At length he said, "The best. . . . Nobody's ever said anything like that about me before."

"Oh, you have a good heart, Mr. Steinbrenner. I can see that. I know you'll help me, sir." He dabbed at his eyes with a handkerchief.

"I haven't been all torn up inside like this since the time they took away my teddy bear," he said, picking up the phone and asking his receptionist to step in.

"Yes, Mr. Steinbrenner?" said the receptionist.

"You're fired," he said.

"May I ask why?"

"For letting in people who remind me of the time they took my teddy bear away. I can't run a baseball team while I'm wondering whatever happened to that dear old teddy bear of mine."

When the receptionist had gone, I expressed admiration for the ease and rapidity with which he had conducted the firing. "Why, the receptionist didn't even call you a brute or an ingrate," I said.

"She didn't dare," said Mr. Steinbrenner. "If she had, she would have blown her chances of managing the Yankees."

I couldn't believe that, after firing her from a receptionist's job, he would hire her back to manage the team.

"Why not?" he asked. "At the rate I fire managers, I can't afford to be picky. Which reminds me—"

He dialed the phone. "I'm calling a sportswriter pal," he whispered. Then: "This is George, Sol. . . . Yeah, terrible about that last road trip. I've got it from the horse's mouth the Yankees are looking for a new manager. . . . Don't quote me."

He hung up. I felt radiant with hero worship. Mr. Steinbrenner was not only going to fire the manager; he was letting me know how he did it. "That will be headlines in the paper tomorrow," I said.

"You bet your sweet patootie," he said. "It'll put the Yankees back on page one, stir up the fans, get the old turnstiles clicking faster. When you fire somebody, son, fire with a purpose. It's good for the box office."

"You're the greatest, Mr. Steinbrenner."

"Now don't go getting me all choked up again," he said.

I saw this was the moment to push my case. "If it's not asking too much," I said, "could I come in some day and fire somebody for you while you watched me to make sure I'm doing it right?"

He rose from his desk and embraced me. "I like you, kid. You could be good, really good," he said. "I'm putting you on the payroll as junior assistant in charge of minor firings. Be in here tomorrow morning early and I'll let you fire a couple of peanut vendors."

I was too overcome to trust my voice, so I merely nodded, sniffled, and moved to the door.

"Before you go," he said.

"Yes."

"About this manager I've got to fire—do you know who's managing the Yankees this week?"

Not wanting to blow my big chance by revealing that I didn't follow baseball, I gave him the name of the only baseball manager I could remember. "It's Earl Weaver," I said.

As I left, he had Weaver on the telephone. "Earl, baby," he was saying, "you're through. Drop by the cashier's window and pick up your paycheck. . . ."

I reported early next morning to fire peanut vendors. Mr. Steinbrenner led in the first, then stood behind me to observe my technique. The peanut vendor was a small, cuddly fellow with plump, round cheeks and a great deal of hair.

"Vendor," I snarled, and then paused.

"Yes sir. Bag of peanuts, sir?"

"What are you waiting for?" asked Mr. Steinbrenner. "Give him the ax."

"I can't," I said.

"Can't! Why not?"

"He reminds me of my dear old teddy bear," I said.

I heard Mr. Steinbrenner snuffle and suppress a sob behind me. Then: "Nobody can talk about teddy bears around me and get away with it," he said in a voice hoarse with sorrow. "You're fired."

I was leaving the Stadium when a guard said Mr. Steinbrenner wanted me on the phone. "Give me your phone number, kid," he said. "I'm going to need some new managers next spring."

James Baldwin

The Fight: Patterson vs. Liston

The night before the 1962 heavyweight championship fight, Hugh Hefner entertained a crowd at the Playboy mansion in Chicago, with its indoor swimming pool and ornate fittings, and a scramble of "bunnies." In the assemblage were writers covering the fight, not beat reporters but people like Norman Mailer, Budd Schulberg, Gay Talese, and James Baldwin, who was working for Playboy. *Baldwin came up to an acquaintance, a brilliant smile lighting up his storm-tossed face, and said, "Why am I here? I don't belong." Baldwin, the author of such books as* Go Tell It on the Mountain, Nobody Knows My Name, *and* The Fire Next Time, *books that were "perfectly placed," wrote one critic, "often with resounding significance," had never written about sports, but he did belong. In this piece, Baldwin, who died in 1990, writes, "The world of sports, in fact, is far from being as simple as the sports pages often make it sound." Which, of course, is the point of this book, too.*

We, the writers—a word I am using in its most primitive sense—arrived in Chicago about ten days before the baffling, bruising, an unbelievable two minutes and six seconds at Comiskey Park. We will get to all that later. I know nothing whatever about the Sweet Science or the Cruel Profession or the Poor Boy's Game. But I know a lot about pride, the poor boy's pride, since that's my story and will, in some way, probably, be my end.

There was something vastly unreal about the entire bit, as though we had all come to Chicago to make various movies and then spent all our time visiting the other fellow's set—on which no cameras were rolling. Dispatches went out every day, typewriters clattered, phones rang; each day, carloads of journalists invaded the Patterson or Liston camps, hung around until Patterson or Liston appeared; asked lame, inane questions, always the same questions, went away again, back to those telephones and typewriters; and informed a waiting, anxious world, or at least a waiting, anxious editor, what Patterson and Liston had said or done that day. It was insane and desperate, since neither of them ever really *did* anything. There wasn't anything for them *to* do, except train for the fight. But there aren't many ways to describe a fighter in training—it's muscle and sweat and grace, it's the same thing over and over—and since neither Patterson nor Liston were doing much boxing, there couldn't be any interesting thumbnail sketches of their sparring partners. The "feud" between Patterson and Liston was as limp and tasteless as British roast lamb. Patterson is really far too much of a gentleman to descend to feuding with anyone, and I simply never believed, especially after talking with Liston, that he had the remotest grudge against Patterson. So there we were, hanging around, twiddling our thumbs, drinking Scotch, and telling stories, and trying to make copy out of nothing. And waiting, of course, for the Big Event, which would justify the monumental amounts of time, money, and energy which were being expended in Chicago.

Neither Patterson nor Liston have the *color,* or the instinct for drama which is possessed to such a superlative degree by the marvelous Archie Moore, and the perhaps less marvelous, but certainly vocal, and rather charming Cassius Clay. In the matter of color, a word which I am not now using in its racial sense, the Press Room far outdid the training camps. There were not only the sports writers, who had come, as I say, from all over the world: there were also the boxing greats, scrubbed and sharp and easygoing, Rocky Marciano, Barney Ross, Ezzard Charles, and the King, Joe Louis, and Ingemar Johansson, who arrived just a little before the fight and did not impress me as being easygoing at all. Archie Moore's word for him is "desperate," and he did not say this with any affection. There were the ruined boxers, stopped by an unlucky glove too early in their careers, who seemed to be treated with the tense and embarrassed affection reserved for faintly unsavory relatives, who were being used, some of them, as sparring partners. There were the managers and trainers, who, in public anyway, and with the exception of Cus D'Amato, seemed to have taken, many years ago, the vow of silence. There were people whose functions were mysterious indeed, certainly unnamed, possibly unnamable, and, one felt, probably, if undefinably, criminal. There were hangers-ons and protégés, a singer somewhere around, whom I didn't meet, owned by Patterson, and another singer owned by someone else—who couldn't sing, everyone agreed, but who didn't have to, being so loaded with personality—and there were some improbable-looking women, turned out, it would seem, by a machine shop, who didn't seem, really, to walk or talk, but rather to gleam, click, and glide, with an almost soundless meshing of gears. There were some pretty incredible girls, too, at the parties, impeccably blank and beautiful and rather incredibly vulnerable. There were the parties and the post mortems and the gossip and speculations and recollections and the liquor and the anecdotes, and dawn coming up to find you leaving somebody else's house or somebody else's room or the Playboy Club; and Jimmy Cannon, Red Smith, Milton Gross, Sandy Grady, and A. J. Liebling; and Norman Mailer, Gerald Kersh, Budd Schulberg, and Ben Hecht—who arrived, however, only for the fight and must have been left with a great deal of time on his hands—and Gay Talese (of the *Times*), and myself. Hanging around in Chicago, hanging on the lightest word, or action, of Floyd Patterson and Sonny Liston.

I am not an *aficionado* of the ring, and haven't been since Joe Louis lost his crown—*he* was the last great fighter for me—and so I can't really make comparisons with previous events of this kind. But neither, it soon struck me, could anybody else. Patterson was, in effect, the *moral* favorite—people *wanted* him to win, either because they liked him, though many people didn't, or because they felt that his victory would be salutary for boxing and that Liston's victory would be a disaster. But no one could be said to be enthusiastic about either man's record in the ring. The general feeling seemed to be that Patterson had never been tested, that he was the champion, in effect, by default; though, on the other hand, everyone attempted to avoid the conclusion that boxing had fallen on evil days and that Patterson had fought no worthy fighters because there were none. The desire to avoid speculating too deeply on the present state and the probable future of boxing was responsible, I think, for some very odd and stammering talk about Patterson's per- sonality. (This led Red Smith to declare that he didn't feel that sports writers had any business trying to be psychiatrists, and that he was just going to write down who hit whom, how hard, and where, and the hell with why.) And there was very sharp disapproval of the way he has handled his career, since he has taken over most of D'Amato's functions as a manager, and is clearly under no one's orders but his own. "In the old days," someone complained, "the manager told the fighter what to do, and he did it. You didn't have to futz around with the guy's *tem-*

perament, for Christ's sake." Never before had any of the sports writers been compelled to deal directly with the fighter instead of with his manager, and all of them seemed baffled by this necessity and many were resentful. I don't know how they got along with D'Amato when he was running the entire show—D'Amato can certainly not be described as either simple or direct—but at least the figure of D'Amato was familiar and operated to protect them from the oddly compelling and touching figure of Floyd Patterson, who is quite probably the least likely fighter in the history of the sport. And I think that part of the resentment he arouses is due to the fact that he brings to what is thought of—quite erroneously—as a simple activity a terrible note of complexity. This is his personal style, a style which strongly suggests that most un-American of attributes, privacy, the will to privacy; and my own guess is that he is still relentlessly, painfully shy—he lives gallantly with his scars, but not all of them have healed—and while he has found a way to master this, he has found no way to hide it; as, for example, another miraculously tough and tender man, Miles Davis, has managed to do. Miles's disguise would certainly never fool anybody with sense, but it keeps a lot of people away, and that's the point. But Patterson, tough and proud and beautiful, is also terribly vulnerable, and looks it.

I met him, luckily for me, with Gay Talese, whom he admires and trusts, I say luckily because I'm not a very aggressive journalist, don't know enough about boxing to know which questions to ask, and am simply not able to ask a man questions about his private life. If Gay had not been there, I am not certain how I would ever have worked up my courage to say anything to Floyd Patterson—especially after having sat through, or suffered, the first, for me, of many press conferences. I only sat through two with Patterson, silently, and in the back—he, poor man, had to go through it every day, sometimes twice a day. And if I don't know enough about boxing to know which questions to ask, I must say that the boxing experts are not one whit more imaginative, though they were, I thought, sometimes rather more insolent. It was a curious insolence, though, veiled, tentative, uncertain—they couldn't be sure that Floyd wouldn't give them as good as he got. And this led, again, to that curious resentment I mentioned earlier, for they were forced, perpetually, to speculate about the man instead of the boxer. It doesn't appear to have occurred yet to many members of the press that one of the reasons their relations with Floyd are so frequently strained·is that he has no reason, on any level, to trust them, and no reason to believe that they would be capable of hearing what he had to say, even if he could say it. Life's far from being as simple as most sports writers would like to have it. The world of sports, in fact, is far from being as simple as the sports pages often make it sound.

Gay and I drove out, ahead of all the other journalists, in a Hertz car, and got to the camp at Elgin while Floyd was still lying down. The camp was very quiet, bucolic, really, when we arrived; set in the middle of small, rolling hills; four or five buildings, a tethered goat—the camp mascot; a small green tent containing a Spartan cot; lots of cars. "They're very car-conscious here," someone said of Floyd's small staff of trainers and helpers. "Most of them have two cars." We ran into some of them standing around and talking on the grounds, and Buster Watson, a close friend of Floyd's, stocky, dark, and able, led us into the Press Room. Floyd's camp was actually Marycrest Farm, the twin of a Chicago settlement house, which works, on a smaller scale but in somewhat the same way, with disturbed and deprived children, as does Floyd's New York alma mater, the Wiltwyck School for Boys. It is a Catholic institution—Patterson is a converted Catholic—and the interior walls of the building in which the press conferences took place were decorated with vivid mosaics, executed by the children in colored beans, of various biblical events. There was an extraordinarily effective crooked cross, executed in charred wood, hanging high on one of the walls. There were two doors to the building in which the two press agents worked, one saying *Caritas,* the other saying *Veritas.* It seemed an incongruous setting for the life being lived there, and the event being prepared, but Ted Carroll, the Negro press agent, a tall man with white hair and a knowledgeable, weary, gentle face, told me that the camp was like the man. "The man lives a secluded life. He's like this place—peaceful and far away." It was not all that peaceful, of course, except naturally; it was otherwise menaced and inundated by hordes of human beings, from small boys, who wanted to be boxers, to old men who remembered Jack Dempsey as a kid. The signs on the road, pointing the way to Floyd Patterson's training camp, were perpetually carried away by souvenir hunters. ("At first," Ted Carroll said, "we were worried that maybe they were carrying them away for another reason—you know, the usual hassle—but no, they just want to put them in the rumpus room.") We walked about with Ted Carroll for a while and he pointed out to us the house, white, with green shutters, somewhat removed from the camp and on a hill, in which Floyd Patterson lived. He was resting now, and the press conference had been called for three o'clock, which was nearly three hours away. But he would be working out before the conference.

Gay and I left Ted and wandered close to the house. I looked at the ring, which had been set up on another hill near the house, and examined the tent. Gay knocked lightly on Floyd's door. There was no answer, but Gay said that the radio was on. We sat down in the sun, near the ring, and speculated on Floyd's training habits, which kept him away from his family for such long periods of time.

Presently, here he came across the grass, loping, rather, head down, with a small, tight smile on his lips. This smile seems always to be there when he is facing people and disappears only when he begins to be comfortable. Then he can laugh, as I never heard him laugh at a press conference, and the face which he watches so carefully in public is then, as it were, permitted to be its boyish and rather surprisingly zestful self. He greeted Gay, and took sharp, covert notice of me, seeming to decide that if I were with Gay, I was probably all right. We followed him into the gym, in which a large sign faced us, saying *So we being many are one body in Christ.* He went through his workout, methodically, rigorously, pausing every now and again to disagree with his trainer, Dan Florio, about the time—he insisted that Dan's stopwatch was unreliable—or to tell Buster that there weren't enough towels, to ask that the windows be closed. "You threw a good right hand that time," Dan Florio said; and, later, "Keep the right hand *up. Up!*" "We got a floor scale that's no good," Floyd said, cheerfully. "Sometimes I weigh two hundred, sometimes I weigh 'eighty-eight." And we watched him jump rope, which he must do according to some music in his head, very beautiful and gleaming and far away, like a boy saint helplessly dancing and seen through the steaming windows of a storefront church.

We followed him into the house when the workout was over, and sat in the kitchen and drank tea; he drank chocolate. Gay knew that I was somewhat tense as to how to make contact with Patterson—my own feeling was that he had a tough enough row to hoe, and that everybody should just leave him alone; how would *I* like it if I were forced to answer inane questions every day concerning the progress of my work?—and told Patterson about some of the things I'd written. But Patterson hadn't heard of me, or read anything of mine. Gay's explanation, though, caused him to look directly at me, and he said, "I've seen you someplace before. I don't know where, but I know I've seen you." I hadn't seen him before, except once, with Liston, in the Commissioner's office, when there had been a spirited fight concerning the construction of Liston's boxing gloves, which were "just about as flat as the back of my hand," according to a sports writer, "just like wearing no gloves at all." I felt certain, considering the number of people and the tension in that room, that he could not have seen me *then*—but we do know some of the same people, and have walked very often on the same streets. Gay suggested that he had seen me on TV. I had hoped that the contact would have turned out to be more personal, like a mutual friend or some activity connected with the Wiltwyck School, but Floyd now remembered the subject of the TV debate he had seen—the race problem, of course—and his face lit up. "I *knew* I'd seen you somewhere!" he said, triumphantly, and looked at me for a moment with the same brotherly pride I felt—and feel—in him.

By now he was, with good grace but a certain tense resignation, preparing himself for the press conference. I gather that there are many people who enjoy meeting the press—and most of them, in fact, were presently in Chicago—but Floyd Patterson is not one of them. I think he hates being put on exhibition, he doesn't believe it is real; while he is terribly conscious of the responsibility imposed on him by the title which he held, he is also afflicted with enough imagination to be baffled by his position. And he is far from having acquired the stony and ruthless perception which will allow him to stand at once within and without his fearful notoriety. Anyway, we trailed over to the building in which the press waited, and Floyd's small, tight, shy smile was back.

But he has learned, though it must have cost him a great deal, how to handle himself. He was asked about his weight, his food, his measurements, his morale. He had been in training for nearly six months ("Is that necessary?" "I just like to do it that way"), had boxed, at this point, about 162 rounds. This was compared to his condition at the time of the first fight with Ingemar Johansson. "Do you believe that you were overtrained for that fight?" "Anything I say now would sound like an excuse." But, later, "I was careless—not overconfident, but careless." He had allowed himself to be surprised by Ingemar's aggressiveness. "Did you and D'Amato fight over your decision to fight Liston?" The weary smile played at the corner of Floyd's mouth, and though he was looking directly at his interlocutors, his eyes were veiled. "No." Long pause. "Cus knows that I do what I want to do—ultimately, he accepted it." Was he surprised by Liston's hostility? No. Perhaps it had made him a bit more determined. Had he anything against Liston personally? "No. I'm the champion and I want to remain the champion." Had he and D'Amato ever disagreed before? "Not in relation to my opponents." Had he heard it said that, as a fighter, he lacked viciousness? "Whoever said that should see the fights I've won without being vicious." And why was he fighting Liston? "Well," said Patterson, "it was my decision to take the fight. You gentlemen disagreed, but you were the ones who placed him in the Number One position, so I felt that it was only right. Liston's criminal record is behind him, not before him." "Do you feel that you've been accepted as a champion?" Floyd smiled more tightly than ever and turned toward the questioner. "No," he said. Then, "Well, I have to be accepted as the champion—but maybe not a good one." "Why do you say," someone else asked, "that the opportunity to become a great champion will never arise?" "Because," said Floyd, patiently, "you gentlemen will never let it arise." Someone asked him about his experiences when boxing in Europe—what kind of reception had he enjoyed? Much greater and much warmer than here, he finally admitted, but added, with a weary and humorous caution, "I don't want to say anything derogatory about the United States. I am satisfied." The press seemed rather to flinch from the purport of this grim and vivid little joke, and switched to the subject of Liston again. Who was most in awe of whom? Floyd had no idea, he said, but, "Liston's confidence is on the surface. Mine is within."

And so it seemed to be indeed, as, later, Gay and I walked with him through the flat, midwestern landscape. It was not exactly that he was less tense—I think that he is probably always tense, and it is that, and not his glass chin, or a lack of stamina, which is his real liability as a fighter—but he was tense in a more private, more bearable way. The fight was very much on his mind, of course, and we talked of the strange battle about the boxing gloves, and the Commissioner's impenetrable and apparent bias toward Liston, though the difference in the construction of the gloves, and the possible meaning of this difference, was clear to everyone. The gloves had been made by two different firms, which was not the usual procedure, and, though they were the same standard eight-ounce weight, Floyd's gloves were the familiar, puffy shape, with most of the weight of the padding over the fist, and Liston's were extraordinarily slender, with most of the weight of the padding over the wrist. But we didn't talk only of the fight, and I can't now remember all the things we *did* talk about. I mainly remember Floyd's voice, going cheerfully on and on, and the way his face kept changing, and the way he laughed; I remember the glimpse I got of him then, a man more complex than he was yet equipped to know, a hero for many children who were still trapped where he had been, who might not have survived without the ring, and who yet, oddly, did not really seem to belong there. I dismissed my dim speculations, that afternoon, as sentimental inaccuracies, rooted in my lack of knowledge of the boxing world, and corrupted with a guilty chauvinism. But now I wonder. He told us that his wife was coming in for the fight, against his will "in order," he said, indescribably, "to *console* me if—" and he made, at last, a gesture with his hand, downward.

Liston's camp was very different, an abandoned racetrack in, or called, Aurora Downs, with wire gates and a uniformed cop, who lets you in, or doesn't. I had simply given up the press conference bit, since they didn't teach me much, and I couldn't ask those questions. Gay Talese couldn't help me with Liston, and this left me floundering on my own until Sandy Grady called up Liston's manager, Jack Nilon, and arranged for me to see Liston for a few minutes alone the next day. Liston's camp was far more outspoken concerning Liston's attitude toward the press than Patterson's. Liston didn't like most of the press and most of them didn't like him. But I didn't, myself, see any reason why he *should* like them, or pretend to—they had certainly never been very nice to him, and I was sure that he saw in them merely some more ignorant, uncaring white people, who, no matter how fine we cut it, had helped to cause him so much grief. And this impression was confirmed by reports from people who *did* get along with him—Wendell Phillips and Bob Teague, who are both Negroes, but rather rare and salty types, and Sandy Grady, who is not a Negro, but is certainly rare, and very probably salty. I got the impression from them that Liston was perfectly willing to take people as they were, if they would do the same for him. Again, I was not particularly appalled by his criminal background, believing, rightly or wrongly, that I probably knew more about the motives and even the necessity of this career than most of the white press could. The only relevance Liston's—presumably previous—associations should have been allowed to have, it seemed to me, concerned the possible effect of these on the future of boxing. Well, while the air was thick with rumor and gospel on this subject, I really cannot go into it without risking, at the very least, being sued for libel; and so, one of the most fascinating aspects of the Chicago story will have to be left in the dark. But the Sweet Science is not, in any case, really so low on shady types as to be forced to depend on Liston. The question is to what extent Liston is prepared to cooperate with whatever powers of darkness there are in boxing; and the extent of his cooperation, we must suppose, must depend, at least partly, on the extent of his awareness. So that there is nothing unique about the position in which he now finds himself and nothing unique about the speculation which now surrounds him.

I got to his camp at about two o'clock one afternoon. Time was running out, the fight was not more than three days away, and the atmosphere in the camp was, at once, listless and electric. Nilon looked as though he had not slept and would not sleep for days, and everyone else rather gave the impression that they wished they could—except for three handsome Negro ladies, related, I supposed, to Mrs. Liston, who sat, rather self-consciously, on the porch of the largest building on the grounds. They may have felt as I did, that training camps are like a theater before the curtain goes up, and if you don't have any function in it, you're probably in the way.

Liston, as we all know, is an enormous man, but surprisingly trim. I had already seen him work out, skipping rope to a record of "Night Train," and, while he wasn't nearly, for me, as moving as Patterson skipping rope in silence, it was still a wonderful sight to see. The press has really maligned Liston very cruelly, I think. He is far from stupid; is not, in fact, stupid at all. And, while there is a great deal of violence in him, I sensed no cruelty at all. On the contrary, he reminded me of big, black men I have known who acquired the reputation of being tough in order to conceal the fact that they weren't hard. Anyone who cared to could turn them into taffy.

Anyway, I liked him, liked him very much. He sat opposite me at the table, sideways, head down, waiting for the blow: for Liston knows, as only the inarticulately suffering can, just how inarticulate he is. But let me clarify that: I say suffering because it seems to me that he has suffered a great deal. It is in his face, in the silence of that face, and in the curiously distant light in the eyes—a light which rarely signals because there have been so few answering signals. And when I say inarticulate, I really do not mean to suggest that he does not know how to talk. He is inarticulate in the way we all are when more has happened to us than we know how to express; and inarticulate in a particularly Negro way—he has a long tale to tell which no one wants to hear. I said, "I can't ask you any questions because everything's been asked. Perhaps I'm only here, really, to say that I wish you well." And this was true, even though I wanted Patterson to win. Anyway, I'm glad I said it because he looked at me then, really for the first time, and he talked to me for a little while.

And what had hurt him most, somewhat to my surprise, was not the general press reaction to him, but the Negro reaction. "Colored people," he said, with great sorrow, "say they don't want their children to look up to me. Well, they ain't teaching their children to look up to

Martin Luther King, either." There was a pause. "I wouldn't be no bad example if I was up there. I could tell a lot of those children what they need to know—because—I passed that way. I could make them *listen.*" And he spoke a little of what he would like to do for young Negro boys and girls, trapped in those circumstances which so nearly defeated himself and Floyd, and from which neither can yet be said to have recovered. "I tell you one thing, though," he said, "if I was up there, I wouldn't bite my tongue." I could certainly believe that. And we discussed the segregation issue, and the role, in it, of those prominent Negroes who find him so distasteful. "I would never," he said, "go against my brother—we got to learn to stop fighting among our own." He lapsed into silence again. "They said they didn't want me to have the title. They didn't say that about Johansson." "They" were the Negroes. "*They* ought to know why I got some of the bum raps I got." But he was not suggesting that they were *all* bum raps. His wife came over, a very pretty woman, seemed to gather in a glance how things were going, and sat down. We talked for a little while of matters entirely unrelated to the fight, and then it was time for his workout, and I left. I felt terribly ambivalent, as many Negroes do these days, since we are all trying to decide, in one way or another, which attitude, in our terrible American dilemma, is the most effective: the disciplined sweetness of Floyd, or the outspoken intransigence of Liston. *If I was up there, I wouldn't bite my tongue.* And Liston is a man aching for respect and responsibility. Sometimes we grow into our responsibilities and sometimes, of course, we fail them.

I left for the fight full of a weird and violent depression, which I traced partly to fatigue—it had been a pretty grueling time—partly to the fact that I had bet more money than I should have—on Patterson —and partly to the fact that *I* had had a pretty definitive fight with someone with whom I had hoped to be friends. And I was depressed about Liston's bulk and force and his twenty-five-pound weight advantage. I was afraid that Patterson might lose, and I really didn't want to see that. And it wasn't that I didn't like Liston. I just felt closer to Floyd.

I was sitting between Norman Mailer and Ben Hecht. Hecht felt about the same way that I did, and we agreed that if Patterson didn't get "stopped," as Hecht put it, "by a baseball bat," in the very beginning—if he could carry Liston for five or six rounds—he might very well hold the title. We didn't pay an awful lot of attention to the preliminaries—or I didn't; Hecht did; I watched the ball park fill with people and listened to the vendors and the jokes and the speculations: and watched the clock.

From my notes: Liston entered the ring to an almost complete silence. Someone called his name, he looked over, smiled, and winked. Floyd entered, and got a hand. But he looked terribly small next to Liston, and my depression deepened.

My notes again: Archie Moore entered the ring, wearing an opera cape. Cassius Clay, in black tie, and as insolent as ever. Mickey Allen sang "The Star-Spangled Banner." When Liston was introduced, some people boo'd—they cheered for Floyd, and I think I know how this made Liston feel. It promised, really, to be one of the worst fights in history.

Well, I was wrong, it was scarcely a fight at all, and I can't but wonder who on earth will come to see the rematch, if there is one. Floyd seemed all right to me at first. He had planned for a long fight, and seemed to be feeling out his man. But Liston got him with a few bad body blows, and a few bad blows to the head. And no one agrees with me on this, but, at one moment, when Floyd lunged for Liston's belly— looking, it must be said, like an amateur, wildly flailing—it seemed to me that some unbearable tension in him broke, that he lost his head. And, in fact, I nearly screamed, "Keep your head, baby!" but it was really too late. Liston got him with a left, and Floyd went down. I could not believe it. I couldn't hear the count and though Hecht said, "It's over," and picked up his coat, and left, I remained standing, staring at the ring, and only conceded that the fight was really over when two other boxers entered the ring. Then I wandered out of the ball park, almost in tears. I met an old colored man at one of the exits, who said to me, cheerfully, "I've been robbed," and we talked about it for a while. We started walking through the crowds and A. J. Liebling, behind us, tapped me on the shoulder and we went off to a bar, to mourn the very possible death of boxing, and to have a drink, with love, for Floyd.

Roger Bannister

The Four-Minute Mile

"Failure is as exciting to watch as success, provided the effort is absolutely genuine and complete. But the spectators fail to understand—and how can they know?—the mental agony through which an athlete must pass before he can give his maximum effort." This is Dr. Roger Bannister, summing up the ultimate breath any great athlete must expel before the effort to surpass an impossible standard. The barrier Bannister set out to break, on May 8, 1954, was the most forbidding in all of athletics at the time: the four-minute mile. Roger Bannister writes—and a writer he is, along with his other gifts—of the dream unfolding.

> Now bid me run,
> And I will strive with things impossible.
>
> —Julius Caesar

I expected that the summer of 1954 would be my last competitive season. It was certain to be a big year in athletics. There would be the Empire Games in Vancouver, the European Games in Berne, and hopes were running high of a four-minute mile.

The great change that now came over my running was that I no longer trained and raced alone. Perhaps I had mellowed a little and was becoming more sociable. Every day between twelve-thirty and one-thirty I trained on a track in Paddington and had a quick lunch before returning to hospital. We called ourselves the Paddington Lunch Time Club. We came from all parts of London and our common bond was a love of running.

I felt extremely happy in the friendships I made there, as we shared the hard work of repetitive quarter-miles and sprints. These training sessions came to mean almost as much to me as had those at the Oxford track. I could now identify myself more intimately with the failure and success of other runners.

In my hardest training Chris Brasher was with me, and he made the task very much lighter. On Friday evenings he took me along to Chelsea Barracks where his coach, Franz Stampfl, held a training session. At weekends Chris Chataway would join us, and in this friendly atmosphere the very severe training we did became most enjoyable.

In December, 1953, we started a new intensive course of training and ran several times a week a series of ten consecutive quarter-miles, each in 66 seconds. Through January and February we gradually speeded them up, keeping to an interval of two minutes between each. By April we could manage them in 61 seconds, but however hard we tried it did not seem possible to reach our target of 60 seconds. We were stuck, or as Chris Brasher expressed it—"bogged down." The training had ceased to do us any good and we needed a change.

Chris Brasher and I drove up to Scotland overnight for a few days' climbing. We turned into the Pass of Glencoe as the sun crept above the horizon at dawn. A misty curtain drew back from the mountains and the "sun's sleepless eye" cast a fresh cold light on the world. The air was calm and fragrant, and the colors of sunrise were mirrored in peaty pools on the moor. Soon the sun was up and we were off climbing. The weekend was a complete mental and physical change. It probably did us more harm than good physically. We climbed hard for the four days we were there, using the wrong muscles in slow and jerking movements.

There was an element of danger too. I remember Chris falling a short way when leading a climb up a rock face depressingly named "Jericho's Wall." Luckily he did not hurt himself. We were both worried lest a sprained ankle might set our training back by several weeks.

After three days our minds turned to running again. We suddenly became alarmed at the thought of taking any more risks, and decided to return. We had slept little, our meals had been irregular. But when we tried to run those quarter-miles again, the time came down to 59 seconds!

It was now less than three weeks to the Oxford University versus A.A.A. race, the first opportunity of the year for us to attack the four-minute mile. Chris Chataway had decided to join Chris Brasher and myself in the A.A.A. team. He doubted his ability to run a three-quarter-mile in three minutes, but he generously offered to attempt it.

I had now abandoned the severe training of the previous months and was concentrating entirely on gaining speed and freshness. I had to learn to release in four short minutes the energy I usually spent in half an hour's training. Each training session took on a special significance as the day of the Oxford race drew near. It felt a privilege and joy each time I ran a trial on the track.

There was no longer any need for my mind to force my limbs to run faster—my body became a unity in motion much greater than the sum of its component parts. I never thought of length of stride or style, or even my judgment of pace. All this had become automatically ingrained. In this way a singleness of drive could be achieved, leaving my mind free from the task of directing operations so that it could fix itself on the great objective ahead. There was more enjoyment in my running than ever before, a new health and vigor. It was as if all my muscles were a part of a perfectly tuned machine. I felt fresh now at the end of each training session.

On April 24 I ran a three-quarter-mile trial in three minutes at Motspur Park with Chataway. I led for the first two laps and we both returned exactly the same time. Four days later I ran a last solo three-quarter-mile trial at Paddington. Norris McWhirter, who had been my patient timekeeper through most of 1953, came over to hold the watch.

The energy of the twins, Norris and Ross McWhirter, was boundless. For them nothing was too much trouble, and they accepted any challenge joyfully. After running together in Oxford as sprinters they carried their partnership into journalism, keeping me posted of the performances of my overseas rivals. They often drove me to athletics meetings, so that I arrived with no fuss, never a minute too soon or too late. Sometimes I was not sure whether it was Norris or Ross who held the watch or drove the car, but I knew that either could be relied upon.

For the trial at Paddington there was as usual a high wind blowing. I would have given almost anything to be able to shirk the test that would tell me with ruthless accuracy what my chances were of achieving a four-minute mile at Oxford. I felt that 2 minutes 59.9 seconds for the three-quarter-mile in a solo training run meant 3 minutes 59.9 seconds in a mile race. A time of 3 minutes 0.1 second would mean 4 minutes 0.1 seconds for the mile—just the difference between success and failure. The watch recorded a time of 2 minutes 59.9 seconds! I felt a little sick afterward and had the taste of nervousness in my mouth. My speedy recovery within five minutes suggested that I had been holding something back. Two days later at Paddington I ran a 1 minute 54 second half-mile quite easily, after a late night, and then took five days' complete rest before the race.

I had been training daily since the previous November, and now that the crisis was approaching I barely knew what to do with myself. I spent most of the time imagining I was developing a cold and wondering if the gale-force winds would ever drop. The day before the race I slipped on a highly polished hospital floor and spent the rest of the day limping. Each night in the week before the race there came a moment when I saw myself at the starting line. My whole body would grow nervous and tremble. I ran the race over in my mind. Then I would calm myself and sometimes get off to sleep.

Next day was Thursday, May 6, 1954. I went into the hospital as usual, and at eleven o'clock I was sharpening my spikes on a grindstone in the laboratory. Someone passing said, "You don't really think that's going to make any difference, do you?"

I knew the weather conditions made the chances of success practically nil. Yet all day I was taking the usual precautions for the race, feeling at the same time that they would prove useless.

I decided to travel up to Oxford alone because I wanted to think quietly. I took an early train deliberately, opened a carriage door, and, quite by chance, there was Franz Stampfl inside. I was delighted to see him, as a friend with the sort of attractive cheerful personality I badly needed at that moment. Through Chris Brasher, Franz had been in touch with my training program, but my own connection with him was slight.

I would have liked his advice and help at this moment, but could not bring myself to ask him. It was as if now, at the end of my running career, I was being forced to admit that coaches were necessary after all, and that I had been wrong to think that the athlete could be sufficient unto himself.

In my mind there lurked the memory of an earlier occasion when I had visited a coach. He had expounded his views on my running and suggested a whole series of changes. The following week I read a newspaper article he wrote about my plans, claiming to be my adviser for the 1952 Olympics. This experience made me inclined to move slowly.

But Franz is not like this. He has no wish to turn the athlete into a machine working at his dictation. We shared a common view of athletics as a means of "recreation" of each individual, as a result of the liberation and expression of the latent power within him. Franz is an artist who can see beauty in human struggle and achievement.

We talked, almost impersonally, about the problem I faced. In my mind I had settled this as the day when, with every ounce of strength I possessed, I would attempt to run the four-minute mile. A wind of gale force was blowing which would slow me up by a second a lap. In order to succeed I must run not merely a four-minute mile, but the equivalent of a 3 minute 56 second mile in calm weather.

I had reached my peak physically and psychologically. There would never be another day like it. I had to drive myself to the limit of my power without the stimulus of competitive opposition. This was my first race for eight months and all this time I had been storing nervous energy. If I tried and failed I should be dejected, and my chances would be less on any later attempt. Yet it seemed that the high wind was going to make it impossible.

I had almost decided when I entered the carriage at Paddington that unless the wind dropped soon I would postpone the attempt. I would just run an easy mile in Oxford and make the attempt on the next possible occasion—ten days later at the White City in London.

Franz understood my apprehension. He thought I was capable of running a mile in 3 minutes 56 seconds, or 3:57, so he could argue convincingly that it was worthwhile making the attempt. "With the proper motivation, that is, a good reason for wanting to do it," he said, "your mind can overcome any sort of adversity. In any case the wind might drop. I remember J. J. Barry in Ireland. He ran a 4 minute 8 second mile without any training or even proper food—simply because he had the will to run. Later in America, where he was given every facility and encouragement, he never ran a fast race. In any case, what if this were your only chance?"

He had won his point. Racing has always been more of a mental than a physical problem to me. He went on talking about athletes and performances, but I heard no more. The dilemma was not banished from my mind, and the idea left uppermost was that this might be my only chance. "How would you ever forgive yourself if you rejected it?" I thought, as the train arrived in Oxford. As it happened, ten days later it was just as windy!

I was met at the station by Charles Wenden, a great friend from my early days in Oxford, who drove me straight down to Iffley Road. The wind was almost gale force. Together we walked round the deserted track. The St. George's flag on a nearby church stood out from the flagpole. The attempt seemed hopeless, yet for some unknown reason I tried out both pairs of spikes. I had a new pair which were specially made for me on the instructions of a climber and fell walker, Eustace

Thomas of Manchester. Some weeks before he had come up to London and together we worked out modifications which would reduce the weight of each running shoe from six to four ounces. This saving in weight might well mean the difference between success and failure.

Still undecided, I drove back to Charles Wenden's home for lunch. On this day, as on many others, I was glad of the peace which I found there. Although both he and his wife Eileen knew the importance of the decision that had to be made, and cared about it as much as I did myself, it was treated by common consent as a question to be settled later.

The immediate problem was to prepare a suitable lunch, and to see that the children, Felicity and Sally, ate theirs. Absorbed in watching the endless small routine of running a home and family, I could forget some of my apprehensions. Charles Wenden had been one of the ex-service students in Oxford after the war, and some of my earliest running had been in his company. Later his house had become a second home for me during my research studies in Oxford, and the calm efficiency of Eileen had often helped to still my own restless worries. Never was this factor so important as on this day.

In the afternoon I called on Chris Chataway. At the moment the sun was shining, and he lay stretched on the window seat. He smiled and said, just as I knew he would, "The day could be a lot worse, couldn't it? Just now it's fine. The forecast says the wind may drop toward evening. Let's not decide until five o'clock."

I spent the afternoon watching from the window the swaying of the leaves. "The wind's hopeless," said Joe Binks on the way down to the track. At five-fifteen there was a shower of rain. The wind blew strongly, but now came in gusts, as if uncertain. As Brasher, Chataway and I warmed up, we knew the eyes of the spectators were on us; they were hoping that the wind would drop just a little—if not enough to run a four-minute mile, enough to make the attempt.

Failure is as exciting to watch as success, provided the effort is absolutely genuine and complete. But the spectators fail to understand—and how can they know—the mental agony through which an athlete must pass before he can give his maximum effort. And how rarely, if he is built as I am, he can give it.

No one tried to persuade me. The decision was mine alone, and the moment was getting closer. As we lined up for the start I glanced at the flag again. It fluttered more gently now, and the scene from Shaw's *Saint Joan* flashed through my mind, how she, at her desperate moment, waited for the wind to change. Yes, the wind was dropping slightly. This was the moment when I made my decision. The attempt was on.

There was complete silence on the ground . . . a false start . . . I felt angry that precious moments during the lull in the wind might be slipping by. The gun fired a second time. . . . Brasher went into the lead and I slipped in effortlessly behind him, feeling tremendously full of running. My legs seemed to meet no resistance at all, as if propelled by some unknown force.

We seemed to be going so slowly! Impatiently I shouted "Faster!" But Brasher kept his head and did not change the pace. I went on worrying until I heard the first lap time, 57.5 seconds. In the excitement my knowledge of pace had deserted me. Brasher could have run the first quarter in 55 seconds without my realizing it, because I felt so full of running, but I should have had to pay for it later. Instead, he had made success possible.

At one and a half laps I was still worrying about the pace. A voice shouting "Relax" penetrated to me above the noise of the crowd. I learnt afterward it was Stampfl's. Unconsciously I obeyed. If the speed was wrong it was too late to do anything about it, so why worry? I was relaxing so much that my mind seemed almost detached from my body. There was no strain.

I barely noticed the half-mile, passed in 1 minute 58 seconds, nor when, round the next bend, Chataway went into the lead. At three-quarters of a mile the effort was still barely perceptible; the time was 3 minutes 0.7 second, and by now the crowd was roaring. Somehow I had to run that last lap in 59 seconds. Chataway led round the next bend and then I pounced past him at the beginning of the back straight, three hundred yards from the finish.

I had a moment of mixed joy and anguish, when my mind took over. It raced well ahead of my body and drew my body compellingly forward. I felt that the moment of a lifetime had come. There was no pain, only a great unity of movement and aim. The world seemed to stand still, or did not exist. The only reality was the next two hundred yards of track under my feet. The tape meant finality—extinction perhaps.

I felt at that moment that it was my chance to do one thing su-premely well. I drove on, impelled by a combination of fear and pride. The air I breathed filled me with the spirit of the track where I had run my first race. The noise in my ears was that of the faithful Oxford crowd. Their hope and encouragement gave me greater strength. I had now turned the last bend and there were only fifty yards more.

My body had long since exhausted all its energy, but it went on running just the same. The physical overdraft came only from greater willpower. This was the crucial moment when my legs were strong enough to carry me over the last few yards as they could never have done in previous years. With five yards to go the tape seemed almost to recede. Would I ever reach it?

Those last few seconds seemed never-ending. The faint line of the finishing tape stood ahead as a haven of peace, after the struggle. The arms of the world were waiting to receive me if only I reached the tape without slackening my speed. If I faltered, there would be no arms to hold me and the world would be a cold, forbidding place, because I had been so close. I leapt at the tape like a man taking his last spring to save himself from the chasm that threatens to engulf him.

My effort was over and I collapsed almost unconscious, with an arm on either side of me. It was only then that real pain overtook me. I felt like an exploded flashlight with no will to live; I just went on existing in the most passive physical state without being quite unconscious. Blood surged from my muscles and seemed to fell me. It was as if all my limbs were caught in an ever-tightening vice. I knew that I had done it before I even heard the time. I was too close to have failed, unless my legs had played strange tricks at the finish by slowing me down and not telling my tiring brain that they had done so.

The stop-watches held the answer. The announcement came—"Result of one mile . . . time, three minutes"—the rest lost in the roar of excitement. I grabbed Brasher and Chataway, and together we scampered round the track in a burst of spontaneous joy. We had done it—the three of us!

We shared a place where no man had yet ventured—secure for all time, however fast men might run miles in future. We had done it where we wanted, when we wanted, how we wanted, in our first attempt of the year. In the wonderful joy my pain was forgotten and I wanted to prolong those precious moments of realization.

I felt suddenly and gloriously free of the burden of athletic ambition that I had been carrying for years. No words could be invented for such supreme happiness, eclipsing all other feelings. I thought at that moment I could never again reach such a climax of single-mindedness. I felt bewildered and overpowered. I knew it would be some time before I caught up with myself.

John Betjeman

Seaside Golf

Sir John Betjeman was England's poet laureate from 1972 until his death in 1984. Though academic critics tended to disparage his works, Betjeman was read with pleasure by his countrymen, appreciative of his celebration of the English countryside and ordinary provincial life. He was an authority on Victorian architecture, too, and a golfer as you might guess from this evocation of an unbeatable combination—soaring drives and "sea sounds in the air."

How straight it flew, how long it flew,
It cleared the rutty track
And soaring, disappeared from view
Beyond the bunker's back—
A glorious, sailing, bounding drive
That made me glad I was alive.

And down the fairway, far along
It glowed a lovely white;
I played an iron sure and strong
And clipp'd it out of sight,
And spite of grassy banks between
I knew I'd find it on the green.

And so I did. It lay content
Two paces from the pin;
A steady putt and then it went
Oh, most securely in.
The very turf rejoiced to see
That quite unprecedented three.

Ah! seaweed smells from sandy caves
And thyme and mist in whiffs,
In-coming tide, Atlantic waves
Slapping the sunny cliffs,
Lark song and sea sounds in the air
And splendor, splendor everywhere.

H. G. Bissinger

The Ambivalence of Ivory

H. G. Bissinger's best-selling book, Friday Night Lights, *created friction in Odessa, Texas, when it was published in 1990. The townspeople of this football-mad West Texas city didn't much like Bissinger's depiction of that high school madness, the insatiable hunger for winning, not just winning a game but winning a state championship. The author, a Pulitzer Prize recipient, spent a year in Odessa, mostly with the football players of Permian High, and his book skillfully explores the curious dynamics of the town itself and the inner feelings of those young athletes. This excerpt concerns Ivory Christian, a linebacker. Christian has undergone a conversion; he has given up all his wildness, except for football, his ticket to college. Indeed, Christian was the only member of the Permian team to receive an athletic scholarship to a big-time college, Texas Christian University. But after a promising freshman year, he left school and returned to Odessa.*

There were moments when Ivory Christian loved the game he tried so much to hate.

You could tell by the very way he lined up at the middle linebacker position, up on the balls of his feet in a cocked crouch, fingers slicing slowly through the air as if trying to feel the very flow of the play, elbows tucked and ready to fire off the snap of the ball in a mercuric flash.

He even liked it sometimes during the early morning workouts that were held twice a week before classes started inside the school gymnasium. The players ran at full strength under the angry glaze of the lights, the first-string offense and defense going against so-called scout teams simulating the offense and defense of the coming week's opponent.

No one was supposed to tackle, but every now and then Ivory pounced out of his crouch and drew a bead on some poor junior running back unfortunate enough to have become the focal point of his frustration and the need to unleash it on someone. As the unsuspecting prey went around the end, still adjusting to the slightly surreal notion of practicing football indoors on a basketball court at seven-twenty in the morning, Ivory just smacked him. There was the jarring pop of helmet against helmet, and then the trajectory of the underclassman as he went skittering across the gleaming gym floor like a billiard ball hopping over a pool table after a wild cue shot. Ivory then sauntered back to the huddle as if he were walking down the runway at the Miss America contest, basking in the glow of ultimate victory but careful not to show too wide a smile because he had, after all, a reputation for self-restraint to keep up.

Much of the time Ivory fought to rid football from his life, to call a merciful halt to the practices, the dreaded gassers, the reading of page after page of plays and game plans, the endless demands on his time. He liked the games, there was no denying that, but it was hard not to find the rest of it pointless.

There were other coaches around the league who drooled over Ivory's size and speed (195 pounds and growing with a 4.7 in the forty) and his strength (he could bench-press 275 pounds as a sixteen-year-old). They thought he had major-college talent written all over him, but Ivory didn't. He was so sure of it he wasn't even going to bother to take the SAT or ACT entrance exams, which made it virtually impossible for him to get a major-college scholarship even if anyone was interested.

Maybe it would have been different if the coaches had let him start at middle linebacker his junior year. He had had the talent for it, there was little question about that, but the coaches simply didn't trust Ivory at the show position of the Permian defense. They switched him to offensive guard, and he played it brilliantly.

But something snapped in Ivory after middle linebacker was wrested from him. The common explanation, he wasn't rah-rah enough, didn't make any sense to him, although the coaches were hardly the only ones who found him to be stubborn and headstrong. But the way Ivory saw it, they just wanted to deprive him of glory, of what was rightfully his.

And where was all this rah-rah stuff supposed to come from? Was it simply expected that he would become indoctrinated into the blinding passion of the Mojo mystique just like everyone else? He was aware of it—everybody in town was—but up until the sixth grade Permian was off-limits to him because the school system was segregated.

If you lived on the Southside, as Ivory's family did, there was no way of going there. Instead, the big school in town was Ector, which wasn't too far from his home. Ector didn't have the football tradition that Permian had. But it had won State twice in basketball, residents of the Southside packing the tiny school gym to the rafters with twelve hundred fans while others who couldn't get in climbed the roof and stared in the windows. That was the tradition Ivory had grown up with, not Mojo.

Relegated to the position of guard, he had played football out of a dutiful sense of obligation, because it made his father proud and also because it somehow seemed his destiny to do so, regardless of what he thought about it. After all, if you were a strong, fast black kid in Odessa, what else were you encouraged to do? What other outlet did you possibly have? When you looked around, where else did you see a single black role model, except in church?

He had talked with his father, Ivory senior, about it, and he told him he wasn't sure he wanted to play college ball even if he had the chance. The way the words came out of his mouth, so flat and dispirited, Ivory senior thought his son might be burned out on the whole thing altogether, the rigors of being seriously involved in football since the age of nine finally getting to him. He had been playing the game for eight years, as long as it took to go to medical school, serve an internship, and complete a residency, but what loomed down the road because of it?

Ivory couldn't see a thing.

His father had played football in Odessa in the sixties when there was an all-black high school in town called Blackshear. The team had played in its own stadium on the Southside, with equipment that looked like something used in a junior high, and it played in the high school version of the Negro League, its opponents the all-black schools of Amarillo and Lubbock and Midland. Those were the days of strict segregation, and the idea of playing for Permian was of course almost inconceivable.

Ivory senior took great pride in his son's accomplishments. In the back of his mind it was probably hard not to think about what football could do for his son and how it could make him the first member of the Christian family ever to go to college. But Ivory senior, who drove a truck for a living, wasn't going to push him. He would abide by his son's decision if Ivory chose not to play football anymore after high school. He also knew his son was a teenager going through changes who had, perhaps for the first time, found there might be something else in life besides football to fill up the empty spaces of Odessa that loomed as large as skyscrapers.

It had come to Ivory in a dream. When he related it to his father he talked about being in a narrow tunnel with a tiny light that he could barely see but he knew he had to find no matter how difficult it was.

To Ivory, the message of the dream was crystal clear. He was living his life wrong, emphasizing all the wrong things, football and hanging out in the streets with his friends and alcohol and marijuana. The day after he had the dream he went to church with a hangover on his breath and Jesus in his heart, as he later described it. He told the pastor at his church, Rose of Sharon Missionary Baptist, about the dream and how he was convinced that it had been a calling to preach and become part of God's ministry.

Pastor Hanson welcomed Ivory's conversion. He knew that Ivory was an influential kid whose actions made a tremendous impression on his peers. But there was something worrisome about it, and he didn't want Ivory moving from one world of isolation into another where the only difference was the level of standards.

Before, Ivory had displayed undisguised contempt for just about everything, an attitude of what Hanson perceived as arrogance. Now he displayed a rigid righteousness that made him almost a kept prisoner. At home he hardly communicated with anyone but went immediately to his tiny room, where he listened to the gospel music of James Cleveland. He went on this way for hours on end, until his mother began to worry and think there was something wrong with him. Why was he so withdrawn, so quiet?

As the result of his conversion, he hated alcohol and had contempt for those who touched it. He also hated swearing, and other players in the locker room figured it was better to abide by his wishes rather than run the risk of messing with him. Before his calling to the ministry he had dated. Now he started grilling girls about their habits to see if their moral standards were high enough for him.

"Not everyone you meet is going to be a jam-up Christian," Hanson told him. "They may drink a beer, they may go to a concert. You can still be Ivory, you can be eighteen years old. You don't have to be forty years old. You don't have to isolate yourself."

But Ivory's metamorphosis was total, a far cry from the days when he had led the chorus of laughter in response to the church teachings about fornication. And rarely had Hanson seen anyone with as instinctive a gift for preaching. He was amazed at Ivory's comprehension and interpretation of the Scripture and his ease in the pulpit, the absolute fearlessness he showed in getting up before the congregation and preaching the word of God with those square shoulders that did make him look as though he was born to be a linebacker.

Wearing a blue suit with a little trim of white handkerchief sticking out of the breast pocket, Ivory made a striking figure, his poise like that of someone thirty years old instead of seventeen. He truly seemed at peace in these moments, able at last to lose himself in something without anguish and ambivalence. He rocked back and forth and nodded his head as Hanson gave the altar prayer one Sunday. Moments later he was introduced as "the Reverend Ivory Christian." The very ring of it sounded stirring and wonderful, and it was amazing to see this teenager who showed almost no enthusiasm about anything, who responded to almost everything with the shrug of an octogenarian ready to die, take the pulpit. He started softly but the exhortations of the congregation— "Talk! Talk!" and "Alright! Alright!" and "Take your time, son! Take your time!"—got him going in a sweet and easy rhythm. He connected with the congregation and they connected with him as he stood beneath a mural of the black Jesus and talked about his conversion:

> When you let go of this world, Jesus puts a certain joy in your heart. Do we really love him enough to say no to the world?

Ivory let go of drinking. He let go of hanging out in the streets. He let go of parties. He let go of cussing. He let go of every former vestige in his life, except football. It still lingered as his perpetual, unconquerable nemesis. He tried to let go of that too, and he talked to Hanson about quitting football altogether because he felt it conflicted with his calling, and he didn't want anything to get in the way of that. But Hanson gently coaxed him not to drop football too fast. It was there, and it had a place in Ivory's life whether he liked it or not. "If playing football can get you to college, if playing football can get you an education, then play football," Hanson told him.

And no matter how much Ivory tried to hate it and belittle it and scoff at it, something took hold of him on game day as surely powerful as spreading the word of Jesus. Everyone on the team experienced butterflies, but no one got them as badly as he did.

It hadn't happened in the first game of the season against El Paso Austin, because everyone knew that El Paso Austin was a terrible team. But it did happen in the second game, in a stadium 530 miles east of Odessa in Marshall, Texas.

As assistant coach Randy Mayes went over the list of the myriad responsibilities of the linebackers one final time, the drone of his footballese a numbing wash in the bloated air, Ivory's legs began to shake. He started sweating and his complexion turned wan. The more Mayes read from the piece of paper he had prepared, which was based on hours of review of several Marshall game films where every play was diagrammed and analyzed for type, formation, and hash tendency, the worse Ivory looked, as if he was drowning in the expectations of what he had to do.

The alien atmosphere of everything, the strange space he and his teammates occupied underneath the decrepit flanks of the bleachers with its spotted shadows and jutting angles, the crackling screech of "Anchors Away" over and over again on the ancient loudspeaker system to an absolutely empty stadium, the tortuous buildup of heat and humidity like the cranking of a catapult, only magnified the tension.

"You okay?" Mayes asked him.

"I need to throw up," he said.

"Go throw up."

And off he went, trying to exorcise the demon of football.

Perhaps it was the distance that separated the two schools and the fact that Permian, at a cost of $20,000 to the school district, had chartered a 737 jet to get to Marshall.

Perhaps it was the breakfast at Johnny Cace's Seafood and Steakhouse, where he sat in the corner with the other black players and helped himself to heaping buffet-style portions of scrambled eggs and biscuits and chicken-fried steak.

Perhaps it was how some of the shoe-polish signs on the rear windows of cars in Marshall rhymed MOJO with HOMO, or the way the Marshall Mavericks slumped against the doorway of the locker room in their letter jackets when the Permian players arrived, their arms folded, the looks on their faces smug and sullen and smirking, as if to say, *So this is big, bad Mojo, the pride of West Texas. They look like a bunch of pussies to me.*

But probably it was the thought of O-dell, as he had been called all that week during practice, staring across from him in the Marshall backfield.

Odell Beckham, the stud duck of the Mavericks, number 33, six feet, 194 pounds, 4.5 speed in the forty, punishing, quick, able to take it up and out to the outside, a guaranteed lock for a major-college scholarship. *O-dell.* Everywhere Ivory went, everywhere he looked, that's all he seemed to hear about. *O-dell.* Watch him do this on the film. *O-dell.* Read about him doing that on the scouting report. *O-dell.* Listen to this publication calling him the third best running back in the state. *O-dell.* Could any player possibly be that good, that awesome, that intimidating? Were the rumors true that he had walked on water against the Nacogdoches Dragons and had simply flown across the field like the Flying Nun against the Texarkana Tigers?

Inside the locker room of the Marshall Mavericks, where a sign in thick red letters on the Coke machine read THERE'S NOTHING THAT COMES EASY THAT'S WORTH A DIME. AS A MATTER OF FACT, I NEVER SAW A FOOTBALL PLAYER MAKE A TACKLE WITH A SMILE ON HIS FACE, Ivory went through his physical upheaval, as far removed from the cocoon of the Rose of Sharon pulpit as he ever could be.

He wasn't preaching now. He was playing football.

Tom Boswell

Mr. Jack Nicklaus

"Games are about who won, who lost and how. But they're also about what's right, what's wrong and why," writes Tom Boswell, who has been covering a wide variety of games and the people who play them for The Washington Post *for over two decades. What's right about the games, according to Boswell, is Jack Nicklaus. Of all the athletes he has covered in his time, Nicklaus, Boswell feels, just might be the closest thing to a genuine hero.*

All in all, it's probably good that Jack Nicklaus never completely lost his love handles, always had a squeaky voice, couldn't tell a joke, was color-blind, couldn't resist raiding the refrigerator for ice cream and had a lousy sand game. (Yes, and he backslid a thousand times on the damn cigarettes, too.)

Otherwise, in the distant future when his career and his legend are discussed, few would be able to believe that such a person—almost embarrassingly close to being an ideal competitor and sportsman—could actually have existed. In fact, as he ages, it might be helpful if Nicklaus would do something wrong—get a parking ticket or make a bad business deal—just so his psychobiographers won't have to throw up their hands in despair.

Few careers, in any walk of life, have started so spectacularly, then continued steadily upward, almost without interruption, for so long. Success, which has ruined many, only refueled Nicklaus. Each piece of good fortune seemed to be reinvested at compound interest. Neither twenty major golf championships, spread over twenty-seven years from 1959 to 1986, nor a personal empire worth hundreds of millions of dollars seemed to disorient this son of a Midwestern drugstore pharmacist. He took himself seriously, but not as seriously as his responsibilities—to his talent, his sport, his family, even his public image.

Yet, just as soon as you started to think you had his diligent dutiful character pinned down and encircled, word would seep back to the PGA Tour that Nicklaus the Practical Joker had struck again, usually in some new installment of his lifelong battle with his friend John McCormack, a tournament director.

Once, after blowing a tournament that McCormack had run, the eternally stoic, always utterly self-controlled Nicklaus walked calmly into McCormack's office and destroyed everything in the room, right down to the picture frames.

After the sounds of smashing and crashing had stopped, Nicklaus walked out, composed and smiling, leaving McCormack and the rest of the golf world to wonder—and never find out—whether his true feelings had been rage or amusement.

Even Nicklaus recognized the problem of living such a relentlessly mythological life. (Let's see, is that five Masters and six PGAs that I've won or six Masters and five PGAs?) Once, while playing in the '75 Doral Open, he sank a 76-yard wedge shot for an eagle at the 10th, then, two holes later, he holed a 77-yard shot for another eagle to take the lead. No TV cameras were on him. His gallery, on a remote part of the course, was only a hundred people. For once, he was almost unobserved. When the second eagle disappeared, Nicklaus dropped his club and began spinning around in circles like a little boy who makes himself dizzy until he falls down. He finally stopped before he flopped.

After his round, after he had won again, he was asked why he had gotten such an attack of silliness. "When I made the second one, it just all felt so crazy," he said. "I was almost beginning to believe some of the stuff you guys write about me."

For such a down-to-earth man (sometimes even a slightly boring man), to become so genuinely heroic almost seems like a joke on the rest of us. Everybody talks about maturing—getting better, not older. More than any athlete of his era, Nicklaus did it.

In the 1960s, as he surpassed Arnold Palmer and established himself as a Goliath of golf, Nicklaus was a sports hero but nothing more. Call him Fat Jack. Then, the young, tubby and titanically powerful Nicklaus may have been the most awesome golfer who ever lived. Bobby Jones watched Nicklaus as his towering 300-yard drives airmailed the farthest fairway traps and as his iron shots from the rough snapped back with mystical backspin. Jones's pronouncement: "Jack Nicklaus plays a game with which I am not familiar."

In the 1970s, as he lost weight and, to his shock, turned from a frumpy fashion frog into a cover boy, Nicklaus established himself as the greatest and most dignified of all golf champions. Slowly, he became a true national hero: the Golden Bear. He not only carried his sport; to most people he actually *was* his sport.

Finally, in the 1980s, when he re-created himself once more as an aging, flawed and beloved everyman—winning the Masters at the age of forty-six with his adult son as a caddie—he became a world hero: the Olden Bear.

Perhaps someday we will learn that Nicklaus was, in some respect, not entirely what he appeared to be. In an age when athletes often seem to be made entirely of clay, Nicklaus remained almost too good to be true for decades at a time. Not "too good" in the Goody Two-Shoes sense. (Ask McCormack about the morning he woke up to discover that "somebody" had ordered that his entire front lawn be buried under several tons of horse shit.) But "too good" in the sense of too decent, too organized, too creative, too lucky, too smart in business, too good a father to his five hell-raising children, too solid a husband, too wise in his self-analysis, too gracious in defeat, too cheerfully and generously joyful in victory.

How'd this guy get so squared away, so sane, so productive? How come his children didn't hate him? How come the small-print news items always said, "Third-round leader Jack Nicklaus flew home last night in his private jet to watch a Little League game, attend a school play and grill a few steaks in the backyard. He will return in time for Sunday's final round." How could this guy, by age thirty, be on vacation more than half the year so he could raise his family, yet still crush everybody's bones? Chi Chi Rodriguez called him "a legend in his spare time."

Where's the divorce, the scandal? How come, for thirty years and still counting, Jack always looked at Barbara as though she were the real reason for it all. And she looked at him like she was fairly proud, but like she might also have to grab him by the ear and straighten him out at any moment. Once, in the late '70s, I stepped into a hotel elevator and caught the old married Nicklauses doing a little necking between floors.

Why weren't his foes—men that he inevitably diminished—insanely jealous of him? How many victories did he take from Arnold Palmer, Lee Trevino, Tom Watson, Seve Ballesteros and Greg Norman? Yet many of his adversaries became his true friends, all were his admirers and some, like Norman, practically worshipped him and sought his advice —which he always gave. Perhaps only Watson, the Stanford psychology major, kept a prickly distance and successfully resisted Nicklaus's subtle seduction. Almost all Watson's greatest victories, in particular the '82 U.S. Open, the '77 and '81 Masters and the '77 British Open, were snatched directly from Nicklaus in confrontations which, while formally respectful, had a certain amount of tangy spin and edged byplay. Once, the pair even went jaw to jaw in the scorer's tent behind the 72nd green at the Masters because Watson thought that Nicklaus, playing ahead, had been waving derisively at him (Take that, kid) as he pulled the ball from the cup after a birdie.

How could Nicklaus set out to build a fabulous golf course and a great tournament in his hometown—the Memorial in Columbus, Ohio —and have it work right off the bat? Okay, having amassed a fortune estimated at several hundred million dollars doesn't hurt. The proud bear, son of a pharmacist, would have used dollar bills to fertilize Muirfield if that's what it took. But it's also true that Nicklaus the course designer and tournament director was as much an instant success as Nicklaus the teenage superstar.

Perhaps part of the reason is that Nicklaus was, and remains, a man who is inspired by failure, or even the thought of failure. Defeat always prodded his bearish nature into slow, inexorable, productive action. For example, in the spring of 1980, Nicklaus, then forty, had been in a two-year slump. "Is Nicklaus Washed Up?" was the standing headline. "I'm sick of playing lousy," said Nicklaus publicly. "I've just been going through the motions for two years. First, it irritates you, then it really bothers you, until finally you get so damn blasted mad at yourself that you decide to do something about it. I've decided to do something. And I will. Or I'll quit."

Privately, he was even more blunt. At about this time, I casually mentioned to Nicklaus how nice it was that Lee Trevino had made a strong comeback the previous two years. "Yes," said Nicklaus, suddenly grabbing me by both shoulders, "it's almost as nice as this year when Nicklaus made his great comeback."

That year, Nicklaus won the U.S. Open and the PGA. No player since has won two major tournaments in the same season.

Typically, Nicklaus loved periods of struggle even better than those periods when his game was ticking smoothly. "These are interesting times," he said during one of his slumps. "The game is most fun when you are experimenting. One day you're great, the next day scatterload. But you're learning. No, that's not right. I probably have forgotten more about golf than I will ever learn. What you do is remember some of the things you thought you'd never forget."

Because he never feared failure, or experimentation, Nicklaus seemed especially suited to golf—the game of perpetual humiliation and embarrassment. Nicklaus approached his whole game, perhaps his whole life, the same way he lined up a putt. Slowly, confidently and from every angle. When the ball went in the hole, he would give a pleasant perfunctory smile—mostly to please his gallery, since he'd expected to make it anyway. When he missed, his look of fierce, sometimes forbidding concentration deepened as he analyzed the problem. What had he forgotten? The grain of the grass, the evaporation of the dew? This was a man who once explained casually that he had chosen an odd-shaped putter because it combined "the largest possible moment of inertia and the smallest dispersion factor."

"When you lip out several putts in a row, you should never think that means that you're putting well and that 'your share' are about to start falling," Nicklaus once said in the mid-'70s when he was at the peak of his powers. "The difference between 'in' and 'almost' is all in here. If you think the game is just a matter of getting it close and letting the law of averages do your work for you, you'll find a different way to miss every time. Your frame of reference must be exactly the width of the cup, not the general vicinity. When you're putting well, the only question is what part of the hole it's going to fall in, not if it's going in."

Whether Nicklaus or Jones in his heyday was the greatest golfer of the twentieth century is a question that they will probably have to decide at match play over the next few ones in the Elysian Fields. Perhaps Nicklaus will be allowed a millennium to practice with hickory shafts, while Jones will be given a few thousand years to decide whether graphite, beryllium or square grooves suits his taste.

It will not require eternity, however, to decide which man had the greatest golf career of the twentieth century. On that score, Jones, the amateur who retired at twenty-eight with no worlds to conquer, abdicated the crown. At a comparable age, Nicklaus also ruled his sport. But he kept competing at or near the mountaintop until he was past forty-five, accomplishing more great feats at later ages than any player.

Only Jones was as dominant in his youth as the 215-pound Fat Jack, who won his first U.S. Amateur at nineteen, his first U.S. Open at twenty-two, and then quickly added his first Masters and PGA at twenty-three.

(In the first 34 major championships of his pro career, Nicklaus had 7 victories, 18 trips to the top three and 20 majors in the top seven.)

No one, however, was ever as consistently exceptional in his thirties as the trimmed-down and glamorous Golden Bear. He took a physique and a game that others thought was the best of all time and radically remodeled them in the interests of consistency and longevity. And he actually got a little better. In what we might call the middle third of his career, starting with his 1970 win at the British Open, Nicklaus had 8 wins and 20 finishes in the top three in a span of 33 majors. He also finished fourth 4 times and was in the top ten in the majors 31 times in those 33 events. Feel free to do a double take. That streak is beyond comparison and almost beyond belief. In that period, Nicklaus also won the TPC and the Tournament of Champions—perhaps the next most prestigious events—three times each.

Finally, only Ben Hogan, after his car wreck, was as inspirational at the end of his career as Nicklaus, who was, by then, a ridiculously beloved Olden Bear.

Most golf fans assume that Nicklaus's greatest accomplishment in his own eyes was his record in the majors. In his first twenty-five years as a pro, from 1961 through 1986, Nicklaus played in exactly 100 majors. He had 18 wins, 18 runners-up, 9 third places and 66 visits to the top ten. Yet ask Nicklaus if his play in golf's biggest events is, in fact, his defining accomplishment, and he balks. He knows that what he's done in the majors is bound, hand and foot, with something vague, yet of broader importance.

"Basically, the majors are the only comparisons over time . . . played on the same courses for generations. All the best players are always there. But I'm just as proud of the whole way I've managed my career, the longevity of it. . . . You only have so much juice. You try to keep what you've got left so you can use it when it means the most."

Nicklaus has illustrated—as vividly as any public figure in our national life—how to manage talent over time; how to organize a balanced and productive life; how to continually revitalize our enthusiasm for our work. To many, Nicklaus is a symbol of successful labor. Yet he is also a marvelous symbol of creative laziness. By age twenty-five, he was already cutting back his tournament appearances. By thirty, he barely played twenty times a year.

However, when he worked, he concentrated utterly. No player ever changed his game more radically than Nicklaus after his weight loss, then again after his thirty-fifth birthday when he, essentially, tinkered with every aspect of his swing to create a more aesthetically pleasing whole. No other player ever attacked the short game after his fortieth birthday and improved immeasurably—partly because he had been so bad for so long. And nobody else ever tore apart his putting, and came out with a new, goofy-looking kind of putter, after age forty-five—then win the Masters with it.

As Nicklaus recedes from golf's center stage, his victories in athletic old age now seem to hold us most tightly. Why? Because they prove that—as we suspected and very much prefer to believe—he was a special person, not just a special athlete. By craft and canniness, he discovered a succession of temporary stays against age and self-doubt—almost against mortality itself. And, repeatedly, he prevailed. With dignity. With easy good grace. With many of the qualities that seem to lose their substance unless some special person can live them out, embody them on his own terms.

"If you don't mind, I'm just going to stand here and enjoy this," said Nicklaus at his mass press conference after his shocking Jack Is Back victory in the '80 U.S. Open at Baltusrol.

When he finally spoke, he said, "I have to start with self-doubt. I kept wondering all week when my wheels would come off like they have for the last year and a half. But they never came off. When I needed a crucial putt, or needed to call on myself for a good shot, I did it. And those are the things I have expected from myself for twenty years.

"I've wondered if I should still be playing this silly game. . . . You see guys who have been winners who get to the point where they ought to get out of their game. They are the last to know. They make themselves seem pathetic. It hurts to think that that is you. . . .

"Once a time is past, it's past. I'll never be 215 pounds, hit it so far or have my hair so short again as I did when I was here in 1967 [and won the Open at Baltusrol]. You can never return. I've lost the '60s and '70s. We all have. I'm not the same. I have to look to the future. I have to see what skills I have now. I have to find out what is in store for Jack Nicklaus in the '80s. I can't look backwards, because that man doesn't exist anymore."

Nicklaus tests himself in opposition not to any one man but to everyone in his game simultaneously. He measures himself by only one standard—the attempt to be the best golfer who ever lived and the best who ever will live.

Throughout his career, Nicklaus has confronted his own limits and flaws with less desire to blink or turn away than any golfer, perhaps any athlete, of his time. Only reality interested him, not self-delusion. When thwarted by bad luck or injury, poor performance or better foes, he suffered, accepted his situation, regrouped and then relentlessly returned.

His greatest return—unless, of course, he wins the British Open on the Old Course at the age of seventy-five—came at the 1986 Masters in what, by something approaching consensus, was the Golf Event of the Century.

That moment, as Nicklaus walked up the final fairway at Augusta National, became the frontispiece in a whole generation's book of sports memories. The place of respect that the Louis-Schmeling fight, for example, may have held for our grandfathers, that image of Nicklaus achieved for millions. In the last half century, perhaps only the U.S.-U.S.S.R. Olympic hockey game of 1980 had a comparable transcendent power over the general non-sporting public.

An exemplary man, a full and rounded adult, was doing an almost impossible athletic deed, and doing it with amazing cheerful grace—ignoring every odd, lovin' every minute of it, waving his putter to the crowd like a scepter. Yet Nicklaus later freely admitted what everyone could see—that he had tears in his eyes "four or five times" as he played, so moved was he by the standing ovations that swept him along through every hole of a tumultuous, cascadingly dramatic final nine.

Despite all that emotion, despite the depths of his famous concentration on every swing, Nicklaus also walked between shots at times with a bemused, almost disbelieving expression on his face—as though he were sharing an inside joke with the world, but not with his competitors, who could only see his closing scores being posted. Starting at the 9th: birdie, birdie, birdie, bogey, birdie, par, eagle, birdie, birdie and finally one more par as his last long birdie putt stopped in front of the hole—one inch from a 29 on the homeward nine.

Of all his victories, all his glory days, this was the most accessible. After all, Nicklaus had spent nearly two years reading stories about how he should stop embarrassing himself and retire. All around him, eyes were being turned away. He arrived at the Masters, for the first time in his career, almost an object of pity. Nicklaus actually stuck a "Jack Should Quit" story to his refrigerator door during Masters week.

"I kept saying to myself, 'Done. Washed up. Finished.' I was trying to make myself mad, but it didn't really work too well because I thought it might be true."

As he walked the closing holes, Nicklaus was talking to himself some more, but the words were very different. The crowds had him crying, something that had happened to him at the '78 British Open and '80 U.S. Open—two of his previous premature valedictories. "We have to play golf. This isn't over," he kept telling himself. "What I really don't understand is how I could keep making putts in the state I was in. I was so excited I shouldn't have been able to pull it back at all, much less pull it back like I wanted to. But I did. One perfect stroke after another. When I don't get nervous, I don't make anything. Maybe I've been doing it backwards."

Bobby Jones was certainly golf's best player/writer, but Nicklaus may have been its best extemporaneous player/talker. He wasn't funny or colorful or charismatic. Instead, he seemed to have a rarer gift— simple, unadorned insight. He knew exactly what was on his mind and, whenever politic, he said exactly that. He spoke almost without spin— no double meaning or hidden agenda. His words were a pane of glass that revealed an analytical, well-lit and fairly guileless mind. Of course, maybe it's only decent for a fellow to be candid and sporting when he can spot the world one-a-side by the age of twenty-one.

Nicklaus never gave a better press conference than describing how he agonized while watching Greg Norman's final 15-foot par putt at the 72nd hole which would have forced a playoff. Nicklaus had never before rooted against a foe.

"I was sitting watching TV as Norman kept making birdies. So when he came to the last putt, I said, 'Maybe I'll stand up.' I like to win golf tournaments with my clubs, not on other people's mistakes. But when you're coming to the finish . . . I'm in the December of my career . . . Well, somebody did something to me at Pebble Beach as I remember," said Nicklaus, recalling Tom Watson's 71st-hole chip-in at the '82 U.S. Open.

Perhaps the '86 Masters crystallized three aspects of Nicklaus's character which—independent of his enormous talent—will be remembered and revered as long as golf is played.

First, Nicklaus was appreciated as a man who loved his family as much as, and probably more than, his fame.

"To have your own son with you to share an experience like that is so great for him, so great for me. I have great admiration for him. He's done a wonderful job of handling the burden of my name," said Nicklaus of son Jack Jr., twenty-four. ". . . If it wasn't for my kids, I probably wouldn't be playing now. You've got to have a reason for doing things. Last time I won [at the '84 Memorial], Jackie caddied for me."

Second, his late-career success demonstrated Nicklaus's ability to accept the fact that golf is an unmasterable game. That knowledge was his key to being a master. Instead of searching for the perfect method or clinging to what had worked in the past, Nicklaus constantly reworked and remolded his game, enjoying the very same process of perpetual loss and rediscovery that panicked and infuriated other players. In the two weeks before the '86 Masters, Nicklaus had made key changes in his full swing and his chipping method and was using a new putter.

Finally, Nicklaus's old-age triumphs exhibited to everyone the unmistakably clean core of his competitiveness. A regal sense of joy in combat, which is the heart of great sportsmanship, was evident throughout those victories. Nicklaus was having fun, expressing his best gifts, actually enjoying the same kinds of pressure which crush so many people in so many walks of life. And he was doing it long after he should have been washed up.

By the end, with many of his golfing gifts gone but his character intact, Nicklaus's play seemed to speak for itself: "This is life. Look how hard it is. Look how great it is."

Jim Bouton

Hey, *Ball Four*

There has been life after Ball Four *for Jim Bouton. A renaissance man to begin with, Bouton had a post-major-league career that included pitching stints at various levels lower than the majors. He also became a funny, saturnine, first-rate television reporter, acted in movies and television shows, and ended up an entrepreneur of note for inventing, along with his partner, a new bubble gum called Big League Chew. But Bouton's name will always and forever be associated with the book that unlocked the musty secrets of the fraternity of sports (see Introduction). This excerpt comes from an updated version of* Ball Four, *published in 1981, with Bouton remembering how it all began to happen to him, and the curious consequences of his book of revelations.*

There was a time, not too long ago, when school kids read *Ball Four* at night under the covers with a flashlight because their parents wouldn't allow it in the house. It was not your typical sports book about the importance of clean living and inspired coaching. I was called a Judas and a Benedict Arnold for having written it. The book was attacked in the media because among other things, it "used four-letter words and destroyed heroes." It was even banned in a few libraries because it was said to be "bad for the youth of America."

The kids, however, saw it differently. I know because they tell me about it now whenever I lecture on college campuses. They come up and say it was nice to learn that ballplayers were human beings, but what they got from the book was moral support for a point of view. They claim that *Ball Four* gave them strength to be the underdog and made them feel less lonely as an outsider in their own lives. Or it helped them to stand up for themselves and see life with a sense of humor.

Then they invariably share a funny story about a coach or teacher who reminds them of someone in the book.

In some fraternities and dorms they play Ball Four Trivia, or Who Said That?, quoting characters from the book. And there is always someone who claims to hold the campus record for reading it 10, 12, or 14 times. Then they produce dog-eared copies for me to sign. I love it.

Sometimes when people compliment me about my book I wonder who they're talking about. A librarian compared _Ball Four_ to the classic _The Catcher in the Rye_ because she said I was an idealist like Holden Caulfield who "viewed the world through jaundice colored glasses." Teachers have personally thanked me for writing the only book their nonreading students would read. And one mother said she wanted to build me a shrine for writing the only book her son ever finished.

The strangest part is that apparently there is something about the book which makes people feel I'm their friend. I'm always amazed when I walk through an airport, for example, and someone I've never met passes by and says simply, "Hey, _Ball Four._" Or strangers will stop me on the street and ask how my kids are doing.

Maybe they identify with me because we share the same perspective. One of my roommates, Steve Hovley, said I was the first fan to make it to the major leagues. _Ball Four_ has the kinds of stories an observant next door neighbor might come home and tell if he ever spent some time with a major league team. Whatever the reasons, it still overwhelms me to think that I wrote something which people remember.

I certainly didn't plan it this way. I don't believe I could have produced this response if I had set out to do it. In fact, ten years ago when I submitted the final manuscript I was not optimistic. My editor, Lenny Shecter, and I had spent so many months rewriting and polishing that after awhile it all seemed like cardboard to us. What's more, the World Publishing Company wasn't too excited either. They doubted there was any market for a diary by a marginal relief pitcher on an expansion team called the Seattle Pilots.

With a first printing of only 5,000 copies I was certain that _Ball Four_ was headed the way of all sports books. And then a funny thing happened. Some advance excerpts appeared in _Look_ magazine and the baseball establishment went crazy. The team owners became furious and wanted to ban the book. The Commissioner called me in for a reprimand and announced that I had done the game, "a grave disservice." Sportswriters called me names like "traitor" and "turncoat." My favorite was "social leper." Dick Young of the _Daily News_ thought that one up.

The ballplayers, most of whom hadn't read it, picked up the cue.

The San Diego Padres burned the book and left the charred remains for me to find in the visitors clubhouse. While I was on the mound trying to pitch, players on the opposing teams hollered obscenities at me. I can still remember Pete Rose, on the top step of the dugout screaming, "Fuck you, Shakespeare."

All that hollering and screaming sure sold books. *Ball Four* went up to 200,000 in hardcover, 3 million in paperback, and got translated into Japanese. I was so grateful I dedicated my second book (*I'm Glad You Didn't Take It Personally*) to my detractors. I don't think they appreciated the gesture.

One way I can tell is that I never get invited back to Oldtimers' Days. Understand, *everybody* gets invited back for Oldtimers' Day no matter what kind of rotten person he was when he was playing. Muggers, drug addicts, rapists, child molesters, all are forgiven for Oldtimers' Day. Except a certain author.

The wildest thing is that they wouldn't forgive a cousin who made the mistake of being related to me. Jeff Bouton was a good college pitcher who dreamed of making the big leagues someday. But after *Ball Four* came out a Detroit Tiger scout told him he'd never make it in the pros unless he *changed his name!* Jeff refused, and a month after he signed he was released. For the rest of his life, he'll never know if it was his pitching or his name.

I believe the overreaction to *Ball Four* boiled down to this: People simply were not used to reading the truth about professional sports.

The owners, for their part, saw this as economically dangerous. What made them so angry about the book was not the locker room stories but the revelations about how difficult it was to make a living in baseball. The owners knew that public opinion was important in maintaining the controversial reserve clause which teams used to control players and hold down salaries. They lived in fear that this special exemption from the anti-trust laws, originally granted by Congress and reluctantly upheld in the courts, might someday be overturned.

To guard against this, the Commissioner and the owners (with help from sportswriters), had convinced the public, the Congress, and the courts—*and* many players!—that the reserve clause was crucial in order to "maintain competitive balance." (As if there was competitive balance when the Yankees were winning 29 pennants in 43 years.) The owners preached that the reserve clause was necessary to stay in business, and that ballplayers were well paid and fairly treated. (Mickey Mantle's $100,000 salary was always announced with great fanfare while all the

$9,000 and $12,000 salaries were kept secret.) The owners had always insisted that dealings between players and teams be kept strictly confidential. They knew that if the public ever learned the truth, it would make it more difficult to defend the reserve clause against future challenges.

Which is why the owners hated _Ball Four_. Here was a book which revealed, in great detail, just how ballplayers' salaries were "negotiated" with general managers. It showed, for the first time, exactly how owners abused and manipulated players by taking advantage of their one way contract.

It turned out the owners had reason to be afraid. It may be no coincidence that after half a century of struggle the players won their free agency shortly after the publication of _Ball Four_. No one will know what part the book may have played in creating a favorable climate of opinion. I only know that when Marvin Miller asked me to testify in the Messersmith arbitration case which freed the players, I quoted passages from _Ball Four_.

The sportswriters, on the other hand, were upset at almost all the other things _Ball Four_ revealed. Chief among these being that ballplayers will, on occasion, take pep pills, get drunk, stay out late, talk dirty, have groupies, and be rude to fans. The irony here, of course, is that if the _sportswriters_ had been telling what went on in baseball there would have been no sensation around my book.

By establishing new boundaries, _Ball Four_ changed sports reporting at least to the extent that, after the book, it was no longer possible to sell the milk and cookies image again. It was not my purpose to do this, but on reflection, it's probably not a bad idea. I think we are all better off looking across at someone, rather than up. Sheldon Kopp, the author and psychologist, wrote, "There are no great men. If you have a hero, look again: you have diminished yourself in some way." Besides, you can get sick on too much milk and cookies.

T. Coraghessan Boyle

The Hector Quesadilla Story

Una más *for Hector Quesadilla; one more season for the burrito-gorging grandfather, for the professional hitter with the .296 lifetime average. And on his birthday, the* viejo's *extended family is present for his last glorious moment in an interminable career. But how can that career come to a close when the game never ends? The recipient of the PEN/Faulkner Award for his novel* World's End, *T. Coraghessan Boyle also won the John Train Humor Prize for this 1984 story.*

He was no Joltin' Joe, no Sultan of Swat, no Iron Man. For one thing, his feet hurt. And God knows no legendary immortal ever suffered so prosaic a complaint. He had shinsplints too, and corns and ingrown toenails and hemorrhoids. Demons drove burning spikes into his tailbone each time he bent to loosen his shoelaces, his limbs were skewed so awkwardly his elbows and knees might have been transposed and the once-proud knot of his frijole-fed belly had fallen like an avalanche. Worse: he was old. Old, old, old, the graybeard hobbling down the rough-hewn steps of the Senate building, the Ancient Mariner chewing on his whiskers and stumbling in his socks. Though they listed his birthdate as 1942 in the program, there were those who knew better: it was way back in '54, during his rookie year for San Buitre, that he had taken Asunción to the altar, and even in those distant days, even in Mexico, twelve-year-olds didn't marry.

When he was younger—really young, nineteen, twenty, tearing up the Mexican League like a saint of the stick—his ears were so sensitive he could hear the soft rasping friction of the pitcher's fingers as he massaged the ball and dug in for a slider, fastball, or changeup. Now he could barely hear the umpire bawling the count in his ear. And his legs. How they ached, how they groaned and creaked and chattered, how they'd gone to fat! He ate too much, that was the problem. Ate prodigiously, ate mightily, ate as if there were a hidden thing inside him, a creature all of jaws with an infinite trailing ribbon of gut. Huevos con chorizo with beans, tortillas, camarones in red sauce and a twelve-ounce steak for breakfast, the chicken in mole to steady him before afternoon games, a sea of beer to wash away the tension of the game and prepare his digestive machinery for the flaming machaca and pepper salad Asunción prepared for him in the blessed evenings of the home stand.

Five foot seven, one hundred eighty-nine and three-quarters pounds. Hector Hernán Jesus y María Quesadilla. Little Cheese, they called him. Cheese, Cheese, Cheesus, went up the cry as he stepped in to pinch-hit in some late inning crisis, Cheese, Cheese, Cheesus, building to a roar until Chavez Ravine resounded as if with the holy name of the Savior Himself when he stroked one of the clean line-drive singles that were his signature or laid down a bunt that stuck like a finger in jelly. When he fanned, when the bat went loose in the fat brown hands and he went down on one knee for support, they hissed and called him *Viejo.*

One more season, he tells himself, though he hasn't played regularly for nearly ten years and can barely trot to first after drawing a walk, One more. He tells Asunción too: One more, One more, as they sit in the gleaming kitchen of their house in Boyle Heights, he with his Carta Blanca, she with her mortar and pestle for grinding the golden petrified kernels of maize into flour for the tortillas he eats like peanuts. *Una más,* she mocks. What do you want, the Hall of Fame? Hang up your spikes Hector.

He stares off into space, his mother's Indian features flattening his own as if the legend were true, as if she really had taken a spatula to him in the cradle, and then, dropping his thick lids as he takes a long slow swallow from the neck of the bottle, he says: Just the other day driving home from the park I saw a car on the freeway, a Mercedes with only two seats, a girl in it, her hair out back like a cloud, and you know what the license plate said? His eyes are open now, black as pitted olives. Do you? She doesn't. Cheese, he says. It said Cheese.

Then she reminds him that Hector Jr. will be twenty-nine next month and that Reina has four children of her own and another on the way. You're a grandfather, Hector—almost a great-grandfather if your son ever settled down. A moment slides by, filled with the light of the sad waning sun and the harsh Yucatano dialect of the radio announcer. *Hombres* on first and third, one down. *Abuelo,* she hisses, grinding stone against stone until it makes his teeth ache. Hang up your spikes, *abuelo.*

But he doesn't. He can't. He won't. He's no grandpa with hair the color of cigarette stains and a blanket over his knees, he's no toothless old gasser sunning himself in the park—he's a big leaguer, proud wearer of the Dodger blue, wielder of stick and glove. How can he get old? The grass is always green, the lights always shining, no clocks or periods or halves or quarters, no punch-in and punch-out: This is the game that never ends. When the heavy hitters have fanned and the pitchers' arms gone sore, when there's no joy in Mudville, taxes are killing everybody and the Russians are raising hell in Guatemala, when the manager paces the dugout like an attack dog, mind racing, searching high and low for the canny veteran to go in and do single combat, there he'll be—always, always, eternal as a monument—Hector Quesadilla, utility infielder, with the .296 lifetime batting average and service with the Reds, Phils, Cubs, Royals, and L.A. Dodgers.

So he waits. Hangs on. Trots his aching legs round the outfield grass before the game, touches his toes ten agonizing times each morning, takes extra batting practice with the rookies and slumping millionaires. Sits. Watches. Massages his feet. Waits through the scourging road trips in the Midwest and along the East Coast, down to muggy Atlanta, across to stormy Wrigley and up to frigid Candlestick, his gut clenched round an indigestible cud of meatloaf and instant potatoes and wax beans, through the terrible nightgames with the alien lights in his eyes, waits at the end of the bench for a word from the manager, for a pat on the ass, a roar, a hiss, a chorus of cheers and catcalls, the marimba pulse of bat striking ball and the sweet looping arc of the clean base hit.

And then comes a day, late in the season, the homeboys battling for the pennant with the big-stick Braves and the sneaking Jints, when he wakes from honeyed dreams in his own bed that's like an old friend with the sheets that smell of starch and soap and flowers, and feels the pain stripped from his body as if at the touch of a healer's fingertips. Usually he dreams nothing, the night a blank, an erasure, and opens his eyes on the agonies of the martyr strapped to a bed of nails. Then he limps to the toilet, makes a poor discolored water, rinses the dead taste from his mouth and staggers to the kitchen table where food, only food, can revive in him the interest in drawing another breath. He butters tortillas and folds them into his mouth, spoons up egg and melted jack cheese and frijoles refritos with the green salsa, lashes into his steak as if it were cut from the thigh of Kerensky, the Atlanta relief ace who'd twice that season caught him looking at a full-count fastball with men in scoring position. But not today. Today is different, a sainted day, a day on which sunshine sits in the windows like a gift of the Magi and the chatter of the starlings in the crapped-over palms across the street is a thing that approaches the divine music of the spheres. What can it be?

In the kitchen it hits him: pozole in a pot on the stove, carnitas in the saucepan, the table spread with sweetcakes, buñuelos and the little marzipan *dulces* he could kill for. *Feliz cumpleaños,* Asunción pipes as he steps through the doorway. Her face is lit with the smile of her mother, her mother's mother, the line of gift-givers descendant to the happy conquistadors and joyous Aztecs. A kiss, a *dulce* and then a knock at the door and Reina, fat with life, throwing her arms around him while her children gobble up the table, the room, their grandfather, with eyes that swallow their faces. Happy birthday, Daddy, Reina says, and Franklin, her youngest, is handing him the gift.

And Hector Jr.?

But he doesn't have to fret about Hector Jr., his firstborn, the boy with these same great sad eyes who'd sat in the dugout in his Reds uniform when they lived in Cincy and worshiped the pudgy icon of his father until the parish priest had to straighten him out on his hagiography, Hector Jr. who studies English at USC and day and night writes his thesis on a poet his father has never heard of, because here he is, walking in the front door with his mother's smile and a store-wrapped gift—a book, of course. Then Reina's children line up to kiss the *abuelo*—they'll be sitting in the box seats this afternoon—and suddenly he knows so much: He will play today, he will hit, oh yes, can there be a doubt? He sees it already. Kerensky, the son of a whore. Extra innings. Koerner or Manfredonia or Brooksie on third. The ball like an orange, a mango, a muskmelon, the clean swipe of the bat, the delirium of the crowd, and the gimpy *abuelo,* a big leaguer still, doffing his cap and taking a tour of the bases in a stately trot, Sultan for a day.

Could things ever be so simple?

In the bottom of the ninth, with the score tied at five and Reina's kids full of Coke, hotdogs, peanuts, and ice cream and getting restless, with Asunción clutching her rosary as if she were drowning and Hector Jr.'s nose stuck in some book, Dupuy taps him to hit for the pitcher with two down and Fast Freddie Phelan on second. The eighth man in the lineup, Spider Martinez from Muchas Vacas, D.R., has just whiffed on three straight pitches and Corcoran, the Braves' left-handed relief man, is all of a sudden pouring it on. Throughout the stadium a hush has fallen over the crowd, the torpor of suppertime, the game poised at apogee. Shadows are lengthening in the outfield, swallows flitting across the face of the scoreboard, here a fan drops into his beer, there a big mama gathers up her purse, her knitting, her shopping bags and parasol and thinks of dinner. Hector sees it all. This is the moment of catharsis, the moment to take it out.

As Martinez slumps toward the dugout, Dupuy, a laconic, embittered man who keeps his suffering inside and drinks Gelusil like water, takes hold of Hector's arm. His eyes are red-rimmed and paunchy, doleful as a basset hound's. Bring the runner in, Champ, he rasps. First pitch fake a bunt, then hit away. Watch Booger at third. Uh-huh, Hector mumbles, snapping his gum. Then he slides his bat from the rack—white ash, tape-wrapped grip, personally blessed by the Archbishop of Guadalajara and his twenty-seven acolytes—and starts for the dugout steps, knowing the course of the next three minutes as surely as his blood knows the course of his veins. The familiar cry will go up—Cheese, Cheese, Cheesus—and he'll amble up to the batter's box, knocking imaginary dirt from his spikes, adjusting the straps of his golf gloves, tugging at his underwear and fiddling with his batting helmet. His face will be impenetrable. Corcoran will work the ball in his glove, maybe tip back his cap for a little hair grease and then give him a look of psychopathic hatred. Hector has seen it before. Me against you. My record, my career, my house, my family, my life, my mutual funds and beer distributorship against yours. He's been hit in the elbow, the knee, the groin, the head. Nothing fazes him. Nothing. Murmuring a prayer to Santa Griselda, patroness of the sun-blasted Sonoran village where he was born like a heat blister on his mother's womb, Hector Hernán Jesus y María Quesadilla will step into the batter's box, ready for anything.

But it's a game of infinite surprises.

Before Hector can set foot on the playing field, Corcoran suddenly doubles up in pain, Phelan goes slack at second and the catcher and shortstop are hustling out to the mound, tailed an instant later by trainer and pitching coach. First thing Hector thinks is a groin pull, then appendicitis, and finally, as Corcoran goes down on one knee, poison. He'd once seen a man shot in the gut at Obregon City, but the report had been loud as a thunderclap and he hears nothing now but the enveloping hum of the crowd. Corcoran is rising shakily, the trainer and pitching coach supporting him while the catcher kicks meditatively in the dirt, and now Mueller, the Atlanta *cabeza,* is striding big-bellied out of the dugout, head down as if to be sure his feet are following orders. Halfway to the mound, Mueller flicks his right hand across his ear quick as a horse flicking its tail, and it's all she wrote for Corcoran.

Poised on the dugout steps like a bird dog, Hector waits, his eyes riveted on the bullpen. Please, he whispers, praying for the intercession of the Niño and pledging a hundred votary candles—at least, at least. Can it be? Yes, milk of my Mother, yes—Kerensky himself strutting out onto the field like a fighting cock. Kerensky!

Come to the birthday boy, Kerensky, he murmurs, so certain he's going to put it in the stands he could point like the immeasurable Bambino. His tired old legs shuffle with impatience as Kerensky stalks across the field, and then he's turning to pick Asunción out of the crowd. She's on her feet now, Reina too, the kids come alive beside her. And Hector Jr., the book forgotten, his face transfigured with the look of rapture he used to get when he was a boy sitting on the steps of the dugout. Hector can't help himself: He grins and gives them the thumbs-up sign.

Then, as Kerensky fires his warm-up smoke, the loudspeaker crackles and Hector emerges from the shadow of the dugout into the tapering golden shafts of the late-afternoon sun. That pitch, I want that one, he mutters, carrying his bat like a javelin and shooting a glare at Kerensky, but something's wrong here, the announcer's got it screwed up: BATTING FOR RARITAN, NUMBER THIRTY-NINE, DAVE TOOL. What the—? And now somebody's tugging at his sleeve and he's turning to gape with incomprehension at the freckle-faced batboy, Dave Tool striding out of the dugout with his big forty-two ounce stick, Dupuy's face locked up like a vault and the crowd, on its feet, chanting Tool, Tool, Tool! For a moment he just stands there, frozen with disbelief. Then Tool is brushing by him and the idiot of a batboy is leading him toward the dugout as if he were an old blind fisherman poised on the edge of the dock.

He feels as if his legs have been cut from under him. Tool! Dupuy is yanking him for Tool? For what? So he can play the lefty-righty percentages like some chess head or something? Tool, of all people. Tool, with his thirty-five home runs a season and lifetime B.A. of .234, Tool who's worn so many uniforms they had to expand the league to make room for him, what's he going to do? Raging, Hector flings down his bat and comes at Dupuy like a cat tossed in a bag. You crazy, you jerk, he sputters. I woulda hit him, I woulda won the game. I dreamed it. And then, his voice breaking: It's my birthday for Christ's sake!

But Dupuy can't answer him, because on the first pitch Tool slams a real worm burner to short and the game is going into extra innings.

By seven o'clock, half the fans have given up and gone home. In the top of the fourteenth, when the visitors came up with a pair of runs on a two-out pinch-hit home run, there was a real exodus, but then the Dodgers struck back for two to knot it up again. Then it was three up and three down, regular as clockwork. Now, at the end of the nineteenth, with the score deadlocked at seven all and the players dragging themselves around the field like gutshot horses, Hector is beginning to think he may get a second chance after all. Especially the way Dupuy's been using up players like some crazy general on the western front, yanking pitchers, juggling his defense, throwing in pinch runners and pinch hitters until he's just about gone through the entire roster. Asunción is still there among the faithful, the foolish, and the self-deluded, fumbling with her rosary and mouthing prayers for Jesus Christ Our Lord, the Madonna, Hector, the hometeam, and her departed mother, in that order. Reina too, looking like the survivor of some disaster, Franklin and Alfredo asleep in their seats, the niñitas gone off somewhere—for Coke and dogs, maybe. And Hector Jr. looks like he's going to stick it out too, though he should be back in his closet writing about the mystical so-and-so and the way he illustrates his poems with gods and men and serpents. Watching him, Hector can feel his heart turn over.

In the bottom of the twentieth, with one down and Gilley on first —he's a starting pitcher but Dupuy sent him in to run for Manfredonia after Manfredonia jammed his ankle like a turkey and had to be helped off the field—Hector pushes himself up from the bench and ambles down to where Dupuy sits in the corner, contemplatively spitting a gout of tobacco juice and saliva into the drain at his feet. Let me hit, Bernard, come on, Hector says, easing down beside him.

Can't, comes the reply, and Dupuy never even raises his head. Can't risk it, Champ. Look around you—and here the manager's voice quavers with uncertainty, with fear and despair and the dull edge of hopelessness—I got nobody left. I hit you, I got to play you.

No, No, you don't understand—I'm going to win it, I swear.

And then the two of them, like old bankrupts on a bench in Miami Beach, look up to watch Phelan hit into a double play.

A buzz runs through the crowd when the Dodgers take the field for the top of the twenty-second. Though Phelan is limping, Thorkelsson's asleep on his feet and Dorfman, fresh on the mound, is the only pitcher left on the roster, the moment is electric. One more inning and they tie the record set by the Mets and Giants back in '64, and then they're making history. Drunk, sober, and then drunk again, saturated with fats and nitrates and sugar, the crowd begins to come to life. Go Dodgers! Eat shit! Yo Mama! Phelan's a bum!

Hector can feel it too. The rage and frustration that had consumed him back in the ninth are gone, replaced by a dawning sense of wonder—he could have won it then, yes, and against his nemesis Kerensky too—but the Niño and Santa Griselda have been saving him for something greater. He sees it now, knows it in his bones: He's going to be the hero of the longest game in history.

As if to bear him out, Dorfman, the kid from Albuquerque, puts in a good inning, cutting the bushed Braves down in order. In the dugout, Doc Pusser, the team physician, is handing out the little green pills that keep your eyes open and Dupuy is blowing into a cup of coffee and staring morosely out at the playing field. Hector watches as Tool, who'd stayed in the game at first base, fans on three straight pitches, then he shoves in beside Dorfman and tells the kid he's looking good out there. With his big cornhusker's ears and nose like a tweezer, Dorfman could be a caricature of the green rookie. He says nothing. Hey, don't let it get to you, kid—I'm going to win this one for you. Next inning or maybe the inning after. Then he tells him how he saw it in a vision and how it's his birthday and the kid's going to get the victory, one of the biggest of all time. Twenty-four, twenty-five innings maybe.

Hector had heard of a game once in the Mexican League that took three days to play and went seventy-three innings, did Dorfman know that? It was down in Culiacán. Chito Martí, the converted bullfighter, had finally ended it by dropping down dead of exhaustion in centerfield, allowing Sexto Silvestro, who'd broken his leg rounding third, to crawl home with the winning run. But Hector doesn't think this game will go that long. Dorfman sighs and extracts a bit of wax from his ear as Pantaleo, the third string catcher, hits back to the pitcher to end the inning. I hope not, he says, uncoiling from the bench, my arm'd fall off.

Ten o'clock comes and goes. Dorfman's still in there, throwing breaking stuff and a little smoke at the Braves, who look as if they just stepped out of *Night of the Living Dead*. The hometeam isn't doing much better. Dupuy's run through the whole team but for Hector, and three or four of the guys have been in there since two in the afternoon; the rest are a bunch of ginks and gimps who can barely stand up. Out in the stands, the fans look grim. The vendors ran out of beer an hour back, and they haven't had dogs or kraut or Coke or anything since eight-thirty.

In the bottom of the twenty-seventh Phelan goes berserk in the dugout and Dupuy has to pin him to the floor while Doc Pusser shoves something up his nose to calm him. Next inning the balls-and-strikes ump passes out cold and Dorfman, who's beginning to look a little fagged, walks the first two batters but manages to weasel his way out of the inning without giving up the go-ahead run. Meanwhile, Thorkelsson has been dropping ice cubes down his trousers to keep awake, Martinez is smoking something suspicious in the can and Ferenc Fortnoi, the third baseman, has begun talking to himself in a tortured Slovene dialect. For his part, Hector feels stronger and more alert as the game goes on. Though he hasn't had a bite since breakfast he feels impervious to the pangs of hunger, as if he were preparing himself, mortifying his flesh like a saint in the desert.

And then, in the top of the thirty-first, with half the fans asleep and the other half staring into nothingness like the inmates of the asylum of Our Lady of Guadeloupe where Hector had once visited his halfwit uncle when he was a boy, Pluto Morales cracks one down the first base line and Tool flubs it. Right away it looks like trouble, because Chester Bubo is running around right field looking up at the sky like a bird-watcher while the ball snakes through the grass, caroms off his left foot and coasts like silk to the edge of the warning track. Morales meanwhile is rounding second and coming on for third, running in slow motion, flat-footed and hump-backed, his face drained of color, arms flapping like the undersized wings of some big flightless bird. It's not even close. By the time Bubo can locate the ball, Morales is ten feet from the plate, pitching into a face-first slide that's at least three parts collapse and that's it, the Braves are up by one. It looks black for the hometeam. But Dorfman, though his arm has begun to swell like a sausage, shows some grit, bears down and retires the side to end the historic top of the unprecedented thirty-first inning.

Now, at long last, the hour has come. It'll be Bubo, Dorfman, and

Tool for the Dodgers in their half of the inning, which means that Hector will hit for Dorfman. I been saving you, Champ, Dupuy rasps, the empty Gelusil bottle clenched in his fist like a hand grenade. Go on in there, he murmurs and his voice fades away to nothing as Bubo pops the first pitch up in back of the plate. Go on in there and do your stuff.

Sucking in his gut, Hector strides out onto the brightly-lit field like a nineteen-year-old, the familiar cry in his ears, the haggard fans on their feet, a sickle moon sketched in overhead as if in some cartoon strip featuring drunken husbands and the milkman. Asunción looks as if she's been nailed to the cross, Reina wakes with a start and shakes the little ones into consciousness and Hector Jr. staggers to his feet like a battered middleweight coming out for the fifteenth round. They're all watching him. The fans whose lives are like empty sacks, the wife who wants him home in front of the TV, his divorced daughter with the four kids and another on the way, his son, pride of his life, who reads for the doctor of philosophy while his crazy *padrecito* puts on a pair of long stockings and chases around after a little white ball like a case of arrested development. He'll show them. He'll show them some *cojones,* some true grit and desire: The game's not over yet.

On the mound for the Braves is Bo Brannerman, a big mustachioed machine of a man, normally a starter but pressed into desperate relief service tonight. A fine pitcher—Hector would be the first to admit it— but he just pitched two nights ago and he's worn thin as wire. Hector steps up to the plate, feeling legendary. He glances over at Tool in the on-deck circle, and then down at Booger, the third base coach. All systems go. He cuts at the air twice and then watches Brannerman rear back and release the ball: Strike one. Hector smiles. Why rush things? Give them a thrill. He watches a low outside slider that just about bounces to even the count, and then stands there like a statue as Brannerman slices the corner of the plate for strike two. From the stands, a chant of *Viejo, Viejo,* and Asunción's piercing soprano, Hit him, Hector!

Hector has no worries, the moment eternal, replayed through games uncountable, with pitchers who were over the hill when he was a rookie with San Buitre, with pups like Brannerman, with big leaguers and Hall of Famers. Here it comes, Hector, ninety-two m.p.h., the big *gringo* trying to throw it by you, the matchless wrists, the flawless swing, one terrific moment of suspended animation—and all of a sudden you're starring in your own movie.

How does it go? The ball cutting through the night sky like a comet, arching high over the centerfielder's hapless scrambling form to slam off the wall while your legs churn up the base paths, rounding first in a gallop, taking second and heading for third . . . but wait, you spill hot coffee on your hand and you can't feel it, the demons apply the live wire to your tailbone, the legs give out and they cut you down at third while the stadium erupts in howls of execration and abuse and the *niñitos* break down, faces flooded with tears of humiliation, Hector Jr. turning his back in disgust, and Asunción raging like harpie, *Abuelo! Abuelo! Abuelo!*

Stunned, shrunken, humiliated, you stagger back to the dugout in a maelstrom of abuse, paper cups, flying spittle, your life a waste, the game a cheat, and then, crowning irony, that bum Tool, worthless all the way back to his washerwoman grandmother and the drunken muttering whey-faced tribe that gave him suck, stands tall like a giant and sends the first pitch out of the park to tie it. Oh, the pain. Flat feet, fire in your legs, your poor tired old heart skipping a beat in mortification. And now Dupuy, red in the face, shouting: The game could be over but for you, you crazy gimpy old beaner washout! You want to hide in your locker, bury yourself under the shower room floor, but you have to watch as the next two men reach base and you pray with fervor that they'll score and put an end to your debasement. But no, Thorkelsson whiffs and the new inning dawns as inevitably as the new minute, the new hour, the new day, endless, implacable, world without end.

But wait, wait: Who's going to pitch? Dorfman's out, there's nobody left, the astonishing thirty-second inning is marching across the scoreboard like an invading army and suddenly Dupuy is standing over you —no, no, he's down on one knee, begging. Hector, he's saying, didn't you use to pitch down in Mexico when you were a kid, didn't I hear that someplace? Yes, you're saying, yes, but that was—

And then you're out on the mound, in command once again, elevated like some half-mad old king in a play, and throwing smoke. The first two batters go down on strikes and the fans are rabid with excitement, Asunción will raise a shrine, Hector Jr. worships you more than all the poets that ever lived, but can it be? You walk the next three and then give up the grand slam to little Tommy Oshimisi! Mother of God, will it never cease? But wait, wait, wait: Here comes the bottom of the thirty-second and Brannerman's wild. He walks a couple, gets a couple out, somebody reaches on an infield single and the bases are loaded for you, Hector Quesadilla, stepping up to the plate now like the Iron Man himself. The wind-up, the delivery, the ball hanging there like a *piñata,* like a birthday gift, and then the stick flashes in your hands like an archangel's sword, and the game goes on forever.

Bill Bradley

After the Applause

In the early 1960s, Sport *Magazine ran a story on a reigning pro basketball player of the day, Easy Ed McCauley of the St. Louis Hawks. Shortly afterward, the editor received a fan letter from a young man who had attended McCauley's summer camp and learned much about the game and other things, too, he said, from McCauley. The letter writer was Bill Bradley, even then politically astute. He became more so at Princeton where he excelled in both basketball and academics. From Princeton, he made a stop at Oxford as a Rhodes scholar, and then went on to a fulfilling career with the New York Knicks. In this selection from his insightful autobiography,* Life on the Run, *Bradley muses on how he might handle life after his "addiction" comes to an end. The way he has done so is on public record.*

There is terror behind the dream of being a professional ballplayer. It comes as a slow realization of finality and of the frightening unknowns which the end brings. When the playing is over, one can sense that one's youth has been spent playing a game and now both the game and youth are gone, along with the innocence that characterizes all games which at root are pure and promote a prolonged adolescence in those who play. Now the athlete must face a world where awkward naiveté can no longer be overlooked because of athletic performance. By age thirty-five any potential for developing skills outside of basketball is slim. The "good guy" syndrome ceases. What is left is the other side of the Faustian bargain: To live all one's days never able to recapture the feeling of those few years of intensified youth. In a way it is the fate of a warrior class to receive rewards, plaudits, and exhilaration simultaneously with the means of self-destruction. When a middle-aged lawyer moves more slowly on the tennis court, he makes adjustments and may even laugh at his geriatric restrictions because for him there remains the law. For the athlete who reaches thirty-five, something in him dies; not a peripheral activity but a fundamental passion. It necessarily dies. The athlete rarely recuperates. He approaches the end of his playing days the way old people approach death. He puts his finances in order. He reminisces easily. He offers advice to the young. But, the athlete differs from an old person in that he must continue living. Behind all the years of practice and all the hours of glory waits that inexorable terror of living without the game.

I have often wondered how I will handle the end of my playing days. No one really knows until that day comes. DeBusschere says that as long as one doesn't puff up with the unnatural attention given a pro athlete, and keeps a few good friends, the adjustment should be easy. I don't know if he really believes it. Tom Heinsohn says you don't realize how much you love the game until you miss it. Forced into a premature retirement by injury, he yearned for the life again so much that he took a 75 percent cut in salary to coach the Celtics. One retired player told me he noticed the end at home in his relationship with his wife. The fears and resentment that were formerly projected into the team now fall on wife and children, making life miserable for all. Holzman says that he never regretted the end, for when it came he had had enough basketball and wanted out. In my case, I've been preparing for the end since my first year, but even so I can only hope that I will manage easily the withdrawal from what Phil Jackson calls "my addiction."

When DeBusschere announced his retirement after getting a ten-year contract to become General Manager of the New York Nets, many newspapers said that he was retiring at his best. Once, after a speech I gave, a man came up to me and said, "Retire while you're still at the top. Whizzer White did it. Jim Brown did it. Bill Russell did it." DeBusschere talks about how sad he felt for Willie Mays struggling at the end of his brilliant career. He calls Mays' play embarrassing. He also says of several players that they played one year too long.

In the same way that it is difficult to watch your father grow old, it's difficult to watch your favorite player become increasingly unable to do the small things that made you admire him. But unless a man has a better opportunity, why should he stop doing something he loves? Fans want stars to retire on top in part to protect their fantasies. That makes no sense; consider Jerry West or Oscar Robertson, whose last two years of struggle didn't diminish the twelve previous years of achievement. In a way it made them more likable than if they had sought to retain an heroic level through early retirement. The decline is sad but human, for it is the one thing that strikes ineluctably in professional sports. To miss it makes a pro's experience incomplete.

The end of a player's career is the end of the big money and big publicity, and at that point the future depends on past prudence and levelheadedness. The specter of Joe Louis or Sugar Ray Robinson haunts many players. DeBusschere believes that of all the Knicks Frazier will have the most difficulty adjusting to the post-playing days. I'm not so sure. "My biggest motivation not to go broke," says Frazier, "doesn't come from the example of Sugar Ray or Joe Louis, but from my father. When he lost all of his money, he lost everything. The new 'Caddies' and other presents that used to arrive at the house stopped coming. I hold back spending too much money more than I would if I hadn't been around when something happened to my father." Frazier clearly has thought about the change of living standard but DeBusschere wonders also whether Clyde can adjust to a life of less publicity after nearly ten years in the New York spotlight. Though his life seemingly focuses on externals, and remains naively vulnerable to the quixotic taste of strangers, I believe Clyde does seem to understand the precarious path he treads and he confidently prepares for the end with little concern for the potential terror. Maybe no fall can be as hard and damaging as that which he witnessed his father take many years before.

Perhaps the last word on the end of a player's career comes from Danny Whelan. "When the fan is kissing your ass and telling you that you're the greatest," says Danny, "he hates you. They want to get you down on their level and they can't when you're on the top. After you retire just go to that guy who was buying you drinks when you were a player and ask him for a job. He'll show you the door. The fan likes to step on a player after he's finished playing if he gets a chance. A good example is Sweetwater Clifton. Just the other night some guy says he remembers Sweets with the Knicks and asks me if I know what he's doing. I shut up. If I had told him that he's driving a cab in Chicago the guy would have got his nuts off. Players would be better off to change their names and start anew."

Jimmy Breslin

The Good Life of Mr. Fitz

In the early 1960s, Jimmy Breslin was told over the telephone that certain members of the Green Bay Packers' family—Paul Hornung and Fuzzy Thurston among them—were enraged about a piece Breslin had written for The Saturday Evening Post *documenting the Packer players' off-the-field follies. The phone caller told Breslin, "If you come around again they said they'd punch you out." Silence from the telephone for a long moment and then the inimitable Breslin voice, a little squeakier than usual: "Ah . . . slip and counter." The irrepressible Jimmy Breslin has been doing that throughout his notable career as a ranking urban journalist and chronicler of other people's lives, as in his well-received biography of Damon Runyon. Another of Breslin's favorite subjects that became a book was the legendary horseracing trainer Sunny Jim Fitzsimmons. Here, from* Sunny Jim, *is a taste of Mr. Fitz's good life.*

By the spring of 1951, Sunny Jim Fitzsimmons was approaching his seventy-seventh birthday and people were calling him ancient. He had lived a full life, and now it was becoming serene. He was at the barn each morning with the hay and ammonia smell opening his eyes and flaring his nostrils as it always had, and then he would train his horses, have something to eat, take a nap and wake up for the afternoon's racing. There was almost no change. You could spend a day with him, then come back six months later and it still would be the same. He would be walking around the stable area, bent almost in half over an aluminum crutch under his right arm. Arthritis has his back bowed and hardened so that he looks like a man carrying a beer keg on his back. He would keep looking up to see ahead of him and he would snap orders to stablehands taking care of the 45 valuable thoroughbreds under his command. Then in the afternoon he would sit at his favorite spot along the rail and watch his horses run and win or lose he would not get excited. He was in the big money; as big as there is in sports. It was a life he had earned by spending years scratching for meal money.

It was a good life for Mr. Fitz. Every day of it. And on June 21, 1951, it all started to fall apart. The day didn't seem to be a bad one. It was a soft spring morning at Aqueduct, the horses were on the track and Mr. Fitz was along the rail watching them. The phone rang in the cottage and a boy yelled out that it was for Mr. Fitz. He walked to the cottage, grumbling about being bothered when he was in the middle of his work. He picked up the phone.

"Yes," he said.

A man's voice on the other end said he was a policeman and that he had just been called in because of a death in the house and he wasn't sure of who was who in the family but he did know that Sunny Jim Fitzsimmons, the horse trainer—well, his wife had just died and he had been told to call somebody at the stable here and tell them.

It was as simple as that. When Mr. Fitz got home there was a police car and an ambulance in front of the house and inside there was a doctor who was saying, in the gentle tones they always use at such times, that it had been very quick; a heart attack; no pain; just one of those things that happens very quickly . . . at her age, you know. Jennie Fitzsimmons, Mr. Fitz's brick, was dead in her room upstairs. There was nothing to do but call the undertaker.

William Woodward, the New York banker whose horses Mr. Fitz had trained for over a quarter century, died during this period, too. Woodward had become a friend of Mr. Fitz's; the anything-goes kind of friend that you can only have after years of close association. Then George (Fish) Tappen, who had grown up with Mr. Fitz, died. Fish had been a part of Mr. Fitz's racing life for all but one or two years of his career. And the Bradys, who for twenty years kept house for Mr. Fitz, also died. Oh, maybe there was six months before Woodward went and another six months or so might have passed before Tappen and the Bradys went. But to Mr. Fitz it seemed like everything had turned into a dark blue suit and the smell of flowers they put around a casket, and the life he had worked for so hard was disappearing around him.

People who live to be very old always say it is the easiest thing in the world to let go when your friends are going. And once you let go and lose interest in what is going on, it doesn't take long for the end to come.

This seemed to some to be what was happening with Mr. Fitz. Or maybe they just thought it was happening because they were looking for it. Anyhow, he seemed to be thinking more about the past than the present or future, and this wasn't like his usual self.

Then some claimed it started to show in the horses. They pointed to the winnings being off. But who could be sure of the reason? There are an awful lot of ifs and buts and maybes in this game.

One thing you can say for sure. Circumstances had changed, too. When William Woodward, Sr., died in 1952 his son Bill took over the stable. Through most of his life, the young Woodward had been around the horses only sparingly. Now he became interested in them and after spending a few days at the stable, then watching horses run in races, he was getting the feeling a man always gets when he is around good horses. Mr. Fitz thought he was a fine boy. But Mr. Fitz was seventy-seven and he had had twenty-seven years of working with a man he had come to think of as a friend and now he had to start all over again with somebody else. It was not easy.

Then something really did happen, and it made all the difference. On his last trip to Belair Stud with Woodward, Sr., Mr. Fitz had looked over the crop of weanlings, leggy little things with almost no bodies to them at all, and Woodward pointed to one of them and said that if everything went well this was a horse he wanted to send to the races in England.

"He is by Nasrullah out of Segula," Woodward said. "I like the breeding."

"He looks fine," Mr. Fitz said.

The next year Woodward was dead, his son was in charge and all of the racing was to be in America. One bright afternoon in the early fall, the young Woodward and Mr. Fitz were in a car which turned into the gravel driveway, bordered by fieldstone fence, of Belair Stud Farm. They were going to look at the yearlings which were about to be broken for racing and the weanlings which still had a year to go before this could be done.

At one enclosure, Woodward and Mr. Fitz got out and walked to the fence rail to look at a group of horses—mares, each with a weanling. When you are at a horse farm and you stand at a rail like this, you rap on the wood to make a noise and then one by one the mares and their yearlings lope toward you. If the weanling gets too close to these strangers at the fence, the mare sticks her head between the weanling and the fence and pushes her offspring away from the strangers he is too small to deal with. Now and then one of the weanlings will dart away from a mare, move as fast as he can in one jumble of long legs, then stop, flick the hind legs up in a little kick, wheel again, get the jumble of legs going, then dart back and put his head under the mare's stomach for a coffee break. You can watch them running around like this for hours.

If Sunny Jim needed a lift at this time in his life, it might well come from these fenced-in fields of soft dirt and deep grass with young horses running in them. Through all of his years, he had taken care of horses, good ones and bad ones, sound ones and ones with injuries nobody else wanted to bother with, and they had shaped his life. Maybe what he needed now, without even knowing it, was to have a big one going for him. The kind of horse that can put that little extra bit of excitement inside you. What was needed, simply was a horse that could make it a fair test between Sunny Jim Fitzsimmons and the calendar. The horse was in the next field.

He was a big, sturdy-legged, inquisitive yearling who came to the fence as Mr. Fitz and Woodward walked up, then wheeled and pounded back toward the center of the field, his feet sending clods of dirt into the air. He would not be two years old until the end of the year, but he had a chest on him and his legs looked like they could kick their way through a brick wall. You look at a horse such as this and it does something to you, even if you are not used to seeing horses. And Mr. Fitz looked at him and asked Woodward which one was that colt out there.

"You saw him with my father," Woodward said. "He's by Nasrullah out of Segula. That's the one my father wanted to send to England."

"Oh, yes," Mr. Fitz said. "Good-lookin' kind of a colt. Good runnin' action. Look at that. Uses two leads at this stage. Big, too. Gonna be extra big. Oh, you can see he could be a real useful horse. Course you don't know what's inside him. Heart, lungs. You don't know that. But he looks real nice right now, don't he?"

"We have him nominated for everything," Woodward said.

"That's good. You never can tell."

Then they left and Mr. Fitz went back to New York to take care of his horses, but on the way back he was thinking a little bit about the horse. There was this one double-sized stall he had at Aqueduct. It used to be two stalls, but he had broken it into one for Johnstown. Remember that? Sure. Johnstown couldn't fit in an ordinary stall. Still got that extra big stall. Yes, it would be a good place to put this colt when he came to the track. He'd need it. You could see he was going to grow into a real big-sized horse. He had wide hips. Good, wide head, too. Plenty of spirit to him. Looked like he wanted to take your shoulder off. He walked with a little swagger, too. Didn't mope around, sloppy-like. Well, I've been wrong before lookin' at horses like this. So has everybody else. There's only one way to tell, though. Get him to racin' and see what happens. You won't know for a long time. This one seems to have something you could go to work on, though.

So he began to think ahead again, to the day when he would get this colt on the race track and see what could be done with him. This was 1953 and he was seventy-nine, but now he definitely had something to keep him going.

Woodward named the horse Nashua. You could stick your fist down the horse's throat, down to where the jaw comes out of the neck, and there would be plenty of room for it because this was a horse with a big windpipe and he could take in enough air to run for a month. He was sent out to a Westbury, Long Island, horse farm owned by John (Shipwreck) Kelly. Bill McCleary, one of Mr. Fitz's exercise boys, went out there to break the horse for racing. This was only the fall and it would be months before Nashua got to the races and the first year wouldn't be that important because a lot of times a horse doesn't come around until he is three years old. This is what makes being with horses beautiful. You are always waiting for something in the future and now, as Nashua learned how to get into a starting gate and how to run around turns, Mr. Fitz was waiting and looking ahead.

The stable shipped to Florida and in February, at Hialeah, he had Nashua on the track working. People saw the horse and they asked Mr. Fitz about him. The answer was what it should be.

"Like him?" Mr. Fitz said. "I don't know whether I like him or not. He's only a baby and we got a long way to go. He looks like he might be a good one, but how do I know? I can't tell if there's anything wrong with him. He can't tell me, either. He can't talk, you know. And I can't see inside him to find out what kind of a motor he's got. I hope he's good. But I don't know what he's going to be." He then kept on with an old-time Fitzsimmons monologue on horses and life and how little any-body knows about what's going to happen. After he was through, he gave a groom hell for throwing out too much straw while mucking out a stall and he was making demands on everybody else around him and that crutch was banging onto the ground hard when he walked. He was not interested in what happened yesterday.

Later in the year, in October, after Nashua had won several races and had lost a couple because he was green and ran that way, Mr. Fitz was standing in the infield at Belmont Park with his son John and grandson Jimmy and far up to the right Eddie Arcaro was sitting quietly on Nashua after they finished a warm-up and the horse was walking toward the starting gate. The race was the Futurity. It was to be run on a strip known as the Widener Chute. This was a running strip which bisected the main track. The horses would come straight down it to the finish line, with no turns. Because of the chute's angle to the stands, it was nearly impossible for anybody in the crowd to make out who was ahead in a race. Mr. Fitz had always watched Futurities down the chute and it didn't bother him. He knew what to look for.

When the race went off, he saw what he wanted. There were good horses in this race . . . a horse called Summer Tan, another called Royal Coinage, a good sprinter named King Hairon, and he could be tough because the race was only for six furlongs. They all came down fast. Mr. Fitz stood quietly, with the crutch under his right arm. He watched the field as it moved along. Halfway down the chute, somewhere around the pole that said there were three furlongs left, Nashua let it go. His stride became longer. His head stuck out. He was working now. Running like a big one. The horses around started to slip back. Then a little growl came from the bottom of Mr. Fitz's throat. Then he growled again.

"Look at how he lowers his belly and goes to work," Mr. Fitz said. There was a spark in his voice. The years had no meaning to them now. This was Sunny Jim Fitzsimmons, age anything, and he had a big horse.

Nashua slammed down the chute and won by a long neck. Arcaro, a big grin on his face, brought the horse back to the winner's circle. Woodward was there and so were the photographers and there were big trophies for everybody, and Arcaro was saying that this big dude is a real runner.

Mr. Fitz was walking out of the infield. A brown-uniformed Pinkerton swung open a part of the rail so he could walk through and as Mr. Fitz came up the Pinkerton said, "Congratulations, Mr. Fitz. Looks like a real good one, doesn't he?"

"Thank you. Oh, he looked all right today. But we got a long way to go, you know. I want to get back to the barn and see what he looks like right now."

Mr. Fitz walked through the gap onto the track and headed for the car in the parking lot so John could drive him back to the barn and he could have the groom walk Nashua around in front of him so he could look close and make sure the horse came out of it all right. Then he would sit down and watch them rub the sweat off the horse and cool him out with water and he'd have plenty of orders to give. No, he was certainly not going into the winner's circle. The barn was his winner's circle.

And as Mr. Fitz made his way across the track, Slim Sully leaned against the iron rail around the crowded winner's circle and looked at Nashua. Then Sully pointed over to Mr. Fitz and he smiled.

"Look at him," Sully was saying. "In what other business could an eighty-year-old man win something called the Futurity?"

Everybody used the line the next day in the papers. It was more than just a line. Mr. Fitz, they knew then, had a future going for him after that race and because of this, when you talk to a friend of Mr. Fitz's today about Nashua, the friend will smile a little and talk a lot about the horse and remember a lot of things about him. All of them will. Nobody ever will forget the part Nashua played in Mr. Fitz's life.

Jimmy Cannon

Archie

Jimmy Cannon looked like a little man because he was short and wore his spiky salt-and-pepper hair short, and he didn't have the presence, say, of some short guys, like Dustin Hoffman. But when the smile came to his ravaged face, full of deep pink capillaries, and the words came out, this true balladeer of the sporting life turned tall. David Halberstam remembered meeting Cannon and being "stunned by the almost unbearable quality of his loneliness." But he was too well loved to be consistently lonely. His special friends were people like Joe DiMaggio, Marlene Dietrich, Joe Louis, Hemingway, and Sinatra. Cannon strummed his music almost every day of the week in one or another New York newspaper. This love song to a considerable boxer of his time, Archie Moore, shows you the spell Cannon could cast over his subject.

Someone should write a song about Archie Moore who in the Polo Grounds knocked out Bobo Olson in three rounds. I don't mean big composers such as Harold Arlen or Duke Ellington. It should be a song that comes out of the backrooms of sloughed saloons on night-drowned streets in morning-worried parts of bad towns.

The guy who writes this one must be a piano player who can be dignified when he picks a quarter out of the marsh of a sawdust floor. They're dead, most of those piano players, their mouths full of dust instead of songs. But I'll bet Archie could dig one up in any town he ever made.

What Archie Moore is should be told in music because this is a guy who understands the truth of jazz. It must be a small song, played with a curfew-cheating stealth and sung in those butt-strangled voices the old guys had. There shouldn't be any parts for fiddles or horns because the kind of music I mean doesn't live in halls or theaters. It's the personal music those old men talked, more than crooned, when they were entertaining themselves to fight the loneliness.

It would have to be a hell of a song at that to grab Archie Moore. There must be in it the embarrassment of decent people ducking into pawn shops. It has to have that because Moore didn't get out of hock until last night when he scored his biggest pay night. It would have to catch sounds a man hears lying in a flea bag bed on a summer night in a slum.

Traveling second class and getting pushed around and borrowing would be in that song. It would define how a man of great skills suffers in obscurity in places like Tasmania because Archie Moore stiffened Frank Lindsay in that burg back in '40. The pug's fear of age would be in and knowing what you have is turning rotten with the years.

It isn't the blues I mean or boogie-woogie or bop. It's the kind of lament Tommy Lyman still sings in the basements of big cities. Anyplace the hustlers hung out, in any town, you used to get music like that. It belonged to them. They were songs about guys mad with booze or going crazy over a wrong broad or getting trimmed with shaved dice. Always, the guys in the song were broke. This was for those who had been betrayed or taken, mauled by junk or doing time on a wrong rap. The music's dead with the dead men and a lot of them had to be buried in the city bone yard on the cuff. If one of them's alive, Archie would know where to find him.

There he was last night, Archie Moore, the light-heavyweight champion of the world, who has fought in the Garden only once. The trash of the fight racket got there and pulled down scores. But Archie was boxing Joe Delaney in a joint called Adelaide in Australia. This was a nice one last night. It was no trouble at all for Archie.

There was all that guff about Olson being too quick, too agile, too young for Archie. So Archie let his 'stach grow and that horn player's beard up under his lip and put on his gold-lined, cream-colored silk bath-robe and walked down into the ring. He was like a master of ceremonies standing in his corner, using both his mitts to shake hands with the pugs who were introduced. This was the easiest one they ever gave him. Generally, Archie looked stunted and flabby when you compared him to the guy he was fighting.

Middleweights don't con Archie even when they're champions. So Olson took the first round. Anyway, I gave it to him. But Archie had him measured and they should put that in the song, too. The night was clammily hot and Archie's a chubby guy even when he makes 175 and drains off the fat. Poor old Archie, they said. This kid will come in such a rush he'll make him back up.

But there was Olson backing up in the first round. Sure, he jabbed and he put a few combinations together. I saw that right Olson hit Archie with. But did you notice what happened when Archie took the shot with his right? The middleweight shuddered. He was gleaming with sweat and pale. He moved into the haven of a clinch.

It was very plain in the second. All Archie needed was one. He would get the range and let it go. So he stalled around, sneaking behind his crossed arms. He jabbed and blocked punches. Olson slipped some blows but Archie was in no hurry. Couple of times Olson nailed him but a hook told him that he was in there with the pawn shop champion who was trying to get out of hock.

The third only lasted a minute and nineteen seconds and that includes the ten Ruby Goldstein, the referee, counted. The right hand lead started Olson and then a right set him up. Then it was a left hook and Olson was down and numb. The second in Archie's corner began to unwrap the gold-lined robe. Olson was crawling across the ring. And then it was over.

But it isn't in this piece. It can't be. I don't know what Moore endured since '36, including the operation that put the welted scar on his belly. They tried to lose him and shut him out. They ran out on him and kept him poor. They forced him to fight in remote places. But now he's here. Marciano's got to be next. And that should be in the song.

Barnaby Conrad

The Death of Manolete

Here is a case of matching the perfect author with the perfect subject. For Barnaby Conrad was a bullfighter himself and later became a talented painter of matadors and bulls. But he earned his considerable reputation as the poet laureate of the sport. Manolete had a shorter career at his profession. In his eight years as a senior matador, beginning in 1939, Manolete was the King of the Matadors and Spain's national hero. But by 1946 he was wearing down, a man of twenty-nine who looked forty. In July of that year he was gored, and rushed back too early to fight the bulls. Then it was August 27, and he was facing a big bull named Islero. Barnaby Conrad tells the story of Manolete's Pass of Death.

Manuel Laureano Rodriguez y Sanchez, called Manolo by his friends, "The Monster" by the press, and known to the adoring public of three continents as Manolete, the world's greatest bullfighter, was drunk. A stranger might not have noticed it, but I knew he didn't talk this much or this confidentially. Especially when sober.

"I'm quitting," he said in his low Cordoban accent. He said it vehemently, as though expecting someone to come back with "Oh, yeah?"

He stood up, glancing over at his mistress, and went to the window of my apartment. He stared out at the Peruvian sunset and nervously shook the ice in his empty glass as though it were dice.

"I tell you, *compadre,* I'm through with it all. I'm going back to Spain and cut off the pigtail forever. I've made more money than five generations of my family put together, but I've never had time to spend it. I'm young. Twenty-nine's not old. I've had my horn wounds, but I'm still in one piece, *gracias a Dios.*"

A short scar notched the left side of his chin, and he put his fingers to it unconsciously. His face, ugly when analyzed feature by feature, was sad and drawn and old, yet at the same time it was compelling and majestic. If he were to walk into any café in any part of the world, people would immediately ask: Who is this gaunt young-old man—for he had the look and aura of Number One. Hod-carrier, dancer, artist, banker, one might not know—only that he was the best in his field.

He ran long fingers over the black hair that had a wide path of gray down the center. "I've been able to spend about three months on my place in Cordoba in all the years I've owned it. I'm going back and enjoy it—never look at another bull except from up in the stands."

He went out to the pantry for another drink, and I turned to Antonia Bronchalo, for several years his "fiancée." She was pretty and seemed like a nice girl, but people said she was hard as Toledo steel. She'd made a few Spanish movies under the name of Lupe Sino, but she was no star. Her fame would always rest in the fact that she was loved by important men—lots of them.

"What do you think," I asked. "Will he quit?"

She smiled. "He's told me for several months now that he'll give it up the moment we get back to Spain and that we'll get married and raise bulls and half a dozen little Manoletes. He's starting to slip. He should get out quick, alive. But they'll never let him." She looked up at the portrait I had done of him. "That pretty gold uniform means excitement and money to too many people for them ever to let him take it off. They'll kill him first."

She was right. When Manolete arrived back in Spain in the spring of 1947, he received a tremendous reception. As the papers put it, no one since the conquistadors had so successfully carried the glories of Spain to the New World. Then, after he announced he was going to retire, they set about to kill him.

It's hard for Americans to understand why all this fuss about one bullfighter. But he wasn't just a bullfighter to the Spaniards. He was their only national and international hero. We have Eisenhower, Gable, Grable, DiMaggio and hundreds of others, but they just had Manolete. And when he was killed, he died such a beautiful dramatic Spanish death that I swear, in spite of the great funeral, the week of national mourning, the odes, the dirges, the posthumous decorations by the government, that in his heart of hearts every Spaniard was glad that he had died.

He even looked Quixotic. Ugly in photos, cold and hard in the bull ring, he had tremendous magnetism, warmth, and gentle humor among his friends. Once in Peru I took a blasé American college girl to watch Manolete in the ceremony of preparing for a fight, though she protested she had no interest in a "joker who hurts little bulls."

"Excuse me, Señorita, if I don't talk much," he said with his shy smile as they worried his thin frame into the skin-tight uniform, "but I am very scared."

After that he didn't say more than ten words to her. But she walked out of the room dazed. "That," she announced, "is the most attractive man in the world."

"To fight a bull when you are not scared is nothing," another bull-fighter once said, "and to not fight a bull when you are scared is nothing. But to fight a bull when you are scared—that is something."

Manolete told me: "My knees start to quake when I first see my name on the posters and they don't stop until the end of the season."

But there was never any real end of the season for him. In 1945, for example, he fought ninety-three fights in Spain in six months, about one every other day. This meant body-racking travel, for he would fight in Barcelona one day, Madrid the next, and then maybe Lisbon the day after. He would snatch some sleep in the train or car and sometimes had to board a plane with his ring outfit still on. Then followed Mexico's season and Peru's season and when he got through with those it was March again and time for the first fights in Valencia.

What, then, made him run? What made him The Best?

Money was the obvious thing. In his eight years as a senior matador he made approximately four million American dollars. In his last years he was getting as high as $25,000 per fight, about $400 for every minute he performed, and he could fight where, when, and as often as he liked. His yearly income was slightly abetted by such things as a liqueur called Anis Manolete, dolls dressed in costume with his sad face on them, testimonials for cognac ads, songs about him, and a movie called *The Man Closest to Death.*

Yet it wasn't the money; people seldom risk their necks just for money. It was that he needed desperately to be someone—something great.

He was born in Cordoba, Spain, in 1917, in the heart of the bull-fighting country. His great uncle, a minor-league bullfighter, was killed by a bull, one of the dreaded Miura breed that years later was to kill Manuel. His mother was the widow of a great matador when she married Manuel's father, also a bullfighter. He began to go blind, kept fighting as long as he could distinguish the shape of the bull, and finally died in the poorhouse when Manuel was five years old.

The family was always hungry-poor. Manuel was a frail child, having had pneumonia when a baby, and could contribute little to his mother's support. But he started carrying a hod as soon as he was big enough to tote one.

His two sisters stood the hunger as long as possible and then they started making money in a profession even older than bullfighting. This was the secret of the driving force behind Manuel. He never got over it. He resolved to make enough money somehow so that his family would never have to worry again, and to become an important enough person so that his sisters' shame would be blurred. Bullfighting is the only way in Spain for a poor boy to become great. "Matadors and royalty are the only ones who live well," they say. Young Manuel decided to become the greatest bullfighter who ever lived.

He was twelve and working as a plasterer's assistant on the Sotomayor ranch when he got his first chance. They raised fighting bulls, that special savage breed of beast, originally found only on the Iberian peninsula, that can kill a lion or tiger easily and which the Caesars used to import for the Coliseum orgies. Little Manuel begged so persistently to be allowed to fight that finally the Sotomayors put him in the corral with a cape and a yearling. Manuel, an awkward, skinny kid in short pants, was knocked down every time he went near the little animal. If the animal had had sharp horns instead of stubs, he would have been killed twenty times; instead he was just a mass of bruises by the time he limped out of the ring. He decided to go back to plastering.

But he couldn't stay away from the bulls. In the next few years he got out with the calves every time he could, even after he had been badly wounded, at thirteen, by a young bull. There are always backseat bullfighters around a ranch and they told him some of the mistakes he was making. He learned fairly fast but he was no genius. He was awkward and tried to do the wrong kind of passes for his build. However, he was brave and took it so seriously that he finally persuaded someone to give him a fight with small bulls in Cordoba's big Plaza de Toros under the *nom de toreau* of Manolete.

In his debut he was clumsy, but so brave and obviously trying so hard that the home folks applauded the sad-faced gawk. It was the greatest day of his life. Flushed with success, he and two other boys scraped their money together, formed a team called the Cordoban Caliphs, and set out to make their fortune. They wangled some contracts fighting at night and in cheap fairs and traveled around Spain for a year. Manolete was almost the comic relief of the outfit. The crowds would laugh at his skinny frame, made more awkward by the fancy passes he was trying. His serious, ugly face and his earnestness made it all the funnier.

"He looks as dreary as a third-class funeral on a rainy day," they'd say. But they couldn't laugh at the way he killed. He was so anxious to do well that when it came time to dispatch his enemy, Manolete would hurl himself straight over the lowered head, the horn missing his body by inches, to sink the sword up to the hilt between the shoulders.

"He's going to get killed that way some day," said the experts, prophetically.

His career, if you could call it that at this point, was interrupted by his being drafted into the army. After his discharge a year later he resumed fighting without the other two Caliphs. Then came the turning point in his life, for Camara spotted him.

José Flores Camara, a bald, dapper little man of thirty-five with omnipresent dark glasses, might have become the greatest bullfighter of all time except for one thing: He was a coward. He displayed more grace and knowledge of bull psychology than anyone had ever seen before. He had the build and he knew all about the different fighting habits of bulls and the rest of the complicated science of tauromachy. The only thing he couldn't do was keep his feet from dancing back out of the way when the bull charged, which is the most important thing in bullfighting.

When he happened to see Manolete gawking around a small-town ring, he knew that here was someone who could be everything that he had failed to be. With his expert eye he saw what the crowd didn't, that the boy wasn't really awkward, but that he was trying the wrong passes for his build and personality. Camara figured that with his brains and Manolete's blood they could really go places. He signed up the astonished young man for a long, long contract.

Camara remade Manolete. He took him out to the ranches and showed him what he was doing wrong. He made him concentrate on just the austere classic passes, none of the spinning or cape-twirling ones. With the cape he showed him how to do beautiful show veronicas, finishing with a half-veronica. It was the only pass, of the dozens that exist, that Manolete would ever do again with the cape. With the small muleta cape used with the sword, Camara let him do only four passes. He showed him how to hold himself regally, how to give the classic passes with a dignity never before seen in the ring.

When Camara thought he was ready, he launched his protégé. It took a little while for people to appreciate what they were witnessing, but soon they came to realize that here was a revolutionary, a great artist. His repertory was startlingly limited, but when he did the simple veronica the cape became a live thing in his hands, and the easy flow of the cloth, the casual way it brought the bull's horns within a fraction of an inch of his legs, was incredibly moving. Heightening the effect was the serious mien and the cold face, not unlike Basil Rathbone's, that gave a feeling of tragedy every time he went into the ring. No one laughed at him now. Camara had made a genius out of a clown. And always the nervous little man with his dark glasses was behind the fence while his protégé was out with the bull watching every move and saying: "Careful, Manolo, this one will hook to the left," or "Take him on the other side, he has a bad eye" or "Fight him in the center, he swerves when he's near the fence." And Manolete kept learning and learning.

If his first year was successful, his second was sensational. It seemed as though Spain had just been waiting for his kind of fighting. His honest and brave style seemed to show up the fakery that the cape-twirlers had been foisting upon the public. In 1939 he took "the alternative" and became a senior matador, fighting older and larger bulls. From then on his rise was dizzy, for every fight and every season seemed better than the last one.

By 1946 he was the king of matadors and Mexico beckoned with astronomical contracts, the highest prices ever paid a bullfighter. Spectators thought they were lucky to get a seat for $100 for his first fight in Mexico City. It was the greatest responsibility a matador ever had, and he gave them their money's worth, although he was carried out badly wounded before the fight was half over. He came to before they got him to the ring infirmary, shook off the people who tried to stop him, and lurched back into the ring to finish the bull, before collapsing.

After he recovered he went on to fight all over Mexico and South America. When I saw him in Lima he was exhausted. Most bullfighters can give a top performance one day and then get away with a few safe, easy ones. But not Manolete. To preserve his fabulous reputation he had to fight every fight as though it were his first time in the Madrid Plaza.

But the machine was wearing down. Though he was only twenty-nine, he looked forty. He was drinking a lot, and not mild Spanish wine but good old American whisky. His timing was beginning to go off. I remember once in Peru he took nine sword thrusts to kill a bull, and he left the ring with tears running down his cheeks.

Even Camara, who enjoyed having his wallet filled through risks taken by someone else, thought it was time to quit. But the public makes an idol and then it tires of what it has made and destroys the idol. When Manolete returned to Spain and announced that he was going to retire, he found he had slipped from public grace. The people were saying that he had dared only to fight small bulls and that this new young Luis Miguel Dominguin was better and braver. Manolete had been on top too long. They wanted someone new. They amused themselves by changing the words of the once-popular eulogizing song "Manolete" to: "Manolete, you couldn't handle a robust field mouse if confronted by one in the bathroom."

"Quit," Camara advised him. "Quit," said Luis Miguel, who would then be cock of the roost. "Quit," said the other bullfighters who then wouldn't look so clumsy and cowardly.

Manolete had too much pride to quit under fire. He said he would have one last season, just a few short months, with the largest bulls in Spain, and fighting with any fighters the promoters wished to bill him with. He wanted to retire untied and undefeated.

His first fight was in Barcelona, and the critics said he had never been greater. Then Pamplona, and he was even better than at Barcelona. It looked as though everyone was wrong, that he was in his prime.

Then, on July 16, he was wounded, in Madrid. The wound wasn't serious, but he left the hospital too soon to go on a vacation in the mountains with Antonia. He began fighting again long before he should have; it was as though he were afraid that if he missed any of these last contracts there would always be some people who would remain unconvinced that he was still The Best.

The next fights were not good. He just wasn't up to it physically, and he wasn't helping himself by the way he was drinking. He would stay up all night with a bottle of whisky, not go to bed, and try to fight the next afternoon. They say he drank because of Antonia, because he knew she was a girl "of a bad style" and a gold digger, but that he loved her and couldn't break off with her and hated himself for loving her. A friend of his said, "She dragged poor Manolo through the Street of Bitterness with her cheapness."

Also the crowds' new attitude toward him was intolerable, not because of egotism but because of his professional pride. Now they were always prone to applaud the other matadors more, no matter how close Manolete let death come.

"They keep demanding more and more of me in every fight," he complained. "And I have no more to give."

The Manolete myth had grown bigger than the real Manolete,

and the people were angry at him instead of at themselves for having created it.

Then came August 27, and the fight in Linares. It was extremely important to him that he be good this afternoon. First, because it was near his home town; second, because Luis Miguel Dominguin was on the same program; third, because the bulls were Miuras, the famous "bulls of death" that have killed more men than any other breed in existence. People claimed that Manolete was scared of Miuras and had always avoided fighting them.

Since it was midsummer and the sun shines till 9 in Andalusia, the fight didn't begin until 6:30. It began like any other of his fights—the stands jammed with mantilla-draped señoritas and men with the broad-brimmed someros cocked over one eye. There was an excitement in the air because of the Miuras and the known rivalry between Dominguin and Manolete.

Gitanillo did well by the first bull and received applause and hand-kerchief waving, which meant the audience wanted him to be granted an ear of the dead bull as a token of a good performance. But the president was hard to please and refused to grant it.

The second bull was Manolete's. It was dangerous and unpredict-able, but Manolete was out to cut an ear. He made the animal charge back and forth in front of him so closely and gracefully that even his detractors were up out of their seats, yelling. But when it came time to kill, he missed with the first thrust. The second dropped the bull cleanly and the crowd applauded wildly, but he had lost the ear.

The trumpet blew, and it was Luis Miguel's turn. This was an im-portant fight to him also. He wanted to show up the old master in his own province. He wanted to show them who could handle Miuras better than anyone in the world.

He strode out into the arena, good-looking, smug, twenty years old. Manolete was through—here was the new idol, here was the king of the rings!

He had the crowd roaring on the first fancy, twirling passes with the big cape. He put in his own *banderillas* superbly to win more ap-plause. With the muleta, the little cape that is draped over the sword for the last part of the fight, he unfurled all of his crowd-pleasing tricks, dropping to his knees for two passes and even kissing the bull's forehead at one moment. He lined the bull up, thrust the sword in between the withers halfway up to the hilt, and the animal sagged down dead. The crowd cheered and waved their handkerchiefs until the president granted Dominguin an ear.

Manolete had watched the entire performance from the passageway, with no change of expression. Those tricks and cape twirls were not his idea of true bullfighting. He would show the crowd what the real thing was if it killed him.

After Gitanillo's mediocre performance with his second animal, Manolete saw the toril gate swing open and the last bull of his life came skidding out of the tunnel. It was named Islero, and it was big and black with horns as sharp as needles. The moment Camara saw it hooking around the ring, he sucked in his breath and said to Manolete: "*Malo*—bad, bad. It hooks terribly to the right." That is a dread thing, for a matador must go over to the right horn to kill. "Stay away from this one, *chico*."

But Manolete was determined to give the best performance of his life. He caught the collar of the cape in his teeth and held it while he got the big scarlet cloth right in his hands. Then he slid through the opening in the fence and called the bull.

"Toro, hah, torooo!" he called in his deep voice, holding the cape out in front of him and shaking it.

The animal wheeled at the voice, its tail shot up, and it charged across the ring. As it reached the cloth the man didn't spin or swirl the cape around him or dance around the way that Luis Miguel had done. He merely planted his feet and swung the cape slowly in front of the bull's nose, guiding the great head with the tantalizing cloth so that the left horn went by his legs ten inches away. Without moving his feet, he took the bull back in another charge and the right horn stabbed six inches away from his thighs. Five more perfect classic veronicas, each closer than the other, finishing with a half-veronica that was so close that the bull's neck hit him and nearly knocked him off balance. He turned his back on the bewildered animal and looked up at the crowd that was cheering deliriously, a crowd that had been shown the difference between truth and fakery.

With the muleta cape, his forte, he worked in even closer, until the crowd was shouting, "No, no!" Camara was shouting with them, for Manolete was passing the animal just as closely on the right side as the left. But the man didn't pay any attention. He did the Pass of Death and his own pass, the dangerous "manoletina." He did fifteen suicidal "natural" passes, the one where the sword is taken out of the cape and only the limp bit of rag is used to divert the bull's charge away from the body. Then he did his famous trade-mark—the fantastic pass where he looked disdainfully away from the bull up into the stands as the animal thundered by. It seemed as though the bull couldn't miss, but it did. By now the crowd was hoarse from cheering the domination that the man had acquired over the wild beast.

It was time to kill. As he was lining up the Miura so that the feet would be together and the shoulder blades open, Camara and his *banderilleros* were yelling: "Stay away from him, man! Off to the side and get away quick!"

But Manolete had to finish this one right. He wasn't going to spoil the performance by running off to the side and stabbing it in the lungs. He was going to head in straight, get the sword in, give the bull a fair shot at him, and hope to God it wouldn't hook to the right.

He stood in front of the Miura, sighted down the blade, rose on the toes of one foot, and as the bull lunged forward, Manolete hurled himself straight over the lowered right horn. The sword was sinking in, the horn cutting by him. But suddenly the bull wrenched its head to the right and drove the horn deep into the man's groin. Manolete was flung high into the air, trying to fight the horn out of his body, and then was slammed to the sand. The bull spiked at him twice on the ground and then staggered, choked, and flopped over dead, the sword up to the red hilt between its shoulder blades.

The pool of blood on the sand told them the man was mortally wounded. Camara and the *banderilleros* picked up the unconscious form and rushed him down the passageway to the ring infirmary. He came to on the operating table and gasped weakly: "Did it die?"

"*Sí, chico, sí,*" said Camara, tears raining down his cheeks.

"It died and they didn't give me anything?" Manolete said, trying to raise himself from the table.

"They gave you everything, Matador," said a *banderillero,* putting his cigarette between the wounded man's lips. "Everything—both ears and tail."

He smiled and lay back.

Antonia arrived from Granada at 3:30 in the morning and demanded a deathbed wedding ceremony, but his friends wouldn't allow it; Manolete's money would go to his family.

At 5 in the morning he moaned: "Doctor, I can't feel anything in my right leg." The doctor assured him he would be well in no time. Then: "Doctor, I can't feel anything in my left leg." He gave a cry and said: "I can't see!" and he was dead.

An old *banderillero* staring at the corpse said dully: "They kept demanding more and more of him, and more was his life, so he gave it to them."

Robert W. Creamer

George Ruth's First Day as a Professional

Robert W. Creamer, a founding editor of Sports Illustrated, *spent more than thirty years working on other people's prose, and sometimes his own. His biography of Babe Ruth,* Babe, *was published in 1974. It was a triumph;* Time *magazine called it "the first really adult biography of the Babe as well as one of the best, and least sentimental, books about a great sports figure ever written." Here is George Ruth, still playing for his "orphanage" team—St. Mary's of Baltimore. But not for long.*

The Xaverians who ran St. Mary's, Ruth's school, also ran Mount St. Joseph's College in Baltimore. Mount St. Joseph's varsity baseball team played colleges such as Villanova, Manhattan, Western Maryland and Seton Hall. Its star in 1912 and 1913 was a tall righthanded pitcher named Bill Morrisette, a Baltimore boy. In 1912 Morrisette attracted attention by carrying a no-hitter into the seventh inning against Washington College of Chestertown, Maryland, and by striking out a dozen men. In the spring of 1913 he pitched a one-hitter against Western Maryland. The Xaverians at Mount St. Joseph's, particularly Brother Gilbert, the baseball coach, did a little fraternal boasting to their confreres at the Industrial School about young Morrisette. The brothers at the Home countered by talking up young George Ruth. Inevitably, according to the old stories, the brothers arranged a game between the two institutions, with Morrisette and Ruth to meet *mano a mano.*

Enter Jack Dunn. Dunn was the owner and manager of the Baltimore Orioles, then of the International League. Part of his ball club's income came, of course, from gate receipts, but another and considerable source of money was derived from the sale of his players to major league teams. Minor league clubs were independently owned, for the most part, and only a few players in the minors had strings tying them to a major league team. The major leaguers could draft players from the minors in the off-season, paying a set sum for each player so drafted, but a minor league operator could and usually did sell outstanding players for better prices before the draft got them. To assure a steady supply of talent for their teams and eventually for the big league market, shrewd operators like Dunn were constantly on the watch for good young ballplayers. The major league executives were generally willing to leave such grass-roots scouting to the minor leaguers, contenting themselves with plucking the fruit after it had ripened.

Dunn knew about Morrisette—he later signed him to a Baltimore contract—as he did about most of the good young ballplayers in the area. He knew about Ruth too.

The story of the Ruth-Morrisette game, in 1913, or the legend of it, had a splendid melodramatic overlay. For one thing, the boys at the Home had a classic reverse-snobbery contempt for Mount St. Joe's, "the rich school down the road," and they wanted desperately to win. For another, it was a very big event in their colorless lives. It was to be a holiday, and there would be a big crowd. Everybody at St. Mary's—the boys, the brothers, the lay members of the staff—would be there. A large body of students and faculty from Mount St. Joe's was coming, and there would be some specially invited guests, including of course, Dunn, who was a particular celebrity to the boys because of his position as owner and manager of the Orioles. St. Mary's looked forward to the big day as though it were Christmas.

On the big day there were flags and bunting everywhere. The school buildings and the grounds and the ballfield had been swept and scrubbed and polished. The anticipated crowd was there, and, to the exultation of the boys, Ruth and St. Mary's walloped Morrisette and Mount St. Joe's, 6–0, with Ruth striking out twenty-two batters during his shutout. After the game Dunn and young Ruth went into Brother Paul's office and talked for two hours, and the following February, a couple of weeks before the Orioles were to leave for spring training, Dunn came to St. Mary's again and signed George Ruth to a professional contract.

When it came time to go south for spring training in 1914, Dunn's roster was rich in experience. Of the eight men, not including pitchers, in his set lineup (there was no platooning then) five were in their thirties and a sixth was twenty-eight; all six had had major league experience. The two younger men in the lineup had played with the Orioles before, and one was in his fourth minor league season. The two best pitchers had been in the majors too. Thus it was no team of green young kids that George Ruth was joining when he came out of St. Mary's Industrial School. Jack Dunn's Orioles were seasoned professionals.

George said goodbye at St. Mary's on Friday and spent the weekend at his father's home over the saloon on Conway Street, a block from the harbor. His instructions were to report to Dunn at the Kernan Hotel on Monday afternoon; about a dozen pitchers and catchers would assemble there and leave Monday night from Union Station for the trip to Fay-etteville, North Carolina, where the Orioles were going to train. Ben Egan, a big catcher who acted as Dunn's field captain, would be in charge of this advance squad. Dunn would follow a week later with the balance of the team.

The weather that weekend in Baltimore was unpleasant: freezing temperatures, overcast sky, snow scattered here and there. On Sunday it became even colder, the temperature falling into the teens. The wind picked up and it began to snow. By nightfall Baltimore was in the midst of a blizzard, part of a huge storm that struck the entire northeast. In New York winds reached 82 miles an hour, and in Baltimore, where 12 inches of snow fell, the gale blew tin roofs off sheds, shutters off houses and even the steeple off a Methodist church. Windows were shattered, fences were blown down and streets were garnished with bricks and plaster. Earth tremors, an eerie coincidence, were felt in Druid Hill Park in the northern part of the city. The storm, the worst in twenty-five years, raged through the night and did not slacken and stop until Monday morning. Baltimore looked like a war-devastated city, with train and telephone and telegraph service disrupted and snow-filled streets choked with debris.

Through this mess George Ruth made his way to the Hotel Kernan to become a professional ballplayer. Not all the players had been able to reach Baltimore, because of the storm, and Dunn had to alter his plans slightly. Ben Egan, for instance, was snowbound at his home in upstate New York, and Dunn put the squad under the command of Scout Steinmann, an ex-ballplayer who was scout, coach and general handy-man around the club. Doc Fewster, the trainer, was in the party too, and so were a couple of young Baltimore newspapermen who had been assigned to cover the Orioles' camp. Of the twelve players in the group, two were catchers and the rest pitchers. Along with Ruth, there were three other young Baltimore boys: Morrisette, Allen Russell and a left-handed pitcher the reporters took delight in calling Smoke Klingelhoefer. Dunn bustled his men over to Union Station, worrying that the effects of the storm might delay the scheduled departure from Baltimore or the anticipated connection with an Atlantic Coast Line train leaving Washington at nine. Things seemed very uncertain and no one really expected to be in Fayetteville the next morning on schedule.

But railroads did miraculous things in those days—like leaving on time and arriving on time even in the aftermath of a blizzard. The Orioles left Union Station on schedule and arrived at Fayetteville without incident at seven-thirty in the morning. For George Ruth the uneventful train ride was far more exciting than the snowstorm; it was the first time he had ever been on a train. Some of the experienced travelers in the group explained the mysteries of an upper berth to the greenhorn, including the proper use of the odd little undersized hammock that hung over the berth. With profound baseball humor they neglected to tell him it was for his clothes, to keep them from falling out of the berth during the night. "That's for pitchers, George," he was told. "It's to rest your pitching arm in while you sleep." When Ruth went to bed he tried his best to sleep with his left arm suspended in the hammock.

In Fayetteville the players were disappointed to find that it was damp and cold, the temperatures barely above freezing. As they creaked their way to the Lafayette Hotel (Ruth's pitching arm stiff from its night in the hammock) they assumed, with regret, that there would be no baseball that day. But as the morning wore on, the sun came out and the temperature climbed, and after they settled in at the Lafayette and unpacked, Steinmann took them over to the Fair Grounds and had them work out for an hour or so, just lobbing baseballs back and forth. The stiffness soon left Ruth's arm. Fresh from the spartan life of the school, he was in marvelous shape: twenty years old, 180 lean hard pounds beautifully distributed over his six feet two inches. He had exceptionally broad shoulders and long arms, and when he wheeled and threw, the ball whipped across the diamond. He began to show off a little, throwing the ball faster than he should have the first day of practice, and Steinmann told him to let up, to take it easy. In the afternoon the temperature soared to 75 and the outfield, soggy in the morning, dried out sufficiently to let the team shag fly balls. There were still puddles—Klingelhoefer splashed through a big one as he raced after a ball—but the players reveled in the sun. Steinmann had planned to follow Dunn's practice of having the players run around the horse track at the Fair Grounds at the end of the workout, but the track was still thick with mud. So Scout had them job the mile back to the hotel instead of walking or riding back in carriages.

It was sunny and hot again the next day. The players took batting practice and hit fungoes to the outfield. The track dried out and everyone ran a lap before heading back to the hotel. Everything was going beautifully. It had been a good two days of work.

But Thursday it rained all day. Steinmann went over to the city hall and arranged with the mayor for the use of the armory, the biggest building in Fayetteville, and the players worked out there as best they could. They were tossing baseballs back and forth when a loud jovial yell filled the place. "It's Egan!" one of the veterans said. Ben Egan, tall, cheerful, fiery, had just arrived from Baltimore, and he lifted them all with his presence. Ruth liked him at once. Egan talked to Steinmann and the newspapermen and watched the players as they worked out. He was impressed with the way Ruth threw the ball, he said.

On Friday it was still wet. Egan took three of the pitchers out back of the hotel to have a catch, but the rain started again and everyone ended up back in the armory.

But on Saturday, along with a warm sun, there was a brisk wind that dried the field like blotting paper, and the stage was set for George Ruth's first big day in professional baseball. Egan and Steinmann decided to divide the squad into two teams and play a seven-inning scrub game. Word got around and a couple of hundred townspeople came over to the Fair Grounds to watch. Steinmann called his team the Sparrows. A pitcher named Cranston pitched and a catcher named Potts caught, which seems normal enough, but otherwise the lineup was chaotic. Old Steinmann played first base; Danforth, who was lefthanded, was at second; Lidgate, the catcher, was at shortstop; and Lamotte, a pitcher, was at third base. Caporel, McKinley and Morrisette, all pitchers, were in the outfield. Egan's team, called the Buzzards, had Jarman pitching and Hurney catching, their natural positions; but Egan had himself at first base and Lefty Cottrell was at second. Ruth played shortstop, which gave the Buzzards a lefthanded double-play combination, and Russell played third base. Klingelhoefer was in left field; Roger Pippen, a young Baltimore sportswriter, was in center; and John Massena, an aspiring unknown, was in right. These were the dramatis personae of Ruth's first game as a professional.

The Buzzards scored a run in the first inning, and the Sparrows tied it in their half of the first. Egan hit a double with the bases loaded in the second inning that scored three runs, and Cottrell followed with a single, scoring Egan. Then, as Pippen wrote in the story of the game he wired to Baltimore that night, "The next batter made a hit that will live in the memory of all who saw it. That clouter was George Ruth, the southpaw from St. Mary's school. The ball carried so far to right field that he walked around the bases." He crossed home plate before Morrisette, of all people, picked up the ball in the cornfield that grew beyond the ballfield in deepest right.

The Fayetteville fans—those at the game and those who were told about it later—were astounded by Ruth's tremendous drive. For years they had been talking about a home run that Jim Thorpe, the Carlisle Indian, had hit when he played with the Fayetteville team in the Carolina League. Thorpe's home run, they had enjoyed telling the Baltimore players, was by far the longest ever seen at the Fair Grounds. Now, with some awe, they agreed that Ruth's homer had gone 60 feet farther than Thorpe's. The *Baltimore Sun* next day had a headline in its Sunday sports section that anticipated the future: "HOMER BY RUTH FEATURE OF GAME." And the *American,* more picturesque, said, "RUTH MAKES MIGHTY CLOUT." The date was Saturday, March 7, 1914. It was Ruth's fifth day as a professional, his first game, his second time at bat.

Later that spring, back in Baltimore, Babe Ruth went up against the major-league Brooklyn Dodgers. An exhibition game, they called it, but it was more than that. Dunn had been saving Ruth to pitch against the Dodgers at Back River Park, a racetrack east of downtown Baltimore beyond the city limits, which Dunn used on Sundays because of a city ordinance that prohibited professional ballgames in Baltimore on Sunday. Ruth pitched strongly at Back River, holding the Dodgers hitless for several innings as the Orioles opened up a big lead, and then coasting to a 10–6 victory. On his first time at bat he hit a fly ball deep to right field that was caught after a long run by Casey Stengel, the Dodgers' twenty-three-year-old right fielder. When Ruth came up again, Stengel played deeper, but Ruth hit the ball over his head anyway for a triple. Casey never forgot that.

"We had never heard of him," Casey said more than half a century later, "but that was nothing in those days. He was a good looking kid, big, rugged, had a good arm. He wore his hair parted in the middle and it came down with a couple of little spit curls on each side of his forehead.

He had good stuff, a good fast ball, a fine curve—a dipsy-do that made you think a little. When he hit that long fly I was embarrassed. Me, a big leaguer, underplaying him. But no one had ever heard of him—especially as a batter. Wilbert Robinson was managing us, and he was all upset. You know what he told me when I got back to the bench? He said, 'If I was you, Stengel, and I saw a man hit a couple of those baseballs in batting practice, I wouldn't play him with such a short field.' I was burned. The next time the kid came up, I went back 25 feet. Maybe it was 30 feet or 35 feet, but I was back there. I put my glove up to my mouth and yelled over to our center fielder, 'Hey, do you think Grapefruit'—that's what we called Robby—'do you think Grapefruit thinks I'm back far enough now?' My God, if he doesn't hit one a mile. I was young and I could run. I could fly. Believe me, I could fly. I could go and catch a ball pretty good. But this one—this one was over my head.

"We lost the game. The kid beats us pitching and he beats us batting. That's when I first saw Ruth. I would say I was impressed."

Robert Daley

The Knee

Robert Daley, an accomplished and prolific novelist, was also at one time a deputy police commissioner in New York City and, earlier, a public relations man for the New York Giants. Out of that experience Daley wrote his first novel, Only a Game. *This excerpt concerns the most dreaded common injury a football player can suffer and, in this compelling story, its effect on victim and team alike.*

"**G**ive me the ball," says Finney, tight-lipped.

Finney weighs 225, and is the biggest man in the backfield. But he is a rookie, and Pennoyer never calls on rookies in tight spots. Nonetheless, the other two backs are winded, and smaller than Finney besides. And Finney wants the ball.

Against his better judgment, Pennoyer calls Finney's number.

At the snap the two lines surge up. The noise is tremendous. Finney smashes in where there is no hole at all, then rolls off, looking for daylight. Hands and arms grapple with him. He wrestles forward, fighting for the desperately needed yard.

A white uniform curled into a fetal position hurls itself at the side of Finney's still planted leg.

There is a pop and a scream. The ball squirts loose. Men dive for it.

When they get up Finney lies on the turf alone, moaning. The players of both teams stand several paces away, staring at him.

Duke Craig, knowing at once what has happened to Jimmy Finney, thinks: It hurts so much you can't even writhe or squirm. You are rigid

111

with pain. Craig shuts his eyes, as if to block off the low sustained moan coming from Finney. As always, it sounds like it is coming from a wounded animal, not a man.

Both teams back off ten yards from where Finney lies. No one looks at him. Then both teams remember that the ball has changed hands; the Browns have recovered the fumble. The old personnel straggles off the field, as the new personnel runs on.

Pete, the trainer, has reached Finney's side, where he attempts to remove the injured player's helmet. Finney's mouth is tightly shut; he has stopped moaning. The helmet won't come off easily; when Pete yanks at it, Finney screams. Dr. Flaherty, a lumbering little man with a black bag, reaches Finney and kneels beside him, fingering Finney's knee. Each time he touches it, Finney's teeth bare, and he gasps. The two fresh teams stand twenty yards apart; no one looks at the group formed by Finney, Pete, Dr. Flaherty, and the other trainer, Paul. Most stare at the ground or off into the stands.

Craig watches from the sideline. His helmet is off. He rubs his sweaty face. All the old memories come flooding back.

Am I through?

Though you have never had a knee injury before, you know immediately what has happened to you. It hurts so much it isn't even localized; every nerve in your body screams with pain. The pain is absolutely exquisite.

So is the fear.

Am I through?

Will I ever play again?

Is my life over?

Craig swallows hard. For a football player there is a loneliness that no one who has not been in that position can even conceive of.

The two husky trainers have Finney by the shoulders. Two substitutes have run on to grasp Finney's legs. When they lift him, Finney screams. The substitutes look back, alarmed, and adjust their grips on his legs. Dr. Flaherty waddles ahead. As they near the bench, Craig sees Finney's face. The sweat is running down Finney's nose and his teeth are clenched tight. Nonetheless, when they set him down, he gives another muffled scream.

Craig looks away. His eyes fill with sweat, or is it tears?

On the field the Big Red defense gives ground grudgingly, but concentration is lost. Inexorably the Browns grind their way down to and over the goal line. With less than five minutes remaining in the game, the Browns lead 20–14.

Finney's replacement is Donald Fox, a second stringer every year he has been in the league. He has a second-stringer's mentality, and eyes that say: In a tight spot, you better give the ball to someone else, I might screw up. Not: Give me the ball, I can make it for us. Fox isn't comfortable under pressure. He is embarrassed. Pennoyer knows this.

Fox is big and fast with many skills, and Pennoyer knows how to use them, but they disappear inside the twenty-yard line, and Slade isn't too brave inside the twenty either. This is one more detail Pennoyer, who already has too much to remember, has to keep in mind. His only clutch back is Craig, who has already carried twenty times, and whose bones must feel like jelly by now. But there is a communion between Pennoyer and Craig. They understand each other, and what needs to be done. The two of them together are a team within a team. Now, as the remaining minutes dribble away, they put strength, and most of all faith, back into this team.

Pennoyer sends out five receivers. The fifth and last is Craig, who delays until the other four have taken their men deep, then filters into the empty short zone and takes Pennoyer's pass. He gains eighteen yards before the pursuit runs him down.

"Way to go, Big Red, way to go."

Craig is hollering and clapping as he runs back to the huddle.

Now Fox carries three times to another first down. Then Slade catches the Browns in a blitz, and, on a draw play gains twelve yards. The team begins to believe.

Pennoyer sends his backs hammering at the line, but the Browns get tough. He passes again, but the ball is batted down. On third and eight Slade catches one for a first down on the ten.

The official signals two minutes left in the game. Pennoyer trots to the sidelines for instructions from Coach Dreuder. Time is not a factor. Two minutes is ample to make ten yards and the winning touchdown.

Pennoyer sends Craig into the line. Shrugging and wrestling, he gets to the three-yard line. On the next play, Slade fumbles the handoff and loses three yards. It is third down and six. Pennoyer calls time out. He confers with Dreuder. They decide on a crossing pattern, Slade on one side and the split end on the other crossing in the end zone, with Pennoyer throwing probably to Slade. The clock shows a minute, forty-six seconds to play.

The play unfolds. Slade is open as Pennoyer fires the ball, but Number 40 makes a sensational play and bats the ball down.

It is fourth down, six yards to go.

Last chance.

The noise is tumultuous. Pennoyer barks signals, but the noise is so great his flankers can't hear them. He raises his hands for quiet. The official waves a time out. Pennoyer calls his team back into the huddle. His voice there is as monotonous as always. He calls the same play. There is no emotion in his face or voice, yet the game will be won or lost on this one play.

He has called a swing pass to Craig. As the lines collide with a crash, Craig loops into the right flat. But Number 40 has read the play and is there. So is the linebacker, who embraces Craig a moment after Craig grabs the ball. But Craig brings his free arm up under the tackle in what is virtually an uppercut, and the tackle is broken. The linebacker sprawls on the turf and Craig has only Number 40 to beat. He whirls, darts toward the center of the goalposts, then suddenly veers back for the corner. Number 40 hits him, but Craig does not intend to be stopped and Number 40 has left his feet too early. Craig drags him into the end zone for the touchdown.

On the bench, his teammates mob Craig. Even Pennoyer grins and hugs him.

They lead, 21–20, with a minute and thirty-five seconds to play.

The men on the bench watch anxiously as Jones kicks off—a scary play at best. Here a good runback could ruin them.

Jones has tried to kick it away from Number 32, but that is where the ball drops anyway, and the man makes a brilliant runback of sixty-two yards. With a minute and twenty-two seconds left, the Browns are close enough for a long field goal, and have all their time-outs left besides.

Number 32 hits the line. Bulling and fighting, he gains six yards and the Browns immediately call time-out to stop the clock.

On second down, Number 48 sweeps left end for five yards. The Browns call another time-out. The ball is on the Big Red's twenty-seven-yard line, and there is one minute to play. On the Big Red bench, players are pleading and exhorting their teammates.

"Be big out there."

"Get *TOUGH*." The last word is a beseeching kind of shout.

Two passes fail. A third gains twelve yards before the receiver steps out of bounds. The Browns are on the nineteen-yard line, easy field-goal range now, with thirty-six seconds to play.

Number 32 hits the line, but is stopped. The Browns call their final time-out to stop the clock.

Number 76 trots onto the field to try for the winning field goal from point-blank range.

At the sideline, Dreuder has his arm around Lincoln Hamilton, president of the Mau Mau Club, and the Big Red's offensive captain. He sends the big lineman into the game.

Coach Dreuder stands gnawing his fingernails as the teams line up for the field-goal attempt. Behind him some players are reconciled to the defeat and sit with heads down, not wanting to watch. Others pace up and down, agonized expressions on their faces, exhorting their teammates on the field.

The crowd noise swells, the ball is snapped. The lines converge and rise up. Hamilton bulls into the center of the line, then smashes through, and as the ball starts to soar throws himself across its line of flight.

The ball strikes the side of his helmet and caroms off sideways. The crowd roar subsides into the sighs and muttering of 84,000 people.

Springing up, Hamilton shakes himself off, and, helmet in hand, his knotty skull illuminated by grinning teeth, jogs back to the bench, where he is hugged and pummeled by his teammates.

In the Big Red dressing room, Hamilton is still being embraced by his teammates.

Photographers snap pictures of Craig and Hamilton, both of them half naked, with their arms around each other. Pennoyer is brought on. He is photographed pouring orange soda over his head.

Presently the dirty ankle tape forms a mound in the center of the floor, the last photographer leaves, and Craig goes through to take his shower.

As he crosses through the trainers' room, he sees that Dr. Flaherty has prepared a hypodermic syringe for Jimmy Finney's knee. A few drops pop from the needle as Doc holds it to the light.

In an instant, Craig sees the old scene, hears the old voices.

"I don't like the look of your knee, Duke. I don't like it at all."

"It *is* a bit swollen."

"We're going to have to aspirate it."

Craig, who didn't know the meaning of this word, was afraid to ask.

Dr. Purcell, the university doctor, was an irascible little man with a raspy voice. First he shot the knee with Novocain, further scaring young Craig, though it did not hurt.

Then Dr. Purcell prepared a syringe the size of a small football pump. Craig, watching this, licked his lips. Dr. Purcell had to push hard to get the big needle into the knee cavity. It made a tearing noise. He worked it around in there, while Craig wiped sweat off his forehead.

Dr. Purcell attempted to withdraw fluid, but nothing happened. The glass pump did not fill up.

Angrily, Dr. Purcell yanked the needle out, ripped it off the glass pump, and threw it on the floor.

"Nurse, goddamit—"

This time when the needle went in, Craig could hear something grating.

"Doc, I think you're touching bone in there."

"Shut up."

Craig was sweating freely now. Again Dr. Purcell attempted to withdraw fluid. Again the syringe did not fill up. Dr. Purcell, furious, began pushing and wiggling the syringe.

"Doc, are you sure you're not touching bone?"

Dr. Purcell, cursing, was wiggling the syringe. Craig imagined the needle scraping the bone inside his knee.

"Doc, I think you're touching bone."

"Bullshit."

The glass football pump began to fill up with watery blood. Dr. Purcell gave a sigh of pleasure: "Ah, there we go—"

Craig, who was nineteen at the time and had been hoping against hope all week that the worst was over, fainted.

"That's it, Jimmy, baby," soothes Dr. Flaherty, "little Novocain to kill the pain so we can get you home."

As he draws the needle out of the inner side of Finney's knee, Craig can hear the same old soft tearing noise.

"That'll hold you till we get you into the hospital, Jimmy, baby. You don't want to go into a hospital here in Cleveland, do you, Jimmy, baby?"

Dr. Flaherty rubs the skin with an antiseptic. "Don't worry about a thing, Jimmy, baby."

Craig goes into the shower. He stands under water as hot as he can stand it, his eyes closed, the water washing down what feel like seams of age in his face.

Pete helps Finney dress. Finney's knee is bulky under Ace bandages. Pete fetches baggy sweat pants to wear in place of trousers. Pete then gets a pair of adjustable crutches out of a gear trunk, measures them by eye to Finney's height, and screws them together.

"Think you can get on the bus with these, Jimmy?"

Finney nods. He seems afraid that if he tries to speak he might weep.

The trainer knows this. But there is nothing he can do. He pats the boy on the back.

"I'll get you an ice bag, Jimmy."

On the plane, nobody wants to sit next to Finney. He lowers himself into a front-row seat next to the porthole. The place next to him stays empty.

Behind Finney there is much loud laughter and calling across seats. The stewardesses pass out the first round of beer as soon as the plane lifts off. Players stand in the aisle in stocking feet, ties loose and shirts open. Some are still sweating. In conversation, they go over every play, congratulating and praising each other, gloating over the victory.

Finney sits alone in the front of the plane, staring out the porthole.

At last Craig goes forward and sits beside him.

"I've got some books home on the human knee, Jimmy. Perhaps you'd like to see them."

But Finney does not turn from the window.

Craig tries a new tack. "Did you know that guys with long torsos and short legs never get knee injuries?"

No answer.

"Very rarely," Craig says.

Craig adds: "If you're one of these guys who can't touch his toes, a really stiff kind of guy, then you'll probably never get a knee injury either."

No answer.

"Lots of times I've wished I was such a guy." Craig gives a laugh. "Of course that would make you a lineman, and you'd get your brains scrambled instead."

Craig hopes for a smile, but when Finney turns from the window, his eyes are damp, and he looks close to tears.

"I know a lot about knees," Craig offers. "I've been treated by about half the knee specialists in the country."

When Finney does not answer, Craig says: "Do you want me to go away?"

"No," Finney says in a husky voice.

Craig says brightly: "The knee is a little like two baseballs sitting one on top of the other, with a ring of, like, felt in between so the top one won't roll off. The felt is the cartilage. Actually it's in two pieces, two semicircles, one on the inner side of the knee called the medial meniscus, and one on the outer side called the lateral meniscus."

Craig, like most players who have had knee injuries, knows the anatomy of the knee like a surgeon.

"Well, there are also four important ligaments tying the two baseballs, the knee, together: one down the inner side of the knee, and one down the outer side, both about two inches long; and two short tough ones inside the knee joint itself, inside the ring of cartilage. They're called the cruciate ligaments, because they cross."

Craig says: "The usual football injury is to the inner side ligament, which becomes stretched or torn completely, and to the cartilage there which can be torn. The ligament, if it's torn, can be sewn together with catgut or silk, and it will heal. If it's only stretched it will heal by itself. The cartilage never heals and has to be cut out. You can live without it," he tells Finney.

You have to learn to, Craig thinks. Because the damaged, well, feel of it is always there. There is noise in it, fluid in it, and frequently pain in it. When you are tired you will limp, and then your pride in your body will make you push back on that heel so the limp won't show—and that hurts. You must exercise every day or lose flexibility of the knee joint, and you realize that when you are older and don't have time for the exercises or they hurt too much, then you may start, like many of the old players, to limp permanently.

The fear of re-injury never leaves you, and that is a formidable psychological barrier in itself. Wrapped in so much tape you'll never have quite as much speed again, and by the end of each season your leg will be as raw from the tape as a bad sunburn all the time. You will dread putting the tape on there before each game, knowing that once the game is over, you must somehow get it off.

In the films you will notice that you are not making the sharp cut you used to make, and they are nailing you where formerly you went for good yardage. You must work out substitutes: shoulder fakes instead of hip fakes, for instance. You can only cut one way, because you only have one strong leg to push off on.

"So your knee winds up with a couple of scars," says Craig cheerfully. "You didn't want to go into that box on the ground in a hundred percent condition, did you?"

Finney watches Craig intently.

"It's an easy operation, only a little over twenty-five minutes, usually. Then you're in a cast about two weeks, then you start walking on crutches." Craig thinks: And then the exercises start, the pain will be beautiful, and if you can't do the exercises because you can't stand the pain, then we will never hear of you again.

"Listen," Craig says earnestly, "it's not the end of the world. You can come back from this, that's the main thing."

Finney, his leg bulky under the sweat pants, licks dry lips.

Behind Craig, his teammates celebrate the victory. He longs to join them, to listen to the talk and jokes, to relive the good plays, to swill the two cans of beer per man which are enough to get a dehydrated player quite drunk. But he must give this up; he can't leave Finney alone now.

"When I got hit and went down," Craig says, "I couldn't believe it could have happened to me. I knew right away what it was."

After a moment, Finney says: "So did I."

"The pain was so bad I thought I would black out."

"It was the worst pain I've ever had."

"I know a doctor who says a knee injury doesn't rank too high in the scale of human pain."

"He never had a knee injury."

"I was running down under a punt. It was the second punt of the game. I made the mistake of looking up for the ball, and somebody hit me that I didn't even see. My cleats caught in the grass and he came rolling across my knee." After a moment, Craig adds soberly: "Mine popped just as loud as yours."

Finney says: "It sure does make a frightening noise. I think it's the most horrible thing I ever heard."

Craig does not want to live through it again, but it all comes back so vividly that he blinks his eyes.

Running. Looking up for the punt. Heavy breathing that he did not hear in time. The shock of impact, followed by the ligament snapping with a report like a gunshot. Then the flood of pain.

"The coach came running over to where I lay. You know what he said?"

"What?"

"He turned to the bench and shouted, 'Get me another halfback.' "

Finney smiles.

Craig heard that, without being aware of what it was. The stadium was jammed and noisy, but he could not see it or hear it. He floated blind and deaf on clouds of pain and fear.

"Get him off here, quick," the coach ordered, for he wanted to save the time out, if possible. Four substitutes hustled Craig off the field.

He sat in almost intolerable pain at the end of the bench. When the game ended, two players lifted him under the arms, but the pain was so great he could not support himself, and two others lifted his knees. He must have moaned or screamed for he remembers that the boy's face turned in surprise, and he then sought a grip which did not involve the injured knee. But there was no such grip; Craig's lower leg dangled and swung all the way to the locker room.

His knee was too swollen to get his pants off. After a while they stopped trying and carried him out to someone's car. At the hospital, the pants were cut off him. A doctor twisted the knee this way and that, and he screamed.

He heard them talking about an operation. He wanted his parents to be there. He was aware inside his pain and fear that his parents would have no influence on the decision to be made; they were three hundred miles away. The coach would decide.

The surgeon explained how the operation would be done. One simple incision, one cartilage removed.

"Just one cartilage, Doctor?" Craig felt towering relief. If it was only one cartilage, he felt sure he would play again.

The next day the surgeon drew diagrams, trying to soothe Craig, who was then nineteen years old. For the first time Craig heard certain words: ". . . simple excision of the medial meniscus . . ."

But he must have awakened on the operating table, because as he came out of the ether he was aware they had cut out both. Tears streamed down his face.

"You sonuva bitch, you cut both of them out."

"You're going to be fine, son."

"You promised you'd only cut one out. You promised."

"You're going to be fine, son."

"Why didn't you kill me, too."

The pain after the operation seemed worse than before. He remembers a lady who, visiting the patient in the next bed, came over to console him. But his pain was so intense that when she bent down over his bed, he couldn't see her.

No position was comfortable. There was no way he could lay his cast to make the pain less, and at night he could not sleep. Night after night he lay alone with his rage, frustration, exhaustion, pain, worry. But I was supposed to be All-American this year, he thought once, and started to cry. When he had wept enough he at last fell into a doze—only to be jolted awake later by another burst of pain.

Craig, remembering, thinks: Pain is hard to remember, usually. But the pain of a knee injury to a football player lasts so long and recurs so often that he never forgets it.

"Jimmy, you come back, or you don't come back depending on how much suffering you're willing to go through after they take the cast off."

By the time Craig's cast was removed the muscles of his thigh had atrophied slightly, especially the ones on top, so that he was unable to straighten his leg against the strong underneath tendons. The joint was full of fluid. He would sit for hours in the whirlpool bath, which was very boring, and he would sit for more hours under infrared heat, which was both boring and painful. The trainer would give him lengthy, hard-thumbed massages every day, trying to work the fluid out of the knee, massaging away from the swollen knee joint, trying to force the fluid upward into the thigh, downward into the calf.

"This is gonna hurt, kid."

Craig nodded. The trainer's thumbs dug into Craig's knee, which was swollen hard. Despite himself, Craig winced.

"I gotta push hard, kid."

Craig bit down on his lip. "I know it."

"It don't do no good otherwise."

He was willing to pay any price if he could play football again. He vowed that the world had not heard the last of Duke Craig. He lifted weights with his bad leg while lying on his back, the weights attached to an iron boot which was strapped to his foot. He climbed up and down the stadium steps, all the way to the topmost row, ZZ, a thousand times, perhaps more, sometimes pausing at the top to gaze wistfully down on his former teammates as they practiced for Saturday's game with S.M.U. or the Aggies or Baylor.

"Hello up there."

It was the team clown, his hands cupped to his mouth. Some other boys waved up at him.

After a moment, Craig called: "Hello down there." He knew some jovial response was called for, and this was the most jovial he could think of.

He missed being part of the team as much as he missed playing. The boys scrimmaging down on the field were still his teammates of course, but not really, for each Saturday they won or lost without him. The desire to be one of them was an ache inside him.

There were periods of stupendous gladness when he thought he noticed full flexibility returning to his knee; he could almost feel himself running on it again, visualize himself scoring touchdowns. And there were relapses, when he had done too much and the knee filled up and in his despair he thought hopelessly: What's the use, I'll never be able to play football again.

Craig tells Finney: "I only missed one season, and I've had eleven others since, Jimmy. It's up to you. How much do you want to come back? The guys who don't come back are the ones not willing to suffer."

An oversimplification. What about the knees that are too chewed up inside? What about the players who can't bring themselves to trust this "new" knee, or are unlucky and get a second shot in the same place? What about the surgeons who do a poor job? The surgeons never admit it, but that is why some players don't come back.

Those who do come back are not the same, Craig thinks. If you ignore the knee, you won't last long, and if you worry about it too much, you won't last long either. You must change your game to protect the knee, and usually alter your stride slightly, too. One leg or the other is sore all the time, the weak leg because it is weak, or the strong one because you have been putting too much strain on it trying to protect the other. Your body gets as used to pain as a woman's, but that doesn't mean you enjoy it.

The injured knee is always there, and every blow on it will make you miss several games. Each time you feel the sudden scalding pain which by now no longer surprises you, you will think hopelessly: Here we go again. The iron boot, the massages, the endless climbs of grandstand steps, the whirlpools and heat; the weeks of not being part of the team anymore, for they have closed ranks, and go into each game without you.

In training camp each summer, you are always lame for the first month. Perhaps, like Craig, you cannot bear being treated with pity—the constant: How's the leg, Duke? And so you begin to pretend that "the" leg is really fine, you're just trying to sneak out of practices. You acquire a reputation for malingering, but anything is preferable to seeming fragile.

He does not mention this to Finney.

"The only problem afterward is that your knee may lock on you sometimes, Jimmy. I remember once against the Redskins, it locked when I was down in the three-point stance and Pennoyer had already started the cadence. Pennoyer is hollering: hut-one, hut-two, hut-three, and my knee is locked. The snap signal is four, and I'm kicking my leg out behind me trying to free my locked knee before Pennoyer can count to four."

Finney laughs—his first genuine laugh.

Craig, pleased that he has helped Finney this much at least, says: "I wonder what *that* looked like from the grandstand."

It wasn't funny at the time. It sent him making the rounds of the orthopedic surgeons, hoping one of them had some secret cure for Duke Craig's knee.

He does not mention this to Finney either.

Behind them, the beer has started to take effect. The players, some of them exhausted and all of them dehydrated, are becoming boisterous. The stewardesses move down the aisle serving filet mignon dinners.

Craig may have helped, but Finney does not touch his meal. Presently the stewardess, who is about as young as Finney, pretty, with a mouthful of big white teeth, leans over him saying: "A big strong boy like you has gotta eat. Why, you'll die if you don't eat."

Finney tries to smile for her, but his smile falls apart. She removes the tray, perplexed, wondering if her makeup is not on straight, or something.

Now the plane starts its landing approach, and the seat-belt lights come on.

As Finney turns from the window, Craig sees that his teeth are clenched tight and his brow beaded with sweat. The Novocain is wearing off.

"I'll get Doc," Craig says.

Finney grabs his arm. "I'll be—all right."

The runway rises up under the landing lights. All the players suck in a chestful of air, holding it. As the plane touches down, all the players expel that air.

"The only way to travel," they sing out with one voice. This is ritual for every landing. They laugh and applaud themselves.

Finney's hands, gripping the armrests, are white.

"I'll get Doc."

Craig stands. "Doc!"

The stairs bump against the plane. The players crowd toward the doors.

Doc Flaherty leans over Finney. "What's the matter, Jimmy?" To the trainer, who is leaning low to peer out the porthole, the physician says: "Do you see the ambulance, Pete?"

"It's there, Doc."

"Let's get him off."

As the two trainers and Jimmy Finney's legs come through the door of the plane, Finney screams. Floodlights have come on, and in their glare, the players, watching, can see that Finney is weeping.

A player's voice out of the gloom says: "Jimmy's one tough guy. It must really hurt."

The stretcher is lifted into the ambulance, and the door slams shut.

Frank Deford

The Depression Baby

In 1976, after Frank Deford wrote this story about basketball coach Al McGuire, the subject said, "I would say that Deford is the most sensitive writer I've ever worked with. He seems to know what you're going to say before you say it. Before long, it's like talking to your wife." Deford is more than a skilled interviewer. He is one of the finest contemporary writers on sports: a star at Sports Illustrated *for many years, the founding editor of* The National *(a daily sports newspaper that lived too short a life), and a novelist (*Everybody's All-American, *among others). So here is Al McGuire, at Marquette University, before he made himself into a television commentator. And here, too, is Frank Deford at his best.*

In Al McGuire's office at Marquette, images of sad clowns abound. Pictures, all over the place, of sad clowns. Everybody must ask him about them. McGuire is touted to be a con, so the sad clowns have got to be a setup. Right away, commit yourself to those sad clowns, you're coming down his street. *Hey, buddy, why do you have a banana in your ear? Because I couldn't find a carrot.* Zap, like that. And yet, how strange an affectation: sad clowns. Obviously, they must mean something. It cannot be the sadness, though. Of all the things this fascinating man is—and clown is one—he is not sad.

Another thing he is, is street smart. McGuire has grown up and left the pavement for the boardrooms, so now when he spots this quality in others, he calls it "credit-card-wise." One time in a nightclub, when the band played "Unchained Melody," all the 40-year-olds in the place suddenly got up and packed the floor, cheek to cheek. Nostalgia ran rampant. Right away, Al said, "Summer song. This was a summer song when it came out. Always more memories with summer songs."

Perfect. He got it. Right on the button. Of course, this is a small thing. A completely insignificant thing. But the point is, he got it just right. And this is a gift. It is McGuire's seminal gift, for all his success flows from it. The best ballplayers see things on the court. McGuire lacked this ability as an athlete, but he owns it in life. Most people play defense in life, others "token it" (as Al says), but there are few scorers, and even fewer playmakers, guys who see things about to open up and can take advantage. McGuire is one of life's playmakers. He perceives. He should be locked in a bicentennial time capsule so that generations yet unborn will understand what this time was really like. There will be all the computers and radar ovens and Instamatics, and McGuire will pop out from among them in 2176 and say, "If the waitress has dirty ankles, the chili will be good." And, "Every obnoxious fan has a wife home who dominates him." And, "If a guy takes off his wristwatch before he fights, he means business." And, "Blacks will have arrived only when we start seeing black receptionists who aren't good-looking."

Words tumble from his mouth. He's a lyrical Marshall McLuhan. Often as not, thoughts are bracketed by the name of the person he is addressing, giving a sense of urgency to even mundane observations: "Tommy, you're going to make the turn here, Tommy." "Howie, how many of these go out, Howie?" And likewise, suddenly, late at night, apropos of nothing, unprompted, spoken in some awe and much gratitude: "Frank, what a great life I've had, Frank."

This starts to get us back to the sad clowns. The key to understanding McGuire is to appreciate his unqualified love of life, of what's going on around him. e.e. cummings: "I was marvelously lucky to touch and seize a rising and striving world; a reckless world, filled with the curiosity of life herself; a vivid and violent world welcoming every challenge; a world hating and adoring and fighting and forgiving; in brief, a world which was a world." Al McGuire: "Welcome to my world." With him everything is naturally vivid and nearly everything is naturally contradictory, the way it must be in crowded, excited worlds.

So with the clowns. It is not the sadness that matters, or even the clownishness. It is the *sad clown,* a contradiction. By definition, can there be such a thing as a sad clown? Or a wise coach? "Sports is a coffee break," McGuire says. And Eugene McCarthy once observed, "Coaching is like politics. You have to be smart enough to know how to do it, but dumb enough to think it is important."

Now, if all of the foregoing has tumbled and twisted and gone in fits and spurts, that's what it is like being around Al McGuire. His business, making money (it includes coaching as a necessary evil), comes ordered and neat, hermetic—to use his word, *calculated*—but everything else veers off in different directions, at changing speeds, ricocheting. Actually, all of that is calculated, too, only we cannot always fathom to what purpose. For example, later on here McGuire is going to expound at length on how he is not only sick of coaching but how he no longer applies himself to the task, and how Marquette could be virtually unbeatable if he just worked harder. Now, these remarks were made thoughtfully and have been repeated and embellished on other occasions. Obviously, they are going to come back to haunt him. Other recruiters are going to repeat them to prospects. If Marquette loses a couple of games back-to-back, the press and the alumni and the students and even those warm and wonderful fans who don't have shrews for wives are going to throw this admission back in his face. And he knows this, knew it when he spoke. So maybe you can figure out why he said what he did. Probably it has something to do with tar babies. Somehow he figures that other people who slug it out with him in his world are going to get stuck.

People are dazzled by McGuire, by his colorful language and by the colorful things he does—riding motorcycles at his age, which is 48, or going off on solitary trips to the four corners of the globe. That stuff is all out front, hanging out there with the clown pictures, so people seize upon it and dwell on this "character." They miss the man. First off, he is a clever entrepreneur, a promoter, a shrewd businessman, an active executive of a large sports equipment company (vice-president of Medalist Industries). This interests him much more than the baskets. "And I have an advantage," he says, "because people have a false impression from reading about me. They expect one thing and suddenly find themselves dealing with a very calculating person. I scare them. I want to skip the French pastry and get right down to the numbers."

The fans and the press think of McGuire as the berserk hothead who drew two technicals in an NCAA championship game, or the uncommonly handsome, dapper sharpie, pacing, spitting, playing to the crowd, cursing his players, themselves attired in madcap uniforms resembling the chorus line in *The Wiz*. The fans and the press overlook the fact that McGuire's Marquette teams have made the NCAA or the NIT ten years in a row, averaging twenty-five wins a season the last nine, and they got there by concentrating on defense, ice-picking out victories by a few points a game. As a coach, you can't much control an offense: *They just weren't going in for us tonight.* A defense is a constant, seldom fluctuating, always commanding. Just because people see Al McGuire's body on the bench, they assume that is he, carrying on. You want to see Al McGuire, look out on the court, look at the way his team plays, calculating. McGuire will play gin rummy against anybody; he won't play the horses or a wheel in Vegas; he won't play the house. You play him, his game, his world. "People say it's all an act, and maybe it is," he says. "Not all of it—but I don't know myself anymore whether I'm acting. Not anymore. I don't know. I just know it pleases me."

The motorcycle, for example, gets involved here. McGuire adores motorcycling. Most mornings at home in Milwaukee, he rises at seven and tools around for a couple of hours on his Kawasaki. Before the regionals in Louisiana last year, he rented a bike and went to a leper hospital. So the motorcycle business is for real. Also, it is French pastry. Let us look at McGuire vis-à-vis more important things; for example, cars and women.

Now, most coaches adore automobiles and have no rapport with women. That is not to say that they don't like sex; it is to say that they tolerate women because women provide sex. But they don't enjoy the company of women. They don't like them *around.* This is what upsets them about women's athletics, not the money it's going to take from men's sports. Just that they're going to be around. On the other hand, American coaches are nuts about cars. Cars count. The most important thing to coaches is to get a courtesy car to drive around town in. This is the sign of being a successful coach. Almost any American coach will sign for $10,000 less if you give him the use of a $6,500 car.

Naturally, being one of the most famous and successful basketball coaches in the land, Al McGuire has a courtesy car. It is a Thunderbird. He gets a fresh one every two years. But, unlike other coaches, he has no relationship with his car. It doesn't mean anything to him. Last February, after a whole winter of driving the thing, 3,200 miles' worth, he still didn't have any idea how to turn on the heat. He had to be shown. And while he can whip around on his motorcycle, he is nearly incompetent as an automobile driver. While driving, he can become oblivious to the fact that he is driving. Sometimes he hunches over the wheel, sort of embracing it, and lets the car carry him and his country music along. Other times he takes both hands off the wheel to properly gesticulate. As a rule, he stops at all stop signs, including those that face down the other road of an intersection. This leads to some confusion in the cars behind the courtesy Thunderbird. Or sometimes, when a topic especially involves him, the car will sort of drift to a halt as he is talking. Just kind of peter out by the side of the road.

But as he does not fraternize with cars, so is he the rare coach who enjoys and appreciates women. This is not telling tales out of school. This has nothing to do with his marriage, which is going on twenty-seven years. This has to do with women generically. "I get along with women better than I do with men," Al says, simply enough. Whenever he talks to a woman he knows, he takes her hands gently in his and confides in her. But understand, the consummate calculator doesn't flash those green eyes just to be friendly. There are many ways to be credit-card-wise. "I've always believed that if you get women involved in anything, it will be a success," McGuire says. "Frank, most men in America are dominated by women, Frank."

He is not. He and Pat McGuire share a marriage that is not unlike the way he coaches. They do not crowd one another. In the twenty-six years he has been married, he has never used a house key. When he comes home, Pat must let him in. When it is late, which it often is, she is inclined to say, "Where have you been?" He replies, "Pat, were there any calls for me, Pat?" When Marquette is on the road, McGuire never sits in the game bus waiting for it to leave. He waits in a bar for the manager to come in and tell him everyone is aboard. Then, if someone was late, he doesn't know. "A lot of coaching is what you choose *not* to do, *not* to see," McGuire says. "This is hypocritical, of course, but it is also true."

This, however, is not to suggest that Pat McGuire puts up with him completely. Like her husband, she is not crazy about all kinds of surprises. This leads to the Al McGuire First Rule of Marriage: when you have something unsettling to tell your wife, advise her thereof just before you go into the bathroom. Thus, when Al decides to take off for Greece or the Yukon or any place where "I can get away from credit cards and free tickets," he announces the trip to Pat as he walks down the hall. "Yes?" she answers. "I'm going to Greece tomorrow for two weeks," he calls out. "What?" she says, afraid she has heard him correctly again. She has. Then he repeats the message and closes the bathroom door. This has worked, more or less, for twenty-six years. Is it at all surprising that his unorthodoxy has succeeded so well at Marquette for a mere twelve?

Now that you are more than somewhat confused, let us go back to his beginning. Al McGuire is influenced by his family and his heritage.

He was born on September 7, 1928, in the Bronx but grew up in the Rockaway Beach section of Queens, where his family ran a workingman's bar. It was a club, a phone, a bank; they cashed paychecks. There were fifty-six saloons in seven blocks, meaning a) the McGuires had a lot of competition, but b) they were in the right business for that particular constituency. Al was named for Al Smith, then running as the first major Catholic presidential candidate. Al Smith was the quintessential New Yorker. He was fervently opposed to Prohibition, he wore a derby hat and said such strange words as "raddio" for what brought us *Amos 'n' Andy*. The namesake McGuire, removed from New York for two decades now, first in North Carolina, then in Milwaukee, still honors the other Al by talking Noo Yawkese. The *r*'s in the middle of many words evaporate. Thus, the fowuds play in the conner, whence they participate in pattuns. And there is the occasional awreddy and youse and den (for then), and the missing prepositions so reminiscent of that disappearing subway culture: down Miami; graduated high school.

McGuire also claims to have enriched the language. It was his interest in the stock market, he says, that brought the term blue chip into sports ("But I wasn't famous enough at the time to get credit for it"). Likewise, "uptick," for when a stock/team advances. Gambling, a familiar pursuit of his father's, an illness for his legendary older brother John, provided "the minus pool" (for losers), "a push" (a standoff), and "numbers," the word McGuire invariably uses for dollars. "What are the numbers?" is a common McGuire expression. Then, from the old sod, there are the adages: "Never undress until you die" (always save something, or, "Squirrel some nuts away"). "Congratulate the temporary" (live for the moment, or, "Go barefoot in the wet grass"). He has recently developed an interest in antiques, which he hunts down on his motorcycle forays, and promises us new terms from antiquing soon.

But it is his imagery, original and borrowed, that is the most vivid McGuire. Seashells and balloons: happiness, victory. Yellow ribbons and medals: success in recruiting. Memos and pipes: academia. Hot bread and gay waiters: guaranteed, a top restaurant. A straw hat in a blizzard: what some people, like the NCAA, will provide you with. Even a whale comes up for a blow sometimes: advice to players who can't get their minds off women. Hot lunch for orphans: a giveaway, some sort of PR venture. French pastry: anything showy or extraneous, such as small talk or white players. Keepers: good-looking broads (you don't throw them back). Closers: people who get by the French pastry and complete a deal, e.g., yours truly, Al McGuire. Guys who charge up the hill into a machine gun: most X-and-O coaches; see also "Brooks Brothers types" and "First Communion guys." Welcome to my world: come uptown with me.

Moreover, McGuire has begun more and more to turn nouns into verbs. Thus, to "rumor it out" is what a smart executive does when he keeps his ear to the ground. And: "Guys like Chones and Meminger magnet kids for us." Or: "You've got to break up cliques or you'll find players husband-and-wifing it out on the court." Or: "If you haven't broken your nose in basketball, you haven't really played. You've just tokened it."

It is the custom at Marquette to let teammates fight, to encourage fights, for that matter, until the day the season opens. McGuire lets them go a minute. One day he stood there, biting his lip for the required time while an older player beat his son Allie, a pretty fair guard, all to hell. This policy is calculated to let frustrations out, draw the team together. Calculated. For he has no stomach for it. McGuire has seen all he would ever want of fighting.

It was an old Irish thing. His father, John, Sr., delighted in it. What more could a man want than to sip a beer and watch his boys mix it up? If not large for a basketball player—6′ 3″—McGuire was a big kid in a saloon, and he worked behind the bar from an early age. It was the bartender's job to break up fights. If you hired a bouncer, the trouble was he was liable to start fights himself; otherwise, he couldn't justify his job. So, fight started, the barkeep had to come over the bar. Feet first. Always come feet first. Or, if the action was slack, a slow Tuesday or whatnot, old John McGuire might drum up a fight for one of his own boys, and they would "go outside" to settle things.

Al McGuire played ball the same way. His older brother Dick, now a Knick scout, was the consummate Noo Yawk player for St. John's and the Knicks—a slick ball handler and passer. Al was what he himself calls a dance-hall player. He was good enough to star as a college player, at St. John's, but as a pro could only hang on as an enforcer for three seasons with the Knicks. Once he grabbed Sid Borgia, the famous official, in what was described by horrified observers as "a boa constrictor grip." Counting two technicals, he got eight fouls in less than a quarter in one game. He boasted that he could "stop" Bob Cousy in his heyday, which he could, after a fashion, halting the action by fouling Cousy or the guy who set picks for him. It was McGuire's big mouth that first sold out the Boston Garden for the Celtics. They paid to see the brash Irishman try to stop their Celtic. In the off-season McGuire would go back to Rock-

away, tend bar, and go outside when his father asked for such diver-
tissement.

"We all thought it was so romantic," he says, "so exciting, but,
Frank, looking back, it wasn't, Frank." Not long ago McGuire was in a
joint in Greenwich Village. A few tables over, there was an argument.
The guy took off his watch. It took six, seven guys to subdue him. McGuire
turned to the businessman he was with. "He'll be back," he said. He had
seen it so many times. Sure enough, in a little while the guy was back,
and there was another mess. The next morning, at breakfast, McGuire
began thinking about the previous night's incident, and just like that,
he threw up. "Maybe it was the orange juice," he says, "but I don't think
so. It was what that fight made me remember. It scared me. I don't want
those memories."

One time, when he was about 24 or 25, his father got him to go
outside with a guy. "I was handling him, but I couldn't put him away,"
McGuire says, "and I knew I couldn't get away with this." He was very
relieved when the cops came and broke it up. Al went back into the bar
and told his father, "Dad, that's it, Dad. I'm never gonna go outside
again." And he never did. His father sulked for a month or more. It was
not long after that that Al decided all of a sudden he could be very
successful in life at large.

But money, or the lack of it, has influenced Al McGuire more than
taking guys outside. Some people who grew up in the Depression are
that way. The McGuires had food on the table; they weren't on the dole.
Still, money was a concern. Of the sons, John, now 52, was considered
the clever one. And he was, except for the gambling. He has adapted
well; he runs a gay bar now. Dick, 50, was considered the bright one. At
an early age he could do the *New York Times* crossword. Al, the youngest,
was dismissed as a glib scuffler. Everybody, himself included, figured he
would become an Irish cop, an FBI man if he got lucky. He was scheduled
to take an FBI physical one day but played golf instead. He thought he
had blown a great chance in life and, remorseful, on his way home he
stopped his car on the Cross Bay Bridge, got out, and chucked his clubs,
the cart, the whole business, in the water. It was a little while later, when
he was an assistant coach at Dartmouth, that he decided he could be a
success, he could make money.

You see, even when nobody figured Al for anything, the family let
him handle the books. The kid was at home with the numbers. And then
one day at Dartmouth, where it snowed a lot, he was alone, and had
time to think, and he figured out he had more talent with the numbers

than with the baskets. "Since then I've never had any trouble making money," he says. "All I have to do is sit down and think. I believe I can do anything in that area."

Since then, while he has coached every year, while it is his profession, coaching has never been the ultimate. As a consequence, he is not vulnerable there. McGuire often says (indeed, he doth protest too much), "I've never blown a whistle, looked at a film, worked at a blackboard or organized a practice in my life." Which is true, and which drives other coaches up the wall. But McGuire, the anti-coach, regularly discusses land mortgages, Medalist shoulder-pad marketing, and his theories on the short-range future of municipal bonds. Intellectually, temperamentally, what is the difference between a fascination with a high-post back door and a short-term bond yield?

And yet, McGuire is only hung up on the numbers in the abstract. *The numbers:* It is a euphemism, like the Victorians using "limbs" for legs. Real money doesn't mean anything to him. He carries it all scrunched up in his pocket: bills, credit cards, notes, gum wrappers, identification cards, all loose together. He takes out the whole mess and plops it on the counter. "Take what you want," he says. A credit card? Two dollars and sixty-three cents for breakfast? My driver's license? Take whatever you want. The Depression baby just wants to know that the money in the bank is solid and permanent. *Never undress until you die.*

"I must be the highest-paid coach in the country," he says. "I wanted it. I thought it would be a goose for basketball. I don't mean just what I get from Marquette. I mean all the numbers. If anybody put all the numbers together it would amaze people. But understand: It hasn't changed me. I've always lived the same. My friends are still hit-and-run types. I eat the same as ever, drink the same, clown around the same. My wife still wears Treasure Island dresses."

He is not friendly with many coaches. Hank Raymonds has been beside him on the bench all twelve years at Marquette and has never had a meal at the McGuires'. Raymonds and young Rick Majerus do the Xs and Os, the trench work. McGuire believes in "complementary" coaches, as he does in complementary players, units that support each other's efforts, not duplicate them. "I can drink enough cocktails for the whole staff," McGuire says. "I don't need another me."

His assistants (McGuire, out of respect and guilt, has taken to calling them "co-coaches") understand his soft-shoe. One asks Majerus: What is it above all about McGuire? We are so used to hearing about the originality, the insouciance, the motorcycle flake, the ability to get along with black players—what is it really with McGuire? "The one main thing," Majerus answers, "is this insecurity Al has about money. Still. I guess he'll always be that way."

There was a group with McGuire a couple of winters ago after a road game. As always, he wouldn't countenance any talk about basketball, but soon enough he brought up the subject of the numbers. Typically, it was the woman in the gathering that he turned to, confided in. Speaking softly, as he does on these occasions, he told her he thought he had things worked out OK for his three kids, for Pat. They were going to have enough. For a Depression baby this made him feel good, he said. But what if he accumulated more money, the woman asked him, what would he do with that?

McGuire was not prepared for the question. He thought for a moment. "A park," he said then. "With what's left, I'd like to see them build a park for poor people."

To most everybody in the business, McGuire is a nagging aberration. Listening to him lecture 500 coaches at a Medalist clinic, Chuck Daly of Penn whispers, "If the rest of us operated his way, we'd be out of business." That is the conventional wisdom. But before he said that, Daly made another observation: "Al's logic is on a different level, above everybody else's." And that is the conventional wisdom, too. So wait a minute. If McGuire wins twenty-five a year and he has the logic, he obviously has the right way. That is logical. Nonetheless, he remains the only coach who waits in the bar, and he stays frustrated that coaches have such low esteem and little security.

"Coaches are so scared," he says. "Every day, practice starts: gimme three lines, gimme three lines. You come out and say gimme two lines, everybody will look at you like you just split the atom. Me, whether it's business or coaching, I'm so pleased when I look like a fool. When I don't do foolish things, make foolish new suggestions, I'm not doing my job. I'm just another shiny-pants bookkeeper.

"The trouble with coaching, the prevailing image, is that coaching is like what you had in high school, because that is the last place where most people were involved with coaching. But coaching college is not pizza parties and getting the team together down at the A and W stand. People can't understand my players screaming back at me, but it's healthy. Also, I notice that the screaming always comes when we're fifteen, twenty ahead. When it's tied, then they're all listening very carefully to what I have to say."

Many adult coaches demand unquestioning loyalty from 20-year-old kids. As McGuire points out, some of the most successful coaches even refuse to accept kids with different philosophies, conflicting egos. "Dealing with problems, with differences—that is what coaching is," he says. "Running pattuns is not coaching." He does not believe that character can be "built" with haircuts and Marine routines and by coaches so insecure that their players can never challenge them.

Off the court, McGuire sees his players only when they come to him in distress. He would be suspicious of any college kid who wanted to be buddy-buddy with a middle-aged man, and vice versa. "I don't pamper," he says. "These guys are celebrities in their own sphere of influence—top shelf, top liquor. Everybody around them touches them with clammy hands. That's the only word: clammy. Well, they don't get that from me." Often, he doesn't even bother to learn their names. For much of last season the starting center, Jerome Whitehead, was called Chapman. Sometimes McGuire has stood up to scream at a player and then had to sink back down because he couldn't remember the kid's name.

"Look, if you're into coaching heavy, into the blackboard, if you're gonna charge up the hill into the machine guns, then you might as well stay at St. Ann's in the fifth grade," he says. "Because coaching up here is something else. You're gonna have to deal with the fifth column, the memos and pipes. And you're gonna get fired. The trouble is, every coach thinks he has the new wrinkle and is gonna last forever. Coaching is a mistress, is what it is. If a job opened up in Alaska tomorrow, two hundred fifty guys from Florida would apply, and they wouldn't even ask about the numbers, and they wouldn't ask their wife, either, like they wouldn't about any mistress.

"But to the players you ain't a love affair. You're just a passing fancy to them. It's pitiful, too, because about every coach who leaves makes better numbers on the outside."

Everyone assumes McGuire gets along with his players—especially the inner-city blacks—because of his unique personality. It counts, to be sure; every charmer is an overlay. But look past the French pastry and his calculation surfaces again—just as he promises. No con works unless the conned party figures he is the one really getting the edge. McGuire settles for a push. "They get and I get," he says. While the players don't get an uncle-coach, they get, as McGuire calls it, "a post-recruiter." He virtually forces them to get a diploma, and he hustles them up the richest pro contracts or good jobs in business. It is surely not just a coincidence that McGuire has thrived during the years when the big-money pro war was on. He has been a cash coach in a cash-and-carry era. On one occasion the Marquette provost had to personally intercede to stop McGuire from pressuring the sports PR man about withholding unfavorable statistics that might harm a player's pro chances.

Shamelessly, McGuire promotes his seniors, a ploy that keeps a kid hustling, playing defense, giving up the ball for his first three seasons, so he will get the ball and the shots (and maybe then the big numbers) his final year. Already, in anticipation of this season, McGuire has begun to protest that Butch Lee, a junior guard, got too much publicity as the star of the Puerto Rico Olympic team. Bo Ellis, a senior, is scheduled to get the ink this time around.

The McGuire Arrangement is, basically, us against them—"The only two things blacks have ever dominated are basketball and poverty"— and it works because he tends bar for everybody. Nobody ever fussed with McGuire more than last year's ball handler, Lloyd Walton. "Sit down!" he would scream at his coach all through games. Says Walton, "He figures your problems are his problems. Hey, I've had a black coach in summer ball, but I never had the rapport with him I had with Al."

When McGuire learned one November night back in 1968 that revolutionaries on campus were pressuring the black players to quit because they were being "exploited," he met with the players in a motel room sometime after 2 A.M. He didn't go long on philosophy. He told them he would support their decision if they left and gave up their scholarships, but he also reminded them that there were more where they came from—maybe not so good, but they weren't Marquette basketball. He was.

Then he faced down the radicals. The smooth-talking theorists he screamed at. The tough guys he ridiculed. He suggested to an idealistic white coed that she should take one of the black players home to her suburb for Thanksgiving. To a priest, he snarled, "Don't come after these kids from the Jesuit house. You never bought a pound of butter in your life, and you're asking them to be kamikaze pilots." By 4:30 A.M. when Pat came to the doorbell to let him in, the revolution was dead.

The relationship between Marquette and McGuire is a curious one and, it seems, a push. Marquette is one of the few Catholic schools left that compete, year after year, with the huge state institutions. For that matter, Marquette is the only private school of any stripe that is always right there at the top. The Warriors not only sell out for the season, they do it head to head, in the same building, against the Milwaukee Bucks, a first-class pro team.

Never mind the ratings: Basketball pays a lot of bills at Marquette. It retired the oppressive old football debt. And McGuire must be reckoned with; for several years now he has been athletic director as well as coach. Of course, there are certain Marquette elements leery of the image of the school being filtered through the McGuire prism.

What the nation sees of Marquette University is a self-proclaimed hustler, ranting and raving at the establishment, running a team of ghetto blacks dressed in wild uniforms. What is this, some kind of desperado vocational school? In fact, Marquette is a relatively subdued place, Jesuit, stocked for the most part by white middle-class midwestern Catholics who end up as schoolteachers. Typically, McGuire—who sent all three of his children there—guarantees that it must be good academically or it couldn't get by charging such high tuition numbers.

While the coach and the school do share the same religion, McGuire does not get faith confused with the pattuns or the players who execute them. His only public concession to Catholicism, such as it is, is his pregame exhortation, which went like this last season, all in one breath: "All-right-let's-show-them-we're-the-number-two-team-in-the-country-and-beat-the-shit-out-of-them-Queen-of-Victory-pray-for-us."

Mostly the Jesuit fathers confine themselves to second-guessing the coach's substitutions rather than the morality of his antics. Says Father William Kelly, an associate professor of theology, "Al does use a few cultural expressions that some might find flippant—'Hail Mary shot,' that sort of thing—but he is not sacrilegious in the traditional faith context. He has just found congeniality in colloquialism. In fact, in terms of his ideals and his faith, he is very much a man of the Church. He is really a very conservative Catholic, if not necessarily a very good one. But Al is loyal and deep in his faith. He is competitive, but when he loses there is no blame. And he always points toward other, more important things."

Ay, there's the rub. The man has never really relished coaching, and with each succeeding season has cared for it less. When the call came, out of the blue, to interview for the Marquette opening ("They were desperate, obviously; otherwise they would have taken a First Communion guy"), he was drifting into real estate and other ventures, coaching with his left hand at little Belmont Abbey College in North Carolina. He went 6–19 and 6–18 his last two years there and was preparing to leave coaching altogether.

He appears to be approaching that estate again. In many ways, as he is the first to admit, Marquette basketball survives on his reputation and the hard work of Raymonds and Majerus. McGuire deigns to make only one recruiting visit a year ("The kids know more about me now than I know about them, but even though I don't work at it, I'm the best recruiter in the world"), and, invariably—eleven years out of thirteen —he gets his ace with his one-shot road show. He is often late for practice; sometimes he doesn't even know where the team is practicing. He gets older and smarter, but for a coach time stands still. The kids are always 19 going on 20, and most coaches and fans are one-track zombies; the Germans have the best word for them: *Fachidioten*—specialty idiots. McGuire would rather talk about how his new uniforms will televise than about his player prospects. When he gets to the Arena floor, the first things he checks are the four most distant corner seats —the worst ones in the house. If they are sold, he figures he has done it again. Then, only then, does he come to life as a coach. For two hours.

"I hate everything about this job except the games," McGuire says. "Everything. I don't even get affected anymore by the winning, by the ratings, those things. The trouble is, it will sound like an excuse because we've never won the national championship, but winning just isn't all that important to me. I don't know why exactly. Maybe it's the fear, the fear of then having to repeat. You win once, then they expect you to win again. On the other hand, I found out when I got those two technicals in the NCAA finals that people sympathized with me for making an ass out of myself. I get thirty-five million people looking at me, I can't help it, I immediately become an ass. People relate to that.

"But, Frank, I'm not doing the job anymore, Frank. I never liked coaching, but at least I should be available more. I should be more courteous to my staff. I should have a more orderly process with the university. Maybe it's the repetition. You take the clinics we do for Medalist. They're almost a success, but now, just when they're getting to be that, I don't have no thrill anymore. I wonder about myself. Can I be a success in anything permanently? Anything permanent?

"I figure I'm wrong eighty percent of the time, but it takes too much time to be right. I won't pay that price with my life. I'm jealous of guys like Dean Smith, Bobby Knight. I'm jealous of their dedication. I wish I had it. I admire the way their teams are dressed, the way their kids handle themselves. At the regionals last year one of our kids came down to lunch barefoot. But I just don't like coaching that much to put the time in on a thing like that. It's not my world. I run my team the only way I can run it and still keep my life.

"I'm ready to get out. It's just the numbers. So many of my numbers depend on me coaching. I'm scared to get out. Fear there, too. So maybe it's time I concentrated on coaching just for one year. It's been long enough I haven't concentrated. Frank, we could have a destructive machine if I worked at it. A destructive machine, Frank."

Is he acting now? It certainly doesn't seem so. The green eyes are neither twinkling nor blazing theatrically, the way they do when they signal routines. By happenstance, McGuire has been momentarily distracted. He came to an out-of-town place under the impression it was a greasy-spoon Mexican joint, but it has turned out, instead, to be a fancy-Dan supper club. With floor show. With table linen, yet. McGuire, in his sneakers and sport shirt, wasn't figuring on this—and place, setting the stage, is very important to him.

He wants to recruit around the kitchen table. Depression babies are kitchen guys, not parlor people. When a player comes to talk to him, get him out of the office, out of Marquette; get him down into some back-alley saloon. Welcome to my world. Visitors are escorted to an oil-cloth-covered dining-room table in the back of a rundown Mexican bodega for a home-cooked meal. Or he just walks with people. Nobody anymore walks along and talks except for Al McGuire. Right away, the other guy is off stride, in the minus pool. You know what it must come from? From the going outside to fight guys. The meanness is out of it, but it's the same principle, same game. OK, let's you and me go outside. Let's go in here. Let's drive out to this lake I know. Let's go to this guy's apartment. Let's go to this little Chinese place. Let's take a walk.

Everybody makes such a to-do about Al McGuire's exotic travels. Big deal: New Zealand. What is that? Anybody can go to New Zealand. That is the diversion, his escape, the smoke screen. Look at his world. That is the truly exotic one. How could a guy so Noo Yawk fit in so well in Milwaukee, or in Carolina before that? It's easy. Wherever McGuire is, he constructs a whole universe out of selected bars and restaurants, places to walk, acquaintances, teddy bears and zanies, places to drive, back rooms and penthouses, motorcycles and country music jukeboxes. Tall guys with broken noses are also a part of this community. There is a cast and there are sets—everything but a zip code.

Nobody else is permitted to see it all. He tells his secretaries when he hires them: two years. After two years, no matter how good you are—especially if you're good—out. *It's 3 A.M., where have you been? Pat, any calls for me, Pat?* The only person who lives in Al McGuireland is Al McGuire. Cynics and the jealous take a look at the characters who pass through, and they check out his con and whisper that he is really an ice-cold man who surrounds himself with bootlickers and sycophants. But that is not true. On the contrary. Sure, they all play up to McGuire—remember now, charmers are an overlay—but he has a need for them, too. Not just the players and the coaches, but all the people and places in Al McGuireland are complementary. Like his players, all retain their individuality and integrity. That's the whole point: Otherwise they're no good to him. Lloyd Walton screaming back is the Lloyd Walton that McGuire wants, in the same way that sometimes he selects a fleabag hotel precisely because he wants a fleabag hotel.

The one permanent thing is the numbers. They are distant and bland, to be sure, but they provide permanency. The other things—the people and the places and the basketball games—are vivid and dear, but they consume too much of him to be sustained. And critics say it is all an act. McGuire wonders himself. But, no, he is not acting. He is directing all the time. Al, you're a director, Al. You're always running pattuns.

Don DeLillo

Game Day

The only description on Don DeLillo's "business" card, besides his name, are the words "I don't want to talk about it." DeLillo has always insisted on letting his words speak for himself, as they have, in a most haunting way, over two decades, beginning in 1971. A theme of his 1985 National Book Award–winning novel White Noise, *"American magic and dread," echoes through all of his novels. DeLillo's second novel,* End Zone, *published in 1972, was possibly the first existential novel about football. In this excerpt, Logos College of West Texas travels to play West Centrex Biotechnical Institute. A sleepless night, a restless day, and now it is time for the kickoff.*

The football team filled two buses and rode a hundred and twenty miles to a point just outside the campus of the West Centrex Biotechnical Institute. There the buses split up, offense to one motel, defense to another. We had steak for dinner and went to our rooms. All evening we kept visiting each other, trying to talk away the nervousness. Finally Sam Trammel and Oscar Veech came around and told us to get to bed. There were three men to a room. The regulars got beds; the substitutes were assigned to cots. Bloomberg and I had a reserve guard, Len Skink, sharing our room. For some reason Len was known as Dog-Boy. In the darkness I listened to the cars going by. I knew I'd have trouble sleeping. A long time passed, anywhere from an hour to three hours or more.

"Is anybody awake?" Len said.

"I am."

"Who's that?" he said.

"Gary."

"You scared me. I didn't think anybody would be awake. I'm having trouble sleeping. Where's Bloomers?"

"He's in bed."

"He doesn't make a sound," Len said. "I can't hear a single sound coming from his bed. A big guy like that."

"That means he's asleep."

"It's real dark in here, isn't it? It's as dark with your eyes open as when they're closed. Put your hand in front of your face. I bet you can't see a thing. My hand is about three inches from my face and I can't see it at all. How far is your hand, Gary?"

"I don't know. I can't see it."

"We better get some sleep. This stuff isn't for me. I remember the night I graduated high school. We stayed up all night. That was some night."

"What did you do?"

"We stayed up," he said.

In the morning we went out to the stadium, suited up without pads or headgear and had an extra mild workout, just getting loose, tossing the ball around, awakening our bodies to the feel of pigskin and turf. The place seemed fairly new. It was shaped like a horseshoe and probably seated about 22,000. Our workout progressed in virtual silence. It was a cool morning with no breeze to speak of. We went back in and listened to the coaches for a while. Then we rode back to the motels. At four o'clock we had our pregame meal—beef consommé, steak and eggs. At five-thirty we went back out to the stadium and slowly, very slowly, got suited up in fresh uniforms. Nobody said much until we went through the runway and took the field for our warmup. In the runway a few people made their private sounds, fierce alien noises having nothing to do with speech or communication of any kind. It was a kind of frantic breathing with elements of chant, each man's sound unique and yet mated to the other sounds, a mass rhythmic breathing that became more widespread as we emerged from the runway and trotted onto the field. We did light calisthenics and ran through some basic plays. Then the receivers and backs ran simple pass patterns as the quarterbacks took turns throwing. Off to the side the linemen exploded from their stances, each one making his private noise, the chant or urgent breathing of men in preparation for ritual danger. We returned to the locker room in silence and listened to our respective coaches issue final instructions. Then I put on my helmet and went looking for Buddy Shock. He and the other linebackers were still being lectured by Vern Feck. I waited until the coach was finished and then I grabbed Buddy by the shoulder, spun him around and hit him with a forearm across the chest, hard. He answered with three open-hand blows against the side of my helmet.

"Right," I said. "Right, right, right."

"Awright. Aw-*right,* Gary boy."

"Right, right, right."

"Awright, aw-*right.*"

"Get it up, get it in."

"Work, work, work."

"Awright."

"Awright. Aw-riiiight."

I walked slowly around the room, swinging my arms over my head. Some of the players were sitting or lying on the floor. I saw Jerry Fallon and approached him. He was standing against a wall, fists clenched at his sides, his helmet on the floor between his feet.

"Awright, Jerry boy."

"Awright, Gary."

"We move them out."

"Huh huh huh."

"How to go, big Jerry."

"Huh huh huh."

"Awright, awright, awright."

"We hit, we hit."

"Jerry boy, big Jerry."

Somebody called for quiet. I turned and saw Emmett Creed standing in front of a blackboard at the head of the room. His arms were crossed over his chest and he held his baseball cap in his right hand. It took only a few seconds before the room was absolutely still. The cap dangled from his fingers.

"I want the maximal effort," he said.

Then we were going down the runway, the sounds louder now, many new noises, some grunts and barks, everyone with his private noise, hard fast rhythmic sounds. We came out of the mouth of the tunnel and I saw the faces looking down from both sides, the true, real and honest faces, Americans on a Saturday night, even the more well-to-do among them bearing the look of sharecroppers, a vestigial line of poverty wearing thin but still present on every face, the teen-agers looking like prewar kids, 1940, poorly cut short hair and a belligerent cleanliness. After the introductions I butted pads with Bobby Hopper and then bounced up and down on the sideline as we won the coin toss. The captains returned and we all gathered together around Creed, all of us making noises, a few prayers said, some obscenities exchanged, men jumping, men slapping each other's helmets. Creed said something into all the noise and then the kick-return team moved onto the field. I glanced across at Centrex. They looked big and happy. They were wearing red jerseys with silver pants and silver helmets. We wore white jerseys with green pants and green and white helmets. My stomach was tight; it seemed to be up near my chest somewhere. I was having trouble breathing and an awful sound was filling my helmet, a sound that seemed to be coming from inside my head. I could see people getting up all over the stadium and the cheerleaders jumping and a couple of stadium cops standing near an exit. I could see the band playing, the movements of the band members as they played, but I couldn't hear the music. I looked down to my right. Bobby Iselin and Taft Robinson were the deep men. Speed and superspeed. About sixty-eight yards upfield the kicker raised his right arm, gave a little hop, and began to move toward the ball.

James Dickey

The Bee

James Dickey will probably be remembered most for his stunning novel Deliverance. *But maybe not. He is a poet first, and a major poet. In 1966 Dickey won the National Book Award for a volume of his poetry, and he has received numerous other literary honors. Dickey is also a sports fan and has written many poems on sports, especially football. This one is a prime example of James Dickey's art.*

To the football coaches of Clemson College, 1942

One dot
Grainily shifting   we at roadside and
The smallest wings coming   along the rail fence out
Of the woods   one dot   of all that green. It now
Becomes flesh-crawling   then the quite still
Of stinging. I must live faster for my terrified
Small son   it is on him. Has come. Clings.

Old wingback, come
To life. If your knee action is high
Enough, the fat may fall in time   God damn
You, Dickey, *dig*   this is your last time to cut
And run   but you must give it everything you have
Left, for screaming near your screaming child is the sheer
Murder of California traffic: some bee hangs driving

Your child
Blindly onto the highway. Get there however

Is still possible. Long live what I badly did
At Clemson   and all of my clumsiest drives
For the ball   all of my trying to turn
The corner downfield   and my spindling explosions
Through the five-hole over tackle. O backfield

Coach Shag Norton,
Tell me as you never yet have told me
To get the lead out   scream whatever will get
The slow-motion of middle age off me   I cannot
Make it this way   I will have to leave
My feet   they are gone   I have him where
He lives   and down we go singing with screams into

The dirt,
Son-screams of fathers   screams of dead coaches turning
To approval   and from between us the bee rises screaming
With flight   grainily shifting   riding the rail fence
Back into the woods   traffic blaring past us
Unchanged, nothing heard through the air-
conditioning glass   we lying at roadside full

Of the forearm prints
Of roadrocks   strawberries on our elbows as from
Scrimmage with the varsity   now we can get
Up   stand   turn away from the highway   look straight
Into trees. See, there is nothing coming out   no
Smallest wing   no shift of a flight-grain   nothing
Nothing. Let us go in, son and listen

For some tobacco-
mumbling voice in the branches   to say "That's
a little better,"   to our lives still hanging
By a hair. There is nothing to stop us   we can go
Deep   deeper   into elms, and listen to traffic die
Roaring, like a football crowd from which we have
Vanished. Dead coaches live in the air, son   live

In the ear
Like fathers, and *urge*   and *urge*. They want you better
Than you are. When needed, they rise and curse you they scream

When something must be saved. Here, under this tree,
We can sit down. You can sleep, and I can try
To give back what I have earned by keeping us
Alive, and safe from bees: the smile of some kind

Of savior—
Of touchdowns, of fumbles, battles,
Lives. Let me sit here with you, son
As on the bench, while the first string takes back
Over, far away   and say with my silentest tongue, with the man-
creating bruises on my arms   with a live leaf a quick
Dead hand on my shoulder, "Coach Norton, I am your boy."

Ken Dryden

Goalies Are Different

A member of the Hockey Hall of Fame and a longtime goaltender for the Montreal Canadiens, Ken Dryden was always considered one of the more cerebral players in the National Hockey League. He read impressive tomes, kept a journal, attended law school; he did things other hockey players did not do. But his teammates allowed Dryden his idiosyncrasies, his frequent introspection, his deviations from team camaraderie because he was a goalie and . . . after all . . . goalies are just different. In this selection from The Game, *Dryden's memoir of his final season as a player, he explains the unusual constitution needed to stand in front of a small net and use the padded body to prevent a hard, flat rubber disc shot at incredibly high speeds from getting past him and into that net.*

I have always been a goalie. I became one long enough ago, before others' memories and reasons intruded on my own, that I can no longer remember why I did, but if I had to guess, it was because of Dave. Almost six years older, he started playing goal before I was old enough to play any position, so by the time I was six and ready to play, there was a set of used and discarded equipment that awaited me—that and an older brother I always tried to emulate.

I have mostly vague recollections of being a goalie at that time. I remember the spectacular feeling of splitting and sprawling on pavement or ice, and feeling that there was something somehow noble and sympathetic about having bruises and occasional cuts, especially if they came, as they did, from only a tennis ball. But if I have one clear image that remains, it is that of a goalie, his right knee on the ice, his left leg extended in a half splits, his left arm stretching for the top corner, and, resting indifferently in his catching glove, a round black puck.

It was the posed position of NHL goalies for promotional photos and hockey cards at the time and it was a position we tried to re-enact as often as we could in backyard games. There was something that looked and felt distinctly major league about a shot "raised" that high, and about a clean, precise movement into space to intercept it. Coming as it did without rebound, it allowed us to freeze the position as if in a photo, extending the moment, letting our feelings catch up to the play, giving us time to step outside ourselves and see what we had done. In school, or at home, with pencil and paper, sometimes thinking of what I was doing, more often just mindlessly doodling, I would draw pictures of goalies, not much more than stick figures really, but fleshed out with parallel lines, and always in that same catching position. Each year when my father arranged for a photographer to take pictures for our family's Christmas card, as Dave and I readied ourselves in our nets, the shooter was told to shoot high to the glove side, that we had rehearsed the rest.

To catch a puck or a ball—it was the great joy of being a goalie. Like a young ballplayer, too young to hit for much enjoyment but old enough to catch and throw, it was something I could do before I was big enough to do the rest. But mostly it was the feeling it gave me. Even now, watching TV or reading a newspaper, I like to have a ball in my hands, fingering its laces, its seams, its nubby surface, until my fingertips are so alive and alert that the ball and I seem drawn to each other. I like to spin it, bounce it, flip it from hand to hand, throw it against a wall or a ceiling, and catch it over and over again. There is something quite magical about a hand that can follow a ball and find it so crisply and tidily every time, something solid and wonderfully reassuring about its muscular certainty and control. So, if it was because of Dave that I became a goalie, it was the feeling of catching a puck or a ball that kept me one. The irony, of course, would be that later, when I finally became a real goalie instead of a kid with a good glove hand, when I learned to use the other parts of a goaltender's equipment—skates, pads, blocker, stick—it could only be at the expense of what had been until then my greatest joy as a goalie.

I was nineteen at the time. It surely had been happening before then, just as it must before any watershed moment, but the time I remember was the warm-up for the 1967 NCAA final against Boston University. For the first few minutes, I remember only feeling good: a shot, a save, a shot, a save; loose, easy, the burn of nerves turning slowly to a burn of exhilaration. For a shot to my right, my right arm went up and I stopped it with my blocker; another, low to the corner, I kicked away with my pad; along the ice to the other side, my skate; high to the left, my catching glove. Again and again: a pad, a catching glove, a skate, a stick, a blocker, whatever was closest moved, and the puck stopped. For someone who had scooped up ice-skimming shots like a shortstop, who had twisted his body to make backhanded catches on shots for the top right corner, it was a moment of great personal triumph. I had come of age. As the warm-up was ending, I could feel myself becoming a goalie.

Goaltending is often described as the most dangerous position in sports. It is not. Race drivers die from racing cars, jockeys die, so do football players. Goalies do not die from being goalies. Nor do they suffer the frequent facial cuts, the knee and shoulder injuries, that forwards and defensemen often suffer. They stand as obstacles to a hard rubber disc, frequently shot at a lethal speed, sometimes unseen, sometimes deflected; the danger to them is obvious, but it is exaggerated— even the unthinkable: a goalie diving anxiously out of the way of a 100 m.p.h. slap shot, the shooter panicking at his own recklessness, the fans "ah"-ing at the near miss. Except for that one, feared time, the time it doesn't happen that way, when the puck moves too fast and the goalie too slow, and, hit in the head, he falls frighteningly to the ice. Moments later, up again, he shakes his head, smiling as others slowly do the same, again reminded that he wears a mask which at other times he sees through and forgets. The danger of playing goal is a *potential* danger, but equipment technology, like a net below a trapeze act, has made serious injury extremely unlikely.

From the time I was six years old, until as a freshman at Cornell I was required to wear a mask, I received fifteen stitches. Since then I have had only four—from a Dennis Hull slap shot that rebounded off my chest, hitting under my chin, in my first playoff year. I have pulled groins and hamstrings, stretched, twisted, and bruised uncounted times various other things, sent my back into spasm twice, broken a toe, and torn the cartilage in one knee. In almost eight years, after more than 400 games and 1000 practices, that's not much.

Yet, I am often afraid. For while I am well protected, and know I'm unlikely to suffer more than a bruise from any shot that is taken, the puck hurts, constantly and cumulatively: through the pillow-thick leg pads I wear, where straps pulled tight around their shins squeeze much of the padding away; through armor-shelled skate boots; through a catching glove compromised too far for its flexibility; with a dull, aching nausea from stomach to throat when my jock slams back against my testes; and most often, on my arms, on wrists and forearms especially, where padding is light and often out of place, where a shot hits and spreads its ache, up an arm and through a body, until both go limp and feel lifeless. Through a season, a puck hurts like a long, slow battering from a skillful boxer, almost unnoticed in the beginning, but gradually wearing me down, until two or three times a year, I wake up in the morning sore, aching, laughing/moaning with each move I make, and feel a hundred years old. It is on those days and others that when practice comes, I shy away.

The puck on his stick, a player skates for the net. Deep in my crouch, intent, ready, to anyone watching I look the same as I always do. But, like a batter who has been knocked down too many times before, when I see a player draw back his stick to shoot, at the critical moment when concentration must turn to commitment, my body stiffens, my eyes widen and go sightless, my head lifts in the air, turning imperceptibly to the right, as if away from the puck—I bail out, leaving only an empty body behind to cover the net. I yell at myself as others might ("you chicken"). I tell myself reasonably, rationally, that lifting my head, blanking my eyes, can only put me in greater danger; but I don't listen. In a game, each shot controlled by a harassing defense, with something else to think about I can usually put away fear and just play. But in practice, without the distraction of a game, seeing Tremblay or Lambert, Risebrough, Chartraw, or Lupien, dangerous, uncontrolled shooters as likely to hit my arms as a corner of the net, I cannot. In time the fear gradually shrinks back, manageable again, but it never quite goes away.

I have thought more about fear, I have been afraid more often, the last few years. For the first time this year, I have realized that I've only rarely been hurt in my career. I have noticed that unlike many, so far as I know, I carry with me no permanent injury. And now that I know I will retire at the end of the season, more and more I find myself thinking—*I've lasted this long: please let me get out in one piece.* For while I know I am well protected, while I know it's unlikely I will suffer any serious injury, like every other goalie I carry with me the fear of the *one big hurt* that never comes. Recently, I read of the retirement of a race-car driver. Explaining his decision to quit, he said that after his many years of racing, after the deaths of close friends and colleagues, after his own near misses, he simply "knew too much." I feel a little differently. I feel I have known all along what I know now. It's just that I can't forget it as easily as I once did.

Playing goal is not fun. Behind a mask, there are no smiling faces, no timely sweaty grins of satisfaction. It is a grim, humorless position, largely uncreative, requiring little physical movement, giving little physical pleasure in return. A goalie is simply there, tied to a net and to a game; the game acts, a goalie reacts. How he reacts, how often, a hundred shots or no shots, is not up to him. Unable to initiate a game's action, unable to focus its direction, he can only do what he's given to do, what the game demands of him, and that he must do. It is his job, a job that cannot be done one minute in every three, one that will not await rare moments of genius, one that ends when the game ends, and only then. For while a goal goes up in lights, a permanent record for the goal-scorer and the game, a save is ephemeral, important at the time, occasionally when a game is over, but able to be wiped away, undone, with the next shot. It is only when a game ends and the mask comes off, when the immense challenge of the job turns abruptly to immense satisfaction or despair, that the unsmiling grimness lifts and goes away.

If you were to spend some time with a team, without ever watching them on the ice, it wouldn't take long before you discovered who its goalies were. Goalies are different. Whether it's because the position attracts certain personality types, or only permits certain ones to succeed; whether the experience is so intense and fundamental that it transforms its practitioners to type—I don't know the answer. But whatever it is, the differences between "players" and "goalies" are manifest and real, transcending as they do even culture and sport.

A few years ago, at a reception at the Canadian Embassy in Prague, the wife of Jiri Holecek, former star goalie for Czechoslovakia, was introduced to Lynda, and immediately exclaimed, "The players think my Jiri's crazy. Do they [my teammates] think your husband's crazy too?" (No more of the conversation was related to me.) For his book on soccer goalies, English journalist Brian Glanville chose as his title *Goalkeepers Are Different*. It is all part of the mythology of the position, anticipated, expected, accepted, and believed; and in many ways real.

Predictably, a goalie is more introverted than his teammates, more serious (for team pictures, when a photographer tells me to smile, unsmilingly I tell him, "Goalies don't smile"), more sensitive and moody ("ghoulies"), more insecure (often unusually "careful" with money; you might remember Johnny Bower and I *shared* a cab). While a goalie might sometimes be gregarious and outgoing, it usually manifests itself in binges—when a game is over, or on the day of a game when he isn't playing—when he feels himself released from a game. Earlier this season, minutes before a game with the Rangers in the Forum, Robinson looked across the dressing room at me and asked, "Who's playing?" Before I could answer, Shutt yelled back, "I'll give ya a hint, Bird," he said. "Bunny's in the shitter puking; Kenny hasn't shut up since he got here." While teams insist on togetherness, and on qualities in their teammates that encourage it both on and off the ice, a goalie is the one player a team allows to be different. Indeed, as perplexed as anyone at his willingness to dress in cumbrous, oversized equipment to get hit by a puck, a team allows a goalie to sit by himself on planes or buses, to disappear on road trips, to reappear and say nothing for long periods of time, to have a single room when everyone else has roommates. After all, *shrug*, he's a goalie. What can you expect? Flaky, crazy, everything he does accepted and explained away, it offers a goalie wonderful licence. It was what allowed Gilles Gratton to "streak" a practice, and Gary Smith to take showers between periods. In many ways, it is also why my teammates accepted my going to law school.

Good goalies come in many shapes, sizes, and styles. So do bad goalies. A goalie is often plump (Savard, a defenceman, always insists "I like my goalies fat"), sometimes unathletic, and with reflex reactions surprisingly similar to those of the average person (recently at a science museum, with a flashing light and a buzzer I tested my eye-hand reactions against Lynda's; she was slightly faster). While most might agree on what the ideal physical and technical goalie-specimen might look like, it almost certainly would be a composite—the physical size of Tretiak, the elegance of Parent, the agility of Giacomin or Cheevers, the bouncy charisma of Vachon or Resch—with no guarantee that *supergoalie* would be any good. For while there are certain minimum standards of size, style, and agility that any goalie must have, goaltending is a remarkably aphysical activity.

If you were to ask a coach or a player what he would most like to see in a goalie, he would, after some rambling out-loud thoughts, probably settle on something like: consistency, dependability, and the ability to make the big save. Only in the latter, and then only in part, is the physical element present. Instead, what these qualities suggest is a certain character of mind, a mind that need not be nimble or dextrous, for the demands of the job are not complex, but a mind emotionally disciplined, one able to be focused and directed, a mind under control. Because the demands on a goalie are mostly mental, it means that for a goalie the biggest enemy is himself. Not a puck, not an opponent, not a quirk of size or style. Him. The stress and anxiety he feels when he plays, the fear of failing, the fear of being embarrassed, the fear of being physically hurt, all are symptoms of his position, in constant ebb and flow, but never disappearing. The successful goalie understands these neuroses, accepts them, and puts them under control. The unsuccessful goalie is distracted by them, his mind in knots, his body quickly following.

It is why Vachon was superb in Los Angeles and as a high-priced free-agent messiah, poor in Detroit. It is why Dan Bouchard, Tretiak-sized, athletic, technically flawless, lurches annoyingly in and out of mediocrity. It is why there are good "good team" goalies and good "bad team" goalies—Gary Smith, Doug Favell, Denis Herron. The latter are spectacular, capable of making near-impossible saves that few others can make. They are essential for bad teams, winning them games they shouldn't win, but they are goalies who need a second chance, who need the cushion of an occasional bad goal, knowing that they can seem to earn it back later with several inspired saves. On a good team, a goalie has few near-impossible saves to make, but the rest he must make, and playing in close and critical games as he does, he gets no second chance.

A good "bad team" goalie, numbed by the volume of goals he cannot prevent, can focus on brilliant saves and brilliant games, the only things that make a difference to a poor team. A good "good team" goalie cannot. Allowing few enough goals that he feels every one, he is driven instead by something else—the penetrating hatred of letting in a goal.

The great satisfaction of playing goal comes from the challenge it presents. Simply stated, it is to give the team what it needs, when it needs it, not when I feel well-rested, injury-free, warmed-up, psyched-up, healthy, happy, and able to give it, but when *the team* needs it. On a team as good as the Canadiens, often it will need nothing; other times, one good save, perhaps two or three; maybe five good minutes, a period, sometimes, though not often, a whole game. Against better teams, you can almost predict what and when it might be; against the rest, you cannot. You simply have to be ready.

During my first two years with the team, for reasons none of us could figure out, we would start games slowly, outplayed for most of the first period, occasionally for a little longer. It happened so regularly that it became a pattern we anticipated and prepared for, each of us with a special role to play. Mine was to keep the score sufficiently close in the first period, usually to within one goal, so as not to discourage any comeback—their role—that otherwise we would almost certainly make. We were a good combination. I could feel heroically beleaguered the first period, all the time knowing that it would end, that we would soon get our stride, and when we did that I would become a virtual spectator to the game.

That has changed. It began to change the next season, and for the last four years, the change has been complete. A much better team than earlier in the decade, it needs less from me now, just pockets of moments that for me and others sometimes seem lost in a game. But more than that, what it needs now is not to be distracted—by bad goals, by looseness or uncertainty in my play. It needs only to feel secure, confident that the defensive zone is taken care of; the rest it can do itself.

It makes my job different from that of every other goalie in the NHL. I get fewer shots, and fewer *hard* shots; I must allow fewer goals, the teams I play on must win Stanley Cups. Most envy me my job, some are not so sure. Once Vachon, my predecessor in Montreal, in the midst of one of his excellent seasons in Los Angeles, told me that he wasn't sure he would ever want to play for the Canadiens again, even if he had the chance. He said he had come to enjoy a feeling he knew he would rarely have in Montreal—the feeling of winning a game for his team—and he wasn't sure how well he could play without it. In a speech a few years ago, my brother talked about the heroic self-image each goalie needs and has, and is allowed to have because of the nature and perception of his position. "A solitary figure," "a thankless job," "facing an onslaught," "a barrage," "like Horatio at the bridge"—it's the stuff of backyard dreams. It is how others often see him; it is how he sometimes sees himself. I know the feeling Vachon described because I felt it early in my career, when the team wasn't as good as it is now. It is a feeling I have learned to live without.

But something else has changed, something that is more difficult to live without. Each year, I find it harder and harder to make a connection between a Canadiens win and me—nothing so much as my winning a game for the team, just a timely save, or a series of saves that made a difference, that arguably made a difference, that *might* have made a difference, that, as with a baseball pitcher, can make a win feel mine and ours. But as the team's superiority has become entrenched, and as the gap between our opponents and us, mostly unchanged, has come to seem wider and more permanent, every save I make seems without urgency, as if it is done completely at my own discretion, a minor bonus if made, a minor inconvenience, quickly overcome, if not.

A few months ago, we played the Colorado Rockies at the Forum. Early in the game, I missed an easy shot from the blueline, and a little unnerved, for the next fifty minutes I juggled long shots, and allowed big rebounds and three additional goals. After each Rockies goal, the team would put on a brief spurt and score quickly, and so with only minutes remaining, the game was tied. Then the Rockies scored again, this time a long, sharp-angled shot that squirted through my legs. The game had seemed finally lost. But in the last three minutes, Lapointe scored, then Lafleur, and we won 6–5. Alone in the dressing room afterwards, I tried to feel angry at my own performance, to feel relieved at being let off the uncomfortable hook I had put myself on, to laugh at what a winner could now find funny; but I couldn't. Instead, feeling weak and empty, I just sat there, unable to understand why I felt the way I did. Only slowly did it come to me: I had been irrelevant; I couldn't even lose the game.

I catch few shots now, perhaps only two or three a game. I should catch more, but years of concussion have left the bones in my hand and wrist often tender and sore, and learning to substitute a leg or a stick to save my hand, my catching glove, reprogrammed and out of practice, often remains at my side. Moreover, the game has changed. Bigger players now clutter the front of the net, obstructing and deflecting shots, or, threatening to do both, they distract a goalie, causing rebounds, making clean, precise movements into space—commitments to a single option unmindful of possible deflection or rebound—an indulgence for which a price is too often paid. What I enjoy most about goaltending now is the game itself: feeling myself slowly immerse in it, finding its rhythm, anticipating it, getting there before it does, challenging it, controlling a play that should control me, making it go where I want it to go, moving easily, crushingly within myself, delivering a clear, confident message to the game. And at the same time, to feel my body slowly act out that feeling, pushing up taller and straighter, thrusting itself forward, clenched, flexed, at game's end released like an untied balloon, its feeling spewing in all directions until the next game.

I enjoy the role I play—now rarely to win a game, but not to lose it; a game fully in my hands, fully in the hands of my teammates, and between us an unstated trust, a quiet confidence, and the results we want. Our roles have changed, but we remain a good combination, and I find that immensely satisfying.

Stanley Elkin

The Masked Playboy vs. The Grim Reaper

*One of America's most outrageous—and seriously undervalued—contemporary black humorists, Stanley Elkin has written a series of rich novels resounding with dazzling language, sometimes at the expense of plot. Among Elkin's novels, these stand out—*The Dick Gibson Show, The Franchiser, George Mills *(which won the National Book Critics Circle Award for fiction in 1982), and* The MacGuffin, *nominated for a National Book Award in 1991. Here, from Elkin's first novel,* Boswell, *published in 1964, the story of an epic heavyweight wrestling match.*

In the locker room I could hear above me the thin crowd (the rain had held it down) shouting at the referee. It was an unmistakable sound; they thought they saw some infraction he had missed. A strange sound of massed outrage, insular and safe, self-conscious in its anonymity and lack of consequence. If commitment always cost so little, which of us would not be a saint?

I dressed quickly, squeezing uncomfortably and awkwardly into the damp trunks. I laced the high-top silk shoes, fit the mask securely over my head, and buckled the clasp of the heavy silk cape around my throat. Down a row of lockers a couple of college wrestlers I didn't know and who had already fought were rubbing each other with liniment. I went over to them.

"Excuse me, did you see John Sallow?" I asked.

They looked at me and then at each other.

"It's a masked man," one of them said. "Ask him what he wants, Tom."

Tom pretended to hitch up his chaps. "What do you want, masked man?"

"Do you know John Sallow? The wrestler? He's on the card tonight. Have you seen him?"

"He went thataway, masked man," the other said.

I walked away and went into the toilet and urinated. One of the college boys came in. "Hey, Tom," he called. "There's a masked man in a white cape in here peeing."

"Knock it off," I said.

"It's all so corny," the kid said.

"Knock it off," I said again.

"Okay, champ."

"Knock it off."

I went back to my locker. John Sallow was there, one gray leg up on the wooden bench.

"Bogolub tells me you may try to give me some trouble tonight," he said.

"This is my last match," I said. "I'm quitting after tonight." It was true. I hadn't known it was true until I said it. Too often it rained; too often I had to take the streetcar; too often I sat too close to the steamy, seedy poor. I could still see the nurse. I never forgive a face.

There were excited screams and a prolonged burst of applause above us. Sallow looked up significantly. "Upstairs," he said. "You'll be introduced first. I'm the favorite."

"Look," I said, "I wanted to talk to you."

"Upstairs," he said. "Talk upstairs."

I took my place behind two blue-uniformed ushers at gate DD. Some boys just to the right of the entrance kept turning around to look at me. They laughed and pointed and whispered to each other. The ring announcer, in a tuxedo, was climbing through the ropes far in front of me. He walked importantly to the center of the ring, stopping every few steps to turn and pull a microphone wire in snappy, snaking arcs along the surface of the canvas. He tapped the microphone with his fingernail and sent a piercing metal *thunk* throughout the arena. Then, shooting his cuffs and clearing his throat, he paused expectantly. The crowd watched with mild interest. "First I have some announcements," he said. He told them of future matches, reading the names of the wrestlers from a card concealed in his palm. He spoke each wrestler's name with a calm aplomb and familiarity so that their grotesque titles—The Butcher and Mad Russian and Wildman—sounded almost like real names.

Then there was a pause. Jerking more microphone cord into the ring as though he needed all he could get for what he would say next, the announcer began again. "Ladies and gentlemen—In the main event this evening . . . two tough . . . wrestlers . . . both important contenders for the heavyweight champeenship of the world. The first . . . that rich man's disguised son . . . who has danced with debutantes and who trains on champagne . . . the muscled millionaire and eligible bachelor . . . who'd rather rough and tumble than ride to the hounds . . . from Nob Hill and Back Bay . . . from Wall Street and the French Riviera . . . from Newport and the fabled courts of the eastern potentates . . . weighing two hundred thirty-five pounds without the cape but in the mask . . . the one . . . the only . . . *Masked Playboy!*"

I pushed the ushers out of the way and bounded down the long aisle toward the ring. To everyone but the kids who had spotted me earlier it must have looked as though I had run across all the turnpikes from Wall Street, over the bridge across the Mississippi, and through the town to the Arena. Modest but good-natured applause paralleled my course down the aisle, as though I were somehow tripping it off automatically as I came abreast of each row. I leaped up the three steps leading to the ring, hurled over the ropes, unclasped the cape and, arching my shoulders, let it fall behind me in a heap. Then swelling my chest and stretching my long body, I stood on the tips of my high-top silk shoes, seemingly hatched from the cape itself, now a crumpled silken eggshell. The crowd cheered. I nodded, lifted the cape with the point of one shoe, slapped it sharply across one arm and then the other, and then tossed it casually to an attendant beneath me. I grabbed the thick ropes where they angled at the ring post. Without moving my legs I pushed, head down, against the ropes. Snapping my head up quickly I pulled against them. I could feel the muscles climbing my back. I looked like a man rowing in place. I let go of the ropes, dropped my weight solidly on my feet and did deep knee bends. Out of the corner of my eye I could see the ring announcer waiting a little impatiently, but the crowd applauded cheerfully. Suddenly I made a precise military right-face and sprang up onto the ropes, catching the upper rope neatly along my left thigh. I hooked my right foot under the lower rope for balance and folded my arms calmly. I looked like someone on a trapeze—or perhaps like a young, masked sales executive perched casually along the edge of his desk.

I smiled at the ring announcer and waved my arm grandly, indicating that he could continue.

He turned away from me and waited until the crowd was silent. When he began again he sounded oddly sad. "Meeting him in mortal . . . physical . . . one-fall . . . forty-five-minute-time-limit combat tonight . . . is that grim gladiator, ancient athlete, stalking spectral superman, fierce-faced fighter . . . that plague prover . . . that hoary horror . . . that breath breaking . . . hope hampering . . . death dealing . . . mortality making . . . heart hemorrhaging . . . life letting—" For the last few seconds the crowd had been applauding in time with the announcer's rhythms. In a way their applause incited him; they incited each other. Now as he paused, exhausted, there were a few last false claps and then silence.

"Widow making," someone yelled from the crowd.

"Coffin counting," someone else shouted.

"People pounding," the announcer added weakly.

I slid off the rope. "MUR . . . DER . . . ING," I shouted from the center of the ring. "All death is murder!"

Angrily the ring announcer motioned me to get back. By exercising the authority of his tuxedo, he seemed to have regained control. "Ladies and gentlemen," he began again more calmly, "in gray trunks, from the Lowlands, John Sallow . . . The Grim Reaper."

With the rest of the crowd I glanced quickly toward the opposite entrance, but no one was standing there. Through the entrance gate I could see the long, low concession stand and someone calmly spooning mustard onto a hot dog. Then I heard a gasp from the other end of the arena. Sallow had been spotted. I looked around just in time to see him coming in through the same gate I had used. Of course, I thought. Of course.

Sallow walked slowly. As he came down the aisle toward the ring some people, more than I would have expected, began applauding. He has his fans, I thought sadly. Most of the people, though, particularly those near the aisle, seemed to shrink back as he passed them. Recognizing someone, he suddenly stopped, put his hand on the man's shoulder and leaned down toward him, whispering something into his ear. When Sallow started again the person he had spoken to stood and left the auditorium. Sallow came up the three stairs, turned and bowed mockingly to the crowd. They looked at him; he smiled, shrugged, climbed through the ropes and walked to his corner. I tried to catch his eye, but he wouldn't look at me.

"The referee will acquaint the wrestlers with the Missouri rules," the ring announcer said.

The referee signaled for us to meet at the center of the ring. "This is a one-fall match, forty-five-minute time limit," he said. "When I signal one of you to break I want you to break clean and break quickly. Both you men have fought in Missouri before. You're both familiar with the rules in this state. I just want to remind you that if a man for any reason should be out of the ring and not return by the time I count twenty, that man forfeits the fight. Do both of you understand?"

Sallow nodded placidly. The referee looked at me. I nodded.

"All right. Are there any questions? Reaper? Playboy? Okay. Return to your corners and when the bell rings, come out to wrestle."

I had just gotten back to my corner when the bell rang. I whirled around expecting to find Sallow behind me. He was across the ring. I moved toward him aggressively and locked my arms around his neck. Already my body was wet. Sallow was completely dry.

"Don't you even sweat?" I whispered.

He twisted out of my neck lock and pushed me away from him.

I went toward him like a sleepwalker, inviting him to lock fingers in a test of strength. He ignored me, ducked quickly under my out-stretched arms, and grabbed me around the waist. He raised me easily off the floor. It was humiliating. I felt queerly like some wooden religious idol carried in a procession. I beat at his neck and shoulders with the flats of my hands. Sallow increased the pressure of his arms around my body. Desperately I closed one hand into a fist and chopped at his ear. He squeezed me tighter. He would crack my ribs, collapse my lungs. Suddenly he dropped me. I lay on my side writhing on the canvas. I tried to get to the ropes, moving across the grainy canvas in a slow sidestroke like a swimmer lost at sea. The Reaper circled around toward my head and blocked my progress. I saw his smooth, marblish shins and tried to hook one arm around them. It was a trap; he came down quickly on my outstretched arm with all his weight.

"Please," I said. "Please, you'll break my arm."

The Reaper leaned across my body and caught me around the hips. He pressed my thighs together viciously. I could feel my balls grind together sickeningly inside my jock. Raising himself to one knee and then to the other he stood up slowly, so that I hung upside down. He worked my head between his legs. Then, without freeing my head, he moved his hands quickly to my legs and pushed them away from his body, stretching my neck. I felt my legs go flying backwards and to protect my neck tried to force them again to his body. I pedaled dis-gustingly in the air. He grabbed my legs again.

"Please," I screamed. "If you drop me, you'll kill me," I whined.

Again he forced my legs away from his body. Then suddenly he loosened his terrible grip on my head. I fell obscenely from between Death's legs. Insanely I jerked my head up and broke my fall with my jaw. My body collapsed heavily behind me. It was like one of those clumsy auto wrecks in wet weather when cars pile uselessly up on each other. I had to get outside the ropes. I had a headache; I could not see clearly. I was gasping for air, actually shoveling it toward my mouth with my hands. Blindly I forced my body toward where I thought the ropes must be. Sallow saw my intention, of course, and kicked at me with his foot. I could not get to my knees; my only way of moving was to roll. Helplessly I curled into a ball and rolled back and forth inside the ring. Sallow stood above me like some giant goalie, feinting with his feet and grotesquely seeming to guide my rolling. The crowd laughed. Suddenly I kicked powerfully toward the ropes. One foot became entangled in them. It was enough to make the referee come between us. He started counting slowly. I crawled painfully under the ropes and onto the ring's outer apron. "Seven," the referee intoned. "Eight." Sallow grinned and stepped toward me. He came through the ropes after me. The referee tried to pull him back, but he shrugged him off as I got to my feet. "Nine," the referee said. "Ten. One for Reaper. Eleven for Playboy. Two for Reaper. Twelve for Playboy."

The Reaper advanced toward me. I circled along the apron. He pursued me.

"Missouri rules, Missouri rules," I said plaintively.

"Natural law, natural law," he answered.

"Three for Reaper. Thirteen for Playboy."

"Not by default, you bastard," I shouted. I jumped back inside the ropes.

"Four for Reaper."

"Famine, Flood, War, Pestilence," I hissed.

He came through the ropes and the referee stood between us. When Sallow was standing inside the ring the referee clapped his hands and stepped back.

I held out my hands again. I was ready to bring them down powerfully on his neck should he try to go under them. He hesitated, looking at my long fingers.

"Games?" he said. "With me?"

Slowly he put one hand behind his back. He thrust the other toward me, the fingers spread wide as a net. He was challenging me to use both my hands against his one in a test of strength. The crowd giggled.

"Both," I said, shaking my head.

He slid his arm up higher behind his back. He looked like a cripple. I shook my head again. The crowd laughed nervously.

He bent one finger.

"No," I said. "No."

He tucked his thumb into his palm.

I stepped back angrily.

He brought down another finger.

"Use both hands," I yelled. "Beat me, but don't humiliate me."

He closed a fourth finger. The crowd was silent. The single finger with which he challenged my ten pointed at me. He took a step backwards. Now he was not pointing but beckoning.

"Don't you like the odds?" someone shouted. The crowd applauded.

"You stink like shit," I yelled at The Reaper.

"Take my hand," he said quietly. "Try to force it down."

I lost control and hurled myself toward Sallow's outstretched finger. I would tear it off, I thought. He stepped back softly, like one pressing himself politely against a wall to allow someone else to pass through a door. The crowd groaned. I looked helplessly at The Reaper; his face was calm, serene, softly satisfied, like one who has spun all the combinations on a lock and can open it now at his leisure. I braced myself too late. My body, remiss, tumbled awkwardly across the ring. The Reaper had brought his fisted hand from behind his back and now smashed my unprotected ear. I fell against the rope with my mouth open. My teeth were like so many Chiclets in my mouth. I bled on the golden canvas. The Reaper stalked me. He took my head under his arm almost gently and held my bleeding ear against his chest. "I am old," he whispered, "because I am wily. Because I take absolutely nothing for granted—not the honor of others, not their determination, not even their youth and strength."

He would kill me. He had no concern for my life. It was all true— the legends, the myths. Until that moment I hadn't really believed them. He had killed the man in South Africa—and how many others? In all those years how many had he maimed and murdered? He wrestled so that he could demonstrate his cruelty, show it in public, with the peculiarly desperate pride of one displaying his cancerous testicles in a medical amphitheater. His strength, his ancient power, was nothing supernatural. It was his indifference that killed us. And it had this advantage: it could not be shorn; he could not be talked out of it. Our pain was our argument. In his arms, my face turning and turning against the bristles in his armpit, I was one with all victims, an Everyman through loss and deprivation, knowing the soul's martial law, its sad, harsh curfew. Our pain was our argument and, like all pain, it was wasted. What was terrible was his energy. He lived arrogantly, like one who you know will not give way coming toward you down a narrow sidewalk. To live was all his thought, to proliferate his strength in endless war. The vampire was the truest symbol in the give and take of the universe.

I screamed at the referee. "Get him off."

The referee looked down at me helplessly. "It hasn't lasted long enough," he said. "You've only been at it ten minutes. You can't quit now."

"Get him off, God damn it!"

"These people paid for a main event. Give them a main event."

"Get him off. The main event is my death. He means to kill me."

"Take it easier with him, Reaper," the referee said. "Work him toward the ropes. Let him get away a minute."

"Sure," the Reaper said mildly.

"No," I shouted. "No. I quit." I tried to turn my neck toward the crowd. "He's killing me," I yelled. "They won't let me quit." They couldn't hear me above their own roar.

The Reaper gathered me toward him; he grabbed my body—I wasn't even resisting now—and raised me over his head. He pushed me away like a kind of medicine ball and I dropped leadenly at the base of the ring post.

I knew my man now. To treat flesh as though it were leather or lead was his only intention. To find the common denominator in all matter. It was scientific; he was a kind of alchemist, this fellow. Of course. Faust and Mephistopheles combined. *Fist!* I lay still.

"Fight," he demanded.

I didn't answer.

"Fight!" he said savagely.

He could win any time, but he refused. This was a main event for him, too. He had thrown me away to give me a chance to organize a new resistance.

"Will you fight?" he asked dangerously.

"Not with you," I said.

The crowd was booing me.

"All right," he said.

He backed away. I watched him. He was bouncing up and down on the balls of his feet in a queer rhythm. His shoulders raised and lowered rapidly, powerfully. His arms seemed actually to lengthen. He stooped forward and came toward me slowly, swinging his balled metallic fists inches above the canvas. It was his Reaper movement, the gesture that had given him his name. I had never seen it and I watched fascinated. The crowd had stopped booing and was screaming for me to get up. The closer he got the more rapidly his fists swept the canvas, but still his pace toward me was slow, deliberate, almost tedious. He loomed above me like some ancient farmer with an invisible scythe. Now the people in the first rows were standing. They rushed toward the ring, pleading with me to get away. At last my resolution broke. I got clumsily to my knees and stumbled away from him. It was too late; his fists were everywhere. They caught me on the legs, the stomach, the neck, the back, the head, the mouth. I felt like some tiny animal—a field mouse —in tall grass, trampled by the mower. I covered my eyes with my hands and dropped to the canvas, squeezing myself flat against it. I squealed helplessly. A fist caught me first on one temple, then on the other.

I heard the referee shout "That's enough" just before I lost consciousness.

I was unconscious for only a few seconds. Oddly, when I came to my head was clear. I could have gotten up; I could have caught one of those fists and pulled him off balance. But I didn't choose to; I thought of one of those phrases they use for the wars—to struggle in vain. They were always praying that battle and injury and death were not in vain —as though anything purchased at some ultimate cost ought to be worth it. It was a well-meant prayer, even a wise one, but not practical. Life was economics. To be alive was to be a consumer. They made a profit on us always. There were no bargains. I saw that to struggle in vain was stupid, to be on the losing side was stupid, but there was nothing one could do. I would not get up, I thought, I would not even let them know I was conscious. I lay there, calmer than I had ever been in my life.

"He's dead," someone screamed after a moment. "He's dead," someone else shouted. They took it up, made it a chant. "He's dead. He's dead. He's dead."

The police rushed into the ring. They made a circle around The Reaper and moved off with him through the crowd. They were protecting him, I knew. He was not being arrested. What he did in the ring was all right. He was immune to law; law itself said he was immune, like someone with diplomatic status. What did that reduce my death to, I wondered. What did that reduce my death to if my murder was not a murder, not some terrible aberration punishable by law? Missouri rules and natural law worked hand in hand in an awful negation of whatever was precious to human beings. Oh, the dirty athletics of death!

Lying there on the canvas, in the idiotic nimbus of my blood, no longer sure I feigned unconsciousness, or even whether I still lived, one thing was sure: I would not fight—ever again. It was stupid to struggle, stupider still to struggle in vain—and that's all struggle ever amounted to in a universe like ours, in bodies like our own. From now on I would be the guest. I would haunt the captain's table, sweating over an etiquette of guesthood as others did over right and wrong. Herlitz knew his man, who only gradually, and after great pain, knew himself.

If only it isn't too late, I thought; if only it isn't too late to do me any good, I thought, just before I died.

Ralph Ellison

The Battle Royal

*Ralph Waldo Ellison was born in Oklahoma City in 1914. His only
novel,* Invisible Man, *published in 1952, won the National Book
Award for fiction and earned Ellison instant international acclaim.
Today,* Invisible Man *remains one of the most powerfully influential
works of the twentieth century. The novel carries its nameless central character on his odyssey from the rural South to New York,
into an underground retreat to ultimate withdrawal into himself—
his only escape from an irrational society. Early in the narrator's
life, he was forced to participate in a surreal "sporting" experience
that forms one of the most searing episodes of the novel—the Battle
Royal.*

Everyone praised me and I was invited to give the speech at a
gathering of the town's leading white citizens. It was a triumph for
our whole community.

It was in the main ballroom of the leading hotel. When I got there
I discovered that it was on the occasion of a smoker, and I was told
that since I was to be there anyway I might as well take part in the
battle royal to be fought by some of my schoolmates as part of the
entertainment. The battle royal came first.

All of the town's big shots were there in their tuxedoes, wolfing
down the buffet foods, drinking beer and whiskey and smoking black
cigars. It was a large room with a high ceiling. Chairs were arranged in
neat rows around three sides of a portable boxing ring. The fourth side
was clear, revealing a gleaming space of polished floor. I had some
misgivings over the battle royal, by the way. Not from a distaste for
fighting, but because I didn't care too much for the other fellows who

were to take part. They were tough guys who seemed to have no grand-father's curse worrying their minds. No one could mistake their tough-ness. And besides, I suspected that fighting a battle royal might detract from the dignity of my speech. In those pre-invisible days I visualized myself as a potential Booker T. Washington. But the other fellows didn't care too much for me either, and there were nine of them. I felt superior to them in my way, and I didn't like the manner in which we were all crowded together into the servants' elevator. Nor did they like my being there. In fact, as the warmly lighted floors flashed past the elevator we had words over the fact that I, by taking part in the fight, had knocked one of their friends out of a night's work.

We were led out of the elevator through a rococo hall into an anteroom and told to get into our fighting togs. Each of us was issued a pair of boxing gloves and ushered out into the big mirrored hall, which we entered looking cautiously about us and whispering, lest we might accidentally be heard above the noise of the room. It was foggy with cigar smoke. And already the whiskey was taking effect. I was shocked to see some of the most important men of the town quite tipsy. They were all there—bankers, lawyers, judges, doctors, fire chiefs, teachers, merchants. Even one of the more fashionable pastors. Something we could not see was going on up front. A clarinet was vibrating sensuously and the men were standing up and moving eagerly forward. We were a small tight group, clustered together, our bare upper bodies touching and shining with anticipatory sweat; while up front the big shots were becoming increasingly excited over something we still could not see. Suddenly I heard the school superintendent, who had told me to come, yell, "Bring up the shines, gentlemen! Bring up the little shines!"

We were rushed up to the front of the ballroom, where it smelled even more strongly of tobacco and whiskey. Then we were pushed into place. I almost wet my pants. A sea of faces, some hostile, some amused, ringed around us, and in the center, facing us, stood a magnificent blonde—stark naked. There was dead silence. I felt a blast of cold air chill me. I tried to back away, but they were behind me and around me. Some of the boys stood with lowered heads, trembling. I felt a wave of irrational guilt and fear. My teeth chattered, my skin turned to goose flesh, my knees knocked. Yet I was strongly attracted and looked in spite of myself. Had the price of looking been blindness, I would have looked. The hair was yellow like that of a circus kewpie doll, the face heavily powdered and rouged, as though to form an abstract mask, the eyes hollow and smeared a cool blue, the color of a baboon's butt. I felt a desire to spit upon her as my eyes brushed slowly over her body. Her breasts were firm and round as the domes of East Indian temples, and I stood so close as to see the fine skin texture, and beads of pearly perspiration glistening like dew around the pink and erected buds of her nipples. I wanted at one and the same time to run from the room, to sink through the floor, or go to her and cover her from my eyes and the eyes of the others with my body; to feel the soft thighs, to caress her and destroy her, to love her and murder her, to hide from her, and yet to stroke where below the small American flag tattooed upon her belly her thighs formed a capital V. I had a notion that of all in the room she saw only me with her impersonal eyes.

And then she began to dance, a slow sensuous movement; the smoke of a hundred cigars clinging to her like the thinnest of veils. She seemed like a fair bird-girl girdled in veils calling to me from the angry surface of some gray and threatening sea. I was transported. Then I became aware of the clarinet playing and the big shots yelling at us. Some threatened us if we looked and others if we did not. On my right I saw one boy faint. And now a man grabbed a silver pitcher from a table and stepped close as he dashed ice water upon him and stood him up and forced two of us to support him as his head hung and moans issued from his thick bluish lips. Another boy began to plead to go home. He was the largest of the group, wearing dark red fighting trunks much too small to conceal the erection which projected from him as though in answer to the insinuating low-registered moaning of the clarinet. He tried to hide himself with his boxing gloves.

And all the while the blonde continued dancing, smiling faintly at the big shots who watched her with fascination, and faintly smiling at our fear. I noticed a certain merchant who followed her hungrily, his lips loose and drooling. He was a large man who wore diamond studs in a shirtfront which swelled with the ample paunch underneath, and each time the blonde swayed her undulating hips he ran his hand through the thin hair of his bald head and, with his arms upheld, his posture clumsy like that of an intoxicated panda, wound his belly in a slow and obscene grind. This creature was completely hypnotized. The music had quickened. As the dancer flung herself about with a detached expression on her face, the men began reaching out to touch her. I could see their beefy fingers sink into the soft flesh. Some of the others tried to stop them and she began to move around the floor in graceful circles, as they gave chase, slipping and sliding over the polished floor. It was mad. Chairs went crashing, drinks were spilt, as they ran laughing and howling after her. They caught her just as she reached a door, raised her from the floor, and tossed her as college boys are tossed at a hazing, and above her red, fixed-smiling lips I saw the terror and disgust in her eyes, almost like my own terror and that which I saw in some of the other boys. As I watched, they tossed her twice and her soft breasts seemed to flatten against the air and her legs flung wildly as she spun. Some of the more sober ones helped her to escape. And I started off the floor, heading for the anteroom with the rest of the boys.

Some were still crying and in hysteria. But as we tried to leave we were stopped and ordered to get into the ring. There was nothing to do but what we were told. All ten of us climbed under the ropes and allowed ourselves to be blindfolded with broad bands of white cloth. One of the men seemed to feel a bit sympathetic and tried to cheer us up as we stood with our backs against the ropes. Some of us tried to grin. "See that boy over there?" one of the men said. "I want you to run across at the bell and give it to him right in the belly. If you don't get him, I'm going to get you. I don't like his looks." Each of us was told the same. The blindfolds were put on. Yet even then I had been going over my speech. In my mind each word was as bright as flame. I felt the cloth pressed into place, and frowned so that it would be loosened when I relaxed.

But now I felt a sudden fit of blind terror. I was unused to darkness. It was as though I had suddenly found myself in a dark room filled with poisonous cottonmouths. I could hear the bleary voices yelling insistently for the battle royal to begin.

"Get going in there!"

"Let me at that big nigger!"

I strained to pick up the school superintendent's voice, as though to squeeze some security out of that slightly more familiar sound.

"Let me at those black sonsabitches!" someone yelled.

"No, Jackson, no!" another voice yelled. "Here, somebody, help me hold Jack."

"I want to get at that ginger-colored nigger. Tear him limb from limb," the first voice yelled.

I stood against the ropes trembling. For in those days I was what they called ginger-colored, and he sounded as though he might crunch me between his teeth like a crisp ginger cookie.

Quite a struggle was going on. Chairs were being kicked about and I could hear voices grunting as with a terrific effort. I wanted to see, to see more desperately than ever before. But the blindfold was as tight as a thick skin-puckering scab and when I raised my gloved hands to push the layers of white aside a voice yelled, "Oh, no you don't, black bastard! Leave that alone!"

"Ring the bell before Jackson kills him a coon!" someone boomed in the sudden silence. And I heard the bell clang and the sound of the feet scuffling forward.

A glove smacked against my head. I pivoted, striking out stiffly as someone went past, and felt the jar ripple along the length of my arm to my shoulder. Then it seemed as though all nine of the boys had turned upon me at once. Blows pounded me from all sides while I struck out as best I could. So many blows landed upon me that I wondered if I were not the only blindfolded fighter in the ring, or if the man called Jackson hadn't succeeded in getting me after all.

Blindfolded, I could no longer control my motions. I had no dignity. I stumbled about like a baby or a drunken man. The smoke had become thicker and with each new blow it seemed to sear and further restrict my lungs. My saliva became like hot bitter glue. A glove connected with my head, filling my mouth with warm blood. It was everywhere. I could not tell if the moisture I felt upon my body was sweat or blood. A blow landed hard against the nape of my neck. I felt myself going over, my head hitting the floor. Streaks of blue light filled the black world behind the blindfold. I lay prone, pretending that I was knocked out, but felt myself seized by hands and yanked to my feet. "Get going, black boy! Mix it up!" My arms were like lead, my head smarting from blows. I managed to feel my way to the ropes and held on, trying to catch my breath. A glove landed in my mid-section and I went over again, feeling as though the smoke had become a knife jabbed into my guts. Pushed this way and that by the legs milling around me, I finally pulled erect and discovered that I could see the black, sweat-washed forms weaving in the smoky-blue atmosphere like drunken dancers weaving to the rapid drum-like thuds of blows.

Everyone fought hysterically. It was complete anarchy. Everybody fought everybody else. No group fought together for long. Two, three, four, fought one, then turned to fight each other, were themselves attacked. Blows landed below the belt and in the kidney with the gloves open as well as closed, and with my eye partly opened now there was not so much terror. I moved carefully, avoiding blows, although not too many to attract attention, fighting from group to group. The boys groped about like blind, cautious crabs crouching to protect their mid-sections, their heads pulled in short against their shoulders, their arms stretched nervously before them, with their fists testing the smoke-filled air like the knobbed feelers of hypersensitive snails. In one corner I glimpsed a boy violently punching the air and heard him scream in pain as he smashed his hand against a ring post. For a second I saw him bent over holding his hand, then going down as a blow caught his unprotected head. I played one group against the other, slipping in and throwing a punch then stepping out of range while pushing the others into the melee to take the blows blindly aimed at me. The smoke was agonizing and there were no rounds, no bells at three minute intervals to relieve our exhaustion. The room spun round me, a swirl of lights, smoke, sweating bodies surrounded by tense white faces. I bled from both nose and mouth, the blood spattering upon my chest.

The men kept yelling, "Slug him, black boy! Knock his guts out!"

"Uppercut him! Kill him! Kill that big boy!"

Taking a fake fall, I saw a boy going down heavily beside me as though we were felled by a single blow, saw a sneaker-clad foot shoot into his groin as the two who had knocked him down stumbled upon him. I rolled out of range, feeling a twinge of nausea.

The harder we fought the more threatening the men became. And yet, I had begun to worry about my speech again. How would it go? Would they recognize my ability? What would they give me?

I was fighting automatically when suddenly I noticed that one after another of the boys was leaving the ring. I was surprised, filled with panic, as though I had been left alone with an unknown danger. Then I understood. The boys had arranged it among themselves. It was the custom for the two men left in the ring to slug it out for the winner's prize. I discovered this too late. When the bell sounded two men in tuxedoes leaped into the ring and removed the blindfold. I found myself facing Tatlock, the biggest of the gang. I felt sick at my stomach. Hardly had the bell stopped ringing in my ears than it clanged again and I saw him moving swiftly toward me. Thinking of nothing else to do I hit him smash on the nose. He kept coming, bringing the rank sharp violence of stale sweat. His face was a black blank of a face, only his eyes alive —with hate of me and aglow with a feverish terror from what had happened to us all. I became anxious. I wanted to deliver my speech and he came at me as though he meant to beat it out of me. I smashed him again and again, taking his blows as they came. Then on a sudden impulse I struck him lightly and as we clinched, I whispered, "Fake like I knocked you out, you can have the prize."

"I'll break your behind," he whispered hoarsely.

"For *them?*"

"For *me,* sonofabitch!"

They were yelling for us to break it up and Tatlock spun me half around with a blow, and as a joggled camera sweeps in a reeling scene, I saw the howling red faces crouching tense beneath the cloud of blue-gray smoke. For a moment the world wavered, unraveled, flowed, then my head cleared and Tatlock bounced before me. That fluttering shadow before my eyes was his jabbing left hand. Then falling forward, my head against his damp shoulder, I whispered,

"I'll make it five dollars more."

"Go to hell!"

But his muscles relaxed a trifle beneath my pressure and I breathed, "Seven?"

"Give it to your ma," he said, ripping me beneath the heart.

And while I still held him I butted him and moved away. I felt myself bombarded with punches. I fought back with hopeless desperation. I wanted to deliver my speech more than anything else in the world, because I felt that only these men could judge truly my ability, and now this stupid clown was ruining my chances. I began fighting carefully now, moving in to punch him and out again with my greater speed. A lucky blow to his chin and I had him going too—until I heard a loud voice yell, "I got my money on the big boy."

Hearing this, I almost dropped my guard. I was confused: Should I try to win against the voice out there? Would not this go against my speech, and was not this a moment for humility, for nonresistance? A blow to my head as I danced about sent my right eye popping like a jack-in-the-box and settled my dilemma. The room went red as I fell. It was a dream fall, my body languid and fastidious as to where to land, until the floor became impatient and smashed up to meet me. A moment later I came to. An hypnotic voice said FIVE emphatically. And I lay there, hazily watching a dark red spot of my own blood shaping itself into a butterfly, glistening and soaking into the soiled gray world of the canvas.

When the voice drawled TEN I was lifted up and dragged to a chair. I sat dazed. My eye pained and swelled with each throb of my pounding heart and I wondered if now I would be allowed to speak. I was wringing wet, my mouth still bleeding. We were grouped along the wall now. The other boys ignored me as they congratulated Tatlock and speculated as to how much they would be paid. One boy whimpered over his smashed hand. Looking up front, I saw attendants in white jackets rolling the portable ring away and placing a small square rug in the vacant space surrounded by chairs. Perhaps, I thought, I will stand on the rug to deliver my speech.

Then the M.C. called to us, "Come on up here boys and get your money."

We ran forward to where the men laughed and talked in their chairs, waiting. Everyone seemed friendly now.

"There it is on the rug," the man said. I saw the rug covered with coins of all dimensions and a few crumpled bills. But what excited me, scattered here and there, were the gold pieces.

"Boys, it's all yours," the man said. "You get all you grab."

"That's right, Sambo," a blond man said, winking at me confidentially.

I trembled with excitement, forgetting my pain. I would get the gold and the bills, I thought. I would use both hands. I would throw my body against the boys nearest me to block them from the gold.

"Get down around the rug now," the man commanded, "and don't anyone touch it until I give the signal."

"This ought to be good," I heard.

As told, we got around the square rug on our knees. Slowly the man raised his freckled hand as we followed it upward with our eyes.

I heard, "These niggers look like they're about to pray!"

Then, "Ready," the man said. "Go!"

I lunged for a yellow coin lying on the blue design of the carpet, touching it and sending a surprised shriek to join those rising around me. I tried frantically to remove my hand but could not let go. A hot, violent force tore through my body, shaking me like a wet rat. The rug was electrified. The hair bristled up on my head as I shook myself free. My muscles jumped, my nerves jangled, writhed. But I saw that this was not stopping the other boys. Laughing in fear and embarrassment, some were holding back and scooping up the coins knocked off by the painful contortions of the others. The men roared above us as we struggled.

"Pick it up, goddamnit, pick it up!" someone called like a bass-voiced parrot. "Go on, get it!"

I crawled rapidly around the floor, picking up the coins, trying to avoid the coppers and to get greenbacks and the gold. Ignoring the shock by laughing, as I brushed the coins off quickly, I discovered that I could contain the electricity—a contradiction, but it works. Then the men began to push us onto the rug. Laughing embarrassedly, we struggled out of their hands and kept after the coins. We were all wet and slippery and hard to hold. Suddenly I saw a boy lifted into the air, glistening with sweat like a circus seal, and dropped, his wet back landing flush upon the charged rug, heard him yell and saw him literally dance upon his back, his elbows beating a frenzied tattoo upon the floor, his muscles twitching like the flesh of a horse stung by many flies. When he finally rolled off, his face was gray and no one stopped him when he ran from the floor amid booming laughter.

"Get the money," the M.C. called. "That's good hard American cash!"

And we snatched and grabbed, snatched and grabbed. I was careful not to come too close to the rug now, and when I felt the hot whiskey breath descend upon me like a cloud of foul air I reached out and grabbed the leg of a chair. It was occupied and I held on desperately.

"Leggo, nigger! Leggo!"

The huge face wavered down to mine as he tried to push me free. But my body was slippery and he was too drunk. It was Mr. Colcord, who owned a chain of movie houses and "entertainment palaces." Each time he grabbed me I slipped out of his hands. It became a real struggle. I feared the rug more than I did the drunk, so I held on, surprising myself for a moment by trying to topple *him* upon the rug. It was such an enormous idea that I found myself actually carrying it out. I tried not to be obvious, yet when I grabbed his leg, trying to tumble him out of the chair, he raised up roaring with laughter, and, looking at me with soberness dead in the eye, kicked me viciously in the chest. The chair leg flew out of my hand and I felt myself going and rolled. It was as though I had rolled through a bed of hot coals. It seemed a whole century would pass before I would roll free, a century in which I was seared through the deepest levels of my body to the fearful breath within me and the breath seared and heated to the point of explosion. It'll all be over in a flash, I thought as I rolled clear. It'll all be over in a flash.

But not yet, the men on the other side were waiting, red faces swollen as though from apoplexy as they bent forward in their chairs. Seeing their fingers coming toward me I rolled away as a fumbled football rolls off the receiver's fingertips, back into the coals. That time I luckily sent the rug sliding out of place and heard the coins ringing against the floor and the boys scuffling to pick them up and the M.C. calling. "All right, boys, that's all. Go get dressed and get your money."

I was limp as a dish rag. My back felt as though it had been beaten with wires.

When we had dressed the M.C. came in and gave us each five dollars, except Tatlock, who got ten for being last in the ring. Then he told us to leave. I was not to get a chance to deliver my speech, I thought. I was going out into the dim alley in despair when I was stopped and told to go back. I returned to the ballroom, where the men were pushing back their chairs and gathering in groups to talk.

The M.C. knocked on a table for quiet. "Gentlemen," he said, "we almost forgot an important part of the program. A most serious part, gentlemen. This boy was brought here to deliver a speech which he made at his graduation yesterday . . ."

"Bravo!"

"I'm told that he is the smartest boy we've got out there in Greenwood. I'm told that he knows more big words than a pocket-sized dictionary."

Much applause and laughter.

"So now, gentlemen, I want you to give him your attention."

There was still laughter as I faced them, my mouth dry, my eye throbbing. I began slowly, but evidently my throat was tense, because they began shouting, "Louder! Louder!"

"We of the younger generation extol the wisdom of that great leader and educator," I shouted, "who first spoke these flaming words of wisdom: 'A ship lost at sea for many days suddenly sighted a friendly vessel. From the mast of the unfortunate vessel was seen a signal: "Water, water; we die of thirst!" The answer from the friendly vessel came back: "Cast down your bucket where you are." The captain of the distressed vessel, at last heeding the injunction, cast down his bucket, and it came up full of fresh sparkling water from the mouth of the Amazon River.' And like him I say, and in his words, 'To those of my race who depend upon bettering their condition in a foreign land, or who underestimate the importance of cultivating friendly relations with the Southern white man, who is his next-door neighbor, I would say: "Cast down your bucket where you are"—cast it down in making friends in every manly way of the people of all races by whom we are surrounded . . .' "

Frederick Exley

Idols and Obsessions

*"A Fan's Notes is one man's life written with brilliance and insight,"
said James Dickey of Frederick Exley's 1968 "novel." That man's
(Exley's) life had been a turbulent one: frustrating failure, booze,
madness, and debilitating scorn (Exley died in June 1992). But on
Sundays when the New York Giants play football, all is calm and
there is peace in Exley's soul. For it is only football that can temporarily divert the angst that, at times, overwhelms him. A National
Book Award nominee, A Fan's Notes was also selected by Book-
of-the-Month Club, in a celebration of their sixtieth anniversary,
as one of the "sixty enduring novels" published between 1926 and
1986. In this excerpt, we learn the roots of the author's allegiance
to the Giants, witness his first meeting with demigod and alter ego
Frank Gifford, and experience his manic obsession with both the
demigod and the team he plays for.*

I met Steve Owen in the late thirties or early forties, when I was
somewhere between the ages of eight and eleven. I suspect it was
closer to the time I was eight, for I remember very little of what
was said, remembering more the character of the meeting—that it was
not an easy one. My father introduced me to him, or rather my father,
when the atmosphere was most strained and the conversation had
lagged, shoved me in front of Owen and said, "This is my son, Fred."

"Are you tough?" Owen said.

"Pardon, sir?"

"Are you tough?"

"I don't know, sir."

Owen looked at my father. "Is he tough, Mr. Exley?"

Though more than anything I wanted my father to say that I was, I was not surprised at his answer.

"It's too soon to tell."

Owen was surprised, though. He had great blondish-red eyebrows, which above his large rimless glasses gave him an astonished expression. Now he looked baffled. As the meeting had not been a comfortable one to begin with, he said in a tone that signaled the end of the conversation, *"I'm sure he's tough, Mr. Exley."* Turning abruptly on his heels, he walked across the lobby to the elevator of his hotel, where this meeting took place.

This was a few years after my father had quit playing football, when he was managing Watertown's semiprofessional team, the Red and Black. A team which took on all challengers and invariably defeated them, they were so good that—stupefying as it seems—the ostensible reason for our journey to New York had been to discuss with Owen the possibility of the Red and Black's playing in exhibition against the Giants. I say "stupefying" now; but that is retrospectively fake sophistication: I thought we could beat the Giants then, and I use the "we" with the glibness of one who was committed unalterably to the team's fortunes—the water boy. On the wall in the bar of the Watertown Elks' Club hangs a picture of that team; seated on the ground before the smiling, casual, and disinterested players is an anguishingly solemn boy—the solemnity attesting to the esteem in which I held my station. I can still remember with what pride I trotted, heavy water bucket and dry towels in hand, onto the field to minister to the combatants' needs. Conversely, I recall the shame I experienced one day when, the team's having fallen behind, the captain decided to adopt a spartan posture and deprive his charges of water, and he had ordered me back from the field, waving me off when I was almost upon the huddle. My ministrations denied in full view of the crowd, I had had to turn and trot, red-faced, back to the bench. Yes, I believed we could beat the Giants then. Long before Owen so adroitly put my father down, though, I had come to see that the idea of such a contest was not a good one.

The trip began on a depressing note. The night before we were to leave, my father got loaded and ran into a parked car, smashing in the front fenders of our Model A Ford roadster. It was one time—in retrospect—that my father's drinking seems excusable. Such a journey in those days was one of near-epic proportions, made only at intervals of many years and at alarming sacrifices to the family budget; I have no doubt that that night my father was tremulous with apprehension, caught up in the spirit of *bon voyage*, and that he drank accordingly. Be that as it may, because he was drunk he left the scene of the accident; and the next day, fearing that the police might be searching for a damaged car, my mother wouldn't let him take the Ford from the garage. For many hours it was uncertain whether we should make the trip at all; but at the last moment, more, I think, because I had been promised the trip than for any other reason, it was decided we should go on the train.

We rode the whole night sitting up in the day coach, without speaking. My father was hung over, deeply ashamed, and there was a horrifying air of furtiveness hanging over us, as if we were fleeing some unspeakable crime. As a result, the trip—which might have been a fantastic adventure—never rose above this unhappy note. In New York we shared a room at the YMCA (I can remember believing that only the impossibly rich ever stayed in hotels), and the visit was a series of small, debilitating defeats: bland, soggy food eaten silently in barnlike automats; a room that varied arbitrarily between extreme heat and cold; a hundred and one missed subway connections; the Fordham-Pittsburgh game's having been sold out; the astonishment I underwent at no one's knowing my father; and finally, the fact that our meeting with Owen, which I had been led to believe was prearranged, was nothing more than wishful thinking on my father's part.

I don't know how many times we went to Owen's hotel, but each time we were told that he was "out." Each time we returned to the YMCA a little more tired, a little more defeated, and with each trip the Giant players whose names I knew, Strong and Cuff and Leemans and Hein, began to loom as large and forbidding as the skyscrapers. At one point I knew, though I daren't say so to my father, that the idea of such a game was preposterous. Moreover, for the first time in my life I began to understand the awesome vanity and gnawing need required to take on New York City with a view to imposing one's personality on the place. This was a knowledge that came to haunt me in later years.

It was not until my father, his voice weary, suggested that we make one final trip to the hotel that I saw that he, too, was disheartened. All the way there I prayed that Owen would still be "out." I had come to see that the meeting was undesired by him, and I feared the consequences of our imposition. The moment we walked into the lobby, however, the desk clerk (who had, I'm sure, come to feel sorry for us) began furiously stabbing the air in the direction of a gruff-looking, bespectacled, and stout man rolling, seaman-like, in the direction of the elevator—a fury that could only have signaled that it was he, Owen. My father moved quickly across the lobby, stopped him, and began the conversation that ended with Owen's *I'm sure he's tough, Mr. Exley.* As I say, I don't remember a good deal of the conversation prior to my being introduced; I do remember that Owen, too, thought the idea of such a contest ridiculous. Worse than that, my father had already been told as much by mail, and I think that his having made the trip in the face of such a refusal struck Owen as rather nervy, accounting for the uneasiness of the meeting. On Owen's leaving, I did not dare look at my father. It wasn't so much that I had ever lived in fear of him as that I had never before seen any man put him down, and I was not prepared to test his reaction to a humiliation which I had unwittingly caused. Moreover, my father's shadow was so imposing that I had scarcely ever, until that moment, had any identity of my own. At the same time I had yearned to emulate and become my father, I had also longed for his destruction. Steve Owen not only gave me identity; he proved to me my father was vulnerable.

On the subway going up to the Polo Grounds, I was remembering that meeting and contemplating the heavy uneasiness of it all anew when suddenly, feeling myself inordinately cramped, I looked up out of my reverie to discover that the car was jammed and that I had somehow got smack among the members of a single family—an astonishing family, a family so incredible that for the first time in my life I considered the possibility of Norman Rockwell's not being lunatic. They were a father, a mother, a girl about fifteen, and a boy one or two years younger than she. All were dressed in expensive-looking camel's-hair coats; each carried an item that designated him a fan—the father two soft and brilliantly plaid wool blankets, the mother a picnic basket, the girl a half-gallon thermos, and the boy a pair of field glasses, strung casually about his neck—each apparently doing his bit to make the day a grand success. What astonished me, though, was the almost hilarious similarity of their physical appearance: each had brilliant auburn hair; each had even, startlingly white teeth, smilingly exposed beneath attractive snub noses; and each of their faces was liberally sprinkled with great, outsized freckles. The total face they presented was one of overwhelming and wholesome handsomeness. My first impulse was to laugh. Had I not felt an extreme discomfort caused by the relish they took in each other's being—their looks seemed to smother each other in love—and the crowdedness that had caused me to find myself wedged among them, separating them, I might have laughed. I felt not unlike a man who eats too fast, drinks too much, occasionally neglects his teeth and fingernails, is given to a pensive scratching of his vital parts, lets rip with a not infrequent fart, and wakes up one morning to find himself smack in the middle of a *Saturday Evening Post* cover, carving the goddam Thanksgiving turkey for a family he has never seen before. What was worse, they were aware of my discomfort; between basking in each other's loveliness they would smile apologetically at me, as though in crowding about me they were aware of having aroused me from my reverie and were sorry for it. Distressed, I felt I ought to say something—"I'm sorry I'm alive" or something—so I said the first thing that came to my mind. It was a lie occasioned by my reverie, one which must have sounded very stupid indeed.

"I know Steve Owen," I said.

"Really!" they all chimed in high and good-natured unison. For some reason I got the impression that they had not the foggiest notion of what I had said. We all fell immediately to beaming at each other and nodding deferentially—a posture that exasperated me to the point where I thought I must absolutely say something else. Hoping that I could strike some chord in them that would relieve the self-consciousness we all were so evidently feeling, I spoke again.

"I know Frank Gifford, too."

"Really!" came their unabashed reply. Their tone seemed so calculated to humor me that I was almost certain they were larking with me. Staring at them, I couldn't be sure; and we all fell back to smiling idiotically and nodding at each other. We did this all the way to the Bronx where, disembarking, I lost contact with them—for the moment at least—and felt much relieved.

It seems amazing to me now that while at USC, where Gifford and I were contemporaries, I never saw him play football; that I had to come three thousand miles from the low, white, smog-enshrouded sun that hung perpetually over the Los Angeles Coliseum to the cold, damp, and dismal Polo Grounds to see him perform for the first time; and that I might never have had the urge that long-ago Sunday had I not once on campus had a strange, unnerving confrontation with him. The confrontation was caused by a girl, though at the time of the encounter I did not understand *what* girl. I had transferred from Hobart College, a small, undistinguished liberal arts college in Geneva, New York, where I was a predental student, to USC, a large, undistinguished university in Los Angeles, where I became an English major. The transition was not unnatural. I went out there because I had been rejected by a girl, my first love, whom I loved beyond the redeeming force of anything save time. Accepting the theory of distance as time, I put as much of it between the girl and myself as I could. Once there, though, the prospect of spending my days gouging at people's teeth and whiffing the intense, acidic odor of decay—a profession I had chosen with no stronger motive than keeping that very girl in swimming suits and tennis shorts: she had (and this, sadly, is the precise extent of my memory of her) the most breath-taking legs I had ever seen—seemed hideous, and I quite naturally became an English major with a view to reading The Books, The Novels and The Poems, those pat reassurances that other men had experienced rejection and pain and loss. Moreover, I accepted the myth of California the Benevolent and believed that beneath her warm skies I would find surcease from my pain in the person of some lithe, fresh-skinned, and incredibly lovely blond coed. Bearing my rejection like a disease, and like a man with a frightfully repugnant and contagious leprosy, I was unable to attract anything as healthy as the girl I had in mind.

Whenever I think of the man I was in those days, cutting across the neat-cropped grass of the campus, burdened down by the weight of the books in which I sought the consolation of other men's grief, and burdened further by the large weight of my own bitterness, the whole vision seems a nightmare. There were girls all about me, so near and yet so out of reach, a pastel nightmare of honey-blond, pink-lipped, golden-legged, lemon-sweatered girls. And always in this horror, this gaggle of femininity, there comes the vision of another girl, now only a little less featureless than all the rest. I saw her first on one stunning spring day when the smog had momentarily lifted, and all the world seemed hard bright blue and green. She came across the campus straight at me, and though I had her in the range of my vision for perhaps a hundred feet, I was only able, for the fury of my heart, to give her five or six frantic glances. She had the kind of comeliness—soft, shoulder-length chestnut hair; a sharp beauty mark right at her sensual mouth; and a figure that was like a swift, unexpected blow to the diaphragm—that to linger on makes the beholder feel obscene. I wanted to look. I couldn't look. I had to look. I could give her only the most gaspingly quick glances. Then she was by me. Waiting as long as I dared, I turned and she was gone.

From that day forward I moved about the campus in a kind of vertigo, with my right eye watching the sidewalk come up to meet my anxious feet, and my left eye clacking in a wild orbit, all over and around its socket, trying to take in the entire campus in frantic split seconds, terrified that I might miss her. On the same day that I found out who she was I saw her again. I was standing in front of Founders' Hall talking with T., a gleaming-toothed, hand-pumping fraternity man with whom I had, my first semester out there, shared a room. We had since gone our separate ways; but whenever we met we always passed the time, being bound together by the contempt with which we viewed each other's world and by the sorrow we felt at really rather liking each other, a condition T. found more difficult to forgive in himself than I did.

"That?" he asked in profound astonishment to my query about the girl. *"That?"* he repeated dumbly, as if this time—for I was much given to teasing T.—I had really gone too far. *"That,"* he proclaimed with menacing impatience, *"just happens to be Frank Gifford's girl!"*

Never will I forget the contempt he showered on me for asking what to him, and I suppose to the rest of fraternity row, was not only a rhetorical but a dazzlingly asinine question. Nor will I forget that he never did give me the girl's name; the information that she was Gifford's girl was, he assumed, quite enough to prevent the likes of me from pursuing the matter further. My first impulse was to laugh and twit his chin with my finger. But the truth was I was getting a little weary of T. His monumental sense of the rightness of things was beginning to grate on me; shrugging, I decided to end it forever. It required the best piece of acting I've ever been called upon to do; but I carried it off, I think, perfectly.

Letting my mouth droop open and fixing on my face a look of serene vacuousness, I said, "Who's Frank Gifford?"

My first thought was that T. was going to strike me. His hands tensed into fists, his face went the color of fire, and he thrust his head defiantly toward me. He didn't strike, though. Either his sense of the propriety of things overcame him, or he guessed, quite accurately, that I would have knocked him on his ass. All he said, between furiously clenched teeth, was: *"Oh, really, Exley, this has gone too far."* Turning hysterically away from me, he thundered off. It had indeed gone too far, and I laughed all the way to the saloon I frequented on Jefferson Boulevard, sadly glad to have seen the last of T.

Frank Gifford was an All-America at USC, and I know of no way of describing this phenomenon short of equating it with being the Pope in the Vatican. Our local *L'Osservatore Romano, The Daily Trojan,* was a

moderately well-written college newspaper except on the subject of
football, when the tone of the writing rose to an hysterical screech. It
reported daily on Gifford's health, one time even imposing upon us the
news that he was suffering an upset stomach, leading an irreverent
acquaintance of mine to wonder aloud whether the athletic department
had heard about "milk of magnesia, for Christ's sake." We were, it seems
to me in retrospect, treated daily to such breathless items as the variations in his weight, his method of conditioning, the knowledge that he
neither smoked nor drank, the humbleness of his beginnings, and once
we were even told the number of fan letters he received daily from
pimply high school girls in the Los Angeles area. The USC publicity man,
perhaps influenced by the proximity of Hollywood press agents, seemed
overly fond of releasing a head-and-shoulder print showing him the
apparently proud possessor of long, black, perfectly ambrosial locks
that came down to caress an alabaster, colossally beauteous face, one
that would have aroused envy in Tony Curtis. Gifford was, in effect,
overwhelmingly present in the consciousness of the campus, even
though my crowd—the literati—never once to my knowledge mentioned
him. We never mentioned him because his being permitted to exist at
the very university where we were apprenticing ourselves for Nobel
Prizes would have detracted from our environment and been an admission that we might be better off at an academe more sympathetic
with our hopes. Still, the act of not mentioning him made him somehow
more present than if, like the pathetic nincompoops on fraternity row,
we spent all our idle hours singing his praises. Our silence made him,
in our family, a kind of retarded child about whom we had tacitly and
selfishly agreed not to speak. It seems the only thing of Gifford's we
were spared—and it is at this point we leave his equation with the
Bishop of Rome—was his opinion of the spiritual state of the USC campus. But I am being unkind now; something occurred between Gifford
and me which led me to conclude that he was not an immodest man.

Unlike most athletes out there, who could be seen swaggering about
the campus with *Property of USC* (did they never see the ironic, touching
servility of this?) stamped indelibly every place but on their foreheads,
Gifford made himself extremely scarce, so scarce that I only saw him
once for but a few brief moments, so scarce that prior to this encounter
I had begun to wonder if he wasn't some myth created by the administration to appease the highly vocal and moronic alumni who were
incessantly clamoring for USC's Return to Greatness in, as the sportswriters say, "the football wars." Sitting at the counter of one of the

campus hamburger joints, I was having a cup of chicken noodle soup and a cheeseburger when it occurred to me that he was one of a party of three men seated a few stools away from me. I knew without looking because the other two men were directing all their remarks to him: "Hey, Frank, how about that?" "Hey, Frank, cha ever hear the one about . . ." It was the kind of given-name familiarity one likes to have with the biggest man on the block. My eyes on my soup, I listened to this sycophancy, smiling rather bitterly, for what seemed an eternity; when I finally did look up, it was he—ambrosial locks and all. He was dressed in blue denims and a terry-cloth sweater, and though I saw no evidence of *USC* stamped anyplace, still I had an overwhelming desire to insult him in some way. How this would be accomplished with any subtlety I had no idea; I certainly didn't want to fight with him. I did, however, want to shout, "Listen, you son of a bitch, life isn't all a goddam football game! You won't always get the girl! Life is rejection and pain and loss"—all those things I so cherishingly cuddled in my self-pitying bosom. I didn't, of course, say any such thing; almost immediately he was up and standing right next to me, waiting to pay the cashier. Unable to let the moment go by, I snapped my head up to face him. When he looked at me, I smiled—a hard, mocking, so-you're-the-big-shit? smile. What I expected him to do, I can't imagine—say, "What's your trouble, buddy?" or what—but what he did do was the least of my expectations. He only looked quizzically at me for a moment, as though he were having difficulty placing me; then he smiled a most ingratiating smile, gave me a most amiable hello, and walked out the door, followed by his buddies who were saying in unison, "Hey, Frank, what'll we do now?"

My first feeling was one of utter rage. I wanted to jump up and throw my water glass through the plate-glass window. Then almost immediately a kind of sullenness set in, then shame. Unless I had read that smile and that salutation incorrectly, there was a note of genuine apology and modesty in them. Even in the close world of the university Gifford must have come to realize that he was having a fantastic success, and that success somewhat embarrassed him. Perhaps he took me for some student acquaintance he had had long before that success, and took my hateful smile as a reproach for his having failed to speak to me on other occasions, his smile being the apology for that neglect. Perhaps he was only saying he was sorry I was a miserable son of a bitch, but that he was hardly going to fight me for it. These speculations, as I found out drinking beer late into that evening, could have gone on forever. I drank eight, nine, ten, drifting between speculations on the nature of that smile and bitter, sexually colored memories of the girl with the breath-taking legs back East, when it suddenly occurred to me that she and not the girl with the chestnut hair was the cause of all my anger, and that I was for perhaps a very long time going to have to live with that anger. Gifford gave me that. With that smile, whatever he meant by it, a smile that he doubtless wouldn't remember, he impressed upon me, in the rigidity of my embarrassment, that it is unmanly to burden others with one's grief. Even though it is man's particularly unhappy aptitude to see to it that his fate is shared.

Leaving the subway and walking toward the Polo Grounds, I was remembering that smile and thinking again how nice it would be if Gifford had a fine day for Owen, when I began to notice that the red-headed family, who were moving with the crowd some paces ahead of me, were laughing and giggling self-consciously, a laughter that evidently was in some way connected with me. Every few paces, having momentarily regained their composure, they would drop their heads together in a covert way, whisper as they walked, then turn again in unison, stare back at me, and begin giggling all anew. It was a laughter that soon had me self-consciously fingering my necktie and looking furtively down at my fly, as though I expected to discover that the overcoat which covered it had somehow miraculously disappeared. We were almost at the entrance to the field when, to my surprise, the father stopped suddenly, turned, walked back to me, and said that he was holding an extra ticket to the game. It was, he said, the result of his maid's having been taken ill, and that he—no, not precisely he, but the children—would deem it an honor if I—"knowing Owen and all"—sat with them. Not in the least interested in doing so, I was so relieved to discover that their laughter had been inspired by something apart from myself—the self-consciousness they felt at inviting me—that I instantaneously and gratefully accepted, thanked him profusely, and was almost immediately sorry. It occurred to me that the children might query me on my relationship with Owen—perhaps even Gifford—and what the hell could I say? My "relationship" with both of these men was so fleeting, so insubstantial, that I would unquestionably have had to invent and thereby not only undergo the strain of having to talk off the top of my head but, by talking, risk exposure as a fraud.

My fears, however, proved groundless. These people, it soon became evident, had no interest in me whatever, they were so bound up in their pride of each other. My discomfort was caused not by any interest they took in me but by their total indifference to me. Directing me by the arm, father seated me not with the children who, he had claimed, desired my presence but on the aisle—obviously, I thought, the maid's seat (accessible to the hot dogs)—and sat himself next to me, separating me from his wife and children who had so harmoniously moved to their respective seats that I was sure that the family held season tickets. Everyone in place, all heads cranked round to me and displayed a perfect miracle of gleaming incisors.

It had only just begun. The game was no sooner under way when father, in an egregiously cultivated, theatrically virile voice, began—to my profound horror—commenting on each and every play. "That is a delayed buck, a play which requires superb blocking and marvelous timing," or, "That, children, is a screen pass, a fantastically perilous play to attempt, and one, I might add, that you won't see *Mr.* Conerly attempt but once or twice a season"—to all of which the mother, the daughter, and the son invariably and in perfect unison exclaimed, "Really!" A tribute to father's brilliance that, to my further and almost numbing horror, I, too, soon discovered I was expected to pay—pay, I would expect, for the unutterable enchantment of sitting with them. Each time that I heard the *Really!* I would become aware of a great shock of auburn hair leaning past father's shoulder, and I would look up to be confronted by a brilliant conglomeration of snub noses, orange freckles, and sparkling teeth, all formed into a face of beseechment, an invitation to join in this tribute to Genius. I delayed accepting the invitation as long as I could; when the looks went from beseechment to mild reproachment, I surrendered and began chiming in with *Really!* At first I came in too quickly or too late, and we seemed to be echoing each other: *Really! Really!* Though this rhythmical ineptness chafed me greatly, it brought from the family only the most understanding and kindly looks. By the end of the first quarter I had my timing down perfectly and settled down to what was the most uncomfortable afternoon of my life.

This was a superb Detroit team. It was the Detroit of a young Bobby Layne and an incomparable Doak Walker, of a monstrously bull-like Leon Harte and a three-hundred-and-thirty-pound Les Bingaman, a team that was expected to move past the Giants with ease and into the championship of the Western Division. Had they done so—which at first they appeared to be doing, picking up two touchdowns before the crowd was scarcely settled—I might have been rather amused at the constraints placed on me by the character of my hosts. But at one thrilling moment, a moment almost palpable in its intensity, and unquestionably motivated by the knowledge of Owen's parting, the Giants recovered, engaged this magnificent football team, and began to play as if they meant to win. Other than the terrible fury of it, I don't remember the details of the game, save that Gifford played superbly; and that at one precise moment, watching him execute one of his plays, I was suddenly and overwhelmingly struck with the urge to cheer, to jump up and down and pummel people on the back.

But then, there was father. What can I say of him? To anything resembling a good play, he would single out the player responsible and say, "Fine show, Gifford!" or "Wonderful stuff there, Price!" and we would chime in with "Good show!" and "Fine stuff!" Then, in a preposterous parody of cultured equanimity, we would be permitted to clap our gloved right hands against our left wrists, like opera-goers, making about as much noise as an argument between mutes. It was very depressing. I hadn't cheered for anything or anybody in three years—since my rejection by the leggy girl—and had even mistakenly come to believe that my new-found restraint was a kind of maturity. Oh, I had had my enthusiasms, but they were dark, the adoration of the griefs and morbidities men commit to paper in the name of literature, the homage I had paid the whole sickly aristocracy of letters. But a man can dwell too long with grief, and now, quite suddenly, quite wonderfully, I wanted to cheer again, to break forth from darkness into light, to stand up in that sparsely filled (it was a typically ungrateful New York that had come to bid Owen farewell), murderously damp, bitingly cold stadium and scream my head off.

But then, here again was father—not only father but the terrible diffidence I felt in the presence of that family, in the overwhelming and shameless pride they took in each other's being and good form. The game moved for me at a snail's pace. Frequently I rose on tiptoe, ready to burst forth, at the last moment restraining myself. As the fury of the game reached an almost audible character, the crowd about me reacted proportionately by going stark raving mad while I stood still, saying *Really!* and filling up two handkerchiefs with a phlegm induced by the afternoon's increasing dampness. What upset me more than anything about father was that he had no loyalty other than to The Game itself, praising players, whether Giants or Lions, indiscriminately. On the more famous players he bestowed a *Mister,* saying, "Oh, fine stuff, *Mr.* Layne!" or, "Wonderful show, *Mr.* Walker!"—coming down hard on the *Mister* the way those creeps affected by The Theater say *Sir* Laurence Olivier or *Miss* Helen Hayes. We continued our *fine show*'s and *good stuff*'s till I thought my heart would break.

Finally I did of course snap. Late in the final period, with the Giants losing by less than a touchdown, Conerly connected with a short pass to Gifford, and I thought the latter was going into the end zone. Unable to help myself, the long afternoon's repressed and joyous tears welling up in my eyes, I went berserk.

Jumping up and down and pummeling father furiously on the back, I screamed, "Oh, Jesus, Frank! Oh, Frank, *baby! Go! For Steve! For Steve! For Steve!*"

Gifford did not go all the way. He went to the one-foot line. Because it was not enough yardage for a first down, it became fourth and inches to go for a touchdown and a victory, the next few seconds proving the most agonizingly apprehensive of my life. It was an agony not allayed by my hosts. When I looked up through tear-bedewed eyes, father was straightening his camel's-hair topcoat, and the face of his loved ones had been transfigured. I had violated their high canons of good taste, their faces had moved from a vision of charming wholesomeness to one of intransigent hostility; it was now eminently clear to them that their invitation to me had been a dreadful mistake.

In an attempt to apologize, I smiled weakly and said, "I'm sorry— I thought *Mr.* Gifford was going all the way," coming down particularly hard on the *Mister.* But this was even more disastrous: Gifford was new to the Giants then, and father had not as yet bestowed that title on him. The total face they presented to me made me want to cut my jugular. Then, I thought, *what the hell;* and because I absolutely refused to let them spoil the moment for me, I said something that had the exact effect I intended: putting them in a state of numbing senselessness.

I said, my voice distinctly irritable, "Aw, c'mon, you *goofies. Cheer. This is for Steve Owen! For Steve Owen!*"

The Giants did not score, and as a result did not win the game. Gifford carried on the last play, as I never doubted that he would. Wasn't this game being played out just as, in my loneliness, I had imagined it would be? Les Bingaman put his three hundred and thirty pounds in Gifford's way, stopping him so close to the goal that the officials were for many moments undetermined; and the Lions, having finally taken over the ball, were a good way up the field, playing ball control and running out the clock, before my mind accepted the evidence of my eyes. When it did so, I began to cough, coughing great globs into my hands. I was coughing only a very few moments before it occurred to

me that I was also weeping. It was a fact that occurred to father simultaneously. For the first time since I had spoken so harshly to him,
he rallied, my tears being in unsurpassably bad taste, and said, "Look
here, it's *only* a game."

Trying to speak softly so the children wouldn't hear, I said,
"Fuck you!"

But they heard. By now I had turned and started up the steep
concrete steps; all the way up them I could hear mother and the children,
still in perfect unison, screeching *Father!* and father, in the most preposterously modulated hysteria, screeching *Officer!* I had to laugh then,
laugh so hard that I almost doubled up on the concrete steps. My irri-
tation had nothing to do with these dead people, and not really—I know
now—anything to do with the outcome of the game. I had begun to be
haunted again by that which had haunted me on my first trip to the
city—the inability of a man to impose his dreams, his ego, upon the
city, and for many long months had been experiencing a rage induced
by New York's stony refusal to esteem me. It was foolish and childish
of me to impose that rage on these people, though not as foolish, I
expect, as father's thinking he could protect his children from life's
bitterness by calling for a policeman.

Frank Gifford went on to realize a fame in New York that only a
visionary would have dared hope for: he became unavoidable, part of
the city's hard mentality. I would never envy or begrudge him that fame.
I did, in fact, become perhaps his most enthusiastic fan. No doubt he
came to represent to me the realization of life's large promises. But that
is another part of this story. It was Owen who over the years kept bringing
me back to life's hard fact of famelessness. It was for this reason, as
much as any other, that I had wanted to make the trip to Oneida to
make my remembrances. After that day at the Polo Grounds I heard of
Owen from time to time, that he was a line coach for one NFL team or
another, that he was coaching somewhere in Canada—perhaps at Win-
nipeg or Saskatchewan. Wherever, it must have seemed to him the
sunless, the glacial side of the moon. Owen unquestionably came to see
the irony of his fate. His offensively obsessed detractors had been rendered petulant by his attitude that "football is a game played down in
the dirt, and always will be," and within three years after his leaving,
his successors, having inherited his ideas (the umbrella pass-defense
for one), took the Giants to a world championship with little other than

a defense. It was one of the greatest defenses (Robustelli, Patton, Huff, Svare, Livingston, *et al.*) that the game has ever seen, but, for all of that, a championship won by men who played the game where Owen had tenaciously and fatally maintained it was played—*in the dirt.*

After that day at the Polo Grounds, I went the way I must go, a little sluggardly, smiling a smile that mocked myself. If I went wrong, it was because, like Tonio Kröger, there was for me no right way. I lived in many cities—Chicago, Los Angeles, Colorado Springs, Baltimore, Miami—and with each new milieu my jobs grew less remunerative, my dreams more absurdly colored. To sustain them I found that it took increasing and ever-increasing amounts of alcohol. After a time I perceived that I was continually contemplating the world through the bubbling, cerise hue of a wine glass. Awaking one morning in a jail cell in Miami, I was led before a judge on a charge of public intoxication and vagrancy, given a suspended sentence of thirty days on the county farm, told by the judge I was a fatuous lunatic, and ordered to be out of the city of Miami within the hour. I came home then, back to Watertown, and by the autumn of 1958, a brief five years from the autumn I had stood in the Polo Grounds, I was in the Avalon Valley State Hospital for the mentally insane and not particularly interested in the reasons that had brought me there.

William Faulkner

Kentucky: May: Saturday

In 1955, Sports Illustrated *sent William Faulkner to the Kentucky Derby to record his impressions of the pomp and circumstance of the occasion, including the race itself. A year earlier Faulkner had won the Pulitzer Prize for his novel* A Fable. *Four years before that, in 1950, he was awarded the Nobel Prize for literature. Faulkner loved horses; they will endure as long as man does, he says in this piece, using that most famous reference from his Nobel Prize acceptance speech. In 1962, he died from injuries after falling off a horse.*

This saw Boone: the bluegrass, the virgin land rolling westward wave by dense wave from the Allegheny gaps, unmarked then, teeming with deer and buffalo about the salt licks and the limestone springs whose water in time would make the fine bourbon whiskey; and the wild men too—the red men and the white ones too who had to be a little wild also to endure and survive and so mark the wilderness with the proofs of their tough survival—Boonesborough, Owenstown, Harrod's and Harbuck's Stations; Kentucky: the dark and bloody ground.

And knew Lincoln too, where the old weathered durable rail fences enclose the green and sacrosanct pace of rounded hills long healed now from the plow, and big old trees to shade the site of the ancient one-room cabin in which the babe first saw light; no sound there now but such wind and birds as when the child first faced the road which would lead to fame and martyrdom—unless perhaps you like to think that the man's voice is somewhere there too, speaking into the scene of his own nativity the simple and matchless prose with which he reminded us of our duties and responsibilities if we wished to continue as a nation.

And knew Stephen Foster and the brick mansion of his song; no longer the dark and bloody ground of memory now, but already my old Kentucky home.

Even from just passing the stables, you carry with you the smell of liniment and ammonia and straw—the strong quiet aroma of horses. And even before we reach the track we can hear horses—the light hard rapid thud of hooves mounting into crescendo and already fading rapidly on. And now in the gray early light we can see them, in couples and groups at canter or hand-gallop under the exercise boys. Then one alone, at once furious and solitary, going full out, breezed, the rider hunched forward, excrescent and precarious, not of the horse but simply (for the instant) with it, in the conventional posture of speed—and who knows, perhaps the two of them, man and horse both: the animal dreaming, hoping that for that moment at least it looked like Whirlaway or Citation, the boy for that moment at least that he was indistinguishable from Arcaro or Earl Sande, perhaps feeling already across his knees the scented sweep of the victorious garland.

And we ourselves are on the track now, but carefully and discreetly back against the rail out of the way: now we are no longer a handful clotting in a murmur of furlongs and poles and tenths of a second, but there are a hundred of us now and more still coming, all craning to look in one direction into the mouth of the chute. Then it is as if the gray, overcast, slightly moist post-dawn air itself had spoken above our heads. This time the exercise boy is a Negro, moving his mount at no schooled or calculated gait at all, just moving it rapidly, getting it off the track and out of the way, speaking not to us but to all circumambience: man and beast either within hearing: "Y'awl can git out of the way too now; here's the big horse coming."

And now we can all see him as he enters the chute on a lead in the hand of a groom. The groom unsnaps the lead and now the two horses come on down the now empty chute toward the now empty track, out of which the final end of the waiting and the expectation has risen almost like an audible sound, a suspiration, a sigh.

Now he passes us (there are two of them, two horses and two riders, but we see only one), not just the Big Horse of professional race argot because he does look big, bigger than we know him to be, so that most of the other horses we have watched this morning appear dwarfed by him, with the small, almost gentle, head and the neat small feet and the trim and delicate pasterns which the ancient Arab blood has brought to him, the man who will ride him Saturday (it is Arcaro himself) hunched like a fly or a cricket on the big withers. He is not even walking. He is strolling. Because he is looking around. Not at us. He has seen people; the sycophant adulant human roar has faded behind his drumming feet too many times for us to hold his attention. And not at track either because he has seen track before and it usually looks like this one does from this point (just entering the backstretch): empty. He is simply looking at this track, which is new to him, as the steeplechase rider walks on foot the new course which he will later ride.

He—they—go on, still walking, vanishing at last behind the bulk of the tote board on the other side on the infield; now the glasses are trained and the stop watches appear, but nothing more until a voice says: "They took him in to let him look at the paddock." So we breathe again for a moment.

Because we have outposts now: a scattering of people in the stands themselves who can see the gate, to warn us in time. And do, though when we see him, because of the bulk of the tote board, he is already in full stride, appearing to skim along just above the top rail like a tremendous brown hawk in the flattened bottom of his stoop, into the clubhouse turn still driving; then something seems to happen; not a falter nor check though it is only afterward that we realize that he has seen the gate back into the chute and for an instant thought, not "Does Arcaro want us to go back in there?" but "Do I want to turn off here?" deciding in the next second (one of them: horse or man) no, and now driving again, down to us and past us as if of his own intention he would make up the second or two or three which his own indecision had cost him, a flow, rush, the motion at once long and deliberate and a little ungainly; a drive and power; something a little rawboned, not graceless so much as too busy to bother with grace, like the motion of a big working hunter, once again appearing to skim along just above the top rail like the big diminishing hawk, inflexible and undeviable, voracious not for meat but for speed and distance.

Old Abe's weathered and paintless rails are now the white panels of millionaires running in ruler-straight lines across the green and gentle swell of the Kentucky hills; among the ordered and parklike grove the mares with recorded lineages longer than most humans know or bother with stand with foals more valuable head for economic head than slum children. It rained last night; the gray air is still moist and filled with a kind of luminousness, lambence, as if each droplet held in airy suspension still its molecule of light, so that the statue which dominated the scene at all times anyway now seems to hold dominion over the air itself like a dim sun, until, looming and gigantic over us, it looks like gold—the golden effigy of the golden horse, "Big Red" to the Negro groom who loved him and did not outlive him very long, Big Red's effigy of course, looking out with the calm pride of the old manly warrior kings, over the land where his get still gambol as infants, until the Saturday afternoon moment when they too will wear the mat of roses in the flash and glare of magnesium; not just his own effigy, but symbol too of all the long recorded line from Aristides through the Whirlaways and Count Fleets and Gallant Foxes and Citations: epiphany and apotheosis of the horse.

Since daylight now we have moved, converged, toward, through the Georgian-Colonial sprawl of the entrance, the throne's anteroom, to bear our own acolytes' office in that ceremonial.

Once the horse moved man's physical body and his household goods and his articles of commerce from one place to another. Nowadays all it moves is a part or the whole of his bank account, either through betting on it or trying to keep owning and feeding it.

So, in a way, unlike the other animals which he has domesticated —cows and sheep and hogs and chickens and dogs (I don't include cats; man has never tamed cats)—the horse is economically obsolete. Yet it still endures and probably will continue to as long as man himself does, long after the cows and sheep and hogs and chickens, and the dogs which control and protect them, are extinct. Because the other beasts and their guardians merely supply man with food, and someday science will feed him by means of synthetic gases and so eliminate the economic need which they fill. While what the horse supplies to man is something deep and profound in his emotional nature and need.

It will endure and survive until man's own nature changes. Because you can almost count on your thumbs the types and classes of human beings in whose lives and memories and experience and glandular discharge the horse has no place. These will be the ones who don't like to bet on anything which involves the element of chance or skill or the unforeseen. They will be the ones who don't like to watch something in motion, either big or going fast, no matter what it is. They will be the ones who don't like to watch something alive and bigger and stronger than man, under the control of puny man's will, doing something which man himself is too weak or too inferior in sight or hearing or speed to do.

These will have to exclude even the ones who don't like horses—

the ones who would not touch a horse or go near it, who have never mounted one nor ever intend to; who can and do and will risk and lose their shirts on a horse they have never seen.

So some people can bet on a horse without ever seeing one outside a Central Park fiacre or a peddler's van. And perhaps nobody can watch horses running forever, with a mutuel window convenient, without making a bet. But it is possible that some people can and do do this.

So it is not just betting, the chance to prove with money your luck or what you call your judgment, that draws people to horse races. It is much deeper than that. It is a sublimation, a transference: man, with his admiration for speed and strength, physical power far beyond what he himself is capable of, projects his own desire for physical supremacy, victory, onto the agent—the baseball or football team, the prize fighter. Only the horse race is more universal because the brutality of the prize fight is absent, as well as the attenuation of football or baseball—the long time needed for the orgasm of victory to occur, where in the horse race it is a matter of minutes, never over two or three, repeated six or eight or 10 times in one afternoon.

And this too: the song, the brick mansion, matched to the apotheosis: Stephen Foster as handmaiden to the Horse as the band announced that it is now about to be the one 30 minutes past 4 o'clock out of all possible 4 o'clocks on one Saturday afternoon out of all possible Saturday afternoons. The brazen chords swell and hover and fade above the packed infield and the stands as the 10 horses parade to post—the 10 animals which for the next two minutes will not just symbolize but bear the burden and be the justification, not just of their individual own three years of life, but of the generations of selection and breeding and training and care which brought them to this one triumphant two minutes where one will be supreme and nine will be supreme failures—brought to this moment which will be supreme for him, the apex of his life which, even counted in lustra, is only 21 years old, the beginning of manhood. Such is the price he will pay for the supremacy; such is the gamble he will take. But what human being would refuse that much loss, for that much gain, at 21?

Only a little over two minutes: one simultaneous metallic clash as the gates spring. Though you do not really know what it was you heard: whether it was that metallic crash, or the simultaneous thunder of the hooves in that first leap or the massed voices, the gasp, the exhalation—whatever it was, the clump of horses indistinguishable yet, like a brown wave dotted with the bright silks of the riders like chips flowing toward us along the rail until, approaching, we can begin to distinguish individuals, streaming past us now as individual horses— horses which (including the rider) once stood about eight feet tall and 10 feet long, now look like arrows twice that length and less than half that thickness, shooting past and bunching again as perspective diminishes, then becoming individual horses once more around the turn into the backstretch, streaming on, to bunch for the last time into the homestretch itself, then again individuals, individual horses, the individual horse, the Horse: 2:01:⅘ minutes.

And now he stands beneath the rose escarpment above the flash and glare of the magnesium and the whirring film of celluloid immortality. This is the moment, the peak, the pinnacle; after this, all is ebb. We who watched have seen too much; expectation, the glandular pressure, has been too high to long endure; it is evening, not only of the day but the emotional capacity too; Boots and Saddles will sound twice more and condensations of light and movement will go through the motions of horses and jockeys again. But they will run as though in dream, toward anticlimax; we must turn away now for a little time, even if only to assimilate, get used to living with, what we have seen and experienced. Though we have not yet escaped that moment. Indeed, this may be the way we will assimilate and endure it: the voices, the talk, at the airports and stations from which we scatter back to where our old lives wait for us, in the aircraft and trains and buses carrying us back toward the old comfortable familiar routine like the old comfortable hat or coat: porter, bus driver, pretty stenographer who has saved for a year, scanted Christmas probably, to be able to say "I saw the Derby," the sports editor who, having spent a week talking and eating and drinking horse and who now wants only to get home and have a double nightcap and go to bed, all talking, all with opinions, valid and enduring:

"That was an accident. Wait until next time."

"What next time? What horse will they use?"

"If I had been riding him, I would have rode him different."

"No, no, he was ridden just right. It was that little shower of rain made the track fast like California."

"Or maybe the rain scared him, since it don't rain in L.A.? Maybe when he felt wet on his feet he thought he was going to sink and he was just jumping for dry land, huh?"

And so on. So it is not the Day after all. It is only the 81st one.

F. Scott Fitzgerald

The Bowl

Fitzgerald's failures in Hollywood have been well documented, but another major disappointment in the writer's life was his inability to play football for Princeton. His love of the game played by the gentlemen of the Ivy League during the jazz age is clearly evident in "The Bowl." Fitzgerald's only commercially published football story, about a Princeton player jinxed by the wind currents in New Haven's Yale Bowl, first appeared in The Saturday Evening Post *in 1928.*

There was a man in my class at Princeton who never went to football games. He spent his Saturday afternoons delving for minutiae about Greek athletics and the somewhat fixed battles between Christians and wild beasts under the Antonines. Lately—several years out of college—he has discovered football players and is making etchings of them in the manner of the late George Bellows. But he was once unresponsive to the very spectacle at his door, and I suspect the originality of his judgments on what is beautiful, what is remarkable and what is fun.

I reveled in football, as audience, amateur statistician and foiled participant—for I had played in prep school, and once there was a headline in the school newspaper: "Deering and Mullins Star Against Taft in Stiff Game Saturday." When I came in to lunch after the battle the school stood up and clapped and the visiting coach shook hands with me and prophesied—incorrectly—that I was going to be heard from. The episode is laid away in the most pleasant lavender of my past. That year I grew very tall and thin, and when at Princeton the following fall I looked anxiously over the freshman candidates and saw the polite disregard with which they looked back at me, I realized that that particular dream was over. Keene said he might make me into a very fair pole vaulter—and he did—but it was a poor substitute; and my terrible disappointment that I wasn't going to be a great football player was probably the foundation of my friendship with Dolly Harlan. I want to begin this story about Dolly with a little rehashing of the Yale game up at New Haven, sophomore year.

Dolly was started at halfback; this was his first big game. I roomed with him and I had scented something peculiar about his state of mind, so I didn't let him out of the corner of my eye during the whole first half. With field glasses I could see the expression on his face; it was strained and incredulous, as it had been the day of his father's death, and it remained so, long after any nervousness had had time to wear off. I thought he was sick and wondered why Keene didn't see and take him out; it wasn't until later that I learned what was the matter.

It was the Yale Bowl. The size of it or the enclosed shape of it or the height of the sides had begun to get on Dolly's nerves when the team practiced there the day before. In that practice he dropped one or two punts, for almost the first time in his life, and he began thinking it was because of the Bowl.

There is a new disease called agoraphobia—afraid of crowds—and another called siderodromophobia—afraid of railroad traveling—and my friend Doctor Glock, the psychoanalyst, would probably account easily for Dolly's state of mind. But here's what Dolly told me afterward:

"Yale would punt and I'd look up. The minute I looked up, the sides of that damn pan would seem to go shooting up too. Then when the ball started to come down, the sides began leaning forward and bending over me until I could see all the people on the top seats screaming at me and shaking their fists. At the last minute I couldn't see the ball at all, but only the Bowl; every time it was just luck that I was under it and every time I juggled it in my hands."

To go back to the game. I was in the cheering section with a good seat on the forty-yard line—good, that is, except when a very vague graduate, who had lost his friends and his hat, stood up in front of me at intervals and faltered, "Stob Ted Coy!" under the impression that we were watching a game played a dozen years before. When he realized finally that he was funny he began performing for the gallery and aroused a chorus of whistles and boos until he was dragged unwillingly under the stand.

It was a good game—what is known in college publications as a historic game. A picture of the team that played it now hangs in every barber shop in Princeton, with Captain Gottlieb in the middle wearing a white sweater, to show that they won a championship. Yale had had a poor season, but they had the breaks in the first quarter, which ended 3 to 0 in their favor.

Between quarters I watched Dolly. He walked around panting and sucking a water bottle and still wearing that strained stunned expression. Afterward he told me he was saying over and over to himself: "I'll speak to Roper. I'll tell him between halves. I'll tell him I can't go through this any more." Several times already he had felt an almost irresistible impulse to shrug his shoulders and trot off the field, for it was not only this unexpected complex about the Bowl; the truth was that Dolly fiercely and bitterly hated the game.

He hated the long, dull period of training, the element of personal conflict, the demand on his time, the monotony of the routine and the nervous apprehension of disaster just before the end. Sometimes he imagined that all the others detested it as much as he did, and fought down their aversion as he did and carried it around inside them like a cancer that they were afraid to recognize. Sometimes he imagined that a man here and there was about to tear off the mask and say, "Dolly, do you hate this lousy business as much as I do?"

His feeling had begun back at St. Regis' School and he had come up to Princeton with the idea that he was through with football forever. But upper classmen from St. Regis kept stopping him on the campus and asking him how much he weighed, and he was nominated for vice president of our class on the strength of his athletic reputation—and it was autumn, with achievement in the air. He wandered down to freshman practice one afternoon, feeling oddly lost and dissatisfied, and smelled the turf and smelled the thrilling season. In half an hour he was lacing on a pair of borrowed shoes and two weeks later he was captain of the freshman team.

Once committed, he saw that he had made a mistake; he even considered leaving college. For, with his decision to play, Dolly assumed a moral responsibility, personal to him, besides. To lose or to let down, or to be let down, was simply intolerable to him. It offended his Scotch sense of waste. Why sweat blood for an hour with only defeat at the end?

Perhaps the worst of it was that he wasn't really a star player. No team in the country could have spared using him, but he could do no spectacular thing superlatively well, neither run, pass nor kick. He was five-feet-eleven and weighed a little more than a hundred and sixty; he was a first-rate defensive man, sure in interference, a fair line plunger and a fair punter. He never fumbled and he was never inadequate; his presence, his constant cold sure aggression, had a strong effect on other men. Morally, he captained any team he played on and that was why Roper had spent so much time trying to get length in his kicks all season—he wanted him in the game.

In the second quarter Yale began to crack. It was a mediocre team composed of flashy material, but uncoordinated because of injuries and impending changes in the Yale coaching system. The quarterback, Josh Logan, had been a wonder at Exeter—I could testify to that—where games can be won by the sheer confidence and spirit of a single man. But college teams are too highly organized to respond so simply and boyishly, and they recover less easily from fumbles and errors of judgment behind the line.

So, with nothing to spare, with much grunting and straining, Princeton moved steadily down the field. On the Yale twenty-yard line things suddenly happened. A Princeton pass was intercepted; the Yale man, excited by his own opportunity, dropped the ball and it bobbed leisurely in the general direction of the Yale goal. Jack Devlin and Dolly Harlan of Princeton and somebody—I forget who—from Yale were all about the same distance from it. What Dolly did in that split second was all instinct; it presented no problem to him. He was a natural athlete and in a crisis his nervous system thought for him. He might have raced the two others for the ball; instead, he took out the Yale man with savage precision while Devlin scooped up the ball and ran ten yards for a touchdown.

This was when the sports writers still saw games through the eyes of Ralph Henry Barbour. The press box was right behind me, and as Princeton lined up to kick goal I heard the radio man ask:

"Who's Number 22?"

"Harlan."

"Harlan is going to kick goal. Devlin, who made the touchdown, comes from Lawrenceville School. He is twenty years old. The ball went true between the bars."

Between the halves, as Dolly sat shaking with fatigue in the locker room, Little, the back-field coach, came and sat beside him.

"When the ends are right on you, don't be afraid to make a fair catch," Little said. "That big Havemeyer is liable to jar the ball right out of your hands."

Now was the time to say it: "I wish you'd tell Bill—" But the words twisted themselves into a trivial question about the wind. His feeling would have to be explained, gone into, and there wasn't time. His own self seemed less important in this room, redolent with the tired breath, the ultimate effort, the exhaustion of ten other men. He was shamed by a harsh sudden quarrel that broke out between an end and tackle; he resented the former players in the room—especially the graduate captain of two years before, who was a little tight and over-vehement about the referee's favoritism. It seemed terrible to add one more jot to all this strain and annoyance. But he might have come out with it all the same if Little hadn't kept saying in a low voice: "What a take-out, Dolly! What a beautiful take-out!" and if Little's hand hadn't rested there, patting his shoulder.

2.

In the third quarter Joe Dougherty kicked an easy field goal from the twenty-yard line and we felt safe, until toward twilight a series of desperate forward passes brought Yale close to a score. But Josh Logan had exhausted his personality in sheer bravado and he was outguessed by the defense at the last. As the substitutes came running in, Princeton began a last march down the field. Then abruptly it was over and the crowd poured from the stands, and Gottlieb, grabbing the ball, leaped up in the air. For a while everything was confused and crazy and happy; I saw some freshmen try to carry Dolly, but they were shy and he got away.

We all felt a great personal elation. We hadn't beaten Yale for three years and now everything was going to be all right. It meant a good winter at college, something pleasant and slick to think back upon in the damp cold days after Christmas, when a bleak futility settles over a university town. Down on the field, an improvised and uproarious team ran through plays with a derby, until the snake dance rolled over them and blotted them out. Outside the Bowl, I saw two abysmally gloomy and disgusted Yale men get into a waiting taxi and in a tone of final abnegation tell the driver "New York." You couldn't find Yale men; in the manner of the vanquished, they had absolutely melted away.

I begin Dolly's story with my memories of this game because that evening the girl walked into it. She was a friend of Josephine Pickman's and the four of us were going to drive up to the Midnight Frolic in New York. When I suggested to him that he'd be too tired he laughed dryly —he'd have gone anywhere that night to get the feel and rhythm of football out of his head. He walked into the hall of Josephine's house at half-past six, looking as if he'd spent the day in the barber shop save for a small and fetching strip of court plaster over one eye. He was one of the handsomest men I ever knew, anyhow; he appeared tall and slender in street clothes, his hair was dark, his eyes big and sensitive and dark, his nose aquiline and, like all his features, somehow romantic. It didn't occur to me then, but I suppose he was pretty vain—not conceited, but vain—for he always dressed in brown or soft light gray, with black ties, and people don't match themselves so successfully by accident.

He was smiling a little to himself as he came in. He shook my hand buoyantly and said, "Why, what a surprise to meet you here, Mr. Deering," in a kidding way. Then he saw the two girls through the long hall, one dark and shining, like himself, and one with gold hair that was foaming and frothing in the firelight, and said in the happiest voice I've ever heard, "Which one is mine?"

"Either you want, I guess."

"Seriously, which is Pickman?"

"She's light."

"Then the other one belongs to me. Isn't that the idea?"

"I think I'd better warn them about the state you're in."

Miss Thorne, small, flushed and lovely, stood beside the fire. Dolly went right up to her.

"You're mine," he said; "you belong to me."

She looked at him coolly, making up her mind; suddenly she liked him and smiled. But Dolly wasn't satisfied. He wanted to do something incredibly silly or startling to express his untold jubilation that he was free.

"I love you," he said. He took her hand, his brown velvet eyes regarding her tenderly, unseeingly, convincingly. "I love you."

For a moment the corners of her lips fell as if in dismay that she had met someone stronger, more confident, more challenging than herself. Then, as she drew herself together visibly, he dropped her hand and the little scene in which he had expended the tension of the afternoon was over.

It was a bright cold November night and the rush of air past the open car brought a vague excitement, a sense that we were hurrying at top speed toward a brilliant destiny. The roads were packed with cars that came to long inexplicable halts while police, blinded by the lights, walked up and down the line giving obscure commands. Before we had been gone an hour New York began to be a distant hazy glow against the sky.

Miss Thorne, Josephine told me, was from Washington, and had just come down from a visit in Boston.

"For the game?" I said.

"No; she didn't go to the game."

"That's too bad. If you'd let me know I could have picked up a seat—"

"She wouldn't have gone. Vienna never goes to games."

I remembered now that she hadn't even murmured the conventional congratulations to Dolly.

"She hates football. Her brother was killed in a prep-school game last year. I wouldn't have brought her tonight, but when we got home from the game I saw she'd been sitting there holding a book open at the same page all afternoon. You see, he was this wonderful kid and her family saw it happen and naturally never got over it."

"But does she mind being with Dolly?"

"Of course not. She just ignores football. If anyone mentions it she simply changes the subject."

I was glad that it was Dolly and not, say, Jack Devlin who was sitting back there with her. And I felt rather sorry for Dolly. However strongly he felt about the game, he must have waited for some acknowledgment that his effort had existed.

He was probably giving her credit for a subtle consideration, yet, as the images of the afternoon flashed into his mind he might have welcomed a compliment to which he could respond "What nonsense!" Neglected entirely, the images would become insistent and obtrusive.

I turned around and was somewhat startled to find that Miss Thorne was in Dolly's arms; I turned quickly back and decided to let them take care of themselves.

As we waited for a traffic light on upper Broadway, I saw a sporting extra headlined with the score of the game. The green sheet was more real than the afternoon itself—succinct, condensed and clear:

PRINCETON CONQUERS YALE 10–3
SEVENTY THOUSAND WATCH TIGER TRIM
BULLDOG

DEVLIN SCORES ON YALE FUMBLE

There it was—not like the afternoon, muddled, uncertain, patchy and scrappy to the end, but nicely mounted now in the setting of the past:

PRINCETON, 10; YALE, 3

Achievement was a curious thing, I thought. Dolly was largely responsible for that. I wondered if all things that screamed in the headlines were simply arbitrary accents. As if people should ask, "What does it look like?"

"It looks most like a cat."

"Well, then, let's call it a cat."

My mind, brightened by the lights and the cheerful tumult, suddenly grasped the fact that all achievement was a placing of emphasis—a molding of the confusion of life into form.

Josephine stopped in front of the New Amsterdam Theater, where her chauffeur met us and took the car. We were early, but a small buzz of excitement went up from the undergraduates waiting in the lobby—"There's Dolly Harlan"—and as we moved toward the elevator several acquaintances came up to shake his hand. Apparently oblivious to these ceremonies, Miss Thorne caught my eye and smiled. I looked at her with curiosity; Josephine had imparted the rather surprising information that she was just sixteen years old. I suppose my return smile was rather patronizing, but instantly I realized that the fact could not be imposed on. In spite of all the warmth and delicacy of her face, the figure that somehow reminded me of an exquisite, romanticized little ballerina, there was a quality in her that was as hard as steel. She had been brought up in Rome, Vienna and Madrid, with flashes of Washington; her father was one of those charming American diplomats who, with fine obstinacy, try to re-create the Old World in their children by making their education rather more royal than that of princes. Miss Thorne was sophisticated. In spite of all the abandon of American young people, sophistication is still a Continental monopoly.

We walked in upon a number in which a dozen chorus girls in orange and black were racing wooden horses against another dozen dressed in Yale blue. When the lights went on, Dolly was recognized and some Princeton students set up a clatter of approval with the little wooden hammers given out for applause; he moved his chair unostentatiously into a shadow.

Almost immediately a flushed and very miserable young man appeared beside our table. In better form he would have been extremely prepossessing; indeed, he flashed a charming and dazzling smile at Dolly, as if requesting his permission to speak to Miss Thorne.

Then he said, "I thought you weren't coming to New York tonight."

"Hello, Carl." She looked up at him coolly.

"Hello, Vienna. That's just it; 'Hello Vienna—Hello Carl.' But why? I thought you weren't coming to New York tonight."

Miss Thorne made no move to introduce the man, but we were conscious of his somewhat raised voice.

"I thought you promised me you weren't coming."

"I didn't expect to, child. I just left Boston this morning."

"And who did you meet in Boston—the fascinating Tunti?" he demanded.

"I didn't meet anyone, child."

"Oh, yes, you did! You met the fascinating Tunti and you discussed living on the Riviera." She didn't answer. "Why are you so dishonest, Vienna?" he went on. "Why did you tell me on the phone—"

"I am not going to be lectured," she said, her tone changing suddenly. "I told you if you took another drink I was through with you. I'm a person of my word and I'd be enormously happy if you went away."

"Vienna!" he cried in a sinking, trembling voice.

At this point I got up and danced with Josephine. When we came back there were people at the table—the men to whom we were to hand over Josephine and Miss Thorne, for I had allowed for Dolly being tired, and several others. One of them was Al Ratoni, the composer, who, it appeared, had been entertained at the embassy in Madrid. Dolly Harlan had drawn his chair aside and was watching the dancers. Just as the lights went down for a new number a man came up out of the darkness and leaning over Miss Thorne whispered in her ear. She started and made a motion to rise, but he put his hand on her shoulder and forced her down. They began to talk together in low excited voices.

The tables were packed close at the old Frolic. There was a man rejoining the party next to us and I couldn't help hearing what he said:

"A young fellow just tried to kill himself down in the wash room. He shot himself through the shoulder, but they got the pistol away before—" A minute later his voice again: "Carl Sanderson, they said."

When the number was over I looked around. Vienna Thorne was staring very rigidly at Miss Lillian Lorraine, who was rising toward the ceiling as an enormous telephone doll. The man who had leaned over Vienna was gone and the others were obliviously unaware that anything had happened. I turned to Dolly and suggested that he and I had better go, and after a glance at Vienna in which reluctance, weariness and then resignation were mingled, he consented. On the way to the hotel I told Dolly what had happened.

"Just some souse," he remarked after a moment's fatigued consideration. "He probably tried to miss himself and get a little sympathy. I suppose those are the sort of things a really attractive girl is up against all the time."

This wasn't my attitude. I could see that mussed white shirt front with very young blood pumping over it, but I didn't argue, and after a while Dolly said, "I suppose that sounds brutal, but it seems a little soft and weak, doesn't it? Perhaps that's just the way I feel tonight."

When Dolly undressed I saw that he was a mass of bruises, but he assured me that none of them would keep him awake. Then I told him why Miss Thorne hadn't mentioned the game and he woke up suddenly; the familiar glitter came back into his eyes.

"So that was it! I wondered. I thought maybe you'd told her not to say anything about it."

Later, when the lights had been out half an hour, he suddenly said "I see" in a loud clear voice. I don't know whether he was awake or asleep.

3.

I've put down as well as I can everything I can remember about the first meeting between Dolly and Miss Vienna Thorne. Reading it over, it sounds casual and insignificant, but the evening lay in the shadow of the game and all that happened seemed like that. Vienna went back to Europe almost immediately and for fifteen months passed out of Dolly's life.

It was a good year—it still rings true in my memory as a good year. Sophomore year is the most dramatic at Princeton, just as junior year is at Yale. It's not only the elections to the upperclass clubs but also everyone's destiny begins to work itself out. You can tell pretty well who's going to come through, not only by their immediate success but by the way they survive failure. Life was very full for me. I made the board of the Princetonian, and our house burned down out in Dayton, and I had a silly half-hour fist fight in the gymnasium with a man who later became one of my closest friends, and in March Dolly and I joined the upperclass club we'd always wanted to be in. I fell in love, too, but it would be an irrelevancy to tell about that here.

April came and the first real Princeton weather, the lazy green-and-gold afternoons and the bright thrilling nights haunted with the hour of senior singing. I was happy, and Dolly would have been happy except for the approach of another football season. He was playing baseball, which excused him from spring practice, but the bands were beginning to play faintly in the distance. They rose to concert pitch during the summer, when he had to answer the question, "Are you going back early for football?" a dozen times a day. On the fifteenth of September he was down in the dust and heat of late-summer Princeton, crawling over the ground on all fours, trotting through the old routine and turning himself into just the sort of specimen that I'd have given ten years of my life to be.

From first to last, he hated it, and never let down for a minute. He went into the Yale game that fall weighing a hundred and fifty-three pounds, though that wasn't the weight printed in the paper, and he and Joe McDonald were the only men who played all through that disastrous game. He could have been captain by lifting his finger—but that involves some stuff that I know confidentially and can't tell. His only horror was that by some chance he'd have to accept it. Two seasons! He didn't even talk about it now. He left the room or the club when the conversation veered around to football. He stopped announcing to me that he "wasn't going through that business any more." This time it took the Christmas holidays to drive that unhappy look from his eyes.

Then at the New Year Miss Vienna Thorne came home from Madrid and in February a man named Case brought her down to the Senior Prom.

4.

She was even prettier than she had been before, softer, externally at least, and a tremendous success. People passing her on the street jerked their heads quickly to look at her—a frightened look, as if they realized that they had almost missed something. She was temporarily tired of European men, she told me, letting me gather that there had been some sort of unfortunate love affair. She was coming out in Washington next fall.

Vienna and Dolly. She disappeared with him for two hours the night of the club dances, and Harold Case was in despair. When they walked in again at midnight I thought they were the handsomest pair I saw. They were both shining with that peculiar luminosity that dark people sometimes have. Harold Case took one look at them and went proudly home.

Vienna came back a week later, solely to see Dolly. Late that evening I had occasion to go up to the deserted club for a book and they called me from the rear terrace, which opens out to the ghostly stadium and to an unpeopled sweep of night. It was an hour of thaw, with spring voices in the warm wind, and wherever there was light enough you could see drops glistening and falling. You could feel the cold melting out of the stars and the bare trees and shrubbery toward Stony Brook turning lush in the darkness.

They were sitting together on a wicker bench, full of themselves and romantic and happy.

"We had to tell someone about it," they said.

"Now can I go?"

"No, Jeff," they insisted; "stay here and envy us. We're in the stage where we want someone to envy us. Do you think we're a good match?"

What could I say?

"Dolly's going to finish at Princeton next year," Vienna went on, "but we're going to announce it after the season in Washington in the autumn."

I was vaguely relieved to find that it was going to be a long engagement.

"I approve of you, Jeff," Vienna said.

"I want Dolly to have more friends like you. You're stimulating for him—you have ideas. I told Dolly he could probably find others like you if he looked around his class."

Dolly and I both felt a little uncomfortable.

"She doesn't want me to be a Babbitt," he said lightly.

"Dolly's perfect," asserted Vienna. "He's the most beautiful thing that ever lived, and you'll find I'm very good for him, Jeff. Already I've helped him make up his mind about one important thing." I guessed what was coming. "He's going to speak a little piece if they bother him about playing football next autumn, aren't you, child?"

"Oh, they won't bother me," said Dolly uncomfortably. "It isn't like that—"

"Well, they'll try to bully you into it, morally."

"Oh, no," he objected. "It isn't like that. Don't let's talk about it now, Vienna. It's such a swell night."

Such a swell night! When I think of my own love passages at Princeton, I always summon up that night of Dolly's, as if it had been I and not he who sat there with youth and hope and beauty in his arms.

Dolly's mother took a place on Ram's Point, Long Island, for the summer, and late in August I went East to visit him. Vienna had been there a week when I arrived, and my impressions were: first, that he was very much in love; and, second, that it was Vienna's party. All sorts of curious people used to drop in to see Vienna. I wouldn't mind them now—I'm more sophisticated—but then they seemed rather a blot on the summer. They were all slightly famous in one way or another, and it was up to you to find out how. There was a lot of talk, and especially there was much discussion of Vienna's personality. Whenever I was alone with any of the other guests we discussed Vienna's sparkling personality. They thought I was dull, and most of them thought Dolly was dull. He was better in his line than any of them were in theirs, but his was the only specialty that wasn't mentioned. Still, I felt vaguely that I was being improved and I boasted about knowing most of those people in the ensuing year, and was annoyed when people failed to recognize their names.

The day before I left, Dolly turned his ankle playing tennis, and afterward he joked about it to me rather somberly.

"If I'd only broken it things would be so much easier. Just a quarter of an inch more bend and one of the bones would have snapped. By the way, look here."

He tossed me a letter. It was a request that he report at Princeton for practice on September fifteenth and that meanwhile he begin getting himself in good condition.

"You're not going to play this fall?"

He shook his head.

"No. I'm not a child any more. I've played for two years and I want this year free. If I went through it again it'd be a piece of moral cowardice."

"I'm not arguing, but—would you have taken this stand if it hadn't been for Vienna?"

"Of course I would. If I let myself be bullied into it I'd never be able to look myself in the face again."

Two weeks later I got the following letter:

Dear Jeff:
When you read this you'll be somewhat surprised. I have,

actually, this time, broken my ankle playing tennis. I can't even walk with crutches at present; it's on a chair in front of me swollen up and wrapped up as big as a house as I write. No one, not even Vienna, knows about our conversation on the same subject last summer and so let us both absolutely forget it. One thing, though—an ankle is a darn hard thing to break, though I never knew it before.

I feel happier than I have for years—no early-season practice, no sweat and suffer, a little discomfort and inconvenience, but free. I feel as if I've outwitted a whole lot of people, and it's nobody's business but that of your

Machiavellian (sic) friend,
DOLLY.

P.S. You might as well tear up this letter.

It didn't sound like Dolly at all.

5.

Once down at Princeton I asked Frank Kane—who sells sporting goods on Nassau Street and can tell you offhand the name of the scrub quarterback in 1901—what was the matter with Bob Tatnall's team senior year.

"Injuries and tough luck," he said. "They wouldn't sweat after the hard games. Take Joe McDonald, for instance, All-American tackle the year before; he was slow and stale, and he knew it and didn't care. It's a wonder Bill got that outfit through the season at all."

I sat in the stands with Dolly and watched them beat Lehigh 3–0 and tie Bucknell by a fluke. The next week we were trimmed 14–0 by Notre Dame. On the day of the Notre Dame game Dolly was in Washington with Vienna, but he was awfully curious about it when he came back next day. He had all the sporting pages of all the papers and he sat reading them and shaking his head. Then he stuffed them suddenly into the wastepaper basket.

"This college is football crazy," he announced. "Do you know that English teams don't even train for sports?"

I didn't enjoy Dolly so much in those days. It was curious to see him with nothing to do. For the first time in his life he hung around— around the room, around the club, around casual groups—he who had always been going somewhere with dynamic indolence. His passage along a walk had once created groups—groups of classmates who wanted to walk with him, of underclassmen who followed with their eyes a moving shrine. He became democratic, he mixed around, and it was somehow not appropriate. He explained that he wanted to know more men in his class.

But people want their idols a little above them, and Dolly had been a sort of private and special idol. He began to hate to be alone, and that, of course, was most apparent to me. If I got up to go out and he didn't happen to be writing a letter to Vienna, he'd ask "Where are you going?" in a rather alarmed way and make an excuse to limp along with me.

"Are you glad you did it, Dolly?" I asked him suddenly one day.

He looked at me with reproach behind the defiance in his eyes.

"Of course I'm glad."

"I wish you were in that back field, all the same."

"It wouldn't matter a bit. This year's game's in the Bowl. I'd probably be dropping kicks for them."

The week of the Navy game he suddenly began going to all the practices. He worried; that terrible sense of responsibility was at work. Once he had hated the mention of football; now he thought and talked of nothing else. The night before the Navy game I woke up several times to find the lights burning brightly in his room.

We lost 7 to 3 on Navy's last-minute forward pass over Devlin's head. After the first half Dolly left the stands and sat down with the players on the field. When he joined me afterward his face was smudgy and dirty as if he had been crying.

The game was in Baltimore that year. Dolly and I were going to spend the night in Washington with Vienna, who was giving a dance. We rode over there in an atmosphere of sullen gloom and it was all I could do to keep him from snapping out at two naval officers who were holding an exultant post mortem in the seat behind.

The dance was what Vienna called her second coming-out party. She was having only the people she liked this time, and these turned out to be chiefly importations from New York. The musicians, the play-wrights, the vague supernumeraries of the arts, who had dropped in at Dolly's house on Ram's Point, were here in force. But Dolly, relieved of his obligations as host, made no clumsy attempt to talk their language that night. He stood moodily against the wall with some of that old air of superiority that had first made me want to know him. Afterward, on my way to bed, I passed Vienna's sitting room and she called me to come in. She and Dolly, both a little white, were sitting across the room from each other and there was tension in the air.

"Sit down, Jeff," said Vienna wearily. "I want you to witness the collapse of a man into a schoolboy." I sat down reluctantly. "Dolly's changed his mind," she said. "He prefers football to me."

"That's not it," said Dolly stubbornly.

"I don't see the point," I objected. "Dolly can't possibly play."

"But he thinks he can. Jeff, just in case you imagine I'm being pig-headed about it, I want to tell you a story. Three years ago, when we first came back to the United States, father put my young brother in school. One afternoon we all went out to see him play football. Just after the game started he was hurt, but father said, 'It's all right. He'll be up in a minute. It happens all the time.' But, Jeff, he never got up. He lay there, and finally they carried him off the field and put a blanket over him. Just as we got to him he died."

She looked from one to the other of us and began to sob convulsively. Dolly went over, frowning, and put his arm around her shoulder.

"Oh, Dolly," she cried, "won't you do this for me—just this one little thing for me?"

He shook his head miserably. "I tried, but I can't," he said. "It's my stuff, don't you understand, Vienna? People have got to do their stuff."

Vienna had risen and was powdering her tears at a mirror; now she flashed around angrily.

"Then I've been laboring under a misapprehension when I supposed you felt about it much as I did."

"Let's not go over all that. I'm tired of talking, Vienna; I'm tired of my own voice. It seems to me that no one I know does anything but talk any more."

"Thanks. I suppose that's meant for me."

"It seems to me your friends talk a great deal. I've never heard so much jabber as I've listened to tonight. Is the idea of actually doing anything repulsive to you, Vienna?"

"It depends upon whether it's worth doing."

"Well, this is worth doing—to me."

"I know your trouble, Dolly," she said bitterly. "You're weak and you want to be admired. This year you haven't had a lot of little boys following you around as if you were Jack Dempsey, and it almost breaks your heart. You want to get out in front of them all and make a show of yourself and hear the applause."

He laughed shortly. "If that's your idea of how a football player feels—"

"Have you made up your mind to play?" she interrupted.

"If I'm any use to them—yes."

"Then I think we're both wasting our time."

Her expression was ruthless, but Dolly refused to see that she was in earnest. When I got away he was still trying to make her "be rational," and next day on the train he said that Vienna had been "a little nervous." He was deeply in love with her, and he didn't dare think of losing her; but he was still in the grip of the sudden emotion that had decided him to play, and his confusion and exhaustion of mind made him believe vainly that everything was going to be all right. But I had seen that look on Vienna's face the night she talked with Mr. Carl Sanderson at the Frolic two years before.

Dolly didn't get off the train at Princeton Junction, but continued on to New York. He went to two orthopedic specialists and one of them arranged a bandage braced with a whole little fence of whalebones that he was to wear day and night. The probabilities were that it would snap at the first brisk encounter, but he could run on it and stand on it when he kicked. He was out on University Field in uniform the following afternoon.

His appearance was a small sensation. I was sitting in the stands watching practice with Harold Case and young Daisy Cary. She was just beginning to be famous then, and I don't know whether she or Dolly attracted the most attention. In those times it was still rather daring to bring down a moving-picture actress; if that same young lady went to Princeton today she would probably be met at the station with a band.

Dolly limped around and everyone said, "He's limping!" He got under a punt and everyone said, "He did that pretty well!" The first team were laid off after the hard Navy game and everyone watched Dolly all afternoon. After practice I caught his eye and he came over and shook hands. Daisy asked him if he'd like to be in a football picture she was going to make. It was only conversation, but he looked at me with a dry smile.

When he came back to the room his ankle was swollen up as big as a stove pipe, and next day he and Keene fixed up an arrangement by which the bandage would be loosened and tightened to fit its varying size. We called it the balloon. The bone was nearly healed, but the little bruised sinews were stretched out of place again every day. He watched the Swarthmore game from the sidelines and the following Monday he was in scrimmage with the second team against the scrubs.

In the afternoons sometimes he wrote to Vienna. His theory was that they were still engaged, but he tried not to worry about it, and I think the very pain that kept him awake at night was good for that. When the season was over he would go and see.

We played Harvard and lost 7 to 3. Jack Devlin's collar bone was broken and he was out for the season, which made it almost sure that Dolly would play. Amid the rumors and fears of mid-November the news aroused a spark of hope in an otherwise morbid undergraduate body— hope all out of proportion to Dolly's condition. He came back to the room the Thursday before the game with his face drawn and tired.

"They're going to start me," he said, "and I'm going to be back for punts. If they only knew—"

"Couldn't you tell Bill how you feel about that?"

He shook his head and I had a sudden suspicion that he was punishing himself for his "accident" last August. He lay silently on the couch while I packed his suitcase for the team train.

The actual day of the game was, as usual, like a dream—unreal with its crowds of friends and relatives and the inessential trappings of a gigantic show. The eleven little men who ran out on the field at last were like bewitched figures in another world, strange and infinitely romantic, blurred by a throbbing mist of people and sound. One aches with them intolerably, trembles with their excitement, but they have no traffic with us now, they are beyond help, consecrated and unreachable—vaguely holy.

The field is rich and green, the preliminaries are over and the teams trickle out into position. Head guards are put on; each man claps his hands and breaks into a lonely little dance. People are still talking around you, arranging themselves, but you have fallen silent and your eye wanders from man to man. There's Jack Whitehead, a senior, at end; Joe McDonald, large and reassuring, at tackle; Toole, a sophomore, at guard; Red Hopman, center; someone you can't identify at the other guard— Bunker probably—he turns and you see his number—Bunker; Bean Gile, looking unnaturally dignified and significant at the other tackle; Poore, another sophomore at end. Back of them is Wash Sampson at quarter —imagine how he feels! But he runs here and there on light feet, speaking to this man and that, trying to communicate his alertness and his confidence of success. Dolly Harlan stands motionless, his hands on his hips, watching the Yale kicker tee up the ball; near him is Captain Bob Tatnall—

There's the whistle! The line of the Yale team sways ponderously forward from its balance and a split second afterward comes the sound of the ball. The field streams with running figures and the whole Bowl strains forward as if thrown by the current of an electric chair.

Suppose we fumbled right away.

Tatnall catches it, goes back ten yards, is surrounded and blotted out of sight. Spears goes through center for three. A short pass, Sampson to Tatnall, is completed, but for no gain. Harlan punts to Devereaux, who is downed in his tracks on the Yale forty-yard line.

Now we'll see what they've got.

It developed immediately that they had a great deal. Using an effective crisscross and a short pass over center, they carried the ball fifty-four yards to the Princeton six-yard line, where they lost it on a fumble, recovered by Red Hopman. After a trade of punts, they began another push, this time to the fifteen-yard line, where, after four hair-raising forward passes, two of them batted down by Dolly, we got the ball on downs. But Yale was still fresh and strong, and with a third onslaught the weaker Princeton line began to give way. Just after the second quarter began Devereaux took the ball over for a touchdown and the half ended with Yale in possession of the ball on our ten-yard line. Score, Yale, 7; Princeton, 0.

We hadn't a chance. The team was playing above itself, better than it had played all year, but it wasn't enough. Save that it was the Yale game, when anything could happen, anything *had* happened, the atmosphere of gloom would have been deeper than it was, and in the cheering section you could cut it with a knife.

Early in the game Dolly Harlan had fumbled Devereaux's high punt, but recovered without gain; toward the end of the half another kick slipped through his fingers, but he scooped it up, and slipping past the end, went back twelve yards. Between halves he told Roper he couldn't seem to get under the ball, but they kept him there. His own kicks were carrying well and he was essential in the only back-field combination that could hope to score.

After the first play of the game he limped slightly, moving around as little as possible to conceal the fact. But I knew enough about football to see that he was in every play, starting at that rather slow pace of his and finishing with a quick side lunge that almost always took out his man. Not a single Yale forward pass was finished in his territory, but toward the end of the third quarter he dropped another kick—backed around in a confused little circle under it, lost it and recovered on the five-yard line just in time to avert a certain score. That made the third time, and I saw Ed Kimball throw off his blanket and begin to warm up on the sidelines.

Just at that point our luck began to change. From a kick formation, with Dolly set to punt from behind our goal, Howard Bement, who had gone in for Wash Sampson at quarter, took the ball through the center of the line, got by the secondary defense and ran twenty-six yards before he was pulled down. Captain Tasker, of Yale, had gone out with a twisted knee, and Princeton began to pile plays through his substitute, between Bean Gile and Hopman, with George Spears and sometimes Bob Tatnall carrying the ball. We went up to the Yale forty-yard line, lost the ball on a fumble and recovered it on another as the third quarter ended. A wild ripple of enthusiasm ran through the Princeton stands. For the first time we had the ball in their territory with first down and the possibility of tying the score. You could hear the tenseness growing all around you in the intermission; it was reflected in the excited movements of the cheer leaders and the uncontrollable patches of sound that leaped out of the crowd, catching up voices here and there and swelling to an undisciplined roar.

I saw Kimball dash out on the field and report to the referee and I thought Dolly was through at last, and was glad, but it was Bob Tatnall who came out, sobbing, and brought the Princeton side cheering to its feet.

With the first play pandemonium broke loose and continued to the end of the game. At intervals it would swoon away to a plaintive humming; then it would rise to the intensity of wind and rain and thunder, and beat across the twilight from one side of the Bowl to the other like the agony of lost souls swinging across a gap in space.

The teams lined up on Yale's forty-one yard line and Spears immediately dashed off tackle for six yards. Again he carried the ball—he was a wild unpopular Southerner with inspired moments—going through the same hole for five more and a first down. Dolly made two on a cross buck and Spears was held at center. It was third down, with the ball on Yale's twenty-nine-yard line and eight to go.

There was some confusion immediately behind me, some pushing and some voices; a man was sick or had fainted—I never discovered which. Then my view was blocked out for a minute by rising bodies and then everything went definitely crazy. Substitutes were jumping around down on the field, waving their blankets, the air was full of hats, cushions, coats and a deafening roar. Dolly Harlan, who had scarcely carried the ball a dozen times in his Princeton career, had picked a long pass from

Kimball out of the air and, dragging a tackler, struggled five yards to the Yale goal.

6.

Some time later the game was over. There was a bad moment when Yale began another attack, but there was no scoring and Bob Tatnall's eleven had redeemed a mediocre season by tying a better Yale team. For us there was the feel of victory about it, the exaltation if not the jubilance, and the Yale faces issuing from out the Bowl wore the look of defeat. It would be a good year, after all—a good fight at the last, a tradition for next year's team. Our class—those of us who cared—would go out from Princeton without the taste of final defeat. The symbol stood—such as it was; the banners blew proudly in the wind. All that is childish? Find us something to fill the niche of victory.

I waited for Dolly outside the dressing rooms until almost everyone had come out; then, as he still lingered, I went in. Someone had given him a little brandy, and since he never drank much, it was swimming in his head.

"Have a chair, Jeff." He smiled, broadly and happily. "Rubber! Tony! Get the distinguished guest a chair. He's an intellectual and he wants to interview one of the bone-headed athletes. Tony, this is Mr. Deering. They've got everything in this funny Bowl but armchairs. I love this Bowl. I'm going to build here."

He fell silent, thinking about all things happily. He was content. I persuaded him to dress—there were people waiting for us. Then he insisted on walking out upon the field, dark now, and feeling the crumbled turf with his shoe.

He picked up a divot from a cleat and let it drop, laughed, looked distracted for a minute, and turned away.

With Tad Davis, Daisy Cary and another girl, we drove to New York. He sat beside Daisy and was silly, charming and attractive. For the first time since I'd known him he talked about the game naturally, even with a touch of vanity.

"For two years I was pretty good and I was always mentioned at the bottom of the column as being among those who played. This year I dropped three punts and slowed up every play till Bob Tatnall kept yelling at me, 'I don't see why they won't take you out!' But a pass not even aimed at me fell in my arms and I'll be in the headlines tomorrow."

He laughed. Somebody touched his foot; he winced and turned white.

"How did you hurt it?" Daisy asked. "In football?"

"I hurt it last summer," he said shortly.

"It must have been terrible to play on it."

"It was."

"I suppose you had to."

"That's the way sometimes."

They understood each other. They were both workers; sick or well, there were things that Daisy also had to do. She spoke of how, with a vile cold, she had had to fall into an open-air lagoon out in Hollywood the winter before.

"Six times—with a fever of a hundred and two. But the production was costing ten thousand dollars a day."

"Couldn't they use a double?"

"They did whenever they could—I only fell in when it had to be done."

She was eighteen and I compared her background of courage and independence and achievement, of politeness based upon the realities of cooperation, with that of most society girls I had known. There was no way in which she wasn't inestimably their superior—if she had looked for a moment my way—but it was Dolly's shining velvet eyes that signaled to her own.

"Can't you go out with me tonight?" I heard her ask him.

He was sorry, but he had to refuse. Vienna was in New York; she was going to see him. I didn't know, and Dolly didn't know, whether there was to be a reconciliation or a good-by.

When she dropped Dolly and me at the Ritz there was real regret, that lingering form of it, in both their eyes.

"There's a marvelous girl," Dolly said. I agreed. "I'm going up to see Vienna. Will you get a room for us at the Madison?"

So I left him. What happened between him and Vienna I don't know; he has never spoken about it to this day. But what happened later in the evening was brought to my attention by several surprised and even indignant witnesses to the event.

Dolly walked into the Ambassador Hotel about ten o'clock and went to the desk to ask for Miss Cary's room. There was a crowd around the desk, among them some Yale or Princeton undergraduates from the game. Several of them had been celebrating and evidently one of them knew Daisy and had tried to get her room by phone. Dolly was abstracted and he must have made his way through them in a somewhat brusque way and asked to be connected with Miss Cary.

One young man stepped back, looked at him unpleasantly and said, "You seem to be in an awful hurry. Just who are you?"

There was one of those slight silent pauses and the people near the desk all turned to look. Something happened inside Dolly; he felt as if life had arranged his role to make possible this particular question— a question that now he had no choice but to answer. Still, there was silence. The small crowd waited.

"Why, I'm Dolly Harlan," he said deliberately. "What do you think of that?"

It was quite outrageous. There was a pause and then a sudden little flurry and chorus: "Dolly Harlan! What? What did he say?"

The clerk had heard the name; he gave it as the phone was answered from Miss Cary's room.

"Mr. Harlan's to go right up, please."

Dolly turned away, alone with his achievement, taking it for once to his breast. He found suddenly that he would not have it long so intimately; the memory would outlive the triumph and even the triumph would outlive the glow in his heart that was best of all. Tall and straight, an image of victory and pride, he moved across the lobby, oblivious alike to the fate ahead of him or the small chatter behind.

Joe Flaherty

Sympathy for the Devil

A journalist of the Jimmy Cannon school, Joe Flaherty wrote for various New York newspapers, including The Village Voice. *He was a sensitive and warm writer who looked for the good in everybody. So he must have found this assignment, to profile Jake LaMotta, the Raging Bull, a trial, but he managed all right. This piece was written for* Inside Sports *soon after the release of the Martin Scorsese film that was rated in a poll of national critics as the finest film of the 1980s.*

All lives are failures in some degree or another. Somewhere along the line we fudge the pristine youthful dream. Even when we achieve, the compromises we've made, the injuries we've inflicted sully the prize. But most of us can live with this, since we deal in minor declinations of the soul.

Not so with Jake LaMotta. LaMotta's fortunes and misfortunes have been so cosmic they could be considered godlike if it weren't for the sacrilege implied. The ruin he has heaped on himself, and on many of those who've come in contact with him, seems pagan. Those who lament LaMotta would have you believe Attila the Hun would have to move up in class to get it on with Jake.

When you go in search of the good word on LaMotta, no soft, illuminating adjective is forthcoming. Since most of the naysayers are from within boxing, the word is even more damning. The ringed world is awash with evocations of loving motherhood, guiding priests and golden-hearted gladiators. Cauliflower corn pone bows only to the jab as the basic element of boxing.

But when the talk turns to LaMotta's character (his boxing ferocity is always lauded), the usual benediction of holy water turns to spit. The only bow to grace is that no one wants his quotes attributed, though this "nicety" could be interpreted as fear of retribution, since no one believes the 58-year-old LaMotta has mended his savage ways.

Thus, one of the game's gentlest promoters calls LaMotta "a reprehensible, obnoxious, despicable sonnuvabitch," and then apologizes that he has characterized a human being in such a fashion.

To be sure, it's a tough assessment, but even LaMotta wouldn't deny he worked like a bull to earn his unsavory rep. Born on the tough Lower East Side of New York, he and his family moved to the Bronx when he was a boy. In that borough of hills (peaks and valleys in psychological jargon), LaMotta's cyclonic emotions got untracked. Young Jake wasn't one of those angels with dirty faces, a wayward street urchin with tousled hair who pinched apples from outside the grocery store and puckishly threw rocks at schoolhouse windows. Jake's mayhem was main arena: armed robbery, assault, rape.

As a teenager he pummeled the head of the local bookie (whom he liked!) in a robbery attempt and left the man for dead with a crushed skull. Subsequently, the papers falsely reported the bookie's death, and LaMotta did not learn until years later, after he won the middleweight championship, that the bookie, following a hospital stay, had moved to Florida to recuperate. In fairness, LaMotta had ongoing pangs of conscience about "the murder," but the primal concern of the heart was how to beat the rap, not the devil.

The horror his early violence wreaked also didn't stop him, in later years, from battering various wives for "love" and numerous opponents for loot. LaMotta's life has been so unappetizingly gamy, so foully unpalatable, it bends the conventional limits of social understanding, as graphically documented in the film of his life, *Raging Bull.*

Even those who shared the same mean streets can find no sympathy. An Irish trainer from the same boyhood Bronx said, "Look, he just went too far. I grew up there, too. We always hustled a fast buck, put out other guys' lights in fistfights, and even brawled with cops. Hell, the Irish are great cop-fighters. But we stopped short of some things, the animal stuff. Beating people's heads in with weapons and wife-beating, Christ, that's as low as you can get.

"Ask anyone. That bastard didn't even know how to say hello. But don't take my word for it. The Micks are notorious for not having a good word for Wops. Go ask his own kind. His own kind hate him because he was a squealer. He even screwed them. You go ask the Italians what they think. When your own kind hate you, that tells you something."

Indeed, the "wise guys," the sharp money guys who always have leeched on the tit of boxing, long ago wrote off LaMotta for his testimony before the Kefauver Committee that he went into the water for the mob when he fought Billy Fox in Madison Square Garden in 1947. But even before that, he wasn't acceptable. Hustlers who live off "the edge" dislike dealing with a "crazy" man.

Even the Italian-American director Martin Scorsese, while creating a technically beautiful film and coaxing marvelous ensemble acting from his cast, was in a moral quandary about what to make of LaMotta the man. If the film had to stand on redeeming social qualities, *Raging Bull* would have been castrated by the censors. Scorsese, like so many who have faced LaMotta, was overwhelmed with the brutishness of the life and in the end, using Robert DeNiro's great talents, settled for an exposition of poetic rage. The violence is softened by slow motion and an operatic score. This creates the illusion that one is dealing with a demon.

But the frightening thing about LaMotta is that he is very real, and removing him from our orbit with technical skill and art is cleverly slipping the punch. The only way to explore LaMotta's life is to delve into the festering place in his heart of darkness.

The LaMotta you meet today hardly qualifies for a portrait in ferocity. If it weren't for his classically failed soufflé of a face and the thickness of his articulate speech, you wouldn't suspect he had made his living at demolition. His weight is back to the 160-pound middleweight limit, and his manner is deferential. His hands belie their destructive force in that they are small, slim and tapered.

"I should have been an artist, or a fag," he jokes. But the jibe has insight. They look like the hands of someone who would beat helplessly on the chest of a bully.

Only the eyes give a clue to his former life. They are so sad and placid, they almost look burned out. Twin novas which didn't survive the Big Bang, memos to some terrible past.

So you're not surprised when he responds to a question about his current life, "I'm a recluse. I stay at home and read, play cards, and watch television. And I love to cook. I'm a gourmet cook. It's a knack."

His oldest son Jack Jr. (by his second wife, Vikki) concurs: "I'd rather eat at home with him cooking than go out to a fine restaurant."

LaMotta's forays outside are restricted to long walks, infrequent trips to an East Side bar to meet Rocky Graziano, who pulled time with him at reform school when they were in their teens, and some evening blackjack games. "I don't want to go out anymore," he says. "I seen it all, and I had it all. Fame, fortune, Cadillacs. There's nothing out there for me. Besides, I don't like the kind of people I attract."

When asked to elaborate, he has trouble pinning it down. "I don't know. Other people like to go out. It must be me. I dislike a lot of people." He amends, "I don't mean a majority of people, but I see through people. Maybe I'm too cynical. But sometimes I hear the first word out of their mouths, or see a smirk on their faces, and I know they're not sincere. They're jealous or something. Jealousy is a word I use a lot, but I think it's right. Well, I think like that anyway. I guess I attract those kind of people, so I stay home."

The recluse pose is really nothing new, if one applies it to LaMotta's inner emotions. In his fighting days, though public, he was notorious for being a loner in the things that mattered. He managed his own career, ostracized the mob until it promised him a shot at the crown for dumping to Fox, and had the intimate counsel of no one. He viewed his wife of that period, Vikki, with insane jealousy and suspicion, and forced his brother Joey, who worked his corner, "to do my bidding." The adjectives applied to Jake were "suspicious," "paranoiac."

Now divorced from his fifth wife, he is even more insular. The film is a hiatus in this isolation. Jack Jr. is up from North Miami Beach on leave from his job to guide his father through the publicity maze connected with the film. Vikki and his five other children also came to New York for the film's opening and some of the attendant hoopla. But when the stardust settles, he will be back living alone in his Manhattan apartment. The isolation may be complete for a long period if some job offers don't result from the film since LaMotta, in earnest, declares, "I'm now practicing celibacy," which could be construed as the last word on the people one attracts.

Jake attributes his decision on unilateral withdrawal to "the failures of my romantic life." His first marriage broke when he met Vikki, "the love of my life." Vikki left when LaMotta lost all control of his temper, his calorie and alcohol intake, and his ability to find his way home to his wife's bed after his retirement. "I think I suffered a nervous breakdown during that period," he says, "and didn't realize it. I was crazy. I was drinking a bottle or two a day. I owned my own joint [in Miami Beach], the price was right. Plus, there were a lot of broads. I blacked out a lot and didn't remember. I really think I was crazy and didn't know it."

LaMotta seems to be hesitant about going all the way back. His notion is that life would have been fine if he and Vikki could have worked out their problems. If they had been "mature" enough to realize he was going through a bad time after retiring, "the small death" all athletes must face, as the novelist John Updike called it.

Similar is the lament that three marriages broke up because finances were tight, and the one thing he regrets is his dump of the Fox fight. The one thing?

LaMotta deals with his woeful experiences piecemeal, not as the pattern of a life. For LaMotta to have led a conventional life, it seems he would have had to be born in different circumstances, or somehow been able to overcome the ones he was dealt. The latter is no mean trick. The soul is cankered with barnacles of who and what spawned us. Only the imperial George Bernard Shaw had the audacity to state that if he had one thing to change in his life it would have been his parents. And for good reason. There's a reverberation in that shot that might ricochet back to our own siring.

LaMotta makes some earnest attempts. "You know, now I think they brainwashed us. You know, this is your life, you're poor, and this is the way it's going to be. I always felt I didn't deserve good things. I was always guilty. I thought I killed someone, but it was more than that. Years later, I even thought of the way I fought. Letting guys hit me in the face. I didn't have to do that. I think I was brainwashed to be punished."

If you want to find the man, it helps to find the boy, and then the father of the boy. LaMotta's father was an Italian immigrant who beat his kids and beat his wife, and it's safe to say Jake was tutored in raucous romance early. And even though LaMotta hated the bullying, like so many sons of fathers who beat, drank, molested or committed suicide, he replayed the old man's aberrations. The psychiatric statistics are too firm in these areas to be taken as happenstance. In dismal surroundings finesse is lost, you take what is offered.

Since the home life was a microcosm of the neighborhood, he had only to expand the MO of violence. In such neighborhoods the glittering prizes of bread, broads and booze went to the wise guys. "Artists and fags" (same thing really) need not apply.

To anyone who knows those streets, the real triumph is to make it through time-honored devices in the neighborhood, not in the outside world. There's a sense of betrayal when one makes it "legit" and moves away. You turn your back on the highest gutter canonization—"a regular guy." It's not for nothing that artists with such roots can't completely resist the swagger, highlighting the accent, the tough-guy stance. These are love notes thrown back over the barricades from their now "effete" surroundings. Worldly success is so much manure—the real bones are still made back on the block.

LaMotta only seems an aberration to us because he achieved celebrity and money and didn't find the happy life. That is the height of anti-Americanism. But to use Willard Motley's phrase, "Knock on any door," and you could find countless LaMottas—violent, suspicious, self-destructive, who have left disasters in their wake, but there was nobody there to chronicle them. We prefer happy endings to our social neglect: saccharine Sylvester Stallones, pugs who are pussycats or flower girls who end up at Ascot.

But even in the field of achieving and then destroying celebrity, LaMotta is not unique. Streetwise black basketball players with fat NBA contracts still get high on more than slam dunks, and up-from-the-pavement union leaders who have had access to the seats of government can't resist the chance to turn a little change on the side. The outside world might be astonished, but the boys on the block understand all too well. What's felonious to some is "regular" to others.

When LaMotta got the chance, he didn't get out. When he made his score in boxing, his first move was to buy an apartment house in the Bronx for his family (parents, brother, sisters). Obviously, to erect a shrine in such heathen lands as the other boroughs never occurred to him, nor should it have. It had to be accessible for worship by those who lay down turf theology.

Years later, when he was broke and retired and serving time on a Florida chain gang for allowing a teenage prostitute to work his nightclub (he claims innocence about her age and trade), his father sold the apartment house (it was in his name, but Jake's property), deserted his family and moved back to his native Italy alone. That's the caliber of doublebank that makes street legend.

If one knows the code of the streets, wife-beating is no surprise either. Women (mothers exempted) were only revered as sexual trophies. The language of lovemaking sounded like contracts: "bang," "screw"—love delivered from a running board. Jealousy is easy to divine, too. You simply ascribed to others the reason you wanted women. If your own intentions were base, so were the world's.

One has only to remember the photos of Vikki LaMotta then, or to look at her now, to realize her erotic worth as a trophy. At age 50, after giving birth to four children (three by Jake and one by a subsequent marriage that also ended in divorce), she still could make a bishop want to break a stained-glass window.

Vikki realizes the cloud a sexual aura casts. "People see the blonde hair, the face, the beautiful body and look no further. They never search for the dignity. It's like beauty doesn't deserve dignity. My problem with Jake was that he consumed me. He did it in a very beautiful way, but he consumed me. I was only 15 when we met in June 1946, and we were married in November of the same year. In a way you could say Jake kidnapped me."

It's a lovely turn of phrase: "kidnapped me." It evokes Fay Wray and her rough-hewn suitor. "Our marriage was fine when Jake had control. In the beginning he trained me, molded me to be his kind of woman, but later on when I matured and deviated from what he wanted, he couldn't handle it. I watched *Pygmalion* on television the other night, and I saw many similarities."

LaMotta's mad jealousy was fueled by the long periods of sexual withdrawal when he was in training. He believed in the old adage that sexual activity sapped strength. "It was a mistake, but in a way it worked. It made me an animal in the ring. But now I think I should have had it once in a while."

Worse, the intensity of training began to render LaMotta impotent when he wanted to perform. For a man like LaMotta to fail at all, but especially with his "kidnapped" goddess, was excruciating. So instead of swatting airplanes, Jake disfigured opponents such as Tony Janiro, whom Vikki found handsome; his brother, who had introduced Vikki to Jake, and who made the mistake of kissing her warmly whenever they met; and Vikki herself, for offering her cheek to be pecked by friends.

The beatings were serious enough to require medical attention, and when once Vikki retaliated, she said, "It was a mistake. He reacted like a fighter. He came back at me and nearly killed me."

Yet for all this, she claims they had glorious times together (rarely shown in the film), and finds her ex-husband spiritual. "Just look into those sad, soft eyes. Whenever I'm sick, Jake is the first at my bedside. What greater love? I love him dearly. No longer in a sexual way, but who knows? That could come back, though I'm frightened to put the heat back into the relationship. It's so loving and warm now. I just don't think of him in a sexual way. To be blunt, I have no desire to ball him. He doesn't like me to say that, but it's the truth. And I'd need that to get back with him. I'm a woman, and woman means hot. But love him I do, and who knows what the future will bring? That's the exciting thing about the future."

They have stayed in constant contact 34 years. Jake visits Vikki in North Miami Beach (in the home he bought for her) a few times each year and stays at the house. "Separate bedrooms," he is quick to add. He talks to her by phone three or four times a week. And he admits that his continuing affection for Vikki hindered his other marriages. "Aw, they knew," he says. "I'm not smart enough with women to hide anything."

Of course, LaMotta's love for Vikki might be heightened by their golden period together. "We had everything," he says. "Love, home, children, money, the championship, his and hers Cadillac cars."

Their children hint at more solid stuff. The two boys I met, Jack Jr., 33, and Joe, 32, seem well-adjusted and carry no scars. Neither remembers the parental brawls. Those took place in private, and Vikki says that when she was black and blue she retreated behind her bedroom doors until the damage healed. There is a courageous civility about that.

Jack Jr. is sympathetic about the forces that fashioned his father's life. "He grew up in the Depression, and everything was struggle. Everything was denial. His generation had to fight to get out. That's why you don't see fighters with the ferocity of the '40s fighters anymore."

Jake concurs. "The fighters today are spoiled. Only Duran and Muhammad Ali could have stood with the greats of the past. You know, we fought every three weeks. When I started to make money, I couldn't get enough. It was a Depression thing. I'd fight anyone. Then when I made it, I didn't know how to handle it. After all those years of denying myself, I went crazy with everything from booze to broads."

Fight everyone, he did. Nobody puts a knock on LaMotta as a fighter. Harry Markson, the retired president of Madison Square Garden boxing, said, "Outside Sugar Ray Robinson, he was the greatest middleweight of that era. He fought black fighters, both light-heavyweight and middleweight, that no one else would touch. He was fearless."

Much is made of LaMotta's dump to Fox, but many forget he was top-ranked for five years without getting a title shot. And going in the water wasn't his province alone. It is common knowledge that good black fighters of that era often had to swoon for the mob to get bouts. Robinson was one who refused and had to wait until he was 30 to get his crack at the middleweight crown, which, perversely, was granted by LaMotta.

Also, some members of the pious press didn't seem to have the clout to force legitimate showdowns. This wasn't for ignorance of fistic worth, but for the most venal of reasons. You still hear gossip about members of the fourth estate who picked up "envelopes" under the guise that they were gifts for their kids' birthdays, graduations, or some such.

Harry Markson, while making no case for LaMotta's action ("Robinson never did it"), added that boxing commissions were either non-existent or had no clout, and that the press and television didn't have the power they have today. "Let's just say that in that period there was ample skulduggery."

LaMotta's sole defense is that he wanted the crown. "I always hated those creeps and never let them near me. They offered me a hundred thousand to dump, and I refused. I only wanted the title. And even when I went along, I still had to kick back $20,000 under the table to get the fight with Cerdan."

Jake testified before Kefauver when the statute of limitations ran out. In his original affidavit Jake named Blinky Palermo as the fixer, but later testified he didn't know who masterminded the dump. "You know who was around in those days. Palermo, Carbo, draw your own conclusions."

LaMotta, in a way, was like John Dean. He validated the bad news in high places everyone knew about but no one wanted to talk about. Finking, no matter how cleansing, is never appreciated. It isn't strange that LaMotta can recite verbatim Brando's Terry Malloy speech, "I coulda been somebody . . ." from *On the Waterfront* with feeling.

When Jake finished talking about this painful period, Jack Jr. massaged his shoulders into relaxation. "No one knows my father except his family. They only know of him back then. Not what he became. A gentle, sweet man. The ending is the exciting part of his life."

Jake, grandiose as ever, proclaimed, "Now I have the patience of a saint. You'll lose your temper before me."

Joe and Vikki concur. Jake, realizing the "saint" line is as gaudy as his leopard-skin fighter's robe (the material of macho bathing suits in the '40s, though LaMotta didn't add the black slim comb as a final fillip), tempers his canonization: "I still make mistakes, but less and less. Isn't that what life is about? It has to be less and less, if I am going . . . going to . . ." He trails off.

Jack says he finds lessons in his father's life: "There are deep meanings in dad's struggle." LaMotta, where his family is concerned, seems not to have passed on the sins of his father.

Martin Scorsese defends his unrelenting, unprobing film portrait of LaMotta by declaring he didn't want to apply tired psychology, that he found LaMotta to be "elemental man." By which I gather he means a man unfettered by influences. It's a quaint notion: The Abominable Snowman Comes to Mulberry Street. The director's peg tells us more about Scorsese than about LaMotta.

Numerous articles have related that Scorsese was a sickly child, consumed by movies and movie magazines, looking down from his window on those mean streets below. As a man, the same articles tell us, he is still housebound, running endless private tapes of movies in a more spacious, affluent setting. This sequestered life comes through in all Scorsese's films, the art of a meticulous voyeur.

Scorsese gets the mannerisms, the speech patterns, the language and the interiors precisely right. What formed the tableau seems beyond him. From a bedroom window—his first viewfinder—barbaric action in the street with an opera record playing in the background might indeed look like the rites of a primal society.

The only way to dispel reverential awe was to *know* those streets. Saloons and poolrooms were not pagan temples, merely colorful neon way stations in a drab culture. Bright bars were concrete equivalents of the neighborhood's best painted women, and a rack of pool balls cascading under fluorescent lights transported the shooter into a colorful galaxy. People didn't die gothic deaths on those streets. Life was drained by the dullness. If LaMotta's hook were a little slower, his temper a shade less manic, he would have been the Friday night undercard in the local beer joint, not a celebrated "Raging Bull."

For Scorsese to plumb LaMotta's psyche he would have to have a narrative curiosity, and that is not the art of a window kid for whom stories take place down below—on the streets. Talk is the province of the corner guys, the verbal spritzers who gaudily throw it around in lieu of money, dreams or hope.

And, of course, narrative is interruptive. It breaks up, sullies the purity of the scene. To visually oriented artists such as Scorsese, narrative is as sacrilegious as inserting dialogue balloons on a Magritte.

So Scorsese took an astringent tone in his film. With *Raging Bull,* he effectively holds boxing films such as *Champion* and *Body and Soul,* which explored social beginnings, up to ridicule. Through attempts at reason and understanding, these films made overtures to the heart. To Scorsese, obviously, these were cluttered films, weakened by sentiment. So he used his camera as an unsympathetic X-ray machine, the bed boy finally making his bones.

Contrary to stereotype, "housegrown" kids are often filled with confidence. The doting of parents, the coloring books and ice cream brought to bedside, the extra blanket for the precious body, the music spinning in the background are the trappings of tyke kings. Consequently, they learn to manipulate an audience early. So it's not surprising Scorsese couldn't understand LaMotta's self-loathing and lack of confidence. LaMotta was only one of the litter.

Also, LaMotta feared and hated priests early. When Scorsese made a bow to such emotion in his *Mean Streets,* he had Harvey Keitel sacrilegiously bless his whiskey glass, evoking Stephen Dedalus in Joyce's *A Portrait of the Artist as a Young Man.* The Jakes and Studs Lonigans of the world took damnation seriously, not as baroque artistic fodder. To LaMotta, the fear of immolating fire was never aesthetic, it was real: "I felt for some reason my opponent had a *right* to destroy me."

Since street kids get by with hustle, not substance, they always doubt themselves. The leopard skin was worn to keep outside tribes at bay. Street kids feel con, not concreteness, is their deliverance. When you work with con and swagger, the final damnation is going to be your unmasking in the larger world.

When I was first published at age 30, after working the docks for most of my life, I was terrified instead of being elated. When I was at a social function with my betters, Norman Mailer, Robert Lowell, Arthur Miller, I laced myself with booze against the impending mass denunciation I felt would expose me as a cultural body-snatcher. This dread was fortified by the oppressive Catholicism of the '40s and '50s. The most deeply felt commandment was that earthly glitter was suspect; it was tawdry, whorish rouge on both your religion and your roots. God, like the old gang, only dug regular guys.

An operatic score is much too florid for LaMotta's life. It is a cultural pretension, akin to the canard that all the Irish are familiar with Yeats. For LaMotta's odyssey of self-loathing, the Catholic hymn, "Lord, I Am Not Worthy," would have come closer.

Indeed, it is because LaMotta is not "elemental man" that he survived and softened his life. LaMotta is what he is today because he has made intellectual decisions, not visceral ones. Through reading, self-hypnotism and study of various religions, through studying acting and grooming himself as a lecturer—all things foreign to him (and elemental man)—he has found some grace in his life.

These are disciplines of the mind, and LaMotta knows his is a life that has to be sentried. He carries this over to his physical well-being by dieting and shunning booze. His decision to be reclusive and his acquiring the domestic arts of cooking and cleaning are further monitors. In the future, he wants to talk to kids about violence and alcoholism ("I think they'll listen to me") and do charity work in hospitals. "You know, tell people stories, do some recitals from my stage and nightclub act. Make people laugh."

He's a man who declares, "I love to do things. To keep busy. That's why I love Vikki and the kids with me now. I cook every meal. I won't let any of them touch a dish. I love projects." Projects are the Dobermans that prowl his darker impulses.

He is still a man who suspects before he greets. In frustration, Graziano says, "He's very complex, very deep. I tell him to relax, but he can't. I introduce him to someone, and he says, 'Who is he? What does he do? What does he want?' He can't realize it's someone who just wants to meet him. He just don't know. I say hello to the world. He just don't know."

Even now, when someone greets Vikki in public with a kiss, he looks on with distrust, but he doesn't act. Reason has brought him to that simple point. He mistrusts success, as well he should. Every high point in his life has been followed by a crash. The title "nobody is going to take from me" was gone 20 months later, lost to Robinson. From the crown, he went on to divorce, alcoholism and conviction on morals charges. He says now, "I can't be happy, everything is going so well."

Not quite that well. Again, success has a rectal side. The IRS has leaned on him for money accrued from the movie, his fifth wife is suing for an alimony settlement and his brother is suing the entire movie production staff, including Jake, for their portrayal of him. In his most emotional statement, Jake declares, "Aw, that's nothing. It's part of living in this vicious, fuckin', mixed-up, sick world."

To LaMotta's credit, he keeps such dark rage on a tight leash these days. He has learned the elemental lesson of those streets. You can't go back because some unhealed part never leaves. In this world our initial address, like tragedy, forever haunts.

Leonard Gardner

At the Lido Gym

Leonard Gardner was twelve when he was given his first pair of boxing gloves by his father, a former amateur boxer. With his new gloves, Gardner aspired to become a heavyweight champion or an Olympic gold medalist. But by the age of fourteen, he had given up his ring dreams for an equally challenging goal, becoming a writer. His two ambitions came together in 1969 when his first novel, Fat City, *was published. "I have seldom read a novel as beautiful and individual as this one" said Ross MacDonald about* Fat City. *The compact story of small-time fighters in Stockton, California, was widely praised and adapted into a film directed by John Huston, with a screenplay by Gardner himself. In this excerpt a young fighter named Ernie Munger enters the Lido Gym, where he is initiated into the "company of men."*

The Lido Gym was in the basement of a three-story brick hotel with a façade of Moorish arches, columns, and brightly colored tile. Behind the hotel several cars, one tireless and up on blocks, rested among dry nettles and wild oats. In a long, narrow, open-end shed of weathered boards and corrugated steel, a group of elderly men were playing bocce ball with their hats on and arguing in Italian. A large paper bag in his hand, Ernie Munger went down the littered concrete stairs. In a ring under a ceiling of exposed joists, wiring, water and sewage pipes, a Negro was shadowboxing in the light of fluorescent tubes. Three men in street clothes, one bald, one with deeply furrowed cheeks, the third wearing a houndstooth-check hat with a narrow up-turned brim, all turned their faces toward the door. The one with the deeply furrowed cheeks reached Ernie first.

"Want a fight, kid?"

234

"You Ruben Luna?"

"Gil Solis. How much you weigh? You got a hell of a reach. You looking for a trainer?"

They were joined by the man in the hat. A Mexican, as was Solis, he was perhaps forty, his face plump and relaxed, his skin smooth, his smile large, guileless and constant. "I'm Luna. You looking for me?"

"Yeah, I just thought I'd work out. Like to see what you think. Billy Tully told me I ought to come by."

"You know Tully?"

"I boxed with him the other day down at the Y."

"Is he getting in shape? How'd you do, all right? You must of done all right, huh?"

Now the bald man came over, whispering hoarsely, and Luna guided Ernie away with a hand on his shoulder. "Got your stuff there? We'll get you started." They walked on their heels through the shower room, the floor wet from a clogged drain. In a narrow, brick-walled, windowless room smelling of bodies, gym clothes and mildew, several partially dressed Negroes and Mexicans glanced up and went on conversing.

"Look around and find you an empty locker," said Luna. "Better bring a padlock with you next time. Get one of those combination kind. They're hard to pick. I'll be out in the gym when you get your togs on."

A service-station attendant, Ernie removed his leather jacket, oil-spotted khaki pants and shirt. When he came out into the gym in tennis shoes and bathing trunks, Ruben Luna sent him into the ring. With other shadow-boxers maneuvering around him in intent mutual avoidance, their punches accented by loud snuffling, Ernie self-consciously warmed up.

"How'd you like to go a round or two?" Luna asked after he had called him out. "I'm not rushing you now. I'd just like to get a look at you."

"With who?"

"Beginner like you. Just box him like you did Tully. Colored boy over there."

Before a full-length mirror a boy in a Hawaiian-print bathing suit and white leather boxing shoes, his reddish hair straightened, was throwing punches.

Looking at those high white shoes, Ernie pushed his hands into heavy gloves held braced for him by the wrists. He stepped into a leather foulproof cup. A headguard was jerked over his brows. Padded and trussed, his face smeared with Vaseline, a rubber mouthpiece between his teeth, he stood waiting while two squat men punched and grappled in the ring. Then he was following his opponent's dark legs up the steps. For two rounds he punched, bounded and was hit in return, the headguard dropping over his eyes and the cup sagging between his legs. Afterward Ruben Luna leaned over the ropes, contending with Gil Solis for the headguard's buckle.

Stripped of the gloves, Ernie stood on the gym floor, panting and nodding while Ruben, squared off with his belly forward and hat brim up, moved his small hands and feet in quick and graceful demonstrations. "You got a good left. Understand what I mean? Step in with that jab. Understand what I mean? Get your body behind it. Bing! Understand what I mean? You hit him with that jab his head's going back, so you step in—understand what I mean?—hit him again, throw the right. Bing! Relax, keep moving, lay it in there, bing, bing, understand what I mean? Keep it out there working for you. Then feint the left, throw the right. Bing! Understand what I mean? Jab and feint, you keep him off balance. Feinting. You make your openings and step in. Bing, bing, whop! Understand what I mean?"

In the flooded shower room, Ernie was addressed by a small Mexican standing motionless under the other nozzle: "How's the ass up here?"

"Not good. Where you from?"

"L.A."

"How's the ass down there?"

"Good."

Soapless, the two hunched under the hissing spray.

"Are the guys tough in this town?"

"Not so tough. How about down there?"

"Tough."

"Just get here?"

"Yeah, I was in a bar yesterday, this guy's calling everybody a son-of-a-bitch. So I go out and wait for him. He come out and I ask did that include me. Says yeah. So I got him. I mean I just come to town. Some welcome. I don't know, trouble just seems to come looking for me."

Then the man began to sing, repeating a single phrase, his voice rising from bass moans and bellows to falsetto wails. *Earth Angel, Earth Angel, will you be mine?* The song went on in the locker room, the singer, as he put on his clothes, shifting to an interlude of improvisation: *Baby, baaaby, baaaaby, uh baby, uuh, oh yeauh, BAAAAAAABY, I WANT you,* while naked figures walked to and from the showers and steam drifted through the doorway. Drawing on his pants, Ernie, bruised, fatigued and elated, felt he had joined the company of men.

Brian Glanville

The Ancient Mariner

One of the most expert of British writers on sports both as a journalist and as a novelist, Brian Glanville has been a soccer authority for the London Times, *and his novel,* The Rise of Gerry Logan, *is still considered one of the truest novels of that sport. Glanville wrote his first novel at age eighteen.* The Olympian, *published in 1969, was his eleventh. It is the story of Ike Low, a runner, and his guru-like coach, who sets out to make him a world-champion miler.*

The first time I met him, I thought he was a nut case, just a nutty old man hanging around the recreation grounds, leaning over the rails, shouting at people as they come by. Ah, shut up, shut up, you daft old bugger, that's all I thought about him, running past. Next time I come around he was still there, still shouting, and I caught a word or two, "Elbows *down!*" What the hell was it to do with *him?* Running around, I suddenly laughed, I'd suddenly remembered this old man at home that used to wander up and down the High Street, shouting at cars and waving his stick at them like they were people. When I got around, I was still laughing and that made him furious; you ought to have heard him, yelling and carrying on at me, something about "I'll bloody teach you to laugh!" and then, when I'd run past, something about I wouldn't win nothing.

I did two more laps and then I packed it in. In the showers there, in the dressing room, he come in to me. With this little white beard and this look in his eye, very pale eyes, pale blue, I'd never seen eyes like them, he was like a prophet, one of them colored pictures in the Bible at home.

He said, "What were you laughing at?" I said, "Me? I wasn't laughing at nothing." I'd have told him to fuck off, but somehow you couldn't, he was so intense. I said, "I often laugh when I train." "Well," he said, "you're not going to get much training done, not *good* training. Who's your coach?" I said, "I haven't got one. Just the club coach." He said, "Which club?" I said, "Spartacus," and he give this snort; he said, "Fifty years out of date. They couldn't teach a stag to run."

Just looking at him, listening to him, he seemed some sort of crank. In fact, it's funny the way things come full circle, because that's how I come to think of him, a crank, just like a lot of people did then; only there was the time in between, quite a long time, when I didn't think like that; and the time after. I suppose it was what Jill said; in a kind of way, he hypnotized me. There were his eyes, for a start, like I've said, so pale, like he'd spent a long time looking at the sun, and when you got to know him, you could imagine him doing that, just staring at the sun, for a challenge, not willing to be beaten by anything. He hardly ever blinked, just stared at you, almost through you, like some sort of blowtorch, burning away at anything he didn't like, any kind of disagreement with what he believed. And the hollow cheeks and his white tuft of hair and the way he shoved his face forward, into yours.

Alan, that's the sprinter, the bronze medal one, used to call him the Ancient Mariner; he'd say, "By thy long gray beard and glittering eye, now wherefore stopp'st thou me?" but not to Sam, not directly to Sam; it wasn't the kind of thing you could imagine yourself saying to him.

Then, of course, there was his rabbit. In a way, it was never so much what he said, but the tone of it, the rhythm of the words coming and coming at you, nonstop, like a torrent; you went with it, or it just swept you away, anyhow. Even now, I remember parts of what he said, then, standing in that little, dark, cramped dressingroom, dripping water, just out of the shower, while he kept on and on at me. He asked, "What distance do you run?" I said, "Two-twenties, quarters," and he said, "You are built to run the *mile*. You are the perfect combination of ectomorph-mesomorph; long calves, lean, muscular thighs and arms, chest between thirty-seven and thirty-eight, and broad, slim shoulders. A miler is the aristocrat of running. A miler is the nearest to a thoroughbred racehorse that exists on two legs. Look at me: a natural distance runner, wiry and muscular, trained down to gristle. We are the *infantry* of running. Your four-forty and eight-eighty men, these are your cavalry. The sprinters are your shock troops, your commandos."

One of the lads changing over in the corner, someone from another club, said, "What are we, then, mate; the walkers?" and the old boy said,

"The walkers are what Chesterton called the donkey; the Devil's walking parody on all two-footed things," and he give this imitation, strutting up and down the dressing room, sticking out his arse and waggling his shoulders, just like walkers do, till all of us that was in there laughed, and even the walker had to smile.

The old boy said, "I am *not* decrying walkers. Each man to the physical activity that suits him best. I would be prepared to award a gold medal even to *crawlers.* We already have hop, step and jumpers. But there must be proportion in all things. Just as a child learns to crawl, then to walk and then to run, so there is a hierarchy in athletic loco-motion."

To tell the truth, I didn't know what he was on about most of the time, leaving school at fifteen like I had, dead idle, never bothering; he was using words I'd never heard of. But it held you; that was the thing about him. He could hold you.

When I was changed, we went for a cup of tea, or rather *I* had a cup of tea, he had a glass of milk. It was at Lyons, in the Edgware Road; we went and sat at one of those stone-topped tables with the tea slopped all over it and teacups everywhere. He asked me why I drank tea; he said, "An athlete is as good as his diet. Tea is bad. Coffee is bad. Alcohol is worse than either. Do you drink alcohol?" I said, "Well, yes, I have a few beers, now and again," and he slapped the table so loud everybody looked around; it was embarrassing. He said, "You are deliberately poi-soning yourself. You are weakening the natural stimuli provided by the nervous system. The human body provides its own stimulant, and its own stimulant is adrenaline. This stimulant can be induced. Fear pro-duces adrenaline. Anticipation produces adrenaline. But alcohol will clog your brain; it will dull your reflexes; it will affect your lungs; it will undermine your heart. Do you smoke?"

I wanted to say no, which was ridiculous, because who was he, I'd only known him half an hour, and whose life was it, his or mine? Which was something that I'd often find myself asking in the time to come; whose life, whose body was it, his or mine? Till I decided—mine. I said, "Well, just a little." He said, "There is no truce to be made with the cigarette. Tobacco is the body's enemy. What happens to a chimney when it's been used a long time?" I said, "Soot?" and he said, "If you smoke, your lungs are like a chimney. But you can't call the sweep. Have you any cigarettes on you now?" and, when I half nodded, held out his hand, thin with blue veins, long fingers, like a claw, and God knows why,

I put my hand in my pocket and took it out, the packet, with what I had left in it, four or five cigarettes, and put them in his hand, and he crumpled them, his fingers closed around them like the grab of them mechanical cranes they have there in the arcades, in the Charing Cross Road, screwing them up; I should have belted him. But I didn't. I just said, "Hey," then watched while he opened his hand and let them drop out, the scrunched-up fags and the packet, onto the floor, like rubbish.

Then he got on to diet; did I eat meat, I shouldn't eat meat, *he* was a vegetarian, that and milk, only this wasn't *good* milk, it had been through too many processes, the best milk was the milk that was closest to the cow. I said, "A runner needs strength, don't he?" He said, "Press down my arm," and rolled up the sleeve and held it out, his right arm, all knobs and cords and veins like the root of a tree, the kind that grows aboveground, gnarled and twisted. I looked at it, and I didn't feel like touching it. He said, "Go on, try," and I tried, I put both hands on his arm; it felt hard, like wood, no flesh on it at all, and I started pressing. I was only eighteen but strong, very, very fit, and it should have been easy, I felt almost sorry for him. But I couldn't budge it, however hard I pushed, till in the end I was actually standing up; there was sweat running down my forehead, people were staring but it didn't worry me, or rather it did worry me, I had to do it; I was making a fool of myself, and when I looked down suddenly, into his eyes, they had this look in them, a sort of smile—of triumph really—and more than that, like he was saying, "There you are, I told you so, I knew you could never beat me," which made me press down all the harder, still looking at him, but it was no go, he just blinked once, that was all, and in the end, I give up. I sat down.

I said, "I don't know how you do it," and he said, "Not bad on vegetables, eh? Vegetables prevail over meat!" and then, "Strength is not just the strength of the body; it is the strength of the mind. The strength of the will prevails over the weakness of the body. The will drives the body beyond what the body believes it can do. That is why a great athlete must feed not only his body but his mind. How big was Paavo Nurmi? How big was Sidney Wooderson? He was a solicitor, and in a running vest he *looked* like a solicitor, but when he ran, the mind was greater than the body." And on and on. And on and on and on.

"Why were the Greeks the true, original athletes? Because the Greeks were the inventors of the golden mean. They did not neglect the body for the mind. In our age, we have neglected the body for the machine. What we have to do is to rediscover the body, stop poisoning it with false stimulants, stop filling it with noxious substances, stop treating it only as a means of self-indulgent *pleasure*. A plant needs water, and a body needs exercise. If you deprive a plant of water, it dies. If you do not exercise a body, it corrupts, and the mind corrupts with it. Look at the politicians and the scholars and the businessmen. Look at the people who rule our world and tell us what to do. What a travesty of logic! These are people who *have* no bodies, only heads. And many athletes have no heads, but only bodies. A champion is a man who has trained his body *and* his mind, who has learned to conquer pain and to use pain for his own purposes. A great athlete is at peace with himself and at peace with the world; he has fulfilled himself. He envies nobody. Wars are caused by people who have not fulfilled themselves; I have fought in two, and I know. Look—just here, above the navel; that was Flanders. And here, look, on the right shoulder. That was Murmansk. But I bore them no ill will, because I knew I would survive. You can kill the body, but you cannot kill the spirit. There are no limits to what the body can do when the spirit is strong. Twenty years ago, they said a four-minute mile was impossible. I told them then: 'We shall live to see it run in three minutes, forty seconds,' and they laughed. But what has happened? The four-minute mile is now a commonplace. Athletes run it every week. Even schoolboys run it. We shall see a three-forty mile and a nine-second 100 meters and a nine-foot high jump and a twenty-foot pole vault. It all lies in the conception. Once these things have been conceived as possible, they are achieved. And that is why athletics are important, why records are important. Because they demonstrate the scope of human possibility; which is unlimited. The inconceivable is conceived, and then it is accomplished.

"Look at me. It was inconceivable that my one arm should resist the pressure of your two, and yet it did. Now it is inconceivable to you that your two arms could defeat my one. But all this is arbitrary. Matter is arbitrary. It is your will against mine, your spirit against mine. Everything depends on the will. I have been in India and seen a fakir stab himself with knives, plunge knives into his body and pull them out again, without a mark. I have seen them walk on fire. If these men desired, they could lift weights which would make the strongest man in an Olympiad look weak. A man like Vlasov of Russia would look puny, although he was three times their size. So this is why I say to you, train. Look after your body. Temper it with pain. And your body will amaze you; you will do things that you thought impossible. That is why running matters. That is why Olympiads matter. Not for gold medals, those little, worthless disks, but for their inner meaning, what they stand for. The Olympic flame is sacred, because it is the flame of human aspiration."

I got excited, listening to him, understanding some of what he said, not understanding lots of it, but still, like I said, being carried along, as much by how he said it as by what he said. I mean, I was eighteen; who had I ever heard who could talk like that, who could spout ideas like that, who could make you believe in what you could do and what you were doing, the way he did?

Up to then I'd just been running, something to do, a race here, a race there, won a few, lost most of them, not knowing what I really wanted—out of that or anything else. But hearing him in that tea shop, I knew what I wanted and I realized it had been there all the time, only, like, it had come and gone. Sometimes I'd felt it when I was actually in a race, when I knew I'd got it in me to win, when I'd feel this sort of current shoot through me, a sort of ambition; other times it was when I was training, usually alone, in Epping Forest or some mornings on the track, early, when I'd been on night shift and I was there alone; you'd be moving so well, so smooth, your body felt so good, that you knew you could beat anyone on earth, bring 'em all on: Elliott, Bannister, the lot. And now I felt it in me again, even without running, even just sitting; this *knowing* that I could be great, that I wanted to be great—and something else: that he could show me how.

Mind you, you might say that was him, that was his stock-in-trade, which I admit; but what I mean is, that was part of it; if he hadn't had one, he wouldn't have had the other.

Out in the street, the Edgware Road, I hardly noticed the crowds. I was in my blue track suit, very proud of it, just got it, with the club crest on the pocket, and Sam was wearing what he always wore off the track, this gray jersey and a pair of blue jeans—never mind what it was, sun or rain, snow or hail.

I remember we walked across Hyde Park, with him still talking, and passing Speaker's Corner, where they was all talking, too, the blackies and the Irish and the nut cases, and him looking around and saying in this loud voice, "Lunatics, the lot of them, pouring out their prejudice and hatred," and it suddenly came to me that this was what he'd kept reminding me of all the time he was talking—the tone of his voice and the way it was one long speech, with you the audience.

All the way across the park, he was talking, I was listening; I think we both just took it for granted he was going to train me. He'd got three or four he was coaching, he said; one was a miler, one was middle distance, and the others sprinters. Sundays they trained on Hampstead Heath; other days it depended on the light and the time people could get off. He said he had this physical education job with the city council—it was long before he opened his gym for businessmen—and he'd done it a year, and when he got tired of it, he'd change. He said, "If I want money, I can always make it. Money is easy to make. Never let yourself be dominated or deluded by the importance of money; it is secondary. I've been a sailor and a soldier and a farmer and a postman and a travel courier. I have cooked in the finest hotels, and I have worked as a garage mechanic. I have written for newspapers, and I have *sold* newspapers. My dear wife is dead, I have no children, and I can exist with perfect comfort in the open air."

Then he asked me what *I* did, and I told him I was working in this cardboard-box factory, knowing more or less what he'd say—partly, I suppose, because it was what I really felt myself—that it was the wrong job for an athlete, unhealthy, that it wouldn't get me nowhere. I must have had half a dozen jobs, anyway, since I'd left school; working in a bakery, then a butcher's shop, apprentice electrician, trainee telephone engineer, and now the factory—nothing that really interested me.

He said, "A job like that erodes the will and stultifies the body. Go out into the air! Be a bus conductor or a park keeper or a swimming pool attendant or even a road sweeper! Do something that involves the use of the body. How can you hope to run when you spend the whole day standing still? How can you hope to master your own body when your body is the slave of a machine?" And I agreed with him; it all made sense; I didn't see nothing funny in it, his taking it for granted this was what I wanted, to be a great runner, whereas up to now it had just been something I did, where in the winter I played a bit of football over the Marshes.

I promised on Sunday I'd meet him on Hampstead Heath to do some training with him. By this time we'd walked right across the park, over to the bridge across the Serpentine, stood there talking, looking at the water, all the willows hanging over it, then back again, to Hyde Park Corner. Once he'd gone, it all felt a bit strange to me; it wasn't my manor, this part of London, but while you were with him you could be anywhere, you didn't think of where you were. When he shook hands, he held on to my hand very tight and looked at me, like an animal trainer or something, right in the eye; he said, "I can make you a great miler. If you want to be a great miler," then left me standing there, all dazed.

I could have flown home, let alone run, and all that night I couldn't sleep; I was running races, winning medals, hearing his voice come at me out of the dark. I don't suppose I slept above an hour.

We met up by the pond there; I was a few minutes late, and he was sitting on this bicycle, which was something I hadn't expected; I suppose I'd thought that he'd be running with me. There was no one else, just him and me; I mean, none of the other runners he'd said he was training. I'd never seen the Heath before, and it made quite an impression on me, though by the time that afternoon was finished, I wouldn't have cared if I'd never seen it again. But the sun was shining, and everything was this fresh, bright green—the grass, the trees, even the weeds. And not flat, like a park, but rolling—dips and hillocks and mounds and woods, very round and lush, more like the country. I wondered if he lived around there; he'd been very mysterious about where he lived; I imagined him living in a tent or maybe a caravan.

We strolled across the road, him wheeling the bike, and as we reached the other side, the Heath, he took a stopwatch out of his pocket. He said, "Here is your enemy. Here is the beast you have to conquer." There was a course he wanted me to run, he said, one he'd worked out himself, all along the paths, so he could ride beside me. He told me, "We'll see what sort of stamina you've got; then, when we know about that, we can work out a training schedule for you. The needs of every athlete vary, not just between the distance runner and the middle-distance runner, the miler and the sprinter, but from miler to miler, sprinter to sprinter."

So off we went, him on the bike with the watch in his hand, now and then telling me, "Spring!" then, "Stop!" up and down the paths, dodging the little kids and the prams and the people, over stones and sometimes tree roots, till I wished I'd never worn my spikes, down steep slopes into little valleys, up them again the other side. I'd always hated cross-country, always tried to get out of it when the club was doing a cross-country run, and this was killing, the worst I'd ever known, no chance to slow down or take a breather because *he* was there, sometimes beside me, sometimes behind me, sometimes just ahead of me, turning around and calling me on, talking and talking, telling me to go faster, to take longer strides, to hold my head higher, to use more arm action, to keep my elbows closer to my sides, until I hated him; I tried to block out the sound of his voice, just concentrate on a group of trees I could see, try and make out what kind they were, or a cloud with a funny shape, or try and guess how many strides it'd take me to an oak tree or a pond or maybe someone I could see walking.

But it never worked for long; he'd suddenly raise his voice, shouting, "*Sprint!*" or some other order, or else he'd suddenly ride out ahead of me so I couldn't ignore him if I wanted to, not with him there just ahead, his hairy old face bent forward towards mine. Then, just as I was thinking that all I wanted to do was catch up with him and smash him, he'd spin around and disappear behind me. To make matters worse, it was a warm afternoon and I was in my track suit. I wanted to stop and strip it off, yet at the same time I didn't want to ask no favors, I didn't want *nothing* from him, just finish the bloody run and go home and never set eyes on him again. And then there was another feeling I had at the same time as *that,* that this was how he wanted me to think, he wanted me to hate him. I don't know why, but somehow I knew it from the expression on his face, a sort of mocking look, and when I couldn't see him, from the sound of his voice.

Once he asked me, "Are you hot?" and I said, "*I'm* all right," though the sweat was running down my forehead, stinging my eyes, dribbling into my mouth, all salt, trickling out of my armpits, inside my running vest. He said, "It's better for you than a Turkish bath, this is." Once I asked him, "How long we been running?" He said, "Thirty-eight minutes. Are you tired?" I said, "No, not tired," and tried to kid myself I wasn't, but the longer I ran, the worse it got, my mouth so dry, my heart pumping away so loud I reckoned people must be able to hear it for miles around. Then he said, "Want a drink?" and honestly I loved him; he had this plastic bottle in his hand; holding it out to me, he said, "Not too much," it was better than champagne, and then, "You'd better take your track suit off," and I did, I stepped out of it, it had practically stuck to me in places, and with that off and the drink I thought, I'll run for miles, I'll bloody show him, and for a while, maybe for a quarter of an hour or so, it really was a bit better, I was almost beginning to enjoy it, which he probably realized, because soon things started getting harder; there were many more hills to climb, even a run across the grass. He said, "Down into that bowl and up the other side. I'll meet you there, I'll time you," and cycled the long way around the path while I ran down into this dip, then had to climb the bleeding hill, like going through some bloody assault course. He was there at the top with his stopwatch, saying, "Very good, all right, come on," and cycling off, not looking back, leaving me to follow like a dog.

So all this feeling good wore off; after a while I was back where I started, and worse, except for taking off the bloody track suit; my legs aching, my chest aching, my heart thumping and banging away, the only things to look forward to, the only things that kept me going, the drinks of water; but only when he offered them, I'd never ask for them, no matter how I felt, any more than I'd stop till the old bastard said I could stop. Except twice to be sick, when he just stood watching me while it all came heaving out, not saying anything, just standing, waiting for me to go on, while I thought, *Christ I'll die, I'm going to die, my guts are coming out, I'll die.*

In the end it got darker and colder; I was swaying about, almost bumping into people, just not seeing them till they was on top of me, and at last, right at the top of another bloody hill, or maybe one of the same bloody hills, God knows, hearing his voice behind me saying, "Okay, that'll do," and collapsing, bang, right where I was, and bursting into tears, lying there crying and not being able to stop, not even caring, just lying there and crying.

He didn't say a word, just stood there by his bicycle, with his back to me, waiting for me to finish, just like when I was being sick. I don't think I've ever hated anyone the way I hated him then—giving me nothing, when it was him who'd got me in this state. People were walking past, looking at me, one or two of them stopping, but I didn't care about that, either. I heard one of them say, behind me, "Is he all right?" and Sam's voice say, "Yes, he's all right," and I thought, *Who the hell are you to say I'm all right, you old cunt; whose body is it, who did all the bloody running?* till at last I stopped crying, and then I felt ashamed; I didn't want to face him, I buried my head in my arms and went on lying there, hoping that he'd go away, but when I looked up, he was still there, still with his back to me, like he was prepared to stand there forever. So I got up, and as I got up, he turned to me; the watch was still in his hand. He said, "You have run for two hours and seventeen minutes. I would estimate that in the first hour you covered ten and a quarter miles, in the second hour, nine and a half miles, and in the final seventeen minutes, less than two miles, making a total of slightly less than twenty-two miles, which is four miles less than the marathon. That, of course, is only an estimate." Not good or bad or well done or how are you. And still up on his bloody bicycle as we went all the way back across the Heath, my feet so sore I could hardly take a step, my calves aching like someone had been going over them with a truncheon, and him saying, "I do not believe in training to exhaustion. The Zatopek training. Zatopek was a great champion, but his achievements have been surpassed. This was not training; this was a test of stamina and will. There were moments when I doubted your will, but I am satisfied that you gave your maximum. Your maximum can be increased, just as your stamina *must* be increased."

I don't even know how I got home, on a bus I think, sleeping most of the way. That night I dreamed that I was flying. He was in it somewhere. He was doing it.

Peter Goldman

Requiem for a Globetrotter

As a senior editor at Newsweek *for over twenty years, Peter Gold-man wrote many of the magazine's finest cover stories. He is also the author of nine books, including* The Death and Life of Malcolm X *and* Charlie Company, *written with Tony Fuller. The genesis of "Requiem" came as Goldman was preparing a book that he intended as a serious look at the history of the Harlem Globetrotters. The book was never written, but in this story, published by* Sport Magazine *in 1977, we get a pretty good idea of what life was like for the Globetrotters in the late 1950s and early 1960s. And in particular, what life was like for a Trotter named Leon Hillard.*

You get what your hand called for.

—*The Sayings of Leon Hillard*

Somebody showed me in the papers a while ago where Leon got what his hand didn't call for. The headline jumped out at me first —EX-GLOBETROTTER IS KILLED BY WIFE—and then, sickeningly, the picture: the black gnome face with the eyes of a kid who knows a secret and a smile as stealthy as sunrise in the ghetto. *Leon Hillard.* The story told how he got messed up with his Sandra. Yelled at her, chased her downstairs to her mama's, kicked open the door and walked into a .38 slug coming out. There were a couple of perfunctory paragraphs about how he played and later coached for the Harlem Globetrotters for 15 of the years between 1951 and 1972, and how he was deep into youth work in Chicago when he died at 45. His whole life story took up half a column. What more is there to write about a dude who only used to be the Second Baddest Show Dribbler on The Road?

So Leon Hillard, a man of a thousand sayings, had it wrong for once: His hand called for better than what he got. His name, to be sure, has got lost down some back highway of our memory. Mention the Globetrotters and an older fan will come back at you with Goose Tatum and Sweetwater Clifton; a kid with Meadowlark Lemon and Curly Neal; both generations with the apparently ageless Marques Haynes. Leon? He played a lot of his years in Marques' shadow, and a lot more bojangling around what he called the little in-between towns with the Trotter second company while Marques and Curly played Front Street. You can hardly find him in authorized Globetrotter history now—he parted that badly with them. They didn't even send flowers.

But the old Globetrotters remember. Leon knew the Trotter thing better than practically anybody—learned it from Tatum, the moody master, in the 1950s and taught it to a new generation of schoolyard brothers in the '60s and '70s. How to read a crowd from the murmur before you even hit the floor. How to get 'em buttered by getting that ball *hot*—hopping hand-to-hand or hand-to-floor so fast it never wants to cool down. How to drag yourself out with your soul all bruised and legs all floor-burned, and still make people laugh. How to survive "The Road": The short bread, the long bus rides, the ennui of playing the same game every night, the funky phone calls home and back. "Leon had the real rhythm of it," said Bobby Hunter, his friend and Trotter protégé. "If the world had to start up again on the moon, you'd have to have somebody with the book on farming, y'know? Well, Leon would've been the one with the book on the Globetrotters."

And more; Leon had kinds of magic you can't do with a basketball. He could get streetcorner basic—*stern,* he liked to say—about issues of money and dignity; he walked out on the Trotters twice, and helped foment a player strike against them in 1971. *Leon crazy,* some of his less impudent teammates whispered. *A gangster. Got an attitude.* But once the deal was down, he greeted a day like an old friend, with a lopsided grin and a line of pavement-wise chatter. "Was never hushed-up today and ha-ha tomorrow," he told me once. "People asked me, 'Leon—how can you be happy all the time?' And I told 'em, 'I'm not really happy, man, but what the hell. You got to be out here six months on The Road, y'know. Ain't no sense in makin' it difficult.' "

When the Trotters retired him off The Road and back to the streets he came from, *that* was the attitude Leon took with him. His business was franchised fast food, but his thing was kids—most recently and promisingly with a Chicago-based foundation called Athletes For Better

Education. Leon could talk a Blackstone Ranger out of gang-banging or charm a junkie off his jones. " 'Cause they know I know what I'm talkin' about," he guessed. "I'm tellin' 'em what they're doin' around the corner, and they can't figure that out. 'Mr. Hillard, how you know that?' Well, I *been* around that corner when I was their age—that's how I know."

Leon's corner was on Chicago's West Side, where the northbound Chickenwing Express out of Arkansas had deposited his folks early in his boyhood. He came up poor, hungry, scrawny and, like most of the brothers on the block, "a little antiwhite"—the whites in his young experience consisting mostly of creditors and cops. He first picked up a basketball when he was 14, in some Y or Baptist gym or somewhere, and he learned to put it down as an act of survival. "Guys in the neighborhood used to muscle me around. Beat up on little guys. So I learned this dribblin' thang. Did what I saw Marques do, or what I *thought* I saw. Make that ball your trick."

He was just 18 when Abe Saperstein, the founding genius of the Trotters and still the reigning monopolist in black basketball talent, bought him straight out of high school for $350 a month. His mama had to sign the contract and see him off in his tatty backstreet clothes to catch up with the second unit in Johnson City, Tenn. Leon arrived green and scared among men old enough to be his father—"my *grand*father, man"—and jealous enough to freeze him back to the ghetto if they wanted. So he faded into the scenery, shy, silent, grinning his sly grin. "Put myself in a *likable* way, y'know?" Worked on his game, tappy-tapping the ball in a thousand hotel room floors until the guests downstairs howled for the house detective and his own arm hurt from his fingertips to his shoulder. Heard, saw and spoke no evil. *Who, me? Don't know nothin'.*

So the old Trotters adopted him. Called him "Junior." Bunked him with Sam Wheeler, the gifted road-company clown who might have succeeded Goose except that his skin was too light and his dunking hand was missing two and a half fingers. Got him off hot dogs and onto beefsteak to flesh up his frame—a skinny 5-7½ then, a wiry 5-11 even in his prime. Tutored him in show basketball when it wasn't yet all show—when you might still roll into a town all road-weary and find a home team heavy with ringers sitting in their locker room with all the lights out just to scare you. Hipped him to the etiquette of life with Abe—call him "Skip," and laugh at his jokes, and never ever beat him at bid whist. Admitted Leon to the pleasures of life: Sipping, smoking, balling, betting, jiving away the long hours on the bus. Even saw him off to church on Sundays under the wing of a seriously religious teammate—"although," Leon told me, smiling, "*that's* really not The Road. Y'know?"

His real mentor was Tatum, a shambling clown with coal-house skin, saucer eyes, a slappy walk, and a seven-foot wingspan affixed improbably to a six-three body. Goose was two men, Leon always thought—like Pagliacci. Brooding, dark and dangerous as a thunderhead until the moment they put on "Sweet Georgia Brown"; then, a brilliant black-in-blackface anachronism masking his wounds and his rages behind a stretchy minstrelman smile. He was mostly a loner on The Road, out of his own preference and the respect of his teammates for his violent temper. But Goose took to Leon, because Leon *was* likable and—just as important in Tatum's jealous eye—he wasn't Marques Haynes. Goose made Leon and Sam Wheeler his designated drivers, in a Fleetwood he bought from an uppity white dealer in Nashville for $9,000 in pennies. He let them tag along on his night prowls, sometimes buying out a whole nightclub for an evening just for them. He took his women in bunches, and then, when he had sent them home, kept Leon up to dawn just talking. "Teachin' me show business. Tellin' me tales of black."

Leon listened and learned. He rifled Goose's trick bag and, by imitation, mastered it. He cased entertainments from the Ice Capades to the Folies Bergere for what he could borrow. Timing. Movement. *Precision it down.* And he ripened his own game. He flung up rainbow-high two-hand setshots when Abe, a stubborn traditionalist, was around, and funky little one-hand jumpers when he wasn't. Leon set the beat for the rhythm section—the backcourt cats hopping the ball around a tight figure-eight weave and into the hole for Goose or Meadow or whoever to play with. He got his show dribble down to no worse than a bounce or two behind Marques, and good enough for Front Street when Marques cut out on his own. Different, too—streety and jazzy. "Marques was like a melody—da da da dum dee, da da da dum dee," Sam Wheeler said. "Leon was more like a rhythm piece—ditdidditdadadaditditdada."

What Leon never learned was going along. He fell into a kind of love-hate thing with Abe—tight with him and his family, but never at the expense of his own pride. He beat Abe at cards. ("Man, you ain't *supposed* to do that," his roomie Sam told him, but Leon did.) He hooted at Abe's attempts at coaching—instructing the Trotters, for example, to slow down the great George Mikan in an exhibition game by yanking on his pants. He sat stone-faced among the peals of black laughter at Abe's gags. ("Look at this oscar here," Abe would say, annoyed. "Didn't get the joke.") He kept bogarting Abe for better money, and when it wasn't forthcoming he walked away from the Trotters. Twice. In 1958, for a year with a breakaway team organized by Goose; in 1960, to start his own road club, thinking Goose's successor, Meadowlark, would follow. "Can't live without us, man," Leon said. "Cut off the head and the body will die."

Only Meadow didn't follow, and without him Leon and his partner Ducky Moore and their Harlem Ambassadors lasted maybe a year and a half. He had a time of it anyway; once, from a backwater town somewhere, he sent Abe a picture postcard of some cartoon cannibals stewing a missionary, with his own scrawled caption: "Thanks for the family recipe." But taking on the Trotters was more than Leon could manage, or afford. He had become a family man—had married Sandra, his neighborhood sweetie, and fathered the first of his three sons, and he finally had to throw in his hand. Folded the Ambassadors and drifted off with other road clubs, sometimes for shorter wages than Abe paid. What he wouldn't do was go back to the Trotters. Not until they begged him— he carried their come-back telegram around like a card of identity— and not until Abe was dead.

He had gone out smoking, a rebel kid with a Chicago rep, waggling a finger right in Abe's round-eyed face while his teammates scattered for shelter. But all the years of The Road buffed him smooth and broadened him. He would come home summers from Paris or Tokyo or someplace, a West Side brother with a bistro list and an acquaintance with good cognac, and would find the same old dudes sipping wine on the same old corner as if they had never moved. Leon discovered then the distance he had traveled from them. He saw in their eyes that they were dying there, and he didn't want to die with them.

So Leon came back to the Trotters and their mini-conglomerated new Chicago management a different man—road-wise, polished, bilingual in back-street and front-office English. "Not ghettoish, y'know— sophisticated." He did a year show-dribbling, and then the new crowd with the custom leisure suits and the State Street attaché cases made him a player-coach. Handed him the second company, the International Unit, a low-dollar, low-spirited assortment of egos, cliques and attitudes, and told him to whip them into shape.

And Leon did. He got dazzling shows out of the team's veteran star, Showboat Hall, exploiting Boat's genius Trotter hands and working around his mercurial humors. He taught his own game to Pablo Robertson, a playground hero out of Harlem and Loyola, and helped make him a star at the risk of his own future as a player. He got his guys on speaking terms with the white opposition, and—almost as difficult—with each other. He put on one marvelous season, the kind old Trotters talk about like wine-sippers admiring a '62 Lafite Rothschild. "Chanting them on like a witch doctor," one teammate remembered—hop it now, down in, back out, on the money, *bang!*

He did almost too well—got himself promoted against his easy nature to the big team and the staticky company of Meadow George Lemon, by then Goose's successor as clown prince on the court and autocrat of the locker room. Leon handled the Lark Question by accepting him as given, and concentrated instead on bringing along the younger Trotters—the sassy asphalt stylists from Harlem and Brooklyn and Chicago's South Side with their superfly games and their flashpoint sensitivities. *Leon know what time it is,* they told each other, and he hipped them to it. The game and the life. The wisdom of The Road reduced to a thousand sayings:

Pack light.

Travel loose.

Send some home on payday.

Chase them messy gals all night if you want, but stay out of the papers, and save 40 good minutes for me and the customers.

If you got a game, play it. But none of that eye-rollin', Stepin' Fetchit stuff—got nothin' to do with the rest of black people and it demeans *you.*

If a dude makes a mistake, leave him alone—you think he *want* to look bad in front of 10,000 people? I made mistakes, and I *been* here.

Do it right and you won't have to do it over. What goes round comes round.

You get what your hand called for.

Nothin' from nothin' is nothin'.

Leon coached with skill and played with Indian-summer magic—well enough to bring the halftime jugglers and trampolinists back from their dressing rooms to watch him do his thing in the third quarter. What he lacked was a certain entrepreneurial regard for bottom lines, and the distance they require between boss and employee. A lifetime of short checks and tall promises had left him incurably suspicious of every management he ever played for—even when he became part of management himself. His view of proprietors was something like his rule for defensing a dude trying to shake-an-bake his way past you to the basket. "Don't look at the cat's feet, man, cause he'll shuffle on you and get away. Stand back and look at *him*. It's survival."

That stand-back distance, subversive for a player, was downright seditious for a coach. Leon encouraged the help to demand money for value, and hassled the front office for bonuses for them. Once, he even said no. He had just dragged into Dayton at 3 or 4 in the morning, the players bus-weary and heavy-eyed, and there in the hotel lobby was the local promoter sweating and fidgeting over his sluggish ticket sales. "Leon," he said, "you got to put five or six of the guys out on the corner at 8 in the morning and do a little clowning—I got a TV crew lined up." Leon stiffened, knowing it would get him in trouble and not caring. " 'Cause, see," he said, "all the time in the years before, the promoters thought the Globetrotters was *machines*. And we had to act like machines, and I was a part of that. But this time I made a decision." He chuckled. "A *major* decision. I looked back at the guy and said, 'I can't help you.' I said, 'The men are tired.' I said, '*You* got to sell your tickets. What *we* do is come in and do your show.' "

The time finally came when Leon figured you don't even do that— when he and his main man Bobby Hunter and a couple of fellow heretics led the elves out on strike against Santa Claus. Mutinies had been tried before on the Trotters, and Abe had always got the jump on them, dispensing a hundred or so here, shuffling a roster there, once sacking practically his whole team and hiring a new one. So Leon moved stealthily. *Sophisticated.* He talked to the players, one by one, then in little midnight black caucuses. "Y'know, if we stopped tomorrow, they can't get no *white* Globetrotters." He got them a downtown white labor lawyer. He and Hunter collected their grievances and then their signatures on union pledge cards—everybody's, in the end, except Meadowlark's. And finally they dispatched the news to the management, with their ultimatum: "By this date and time, if we do not be recognized as a union, we will not be performin'."

This time, to their own surprise nearly as much as management's, the Trotters were serious—dead serious enough to fold the show one night in Port Huron, Mich., and hunker down in their motel for most of a prime-time month in the late autumn of '71. It was only that first day Leon reminisced about with any real pleasure—the guys painting up their picket signs and peeping out through the venetian blinds at the arena across the street. "People was flockin' there, and we was laughin' all up our sleeves—they thought it was a Globetrotter *joke*." After that it was a siege, a dozen black guys in a motel spending their last checks and watching each other's eyes and wondering if they would wilt before the guys in the leisure suits.

They won, sort of—got their players association recognized, and doubled the average annual wage to something over $30,000, and pried loose some concessions, including meal money and premium pay for doubleheaders. But their victory, and their union, lasted roughly the three-year life of their first contract. Old faces started disappearing, all for reasons accepted in professional sports as sound. Showboat Hall was pronounced too old at 45; Pablo Robertson flunked his team physical; Bobby Hunter, the union president, got beat out of his job in training camp; some bad-ass city kids were cut for economy or supplanted by new recruits from the Southern black colleges. And Leon? Leon was one of the first to go. He couldn't cut it as a player any more, they told him, and the coaching jobs were taken by Meadow and Marques. They sent him home to Sandra and the boys with $14,000 in severance pay, but no pension. He never looked back. *Nothin' from nothin' is nothin'.*

But he did bring something home from The Road—a vocation for kids that he discovered on a Trotter tour a world away from home. "It was Africa—North Africa," he remembered, "and I learned a lesson there. From some kids, orphan kids, the oldest one about 12 years old. Not even brothers or sisters or anything—wasn't no parent over them. Just kids like you see dogs in the street, wanderin' around, tryin' to survive. *For each other.*" Remembering them Leon's eyes began flooding, and his voice thickened. "And it just opened my mind, y'know? 'Cause I didn't know thangs then about humanitarianism.

" 'Cause, see, these kids followed us. Came up behind you and kind of touched on your elbow, and when you turned around, they'd be pointin' at their mouths, goin *ahhhh! Ahhhh!* And people had told us not to give 'em nothin'—'They're thieves, they're this, they're that.' But they followed Sam Wheeler and me to this restaurant—had an open door where you could just go in and see out on the streets. And these kids sat out there on the curb watchin' us eat, y'know, and we felt really bad.

"So when we left the restaurant, they followed us back, and we gave 'em some money anyway, spite of the fact that they told us not to. We got back to the hotel and went up, and we was watchin' them out the window." Leon sniffled loudly. "And they disappeared—we didn't see 'em for 15 or 20 minutes, and then they came back. Sittin' on the curb. They had went to the store and got bread. Meat. And they set there, and this 12-year-old, he divided that bread and that meat into seven pieces.

They didn't argue—'Well, you got more than me!' Just divided it. Survivin' for each other. And I started thinkin'—those kind of kids, y'know, and if they could do that why couldn't *we* do that?" He was weeping now at the memory. "I always stay away from that," he apologized, "but it had a lot to do with my life. Made me want to have somethin' to do with kids' lives."

So Leon went back to the corner, to compete with the dope dealers, the gang-bangers and the storefront Marxist-Leninists for souls. For a while, he answered too many freelance distress calls from too many community groups and playground workers and plain messed-up families. "He was always moving 50 directions at once," Hunter remembers, "and ten minutes late for everything." It was almost as if he thought he could go one on one against death. Once, a lady with a kid on heroin called for help; Leon talked to the boy for four hours, made a few phone calls, and had him in a withdrawal clinic before the night was out. Another time, a street blood came at him with a piece, and Leon kung-fued him with words. "I mean, man, just shoot me, 'cause I'm tellin' you what's real. You done went to the movie and think you're Superfly or somebody, and I'm tellin you where you gonna end up at—one-to-five, boy, a dollar a day, and then you either *gonna* be dead or *wish* you was dead, 'cause you gonna be a vegetable walkin' around in these streets." The blood backed off.

It took Leon until his last year or so to get his act really together —to connect his streety wizardry with people organized to make it last. He tried for a while with the Abe Saperstein Foundation, but it got nearly as heavy working for Abe's ghost as it had been working for Abe. So he cut out, along with Bob Love, then Chicago's reigning black NBA hero, and Chick Sherrer, a close white pal who used to organize basketball camps for the NBA, and they started AFBE—Athletes For Better Education. The centerpiece of their year-round program was a two-week summer getaway for kids off the block, basketball plus saturation three-R academics plus Leonology 101-102—those rudimentary arts of life and survival known more formally as citizenship.

Leon didn't live long enough to get it really grooving, and his heirs at AFBE are left with their might-have-beens. Like the time at the first camp when one kid stole something from another, and the staff called all 125 campers together for a late-night meeting. Love was there, and Artis Gilmore of the Chicago Bulls, and a bunch of college All-Americans, but it was Leon who handled the problem—talked on nonstop for an hour about manhood and responsibility. *Survivin' for each other.* "And he just captured the entire audience," Sherrer remembers. "I mean, like nobody rustled, nobody made a noise, nobody got up to go to the bathroom. And at the end of the discussion, the kid who took whatever it was got up, tears in his eyes, and said, 'I took it.' And gave it back and apologized, and the whole camp just burst into applause."

Leon for the first time had it all—all, that is, except time. He lived out at the edge and knew it, going anywhere, confronting anybody, caring and not caring what happened to him. "I'm gonna go violently," he began saying. "There's too many things out here I can't control." He and his mother were close, in that bonding common to black families, and when she died last year, he dreamed one night that he was going, too. Felt a cleansing steal over him, and saw her standing in the room smiling at him, and suddenly he was face down on the floor, coming awake hollering, "Don't shoot! Don't shoot!"

What he didn't see was where death was coming from. He knew what The Road can do to a family—had seen too many of them come apart over the short bread, the long absences and the seven-day, uptown-Saturday-night atmosphere. He had come back to Sandra with a worldly estate consisting of less than $1,000 a year for all those years away and the mortgage on their two-flat in a fading South Side neighborhood. His youth work couldn't pay the bills, and even when he got his Lemmy's hotdog franchise going on a federal loan secured by his own sweat, economics remained a source of tension in the family. And so did the habits of The Road. Globetrotter men tend to spend their summer furloughs on their best behavior, Leon once told me, because Globetrotter women "know what he been doin' out there." The trouble comes when the men can't leave the life behind—and the gossip attending Leon's death was that he couldn't.

There was talk of another woman; of Leon banging the bottle, though no one who knew him well saw or believed it; or quarrels over love and money so bitter that the Hillards, once devoted, started talking about divorce. The official investigation did not scratch much deeper than the chatter. The fatal shooting of one black person by another is known in the argot of Chicago criminal justice as a nigger disorderly, and there was no evident reason to question Sandra Hillard's story. Yes, she told the police, she and Leon had argued till she walked out on him and took refuge with her mother downstairs. Leon, she said, phoned down and threatened mayhem unless she came home. She didn't, and, as she told it to the police, Leon came storming after her, splintered the door loose from its jamb, and, silhouetted in the empty frame, stopped a slug fired by his own wife from his own gun. It was, under the law, a justifiable homicide—deadly force in self-defense against deadly force.

They gave Leon Hillard a funeral, and everybody came. Or almost everybody; the Globetrotters' home office, since reconglomerated into Metromedia in Los Angeles, kept its silent distance, and only a couple of its currently employed hands showed up. But Bob Love came to help bear Leon's pall, and Ernie Banks, and Bobby Hunter, of course, and Old Sweets Clifton, now a cabbie in Chicago, and a lot of people nobody but Leon ever heard of. In his eulogy, Chick Sherrer mentioned how I had asked Hunter who was Leon's best friend; Hunter had automatically answered that *he* was—then reconsidered and guessed that there would be a lot of competition. There was. The friends of Leon Hillard overflowed the funeral and filled a hundred cars going to the graveyard, seeing Leon to the end of The Road.

Sandy Grady

Cruncher

"A three-beer man . . . but a good boy," is how a local bartender described the Philadelphia Eagles' Chuck Bednarik. A cruncher *he was, the most lasting fame coming to him after he put the ferocious hit on Frank Gifford that ended Gifford's career. In 1960, when this story was written for* Saga *magazine by the then* Philadelphia Bulletin *sports columnist, Sandy Grady, Bednarik was thirty-five years old, coaxed out of retirement and playing most of that championship season for the Eagles as both linebacker and center. An intimate look at the last of pro football's two-way gladiators.*

He didn't need an alarm clock. The big man had his own private clock wound tight. At 8:30 it clanged deep in his mind. The big man shuffled his 230 pounds and stared blinking at the ceiling. He had taken two sleeping pills to sink him into this dreamless coma. Now he fought his way back to life, like a fighter getting off the deck. The big man could hear his four daughters squealing over their toys downstairs—it was the day after Christmas. He could hear the subdued murmur of Philadelphia suburban traffic from outside on Pennsylvania Route 611.

This was going to be the biggest damn day of Chuck Bednarik's life, and suddenly he knew it, and he catapulted out of the bed as if burned. In five hours he would be on the winter-gray turf of Franklin Field. He would have to play almost 60 minutes against Green Bay. If they were 60 good minutes, Philadelphia might win the pro football championship. Bednarik was 35 years old. He had endured jolts and bruises through a dozen games for this moment. Now he had to wad up the whole ball of his middle-aged comeback and gamble it on one hour of action.

"Hey, Chuck," Emma Bednarik called, "I've got coffee and scrambled eggs and toast and jelly and . . ."

She was kidding. It was a ritual. Bednarik scowled at the unshaven, heavy jaw in the mirror. The thought of food almost made him sick. He knew the tension was starting early.

By 9:30 Bednarik was dressed. He went outside to taste the weather, the way a fisherman will sniff the wind before shoving off. Bednarik walked on the lawn, still patched with old snow. The quiet Abington street of $40,000 homes was a long way from the old Bednarik household, hidden in the steel-slag haze of Bethlehem.

He checked the watch: 9:45. The tigers inside him were doing cartwheels now. Even at Bethlehem High he'd felt them some. At Penn during those All-American years, he'd felt the tigers churning a little before the big games. Before each of the 30 missions as a B-24 gunner over Europe, the tigers had somersaulted in Bednarik's stomach. That was different. The 11 pro seasons had quieted the old tigers. Until this year, that is. It had been one helluva season, every game for the money, ten wins, with Bednarik under pressure as a center and linebacker. The tigers flipped inside before every game, but he knew this was going to be the worst.

"Emma, I think I'll drive down and start dressing," said Bednarik.

It was casual as a broker, a salesman, a 9-to-5 clerk telling his wife he was heading for the office. "It's gonna be a cinch, baby," said Bednarik, going out the door. "It's gonna be nice and cold. I could play all day in this weather."

He knew he was lying, backing the maroon Pontiac station wagon out of the garage. He had been tired, racked up and the air coming in hot gasps, a couple of times this year. The first time he'd tried this 60-minute trick, the sultry day in Cleveland, had been no picnic. He'd been mad as hell at Paul Brown or he would never have gone the route. He was 35 and he couldn't lie to his legs. He had retired twice before, but this time he had meant it. He had the good job with the concrete outfit. He was still amazed when he thought about the whole weird deal. Here he was, a beat-up old linebacker, driving to a stadium to play for the National Football League championship, when he should be out hustling concrete.

Bednarik began wheeling faster, beating the cars away from the lights, the tension gnawing. He had to stop Hornung on that option pass play. Hell, Gifford was the best at that play and the Eagles had handled him, hadn't they? He had to watch Starr on those swing passes. There were going to be a lot of trap plays. If somebody sucked in, he'd have to handle Jim Taylor alone. The movies don't lie about Taylor. He runs like hell.

The tigers were doing their acrobatic williwaws inside Bednarik now. Before he reached Franklin Field he'd pick up two candy bars. He needed the energy. He hoped he could get one of them down.

Chuck Bednarik didn't know where the big season began. How do you reach back and put a finger on the flow of time and say, This is where it started? Maybe it began the year he was 16, a skinny kid who wanted to be a fullback, and Jack Butler at Bethlehem High said, "C'mere, Bednarik, you got three days to learn to be a center." Did it start that far back—or the day he came out of the Air Force and decided to go to Penn? Or the day on the train he popped off to Greasy Neale. Bednarik was a rookie then on the 1949 championship Eagles, and Neale was a tough guy, but Bednarik cornered him on the train: "I'm tired of sitting on my butt—play me or trade me to somebody who will." Greasy stuck him in against the Chicago Cardinals, and somehow he avoided getting killed. There were 145 pro games after that one, and Bednarik missed only one. Bednarik liked to remember that. When he could walk, he would play.

But this season had been wildly absurd. It was something Bednarik hardly dared dream after a half-dozen gin-and-tonics. Bednarik knew this shouldn't be a championship team. Too many rookies, too many old guys. Bednarik knew at 35 he shouldn't be playing 60 minutes. Sam Huff, Les Richter, Joe Schmidt—those guys wouldn't do it. Yet here he was.

Maybe it began last spring on the day he went to the Eagles' office. Just a nice, spring day in Philadelphia, the girls swishing along Locust St. in their summer dresses.

"I hear you and Emma have a new baby on the way, Chuck," said Vince McNally. "Congratulations."

"Thanks," said Bednarik. He watched McNally light another cigarette across the desk. McNally is an ex–Knute Rockne quarterback, a trim, white-haired man who is general manager of the Eagles.

"Chuck, you might regret quitting football. All right, so you'll be 35. You're still in great shape."

"I don't want anybody pitying me," said Bednarik. "I couldn't stand to slow up and look like a bum out there."

"Believe me, Chuck," said McNally, his eyes narrowing behind the horn rims, "the Eagles need you this year. I wouldn't make this offer if

I thought you'd slowed up. I think you need us, too, with your new responsibilities."

"I've got a job. It's time I started to earn a living."

McNally lit another cigarette. He picked up an envelope on the desk. He penciled down a figure: $2000. It wouldn't look a decent raise to a baseball player. A pitcher would laugh. A quarterback would laugh. Bednarik is an old lineman. Old linemen don't laugh at two grand.

"You know we haven't made any money," said McNally. "We've had losing teams. Buck Shaw wants you badly. Talk to Emma about it. Think it over."

"I've thought it over," said Bednarik. "Hell, maybe I knew I'd do this all along. Gimme the contract."

McNally stubbed out the cigarette and grinned.

An old lineman's version of hell starts in July. The pro training camps are stuck in alien hamlets of Wisconsin and Minnesota and the Pennsylvania hills. It is supposed to be cool. It never is. The old lineman's enemy is the sun that sweats out the beer and the sirloin steaks and the mashed potatoes. The wind sprints are brutal, and the scrimmages are no rest. There is always a rookie who wants to make a quick reputation. There is always a rookie who wants to knock an old lineman on his sweaty, disgusted, bored, tired rear end.

The Eagles train in Hershey, Pennsylvania. There is the aroma of chocolate on the wind. The hills are green. The heat beats on them in brassy waves. The rookies dress quickly in the gray sweat suits, eager for the calisthenics the old pros hate.

"You're going for a nice vacation," Emma Bednarik said, needling her husband. "You're getting away from the girls and all the racket here. You'll loaf up in those cool hills."

Bednarik groaned. Cool hills. Nuts. He had tried to stay in shape always. A little gin in the summer didn't hurt. He cut down the cigarettes. No bread-and-butter. Plenty of golf. Still it hurt to run the first few days in that damnable sun.

"He's a three-beer man, Chuck Bednarik," said the bartender proudly in one of Hershey's few spas. "Chuck's in here 15 minutes after practice. Whoo-eee, he's hot. Fast as I can draw 'em, he knocks off three draft beers. That's all I see of Chuck Bednarik. He's in bed by 10. Thirsty, but a good boy."

Bednarik was toughening the 240 pounds now. His snapbacks to Norm Van Brocklin were sharp. Bednarik watched the kids passing through camp rapidly as street cars. The Eagles had won seven, lost five, the year before. Buck Shaw needed blocking. He needed a lot of things. The club was too patchy for a title, even with Van Brocklin's arm. Maxie Baughan, a red-haired kid from Georgia Tech, looked tough working at linebacker with Chuck Weber and Bob Pellegrini. Huh, linebacking wasn't Bednarik's worry now, though. He was a center.

"Why don't you come over to the defensive meetings, Chuck," said Jerry Williams, who drew the defense's diagrams. "You can't tell. You may need this stuff someday."

"Okay, I'll drop in," said Bednarik. He did sit through a half-lecture, but he sneaked out the door, restless with the Xs on the blackboard. What did they expect him to do, play 60 minutes?

Chuck Bednarik's season began in Cleveland. The Eagles had played a lot of football before that. They had mildly surprised themselves by winning all five exhibitions. In Philadelphia people snickered that McNally was staging another ticket-selling drive. It looked true when the Browns waffled the Eagles, 41–24, in the home opener. The Eagles went to Dallas and stole one, 27–25. They came home and beat the Cards, then stopped the Lions solidly. The plane ride to Cleveland was quiet. Beating the Browns in their own park was like trying to steal a hunk of beef from a lion.

"Hey, Chuck, get in! Get in! Pelly's hurt!"

Guys were banging Bednarik on his back, shoving him toward the field. It had been the third play of the game. Bednarik had been resting on the bench. A Cleveland run swept out of his line of vision. He didn't see Bob Pellegrini flattened in the violent mob, painfully hurt. When he leaped up, Bednarik knew Pelly was down, though. The fire bell in his mind clanged. Hell, this might be a ball. He hadn't gone both ways since he was at Penn.

"Wait a minute, Chuck." Shaw grabbed his arm. "Don't be a hero. If you get tired, let me know."

Bednarik jammed on the helmet. He took the wide, crouching stance at the left linebacker slot. Tom Brookshier yelled something about a pass pattern. Bednarik didn't hear. He was suddenly embroiled in a gulf of Brown blockers.

They came at him again on the second play. There was a sharp twinge in his thigh. He felt as though he'd been stabbed with an icepick. Bednarik didn't want to limp. He wanted to stay in now.

The Cleveland slotback had lined up on his right. The end, Gern Nagler, was on his left. The slotback feinted a block. Bednarik turned to bounce him off, catching a glimpse of Bobby Mitchell hurtling around his end. What he didn't see was the end, who hit him from the blind side, because this was a play the Browns call "The Clip." Bednarik's 235 pounds somersaulted in the air so viciously he landed on his feet. Somehow he helped Jimmy Carr bring down Mitchell.

Bednarik lay in the grass in front of the Cleveland bench. He didn't really want to move. Then he glanced up and saw Paul Brown. Under the snapbrim hat, Brown was laughing as though Bednarik was the most comic figure since Fatty Arbuckle was hit with his last lemon pie.

"Bednarik," said Brown, "you're too damn old for this game."

Bednarik was off the grass now. Fast. He unleashed a torrent of abuse. His thick neck was red with anger. When someone jostled Bednarik away, Brown wasn't laughing.

"How's the leg, Chuck?" Dr. Mike Mandarino said at the half.

"It's nothing," mumbled Bednarik. "A little muscle pull. Damn, it's hot out there."

They packed ice around the leg, but anger was Bednarik's private antidote for the pain. "Jeez, I called that Brown things I oughta apologize for," said Bednarik in the clubhouse. "Not even my own father could say that to me, though—that I'm an old bum. I'm gonna show that sonofabitch how old No. 60 is."

The chance came quickly. The Eagles had to stop the Browns on the goal stripe. Jimmy Brown came rumbling through the hole, churning high. Bednarik had the open shot, and he hit Brown with every ounce of his anger, lifting him like a sack of sugar. There were 30 seconds left when Bednarik snapped the ball to the field goal kicker, Bobby Walston. Bednarik held the block for the three-count.

"Boot like hell, Cheewah," Bednarik thought.

The wind was in his face, and the posts were 38 yards away, but the kick was good. The Eagles had won, 31–29. Bednarik had made 15 tackles, 11 of them unassisted.

"How d'ya like that Paul Brown?" Bednarik said to Walston as they sat in the clubhouse. "He had a real smirky smile on his face when he left the field."

"Helluva game, Chuck," said Pellegrini.

"Thanks, Gringo," said Bednarik.

He limped off the plane at Philadelphia and skipped the parties. Emma Bednarik had to massage the left thigh until Bednarik could sleep. The long ordeal of Charles Bednarik had begun.

Buck Shaw laughed the next day. "No, I can't expect Bednarik to play 59 minutes the next seven games. Oh, he'd try to do it if I asked.

But that routine would be too tough for a guy 15 years younger than Chuck."

Bednarik wasn't laughing. He woke up with a numb leg. Emma fixed a dish he loves, called "pig-in-a-bag." He didn't want to eat. In the late afternoon, Bednarik and defensive end Ed Khayat hoisted a ladder and hung storm windows on the big house. Bednarik felt better.

The next two weeks were almost a holiday. The Eagles caught Bobby Layne with his dauber down, and they blew through Pittsburgh, 34–7. Bednarik intercepted a pass to set up a touchdown. He was a linebacker now, as Shaw tried to rest him by using rookie Bill Lapham at center. The next game was with the Redskins, who almost blitzed Van Brocklin loose from his handsome teeth before Dutch pulled it out, 19–13.

After the game, Bednarik threw a wingding. The pros, who won't avoid a little fluid celebrating after a victory, said it was the best party of the year. Chuck had 78 people milling through his paneled den in the basement. Bednarik likes gin-and-tonic, a drink associated with Bermuda shorts and sunny beaches. He likes 'em in the snow, if necessary. Usually the Bednarik limit is two. That night he was in a swinging mood.

"I got a lot of trophies in this room," Chuck said to a few of the bulls at the party. "I want one more."

"Which one, Chuck baby?"

"You know damn well which one," said Bednarik. "The big one. See all those team pictures? I want one of the 1960 Eagles. And under it I want it to say, 'N.F.L. CHAMPIONS.' "

"That's a surprise," said somebody. "I thought you wanted it to say, 'To hell with Paul Brown.' "

Bednarik laughed. It was a good party. But the Giants would be ready in Yankee Stadium the next Sunday. The Giants didn't give a damn about Bednarik's dream or the Eagles' 6–1 record. The Giants would be cruel and crafty—they had not overlooked the way the Redskins had blitzed Van Brocklin flat on his satin britches.

Bednarik could have reached into the grab bag of Manhattan and picked any bauble on this crisp, lively Saturday night. Mary Martin was packing them in with *The Sound of Music.* Tammy Grimes had opened a new musical and Ethel Merman was still blaring through *Gypsy.* The taxis hooted through the canyons to the good East Side restaurants, and the night clubs were jumping. But Bednarik is not a bright lights guy. He was in New York to play the Giants and, as usual, the tigers of tension had their claws in him.

So he stood on a corner of Times Square with his roommate, John Nocera, for two hours, watching the swirl of the mob past the hot dog joints on 42nd Street.

"It's a big town, Nose," said Bednarik, unrecognized by the shoals of milling sightseers.

"Yeah? Well, we'll shake it up tomorrow," said Nocera.

Bednarik grunted. "Huh. Know how long since we've beaten these guys over here, Nose? Not since Jim Trimble's first year, 1952, when we caught 'em 14–10. That's eight in a row here. I think about those things, Nose." Bednarik flipped a cigarette, Bogart-style, and headed for the hotel. Maybe he could sleep a little.

The Eagle blocking pattern for a pass has the center sliding back to form one rim of the passer's cup. The halfbacks swing out for a safety valve pass. The Giants had howling success with this gimmick the first half. They roared through it like pillaging Indians. Bednarik, assigned to be a linebacker only, watched in dismay as center Bill Lapham was knocked into inept confusion by the blitz. The Giants gobbled up Van Brocklin like barracuda hitting a wounded porpoise. They led 10–0 at the half. Goodbye, Dreamsville.

"Okay, Sam, the fun's over," Bednarik said to Sam Huff, the Giant linebacker. "The veterans are taking over."

Huff and Bednarik like each other, and Sam grinned at Bednarik's bravado. He knew the Giants could win if they kept the blitz moving. Bednarik had the plan from line coach Nick Skorich to stop it. No more fancy blocking. The halfbacks would stay tight. Bednarik and the other linemen would form a wall. It worked, and Van Brocklin tied it 10–10.

Now Bednarik, back at his full-time job, caught the jungle flavor and smell of the game. Mel Triplett, the good Giant fullback, came through the hole on a slant. Bednarik bombed him, the ball squirted up like a hunk of wet soap, and Carr took it on the fly for a touchdown. It was 17–10, but the Giants were driving back to tie it. They flipped the ball to Gifford, the one guy who could run all the way for the money.

Gifford, a runner who never made a mistake, made a near-fatal one now. He tried to feint Don Burroughs. He took his eye off Bednarik. Chuck hit him chest-high with every ounce of power, trying to shatter the ball loose. Gifford flopped on the turf, inert as stone. Most of the 63,571 fans would not soon forget the sight of Bednarik, dancing wildly over Gifford's body, shaking his fist in conquest, yelling his triumph.

"We got the ball! We got it!" Bednarik was screaming.

The Giant doctor, bent over Gifford, snapped, "Shut up, you damn gorilla. You've almost killed this man." He said worse things, too, and Bednarik suddenly realized Gifford might indeed be hurt.

"You hit him hard, Chuck," said Huff, level-eyed.

"I got excited, Sam," said Bednarik.

"Pros don't get excited, Chuck," said Huff.

In the locker room, though, Huff shrugged off the smashing tackle. Gifford was in the hospital with a severe concussion, his career ended. "It's a tough business," said Huff. "Chuck hit him clean."

Chuck Conerly, the only pro on the field who had been around as long as Bednarik, was burning, though. "Bednarik's a cheap-shot artist," snarled Conerly. "I told him so, too."

"The Giants will take care of Bednarik next week," said a New York writer walking out of Yankee Stadium. "They're mad as hell. The pros know how to handle a guy like that."

All week the telephone rang in the Abington house. Did Bednarik figure the Giants would gang him in revenge for Gifford? "If they do," Bednarik said, "you'll see the biggest coward in the world. I'll run like hell. Nobody's gonna suck me into a fight to get me out of the game. This one we've gotta win."

He sent Gifford a card of apology and a bowl of fruit. It was only a token, though. Bednarik knew the tackle had been hard—but necessary and legitimate. Bednarik vastly enjoys publicity. He loves flash-bulbs popping and the interviews and the headlines and the kids swarming for autographs. Now he was getting a bad rap coast-to-coast for hurting Gifford. He tried to ignore it, but he didn't know how the Giants would react.

Bednarik remembered another old pro, his rookie year, who felled Charlie Trippi and almost crippled him. He remembered the way the Chicago Cardinals waited for this guy until the next game. Then they took turns whacking him with everything, getting 15-yard penalties in bundles. After the game in the runway the old pro was trapped by a half-dozen Cardinals, swinging helmets. Bednarik didn't want this sort of scene with the Giants.

"To hell with it," Bednarik said, "we've got a title to win now. The only Giant who blew his top is Conerly, who's a sour grapes bum with a glorified column in that New York paper."

Bednarik was right. No Giant took a shot at him. They had their opportunities, because before the game, Shaw tapped Chuck on the shoulder pad: "Sorry, Chuck, I'll need you both ways again today." He played almost 60 minutes again, and the Eagles, running as always like

Silky Sullivan on his good days, bellowed back on two Van Brocklin touchdowns to win it, 31–23.

"How'd you like to play 60 minutes, Sam?" Bednarik said sweetly to Huff.

"Man," said Huff, "there ain't that much money in the world."

The cops said there were 15,000 people at the airport. The Eagles had taken the Eastern title in St. Louis, and Bednarik peered in astonishment out the DC-6 window at the mob, the TV flood lights, the bands blaring. Most of the Eagles tried a flank movement, sneaking out the front hatch and running for their cars. Not Bednarik. He had waited 11 years for this crowd.

"I promise you," said Bednarik, "no matter who we play, we'll win the world title for Philadelphia."

Immense roar. He might have offered to abolish taxes and give away free booze. Bednarik, beaming over the bow tie, shuffled through the victory pack, shaking hands, scrawling his name on kids' windbreakers.

There were two left now, the Steelers and the Redskins, meaningless games, and Shaw wanted to keep Bednarik out of them. It was like inviting Jackie Leonard to a cocktail party and forbidding him to tell jokes. Bednarik's No. 60 seemed to appear in the midst of every gang tackle.

"It's not luck, it's instinct," marveled Skorich. "You've heard of people being accident prone, Bednarik is tackle prone. If the play's on his side, he'll get a piece of it. Sure, Huff and Les Richter and Joe Schmidt get the publicity. This guy is the best."

Now it was four days before the Green Bay match. On the snow-lined practice field, the seven bulls made seven puffs of blue vapor in the frozen, bruised air. They looked like seven laundry bags in the grey sweat suits.

"Kamikaze!" yelled Bednarik as the bulls rumbled after an imaginary Green Bay punt receiver.

"Kamikaze!" the bulls bellowed in a ragged chorus.

"Kamikaze, baby, kamikaze!"

Later a guy asked Bednarik who started this curious battle yell. "I did," said Bednarik. "We're like those Japanese pilots. This is our last fight and we're not coming back."

A couple of newspaper types were having a glass of grog to fight off the cold later. One shook his head at Bednarik's theatrics.

"Can you imagine Cousy or Mantle or Spahn or Musial coming up with that kamikaze stuff," he said. "On anybody else it would sound absurd. On Bednarik it sounds normal, because he's really the gung-ho type. He plays for the money, but beneath it all, he's still a soph at Penn, getting ready for Notre Dame."

His companion quaffed the glass. "Yeah, I guess that's one reason I hope Bednarik has one helluva game against Green Bay. He reminds me a little of Archie Moore. Not only the newspaper color. I mean the way Chuck's been beating around for years, playing his guts out, but not getting the championships or the big money or the national acclaim."

"It's like Van Brocklin said," agreed the other. "If he were in New York, they'd build a statue of Bednarik in the centerfield of Yankee Stadium."

"Well, here's a big one Monday."

"To Monday. . . ."

Now Monday's clock ticked loud as a hammer on a tin roof inside Bednarik. It was 10:30. He walked into the Eagles' clubhouse. The stadium above was warming with pale sunlight and early clots of people. Bednarik had a cup of hot chocolate. Other Eagles drifted in. It was explosively quiet. You could hear shoes plop on the concrete.

"We gotta win this one, you jokers," yelled Bednarik. "My wife's already spent the money."

The tension rippled but it did not break. The Eagles dressed in taut silence. No one laughed when Van Brocklin tried to put his left shoe on his right foot a half-dozen times. Bednarik, who sometimes makes fight talks before Eagle games, was wise enough to stay mute. Shaw walked into the cluttered, narrow room and said that no matter what happened against Green Bay, this has been the proudest year of his life. Shaw, too, knew the money and the pride was out in the field now, and no speeches were needed.

"Let's go kick a few tails," said Bednarik. The Eagles clumped out into the pasty sunshine, following the "60" on the green back. The Star-Spangled Banner floated over the jammed arena, and Bednarik felt the tigers inside, snarling and leaping. They did not subside until he hit the first Packer. He hit him hard.

Bednarik had to work like hell the first 15 minutes. The Packers twice got the ball inside the 25. Jim Taylor, their fine fullback, and Paul Hornung, the gifted halfback, had to be stopped. The Eagles scrambled ahead, 10–6, but Hornung threatened to run them out of the park in the second half. It was fourth down. Tough yardage. Hornung stormed right and cut for a hole. Bednarik crunched a shoulder into him with the mindless violence of freight train hitting a sports car. Hornung dropped and twisted in terrible pain. Trainers came running.

"Oh, my God," thought Bednarik. "First Gifford, now this."

In the time out, Bednarik turned to one of the Eagles. "I hit him a good shot. There wasn't nothing wrong with that tackle." They had carried Hornung away, finished with a pinched nerve in the shoulder that hurt like a hundred toothaches.

"You hit him damn good, Chuck," said the Eagle.

The Eagles had a 13–10 lead, but the last nine minutes would be frenzied. The Packers looked for the knockout punch, like a tough fighter losing a decision. Bednarik gobbled up a Max McGee fumble, which helped. Then the clock was spinning in chill blue dusk.

Last play. A pass to Taylor. He came rumbling, knocking down Eagles, 17 yards away from the championship.

"I saw guys bounce off him," Bednarik would say later, bringing back the vivid moment. "I saw Baughan hit and bounce, Burroughs hit and bounce. I said, by God, I'm not gonna bounce, I'm gonna catch him in a bearhug and hold him. I wrestled him down and I held him tight, watching the clock run. Then I said, 'Okay, Taylor, get up. This is one game that's over.' "

Bednarik had made 11 tackles and played 58 minutes and been incredibly good for a shaky antique. He wanted one more gift now: the white Corvette a sports magazine bequeaths to the game's outstanding player. The writers voted for Van Brocklin, though. Somebody told Bednarik.

"Quarterbacks," he said with a shrug. There was no malice. Quarterbacks are part of the lineman's world, like flying elbows and cracked teeth.

He had the picture he wanted for the den now: the three tiers of hard-jawed faces, 37 guys in the green blazers, Bednarik looming over them all in a candy-striped tie, with the legend: "1960 Eagles—World Champions." He had the fame that only a championship can harvest in American sports. He could laugh at Paul Brown for sneering at his age, and he could forget the years he played savage football while other linebackers on winning teams got the acclaim.

One ingredient was left for Bednarik's apple-pie world: the money.

"I've never given you a hard time about the salary," Chuck said, sitting again in Vince McNally's office at Locust and 12th Streets. "You've always had the contract ready and boom-boom I signed."

"True, Chuck," said McNally, beginning to chain smoke, knowing what was coming. "We wanted to pay you more but—"

"I know. You weren't drawing people and couldn't pay big salaries. Only now it's different. You drew 350,000 people. You made money. I played my heart out for you. Nobody else in the league went 60 minutes."

"You did a wonderful job," said McNally. "What's on your mind?"

"This," said Bednarik. It was his time to scribble on the envelope. The figure was close to a $6,000 raise. McNally began to blow smoke in furious clouds. It was a modest request compared to paychecks of Mantle, Mays or Spahn, but pro football doesn't make millionaires of its linemen.

"That's a quarterback's salary," said McNally.

"I'm your quarterback on defense," said Bednarik, stung in his lineman's pride. "Look, Vince, I think I can play another year, either as center or linebacker, not both. But maybe I'm wrong. Maybe I'm too old. Maybe I ought to hang them up."

"Mary," yelled McNally to his secretary, "type me up a contract for Charles Bednarik."

Now he had the respect and the glory and the money, but one moment from the big season stuck in his craw: the tackle that finished Frank Gifford. No one had ever called Bednarik an easy-going football player, but no one had called him a dirty one either. He had seen other bulls get the tag "hatchet man" for banging a star such as Gifford. Bednarik is a rough, swaggering guy, full of noisy gusto about his trade, but he did not like the idea of playing his last years with a gunman's reputation.

On a summer day, Gifford called. He wanted to do an interview for his New York radio show. He congratulated Bednarik on his signing. It was the first time Bednarik had heard from the Giant back since he smashed him to earth in November.

"Before we go on the air, Chuck," Gifford said, "I want to tell you something. I've never resented the way you hit me. It was a good, clean tackle. The whole thing was my fault for not seeing you coming. I'll tell the world that. You've always been tough but you're clean, buddy."

Bednarik hung up the phone, immensely happy. He sat down in the backyard, the newest and fifth Bednarik daughter gurgling in his tattooed arms. The other girls, Charlene, Donna, Pam and Carol, skittered and tumbled on the shady lawn.

"It took a real pro to say what Giff did," Bednarik said. "Did you ever hit a golf ball just right, so it just clicked and shot 250 yards? That's the way the Gifford tackle was. It felt like a feather I hit him with such lucky timing. Not lucky for Giff, though."

"Did you ever have a guy you really wanted to hurt, Chuck? A guy you really hated?"

Bednarik bounced Jacqueline Bednarik softly, thinking. You could almost see his mind shifting from this tranquil yard, the cries of the girls like bright pennants on the muted air, to the cursing, thudding wars of the bulls on a hundred other afternoons.

"Yeah, you get in those situations," he said slowly. "Guys pop you, and you say, 'Damn you, I'll get you for that.' But you don't get the chance for a game or two, and then you've got a feud. Lou Creekmur with the Lions, he was a bad guy, but I never got a shot at him. Don Colo was another I missed. Oh, I skip those team riots if I can. We had two big, bloody things against the 49ers in San Francisco, but I just watched. What's the percentage? I've had to fight some guys, though— and one I remember good was Chuck Noll."

He swung the baby gently against his chest, remembering. Noll was a 220-pound guard for the Browns. On a kickoff he had met Bednarik with an uppercut that had Chuck seeing galaxies of shooting stars. "You'll get yours, buddy!" said Bednarik. He nursed his anger a year, waiting for the moment. It came at Philadelphia in a game the Eagles were losing badly to Cleveland.

"Hey, Frank," Bednarik said to his roommate, Frank Wydo, "let's get that No. 65."

On the kickoff, Wydo hit Noll high and Bednarik creamed him low. Noll came up frothing. "I'll come to the locker room after the game and kill you, Bednarik," he screamed.

"Don't bother," said Chuck. "I'll meet you right here."

Bednarik forgot the incident. The game ended on that precise spot of turf, though. Noll came running, eyes full of fire, yanking off his helmet as he got in firing range.

"That was a mistake, taking off the helmet," said Bednarik. "I dropped him with one shot to the jaw."

The fight had more spectators in Cleveland than some championship matches, because the TV cameras had closed in on the scene. The cameras also caught the Browns helping Noll stagger away—and Bednarik, enraged now, chasing him to the dugout. Bednarik dropped him again with a hook. The Lake Erie TV watchers were so irate that Bednarik had to stay in his hotel room on the Eagles' next visit. Commissioner Bert Bell fined him $50 and demanded he apologize.

"Hey, this thing between me and you has been going on two years," Bednarik said to Noll during a pre-game warmup. "Let's forget it."

Noll put his chin a half-inch from Bednarik's chin.

"—you," he said.

Bednarik shrugged and walked away. Noll grabbed his shoulder and spun him. He stuck out a hand. "Okay," he said, "let's start from scratch, No. 60."

"Wydo hit me like that once," Chuck laughed. "He was later my best buddy and roomie on the Eagles. But this was when he was a Steeler rookie. He clipped me a good shot on the jaw. I asked him what the hell that was for. 'For hitting me in the Penn-Cornell game,' he said. I told him I didn't even know he was on the Cornell squad. We still laugh about it.

"The rookies are the worst, though," said Chuck. "You get to recognize the old cheap-shot artists. You watch 'em close. But the exhibitions are murder, because every green kid from Slippery Rock Tech wants to get a quick reputation belting you on your pants."

In the dying light we worked on a pitcher of ice tea. Bednarik talked of each Eagle team, even the bad ones, with tremendous pride. "He may not remember his own phone number," said Emma, "but I don't think he's ever forgotten an Eagle score, or a touchdown, or a play. That goes for Penn, too."

Over the dozen years, the small failures nag at his mind as well as the larger triumphs. He was fined $50 once for dogging it on a touchdown play and it still rankles.

"We're playing the Steelers and Lynn Chadnois comes around end and Fran Rogell brushes me out. Trimble yells, 'You quit, Bednarik—that'll cost you $50.' I yelled back, 'What about those ten other guys?' I liked Jim but he was going through a rough season. He fined some other guys that day and the ball club turned against him. I never quit."

Bednarik does not hide his job and his booming pride in the career he has carved out of muscle and pain. We walked slowly around the walls of the basement den, swarming with trophies and photos. Bednarik belting a Navy halfback for Penn. Bednarik at an All-America party. Bednarik at a Penn banquet. (The ends gave him a trophy that year for making all of their tackles.)

Bednarik and the crew of the Liberator bomber in which he flew over Europe. ("Sometimes one engine would be shot out, once the tires were blown off, always there seemed to be 100 or 200 flak holes—Lord, we were lucky.") Bednarik wearing a huge cigar and a huge grin after beating the Giants.

"Where do you think you'd be now if it wasn't for football, Chuck?" I asked him.

"I dunno. Working in the steel mill like my dad did, I guess. If the war hadn't come along, I wouldn't have gone to college. I always hung around with older guys in Bethlehem and I was in a hurry to get a job and make some pocket money. John Butler suggested I try to get in Penn. I remember the day I walked into the dining room and George Munger saw me—I was 210 pounds, 6-3, mature compared to those college kids—and Munger's eyes popped. I had to carry mail on the campus, a dollar an hour, though, until I became eligible."

We walked up the stairs and into the quiet dusk.

"If it hadn't been football, though, I think I would have had a good crack at baseball," said Bednarik. "That's what I really regret. In 1952 I worked out before every game with the A's. I'd hit those good pitchers—Shantz and Kellner and Coleman. I got to be a close pal of Gus Zernial and we'd hit homers in batting practice for dimes. I didn't lose money.

"Jimmy Dykes and Art Ehlers—he was the general manager—liked me, I knew. One Sunday night Ehlers called me. They needed a catcher at Ottawa. Hell, yes, I'd go. That was triple-A, and just a step to the majors. But I called McNally and he said no. 'You're the heart of our defense,' he said, 'and I'm not going to let you break a leg in a baseball game.' I'm sorry I never had the chance to prove I could catch in the majors."

Bednarik stood on the front lawn and looked up at the house towering in the circle of trees. Dogwood and holly and ferns lined the walk.

It was a long way from the steel mill, a long way from the profane, sweaty crash of a hundred battles with the bulls in the big arenas.

"Football gave me all this," said Bednarik, standing in the velvet dusk. "I gave everything I had to football, though, and I'm not so old that I haven't got some more to give."

At the moment on the cool suburban street, the tigers inside Chuck Bednarik were still, resting, waiting. The tigers would get their chance.

Arnold Hano

The Catch

When last heard from, in 1992, the seventy-year-old Arnold Hano
and his wife, Bonnie, had joined the Peace Corps and were serving
in Costa Rica. Well, why not? Hano always seems to be in the
appropriate place at the appropriate time. As he was that afternoon
on September 29, 1954, sitting in the bleachers at the Polo Grounds,
watching Willie Mays chase a World Series fly ball by Vic Wertz of
the Cleveland Indians. That catch, and subsequent throw by Mays,
offer compelling evidence of a statement Hano once made about
the champion athlete; that is, someone like Willie Mays: "man
achieving man's potential: blood, muscle, nerve, mind, soul all
integrated into total effort."

And like wolves drawn to our fresh prey, we had already forgotten
him, eyes riveted on Liddle, while off to the side of the plate Vic
Wertz studied the new Giant pitcher and made whatever esti-
mations he had to make.

Wertz had hit three times already; nobody expected more of him.
He had hit one of Maglie's fast balls in the first inning, a pitch that was
headed for the outside corner but Wertz's bat was too swift and he had
pulled the ball for a triple. Then he hit a little curve, a dinky affair that
was either Maglie's slider or a curve that didn't break too well, and drove
it into left field for a single. Finally, he had pulled another outside pitch
that—by all rights—he shouldn't have been able to pull, so far from the
right-field side of the plate was it. But he had pulled it, as great sluggers
will pull any ball because that is how home runs are made. Wertz hadn't
hit a home run on that waist-high pitch on the outside; he had rifled it
to right field for another single.

But that was all off Maglie, forgotten behind a door over five hundred feet from the plate. Now it was Liddle, jerking into motion as Wertz poised at the plate, and then the motion smoothed out and the ball came sweeping in to Wertz, a shoulder-high pitch, a fast ball that probably would have been a fast curve, except that Wertz was coming around and hitting it, hitting it about as hard as I have ever seen a ball hit, on a high line to dead center field.

For whatever it is worth, I have seen such hitters as Babe Ruth, Lou Gehrig, Ted Williams, Jimmy Foxx, Ralph Kiner, Hack Wilson, Johnny Mize, and lesser-known but equally long hitters as Wally Berger and Bob Seeds send the batted ball tremendous distances. None, that I recall, ever hit a ball any harder than this one by Wertz in my presence.

And yet I was not immediately perturbed. I have been a Giant fan for years, twenty-eight years to be exact, and I have seen balls hit with violence to extreme center field which were caught easily by Mays, or Thomson before him, or Lockman or Ripple or Hank Leiber or George Kiddo Davis, that most marvelous fly catcher.

I did not—then—feel alarm, though the crack was loud and clear, and the crowd's roar rumbled behind it like growing thunder. It may be that I did not believe the ball would carry as far as it did, hard hit as it was. I have seen hard-hit balls go a hundred feet into an infielder's waiting glove, and all that one remembers is crack, blur, spank. This ball did not alarm me because it was hit to dead center field—Mays' territory—and not between the fielders, into those dread alleys in left-center and right-center which lead to the bullpens.

And this was not a terribly high drive. It was a long low fly or a high liner, whichever you wish. This ball was hit not nearly so high as the triple Wertz struck earlier in the day, so I may have assumed that it would soon start to break and dip and come down to Mays, not too far from his normal position.

Then I looked at Willie, and alarm raced through me, peril flaring against my heart. To my utter astonishment, the young Giant center fielder—the inimitable Mays, most skilled of outfielders, unique for his ability to scent the length and direction of any drive and then turn and move to the final destination of the ball—Mays was turned full around, head down, running as hard as he could, straight toward the runway between the two bleacher sections.

I knew then that I had underestimated—badly underestimated—the length of Wertz's blow.

I wrenched my eyes from Mays and took another look at the ball, winging its way along, undipping, unbreaking, forty feet higher than Mays' head, rushing along like a locomotive, nearing Mays, and I thought then: it will beat him to the wall.

Through the years I have tried to do what Red Barber has cautioned me and millions of admiring fans to do: take your eye from the ball after it's been hit and look at the outfielder and the runners. This is a terribly difficult thing to learn; for twenty-five years I was unable to do it. Then I started to take stabs at the fielder and the ball, alternately. Now I do it pretty well. Barber's advice pays off a thousand times in appreciation of what is unfolding, of what takes some six or seven seconds—that's all, six or seven seconds—and of what I can see in several takes, like a jerking motion picture, until I have enough pieces to make nearly a whole.

There is no perfect whole, of course, to a play in baseball. If there was, it would require a God to take it all in. For instance, on such a play, I would like to know what Manager Durocher is doing—leaping to the outer lip of the sunken dugout, bent forward, frozen in anxious fear? And Lopez—is he also frozen, hope high but too anxious to let it swarm through him? The coaches—have they started to wave their arms in joy, getting the runners moving, or are they half-waiting, in fear of the impossible catch and the mad scramble that might ensue on the base paths?

The players—what have they done? The fans—are they standing, or half-crouched, yelling (I hear them, but since I do not see them, I do not know who makes that noise, which of them yells and which is silent)? Has activity stopped in the Giant bullpen where Grissom still had been toiling? Was he now turned to watch the flight of the ball, the churning dash of Mays?

No man can get the entire picture; I did what I could, and it was painful to rip my sight from one scene frozen forever on my mind, to the next, and then to the next.

I had seen the ball hit, its rise; I had seen Mays' first backward sprint; I had again seen the ball and Mays at the same time, Mays still leading. Now I turned to the diamond—how long does it take the eyes to sweep and focus and telegraph to the brain?—and there was the vacant spot on the hill (how often we see what is not there before we see what is there) where Liddle had been and I saw him at the third-base line, between home and third (the wrong place for a pitcher on such a play; he should be behind third to cover a play there, or behind home to back up a play there, but not in between).

I saw Doby, too, hesitating, the only man, I think, on the diamond who now conceded that Mays might catch the ball. Doby is a center fielder and a fine one and very fast himself, so he knows what a center fielder can do. He must have gone nearly halfway to third, now he was coming back to second base a bit. Of course, he may have known that he could jog home if the ball landed over Mays' head, so there was no need to get too far down the line.

Rosen was as near to second as Doby, it seemed. He had come down from first, and for a second—no, not that long, nowhere near that long, for a hundred-thousandth of a second, more likely—I thought Doby and Rosen were Dark and Williams hovering around second, making some foolish double play on this ball that had been hit three hundred and thirty feet past them. Then my mind cleared; they were in Cleveland uniforms, not Giant, they were Doby and Rosen.

And that is all I allowed my eyes on the inner diamond. Back now to Mays—had three seconds elapsed from the first ominous connection of bat and ball?—and I saw Mays do something that he seldom does and that is so often fatal to outfielders. For the briefest piece of time— I cannot shatter and compute fractions of seconds like some atom gun—Mays started to raise his head and turn it to his left, as though he were about to look behind him.

Then he thought better of it, and continued the swift race with the ball that hovered quite close to him now, thirty feet high and coming down (yes, finally coming down) and again—for the second time—I knew Mays would make the catch.

In the Polo Grounds, there are two square-ish green screens, flanking the runway between the two bleacher sections, one to the left-field side of the runway, the other to the right. The screens are intended to provide a solid dark background for the pitched ball as it comes in to the batter. Otherwise he would be trying to pick out the ball from a far-off sea of shirts of many colors, jackets, balloons, and banners.

Wertz's drive, I could see now, was not going to end up in the runway on the fly; it was headed for the screen on the right-field side.

The fly, therefore, was not the longest ball ever hit in the Polo Grounds, not by a comfortable margin. Wally Berger had hit a ball over the left-field roof around the four-hundred foot marker. Joe Adcock had hit a ball into the center-field bleachers. A Giant pitcher, Hal Schumacher, had once hit a ball over the left-field roof, about as far out as Berger's. Nor—if Mays caught it—would it be the longest ball ever caught in the Polo Grounds. In either the 1936 or 1937 World Series—I do not recall which—Joe DiMaggio and Hank Leiber traded gigantic smashes to the foot of the stairs within that runway; each man had caught the other's. When DiMaggio caught Leiber's, in fact, it meant the third out of the game. DiMaggio caught the ball and barely broke step to go up the stairs and out of sight before the crowd was fully aware of what had happened.

So Mays' catch—if he made it—would not necessarily be in the realm of the improbable. Others had done feats that bore some resemblance to this.

Yet Mays' catch—if, indeed, he was to make it—would dwarf all the others for the simple reason that he, too, could have caught Leiber's or DiMaggio's fly, whereas neither could have caught Wertz's. Those balls had been towering drives, hit so high the outfielder could run forever before the ball came down. Wertz had hit his ball harder and on a lower trajectory. Leiber—not a fast man—was nearing second base when DiMaggio caught his ball; Wertz—also not fast—was at first when . . .

When Mays simply slowed down to avoid running into the wall, put his hands up in cup-like fashion over his left shoulder, and caught the ball much like a football player catching leading passes in the end zone.

He had turned so quickly, and run so fast and truly that he made this impossible catch look—to us in the bleachers—quite ordinary. To those reporters in the press box, nearly six hundred feet from the bleacher wall, it must have appeared far more astonishing, watching Mays run and run until he had become the size of a pigmy and then he had run some more, while the ball diminished to a mote of white dust and finally disappeared in the dark blob that was Mays' mitt.

The play was not finished, with the catch.

Now another pet theory of mine could be put to the test. For years I have criticized baserunners who advance from second base while a long fly ball is in the air, then return to the base once the catch has been made and proceed to third after tagging up. I have wondered why these men have not held their base; if the ball is not caught, they can score from second. If it is, surely they will reach third. And—if they are swift—should they not be able to score from second on enormously long flies to dead center field?

Here was such a fly; here was Doby so close to second before the catch that he must have practically been touching the bag when Mays was first touching the drive, his back to the diamond. Now Doby could—if he dared—test the theory.

And immediately I saw how foolish my theory was when the thrower was Mays.

It is here that Mays outshines all others. I do not think the catch made was as sensational as some others I have seen, although no one else could have made it. I recall a catch made by Fred Lindstrom, a converted third baseman who had bad legs, against Pittsburgh. Lindstrom ran to the right-center field wall beyond the Giants' bullpen and leaped high to snare the ball with his gloved hand. Then his body smashed into the wall and he fell on his back, his gloved hand held over his body, the speck of white still showing. After a few seconds, he got to his feet, quite groggy, but still holding the ball. That was the finest catch I can recall, and the account of the game in next day's New York *Herald-Tribune* indicated it might have been the greatest catch ever made in the Polo Grounds.

Yet Lindstrom could not have reached the ball Wertz hit and Mays would have been standing at the wall, ready to leap and catch the ball Lindstrom grabbed.

Mays never left his feet for the ball Wertz hit; all he did was outrun the ball. I do not diminish the feat; no other center fielder that I have ever seen (Joe and Dom DiMaggio, Terry Moore, Sammy West, Eddie Roush, Earle Combs, and Duke Snider are but a few that stand out) could have done it for no one else was as fast in getting to the ball. But I am of the opinion that had not Mays made that slight movement with his head as though he were going to look back in the middle of flight, he would have caught the ball standing still.

The throw to second base was something else again.

Mays caught the ball, and then whirled and threw, like some olden statue of a Greek javelin hurler, his head twisted away to the left as his right arm swept out and around. But Mays is no classic study for the simple reason that at the peak of his activity, his baseball cap flies off. And as he turned, or as he threw—I could not tell which, the two motions were welded into one—off came the cap, and then Mays himself continued to spin around after the gigantic effort of returning the ball whence it came, and he went down flat on his belly, and out of sight.

But the throw! What an astonishing throw, to make all other throws ever before it, even those four Mays himself had made during fielding practice, appear the flings of teen-age girls. This was the throw of a giant, the throw of a howitzer made human, arriving at second base— to Williams or Dark, I don't know which, but probably Williams, my memory says Dark was at the edge of the outfield grass, in deep shortstop position—just as Doby was pulling into third, and as Rosen was scampering back to first.

I wonder what will happen to Mays in the next few years. He may gain in finesse and batting wisdom, but he cannot really improve much because his finest talent lies in his reflex action. He is so swift in his reflexes, the way young Joe Louis was with his hands when, cobra-like, they would flash through the thinnest slit in a foe's defense, Louis, lashing Paulino Uzcudun with the first hard punch he threw, drilled into the tiniest opening and crushing the man who had never before been knocked out. That is Mays, too. Making a great catch and whirling and throwing, before another man would have been twenty feet from the ball.

And until those reflexes slow down, Mays must be regarded as off by himself, not merely *a* great ball player, but *the* great ball player of our time.

(I am not discussing his hitting here; for some strange reason— National League-itis, I guess—when I discuss the native ability of a ball player, I invariably narrow my gaze to his defensive ability. DiMaggio was a better hitter in his prime than Mays is now, maybe than Mays ever will be, although no hitter was ever as good as Mays at the same stage of their respective careers—check Ruth, Wagner, Cobb, Hornsby in their second full year of play and you will see what I mean.)

Still, Willie's 1954 season at the plate may have been some freak occurrence. It happens sometimes that a ball player hits all season far above his norm. I am thinking of Ferris Fain who led the league a few years ago, though he had never been an impressive hitter before. My wife inquired about this man Fain, of whom she was suddenly hearing so much. I told her that he was a pretty good ball player, an excellent defensive first baseman, and a fair hitter. She said, "Fair? He's leading the league, isn't he?"

I said, "Yes, but that's a fluke. He's hitting way over his head. Watch what happens next year."*

Or take Carl Furillo hitting over .340 in 1953. Furillo is a fine hitter, a solid .300 hitter who can drive in nearly a hundred runs a season, but .340 is not his normal average. Possibly .345 is nowhere near Mays' norm; nothing in the past had indicated he could hit that high.

I do not list Mays among the great hitters, though I concede that one day we all may. As a fielder, he is already supreme.

So much for Mays and the catch.

---

* The following year Fain led the league again.

Mark Harris

Labor Day Doubleheader

In 1954, a novel was published that was told in the first person by a young, hard-throwing left-handed pitcher named Henry W. Wiggen. The Southpaw *was the name of the novel, and Wiggen's view of the major league game was a fresh one. The ballplayer's life was as mundane as any other job. His teammates were mortal men, bowed by the weight of normal, everyday concerns. In 1956, Wiggen, with "certain of his enthusiasms restrained" by his creator, Mark Harris, followed with another book,* Bang the Drum Slowly. *This was the story of one of those mortal men, a slow-witted, mediocre catcher, Bruce Pearson, who is dying of Hodgkin's disease. Here, from* Bang the Drum Slowly, *is Wiggen's account of Pearson's last game.*

We took 3 out of 4, last times in Boston, Friday, a doubleheader Saturday, and a singleton Sunday, playing to an empty park. I do not think 10,000 people showed up in the 3 days, though I don't know why. Boston was a better club than that. But they weren't winning, and what folks want is a winner, "Never mind good baseball, give us a winner," not loving the game but only loving winning, all these towns screaming for big-league ball that don't know good from bad to begin with. All they know is names. They rather sit home and stare at some big-league catcher's big-name ass on TV and the umpire's ass behind, thinking this is the same thing as *seeing* a ball game, which it is not. It all sounded hollow up there in the empty park, all echoes, and you waited for noise on a good play, but all you heard was somebody clapping here and somebody else clapping about 19,000 miles away, and then 2 more people another 19,000. It was hard to keep remembering that these were ball games we needed, hard to keep hustling, hard to keep remembering we were still in the middle of the race with an awful lot of money riding on a day's work.

It was gloomy up there. I keep thinking it drizzled or at least was cloudy, but I see by the clips that it was not so. It was only a feeling you got in the quiet park, like everybody in the whole of Boston went out of town for the weekend or else died for all you could tell. All the same, we hustled, maybe even hustled more than usual, or else it only sounded that way because you could hear everybody clearer in the quiet, hear the boys calling to themself, hear the singing, almost hear them thinking, see Perry and Coker talking behind their hand across second, see Vincent looking across from left at his brother and doing what his brother said, see Lawyer Longabucco between, also looking at Pasquale, and Pasquale doing their thinking, waving them now in, now back, now left, now right, hear Red calling to George in Spanish, hear Clint and Joe in the coaching boxes, hear them even hustling in the bullpen, see them all picking up their sign and hitting or taking or running or playing it safe, hustling, hustling, so if you seen a movie of it with the date blacked out you would of said it was sometime in April or May, never guessing September. We went back home Sunday night with the cushion at 3½.

In the morning he did not feel too good, Monday, Labor Day. "I will call Doc," I said.

"No," he said.

"Does it feel like the attack?" I said.

"Yes and no," he said. "I feel dipsy. Maybe I will feel better opening the window," and he went and opened it and sat by it and breathed it in and went and put a chew of Days O Work in his mouth and went back and spit down a couple times.

"Maybe it will rain," I said.

"Not soon," he said. "Maybe by night," leaning out and looking both ways and up. He knew if it would rain or not, which I myself do not know without looking at the paper and even then do not know because I forget to look. In the end I never know if it will rain until it begins. But he knew by the way the clouds blew, and he said he felt better now, and he shut the window and called Katie, saying he felt dipsy today, and he said in the phone, "No, I do not think he did" and clapped his hand over the phone and begun to say something to me, and I said, "No.

Tell her no. Tell her I forgot," and she eat him out, and he said, "But, Katie," and then again, "But, Katie, but," until she hung up, and I did not look, and he went on talking, like he was still talking to her, and finally he said, "Well, OK, Katie, and I love you, too" and hung up, all smiles, and we went out to the park and he still did not feel too good, and he told Dutch, and Dutch said, "Well, we can not do without you, but we will try. Will we not try, boys, and make the best of a bad blow?" and the boys all said "Yes siree bob" and "You said it, boss" and "Sure enough" and all, and they hustled out, and me and Bruce laid on the table and listened with Mick.

There was plenty of scrap left in Washington yet. They did not know they were beat. You probably could of even found a little Washington money in town if you looked hard enough, not much, but some, for the town did not know what the Mammoths knew, not knowing the truth, not knowing Washington was beat on August 26, which I personally knew laying in bed and listening to the boys, and knew for sure when Goose shot the light out, knowing what it done to a fellow when he knew, how it made them cut out the horseshit and stick to the job. Washington hustled, jumping Van Gundy for a run in the second and another in the fourth, and we laid there, not moving, only listening, Mick folding towels but not hurrying like he hurries when he is nervous, only sitting there folding one after the other and setting it on the pile and creasing it out and reaching over slowly for the next, the 3 of us as calm as we could be like we were looking at the front end of a movie we already seen the back end of, and you knew who done it, who killed who, and we thought, "Washington, you are dead and do not know it."

George opened our fifth with a single, and they played Perry for the bunt, which he crossed them up and slammed through first and into the opposite field, and it was Pasquale that bunted instead and caught all Washington flat-footed, George scoring and Perry going clear to third and Pasquale winding up at second, for George dumped Eric Bushell in the play at the plate, and they passed Sid to get at Canada, and then they passed *Canada,* not meaning to, and Bruce said he felt better now, and we went down and warmed.

We warmed close to the wall. I remember every now and then he stuck out his hand and leaned against it, and I said, "Still feeling dipsy?" and he said, "No, only a little," and he crouched down again, first sitting on his heels and then flatting out his feet behind him and resting on his knees and looking back over his shoulder to see where Dutch was looking, for Dutch will fine a catcher for catching on his knees. "Maybe it will rain," I said, and he looked up and said "I hope so."

"I am warm," I said, though I was not, and we sat on the bench in the bullpen.

"It is a big crowd," he said. "It is Labor Day, that is what it is," and he took out a chew and broke it in half and give me half a chunk, saying, "Chew a chew, Arthur," which he always asked me and I always turned down except I took it then and chewed it and did not like it much, having no use for tobacco nor liquor, and every time I spit it dribbled down my chin. "Keep your teeth tight shut when you spit," he said.

It run long, for we begun hitting quite a bit, and he said, "You must be getting cold by now," and I said no. "It is getting cold," he said, and he reached around behind him for his jacket except it was not there, and I jiggled the phone, saying, "Send up a jacket for Bruce," and 3 boys sprung up off the bench and raced down the line, Wash and Piney and Herb Macy, and the crowd all begun yelling and pointing, never seeing such a thing before as 3 men all racing for the bullpen like that, and Krazy Kress sent down a note saying, "Author, what the hell??????" and I looked up at the press-box and give Krazy flat palms, same as saying, "What the hell what?"

We started fast in the second game. It was raining a little. Sid hit a home run in the first with Pasquale aboard, Number 42, the first home run he hit since August 17, according to the paper, and Bruce shook his hand at the plate, and Sid stopped and told Bruce, "Wipe off your bat," and Bruce looked at his bat and at Sid, not understanding, not feeling the rain, and Sid took the bat and wiped it off, and Bruce whistled a single in left, the last base hit he ever hit, and made his turn and went back and stood with one foot on the bag and said something to Clint, and Clint yelled for Dutch, and Dutch went out, and they talked. I do not know what about. Dutch only said to me, "Pick up your sign off the bench," and he sent for Doc, and Doc sat in the alley behind the dugout and waited, and the boys sometimes strolled back and sat beside him, asking him questions, "What does he have?" and such as that. They smoked back there, which Dutch does not like you to, saying, "Smoking ain't learning. Sitting on the bench and watching is learning," but he said nothing that day. You knew he wouldn't.

Washington begun stalling like mad in the third, hoping for heavy rain before it become official, claiming it was raining, though the umps ruled it was not. Sy Sibley was umping behind the plate. They stepped out between pitches and wiped off their bat and tied their shoe and blew their nose and gouged around in their eye, saying, "Something is in my eye," and Sy said, "Sure, your eyeball," and they stepped back in. As soon as they stepped back in again I pitched.

He never knew what was coming, curve ball or what. "Just keep your meat hand out of the way," I said, and he said he would but did not. It did not register. He was catching by habit and memory, only knowing that when the pitcher threw it you were supposed to stop it and throw it back, and if a fellow hit a foul ball you were supposed to whip off your mask and collar it, and if a man was on base you were supposed to keep him from going on to the next one. You play ball all your life until a day comes when you do not know what you are doing, but you do it anyhow, working through a fog, not remembering anything but only knowing who people were by how they moved, this fellow the hitter, this the pitcher, and if you hit the ball you run to the right, and then when you got there you asked Clint Strap were you safe or out because you do not know yourself. There was a fog settling down over him.

I do not know how he got through it. I do not even know how yours truly got through it. I do not remember much. It was 3–0 after 4½, official now, and now we begun stalling, claiming it was raining, claiming the ball was wet and we were libel to be beaned, which Washington said would make no difference to fellows with heads as hard as us. Eric Bushell said it to me in the fifth when I complained the ball was wet, and I stepped out and started laughing, "Ha ha ha ho ho ho ha ha ha," doubling over and laughing, and Sy Sibley said, "Quit stalling," and I said I could not help it if Bushell was going to say such humorous things to me and make me laugh. "Tell him to stop," I said. "Ha ha ha ho ho ho ha ha ha."

"What did he say?" said Sy, and I told him, telling him very slow, telling him who Eric Bushell was and who I was, the crowd thinking it was an argument and booing Sy. "Forget it," said he. "Get back in and hit."

"You mean bat," said Bushell. "He never hits," and I begun laughing again, stepping out and saying how could a man bat with this fellow behind me that if the TV people knew how funny he was they would make him an offer.

"Hit!" said Sy. "Bat! Do not stall."

"Who is stalling?" said I, and I stepped back in, the rain coming a little heavier now.

I threw one pitch in the top of the seventh, a ball, wide, to Billy Linenthal. I guess I remember. Bruce took it backhand and stood up and slowly raised his hand and took the ball out of his mitt and started to toss it back, aiming very careful at my chin, like Red told him to, and then everybody begun running, for the rain come in for sure now, and he seen everybody running, but he did not run, only stood there. I started off towards the dugout, maybe as far as the baseline, thinking he was following, and then I seen that he was not. I seen him standing looking for somebody to throw to, the last pitch he ever caught, and I went back for him, and Mike and Red were there when I got there, and Mike said, "It is over, son," and he said "Sure" and trotted on in.

W. C. Heinz

Fighter's Wife

When they speak about the early post–World War II sportswriters, the ones that matter today, the names that always come quickest to mind are Red Smith and W. C. Heinz. Heinz, as has been pointed out in the introduction to this volume, was writing the "new journalism" before the term had been invented. One of his magazine editors caught the essence of this professional when he wrote: "Heinz is a sufferer—a writer with such a respect for writing that every story is a try for a new record, for a cleaner knockout, for a deeper look into life." Here is W. C. Heinz, as defined, writing about what it is like to be married to a fighter at the moment of highest anxiety. The fighter's wife is Norma Unger Graziano.

It was 9:30 in the evening and they would put the fight on shortly after 10 o'clock. There were about a dozen people in the house, all but two of them women, but it was not noisy. They sat in the carpeted, lush living room on the ground floor of the red-brick, two-family house. For an hour, on and off, she had been a part of their small talk, but now she stood up and walked toward the kitchen and got out the ironing board.

"I hope he should retire," her grandmother said. "I hope he should win and retire healthy. He must be healthy for his family. Allus I hope, he should be healthy with my whole heart."

One day, when Norma Unger was seventeen years old, she and her friend Alice and Alice's friend Yolanda were sitting at a table in an ice-

cream parlor on the corner of Seventh Street and Second Avenue. They were having sodas and talking about boys. Yolanda said her brother was coming out of the Army, and she reached into a pocket and came out with two snapshots of him.

"I think you'd like him," she said to Norma while Norma looked at the pictures, "and I think he'd like you. I think it would be fun to arrange a blind date."

That was the first time Norma Unger ever heard of Rocky Graziano, the first time in her life.

"The last time he fought Zale," her mother said, "she had her portable radio and was walking up and down the street, turning it on and off."

"Once she sat in the bathtub all through the fight," her grandmother said.

So they arranged a blind date for the next Saturday night. On Saturday she decided she wanted to do something else, so, still early in the evening, she walked over to Yolanda's house. It was a walkup on First Avenue, and she climbed the steps and rang the bell in the hallway and waited. There was one bulb burning at the ceiling, and after a while Yolanda came downstairs and she explained it to Yolanda. While she was explaining it she heard a noise at the top of the stairs, and there he was, hurrying down the stairs, and she was embarrassed.

"Oh," Yolanda said, stopping him when he got to the foot of the stairs, "this is Norma Unger. Norma, this is my brother, Rocky."

"Hello," she said, looking at him.

"Hello," Rocky said and then he turned. "I'll see you."

He left then, but he was wearing a dark-blue suit and he had on a gray hat, porkpie style. He had nice eyes and a nice smile and a nice face, and that was the first time Norma Unger ever saw Rocky Graziano, the first time in her life.

"The time he won the title in Chicago," her mother said. "You remember how he was getting beaten, and she ran crying into the bedroom and locked the door and when she came out he was middleweight champion."

"I don't know," her grandmother said.

"Every time she does something different," her mother said.

They used to see each other around the neighborhood after that. She saw him in the ice-cream parlor a few times. A couple of times they had sodas together. Alice used to go out then with Terry Young, the fighter, and he was Rocky's friend, so the first date they had was a double date with Alice and Terry. That was when she found out he was a fighter, but nobody had ever heard of him then, and she didn't think much about it. After that they went a lot to the movies. He was always in a happy mood, and he wasn't one of those guys who was always trying to kiss a girl good night, and that helped.

"I don't know," her grandmother said. "I wonder what she does tonight."

"I don't know," her mother said, looking around. "Where'd she go?"

It was the first they had missed her. A couple of her friends, the one named Lucille and the other named Innocent, got up and walked out into the kitchen and found her ironing.

"So?" Innocent said.

"Oh," she said, "just a blouse for Audrey for school tomorrow. I thought I could sneak it in. You know, anything to keep busy."

"That's right," Lucille said. "That's why we should do the dresses."

It was 9:35.

They were married after they had known each other for three months. For a while they had teased one another about getting married. Then one day Rocky met her and said Yolanda was getting married. He said Yolanda was going down for her blood test, and they ought to go along to see what it was like. When they got there with Yolanda they decided to take the blood test themselves. Then, because they had had the blood test, they decided they should get married right away.

She was still only seventeen. They went to City Hall, but a man told them she would have to have her mother's consent. She was afraid to ask her mother or her grandmother, so they walked to the Hudson Tubes and rode to Bayonne, New Jersey. They walked along the street and asked some people until they found a place with big windows in the front and it looked sort of like a real-estate office. It said "Justice of the Peace" on the window, but the man said they would have to have the blood test in Jersey and stay there for a while before he could marry them, so they went back to New York.

She doesn't remember exactly how they managed it. A few days later they started going around to buildings away downtown. They went around to a hundred buildings, it seemed, and finally a man married them.

It was in an office. She had on a beige suit and Rocky had on a dark-blue suit and a white shirt and a dark-blue tie. There were a couple of detectives around the building, and Rocky gave them five dollars each to be witnesses. The ceremony seemed so short. She had never thought anything about a big wedding, because they didn't have the money, but still it seemed so short.

The funny thing is, after Rocky became famous he was fighting in the Garden one night. After the fight he was coming out of the ring, and a man stopped him in the aisle.

"Hey," the man said. "Remember me? I'm your best man."

"Who the hell are you?" Rocky said he said.

"Don't you remember?" the man said, and it was one of the detectives. "I stood up with you when you were married, Rock."

She went into one of the bedrooms then—quietly because Audrey, who is five, and Roxie, who is going on two, were sleeping—and when she came out she had a pile of new girls' dresses in her arms. She dropped them on the table, and she found the sewing basket and she stood there watching, smoking a cigarette, while Lucille and Innocent started to sort through the dresses and, each selecting one, to turn the hems.

It was 9:40.

"I'll take the radio in," Norma said. "I won't listen."

She went to a closet and took out a small radio, the electric cord dangling, and carried it to those sitting in the living room. While she was gone the other two sat sewing, not saying anything.

"She's too nervous," Lucille said finally. "I told her to have some brandy around."

"She doesn't drink," the one named Innocent said.

"She could have some brandy around."

When Norma came back they were silent. She stood, leaning on the sideboard, smoking and just watching them. She is twenty-three now, slim, dark-haired, and she had on a gray-and-green print dress with short sleeves and a flared skirt.

"I called up my husband," Lucille said, sewing, "and he said the whole place is closed down. Everybody went to the fight. Even the bartender went to the fight."

She used to go to see him fight, but that was at first. One day, while they were still just going together, he asked her to walk over to the gym with him to watch him train. It was the gym on Fourteenth Street, and it was the first time she had ever seen any fighters in a ring. She stood in the gray, dusty-looking gym with all the men, watching Rocky box. Then he always wanted her to go with him when he fought, to Fort Hamilton and the Broadway Arena and the Ridgewood Grove. Less and less she liked it, and the first Frankie Terry fight was the last she saw. It was such a bad thing to watch, because they were cursing and even kicking. It was a real free-for-all, and after that she wouldn't go any more, although for a while she used to stand outside the clubs and wait for him to come out.

At first he couldn't understand it. Maybe he thought it meant something else, because he got mad about it once. When she wouldn't go with him for his fight with Leon Anthony he wouldn't fight. They went to a movie together instead that night, and Rocky was suspended by the Boxing Commission because of it. After a while, though, she was able to explain it so he saw it, and now he understands why she doesn't even want to watch him train for a fight.

"What time is it?" the one named Babe said.

"It's nine forty-five," Lucille said.

"You people sew so nice," Babe said.

Babe was standing in the doorway, watching the two at the table. Then she walked into the kitchen and sat down on one of the high red-and-white stools.

"The sewing circle," Norma said. "Boys are so much easier."

"Don't say that," Babe said. "You should see my Joseph."

"They make clothes so nice now," Innocent said, sewing.

"Girls' clothes," Babe said.

"Oh, boys', too," Innocent said.

"I'm getting a nervous stomach," Norma said.

She left them, then, and walked back toward the bedrooms and the bath. It was 9:50 by the kitchen clock.

Their first night they spent in a hotel on Fourteenth Street. Then they went to the flat where Rocky's people lived. They had one bedroom and Rocky's people had the other. There were only four rooms, so Rocky's brother, Lennie, slept in the living room and his sister, Ida, slept in the kitchen. They lived like that for five months, on First Avenue between Eighth and Ninth streets.

For two years after that they lived with her mother and stepfather in Brooklyn. There were only three rooms, so they slept in the living room. When Audrey came the crib was in the living room, too.

"Norma," one of those from the living room said, "what's the number on that little radio?"

It was the one named Lee and she was standing in the doorway, leaning against the frame. Norma had come back into the kitchen and had just been watching the sewing.

"I don't know," Norma said, and the one named Lee left.

"Listen, Norma," Babe said, "he'll come out all right. You know what my husband said: 'We'll carry him home on our shoulders.' Tony says, 'I shouldn't go to the fight, because I get so nervous, but I'm goin' because Rocky is gonna win.'"

"Like my husband," Lucille said. "Dom was cryin' after the last one. Some fellas from Second Avenue found him and said, 'C'mon, we'll take you home.' So tonight he said he didn't care if he was to go or not."

They could hear them tuning the radio in the living room. In the kitchen they could hear music and then a man's voice coming over the radio very loud and then softer. It was 10 o'clock.

"Say," Norma said, "and what do you think you're doing?"

It was Audrey, standing in the doorway that leads to the bedrooms, a small, dark-haired child in a long white nightgown. She was just standing, blinking in the light, rubbing her eyes with the backs of her hands.

"Aah," Babe said.

"You're makin' too much noise," the child said, still rubbing her eyes, her voice small and whining. "You're makin' too much noise."

"Aah," Babe said. "C'mere."

She reached down and picked the child up and, sitting on the stool, she held her on her lap. Still the child rubbed her eyes.

"How do you like school?" Babe said, turning her head down and talking to the child.

"She won't be able to get up," Norma said. "She has to get some sleep."

"She knows something is happening," Innocent said.

"You're makin' too much noise," the child said.

"What happened?" Norma said, looking up. "You can't get it?"

It was Phil, Lee's husband. He was just standing there, dapper and looking at them and smiling.

"We got it," he said, smiling. "I'm goin' in now."

Now they could hear from the radio the voice of Bill Corum. It was Bill Corum all right, the voice just a little hard and sportslike.

"Bill Corum with Don Dunphy bringing you another major sports event for . . ."

"All right," Norma said softly, getting up and going to the child. She took the child from Babe then, and she carried her out.

"He's got to win," Babe said when Norma was gone.

"That's right," Lucille said, sewing.

"He's gonna win," Innocent said.

"Who feels like sewing?" Lucille said, stopping.

"I don't."

"If you stop I will."

They went on sewing though. They were sewing when Norma came back and Norma, standing and watching, lit another cigarette.

"I don't even think it's ten o'clock yet," Lucille said.

"It's after ten," Norma said, "but they have to get the introductions out of the way."

Now, from the radio far off in the living room they could hear the voice of Johnny Addie, the ring announcer. His voice was very clear, but distant, the only sound in the house.

". . . popular middleweight from Cleveland, Chuck Hunter."

"My husband was like this all day," Babe said, moving her hands. "Back and forth, back and forth. He couldn't eat."

". . . middleweight contender from Brooklyn, Vinnie Cidone."

"If anybody wants to go in—" Norma said.

"No," the two at the table said together, shaking their heads.

"I have to go in," Babe said, sliding off the stool.

"If anybody else wants to go in," Norma said, "because I'm gonna close this door."

"No," her mother, a rather short, trim woman, standing in the doorway now, said, "let's take a walk."

"Wait until it starts," Norma said.

". . . the welterweight king, Sugar Ray Robinson!"

"This is the worst part," Lucille said, "waiting for the introductions."

"No," Norma said. "The worst part is waiting through 'The Star Spangled Banner.'"

"All right," her mother said. "Let's go."

". . . the ring officials are assigned here by the New York State Athletic Commission . . ."

Norma went to get a fresh pack of cigarettes, and then they hurried, the three of them, the one seeming almost to fall over the one ahead, through the dining room and through the living room. In the living room those crowded around the small radio looked up and shouted something as the three hurried out the front door.

"We're going for a walk," Lucille said, shouting it back.

". . . from Irvington, New Jersey, wearing black trunks . . . Charley Fusari!"

It was the last thing she heard as she hurried out of her own house and into the night.

She had never, at any time, thought it would be like this. When she was still so young she had listened to the words of Frank Sinatra, but she had always known those were not the truth and that it would never be like that. She had not thought about it much, just that when she did get married it would probably be to some ordinary working guy, and they would live in a little apartment. She could never have known that it would be with a fighter and that they would have two cars and live in their own house, and that she would be driven from it periodically, from her own house, by voices like this.

"It's an advantage I have when he fights in the warm weather," she said. "I can go for nice long walks."

They stood together for a moment under the tree in front of the house. It was a warm, rather humid evening and the street was busy with traffic, the cars shushing by with the lights from their headlights flooding onto the three women in the summer dresses standing under the tree and lighting cigarettes and then starting to walk down the block.

"It's not so warm," her mother said. "I'm cold."

"It isn't really cold," Norma said, "but my teeth are chattering."

"Listen," Lucille said, "you can hear the fight walking along here. Look at them up there."

They could see them sitting on a second-floor sunporch of one of the brick houses, men sitting around, shirt-sleeved, smoking, and through the open windows they could hear, faintly, the voice of Dunphy. They could tell he was calling the fight, but it was impossible to tell what he was saying, and they walked along under the trees, their heels making hard sounds on the pavement.

"Fusari's! . . ."

They heard that much starting by another house, and when Lucille heard it she stopped, dropping back. Then she turned into a driveway, her head forward, and stood motionless.

"Let's walk faster," Norma said.

"All I hear is Graziano, Graziano," her mother said.

"It isn't so much that he wins or loses," Norma said, "but that he doesn't get hurt. Of course, when you win it leaves a better taste, but it's just that he shouldn't get hurt."

Walking along, their heels clicking faster, they could hear Lucille running up behind them now. Then she was with them again, breathing audibly.

"Your husband must be winning," Lucille said. "Your husband must have knocked Fusari down. I heard him say something about the middle of the ring."

"I don't want to hear it," Norma said, walking.

When they came to the corner they stopped for just a moment. Then they turned left and started walking again.

"Who said being a fighter's wife is easy?" Lucille said.

"It's like being in the ring," Norma said.

"She fights right in the ring with him every fight," her mother said, talking to Lucille.

"That's the trouble," Norma said. "You can't get in the ring with him."

"What could you do?" her mother said.

"Well," she said, "if they put Fusari's wife in the ring."

"He just said Fusari's in trouble," Lucille said quickly.

"You heard it?" Norma said.

"Yes."

"I don't know," Norma said. "It's too much."

"That's the funny thing," Lucille said. "Everybody waits for tonight but you."

"I wait for the night after tonight."

They had reached another corner. They turned left again, but the radio was loud from the house on the corner, the whole first floor lighted beyond the stucco steps. They could hear the hysteria of Dunphy's voice, the crowd noises behind it.

"Shall I ask?" Lucille said. "I could ask here if somebody is knocked out."

"No," Norma said. "Never mind."

She kept walking, but her mother and Lucille stopped. Lucille started up the steps, the radio loud and frantic. When she got to the top of the steps a dog started to bark in the house, and then the door opened and a dog, wild-looking, stood there barking.

"No," Lucille said to the dog, holding up her hands and starting to back down. "Never mind."

A boy showed behind the dog then, a boy of about twelve or thirteen. The boy grabbed the dog and the dog stopped barking, the radio loud again.

"We wanted to know—" Lucille said, halfway down the steps but stopping now—"we wanted to know if one fighter was knocked out."

"No," the boy said, "but Fusari is hurt bad. He's gettin' a beating."

"Norma!" Lucille said, hollering it down the block. "Fusari is hurt!"

"Norma!" her mother said, standing on the sidewalk and hollering it. "Rocky's winning!"

"But when?" Norma said, stopping and turning and shouting it back.

The two were running down the block toward her now. They could make out her dress, the light from a street lamp falling on it through the trees.

"It's the fourth round," Lucille said, running up.

"All I hear," her mother said, "is a left by Graziano, a right by Graziano."

They lighted other cigarettes and started to walk again, Norma between them. A car went by and slowed, approaching the corner, and they could hear the car radio coming through the night.

"It's still going on," Norma said.

"All of a sudden it isn't cold any more," her mother said.

"It got warm," Norma said, trying to laugh it.

"That's a funny thing," Lucille said. "Isn't that funny?"

This is a neighborhood of two-family brick homes. There are small neat lawns in front of the houses and low hedges and cement walks up to the front doors.

"We should have gone to a movie," her mother said.

"That's what I did for the Bummy Davis fight," Norma said. "I saw half a movie. You'd think you'd get over it."

"Every fight it gets worse," her mother said. "At first we used to be able to go to the fights."

They were back in front of the house now. They had slowed down and now they stopped. They could hear, although not distinctly, the radio in the house. They seemed reluctant now to leave the house, to start the walk again, when Babe came running out.

"What?" Norma said. "It's over?"

"No," Babe said, standing in front of them, excited, "but Rocky's ahead. He can't seem to get the left, though. They say something on the radio that he can't seem to get the left."

She was shaking her left fist.

"Was Fusari down?" Lucille said.

"No, but in one round the bell saved him, so we hear. Now it's four rounds for Rocky and three for Fusari or something, but Fusari's bleeding now."

"Is Rocky hurt?" the mother said.

"In the third round he was bleeding over his left eye, but it doesn't bother him now. You should hear it, because . . ."

Norma was rocking a little, back and forth, one foot ahead of the other, smoking and looking at Babe and then down the block.

"You should look on it like any other business," her mother said.

"But you can't do it," Norma said.

"Whatever happens happens," her mother said.

Dunphy's voice came from the house again, excited. When it did Lucille turned and ran up the walk toward the house and Babe followed her. Norma and her mother began to walk.

"Babe said that Rocky slipped, that he crossed his feet and slipped."

"He always does that," Norma said. "Clumsy."

"Once he fell off a ladder."

"Audrey was inside the house watching him through the window and all of a sudden he disappeared. When he's introduced he usually falls into the ring."

"It seems so long," her mother said.

"Well, it takes forty minutes if it goes ten rounds. That's a long time."

"You're telling me."

"I should go to the dentist when he fights. That way I can't worry about him."

"Oh-oh, it's still on."

"I want to hear it, but I don't want to hear it."

"That's it. You want to hear the good part of it."

"It must be the tenth round soon."

". . . Fusari's down! . . ."

It had come loudly and quickly and then was gone, from a car passing swiftly. When they heard it they stopped, their feet poised to go on.

"Fusari's down!" her mother said.

"But did he get up?"

". . . a left hook by Graziano. A right by Graziano . . ."

It was from a house and they stood facing the house, their heads turned to hear it. Even then they could hear only some of it.

"Maybe he'll do what he did in the Cochrane fight," Norma said.

"Norma!"

It was a scream from down the block. When they heard it they turned quickly and they could see figures running through the light and shadow, out of the house.

"Norma! Rocky wins! He wins! He wins!"

They ran, running toward the house. As they ran neighbors came running out of houses, appearing at the low hedges along the sidewalk, shouting to them. The street was all noise now, and when she got to the house she was out of breath, and they were swarming around her, hugging her, kissing her, shouting at her, all of them trying to tell her at once. She ran to the radio where the rest were still gathered and she knelt down in front of it, listening now while Corum told again how it had happened, because now she could not get enough.

"What time will he get home?" somebody said.

After the last Zale fight she couldn't help it. Even when she heard them bringing him into the house she couldn't stop crying, because that was the first time he had ever really been knocked out like that.

The night in Chicago when he beat Zale was the other kind of a night. When he came back to the hotel, the mob around him, they went into the bedroom together to wake Audrey to tell her that her father was the middleweight champion of the world. Audrey was three then, and when they woke her and she stood up in the crib and looked at her father she saw the bandages over one eye and the other eye swollen and closed and the welts on his face.

"What happened, Daddy?" Audrey said.

"You see what I said?" he said, bending over and pointing his finger at Audrey. "Now stay outa the gutter."

"I don't know," she said. "You never can tell."

It was almost three hours before he came home. In the three hours more people came. The neighbors came in and the men came back from the fight. They congregated in the kitchen, those who had been there and the others, and they fought it all over again for her, swinging their arms, getting more and more excited. They said the same things over and over, and even those who had been in the house all evening, listening to the radio, kept repeating themselves.

"When I was close to the radio," the one named Lee told her twice, "he was losing, and when I walked away he was always winning. So when I walked away Fusari was down so I stayed away and Rocky won the fight."

She stood out on the terrace in the front for a long time, waiting. A couple of reporters—Jim Jennings and Harold Weissman from the *Mirror*—came and Weissman asked her questions about when she had last seen Rocky and if she had been nervous. Behind her, in the house, the phone rang again and again but others answered it.

"You should go to bed," her grandmother said. "The baby will be up early."

At 1:45 a car pulled up and the mob along the curb and on the sidewalk pressed around it. It was Jack Romeo, and he pushed through them and came up the steps, handing her something in a paper bag.

"What is it?" she said, reaching for it. "A bottle?"

"No," he said. "The gloves."

She heard them along the curb then, calling and applauding. In what light there was she could see him. He had on a white cap, and there was a white towel around his neck. Then he had the towel in his hands, and he was pushing through them, acknowledging them in a thick voice until he climbed the steps and saw her.

"Hello, honey," he said, going to her and kissing her quickly.

They walked into the house together, their friends around. They stood for a minute together in the middle of all of them, Rocky answering Weissman's questions.

"No," Rocky said finally, "I'm gonna take a hot bath now, if you'll excuse me. I mean I'm all sweaty. You know? I gotta relax."

"Sure. Sure," they said.

She walked out with him, then, through the dining room and the kitchen and down the hall to the bathroom to run the water into the tub, to be glad again, finally at two o'clock in the morning, that she was this fighter's wife.

"But don't you want him to retire?" a reporter said to her once. "I mean as soon as you get a little more money?"

She was sitting in a chair in the corner of the room and the reporter was sitting across the room from her.

"No," she said. "I mean that's not up to me. I think a husband should do whatever work he likes to do. I think if a wife sees her husband happy that's enough."

Ed Hinton

Better Hurt Than Dead

The original title of the following piece, which appeared in 1991 in the short-lived sports daily The National, *was "The Last Ride of A.J. Foyt." When Ed Hinton wrote the story, Foyt swore that the 1991 Indianapolis 500, his thirty-fourth, was to also be his last. Foyt, who broke both ankles in a crash in a Milwaukee race the September before, miraculously recovered in time to qualify second for Indy. But early into the big race, which Foyt had won four times, he crashed again. It was a harmless spill with no broken bones or fractures to speak of, but one that eliminated him from the race and thus ruined the storybook farewell this motor-track legend had planned for himself. It was not the way to go, so A.J. Foyt put off those retirement plans to give it yet another shot. Here, then, is the "toughest s.o.b. in racing" as he prepared for what was to be his last ride.*

Eight a.m. and raining on Waller, Texas, out where Texas begins to look like Texas ought to, 40 miles northwest of Houston on the road toward Austin. Around the formica tables at Stockman's Restaurant the cattlemen are brought coffee with the spoons already in the mugs. George Jones is on the jukebox: . . . *and the mem'ries get stronger* . . .

Eight a.m., not 7:59, not 8:01, and an old bull of a man/legend lumbers in, barely walking, his myriad old wounds aching in the damp. As on most mornings when he's home, he has driven a pickup six miles from his ranch to Stockman's for breakfast.

This may be the only place in the world where A.J. Foyt can walk in and nobody feels a vague urge to dive for cover.

He settles 235 pounds into a chair, and he says:

"Iced tea."

Iced tea for breakfast is the mildest of his dietary quirks—hell, he won four Indy 500s on breakfasts of chili and cheeseburgers. While hospitalized with his latest, worst set of injuries, he devoured candy bars and Cokes. His fighter-pilot vision, his uncanny depth perception —a major reason he's still alive—has always flouted warnings to eat vegetables. "Squash, green beans, I don't eat any of that crap."

On a steady diet of fried food, cheese and ice cream, he has endured, even regenerated, as the toughest sonofabitch ever to drive a race car, if not the toughest ever to participate in sports.

But now a heart wound is imminent. The days are dwindling toward the last great ride of the greatest race driver ever: A.J. Foyt's last Indy. The world will have to wait and see how he handles that. Not even he knows, and he will not allow himself to wonder.

He is 56. Been hurting since he was 30. But better hurting than dead—which he should have been since 1965.

"Don't hurry. He's dead," said the first doctor to get to him that Sunday at Riverside, Calif. And that would have been that, and all these years they'd have reminisced about the late, great A.J. Foyt, had not his old hell-raisin' buddy, the second-toughest guy ever to drive a race car, Parnelli Jones, noticed a faint gagging sound from the unconscious body and said, "Well, wait a minute," crawled into the overturned stock car and with his fingers started to dig the mud and sand from A.J. Foyt's mouth and throat so he could breathe again.

Broken back, crushed sternum and bad concussion. And A.J. Foyt's prime as a driver was yet to come: His third and fourth Indy 500 wins, victories in the Daytona 500 stock car race, the 24 Hours of Le Mans sports car race, the 24 Hours of Daytona, the 12 Hours of Sebring— every one of the world's most renowned races except the Grand Prix of Monaco, which he never entered because of his disdain for Formula One racing.

Formula One wasn't considered racing at all by the tough guys around the dirt tracks that loosed A.J. Foyt onto the world and birthed his mean-as-a-bull image. The late Johnny White once recalled what it felt like when a raging young Foyt snatched him by the head as he sat in a sprint car at Williams Grove, Pa.: "I could feel my helmet breaking around my ears—krrrrnch!"

Foyt's is a record of diversified talent, guts and tantrums unequaled in all the world and likely to stand for the ages.

Several rooms—in several places—full of trophies are unnecessary
reminders of his career, considering the head-to-toe museum he walks
around in. Take that scar the breadth of a calf rope, running the length
of his right forearm. That's the ghost of the muscle tissue left hanging
in a guardrail in Michigan in 1980. Those white splotches on his neck
are old skin grafts, from fiery crashes down through the years.

So this latest thing, though it might seem like the physical comeback
of alltime, in all of sport—this matter of A.J. Foyt's feet and legs, gathered
piece by piece out of a dirt embankment last September and now back
under him, functioning, rather than hanging in some wheelchair, or
amputated and buried ahead of him—this was just par for Foyt. This
was not so much miracle, and not so much modern surgery and therapy,
as it was that A.J. Foyt said he was going to keep those feet and legs
and he meant it.

The doctors who got to Foyt last September at Elkhart Lake, Wis.,
were amazed he didn't just pass out from the pain. He was conscious
through it all, from the moment the brakes failed to the instant the car
stuck in the dirt like a dart, its front end torn off and Foyt's lower body
rammed into the earth.

When the doctors got to him, his left femur was sticking up through
the mud and various other parts of both legs and feet were more or less
sprouting up every which way so that the doctors couldn't tell at first
which leg or foot was which, or whether they were still attached to A.J.
Foyt at all. The doctors dug the dirt away with their hands and began
administering morphine, 15 c.c. in all, enough to knock out a mule, and
still it hurt so bad that Foyt rolled his eyes toward Dr. Terry Trammell
and growled, "Just find a goddamn hammer and knock me in the head!"

On this usual morning at Stockman's, A.J. Foyt can grin, even laugh
about all the physical pain, all these years. You want to make him
somber, subdued, start him muttering? Then go ahead. Bring this up:

What do you imagine it's gonna feel like, A.J., when you limp out
there in front of 400,000 people at 11 o'clock on the morning of May 26,
1991 and slide down into that car to start your 34th—and your last—
Indy 500?

He snaps the reflex denial, the defense mechanism with which he
has approached every Indy of his life: "I'm looking at it as just another
race."

Think about it, A.J.: Four Indy 500 wins and 34 straight starts and

400,000 people standing in unison to deliver what amounts to the Nobel Prize of cheers, a thunderous, relentless ovation awarded not for a day nor a single win nor even any near-immortal season, but for lifetime achievement.

He gazes down at the table top. He unwraps his flatware from the paper napkin and doodles with a fork.

"To be truthful with you, I've kind of dialed it out of my mind. Trying to *keep* it out." And here there is a bare hint of warning, a glimmer of the long-ago fiery ire. He pauses.

"It's just—it's gonna be just another race and, I mean, things might change, you know, but like I say, right now, that's . . ." He trails off, turning the fork over and over on the table.

Two p.m. and atypically hot for April in Indianapolis, and every one of the 290,000 seats at Indianapolis Motor Speedway is empty. In all of sports there is no more haunting sight than these, the most massive grandstands on the face of the earth, empty, echoing with the turbo-charged whine of a single car.

In the pits, a handful of people—mostly mechanics in black shirts with white letters reading "A.J. Foyt/Copenhagen Racing"—squint down the track, awaiting the approach of the black dot emitting the distant whine.

A.J. Foyt is here for a private test session, to shake down a new car, but mainly "to test myself . . . to see if I really want to do this." He has to know ahead of time. He doesn't intend to come out here for qualifying on May 11 and make a fool of himself.

Minutes earlier, from inside a "full-face" helmet, his eyes crinkled with suffering as he crammed his 6-foot bulk into the tiny cockpit of the new Lola—a car built in England to accommodate the typical modern-day Indy-car driver, who is about 5-8, 160 pounds. Yet, once settled in, the eyes again became those of a boy, at home, at peace.

And now the black dot grows on the hallowed horizon of Indy's front straightaway, creeping along at a mere 120 mph on a warmup lap. As it crosses the start-finish line, the Lola jumps as A.J. Foyt's rebuilt right foot goes to the floor, unleashing all of the Ilmor-Chevy engine's 700 horsepower. Digital stopwatches begin to blink in the pits, and from the backstretch now you can hear the turbocharger screaming. But suddenly a crewman presses his radio headset closer to his ears, listens, and shouts to the others:

"Heads up! Comin' in."

The black Lola pulls in and the visor goes up on the orange helmet, and inside, A.J. Foyt is laughing. Why is he laughing? Because on this, his very first "hot lap" since last September, the goddamn *brakes* felt like they were going to fail, just like they felt that moment before that other Lola went airborne at Elkhart Lake, just like they felt that moment before the stock car slammed into the embankment at Riverside in '65.

"Had a little flashback out there just now," Foyt says, grinning. "I touched the brake pedal and it went to the floor. Probably just air in the lines, first time out for this car and all. But, tell you what: Let's bleed those brakes again, just to be sure."

And that is as close to afraid as A.J. Foyt will get in this, the test session during which he climbs back on the horse. Not that he hasn't been scared in his time. "I've heard some of the top names in racing say they've never been scared. Bull! Any sonofabitch who's ever been any good has been scared. I've thrilled the [expletive] out of myself on many a lap, and I'm not just talking about the times I've been hurt."

Brakes bled, reworked, checked out, he goes out again. One more shakedown lap, at a mere 197 mph, and then you can hear things start to get serious.

The way you know an Indy car means business is when you can hear it pushing wind before it, a whoosh just ahead of the engine's scream, and now down the front stretch you can hear it, this hurricane with a siren inside it, heralding the comeback of A.J. Foyt, and now there is a whooshwheeeeeee YOW! as he passes, the black Lola moving so fast that your eyes can't follow it smoothly; it sort of jumps and skips across your field of vision. When an Indy car starts to play that jump-skip trick on your eyes, the rule of thumb is that it's doing about 230 mph. And all that can harness that fury safely is the centrifugal force of that sharp left turn into Indy's first corner.

Bobby Rahal, a driver Foyt can't abide—he's one of that fancy-pants new breed—once articulated oh so well what is happening now: "No amount of money in the world can make you go into that first turn at Indy and turn left unless you *want* to."

You can tell by the sound whether a driver backs off the throttle in the first turn, but the whine remains steady. A.J. Foyt's right foot is still on the floor. Stopwatches blink and whooshwheeee YOW! and a pit board is held up so he can see it: 212.5 mph average around the track, and A.J. Foyt is *back,* by God and by Foyt.

Next lap's average is 213.3, and before this test session is done there'll be a lap at 216.6—not bad for a busted-up, overweight, 56-year-old man who hates vegetables and milk—and Steve Watterson is standing there in the pits dumbfounded.

Watterson is the Houston Oilers' special rehabilitation trainer who last November took on the biggest rehab project of his career. You take all the worst lower-body injuries in NFL history, combine them, come up with a 10 Worst list, put them all into one man's body, and that, essentially, was A.J. Foyt when Watterson first laid eyes on him.

In his time around the NFL, Watterson has put Joe Theismann and Ron Jaworski and Bill Burgy back together—"I've worked on some destroyed joints, some compound fractures. But nothing of this magnitude."

Watterson found a man who'd undergone three lengthy, complex rounds of surgery for compound fractures of both legs and bad mangling of both feet. There were skin grafts, steel pins, open wounds everywhere below both knees and numerous masses of scar tissue.

"Both ankles were frozen . . . there was no sensory perception in the feet. I could put his feet in hot water or ice water and he couldn't tell me which was which. . . . When he wanted to walk on the beach I told his wife to get him some of those scuba diving socks, because if he stepped on glass he'd never know it.

"All through the therapy he would tell me—yell at me—'Fix my right foot so it will go *down*. Don't worry about whether I can lift it. In my game, if you lift your right foot, you lose.'

"I've worked with the Olympics. Worked with the NFL. Known some tough men . . . But never have I met anyone tougher than A.J. Foyt."

Four a.m. in a Milwaukee Hospital last September, deep in a relentless, waking, living nightmare. *Damn* that useless morphine that makes you vomit till your stomach is dry and then keeps you heaving until even your diaphragm and ribs are killing you.

A.J. Foyt closes his eyes but there is no sleep. There has been no sleep for days, except under anesthesia during surgery. A decade ago, the ripped open arm "hurt! Godamighty!" when he woke up in the helicopter over Michigan, but this . . . *this!*

Then his daddy comes.

Old Tony Foyt comes in quietly and stands by the bed and surveys the situation. "You're hurt pretty bad," he says. "But everything's going to be all right."

A.J. breathes just a little easier and the dry-heaving stops.

"It'll be all right," his daddy says.

Tony Foyt has been dead since 1983. But through the decades he never failed to be with A.J. when A.J. was hurt bad, and Tony was—is—too solid a chunk of old Czech-German-Texan granite to abandon the boy now.

For two sleepless weeks, every time A.J. Foyt closes his eyes, his daddy will be there.

Months later, A.J. will still "feel like I talked to him . . . like he was right there and he came and talked to me. . . . I don't know—I can't tell you why."

Psychologists have noted that men dying, men in excruciating pain, often dream of their long-dead fathers. Gen. George S. Patton's last utterance was, "Papa?"

Bullish and hardened as A.J. Foyt has always seemed, he has always been at his epicenter just a big old tough kid who loved his mama and daddy more than anything—far more, far deeper, than the average son loves.

"I never really left my parents. I don't know if that's good or bad. I have no regrets.

"My own kids [two sons and a daughter, all grown], I'm close to 'em and yet I'm not close to 'em. You know how it is nowadays. But my mama and daddy—it was more like a partnership than a mama and daddy. Daddy worked with me. We built our own cars. We built the car we won Indy with in '67. In '77 we won with both a car and an engine we'd built ourselves. I'm the only man who's ever won Indy by building his own car and his own motor and then driving the thing himself. I doubt anybody will ever do that again.

"It's still hard to realize that mama's been gone since '81 and daddy since '83." Both died in the month of May, Indy month. "They both waited till I qualified at Indy, waited till I got home [during the two-week lull between qualifying and the race], and closed their eyes."

If ever there was a tougher man than Anthony Joseph Foyt Jr., "A.J.," he was Anthony Joseph Foyt Sr., "Tony." Here's how tough Tony Foyt was: In 1975, he happened to visit his doctor's office for some routine tests, and evidence was discovered that months earlier he'd suffered a massive heart attack. Most men would have dropped dead from the attack. Tony Foyt, if he'd felt a sledgehammer in his chest, hadn't told anyone. He had ignored it, hadn't even broken stride.

But in 1983 there was an ailment not even Tony could ignore—cancer. By February, he was in the hospital dying. He clearly wouldn't live to see another Indy 500. The British Aston-Martin team, and Daytona International Speedway President Bill France Jr., had been asking A.J. to race in the 24 Hours of Daytona. A.J. hadn't driven in a 24-hour race since Le Mans in '67.

"No use in you hangin' around here," Tony said. "Go on down there and run."

The Aston-Martin failed early in the race, but another team owner hurried to A.J. and offered him a chance to switch teams in mid-race, to co-drive with Frenchmen Bob Wollek and Claude Ballot-Lena in a turbo Porsche. A.J. had never driven a Porsche, didn't even know the shift pattern—had to be shown the pattern on another Porsche that had been wrecked.

At dawn, it was foggy, pouring rain. A.J. hadn't raced in the rain in 20 years—he'd been running oval-track races, which aren't run when it's wet.

Wollek roared into the pits, climbed out, and A.J. Foyt got in. He tested the shifter, revved the engine and roared away, and at 200 mph the car was hydroplaning, sending huge roostertails of water skyward. A.J. Foyt was faster than anyone else on the track, faster than all the Englishmen and Italians and Germans with all their years of experience racing in rain.

Foyt, Wollek and Ballot-Lena won. Afterward, the team owner asked how much of the purse A.J. would like.

"None of it," said A.J. "All I want is the trophy."

With it in hand, he boarded his private jet back to Houston. He rushed to the hospital and gave it to his Daddy.

When Tony died, A.J. sank into "a limbo" that would last for years, and sap his pride in racing. He lost interest in everything—his two ranches, his thoroughbred horses, his businesses. "Thank God I wasn't much of a drinker. I probably would have gone on the bottle—become a total alcoholic."

Dazed, distraught, Foyt stood still while Indy car competition soared into high technology. Suddenly, after 25 years as emperor of Indy, his efforts there withered.

"He hasn't kept up with all the testing, technology and development over the past eight years," says retired three-time Indy winner Bobby Unser. "These drivers out here today think, 'Oh, I've raced against

Foyt—he's easy.' But they've never raced against *Foyt.* If they'd ever raced against *Foyt,* they'd be saying 'Yes, sir' and 'No, sir' to him today."

Eleven a.m. on a typically muggy East Texas day and a big red Chevy pickup, the kind with double wheels on the back, is rolling toward Houston with the radar detector on and A.J. Foyt at the wheel, relaxed, remembering.

"One time out at Riverside, NASCAR had this real badass technical inspector who kept messing with Parnelli. Parnelli finally said, 'Show me where my car's illegal.' The inspector stuck his head under the hood, and Parnelli slammed the hood down on his head. Wham!

"Of course they threw Parnelli out. We did some crazy stuff. But we didn't care if they threw us out. See, we were there to run a race, and if they liked us, fine, and if not, [expletive] on 'em."

NASCAR, USAC, CART, didn't matter. Foyt and his running mates, Parnelli Jones and Jim Hurtubise, had come off the meanest dirt tracks in America. Hurtubise was horribly disfigured in a fiery crash at Milwaukee, and when surgeons told him his hands would be immobile for the rest of his life, but that they could shape them however he wanted, he said, "Shape 'em to fit a steering wheel" and went on racing until he died of a heart attack.

"We traveled a lot together, me and Parnelli and Hurtubise. Raised some hell. Had a beer or two." And now A.J. Foyt is smiling, gazing off somewhere into the 1960s.

"One time Parnelli won a race at Cleveland, Ohio. I pulled the truck up to victory lane and said, 'Let's go.' Well, this fan walked by and said to Parnelli, 'I wish you hadn't won today. I wish you'd got killed.' Parnelli took that trophy and slapped the sonofabitch with it. Right there in victory lane. Wham! Right in his face."

Parnelli Jones swears today that "I was the *sane* one of the bunch. Them other two were crazy."

Jones shrugs matter-of-factly: "I've seen A.J. jerk guys out of cars and beat the hell out of 'em, stuff like that. And I don't mean around the race tracks. I mean driving down the street, when people would hassle him . . . I've seen him take care of a couple of 'em at a time.

"One day we were sittin' around the pits at Indy, talkin'," says Jones, "and A.J. says, 'Tell you what: Let's take on Muhammad Ali. You fight him one round and I'll fight him the next. I think we'd kick his ass.' . . . That was A.J.'s idea, not mine . . ."

The racing world waited for years for what would have been the damnedest non-title fight of all time, Foyt vs. Jones, a struggle that likely would have gouged half the bricks out of Indy's front straightaway.

"I knew if we ever got to dukin' it out, there would be some blood shed," says Jones. But it never happened. The closest they ever came was at Ascot Park, a little dirt track outside Los Angeles, over a matter as minuscule—to everyone but Foyt and Jones—as a trophy dash in midget cars.

"I was on the pole," says Jones, "and A.J. started on the outside of me. When the race started, he pinched me off—chopped me real bad —and I spun my car. Afterward, we were standing there jawing at each other, cussin' a mile a minute. We came close to blows. I went back to my crew and said, 'I've had it with Foyt! I'll never talk to the sonofabitch again.' Then, just before the main event, I was down there working on my car, adjusting the chassis, and if I'da seen him coming I'da never let him get his hands on me. But I had my back turned, and all of a sudden I felt this big ol' huggy bear with his arms around me. It was Foyt, grinning. . . . That's the kind of guy Foyt is: He has this great talent for pissin' you off and then coming back and giving you a big hug."

At Indy, Foyt's reputation was so ferocious that all it took was a growl to scatter a crowd.

"One time at Indy," Jones recalls, "Foyt had just come back into his garage after qualifying, and here came all these USAC officials, old guys, to inspect his car. Foyt was sitting on a stool in the garage when they came in, and he screamed, 'GET THE [EXPLETIVE] OUTTA HERE!' and here went all these old guys staggering backwards, getting out of there," and Parnelli Jones is clutching his chest, mimicking guys having heart attacks. "A while later the door cracked open and this old guy peeked in and said, 'Oh, Mr. Foyt? Is it all right if we come check your car?' And these were the *officials.*"

Since his first two Indy 500 wins, in 1961 and '64, the world has been on the lookout for A.J. Foyt. The pinnacle of scrutiny came in 1967, when Ford Motor Co. gathered an armada of American drivers and cars for an all-out assault on Le Mans. Parnelli Jones turned down a spot on the team, figuring "I was too tough on equipment—I had enough trouble making a car last 500 miles, let alone 24 hours." Foyt accepted, seeing Europe's deadliest track as nothing more than "a li'l ol' country road."

Just two weeks earlier, Foyt had won his third Indy, plowing headlong through a smoke-shrouded melee of wrecking cars on the home stretch on the very last lap. Then he flew off to France to co-drive with Dan Gurney in a Ford Mark IV prototype sports car. Before the race, the French media predicted, "The wild young Americans will drive too hard. They will break the car. They will not finish."

They would lead for a total of 23½ hours and win, becoming the only all-American driving team in a thoroughly American car to win Le Mans.

Gurney started the race, and by late afternoon had set the Mark IV's headlights blazing, the international signal to "Move over! Leader coming by!"

When Foyt's first stint came, "I'd only had about four or five laps of practice on the course." It was tantamount to sending an all-pro cornerback out to play one-on-one soccer against Pele. But Foyt would learn fast, on the job. He had come to trust the rowdy, bullish New Zealander Denis Hulme. Foyt roared out of the pits and spotted Hulme's car on the track. "He was already a couple of laps down, but I knew he knew the course. I followed Denny for eight or 10 laps, to familiarize myself with the course, then passed him and went on."

Between midnight and dawn came one of the legendary driving stints in the lore of Le Mans. By the newcomer, A.J. Foyt.

"About 3:30 in the morning, I was supposed to be finishing a four-hour shift. But they couldn't find Gurney in the pits. He'd been to Le Mans before, and he knew what it was like when all that fog started coming in. Man, I was tired. I said, 'Let me out!' They said, 'You gotta do another shift. We can't find Gurney.' I was hurting.

"About 4:30 in the morning was when some of the other Fords wrecked. Going down the Mulsanne Straight [nearly four miles of country highway where speed's only limits are those of horsepower and nerve], a guy blew an engine and turned over and caught fire. The car was upside down and burning right there at the end of the straight, and here was all this smoke and fog and all these cars flying in. I guess you're running about 240 or 250 down the Mulsanne. I downshifted real hard and missed the wreck. But I over-revved the engine and figured we'd warped everything. Turned out the car was fine. When Gurney finally relieved me, I'd driven nearly eight hours straight."

After the race, the European press asked the wild young Americans the "secret" that had won the race for them.

Foyt lifted his right foot toward their faces and said, "*This* won the race."

They asked if he thought winning the world's two greatest races, back to back within a fortnight, would make him famous. Foyt was incredulous. You know, hell, he was already famous in America, the only place that mattered to him. Foyt pointed to his right foot again:

"That *foot* is what made me famous."

Noon at Foyt's racing shop in northwest Houston, and he is sitting on a little midget racer, not very different from the one he was driving on Texas dirt in 1955 when the sprint car moguls discovered him and took him off to Minnesota, where his stardom budded. By 1957, sprint car owners figured the 22-year-old was ready for a crucial test: the high-banked, half-mile oval at Salem, Ind.

"A lot of people wouldn't run the high-banked tracks in sprint cars because it was so dangerous, so if you ran good on the high banks they figured you were fearless and crazy—figured you'd probably be a good Indy driver."

And so in 1958, a crotchety official at the gate to storied Gasoline Alley watched a bullish Texas youth amble up.

"What do you want, boy?" the old man asked.

"I'm a driver."

"What's your name?"

"A.J. Foyt."

"Who do you drive for?"

"Al Dean."

"You got a letter or anything to prove it?"

"Nossir."

"Well, Dean's car isn't in yet. You'll have to come back in a couple of days."

"But, sir, I'm a USAC member."

"I don't care. You can't come in here."

Foyt still laughs about it. "I had to stay outside for two days."

Nobody asks A.J. Foyt for identification at the gates of Gasoline Alley now. Nobody has for 30 years. Not once. He is the living, breathing, singular symbol of the place. After this Indy 500, after A.J. Foyt's last one, "they'll survive, I'm sure . . . But I do believe a lot of people hate to see me go."

All A.J. Foyt has ever known is driving. Tony built him a custom little car to play in when he was 2. One weekend when he was 11, A.J. was home alone with one of the midget cars his Daddy owned. When his Daddy and Mama got home, they "found the whole yard tore up," Tony once recalled. "The grass was all chewed to bits and there were tire gouges all over the place. The swing set we had in the yard had been knocked over. . . . I knew right away that A.J. had got some of his buddies to push him and they'd got that midget fired up." Tony went to the garage and found the car: "He'd caught the thing on fire and had burned up the engine."

Tony went into A.J.'s bedroom and found him pretending to be asleep. Tony stood there seething, but calmed down, knowing "right then, standing there in the kid's bedroom, that he would have to race, that there wasn't going to be any other way."

That was in 1946. And now, there is no telling how A.J. Foyt is going to react when those 400,000 people thunder this coming Indy 500 morning. But there's a very good hint at how he'll feel when he goes back to Indy in '92, not as a driver:

Twelve-thirty p.m. on a balmy winter Sunday at Daytona last February. On crutches, A.J. Foyt hobbles off an elevator into a VIP suite and settles 235 pounds into a plush chair. Far below sit 42 monstrous stock cars, waiting to awaken for the Daytona 500.

As iron a man in stock cars as at Indy, Foyt is sitting out the Daytona 500 for the first time since 1965, when he was laid up with the Riverside injuries.

He is wearing sunglasses. So no other human will ever know what is going on in A.J. Foyt's eyes as the command is given to start engines and the iron thunder rises against the tinted windows of the VIP suite and the cars lumber off the starting grid.

"I damn near got tears in my eyes," is as much as he'll admit later, "watching them drive away . . . I felt like they were leaving me . . . up in those grandstands, where I didn't belong."

John Huston

Fool

John Huston was a man of many talents. Though best known as the director of memorable motion pictures such as The Maltese Falcon, The African Queen, Prizzi's Honor, *and* The Treasure of the Sierra Madre, *Huston was also a fine actor and writer. Sports were a major part of his life as well, and at one time he dabbled in boxing. His fascination with the fight game is evident not only in this short story he wrote in 1929 about honor among sparring partners, but also in his work as the director of the film version of Leonard Gardner's novel* Fat City. *(See page 234.)*

Victor du Lara was a young Italian. He had the shape of head you often see on clever boys. You call it conical. From a small hard jaw it widened upward to a cranium that was round like a bowl. He had a hard mouth, and his eyes were set wide apart. He was short with a strong back, so he could hold like a vise and pound in the clinches. He was a slugger with a lot of native speed. Like a nail he made his own openings, and he followed up fast, hammering like a carpenter.

Victor and myself, and a fellow named Harry who used to second for us, and a friend of Harry's, a man whose name I forget, who had just got out of the army, were all of us on the street car. We were coming away from Madison Square Garden down in Darktown.

Madison Square Garden is a Negro fight arena, named after the big Madison Square Garden in New York.

When I think about that ride I get elated. Something had happened that put me at the dirty end of the stick. I had done something terrible. I want to say that Victor and Harry and the soldier were three men of mercy. They laughed at my sin and didn't rub it in. They let it go at that. Their treatment rid my nature of a lot of rubbish.

Victor du Lara and I had gone as children to the same school, but we had not known each other. That is, we had never been friends. I was a few months younger than he, and that made a great difference. He was the crustiest boy in the school.

The neighborhood of the school was poor. Most of the students were the sons and daughters of low-class Italians and Negroes and Polacks. Beside myself, there was only one other child who could lay any claim to being well raised, and he was slightly effeminate. The Italian boys used to gang him on his way home—not from lack of nerve, for any one of them could have handled him. They only desired to share the pleasure. I envied them.

One night after school I was alone with the tormented fellow. I hoped vicariously to enjoy the companionship of the roughnecks by beating him myself. But it was a heartless effort. He made no resistance. The yard was deserted except for the effeminate boy and me. I had been awkward about starting the fight. He would resent nothing. Finally I pushed him over. When he got up I knocked him down with my fist. Then he sat in the sand, rubbing his eyes and weeping, while blood trickled out of his nose. I threw him my handkerchief and went home.

To and from school, and in the recess periods, Victor jumped rope and shadow boxed. He was the youngest in his room and he was small, but he could teach tricks to anybody in the school. Into the Negroes he put the fear of God. He called them jigaboos. I have seen him step into a group of blacks, measure the largest, and without warning slap him flat-handed. They came to understand that any defense meant twice the punishment. Whenever they gathered there was always one posted to keep a nervous watch for Victor. When he came toward them they'd separate. He never picked on a Negro alone.

In those days all paths led to love and physical supremacy. They were the male and female and they embraced in constant beauty. The youth of the school were hot-blooded. Hardly any of us were graduated without physical experiences of love. At fourteen the Latin girls had swelling breasts. The eighth grade was a hotbed of romance.

Victor wore bracelets on his wrists, and rings too small for his fingers dangled on strings over his chest. The jewelry belonged to girls. It was secured by Victor's plights. He was a vowing lover.

His first professional fight was when he was sixteen. At the athletic club he had one or two starts. But he was full of contempt for the amateur. They tried to give him a bronze medal for clouting the State champion, but Victor said keep it: if he didn't get cash he wouldn't fight. His professional start was out at Monrovia, which is a little fight town about twenty-five miles away from the city. It is quite a fight center. They have several good Negro boys out there. They still have battles royal, which they wisely keep all black. They make up their main events by bringing two good boxers in. The crowds are mixed, but they are mostly white. It is a good tryout place.

Victor boxed a white man, who was getting old and going down. But he had been good in his day, and he had an awful stock of tricks. At Monrovia they like blood. They judge a card by the number of knockouts. The matchmaker out there would rather put a ham and a good boy together than two evenly matched hams. The man Victor was to box had a little reputation, so the matchmaker must have thought it would be that kind of a fight. The State limit was four rounds. Victor forced the going from the first. His opponent was a general, and tried to stall by clinching. But he found that the young Italian was like a riveting machine. He could jar himself loose. Then the man got dirty. In a clinch he rolled the heel of his glove over Victor's nose, and when Victor lowered his head, he gave him his elbows and put his thumbs in his eyes.

Remember, this was Victor's first professional fight. He had boxed up at the athletic club with kids his own age. Here was something new. He'd never been up against a man like this before. What he did showed there was no dog in him. Nothing in Queensberry could help him. So he bared his teeth and caught his man by the throat. Then he hung on. That's the kind of a guy he was.

2.

The beginning of our friendship was one day in the gymnasium he asked me to work out. It's best to be careful of a pickup. If you're known to be any good, and if he isn't afraid of you, he'll usually try to put one over for the crowd.

"All right if you'll take it easy. I only want to sweat."

We boxed nicely. Afterwards I took my rubdown. Victor asked me to be first. While I was being rubbed he talked.

"I'm no good with tall fellows like you unless I go hard. That's the only way I can fight. If you can't box you can't beat a man that won't

fight. There are two kinds of fighters, offensive and defensive. What's
your religion? Are you a Catholic?"

"No," I answered.

"But you believe in God."

"Yes, indeed."

We took our shower together. While the water rained down on him
he stuck out his belly.

"You went to the Lincoln Heights school, didn't you?" he asked.

"Yes," I said. "I remember you. You were in the eighth grade when
I was in the seventh. I only went there one year."

"Are you using your real name?"

"No." I told him what my real name was.

While we were drying he asked if I liked wine. I said that I did, and
he invited me to come over to his house.

"There's no one there but my old lady."

When we got on our clothes I went with him.

His mother was a nice Italian lady, who spoke no English. She sat
with me in the parlor and smiled, while Victor got wine and glasses. I
do not believe she drank any, but only held some in her glass, and smiled
while we drank, which was her Latin breeding.

The ride on the street car that I spoke of at the start was after the
night's bouts at Madison Square Garden, where Victor and I had both
fought.

I want to say that an all-black crowd makes about the best audience
there is. Negroes have a real sense of humor, no mistake. What happened
that night a white audience would never have stood for.

We used to get only fifteen or twenty dollars for a fight out there.
It would have been worth it if we had fought for nothing. The referee
was a Negro who had been a fighter himself. He was the most comic
man I ever saw in a ring. He was a regular actor. It was worth the price
of admission to see that man break up a clinch. He would knock with
his knuckle on a boy's shoulder, very dignified, as though he were knocking at a door. Then when they broke he would thank them, bowing from
the waist. That used to bring down the house.

The way they made up their cards out there was a scream. Two
days in advance they wouldn't know who was going to fight. But the
bills would have been out for a week. How they worked it was they just
threw a lot of fake names on the poster. Then first come, first served.
You could look over the programme, and choose for your own whichever
name you liked best. They introduced me by six different names the
times I fought.

This evening I fought an extra time to fill up a vacant spot on the bill. My first fight was the one I was matched for. It was with a big red-headed boy. They introduced me as Battling Levinsky, which is very funny, as I am neither Russian nor Jew. The first fight was no match. We were stopped in the third round. That black referee stopped more fights than any man I ever saw. Maybe it was because the matches out there were the craziest in the world. But all the boxers were not hams. Occasionally they brought in some good boys who were short on pin money, and two fine young Negroes were developed out there and got their start. Still, almost anybody could get on. At Madison Square I've seen boys fight in those Y. M. C. A. gymnasium pants, and tennis shoes.

The Irish kid whom I boxed that evening wasn't much above that class. He was heavier than I but he could never get inside my long arms. And for all his weight he wasn't even strong. Although I am not a hard hitter, they had to stop us because the Irish boy couldn't take it.

3.

My second match you would never call a fight. It was with Victor to help him out. Everything was agreed upon beforehand. His boy did not show up, and there was no one on the card good enough to match him with. At Madison Square they never heard of a forfeit. He would either lose his twenty dollars, or we would have to pull a fake.

That fight was the funniest thing that ever went in a ring. I was a lightweight and very tall, and Victor du Lara was a welter. As I said there was an all-around understanding—the matchmaker, the referee, even the audience.

To line us up just about as we were, I'll say that Victor was a hard hitter, a slugger with speed. He fought low, weaving his body and swinging them up from his hips, with his whole weight behind each blow. But for all that he was a very clean cut kind of boy. I was tall with long arms, and I knew how to keep them out. I was naturally a straight hitter, right from the start when I had my fights at grammar school. I developed a short jab in my left that was almost automatic. It would work without my thinking of it. The blow was not hard, you understand, but it was stinging and cutting, and it used to make them first mad and then disheartened.

We were introduced and the fight started. No two boys ever came together who could fake less convincingly. Victor with a slugger like himself, or I with the other kind of fighter, a more scientific person, might either of us have stalled it out. But the two of us together trying to bluff were the craziest pair you ever saw.

My left went out automatically, and chopped him right on the nose. I knew what I had done and I climbed into a clinch where I apologized. Victor, as he was a welter, could have killed me.

The Negro crowd knew what had happened. They laughed. If a white audience had been around that ring, we would have been mobbed. But Negroes are either sillier than whites or they have a finer sense of humor. I'll leave it to you.

In the clinch Victor didn't answer me, but only pushed me off. I was frightened and puzzled. I didn't know whether he was angry or just keeping up the bluff. I broke clean and began to dance around. Then he came at me hard, or so I thought.

"I don't like to do this," I thought, "but if he is going to make a real fight of it I'll stay in as long as I can."

So I nailed him again right on the nose.

I heard the crowd yell. It was certainly a peculiar situation. Negroes are quick to see a thing. They could tell about my dilemma.

Victor drove in with a one-two, but I caught both blows on my forearms, and gave him back two short ones right square on his nose. I felt the bone give through the pads on my knuckles. A red clot big as a polliwog came down out of his nostril and hung over his lip. I was certainly afraid. I was worried for fear it was all a great mistake. I grabbed Victor's arm and yelled in his ear over the noise.

"Vic, did I hurt you?"

He said something back, but for the noise I couldn't hear. I tried to see the expression on his face. He was so bloody I couldn't make him out. It was time. I went to my corner worse off than ever. In my corner I decided there was only one thing to do. Rather than take any chance about his meaning business, I'd leave an opening. If he wanted he could knock me cold. It would be better than my picking them off his nose that way, and he trying to do the right thing. I tried to catch his eye across the ring. I thought maybe if he could see me smile at him he might understand.

Harry, the man I spoke of, was my second. He was a friend of Victor's and a friend of mine. As Harry liked us both I thought he might tell me, if he knew, what was going on.

"How does it look?" I asked.

"It looks great," answered Harry. "Nobody ever saw anything like it."

I was all turned around. I believed, or tried to, that Victor wasn't in earnest, that he could lay me out whenever he pleased. But there was the shade of the doubt. My mind was made up to do as I said. I'd leave a spot open; then, if he wanted, he could cut me down. Anyhow I'd know what the game was.

But that is harder to do than you'd think. Your instinct is not to drop your arms and let yourself be plugged. It was certainly nerve-wracking.

The bell had rung and I had come out. I was dancing around.

Everyone was on their feet, yelling their lungs out. The referee was making comic antics. I couldn't see humor in anything. Victor edged toward me. The Negroes pounded their feet and clapped. I never heard such a racket. The referee darted around the ring like a bird. I just danced back and forth.

I thought, "I'll have to end this."

I stepped over and made a wild swing at Victor's head. I expected him to dodge it, and maybe lay me cold on the spot. But it landed, and I never hit a punch more solid.

That almost killed the crowd. They laughed and laughed. I never heard such laughter in my life. I grabbed Victor and clinched. He pushed me away. I just stood there with my hands down.

He looked at me strangely, and backed off a little, lowering his own hands. The referee paused in the center of the ring, and the Negroes all shut their mouths. Everything was at a standstill.

Right then was the strangest moment I ever spent. Victor didn't lead and I didn't. The whole world seemed paralyzed. I had only one thought.

I thought, "I'm a shameful fool! I'm a shameful fool!"

The bell sounded. That crowd released. I mean they let everything loose. Nobody ever heard a yell like that crowd gave. I ran to Victor and threw my arms around him.

Don't believe I'm one of those guys who kisses a boy after he's knocked him hell west and crooked. I never hugged any boy before, and I never have since. I'll leave it to you to understand.

It was only the end of the second round, but the fight was over.

"I didn't cross myself," Victor said. "It was a fake, so I didn't like to cross myself."

We climbed out of the ring and walked down the aisle. Those Negroes got up off their benches and slapped our backs. And I want to say that I never felt anything so comforting as those black hands on me.

To show you the kind of fellows they were, when the manager and referee came back to pay us off they offered me thirty-five dollars.

"For that last fight," I said, "I don't want any money."

"You aren't getting any," the referee said. "The extra fifteen is just a present from the house."

So they made me take the money.

And I want to say right here that I never knew a guy like this Victor. He stood up there and let me break his nose like the shameful fool I was when he could have stretched me unconscious with either hand in less time than it takes to tell it here. That's what I call a man of mercy.

We got dressed and went outside and caught the street car. The soldier who had come with Harry, and Harry were along with Victor and me.

I remembered Victor as he was back in the Lincoln Heights school, when I used to stand back and envy him. Then I thought to myself, "That same guy let me break his nose."

4.

Suddenly I felt happy. I stopped feeling terrible about the thing I'd done. I only felt glad I was with those three guys. I began to talk without there being sense to anything I said. But those three fellows all listened to me as if they wouldn't miss a word. I never had such a time. I sat there with my cap in my lap, bent toward those fellows. When I had anything to say I would put my mouth to the nearest ear and shout. Harry and the soldier talked the same way. I guess we were having what you'd call the social instinct.

The soldier would speak, then Harry or I, then Victor would break in. After that long silence in the ring I certainly wanted to hear him talk.

He said: "Listen. I believe that Christ and Judas were in cahoots. I believe it was all laid out between them. Christ told Judas in private to sell Him for thirty pieces of silver, that if the Jews thought he'd been sold for that much, had suffered on the cross all for thirty pieces of silver, then they would not want to be like Judas and would want to be like Christ. It would make them good. I believe it was all fixed."

"I believe that," said Harry.

"Of course," said Victor. "He was the only one to die with his Lord-and-Master."

The soldier turned to me.

"What do you think? Do you believe that, too?"

"That was it," I said.

Dan Jenkins

The Coach Speaketh

Dan Jenkins is the sportswriter as storyteller. His yarns about the sports world, both fiction and nonfiction, jar the senses like a raucous tailgating party. As a senior writer for Sports Illustrated, *Jenkins wrote more than five hundred articles. In between his outpouring of nonfiction, he found time to write some best-selling novels, including* Semi-Tough, Baja, Oklahoma, *and* Dead Solid Perfect. *In this sampling, which appeared in* Playboy *in 1985, Jenkins gives us his definitive translation of the many-layered language spoken by college football coaches.*

C ollege football coaches have a language of their own, one that can only be understood by sportswriters usually, apart from one or two people on an island in the Netherlands Antilles.

What follow are the statements that most college coaches make to the alumni with their translations in parentheses, courtesy of a world-weary listener:

I've never had a reception like this anywhere, and if your enthusiasm carries over into the season, we'll win our share of games.

(Which one of you rich pricks is going to help me recruit that Swahili over in East Texas?)

I left a great school to come here but I've never backed off from a challenge yet.

(I think I'm going to like the oil business.)

I want the kids to think of me as their father. If they have any problem, big or small, I want them to come to me first.

(Until their eligibility is up.)

My obligation is not only to this university but to everybody connected with it. I'll go anywhere to make a speech and make new friends for this team, this faculty, this administration, this town.

(For a $3,000 fee, plus expenses.)

These kids were pretty good football players at one time. We're going to find out what happened to them.

(The guy who was here ahead of me couldn't coach a bunch of Mexicans in a bean-eating contest.)

I managed to get every assistant coach I went after, and I don't know anybody who's got a more capable or more loyal staff than I do.

(The first one of those assholes who screws up is out of here on a flatbed truck.)

I've told these kids that when we go out there for two-a-days, everybody is starting out equal.

(Except for the first team and they're so far ahead of everybody else, it makes my ass hurt.)

It's time for college coaches to understand that we're in the entertainment business. That's why I'm going to open up our offense.

(Anybody with sense knows you win with defense. I'll castrate the first quarterback who throws a pass inside his own 30-yard line.)

I know we've got some big-name teams on our future schedules, but we can't do anything about it, and personally I think those teams will help get us ready for this tough conference we're in.

(The athletic director who scheduled all this Oklahoma and USC shit ought to have his pecker cut off. I've been in touch with Lamar and Louisiana Tech.)

I don't ever want to hear the word steroid in my presence.

(But I'll drive a stake through the heart of any lineman who don't come back next year weighing 280 or over.)

In 30 years of coaching, on all levels, I've never had a punt blocked.

(One of you recruiters better go out and get me one of them barefooted sons of bitches who can kick it over the iron curtain.)

I want to make it clear to everybody that the kids we recruit are coming here to get an education first and play football second.

(Except from September through December when my job is on the line.)

One of the first things I'm going to do is change the uniforms. I've researched it and discovered that our school colors are actually burnt maroon and royal gray.

(No wonder they couldn't win here. They been dressing like peppermint sticks.)

Nobody was more pleased than the coaching staff when the chancellor announced plans for a new science building.

(That phony cocksucker made a promise to me that we'd get an athletic dorm, a weight room, artificial turf, and new stadium lights before those silly jerks got a new building.)

We could have had that kid but we couldn't live with his SAT scores.

(The little shitass wanted a BMW and two wardrobes, one for fall and one for spring.)

I understand the intent behind the NCAA rule. It's a good rule.

(It's a crock of shit. If I want to give a kid some spending it ain't nobody's business but my own.)

The press has a job to do like everybody else.

(There's one particular sportswriter in this town who's gonna get his baby kidnapped if he don't get off my butt.)

I'm not saying we'll win any championships, but in a year or two I'll bet we have a say in who does.

(If the alumni can buy me them Swahilis I want. Otherwise, it's been nice knowing you.)

Pat Jordan

The Tryout

Pat Jordan was twenty-five years old, with a wife and four kids, when he decided to become a writer. Before that, at age seventeen, the pitcher had signed a $40,000 contract with the Milwaukee Braves. He was a bonus baby. Five years later the fire went out of his arm; he was twenty-two years old and a has-been. No has-been as a writer, though. His third book, A False Spring, *summoned back elegiacally those days of little glory and much frustration including, in this excerpt, his tryout at Yankee Stadium, with would-be team-mates like Mickey Mantle, Yogi Berra, and Whitey Ford looking on.*

While Ray Garland led my brother on a tour of Yankee Stadium, in which everything, even the walls of the Stadium Club, seemed to be done in white with navy pinstripes, I was led to the Yankees' dressing room where I was given the uniform I would wear for my workout. The dressing room was unlike any I had ever seen. It was brightly lighted, spacious and spotless. The walls were white enamel and the floor was covered with a thick carpet. The players' lockers lined the walls. Each was an open-faced stall filled with polished black spikes, fresh-smelling new gloves and smartly pressed pinstriped uniforms. Yogi Berra, squat and homely, was sitting in his underwear on the tiny stool in front of his stall. He was hunched over reading his mail. Elston Howard, with a long pockmarked face the color of light coffee, was sitting in front of his stall talking softly with muscular Moose Skowron. Other players, in various stages of undress, moved about the room or sat by their stalls methodically putting on their uniforms. In the center of the room was a large picnic table with benches on either side. Two fully-uniformed players sat across from one another, heads down, intently autographing the 18 new baseballs in the box between them. They signed each ball with a flourish, dropped it back into the box with a "plunk," and then plucked out another as if a piece of fancy fruit. After a while one of the players got up and left and another slid into his place and began autographing the same balls. Each player had a specific spot on the balls where his signature must go. And the size of his signature usually was proportionate to his fame—the largest flourishes belonging to Mickey Mantle and Yogi Berra and the smaller ones to Bob Grim and Johnny Kucks.

To the left of the dressing room was a small, dark lounge with a leather reclining chair, a sofa, a coffee table and a television set. Whitey Ford, in full uniform, was stretched out in the chair smoking a cigarette and reading the *Wall Street Journal.*

To the right of the dressing room was the trainer's room. Even more spotless and brightly lighted than the dressing room, it fairly gleamed with stainless steel instruments and yards of white gauze and tape. Mickey Mantle was straddling the aluminum whirlpool machine. His left leg was outside the machine's small tub, while his right leg was plunged into the hot, churning waters that had turned his flesh a glowing pink. He used his left leg to balance himself on the floor, making a few awkward little hops every few seconds to retain that balance. He was amazingly short, I noticed, and tightly muscled. His shoulders and chest, and the thigh and calf of his left leg, were wrapped in bandages. He was grinning as I passed. It was a wide, blank grin that lent his puffy face an air of boyish dissipation.

I found an empty stall and began to undress among men who had been my idols since youth and whom I'd known only as names in newsprint and blurred images on a television screen. They did not look so imposing as I had imagined. I was bigger than most of them. As I undressed and put on my pinstriped uniform, I began to feel increasingly at ease. The uniform fit perfectly. I laced my spikes and stood up. I was indistinguishable from the players around me. I could have been any rookie just recalled from Denver or Richmond. I was truly at ease now and unbelievably confident, just as I had been on my last visit to Yankee Stadium as a 12-year-old on Mel Allen's television show. I was positive it was my destiny to be a teammate of these famous men.

I left the dressing room and began walking through the darkened runway that led underneath the concrete stands. Above me, I heard a faint rumbling. The runway became darker and darker as the stands above me graded lower and lower, and then suddenly I stepped through a doorway into the Yankee dugout and was momentarily blinded by the flash of sunlight and cloudless sky and immense expanse of field spread out before me. It took me a minute to catch my breath and for my eyes to adjust to the sudden brightness. Then, I traced the towering, triple-decked stands that surrounded the playing surface everywhere except in centerfield. As the stands rose they curved away from, then out over the field, casting a huge shadow, like the wings of a prehistoric bird, across the dark grass. The centerfield stands were open to the sun and seemed miles away. Behind them on an elevated track a train passed slowly. Only much later would I notice that the paint on those towering stands was faded and peeling, and that the grass which had looked so green was actually rather yellowish and did not cleanly outline the base paths as it should have. Yankee Stadium, as I remember it from that day, was not the most beautiful stadium I would visit. But it was the most majestic, and the memory of that day still chills me.

The playing field was deserted when I stepped onto the grass. The stands were empty also, except for the seats behind each dugout. It was hours before game time. I moved to a pitching rubber alongside home plate and was immediately tossed a baseball by a catcher in a Yankee uniform. I learned later he was Johnny Blanchard, an occasional substitute for Yogi Berra. Blanchard trotted back to the homeplate screen, crouched in front of it and gave me a target. I began to throw. As I did, I saw my brother, Ray Garland, the Yankee pitching coach Jim Turner and two men in business suits, whom I did not know, take seats directly behind the screen where Blanchard crouched.

As I threw, the Yankee and Kansas City players began to emerge from their dugouts like stragglers from a routed army. They started leisurely games of catch and pepper along the firstbase and thirdbase lines. They joked back and forth across home plate while I threw, unnoticed, between them. I was too scared to look either left or right, so I just continued to throw harder and harder until finally I cut loose with my first full-speed fastball. The sound of the ball hitting Blanchard's glove echoed around the stadium. The moment the ball left my hand I knew it was traveling faster than any ball I had ever thrown. I threw another fastball, and another, and another, each one a small explosion of its own. Those tiny explosions so exhilarated me that I failed to notice the Yankee and Kansas City players had stopped their banter. Nor did I notice when they also stopped their games of catch and pepper to just stand quietly and watch me throw. I was not aware of anything, really, except that the ball in my hand was as weightless as styrofoam and my motion had slipped into a groove so natural and smooth and mechanically perfect that it required no effort.

Even as I threw I saw it all—my arm passing above my head at precisely the same angle on each pitch. It was as if I, too, were standing outside myself, watching me throw. I imposed nothing on my talent. It had a will of its own, and all I could do was watch in amazement. This moment, then, was what it was all about. My talent, after all, was simply a diversion. It existed as an end in itself, with no purpose beyond being perfected and enjoyed. Money, victories, strikeouts, batters even, were meaningless. The men evaluating it from behind the screen and the players paying homage to it beside me were also meaningless. Nothing mattered but the simple act of throwing. And since it was only a diversion, once completed it, too, lost all meaning.

I would have gone on like that forever if Blanchard had not stood up and turned to say a few words to the men behind the screen. As he did, he slipped a sponge into his glove. I was suddenly aware of being watched and was momentarily flustered by such attention. The players went back to their games of pepper and I was alone again. I did not wonder what Blanchard was saying about me, but only wished he'd return to his crouch so I could begin throwing again. I feared the moment had been lost.

After showering and dressing, I met my brother and Ray Garland in the office of Johnny Johnston, the Yankees' Farm Director and one of the men who had been watching me throw. The walls of his office were hung with huge blackboards that contained the names, birthdates, records and present teams of every player in the Yankee farm system. When a player was moved from one team to another, his name was moved accordingly. Ray sat on the sofa along the wall and motioned my brother and me to two chairs in front of Johnston's desk. Johnston, a pudgy, bland-looking man with thinning blond hair, sat across from us, his white face expressionless. Unlike the scouts, and like most front-office personnel, Johnston possessed no extensive baseball-playing experience. Nor did he possess any of their warmth, manufactured though it might be. He was a businessman. He leaned forward and clasped his hands. "Impressive," he said in a voice that did not sound impressed. "Very impressive. But you can't tell much from just watching him throw. . . . Still, we liked what we saw. We'll give him three tens. Thirty thousand spread over three years. That's the largest bonus we've offered anyone since Frank Leja."

"I'm sure," my brother said. "But the kid won't sign for a penny less than forty. We know we can get that from any club."

"Maybe," said Johnston. "But the Yankeees are not 'any club.' "

Ray Garland stood up. "He's right, ya know. Jeesus Christ, this *is* the Yankees! Most kids would sign with us for nuthin', much less thirty grand." Johnston nodded and motioned for Ray to sit down.

"It's got to be at least forty," said my brother. "And at that we're willing to take less than we could get from other clubs."

Johnston was silent for a moment and then said, "Three twelves. Thirty-six thousand dollars, and that's our final offer. If you leave here without signing, it'll go down to thirty again."

Ray jumped out of his seat. "Jeesus Christ, he's not kiddin'! That's the way he works. That's more money than even I thought he'd offer!" He turned suddenly toward me and said, "What do you think, Pat? Don't you want to be a Yankee?"

"What?" I said.

"Don't you want to be a Yankee?" Ray asked. Everyone was staring at me. My brother and Johnston had surprised looks on their faces. Johnston said, "Well?"

"I don't know," I said. "I want to play for the Yankees, but . . ." I looked to my brother, who made an almost imperceptible shake of his head. ". . . It's up to my brother." He winked. (Years later when I would remind George about that day in Johnston's office, he'd say to me, "You know, I really wanted to take their final offer. But I knew it wasn't what you wanted." I said, "But it was! It was what I wanted!" He shook his head. "No, it wasn't," he said. "It would have hurt your pride to take less than we'd planned on.")

My brother turned to Johnston and said, "I don't see why the kid's worth thirty-six but not forty right now. I tell you what, we'll compromise. Throw in four years of college tuition and we'll sign." (At the time four years of tuition would have amounted to about $2800.)

Ray Garland smiled and looked to Johnston. Johnston shook his head no. My brother stood up to leave. I stood up. Ray jumped up and ran to the door. He spread his arms across it and said in an ominous voice, "I won't let you leave this room until Pat becomes a Yankee!" The gesture was a grand one, and my brother and I laughed over it on the way back to Connecticut. This was further proof, he said, that the entire proceedings had been carefully orchestrated by Johnston and Ray Garland, and that it was now only a matter of time before they acceded to our wishes.

A week later, we returned to Yankee Stadium only this time it was for a special workout for Hank Greenberg, the former homerun slugger of the Detroit Tigers and, at that time, a vice-president of the Chicago White Sox. Ron Northey, the White Sox scout in our area, had wanted me to work out in Chicago, but George had convinced him it would be more convenient for all of us to wait until the White Sox came to New York. He also figured that if Ray Garland and Johnny Johnston saw me throwing for Greenberg, it would persuade them to produce the additional money we wanted. We had not heard a word from them since that day in Johnston's office. My brother had also formulated a theory that virtually assured me of at least a $50,000 bonus. If the notoriously tight-fisted Yankees offered me $36,000, he said, then freer-spending teams like the Braves or White Sox would almost surely offer more. What neither of us knew at the time, however, was that 1959 was the first year the Yankees began to offer large bonuses. They had lost too many fine prospects to teams like the Braves and White Sox over the past years, prospects who were no longer swayed by Yankee pinstripes. On that day I dressed in Chicago's gray traveling uniform, however, I was still very much impressed by those pinstripes. I had no desire to sign with any team other than the Yankees, and secretly I hoped that Hank Greenberg would not offer the $50,000 my brother now demanded.

The visiting team's dressing room in Yankee Stadium was much smaller and drabber than the home team's. It looked as I'd originally expected a major league locker room to look. Even the White Sox players appeared less impressive than had the Yankees. Many of their names were unfamiliar to me—Barry Latman, Norm Cash, Ray Moore, Earl Battey. Only Early Wynn, barrel-chested and scowling, was recognizable. The rest suffered in comparison to Mantle, Ford and Berra. So did the atmosphere of their locker room. It was raucous and profane, with none of that self-contained and muted efficiency so evident in the Yankees' dressing room. At one point as I dressed, Norm Cash, wearing a towel around his waist, began to prance about the room and yell in a shrill voice, "Call for Mr. Levy! Call for Mr. Levy! Call for Mr. Levy!" He stopped only when Barry Latman, the team's Jewish pitcher, lunged at him. The two men grappled and fell to the floor. It took five of their teammates to separate them. I prayed that Hank Greenberg would not offer me $50,000.

I wanted to throw beside home plate as I had a week before, but Northey said it would be better for me to throw in the left field bullpen. "More privacy," he said. He smiled. "Ray Garland won't get a free peek at you out there." I threw well that day, and would have thrown even better if Greenberg had not stood behind my catcher and unnerved me. When I was sufficiently warmed up, he leaned over my catcher's shoulder like an umpire and said, "Let me see if you got a fastball." He was a huge man with a long, horsey face and bulbous nose. As I began my delivery I was tempted to use his nose as a target. After the pitch he straightened up. "Not bad," he said. "Fair enough for a kid." He spoke with a Bronx accent in a whiney voice that seemed ludicrous coming from such a big man. He continued to call for various pitches and to comment on them throughout the workout. He would have unnerved me even more if I had not caught sight of Ray Garland peeking over the wall that separated the bullpen's occupants from the fans. Ray's furtive looks made me smile, and I relaxed considerably. I began to throw almost as well as I had the week before, and nothing Hank Greenberg said or did could stop me.

Later, I met my brother, Northey and Greenberg in box seats along the thirdbase line. Greenberg was telling George what a great city Chicago was and what a great bunch of guys the White Sox players were. Cash and Latman, too? I was tempted to ask. Finally, he offered us $36,000. I was relieved. I didn't like him much. Maybe it was just his voice that did not seem to fit a man who once hit 58 home runs in a single season. I was disappointed in the same way all those silent film fans must have been the first time they heard John Gilbert in a talkie. Maybe, too, it was the way he had upset me while I was throwing. I suspected it had been deliberate on his part. Or perhaps it was simply my fault. Maybe I expected too much from a man who was no better and no worse than a lot of other men who never hit 58 home runs in one season.

After hearing Greenberg's bid we began to wonder if higher offers would come from other teams. So far we had received but three—$35,000 from the Orioles, $36,000 from the Yankees and $36,000 from the White Sox. Nothing indicated the Milwaukee Braves would offer more. George asked me if I was willing to sign with the Yankees for $36,000 and cancel our flight to Milwaukee. I said yes. That afternoon he called Ray Garland and told him we were ready to sign. We met Ray at the stadium and went directly to Johnston's office. Johnston was in conference, according to his secretary, so we took seats and waited. Ray was unusually quiet. It was almost an hour before Johnston came out of his office. He had his arm around the shoulders of a husky blond youth about my age, and he was congratulating the boy's parents. "You won't be sorry," he said and shook their hands. After they left, Johnston motioned us into his office.

"You win," my brother said with a smile. "The kid wants to sign for thirty-six."

"That's out of the question," said Johnston. "Did you see that boy who just left? His name is Hub King. We just gave him your $36,000. I'm afraid the best we can offer now is $24,000."

"What the hell do you mean?" shouted my brother. "The kid was worth $36,000 a week ago! What makes him worth less than that now? He hasn't gotten worse overnight, has he?"

Johnston didn't say anything for a few minutes. Ray was looking down at the floor. Finally Johnston said, "Well, $24,000, take it or leave it."

We left. On the way to our car Ray said, "I'm sorry about this. There's nothing I can do." Then he shook my hand and wished me luck. It was then, finally, that my brother and I realized that of all the scouts we had known, Ray Garland was probably the most sincere. If only he hadn't been so slick-looking and hadn't talked out of the side of his mouth.

Roger Kahn

The Ten Years of Jackie Robinson

In a 1969 issue of Sport *Magazine, the editor wrote about one of the magazine's key contributors, Roger Kahn. He told about Kahn's prominent career as a writer and then mentioned a book Kahn hoped to write—on the Dodgers of the 1950s, the team he grew up with when he was a sportswriter for the* New York Herald-Tribune. *That item on Kahn concluded: "If the book turns out to be as good as Roger is talking about it now—look out." It turned out better, a rare case of a writer exceeding his aspirations. Write in the word* classic *beside* The Boys of Summer. *The following piece does not come from* The Boys of Summer; *consider it the warm-up for that book. It was written in 1955, a decade after Jackie Robinson broke the color line in baseball. Here's how it was for Jackie Robinson as a pioneer.*

When the Brooklyn Dodgers are at home, Jackie Robinson may visit the United Nations on a Monday afternoon and discuss sociology with a delegate. "There is still a little prejudice in baseball," he will remark, "but we have reached the point where any Negro with major-league ability can play in the major leagues." That Monday night, Robinson may travel to Ebbets Field and discuss beanballs with an opposing pitcher. "Listen, you gutless obscenity," he is apt to suggest, "throw that obscene baseball at my head again and I'm gonna cut your obscene legs in half." If Jackie Robinson is an enigma, the reason may be here. He can converse with Eleanor Roosevelt and curse at Sal Maglie with equal intensity and skill.

As Robinson approaches the end of his tenth and possibly final season in organized baseball, he is known in many ways by many people.

Because in the beginning, Robinson endured outrage and vituperation with an almost magic mixture of humility and pride, there are those who know him as a saint.

Because today, Robinson fights mudslinging with mudslinging, and sometimes even slings mud first, there are those who know him as a troublemaker.

Because Robinson destroyed baseball's shameful racial barrier, there are those who know him as a hero.

Because in the ten seasons Robinson has turned not one shade lighter in color, there are those who know him as a villain.

Although Jackie Robinson is, perhaps, no longer baseball's most exciting player, he is still its most controversial one. The world of baseball is essentially simple. The men in the light uniforms—the home team—are the good guys. They may beat little old ladies for sport, they may turn down requests to visit children in hospitals, but on the field, just so long as their uniforms are white, they are the good guys. The fellows in the dark uniforms are bad. They may defend the little old ladies and spend half their time with the sick, but as soon as they put on gray traveling uniforms, they become the bad guys.

The one modern player who does not fit the traditional pattern is Robinson. He has been booed while wearing his white uniform at Ebbets Field. He has been cheered as a visiting player in Crosley Field, Cincinnati, or Busch Stadium, St. Louis. Robinson is not "of the Dodgers," in the sense that the description fits Pee Wee Reese or Duke Snider. First, Jackie is the Negro who opened the major leagues to his race. Second —but only second—he has been one of the Dodgers' most spectacularly effective stars.

As a ballplayer, Robinson has created one overwhelming impression. "He comes to win," Leo Durocher sums it up. "He beats you."

It is not as a Dodger star but rather as a man that Jackie arouses controversy. Ask one hundred people about Robinson as an individual, and you are likely to get one hundred different impressions.

"They told me when I went to Brooklyn that Robinson would be tough to handle," said Chuck Dressen, who managed the Dodgers from 1951 through 1953. "I don't know. There never was an easier guy for me to manage and there never was nothing I asked that he didn't do. Hit-and-run. Bunt. Anything. He was the greatest player I ever managed."

Walter O'Malley, who replaced Branch Rickey as Dodger president in 1951 but did not replace Rickey as Robinson's personal hero, has a different view. "Robinson," he insisted in an off-guard moment last May, "is always conscious of publicity and is always seeking publicity. Maybe it's a speech he's about to make, or a sale at his store, but when Robinson gets his name in the headlines, you can be sure there's a reason. Why, that business with Walter Alston in spring training, it was ridiculous. It was just another case of Robinson's publicity-seeking."

"I'll say this for Jack," Duke Snider declared. "When he believes something is right, he'll fight for it hard as anybody I ever saw."

"I'm just about fed up with Robinson fights and Robinson incidents and Robinson explanations," admitted a widely syndicated columnist. "He's boring. I'm going to heave a great big sigh of relief when he gets out of baseball. Then I won't have to bother with him any more."

"When I first came up, I was pretty scared by the big leagues," Carl Erskine recalled. "I remember how friendly Jackie was. I was just a kid. It's something you appreciate a whole lot."

"He's the loudest man around," an umpire said. "No, maybe Durocher is just as bad. But Robinson's gotta second guess every call and keep his big mouth going all the time."

"I've got to admire him," Ralph Kiner said. "He had a tough time when he was younger and he was a pretty rough character. That's no secret out on the Coast. But he's gotten over that now. You have to hand it to Robinson. He has come a long way and he's taken a hell of a lot but he's never stopped coming."

On the 1955 Brooklyn Dodgers, Jackie holds a peculiar position. In point of years he is an elder statesman, and in point of spirit he is a club leader. Yet he has no truly close friends among either white or Negro Dodgers.

Jackie is an inveterate card player and when the Dodgers travel, this passion seems to bring him near players with whom he cannot have much else in common. Frequently he plays with Billy Loes, a pitcher who walked out of the blackboard jungle and into the major leagues. Loes is interested in girls and, to a lesser degree, in baseball; he is interested in little else. Jackie's conversations with him occasionally run two sentences long.

"Boy, am I havin' lousy luck," Loes may offer.

"Your deal, Billy," is a typical Robinson reply.

Jackie rooms with Jim Gilliam, the young second-baseman who usually has less to say than any other Dodger. Even when he might have roomed with Joe Black who, like himself, is a fluent and fairly sophisticated college man, he roomed with Gilliam. Robinson and Gilliam, in a sense, are business associates rather than friends, but Gilliam, during a recent burst of conversation, was able to cast a great deal of light on Robinson's relationship with other Negroes both in and out of baseball. "Some of my friends, when they hear I room with Jack, they say 'Boy, you room with him? Ain't he stuck up?' " Gilliam reported. "I tell them the truth. He's been wonderful to me. He told me about the pitchers and stuff like that, and how much I should tip and where I should eat and all that. He ain't been stuck up at all."

Inside the Brooklyn clubhouse, Robinson's position is more of what one would expect. He is a dominant figure. His locker is next to that of Gil Hodges. Next to Hodges' locker is a space occupied by a small gas heater, and on the other side of that sits Pee Wee Reese. As captain, Reese is assigned the only locker in the entire clubhouse that has a door.

Duke Snider is nearby and Reese's locker is one of the gathering points in the clubhouse. (The television set is another and that isn't far from Robinson's locker, either.) During clubhouse conversations, Jackie, like Reese and Erskine, is a club leader.

In many ways Jackie, after ten years, is the natural captain of the Dodgers. He is the team's most aggressive ballplayer and it has been suggested that had Robinson been white he would be captain now. Reese is the most respected of all Brooklyn players, but he doesn't have Robinson's fire.

To this day, a few Dodgers make occasional remarks about color. "Don't you think they're gonna take over baseball in ten years?" a player challenged a newspaperman earlier this year after a long and obviously fruitless conversation. "They can run faster; they'll run us white guys right out of the game." The player spoke sincerely. He has been happy to have Robinson on his side, but he is afraid that Robinson represents a threat. This ambivalent feeling is not uncommon on the Dodgers.

"The players were the easiest part of all," Jackie himself insisted once when reviewing his struggle. "The press and fans made things a whole lot tougher." Robinson tends to say what he wishes were true and offer his wish as truth. The resentment of players obviously was among the most difficult obstacles he had to surmount. Robinson's introduction into the major leagues prompted Dixie Walker to ask that he be traded, and brought the St. Louis Cardinals to the verge of a player strike. A great deal of player resentment still remains, and in some cases Jackie's success has made it even stronger. Naturally, players who resent Robinson do not tell him so. Public proclamations of bigotry have virtually ended in baseball. Yet Jackie's subconscious awareness of resentment, plus the fact that resentment remains, are significant parts of any evaluation of his place on the Dodgers today. There has been integration. It has not been complete.

Jackie Roosevelt Robinson today is grayer, fatter, richer, and far more assured than he was ten years ago. He has built a handsome home set among three acres of rolling Connecticut woodland, but he has developed a nervous stomach. He has acquired considerable presence before a microphone; he is a good speaker.

We talked most recently one morning on a bumpy bus that carried the Dodgers from the Chase Hotel in St. Louis to the city's airport. Robinson is permitted to stay at the Chase and has been for the last two years. It is interesting to note that when the hotel management first suggested to the club that it was time the Negro players checked in at the Chase along with the rest of the Dodgers, certain qualifications were laid down. "They'll have to eat in their rooms," the hotel official said, "and they'll have to agree not to hang around the lobbies and the other public rooms." Told about the offer, Roy Campanella said he would pass it up. Roy wasn't going to stay anywhere he wasn't wanted. Don Newcombe, Jim Gilliam, and Joe Black agreed. But Jackie Robinson said he guessed the terms were all right with him, he would stay at the Chase. It was a wedge, anyway. So he did, and within an amazingly short time the hotel lifted all the bars and quietly passed the word that Jackie should consider himself just another guest and go where he pleased in the hotel and eat where everybody else ate. So now, because Jackie, eight years after he hit the big leagues, long after the "pioneering" days were supposed to be ended, was still willing to humble himself in order to advance the larger cause, all Negro ballplayers are welcome at the Chase—and another barrier has come down. Wherever Jackie goes, he encounters reminders of barriers that no longer exist because of himself.

"We feel," he began, "that . . ."

"Who is we?"

"Rachel and me," Robinson explained. Rachel, his wife, has played a tremendous role in the ten years of Jackie Robinson.

"Anyway," he said, "we feel that those barriers haven't been knocked down because of just us. We've had help. It isn't even right to say *I* broke a color line. Mr. Rickey did. I played ball. Mr. Rickey made it possible for me to play."

Of all the men Robinson has met in baseball, he considers Rickey "the finest, in a class by himself." Before the 1952 World Series, Jackie made a point of specifying that he wanted to win the Series for two people: "Rae and Mr. Rickey." Rickey was then general manager of the Pittsburgh Pirates and O'Malley had succeeded him as Dodger president. "But I wanted to let Mr. Rickey know where he stood in my book," Jackie explained.

"Aside from Mr. Rickey I haven't made any what you call real close friends in baseball," Jackie said. "I mean, I got a lot of respect for fellows. Pee Wee Reese."

I was taking notes on a bouncy bus. "Shall I write Durocher's name here, too?" I asked.

"No," Robinson said. "Don't write down Durocher. But I mean fellows like Gil Hodges. One of my biggest kicks was when I heard Ben Wade talking about me being a team man. It indicated to me a lot of guys have that feeling. I felt pretty happy about it."

"Are you pretty happy about most things?"

Robinson was carrying two large packages on his lap, juggling them as the bus swayed. "I don't think I can be any more contented than I am now," he said. "I've been awfully lucky. I think we've been blessed." He nodded toward the packages. "These are for Rae. Presents. We're very close. Probably it's because of the importance of what I've had to do. We've just gotten closer and closer. A problem comes up for me, I ask Rae. A problem for her, she asks me."

"What does she say about all the fights you get into?"

Jackie grinned. This had come up before. "Whenever I get in a real bad argument, I don't care about O'Malley or anything like that. I'm kinda worried about coming home. What's Rae gonna say? My real judge of anything is my family relations. That's the most important. The house, you know, it wasn't so important to me. Rae, it's something she always wanted for the kids. It's no real mansion. I mean there's only four bedrooms."

"Do *you* think you get involved in too many incidents?"

"If I stayed in a shell," Robinson said, "personally I could be maybe 50 percent better off in the minds of the little people. You know, the people that feel I should mind my place. But people that I know who aren't little, you know, people who are big in their minds, I've lost nothing by being aggressive. I mean that's the way I am, and am I supposed to try to act different because I'm Negro? I've lost nothing being myself. Here in St. Louis, you know how much progress in human relations we've made? Aggressiveness hasn't hurt."

"Suppose, Jack, you were to start in again. Would you be less aggressive? Would you act differently?"

Around Robinson on the bus, his teammates chattered among themselves. None bothered to eavesdrop. "I'll tell you one thing that would
be different," Jackie said. "I sort of had a chip in the beginning. I was
looking for things. Maybe in the early years I kept to myself more than
I should have because of that chip. I think maybe I'd be more—what's
the word?—outgoing. Yeah, I know that. I'd try and make friends
quicker."

Jackie looked at his shoes, then glanced out the bus window. It was
a factory neighborhood. The airport was still twenty minutes away. "I
wouldn't be different about aggressiveness if I was doing it over again,"
he said. "I guess I'm an aggressive guy." Robinson stopped as if he were
waiting for a refutation. "Funny thing," he said when none was offered,
"about this whole business. A lot of times you meet white fellows from
the South who never had a chance to mix. You find them more friendly
than a lot of Northerners. It's the Northerners sometimes who make the
fuss about aggressiveness."

Over the years, Jackie has been asked about retirement frequently.
In 1952 he said difficulty with umpires was making him think of quitting.
Since then he has repeatedly mentioned the thought of retirement from
baseball, but only recently has he secured a high-paying job which is
to start when his playing career ends. Robinson says he is now financially
independent of baseball. He is playing only because he feels he owes
the game a debt which he must repay by remaining in it as long as he
can play well.

"I don't know about next year," he said. "It depends on the ball
club; how much I can help the ball club. I'll be able to tell easy how
much I can help, soon as I see the contract they offer me."

The bus pulled onto a concrete highway and, quite suddenly, the
bouncing stopped. The sun had risen higher and heat was beginning to
settle on St. Louis. It was going to be good to escape. There was only
one other question I wanted to ask Jackie. His answer was not really
satisfactory.

"The toughest stretch since I came into baseball?" he said. "I guess
it was that Williams thing. I ran into Davey Williams at first base and
there I was right in the middle of a big obscene mess again and I figured
when I get home Rachel's gonna be sore and what the hell am I doing
this for? I don't need it. I don't need the money. What for?" Jackie
sometimes gets excited when he recalls something that is important to
him and he seemed about to get angry all over again. Sal Maglie had
thrown at a few Brooklyn hitters one game in May, and Robinson bunted

to get Maglie within spiking distance. Maglie stayed at the mound and, instead, Davey Williams covered first after Whitey Lockman fielded the bunt. Jackie was out easily but he bowled over Williams as he crossed the base. Thereafter Maglie threw no more beanballs, and the Dodgers won the game, but Robinson, praised by some and damned by others, was a storm center again. As he thought of it, his anger rose.

"Wasn't it tougher in the early years?" I asked quickly.

"No," Jackie said. "In the early years I never thought of quitting. There was too much to fight for. With that Williams thing, I was fighting for nothing except to win. That was the toughest stretch I ever had to go through. I mean it."

If Robinson's evaluation of the Williams affair was valid, then he is the recipient of a lot of misplaced credit. Actually, his evaluation was wrong. The hardest thing Robinson ever had to do in baseball was the first thing he had to do—just to be the first Negro in modern history to play organized ball. Almost willingly, he seems to have forgotten a great deal of his difficult past. Rarely now is there talk in baseball of the enormously courageous thing which Jackie accomplished.

On a train between Milwaukee and Chicago, Rube Walker, a reserve Dodger catcher from Lenoir, North Carolina, was talking about beanballs. "I don't like 'em nohow," he said.

"But what we see isn't so bad," said Dixie Howell, the Dodgers' number-three catcher, who lives in Louisville. "I was at Montreal when Robinson first broke in. Man, you never saw nothin' like that. Ev-y time he come up, he'd go down. Man, did they throw at him."

"Worst you ever saw?" asked Walker.

"By a long shot," Howell said.

Ballplayers are not demonstrative and Walker did not react further. This was in a dining car and his next words were merely "pass the salt, please." But he and Howell felt a matter-of-fact professional admiration for one of Jackie Robinson's many talents—his ability to get up from a knockdown pitch unfrightened.

To make a major point of a North Carolinian and a Kentuckian sharing admiration for a Negro would be wrong. After Jackie Robinson's ten years, Walker and Howell are not unique. The point is that after the ten years, Howell still regards the beanballs directed at Robinson by International League pitchers during the 1946 season as the most vicious he has ever seen. Jackie himself never mentions this. He cannot have forgotten it, nor is it likely that he has thrust the memory into his subconscious. But he would like to forget it.

It is no small part of the ten years of Jackie Robinson that nobody any longer bothers to count the number of Negro players who appear on the field in a big-league game. There once was much discussion of what John Lardner called "the 50-percent color line." Branch Rickey described it as "the saturation point." When a major-league club first attempted to field a team of five Negroes and four white players, it was whispered, there would be trouble. There seemed to be an enormous risk in attempting to topple white numerical supremacy on a major-league diamond. Today the Dodgers can start Don Newcombe, Roy Campanella, Sandy Amoros, Jim Gilliam and Robinson without so much as a passing comment.

In October 1945, William O'Dwyer was mayor of New York City, and Harry Truman was a rookie President. Dwight D. Eisenhower was wondering what new field he should try, because World War II had been over for two months. On the 23rd of the month, Branch Rickey announced that the Brooklyn Dodgers had signed a twenty-six-year-old Negro named Jackie Robinson and had assigned him to play for their Montreal farm team.

On the 24th of October, the late William G. Bramham, commissioner of minor-league baseball, had a statement to make. "Father Divine will have to look to his laurels," Bramham told a reporter, "for we can expect Rickey Temple to be in the course of construction in Harlem soon." Exercising iron self-control, Bramham called Rickey no name worse than a carpetbagger. "Nothing to the contrary appearing in the rules that I know of," Bramham said with open anger, "Robinson's contract must be promulgated just as any other."

The day he announced the signing, Rickey arranged for Jackie to meet the press. "Just be yourself," he told him. "Simply say that you are going to do the best you can and let it go at that." Since more than twenty-five newspapermen flocked to the press conference, Robinson could not let it go at that.

"He answered a dozen questions," wrote Al Parsley in the Montreal *Herald,* "with easy confidence but no cocksureness. His was no easy chore . . . he was a lone black man entering a room where the gathering, if not frankly hostile, was at least belligerently indifferent." Robinson handled his chore splendidly; press reaction was generally favorable, although frank hostility was evident throughout much of baseball and in some newspaper columns.

Alvin Garner, the president of the Texas League, announced: "I'm positive you'll never see any Negro players on any teams in the South as long as the Jim Crow laws are in force."

Happy Chandler, commissioner of baseball, refused to comment.

Clark Griffith, president of the Washington Senators, who had long ignored clamor urging him to hire a Negro, suddenly accused Rickey of attempting to become "dictator of Negroes in baseball!"

Jimmy Powers, sports editor of the New York *Daily News,* a tabloid with the largest circulation of any newspaper in America, predicted: "Robinson will not make the grade in the big league this year or next . . . Robinson is a 1000–1 shot."

Red Smith, writing in the now dead Philadelphia *Record,* summarized: "It has become apparent that not everybody who prattles of tolerance and racial equality has precisely the same understanding of the terms."

There was precious little prattling about tolerance in Florida that winter. In late February, Robinson flew from his California home to Daytona Beach, where the Montreal Royals were to train after a week of early drills at Sanford, a smaller town twenty miles distant. Jackie was cheerfully received by newspapermen, Dodger officials, and Clay Hopper, the Mississippi-born manager of the Royals, but he was received in the established Southern tradition by the white citizens of Sanford. After two days of practice at Sanford, Robinson was forced to return to Daytona Beach. Before running him out of town, Sanford civic groups explained: "We don't want no *Nigras* mixing with no whites here."

At Daytona Beach, Jackie lived with a Negro family and encountered only isolated resistance. When the Royals traveled to Deland for an exhibition game with Indianapolis some weeks later, he was given another taste of democracy as it was practiced in Florida during mid-March of 1946. As Robinson slid across home plate in the first inning of the game, a local policeman bolted onto the field.

"Get off the field right now," he ordered Robinson, "or I'm putting you in jail!"

Robinson claims that his first reaction was to laugh, so ludicrous did the situation seem. But he did not laugh. Then, as always in the South, Robinson had attracted a huge crowd, and as he faced the policeman, the crowd rose to its feet. The Indianapolis players, in the field, stood stark still, watching. Then Jackie turned and walked toward the dugout, and Clay Hopper emerged from it.

"What's wrong?" Hopper asked.

"We ain't havin' *Nigras* mix with white boys in this town," the policeman said. "You can't change our way of livin'. *Nigras* and white, they can't sit together and they can't play together and you know damn well they can't get married together."

Hopper did not answer.

"Tell that Nigra I said to git," the policeman said. And Jackie left.

Spring training ended on April 14, and when it did, the burden of living in the South was lifted from Jackie's shoulders. He had made the team, and when the 1946 International League season began, his job was pretty much limited to the field. Jackie had played shortstop for the Kansas City Monarchs when Clyde Sukeforth scouted him for Rickey in 1945, and he had tried out for the Royals as a shortstop. But the Royals owned a capable shortstop named Stan Breard and that, coupled with some questions about the strength of Robinson's arm, prompted a switch. As the 1946 season opened, Jackie Robinson was a second-baseman.

This was the season of the beanballs Dixie Howell remembers. It was the season in which a Syracuse player held up a black cat and shouted: "Hey, Robinson! Here's one of your relatives!" It was the season in which Baltimore players greeted Jackie with vile names and profanity.

But it was also the season in which beanballs so affected Robinson that he batted .349. And rather than answer the Syracuse player with words, Robinson replied with a double that enabled him to score the winning run. Rather than match names with the Baltimore players, he stole home one night and drew an ovation from the Baltimore fans. Probably 1946 was baseball's finest year, for in 1946 it was proved that democracy can work in baseball when it is given a chance.

At times during the 1946 season, Branch Rickey would travel from Brooklyn to Montreal for talks with Robinson. "Always," Rickey once said, "for as long as you are in baseball, you must conduct yourself as you are doing now. Always you will be on trial. That is the cross you must bear."

"I remember the meeting when Rickey said that," a man in the Dodger organization said. "Jackie agreed, too." The man chuckled. "I guess Jack's sort of changed his mind over the years." But it wasn't until the place of Negroes in baseball was assured that Robinson's conduct changed.

Late in the 1946 season, the Dodgers found themselves involved in a close race with the St. Louis Cardinals, and there was pressure applied to Rickey to promote Robinson in August and September. For a while Rickey held his peace, but finally he announced: "Robinson is the property of Montreal and that is where he will stay. Montreal is going to be involved in a playoff and we owe it to our Montreal fans to keep Robinson there." Montreal, with Robinson, won the Little World Series. The Dodgers, without him, lost a pennant playoff to the Cardinals in two consecutive games.

There was little connection between the reason Rickey gave for not promoting Robinson and the reasons that actually existed. As far as he could, Rickey wanted to make Robinson's task easy. To do that he needed time. All through the winter of 1946–47, Rickey met with leaders of the American Negro community. Just as Robinson would be on trial as a major-leaguer, he explained, so would Negroes be as major-league fans. Working directly with Negro groups and indirectly through Negro leaders, Rickey worked to make sure there would be as little friction in the grandstand as possible. While barring Negroes from play, owners had not refused to allow them to buy tickets, of course, and the idea of Negroes in big-league stadiums was nothing new. Yet, with Robinson on the Dodgers, a whole new set of circumstances applied to the old idea. Rickey's caution was rewarded in 1947 and in Robinson's first major-league season there was not one grandstand incident worthy of note.

In another foresighted move, Rickey shifted the Dodger and Montreal training camps to Havana, where the air was free of the fierce racial tensions that throbbed in America's South. Finally, Rickey did not place Robinson on the Dodger roster before spring training started. He wanted the Dodgers first to see Jackie and to recognize what a fine ballplayer he was. Then, Rickey hoped, there would be a sort of mass demand from Dodger players: "Promote Robinson." This just was not to be. Leo Durocher, who was then managing the Dodgers, is a man totally devoid of racial prejudice, but some of Durocher's athletes thought differently.

Dixie Walker wanted to be traded and wanted other Dodgers to join with him in protest against Robinson. Eddie Stanky wasn't sure. Happily, Walker found few recruits, and his evil influence was countered by that of Pee Wee Reese, a Kentucky gentleman. "The first time I heard Robinson had been signed," Reese said, "I thought, what position does he play? Then I found out he was a shortstop and I figured, damn it, there are nine positions on the field and this guy has got to be a shortstop like me. Then I figured some more. Maybe there'd be room for both of us on the team. What then? What would the people down around home say about me playing with a colored boy? I figured maybe they wouldn't like it, and then I figured something else. The hell with anyone that didn't like it. I didn't know Robinson, but I knew he deserved a chance, same as anybody else. It just didn't make any difference what anybody else had to say. He deserved a chance."

While the Dodgers trained in the city of Havana, Montreal drilled at Havana Military Academy, fifteen miles away. The team was quartered at the school dormitory, but Robinson, who had been accompanied by a Negro pitcher named John Wright during 1946 and now was one of four Negroes in the Brooklyn organization, was booked into a Havana hotel. This meant thirty miles of travel daily and Robinson, unable to understand the reason for a Jim Crow pattern in Cuba, asked Rickey about it. "I can't afford to take a chance and have a single incident occur," Rickey answered. "This training session must be perfectly smooth."

For two weeks Montreal played exhibitions with a Dodger "B" squad and then the Royals and the Dodger regulars flew to Panama for a series of exhibitions. Shortly before the trip, Mel Jones, then business manager of the Royals, handed Robinson a first-baseman's mitt. "Listen," Robinson said, "I want to play second base. Didn't I do all right there last year?" Jones said he was sorry. "Just passing an order down from the boss," he said. "Mr. Rickey wants you at first base." Robinson did not do badly at first base in the Panama series, and in the seven games he batted .625 and stole seven bases. This was the demonstration Rickey had awaited. Unprejudiced Dodgers said they were impressed. Prejudiced Dodgers insisted that they were not. "I've seen hot-hittin' bushers before," one said. After the series the teams flew back to Cuba, and late one night Rickey passed along word to Robinson that on April 10 he was to become a Dodger. Eddie Stanky was the Dodger second-baseman. Robinson would have to play first.

Happy Chandler's suspension of Leo Durocher had taken the spotlight away from Robinson by the time April 10 arrived, and in retrospect Jackie insists he was just as glad to have a respite from publicity. The Dodgers had not asked for his promotion and as a whole their reception was cool. Robinson in turn remained aloof.

Jack has dark memories of 1947. He was reading in the club car of a train once while several other Dodgers played poker. Hugh Casey, the pitcher, was having a hard time winning a pot, and finally he got up from the table and walked over to Robinson. Without a word Casey rubbed Robinson's head, then turned and went back to his card game.

In 1947, Burt Shotton, who replaced Durocher, put Robinson second in the Brooklyn batting order. On several occasions Dixie Walker hit home runs with Robinson on base, but at no time did Jackie follow baseball custom and shake Walker's hand at home plate. "I wasn't sure if he'd take my hand," Robinson said, "and I didn't want to provoke anything."

In 1947 the Philadelphia Phillies, under Ben Chapman, rode Robinson so hard that Commissioner Chandler interceded.

But there are other memories of 1947 for Robinson; more pleasant ones. Jeep Handley, a Philadelphia infielder, apologized for Chapman's name-calling. Clyde Sukeforth, a coach under Shotton, never once left Robinson's corner. Hank Greenberg told him: "Let's have a talk. There are a few things I've learned down through the years that can help make it easier for you."

One player on the Chicago Cubs attempted to organize a strike against Robinson, but was unsuccessful. The situation on the St. Louis Cardinals was more serious. Only splendid work by Stanley Woodward, a magnificent newspaperman who at the time was sports editor of the New York *Herald-Tribune,* brought the story to light. Only forthright work by Ford Frick, the president of the National League who has since become baseball commissioner, killed the Cardinal strike aborning.

The original Cardinal plan, as exposed by Woodward, called for a strike on May 6, date of the team's first game against the Dodgers. "Subsequently," Woodward wrote, "the St. Louis players conceived the idea of a general strike within the National League on a certain date." An uncompromising mandate from Frick to the players who were threatening to strike went like this: "If you do this, you will be suspended from the league. You will find that the friends you think you have in the press box will not support you, that you will be outcasts. I do not care if half the league strikes. All will be suspended. . . . This is the United States of America and one citizen has as much right to play as any other."

If, in all the ten years of Jackie Robinson, there was a single moment when the success of his mission became assured, then it was the instant Frick issued this directive. It is impossible to order people to be tolerant, but once the price of intolerance becomes too high, the ranks of the bigots tend to grow slim.

For Robinson, 1947 was very much like 1946. He never argued with an umpire. When Lenny Merullo, a Chicago infielder, kneed him, Jackie checked the punch he wanted to throw. When Ewell Blackwell stopped pitching long enough to call him a long series of names, Robinson said only: "Come on. Throw the ball." Then he singled.

But gradually the web of tension in which Robinson performed began to loosen. In the spring of 1948, the Ku Klux Klan futilely warned him not to play in Atlanta. But by the summer of '48, Robinson had relaxed enough to argue with an umpire. This was in Pittsburgh, and he was joined by Clyde Sukeforth. The two argued so violently that they were ejected.

Robinson became a major-league second-baseman in 1948, but, except for an appearance before the House Committee on Un-American Activities, it was not a notable year for him. Called to Congress to refute Paul Robeson's statement that American Negroes would never fight against the Soviet Union, Robinson delivered an eloquent speech. Rickey and Lester Granger, head of the Urban League, a national Negro organization, helped him write it and applause came from all sides. On the field, however, Robinson slumped. He had grown fat over the winter and not until 1949 was Robinson to regain top form.

The Dodgers finished third in 1948 but in 1949, when Robinson won the batting championship and a Most Valuable Player award, they won the pennant. By '49 Robinson felt free to criticize umpires whenever the spirit moved him; by '50 he was feuding with umpires and Leo Durocher and by '51 he was just about as controversial as he is today.

Currently Robinson will call a newspaperman down when he feels the reporter has been biased or inaccurate. Two seasons ago he had his most interesting argument with a reporter. Dick Young, of the *Daily News,* had written somewhat sharply about Robinson and then made a customary visit to the dugout before a Dodger game in Philadelphia. A few minutes before game-time nearly all the Dodgers were seated in the dugout and Young was standing nearby talking. "If you can't write the truth, you shouldn't write," Robinson shouted quite suddenly from his seat.

Unaware that Robinson was shouting at him, Young continued talking. "Yeah, you, Young," Robinson hollered. "You didn't write the truth."

George Shuba, the Dodger sitting next to Robinson, was studying the floor. Other Dodgers were staring at left field. None was saying anything.

"Ever since you went to Washington, Robinson," Young screamed as he attempted to seize the offensive, "your head has been too big."

"If the shoe fits," Robinson shouted, "wear it."

"Your head is big," Young screamed.

"If the shoe fits wear it," Robinson shouted.

The screaming and shouting continued until game-time, when Young left for the press box and Robinson devoted his attention to his job. "I couldn't let him get away with yelling at me in front of the whole team," Young said later. Relations between the two were cool for a while but time has healed the rift.

This season Robinson called down Francis Stann, a Washington columnist, before an exhibition game in Griffith Stadium. Stann had quoted an anonymous third party as saying that Robinson was about through and Robinson lashed him mercilessly and profanely.

"What good can that possibly do?" someone asked Robinson. "You'll only make an enemy."

"I can't help it," Robinson said. "I get so mad I don't know what I'm saying."

Why get so angry at newspapermen, who as a class are not more bigoted or biased than lawyers, congressmen or physicians? Well, newspapermen have hurt Robinson and in his lifetime Robinson has been hurt more than any man should be.

When a Dodger kicked in the door to the umpires' dressing room at Braves Field late in 1951, a Boston reporter blamed Robinson for the kicking. "I'm sorry, Jackie," the reporter said when he was told the truth. "It was right on the deadline and I didn't have time to check."

Another newspaperman once stole Robinson's name to use as a byline on a story consisting of lies and opinions with which Robinson did not agree. This was during a period of racial tension on the Dodgers and the reporter's piracy put Robinson in the position of lying about the most important cause in his life. No one could take this in stride, of course, but Robinson took it particularly badly.

The rantings at reporters are well-known in the newspaper business and possibly because they have made him a formidable target for all but the most bull-voiced of critics, Robinson has almost reveled in his notoriety. But he gets along with most reporters most of the time and he occasionally makes an effort to help one.

Three springs ago during the period when Robinson was associated with a magazine, he fell to chatting in Miami with a newspaperman whose newspaper had just died. They talked vaguely of baseball for ten minutes before the newspaperman without portfolio ambled off in the general direction of a martini.

"He didn't take any notes," Robinson mused aloud. "I guess I didn't give him a story."

A bystander pointed out that the man's paper had folded. "Well, what's he doing down here?" Robinson asked.

"Looking for a job in baseball, maybe."

"Is he in a bad way?" Robinson said bluntly.

"He's not in a good way."

"Well, look," Robinson said. "He can write, can't he?"

"Sure."

"Well, look," Robinson repeated. "Tell him to go see the fellows at the magazine when he's in New York. I'll let them know he's coming and they'll give him some stories to write."

Robinson and the unemployed newspaperman had never been close. When a different sort of misfortune befell a sportswriter with whom he had been friendly, Robinson's reaction was even more direct and more swift. Telephoning about a luncheon, Robinson asked how things were and the sportswriter mentioned the death of a child.

"Oh, no," Robinson exclaimed. Instantly, he added: "How is your wife?"

"Not too bad."

"Is she home now?" Robinson asked.

"Yes."

"I'm going to call her," Robinson said and, without another word, he hung up.

Later, the sportswriter's wife was explaining how much the call had moved her. "It wasn't just that Jackie called," she said. "It was the way he called. The first thing he said was: 'I hope my bringing this up doesn't upset you, but I just want you to know that I'm sorry.' That was a particularly sensitive thing to say. It was a lovely way to say something that I know must have been very hard for him to say at all."

There are assorted targets for Robinson's current wrath. He is a harsh bench-jockey, and his needling is sharper than it ought to be. Even when he is not angry, he is so intent upon speaking his mind, regardless of whom he may hurt, that he is often indiscreet.

Jackie Robinson will speak his mind. This American Negro born in Georgia, bred in California, loved and hated everywhere, will not sit in the back of a bus or call all white men "Mister." He does not drawl his words and he isn't afraid of ghosts and he isn't ashamed of his skin and he never ever says: "Yowsah, boss." This American Negro, this dark symbol of enlightenment, is proud and educated and sensitive and indiscreet and hot-tempered and warm-hearted.

Those who do not know Robinson will call him "troublemaker." Those who do not understand him will call him "pop-off guy." Perhaps both terms are right. Robinson has made trouble for bigots, more trouble than they could handle.

Branch Rickey, who supposedly is the finest scout in baseball history, chose Robinson with wisdom, that borders upon clairvoyance, to right a single wrong. Robinson had the playing ability to become a superstar, plus the intelligence to understand the significance of his role. He had the fighting temperament to wring the most from his ability and he had the self-control to keep his temper in check. Why has he let himself go?

One excuse might be that he has been called "nigger" a thousand times in ten baseball seasons; another is that he was scarred in his crusade. But, really, Jackie Robinson doesn't need any excuse. If the man rugged enough to break baseball's color line turns out to be a thoroughly rugged man, no one has any license to be surprised.

William Kennedy

Going for a Perfect Game

In 1984, William Kennedy won the Pulitzer Prize for his novel
Ironweed. *And he won more: recognition, finally, for his Albany
novels that, some critics said, reminded them of Joyce's Dublin and
James T. Farrell's Chicago. He has since written a fifth,* Very Old
Bones, *published in 1992 to much acclaim. Following is the opening
chapter from Kennedy's second Albany novel,* Billy Phelan's Greatest Game. *It takes place in a bowling alley, with the title character
matched against the best of the locals.*

Martin Daugherty, age fifty and now the scorekeeper, observed it
all as Billy Phelan, working on a perfect game, walked with the
arrogance of a young, untried eagle toward the ball return,
scooped up his black, two-finger ball, tossed it like a juggler from right
to left hand, then held it in his left palm, weightlessly. Billy rubbed his
right palm and fingers on the hollow cone of chalk in the brass dish
atop the ball rack, wiped off the excess with a pull-stroke of the towel.
He faced the pins, eyed his spot down where the wood of the alley
changed color, at a point seven boards in from the right edge. And then,
looking to Martin like pure energy in shoes, he shuffled: left foot, right
foot, left-right-left and slide, right hand pushing out, then back, like a
pendulum, as he moved, wrist turning slightly at the back of the arc.
His arm, pure control in shirtsleeves to Martin, swung forward, and the
ball glided almost silently down the polished alley, rolled through the
seventh board's darkness, curving minimally as it moved, curving more
sharply as it neared the pins, and struck solidly between the headpin
and the three pin, scattering all in a jamboree of spins and jigs.

"Attaway, Billy," said his backer, Morrie Berman, clapping twice. "Lotta mix, lotta mix."

"Ball is working all right," Billy said.

Billy stood long-legged and thin, waiting for Bugs, the cross-eyed pinboy, to send back the ball. When it snapped up from underneath the curved wooden ball return, Billy lifted it off, faced the fresh setup on alley nine, shuffled, thrust, and threw yet another strike: eight in a row now.

Martin Daugherty noted the strike on the scoresheet, which showed no numbers, only the eight strike marks: bad luck to fill in the score while a man is still striking. Martin was already thinking of writing his next column about this game, provided Billy carried it off. He would point out how some men moved through the daily sludge of their lives and then, with a stroke, cut away the sludge and transformed themselves. Yet what they became was not the result of a sudden act, but the culmination of all they had ever done: a triumph for self-development, the end of something general, the beginning of something specific.

To Martin, Billy Phelan, on an early Thursday morning in late October, 1938, already seemed more specific than most men. Billy seemed fully defined at thirty-one (the age when Martin had been advised by his father that he was a failure).

Billy was not a half-bad bowler: 185 average in the K. of C. league, where Martin bowled with him Thursday nights. But he was not a serious match for Scotty Streck, who led the City League, the fastest league in town, with a 206 average. Scotty lived with his bowling ball as if it were a third testicle, and when he found Billy and Martin playing eight ball at a pool table in the Downtown Health and Amusement Club, the city's only twenty-four-hour gamester's palace, no women, no mixed leagues, please, beer on tap till 4:00 A.M., maybe 5:00, but no whiskey on premises, why then Scotty's question was: Wanna bowl some jackpots, Billy? Sure, with a twenty-pin spot, Billy said. Give you fifty-five for three games, offered the Scotcheroo. Not enough, but all right, said Billy, five bucks? Five bucks fine, said Scotty.

And so it was on, with the loser to pay for the bowling, twenty cents a game. Scotty's first game was 212. Billy turned in a sad 143, with five splits, too heavy on the headpin, putting him sixty-nine pins down, his spot eliminated.

Billy found the pocket in the second game and rolled 226. But Scotty had also discovered where the pocket lurked, and threw 236 to increase his lead to seventy-nine pins. Now in the eighth frame of the final game, the match was evening out, Scotty steady with spares and doubles, but his lead fading fast in front of Billy's homestretch run toward perfection.

Word of a possible 300 game with a bet on it drew the bar stragglers, the fag-end bowlers, the night manager, the all-night pinboys, even the sweeper, to alleys nine and ten in the cavernous old room, spectators at the wonder. No one spoke to Billy about the unbroken string of strikes, also bad luck. But it was legitimate to talk of the bet: two hundred dollars, between Morrie Berman and Charlie Boy McCall, the significance being in the sanctified presence of Charlie Boy, a soft, likeable kid gone to early bloat, but nevertheless the most powerful young man in town, son of the man who controlled all the gambling, all of it, in the city of Albany, and nephew of the two politicians who ran the city itself, all of it, and Albany County, all of that too: Irish-American potentates of the night and the day.

Martin knew all the McCall brothers, had gone to school with them, saw them grow up in the world and take power over it. They all, including young Charlie Boy, the only heir, still lived on Colonie Street in Arbor Hill, where Martin and his father used to live, where Billy Phelan used to live. There was nothing that Charlie Boy could not get, any time, any place in this town; and when he came into the old Downtown alleys with Scotty, and when Scotty quickly found Billy to play with, Charlie just as quickly found Morrie Berman, a swarthy ex-pimp and gambler who would bet on the behavior of bumblebees. A week ago Martin had seen Morrie open a welsher's forehead with a shotglass at Brockley's bar on Broadway over a three-hundred-dollar dart game: heavy bettor, Morrie, but he paid when he lost and he demanded the same from others. Martin knew Morrie's reputation better than he knew the man: a fellow who used to drink around town with Legs Diamond and had hoodlums for pals. But Morrie wasn't quite a hoodlum himself, as far as Martin could tell. He was the son of a politically radical Jew, grandson of a superb old Sheridan Avenue tailor. In Morrie the worthy Berman family strain had gone slightly askew.

The bet between Charlie Boy and Morrie had begun at one hundred dollars and stayed there for two games, with Martin holding the money. But when Morrie saw that Billy had unquestionably found the pocket at the windup of the second game, he offered to raise the ante another hundred; folly, perhaps, for his boy Billy was seventy-nine pins down. Well yes, but that was really only twenty-four down with the fifty-five-pin spot, and you go with the hot instrument. Charlie Boy quickly agreed to the raise, what's another hundred, and Billy then stood up and rolled his eight strikes, striking somberness into Charlie Boy's mood, and vengeance into Scotty's educated right hand.

Martin knew Scotty Streck and admired his talent without liking him. Scotty worked in the West Albany railroad shops, a short, muscular, brush-cut, bandy-legged native of the West End German neighborhood of Cabbagetown. He was twenty-six and had been bowling since he was old enough to lift a duckpin ball. At age sixteen he was a precociously unreal star with a 195 average. He bowled now almost every night of his life, bowled in matches all over the country and clearly coveted a national reputation. But to Martin he lacked champion style: a hothead, generous neither with himself nor with others. He'd been nicknamed Scotty for his closeness with money, never known to bet more than five dollars on himself. Yet he thrived on competition and traveled with a backer, who, as often as not, was his childhood pal, Charlie McCall. No matter what he did or didn't do, Scotty was still the best bowler in town, and bowling freaks, who abounded in Albany, gathered round to watch when he came out to play.

The freaks now sat on folding chairs and benches behind the only game in process in the old alleys, alleys which had been housed in two other buildings and moved twice before being installed here on State Street, just up from Broadway in an old dancing academy. They were venerable, quirky boards, whose history now spoke to Martin. He looked the crowd over: men sitting among unswept papers, dust, and cigar butts, bathing in the raw incandescence of naked bulbs, surrounded by spittoons; a nocturnal bunch in shirtsleeves and baggy clothes, their hands full of meaningful drink, fixated on an ancient game with origins in Christian ritual, a game brought to this city centuries ago by nameless old Dutchmen and now a captive of the indoor sports of the city. The game abided in such windowless, smoky lofts as this one, which smelled of beer, cigar smoke and alley wax, an unhealthy ambience which never-theless nourished exquisite nighttime skills.

These men, part of Broadway's action-easy, gravy-vested sporting mob, carefully studied such artists of the game as Scotty, with his high-level consistency, and Billy, who might achieve perfection tonight through a burst of accuracy, and converted them into objects of com-munity affection. The mob would make these artists sports-page heroes, enter them into the hall of small fame that existed only in the mob mind, which venerated all winners.

After Billy rolled his eighth strike, Scotty stood, danced his bob and weave toward the foul line, and threw the ball with a corkscrewed arm, sent it spinning and hooking toward the one-three pocket. It was a perfect hit, but a dead one somehow, and he left the eight and ten pins perversely standing: the strike split, all but impossible to make.

"Dirty son of a biiiiiitch!" Scotty screamed at the pair of uncooperative pins, silencing all hubbub behind him, sending waves of uh-oh through the spectators, who knew very well how it went when a man began to fall apart at the elbow.

"You think maybe I'm getting to him?" Billy whispered to Martin.

"He can't even stand to lose a fiver, can he?"

Scotty tried for the split, ticking the eight, leaving the ten.

"Let's *get* it now, Scotty," Charlie Boy McCall said. "In there, buddy."

Scotty nodded at Charlie Boy, retrieved his ball and faced the new setup, bobbed, weaved, corkscrewed, and crossed over to the one-two pocket, Jersey hit, leaving the five pin. He made the spare easily, but sparing is not how you pick up pinnage against the hottest of the hot.

Billy might have been hot every night if he'd been as single-minded as Scotty about the game. But Martin knew Billy to be a generalist, a man in need of the sweetness of miscellany. Billy's best game was pool, but he'd never be anything like a national champion at that either, didn't think that way, didn't have the need that comes with obsessive specialization. Billy roamed through the grandness of all games, yeoman here, journeyman there, low-level maestro unlikely to transcend, either as gambler, card dealer, dice or pool shooter. He'd been a decent shortstop in the city-wide Twilight League as a young man. He was a champion drinker who could go for three days on the sauce and not yield to sleep, a double-twenty specialist at the dart board, a chancy, small-time bookie, and so on and so on and so on, and why, Martin Daugherty, are you so obsessed with Billy Phelan? Why make a heroic *picaro* out of a simple chump?

Well, says Martin, haven't I known him since he was a sausage? Haven't I seen him grow stridently into young manhood while I slip and slide softly into moribund middle age? Why, I knew him when he had a father, knew his father too, knew him when that father abdicated, and I ached for the boy then and have ever since, for I know how it is to live in the inescapable presence of the absence of the father.

Martin had watched Billy move into street-corner life after his father left, saw him hanging around Ronan's clubroom, saw him organize the Sunday morning crap game in Bohen's barn after nine o'clock mass, saw him become a pinboy at the K. of C. to earn some change. That was where the boy learned how to bowl, sneaking free games after Duffy, the custodian, went off to the movies.

Martin was there the afternoon the pinboys went wild and rolled balls up and down the middle of the alleys at one another, reveling in a boyish exuberance that went bad when Billy tried to scoop up one of those missiles like a hot grounder and smashed his third finger between that onrushing ball and another one lying loose on the runway. Smash and blood, and Martin moved in and took him (he was fourteen, the same age as Martin's own son is this early morning) over to the Homeopathic Hospital on North Pearl Street and saw to it that the intern called a surgeon, who came and sewed up the smash, but never splinted it, just wrapped it with its stitches and taped it to Billy's pinky and said: That's the best anybody can do with this mess; nothing left there to splint. And Billy healed, crediting it to the influence of the healthy pinky. The nail and some bone grew back crookedly, and Martin can now see the twist and puff of Billy's memorable deformity. But what does a sassy fellow like Billy need with a perfectly formed third finger? The twist lends character to the hand that holds the deck, that palms the two-finger ball, that holds the stick at the crap table, that builds the cockeyed bridge for the educated cue.

If Martin had his way, he would infuse a little of Billy's scarred sassiness into his own son's manner, a boy too tame, too subservient to the priests. Martin might even profit by injecting some sass into his own acquiescent life.

Consider that: a sassy Martin Daugherty.

Well, that may not be all that likely, really. Difficult to acquire such things.

Billy's native arrogance might well have been a gift of miffed genes, then come to splendid definition through the tests to which a street like Broadway puts a young man on the make: tests designed to refine a breed, enforce a code, exclude all simps and gumps, and deliver into the city's life a man worthy of functioning in this age of nocturnal supremacy. Men like Billy Phelan, forged in the brass of Broadway, send, in the time of their splendor, telegraphic statements of mission: I, you bums, am a winner. And that message, however devoid of Christ-like other-cheekery, dooms the faint-hearted Scottys of the night, who must sludge along, never knowing how it feels to spill over with the small change of sassiness, how it feels to leave the spillover there on the floor, more where that came from, pal. Leave it for the sweeper.

Billy went for his ball, kissed it once, massaged it, chalked and toweled his right hand, spat in the spittoon to lighten his burden, bent slightly at the waist, shuffled and slid, and bazoo-bazoo, boys, threw another strike: not *just* another strike, but a titanic blast this time which sent all pins flying pitward, the cleanest of clean hits, perfection unto tidiness, bespeaking power battening on power, control escalating.

Billy looked at no one.

Nine in a row, but still nobody said anything except hey, and yeah-yeah, with a bit more applause offered up. Billy waited for the ball to come back, rubbing his feet on the floor dirt just beyond the runway, dusting his soles with slide insurance, then picked up the ball and sidled back to the runway of alley nine for his last frame. And then he rolled it, folks, and boom-boom went the pins, zot-zot, you sons of bitches, ten in a row now, and a cheer went up, but still no comment, ten straight and his score (even though Martin hadn't filled in any numbers yet) is 280, with two more balls yet to come, twenty more pins to go. Is Billy Phelan ready for perfection? Can you handle it, kid? What will you do with it if you get it?

Billy had already won the match; no way for Scotty to catch him, given that spot. But now it looked as if Billy would beat Scotty without the spot, and, tied to a perfect game, the win would surely make the sports pages later in the week.

Scotty stood up and walked to the end of the ball return to wait. He chalked his hands, rubbed them together, played with the towel, as Billy bent over to pick up his ball.

"You ever throw three hundred anyplace before?" Scotty asked.

"I ain't thrown it *here* yet," Billy said.

So he did it, Martin thought. Scotty's chin trembled as he watched Billy. Scotty, the nervous sportsman. Did saying what he had just said mean that the man lacked all character? Did only relentless winning define his being? Was the fear of losing sufficient cause for him to try to foul another man's luck? Why of course it was, Martin. Of course it was.

Billy threw, but it was a Jersey hit, his first crossover in the game. The ball's mixing power overcame imprecision, however, and the pins spun and rolled, toppling the stubborn ten pin, and giving Billy his eleventh strike. Scotty pulled at the towel and sat down.

"You prick," Morrie Berman said to him. "What'd you say that to him for?"

"Say what?"

"No class," said Morrie. "Class'll tell in the shit house, and you got no class."

Billy picked up his ball and faced the pins for the last act. He called out to Bugs, the pinboy: "Four pin is off the spot," and he pointed to it.

Martin saw he was right, and Bugs moved the pin back into proper position. Billy kissed the ball, shuffled and threw, and the ball went elegantly forward, perfect line, perfect break, perfect one-three pocket hit. Nine pins flew away. The four pin never moved.

"Two-ninety-nine," Martin said out loud, and the mob gave its full yell and applause and then stood up to rubberneck at the scoresheet, which Martin was filling in at last, thirty pins a frame, twenty-nine in the last one. He put down the crayon to shake hands with Billy, who stood over the table, ogling his own nifty numbers.

"Some performance, Billy," said Charlie Boy McCall, standing to stretch his babyfat. "I should learn not to bet against you. You remember the last time?"

"Pool match at the K. of C."

"I bet twenty bucks on some other guy."

"Live and learn, Charlie, live and learn."

"You were always good at everything," Charlie said. "How do you explain that?"

"I say my prayers and vote the right ticket."

"That ain't enough in this town," Charlie said.

"I come from Colonie Street."

"That says it," said Charlie, who still lived on Colonie Street.

"Scotty still has to finish two frames," Martin announced to all; for Scotty was already at alley ten, facing down the burden of second best. The crowd politely sat and watched him throw a strike. He moved to alley nine and with a Jersey hit left the baby split. He cursed inaudibly, then made the split. With his one remaining ball he threw a perfect strike for a game of 219, a total of 667. Billy's total was 668.

"Billy Phelan wins the match by one pin, without using any of the spot," Martin was delighted to announce, and he read aloud the game scores and totals of both men. Then he handed the bet money to Morrie Berman.

"I don't even feel bad," Charlie Boy said. "That was a hell of a thing to watch. When you got to lose, it's nice to lose to somebody who knows what he's doing."

"Yeah, you were hot all right," Scotty said, handing Billy a five-dollar bill. "Really hot."

"Hot, my ass," Morrie Berman said to Scotty. "You hexed him, you bastard. He might've gone all the way if you didn't say anything, but you hexed him, talking about it."

The crowd was already moving away, back to the bar, the sweeper confronting those cigar butts at last. New people were arriving, waiters and bartenders who would roll in the Nighthawk League, which started at 3:00 A.M. It was now two-thirty in the morning.

"Listen, you mocky bastard," Scotty said, "I don't have to take any noise from you." Scotty's fists were doubled, his face flushed, his chin in vigorous tremolo. Martin's later vision of Scotty's coloration and form at this moment was that of a large, crimson firecracker.

"Hold on here, hold on," Charlie McCall said. "Cool down, Scotty. No damage done. Cool down, no trouble now." Charlie was about eight feet away from the two men when he spoke, too far to do anything when Morrie started his lunge. But Martin saw it coming and jumped between the two, throwing his full weight into Morrie, his junior by thirty pounds, and knocking him backward into a folding chair, on which he sat without deliberation. Others sealed off Scotty from further attack and Billy held Morrie fast in the chair with two hands.

"Easy does it, man," Billy said, "I don't give a damn what he did."

"The cheap fink," Morrie said. "He wouldn't give a sick whore a hairpin."

Martin laughed at the line. Others laughed. Morrie smiled. Here was a line for the Broadway annals. Epitaph for the Scotcheroo: It was reliably reported during his lifetime that he would not give a sick whore a hairpin. Perhaps this enhanced ignominy was also entering Scotty's head after the laughter, or perhaps it was the result of *his* genetic gift, or simply the losing, and the unbearable self-laceration that went with it. Whatever it was, Scotty doubled up, gasping, burping. He threw his arms around his own chest, wobbled, took a short step, and fell forward, gashing his left cheek on a spittoon. He rolled onto his side, arms still aclutch, eyes squeezing out the agony in his chest.

The mob gawked and Morrie stood up to look. Martin bent over the fallen man, then lifted him up from the floor and stretched him out on the bench from which he had risen to hex Billy. Martin blotted the gash with Scotty's own shirttail, and then opened his left eyelid. Martin looked up at the awestruck mob and asked: "Anybody here a doctor?" And he answered himself: "No, of course not," and looked then at the night manager and said, "Call an ambulance, Al," even though he knew Scotty was already beyond help. Scotty: Game over.

How odd to Martin, seeing a champion die in the embrace of shame, egotism, and fear of failure. Martin trembled at a potential vision of himself also prostrate before such forces, done in by a shame too great to endure, and so now is the time to double up and die. Martin saw his own father curdled by shame, his mother crippled by it twice: her own and her husband's. And Martin himself had been bewildered and thrust into silence and timidity by it (but was that the true cause?). Jesus, man, pay attention here. Somebody lies dead in front of you and you're busy exploring the origins of your own timidity. Martin, as was said of your famous father, your sense of priority is bowlegged.

Martin straightened Scotty's arm along his side, stared at the closed right eye, the half-open left eye, and sat down in the scorekeeper's chair to search pointlessly for vital signs in this dead hero of very recent yore. Finally, he closed the left eye with his thumb.

"He's really gone," he told everybody, and they all seemed to wheeze inwardly. Then they really did disperse until only Charlie Boy McCall, face gone white, sat down at Scotty's feet and stared fully at the end of something. And he said, in his native way, "Holy Mother of God, that was a quick decision."

"Somebody we should call, Charlie?" Martin asked the shocked young man.

"His wife," said Charlie. "He's got two kids."

"Very tough. Very. Anybody else? What about his father?"

"Dead," said Charlie. "His mother's in Florida. His wife's the one."

"I'll be glad to call her," Martin said. "But then again maybe you ought to do that, Charlie. You're so much closer."

"I'll take care of it, Martin."

And Martin nodded and moved away from dead Scotty, who was true to the end to the insulting intent of his public name: tightwad of heart, parsimonious dwarf of soul.

"I never bowled a guy to death before," Billy said.

"No jokes now," Martin said.

"I told you he was a busher," Billy said.

"All right but not now."

"Screw the son of a bitch," Morrie said to them both, said it softly, and then went over to Charlie and said, "I know he was your friend, Charlie, and I'm sorry. But I haven't liked him for years. We never got along."

"Please don't say any more," Charlie said with bowed head.

"I just want you personally to know I'm sorry. Because I know how close you two guys were. I'da liked him if I could, but Jesus Christ, I don't want *you* sore at me, Charlie. You get what I mean?"

"I get it. I'm not sore at you."

"I'm glad you say that because sometimes when you fight a guy his friends turn into your enemies, even though they got nothin' against you themselves. You see what I mean?"

"I see, and I've got nothing against you, Morris. You're just a punk, you've always been a punk, and the fact is I never liked you and like you a hell of a lot less than that right now. Good night, Morris."

And Charlie Boy turned away from Morrie Berman to study the corpse of his friend.

Martin Daugherty, infused with new wisdom by the entire set of events, communicated across the miles of the city to his senile father in the nursing home bed. You see, Papa, Martin said into the microphone of the filial network, it's very clear to me now. The secret of Scotty's death lies in the simple truth uncovered by Morrie Berman: that Scotty would not give a sick whore a hairpin. And Papa, I tell you that we must all give hairpins to sick whores. It is essential. Do you hear me? Can you understand? We must give hairpins to sick whores whenever they require them. What better thing can a man do?

Stephen King

Brooklyn August

References to baseball, and in particular Boston Red Sox baseball, often find their way into Stephen King's novels of horror. But before King's psychotronic imagination helped propel him to his accustomed spot at the top of the best-seller list, he wrote this uncharacteristically gentle elegy to the game as it was in Brooklyn, circa 1956.

In Ebbets Field the crab-grass grows
(where Alston managed)
row on row
      in a somehow sad twilight
      I still see them, with the green smell
      of just-mown infield grass heavy
      in the dark channels of my nose:
      picked out by the right-field floods, just
      turned on and already assaulted by circling moths
      and bugs on the night shift—
      below, the old men and offduty taxi drivers
      drinking big cups of Schlitz in the 75¢ seats,
      this Flatbush as real as velvet Harlem streets
      where jive hangs suspended in the streets of '56
In Ebbets Field the infield's slow
and seats are empty, row on row
      Hodges crouched over first, glove stretched
      to touch the throw from Robinson at third
      the batters' boxes white as mist against
      the glowing sky-filled evening
      (Mantle homered early, Flatbush is down by 2);

Newcombe trudged past first to a silent shower
Carl Erskine is in now and chucking hard but
Johnny Podres and Clem Labine are heating
in case it goes haywire in the late going
In Ebbets Field they come and go
and play their innings, blow by blow
time's called in the dimness of the 5th
someone threw a bottle at Sandy Amoros in right
he spears it in wordless ballet, hands it
to the groundskeeper;
the faceless fans cry down juicy Brooklyn vowels
on both, who ignore them beautifully
Pee Wee Reese leans on his knees west of second
Campanella gives the sign
with my eyes closed I can see it all
smell eight pm dirt and steamed franks
in crenellated cardboard troughs;
can see the purple evening above the stadium dish
as Erskine winds and throws low-inside:

Maxine Kumin

400-meter Freestyle

*Poet, novelist, teacher, writer of numerous children's books,
Maxine Kumin won the Pulitzer Prize for poetry in 1973 for* Up
Country: Poems of New England. *Here, she pulls you into the last
fifty meters of a water race, and the last surge of that pumping
"plum red heart."*

The gun full swing the swimmer catapults and cracks

                                                s

                                                i

                                                x

feet away onto that perfect glass he catches at

a

n

  d

throws behind him scoop after scoop cunningly moving

                                                t

                                                h

                                                e

water back to move him forward. Thrift is his wonderful

s

e

  c

ret; he has schooled out all extravagance. No muscle

                                                r

                                              i

                                              p

ples without compensation wrist cock to heel snap to

h
i
s
mobile mouth that siphons in the air that nurtures
                                                  h
                                                    i
                                                    m
at half an inch above sea level so to speak.
T
h
  e
astonishing whites of the soles of his feet rise
                                              a
                                                n
                                                d
salute us on the turns. He flips, converts, and is gone
a
l
  l
in one. We watch him for signs. His arms are steady at
                                                    t
                                                    h
                                                    e
catch, his cadent feet tick in the stretch, they know
t
h
  e
lesson well. Lungs know, too; he does not list for
                                              a
                                                i
                                                r
he drives along on little sips carefully expended
b
u
  t
that plum red heart pumps hard cries hurt how soon
                                              i
                                                t
                                                s
near one more and makes its final surge   TIME: 4:25:9

Al Laney

Wills vs. Lenglen

It can fairly be said that Al Laney spanned almost all the major eras of sports in the twentieth century (save the present). He came to New York, a young man just out of the army, at the beginning of the roaring twenties, when, as he himself wrote, "Knees came in and busts went out, and there was a widespread belief that gin made in a bathtub was fit to drink." Almost fifty years later Laney wrote his memoirs of covering all the great tennis stars (mostly for the New York Herald-Tribune*) through the late sixties. Here it is, February 16, 1926, Cannes, France, and a one-hour match between the "queen of queens," Suzanne Lenglen, and her twenty-year-old American opponent, dubbed Little Miss Poker Face, Helen Wills— the only time these tennis immortals were ever to meet. For a certain symmetry, you might read this piece first and then jump to John R. Tunis's short story, "The Mother of a Champion" (page 666). Then you decide which is stranger, truth or fiction.*

The golden sun of the Era of Wonderful Nonsense was somewhat beyond the meridian at the beginning of 1926, but the art of ballyhoo was at the peak. In sports, as in other areas of life, sensational occurrences took place more or less year long, rising to a summit with the defeat of Jack Dempsey by Gene Tunney in another Battle of the Century in September. In tennis the year also was on the flamboyant side, the meeting of two girls, one French, the other American, in an otherwise unimportant tournament on the French Riviera. Only a girls' tennis match, but it was blown up into a titanic struggle such as the world had never seen before. This was to be the only meeting of those transatlantic rivals, Suzanne Lenglen and Helen Wills, and it came on

February 16 in the final round of an ordinary resort tournament at the small Carlton Club in Cannes, of which I had such pleasant memories.

By the time it came off it was of worldwide interest. It probably could have filled Yankee Stadium the way it was built up, but it was played at a not very attractive club of six or so courts, with almost no facilities for dressing and with stands still being hurriedly knocked together when the crowds stormed the place the day of the match.

The thing had been growing for three years or more, ever since the California schoolgirl had begun to demonstrate that she was the best our country ever produced and might be the very best in the world. The only way to find out about that was for her to meet the world champion, and people everywhere, even those who never attended tennis tournaments, were looking forward to that meeting. Miss Wills also seemed to want it, and it was she who came seeking it.

On her first trip to Wimbledon in 1924, Helen would have encountered Suzanne had not the French girl been forced to retire from the tournament after being near collapse at the end of a match with Elizabeth Ryan. The winter before, Suzanne had contracted a slight first touch of hepatitis, the disease of which she died in 1938. Helen went to the final, where she was beaten by Kitty McKane, and since she did not go to Europe at all in 1925, this winter of 1926 was the earliest time a meeting with Suzanne was possible.

So, immediately it was announced from California early in January that Helen, accompanied by her mother, would soon leave for France "to study and play a little tennis," the loud bazoo began to sound. From that moment on, volumes of nonsense were written, and some of the best brains of the writing profession were applied to the matter. The minute details of the past lives of the two young women were published, and Miss Wills, who was barely twenty, was pictured as something of a girlish knight going out to slay the dragon.

By mid-decade the delightful winter-season life along the pleasure stations of the Côte d'Azur had reached the high plateau on which it would remain for a few more pre-Depression years. There had been a great influx of wealthy North American, English, and South American visitors; and refugees from the Russian Revolution who had come through that upheaval with quantities of gold were spending almost as liberally as the grand dukes of old. Every nationality and every type was present—crooks, pimps, great ladies, and prostitutes by the hundreds, famous persons from stage and Hollywood, titled gentlemen from every European country where titles remained intact.

In this world Suzanne Lenglen ruled as the champion of champions, the queen of queens. Never beaten in her own country, she was a truly national figure, and a visit to the Riviera without seeing Suzanne play was like a visit to Rome without seeing St. Peter's. For six years she had reigned unchallenged anywhere, but especially along the Azure Coast from December to March. She played tennis where she pleased, bestowing her favors where she could be induced in one way or another to bestow them, and very often she danced away the night at some brilliant social gathering, where she outshone all the ladies present, of whatever rank or stature.

This short glittering coastline belonged to Suzanne in a certain sense, and the plan of the young girl from California to come and play the tournaments was looked upon as an "invasion" of Suzanne's territory. Mademoiselle Lenglen was reported to have said she thought it "cheeky," although I do not know what the French word for cheeky might be.

Whatever she may have thought about Miss Wills personally, Suzanne certainly did resent the shift of attention from herself to Helen as soon as the American girl arrived in Cannes toward the end of January. For a while then, Miss Wills was the main show, and Lenglen never before had played any but the star's role.

And what a contrast they presented! Between them lay a gap far larger than the distance between the homeland of Miss Wills on the shores of the Pacific and Suzanne's sunny Mediterranean playground. Lenglen, a Latin and an actress to her fingertips, was slender, almost thin, with nothing about her figure suggesting the athlete, but supple, marvelously graceful, and full of accompanying acrobatics calculated to bring cheers from the crowd. An artist with a true sense of the dramatic.

She was far from beautiful. In fact, her face was homely in repose, with a long crooked nose, irregular teeth, sallow complexion, and eyes that were so neutral that their color could hardly be determined. It was a face on which hardly anything was right. And yet, in a drawing room, this homely girl could dominate everything, taking the attention away from dozens of women far prettier or even notorious for one reason or another. She could, in an extraordinary way, make quite fashionable women appear just a little dull, if not actually dowdy, beside her. For an ugly girl she had more charm and vivacity than a hundred pretty girls you might meet. And Suzanne had suitors. Plenty of them.

Miss Wills, on the other hand, presented a picture of a typical young American girl, sturdy, well built, and healthy-looking, with a strong suggestion of girlish simplicity. The picture of her as some sort of avenger was wholly false.

My own arrival from Paris was practically simultaneous with that of Miss Wills's entourage, but since I had to find a place to stay I had to neglect her for a day. I could not afford to put up at any of the big hotels along the Croisette where the sports and political reporters for the big London papers now assigned to the tennis story were staying. What I needed was a small, cheap, and inelegant hotel, of which fortunately there were many hidden away up and down the coast, although at this moment there were not many vacant rooms anywhere. I found one, though, at the Jeanne d'Arc on the Avenue de la Palmeraie, which really was in the village of Golfe Jean, a few miles from the center of Cannes on the way to Nice. It had about a dozen rooms and a large garden where dinner was served under the trees in good weather.

Even after Helen began to play in tournaments there still was no assurance that she and Suzanne would meet on the court. While Helen dodged reporters, Suzanne seemed to be dodging Helen. Lenglen had been playing the tournaments for a month or so, mostly in doubles and mixed doubles, but with the American girl actually on the scene she confined her activity to practicing by day and dancing by night at the Ambassadeurs. She was the one who had everything to lose and she would choose the conditions that suited her. It appeared that she was merely keeping the thing alive and suspenseful so that the Riviera could reap the full benefit. She had no intention of avoiding the challenge, and in plenty of time to get full value from the announcement she sent in her entry for the Carlton tournament.

Meanwhile, Miss Wills, very busy indeed, had captured the Riviera set by the refreshing simplicity and charm of her manner. "*Une petite fille de province,*" the *Éclairer de Nice,* the South of France's biggest paper, called her, and she certainly did give an impression of a simple, rather pretty girl from the suburbs. She had appointments almost daily with Paris dress houses eager to clothe her, and she drove nearly every day to a tournament somewhere, adjusting quickly to the new playing conditions.

After playing at the Gallia tournament at her own hotel, she played the Métropole, also in Cannes, and then, the week before Carlton, she motored to Nice for her matches in the South of France Championships. This was at Lenglen's own home club, and by now everyone, including Suzanne, had seen that here was a real menace. Interest was intense.

By the time the Nice tournament began we all knew that the Carlton would be the big one, so we pressed forward, storming the ramparts of the Gallia, so to speak. Now Miss Wills's new clothes were about ready, so she took a day off from the tournament and we had the experience of standing around outside the Cannes branch of a famous Paris couturier while Helen had her final fittings. She had got us there before the place opened for the day, but our long wait was rewarded when she finally appeared.

It was a different girl who came out of the dress shop. This was an eager schoolgirl in a new frock, and for the first time we saw that Miss Wills was really beautiful. I don't think any of us had realized it before. The news accounts from the Riviera now began to refer to Miss Wills as statuesque, beautiful in the mold of a statue in the classic style.

I do not remember much about the early rounds of the Carlton tournament. In fact, nothing. I remember the mounting excitement as day by day the ladies came closer together and that the atmosphere of a heavyweight championship fight had somehow developed around this amateur tennis match between two nice girls. Only a few of the biggest fights have generated this kind of on-the-scene tension and turmoil.

It would have been hard to choose a more unlikely ground for an event of such worldwide interest. The six courts of the Carlton Club were squeezed into a small plot on a narrow, dirty street behind the Carlton Hotel a few hundred yards back from the Croisette, and a narrow alley ran down one side. Normally there was a "center" court with small wooden stands along one side with seats for perhaps a thousand or so. Behind this was a one-story building, a garage, I think. Outside the grounds on the other side was a small factory of some sort from which came the wasplike buzz of machinery. Beyond and to one side of this were two or three small villas with orange tiles for roofs and with eucalyptus trees in front. High above were the towers of the Carlton Hotel.

It was customary on the Riviera to schedule important matches early in the afternoon so as to be done with play before the sun was low, when a chill came quickly into the Mediterranean air. This one, however, was set for eleven o'clock in the morning. Many wondered at the odd time, but those of us who had played on the Carlton courts suspected why. The six courts were so badly laid out with regard to the sun that just before and just after midday was the only time when the center court was certain to be just right from both ends, although, of course, it was playable in the afternoon.

Anticipating some difficulty about press accommodations and being generally quite nervous about the whole thing, I was up early and at the club before nine o'clock. Already there was a long line waiting for the gates to open. The line stretched four or five abreast down the street beside the club toward the Croisette. I watched it grow until it reached that elegant promenade and was turned by policemen to extend under the palm trees alongside. They said the first people had appeared soon after dawn, and a quick estimate at nine-thirty indicated that already there were more in this line than could possibly get inside. The crowd was orderly for a long time, but the French have not the Englishman's willingness to wait long and placidly in line. There were to be mob scenes in the narrow way where the club had the bad luck to have placed the main gate to the grounds, and there were premonitions of it when I decided a little before ten that I'd better try to get inside myself while I could.

I could not get near the gate I was supposed to enter. The crowd seeking to buy tickets had abandoned its orderly line and was milling about and shouting imprecations at the ticket sellers.

There was a gate on the other side, but another mob was storming it in the narrow confines of the alley. It must have been close to ten-thirty when several photographers, their cameras held high above their heads, formed a flying wedge to get us through in their wake. We made it all right, more easily in the end than I would have thought possible. Probably the voluble crowd knew by now they were not to get in at all, short of knocking the gate down, and had given up.

Once inside another few minutes were consumed trying to find out where I was supposed to sit. I never did. As they used to say at Ebbets Field in the dear dead days, it was everyone for theirself.

As the time for the match to start drew nearer the crowd outside became noisier. We could not see them, but they were there and some still were trying to crash the gate. When it became certain that the majority would not get inside, they began to seek other places. Soon the trees overlooking the place held the more athletic of the frustrated, and the windows of a house nearby were filled. Presently the red tiles on its roof, removed from within, began to disappear and faces to pop through the holes. The roof of the garage was jammed, and people brought ladders to lean against its wall, behind the seats on one side. On every rung halfway to the top someone stood, hands on the shoulders of the one on the rung below. Every roof from which a part of the court could be seen had as many people as it would bear sitting or standing upon it, and every tree limb that would give a precarious perch was occupied. The police, who had gone up the trees with the apparent intention of routing the occupants, took the vacated places and remained to look. It seemed that there must have been a thousand people looking down on the court in these ways, almost as many seeing the match, or some portion of it, from outside as from inside.

The arrival of Suzanne at the clubhouse entrance in her chauffeur-driven car from Nice was hailed by an outburst of cheering outside and the calling of her name. This was followed by a great roar when, someone said, she blew them kisses. Helen had to come only from the nearby Carlton, whose tower windows also were full of people watching. Probably she had preceded Suzanne, who always made certain of her "entrance."

The suspense had begun to mount sharply even before the two girls entered together, making a nice picture for the battalion of photographers that immediately engulfed them. Suzanne came like a great actress making an entrance that stopped the show, with flashing smile, bowing, posing, blowing kisses, full of grace and ever gracious. Helen, walking beside the Queen and, as befits a lady in waiting, just a little to the rear, came in calm, impassive, and unruffled, looking nowhere but in front. She seemed sturdy and placidly unemotional, although she must surely have been nervous. I noted for the first time that Miss Wills had large, capable-looking hands, and I wondered if she really was the talented painter of pictures she was supposed to be. I don't suppose she took either literature or art very seriously at this time.

Suzanne wore a pure white coat with white fur collar over a short white dress and her famous bandeau was of salmon pink. Helen wore her usual tennis costume, middy blouse and pleated white skirt, and she had a dark coat over the arm not full of rackets. When the photographers were induced to retire, and the girls were about to take the court, Helen removed her sweater. Suzanne wore hers all through the match, although the sun now was hot. When the flashing entrance smile had been turned off, it was seen that Suzanne had a somewhat strained, pinched look. There were dark lines and the eyes seemed drawn. She did not look well.

Up to this point I have been calling on perhaps faulty memory, my own and that of others, but once play began I wrote things down and I still have full confidence in what I now write. The notes are not altogether clear as to calligraphy, and some are not meaningful any more, but they tell a story and this is it.

The match lasted exactly one hour. Lenglen opened with a love game on her service, but Helen then began to hit her own faster drives deep, and controlled the back court exchanges just well enough to win the next two games for a 2–1 lead. She had won the champion's service, and when that service game was lost to a scoring shot from Helen's backhand off a fine Lenglen shot, you could sense the realization coming to Suzanne that she was in for a fight. No other girl ever had scored off such a shot. It must have been an unpleasant awakening. She knew now what she was facing. None could know it better. Here was an opponent her equal in controlled driving, and definitely more forceful. Helen's game was based on speed of stroke perfectly controlled, with drives more forceful than any woman and many men. Helen was not, however, Suzanne's equal in resourcefulness.

Helen had hit every backhand shot in these early games across court to the backhand line, often right into the backhand corner. These were shots of high quality, immaculate in their purity of execution, but they were sent to Lenglen's backhand, one of the most accurate and precisely controlled strokes and altogether one of the finest shots ever seen in the game of tennis.

Lenglen was quick to see the advantage it gave her. After losing the second and third games, she began with great confidence to take those booming backhand drives pitching close to her own backhand corner, certainly the hardest and deepest she ever had encountered from another girl. Initially they had surprised her, but she was not now hurried by them and it seemed she even invited them by playing her own shots to Miss Wills's left side. Suzanne took the ball cleanly in the exact center of her racket and with her slightly undercut stroke placed her return to the spot her eye had picked out, very short down each of Miss Wills's sidelines.

This often brought Helen forward, and each time she came she lost the point. These coups were much easier for Suzanne to bring off than would have been similar shots hit deep to her forehand corner, but Miss Wills never attacked that sector with her backhand. She seemed to think at this time that the Lenglen backhand was the wing to attack, and attack it she did with great strength.

In spite of it, though, Suzanne won ten straight points from 2–1 in Miss Wills's favor. She won them with unyielding defense against the hardest thrusts Helen could manage and from which she herself could counterattack with perfectly timed shots. These, placing Miss Wills in a losing position, were designed to draw errors. This was the game of women's tennis such as we would expect these two to play. Miss Wills was playing very well indeed and she was losing, but it took nearly perfect stroking and a well-conceived plan to check her. We expected that Miss Wills, with her equipment, would find the way to alter the course of the play, and she did.

Having lost her service twice and now behind 2–4, she came to the net to volley for the first time in the seventh game and won it with a not very neat but effective push out of reach. Suzanne seemed now to have decided upon her plan of action, however, and to have regained her confidence, which had been disturbed by the unexpectedly strong resistance of the American girl. Helen could win only two points in the next two games as Suzanne captured the first set 6–3 to a great burst of cheering.

This seemed a convincing enough margin, but the set had been played under considerable stress, nevertheless, and Suzanne went to the chair to sip brandy before taking her place for the start of the second. She seemed already tired and nervous. The disturbing noises from the crowd annoyed her much more than they bothered Helen, and several times Suzanne had looked with an appealing gesture toward the spot where a vehicle of some kind had been drawn up alongside the fence with a shouting group sitting on top of it. She had first ordered them to be silent and then, being ignored, had pleaded with them, with the same effect.

Helen began the second set as Suzanne had begun the first, by serving a love game. This was the first time the strong and well-placed American service itself had been a decisive factor, and its sudden increase in power seemed to surprise Lenglen. All Miss Wills's shots, in fact, appeared now to carry more pace, or what the English call "devil" and, choosing well the proper ball on which to hit out, she placed Suzanne altogether on the defensive for a time. The greater speed of stroke of the American girl now was quite noticeable.

Helen went to a lead of 3–1, and she was serving so well it seemed to us unlikely she would lose a service game at all. If she did not, she would win the second set by 6–3, even without breaking the French girl's service again. At one point in the fourth game she had passed Suzanne cleanly at the net with a sharply angled forehand across the body. Suzanne stopped at the chair again for another sip of brandy before returning to her position. This seemed an ominous sign, and we thought that Suzanne never would survive a third set. But it gave her time to consider her position, which was, as a matter of fact, critical. With Miss Wills serving with a 4–1 lead in sight, Suzanne knew well that the capture of the American's service was imperative at this point. She dare not fall behind 1–4.

And then I think Miss Wills made a tactical mistake. Serving for this commanding lead, she appeared deliberately to reduce the pace of the game. Instead of pressing her advantage she began to exchange deep and well-placed but slower drives with Suzanne.

Now, Miss Wills was not equipped to play this kind of game so well as Suzanne. Indeed, no girl that ever lived could do this. No matter where the ball was hit Suzanne could reach it with her marvelously fluid footwork and, given time for the stroke, she was again in control of the play. In such exchanges hers would be the last shot of each rally if it didn't end with an opponent's error. The shots that Helen missed now were those for which she was made to run and strain. Suzanne, for the second time, had a run of two games in which she lost only two points, both well earned by Helen. The score was now 3–3 and now surely the crisis was passed for Suzanne.

How wrong we were!

Now came the longest game of the match. With Helen serving, Suzanne was within a stroke of winning the game at 15–40 for a 4–3 lead and her own service to follow. Ten more points were to be played, however, and then Miss Wills won the game to give her that lead. Helen had brought out her very best game at this crisis, and we saw then the wonderful driving that only she in all the world could command and sustain over the next ten years or so.

The effect on Suzanne of losing this game from a winning position, and against play that indicated she might have met her match at last, was profound and visible. She was clearly surprised at such very strong resistance. She took more brandy before taking up the balls to serve the eighth game.

As the play continued she appeared to falter, although actually she made no mistake in stroking at all. It was the way she looked. She seemed much more nervous, but at 30–all she received a small break that appeared to restore her a little while it depressed her opponent. Suzanne drove to Miss Wills's forehand line a ball that could not have been returned but appeared to have pitched just outside. Cyril Tolley, who was judging the line, gave no sign and then, when Miss Wills looked an inquiry at him, indicated that the ball had been good. If he had given it the other way, as Miss Wills clearly thought he should, she would have been one point away from a 5–3 lead and in Lenglen's present state that might have been decisive.

Miss Wills lost the next point weakly, perhaps, while contemplating what might have been, but she then served very well to reach 5–4. And now for the second time at a critical moment Miss Wills became tentative. And once more Lenglen's great skill at maneuvering an opponent lacking in aggression came to the fore. Again she drew Helen to a forward position where the American girl, unable to find room for her full-blooded drives, hit out or into the net. Suzanne thus won at love a game whose loss would have carried with it the loss of the second set and, very likely, the third also. This was, if partly the result of Miss Wills's strange quietude, even more the true champion's response to danger. It was characteristic, and a few minutes later we were to see an even more impressive demonstration of it.

Having survived these several dangers brilliantly, Suzanne now appeared to be moving straight to victory. She won Miss Wills's service surely, if not easily, from 30–all in the eleventh game and then in the twelfth, serving perfectly to prevent a forcing reply, went straight to match point at 40–15. And then, one stroke away from a two-set victory for Lenglen, there was a long exchange of deep drives at the end of which Miss Wills, finding at last a ball she could flog, sent a screaming forehand toward Lenglen's forehand corner. It had the look of a winning stroke, but the call of "Out" was heard and both players thought the match over.

Suzanne threw into the air the ball she had held in her hand throughout the rally and ran to the net to receive the traditional winner's handshake across the barrier. Before she could reach Helen, the court was full of people, a regular mob scene. They came from all directions, carrying huge baskets of flowers and the photographers swarmed everywhere.

Through this throng of people and flowers, Lord Charles Hope, the lineman, pushed his way to the umpire's chair. Commander Hillyard leaned down to hear what was said amid the bedlam. Sir Charles explained that the ball had been emphatically good, not out. It was not he who had called but some volunteer official, of whom there were hundreds in the stands. Hillyard immediately changed the decision, made the score 40–30, and began an effort that at first seemed futile to clear the court so the match could be resumed. In those pre-loudspeaker days it took some doing. Many minutes passed before the facts could be communicated to the crowd, all of whom were standing and most of whom were shouting.

Confusion still reigned for a while but in time all got back to their places. I could not see Lenglen's face when she first realized the situation. It must have been a study in dejection for she had a sorrowful cast of feature even when in repose and this for her was a tragic development. The highly charged emotional atmosphere had taken its toll of her nervous strength, but she had overcome all, including the strongest game she ever had faced, and come through successfully still queen and still champion at what cost only she probably knew. And now, exhausted from physical effort and nervous strain, she must go back and do it again under even worse strain. All was still uncertain and had to be played for.

And now Mademoiselle Lenglen confirmed and underscored her position as Queen of the Courts and one of the great champions of sports history. Without a word or any outward sign, she walked steadily back to her place, picked up the discarded balls and served. Her face was drawn but even when Miss Wills won the next point, also a match point, and then eventually the game, to draw even again at 6–all, there still was no sign.

When Miss Wills stood within one point of winning the following game, the thirteenth, a point that would have given her the lead at 7–6, there was at last a nervous gesture from Suzanne which seemed to indicate she might now be near collapse. But she steadied herself, recovered her concentration and won the game against the American's service, which was at its biting best now.

And so, serving once more for the match a good quarter-hour after she had thought she had it won, Suzanne came at last to her third match point. It had not been easy to arrive there, for Miss Wills resisted beautifully and with calm judgment. Suzanne had played with nearly perfect strokes, which, under the circumstances, showed a hardihood we none of us suspected in so highly emotional a creature. Then, in sight of the end once more, she reacted. Suzanne served a double fault, so rare a thing with her as to make one wonder if she were not really at the end of her resources.

But once again the champion gathered her remaining strength. This remarkable woman now played with a certainty and restraint, with unshaken nerve and fortitude, that were difficult to believe in the supercharged atmosphere after all that had gone before. Having served the double fault at match point, she then needed two more points to get out from deuce. For the first she fenced with Miss Wills until she drew an error. For the last one of all, her fourth match point, she carefully drew a weak reply from Helen and then she won in the champion's way by hitting a winner. It was, in a word, magnificent.

This time Suzanne did not run to the net. She stood almost in a trance, it seemed, in mid-court, and was there engulfed again by the rush of partisans, photographers, and the baskets of flowers which returned for a monster horticultural display. I doubted she ever would reach the net, where Miss Wills waited to do the honors for the second time, if the photographers had not insisted upon it so they could take a thousand pictures of the kind photographers the world over must have.

Suzanne received an ovation beyond anything even she had previously experienced. Finally they sat her down on a bench at the side of the court and surrounded her with a wall of flowers until only her turbaned head showed above. She was surrounded also by a wall of hundreds of people, including lords and ladies, all pushing forward to congratulate and be near her. And directly behind where Suzanne sat, Helen stood for a few minutes, unnoticed, forgotten, and alone in the midst of the thing. I watched as Miss Wills, with hardly room to extend her arms, pulled on her sweater. Then, still alone, she turned and began quietly to push her way back through the indifferent crowd toward the gate. She disappeared among them and no one seemed to care that she was gone.

I had plenty of time so I watched the scene for a while and then went out and found a seat along the Croisette, where I could sit in the sun and think about the strange match. I have been thinking about it in sunshine and shadow ever since and the conclusion I reached while sitting in the bench in sight of the Mediterranean remain the same today.

I was to see Miss Wills many times afterward winning all her eight Wimbledon titles, all those in Paris and many of those at Forest Hills, besides her yearly Wightman Cup encounters. Suzanne was seen afterward only through the French Championships, which followed in Paris three months later in May, and at her last Wimbledon that June.

My feeling about the Cannes match was then, and is now, that if it had been played under normal conditions Lenglen would have won more easily and more decisively. I think also that if she and Miss Wills had met later that same year, which seemed likely then but turned out not to be, Lenglen also would have won but probably less easily. If they had continued both to play the tournaments through the next years, however, I am certain that Miss Wills would have overtaken Suzanne and passed her.

This does not mean that I place Miss Wills at her peak above Lenglen at hers, for I believe the opposite. But Helen showed at Cannes that she already was close and still improving and Lenglen, never very robust, already probably was declining a little in a tennis sense. She had been queen of Wimbledon for seven years in 1926. Miss Wills first became champion there in 1927 after Suzanne's departure. If we add seven years to that date, we will see Miss Wills in 1934 also seriously challenged by players of lesser talent than her own.

These two wonderful performers were really of different tennis generations, and had they met more they must inevitably have come level and one passed the other, the one going up, the other down. It is ever the fate of even the greatest of champions.

John Lardner

The Roller Derby

In the 1950s, John Lardner wrote a sports column for True *magazine, a men's magazine that had a large audience. Lardner's column was called "It Happened in Sports." The elder editor of this volume was then a child editor at* True, *privileged—and somewhat awestruck—to be able to work with Lardner, mostly just to talk about his choice of subject. When his pieces came in there was nothing to be done with them except perhaps to double-check a fact or two. The language was always perfect. What one always noted about Lardner was that he had an infallible ear for vernacular, which he knew just how to touch up, as well as an exceptional gift for parody. Both virtues are on display here in a story of a postwar sports phenomenon that rates—with maybe a dozen others—as one of Lardner's best.*

I t develops that there are certain parts of this country in which the thing called the Roller Derby is still unknown. The people in such places live in the same state of uneasy innocence as the Indians did before the white man came along, bringing them civilization, uncut whiskey, glass beads for all hands, and two or three new variations of hoof-and-mouth disease.

It's a matter of record that the Indians could not get this kind of civilization fast enough, once they had a look at it, and the same thing is true of the Roller Derby. Those in America who have not yet seen the Derby are sending out loud, clear calls to know what it is all about. The more advanced tribes who have tasted the Derby by television or been exposed to it in person are clamoring and stampeding for more—or so we are told by Mr. Leo A. Seltzer, who sells the stuff to the natives.

Of course, Mr. Seltzer's definition of a stampede is flexible. Back in 1935 B.T. (Before Television), when he tried his first Roller Derby on the public for size, Mr. Seltzer was satisfied with a stampede of three hundred or four hundred people, at any wide place in the road. He did not care how many of them wore shoes. Today, in the age of so-called video, he measures his clients by the million. The incidence of shoes among them is getting higher. Some even wear neckties. In short, Mr. Seltzer feels he has finally got hold of the *bon ton,* and got them where it hurts.

The Roller Derby, mark you, is a sport. Its backers will stand up and raise their right hands and swear it is. And they are right. Defenestration is also a sport, for those who like it (defenestration is pushing people out of windows). So is extravasation (extravasation is bloodletting, with a license). So is lapidation (lapidation is stoning people to death, or near there). So is the grand old game of suttee, which consists of barbecuing live widows over a charcoal fire.

So, for that matter, is wrestling—and here we are getting close to the meat of the matter. For wrestling is the thing that the Roller Derby threatens to replace, in certain ways. When the television business started to warm up, after the war, it was found that many set owners took a morbid interest in the actions of wrestlers like Primo Carnera and Gorgeous George. The more grotesque, the better. Then televised wrestling began to seem a little cold and stately. That was the spot into which the Roller Derby stepped.

Mr. Seltzer and his staff of calculators estimate that of the more than a million new addicts who paid to see his skaters in the last year, 91 per cent were won and brought over by the telecasts of noted television broadcasters like Joe Hasel of WJZ-TV, in New York City, where the Roller Derby broke into Madison Square Garden this year and took its place in Garden history with the Democratic Convention of 1924 (also a sport). That is a pretty solid estimate, that 91 per cent, for Mr. Seltzer did not just pull it out of the air, like a butterfly. He went around to the customers in person, feeling their pulses, and asked them, "What in the world brings you to my place, friend?" Most of them said television, which is good enough for Mr. Seltzer. He now feels that, after thirteen lean years or so, the tide has turned, that the nation is his oyster, that America is about to break out with Roller Derby teams and leagues at every pore.

Your correspondent set out the other day to learn the details of the sport, in behalf of those tribes which have not yet put their wampum on the line to see it. It was a most interesting visit. As I knocked at the door, they were just pulling six inches of light, seasoned timber out of the flank of Miss Marjorie Clair Brashun, daughter of a plumber from St. Paul, Minnesota. Miss Brashun, known to the trade for what seem to be satisfactory reasons as Toughie, is one of the leading female skaters of the Roller Derby troupe. Since she likes to wear wood next to her skin, she had gone on skating for some time before the house doctors learned that she had bumped into the guard rail of the track and acquired a piece of it internally.

The sight of Miss Brashun being defrosted caused a slight argument among the Roller Derby people as to whether she is four feet eleven or four feet ten in height. Personally, I think it might be one or the other. I have never gone close enough to a live rattlesnake to put a tape measure on it, and in the same way I am willing to be an inch or two wrong about Miss Brashun.

"The girls in this sport are tougher than the boys," said Mr. Seltzer.

"That's right," snarled Miss Brashun.

"If the girls have a fight on the track," said Mr. Seltzer, "they go right on fighting after the match, maybe for two or three years. In their spare time they spit in each other's teacups. But the girls have a weakness. They are tender in the coccyx."

The coccyx, it should be said, is a vestigial bone at the southern end of the spine. Women skaters wear a special strip of sponge rubber over this area, since they are always falling upon it and making it ring like a bell. In fact, their uniforms are padded all over, and so are the men's—with hip pads, shoulder pads, and thigh pads, topped off by a helmet borrowed partly from football and partly from Marshal Rommel's Afrika Korps. There is lots of padding, but not enough.

A Mr. Billy Reynolds went to the hospital recently with six breaks in one leg. A Miss Margie Anderson (out of Miami) had twenty-four stitches taken in her shapely Gothic torso. A Miss Virginia Rushing broke her pelvic bone in a warm debate, but went on skating for several weeks before she noticed it. Your correspondent would estimate that the number of stitches embroidered in Mr. Seltzer's troupe each week is about the same as Betsy Ross took in making the first flag.

Before establishing the fact that the Roller Derby is, like cutting throats, a sport, let us glance at its history for a moment. Mr. Seltzer, who operates out of Chicago, is an old dance-marathon man. You can tell by the way he stands erect and looks at the world through clear eyes that he got out of that business long ago. At the peak of the Depression he rounded up a few roller skaters and went on the road with the first Derby. For a while, like Virginia Rushing with her pelvic bone, nobody noticed. Things were tough and slow. Once, among the Southern hills, twenty-two of the skaters were killed in a bus accident. It may be, in view of the way they made their living, that this was an easy and merciful death, but probably not, for the skaters seem to enjoy the work.

Today, old-timers come up to the Derby's doors in each town it plays and introduce themselves as former members of the troupe. Recently a deaf-mute pants presser approached the Seltzer staff and opened conversation with the following written message: "I'm an old Roller Derby ace." He was, at that, and the sight of him reminded Mr. Seltzer that the man was probably responsible for the fact that the Derby today enjoys a strong deaf-mute following wherever it plays.

Now that the show—beg pardon, sport—has struck gold, it plays mostly the big towns in the television belt. It carries a squad of anywhere from thirty skaters up (there were sixty-five at Madison Square Garden), half of them men, half women, and a portable Masonite track which is eighteen laps, or two quarts of blood, to the mile. It also packs a staff of referees, medical men, and penalty boxes. The referees put the skaters into the penalty boxes if the medical men have not previously put them into local hospitals.

There are certain laws of God and man the violation of which, I am told, will get a skater thrown out of the match for the night, but I hesitate to imagine what those could be. The penalty boxes take care of the rest, as in hockey. As in football, blocking is encouraged. As in six-day bike racing, you can jam and sprint at will. As in osteopathy, you can probe for new bones in your fellow man. As in wrestling—well, I was especially interested in the work of a Mr. Silver Rich, who has developed a two-handed kidney punch from behind which puts me strongly in mind of the technique of the five wrestling Duseks from Omaha. It is extremely legal by Roller Derby rules.

The squad is divided into separate teams of boys and girls, the boys playing the boys for fifteen minutes, then the girls playing the girls for fifteen minutes, and so on alternately, while Mr. Seltzer counts the house. In a wholesome, high-spirited way, Mr. Seltzer calls the teams by the names of towns, such as Brooklyn, New York, Philadelphia, and Cleveland. A player like Miss Toughie Brashun (but there are, I am glad to say, no other players like Miss Brashun) will represent Brooklyn in the same way that Mr. Luis Olmo, the Dodger from South America, represents Brooklyn—that is, she wears a Brooklyn shirt.

There is a further similarity, and Happy Chandler can sue me if he likes, between baseball and the skating dodge. The skaters do not like new equipment. They hone, grind, cut, gouge, and chew on their skates and shoes as ballplayers hone their bats, break in their gloves, and cut their shirtsleeves. They sometimes get friends to break in their shoes, and they file down their wooden skate wheels so close that Mr. Seltzer has to supply them with three or four new sets of wheels apiece per evening. The wheels are wooden because metal wheels set up such a vibration that Miss Brashun, for instance, could not hear herself thinking up a plan to murder Miss Gerry Murray, her deadliest rival, in cold blood, if she wore them.

As in bike racing, the fastest skaters on each team sprint for points—one point for passing one rival within two minutes, two points for three, and five points for passing the whole enemy team of five. The other skaters form packs to deter hostile sprinters from passing. At the end of the match, the winning and losing teams split a percentage of the gate on a 60–40 basis and walk, or are carried, home to supper. In their spare time, roller skaters often get married to each other. Miss Brashun is the bride of a skater named Ken Monte, while Miss Murray is Mrs. Gene Gammon in private life. Like other people, skaters have children, and these, Mr. Seltzer hopes, will grow up to be skaters too. The supply is short, and he cannot afford to miss a bet.

That raises the question of where Roller Derby skaters come from. Some of them used to be bike-riders, some of them used to be ice-skaters, some of them used to be ballplayers, and some of them used to be home girls. A Miss Peggy Smalley was a home girl on a high hill in Tennessee when the Roller Derby suddenly surrounded her. The skate shoes they gave her were the first shoes she had ever seen. If it weren't for the skates, she would throw them away. It is claimed that one of the boys in the troupe deserted the St. Louis Cardinal chain for the Derby because he could make more money that way. That may be a gratuitous sneer at baseball, but on the other hand, thinking about the Cardinals, it may be true. Mr. Billy Bogash, recognized as the Ty Cobb of roller skating, makes consistently better than $10,000 a year, and when a good girl skater and a good boy skater have the presence of mind to marry each other, the pair can knock down from $15,000 to $20,000 per annum, as well as everything that gets in their way.

Pending the arrival of the next generation, Mr. Seltzer has got to dig up and train new skaters to keep the market supplied. Toward this end he runs a skating school in Chicago, where prospects are polished at the house's expense. It takes about a year of training to get a skater ready for the "pack," and three years to make a top point-sprinting performer. Like piano teachers who dislike to take on pupils who have learned to play "Yankee Doodle" with one finger, Mr. Seltzer prefers absolutely fresh recruits with no fixed skating tricks and no bad habits. A bad habit in a roller skater, for instance, would be kindness. Those things have got to be pruned out of the subject while he is young.

The new Roller Derby helmets, which were put on view for the first time at Madison Square Garden, are not entirely popular with skaters, especially the ladies (I use the word in a general sense) among them. Neither are all the pads. There is a certain vanity among girl skaters, when they are not too busy tattooing their initials on the shins of the next girl, and they point out that Mr. Seltzer's scheme of padding, while technically useful on the track, does not coincide with nature's scheme. They prefer nature's. As for the helmets, there are two things against them. The ladies like to have their hair float behind them in the breeze when they skate. It looks better. Also, the helmet protects the hair of their victims. A lady skater who cannot sink her hands wrist-deep into the coiffure of an enemy, take a good hold, and pull of the scalp at the roots feels frustrated. She feels that her individual liberties have been violated. She wonders what to do with herself.

"Have a heart," said Miss Toughie Brashun to Mr. Seltzer the other day. "I have my eye on a hair-do that I want to rip open from here to Texas."

"Nothing doing," said the chief sternly. "Helmets will be worn. Safety first. Players desiring concussions must obtain them on their own time. Security and dignity are the rule of the sport."

"That's what you think," muttered Miss Brashun, baring her fangs. The final issue remains in doubt. As we go to press, history awaits the outcome.

Ring Lardner

Champion

When describing Ringgold Wilmer Lardner's stories and sketches of American life during and after that "golden age of sports," critics almost always use the phrase "mordant wit." The reason for this is that it fits Lardner like Alibi Ike's glove. Of all his stories, "Champion"—full of mordancy—is probably his best-known work. The story was made into a popular film starring Kirk Douglas as the malevolent champion, Midge Kelly.

Midge Kelly scored his first knockout when he was seventeen. The knockee was his brother Connie, three years his junior and a cripple. The purse was a half dollar given to the younger Kelly by a lady whose electric had just missed bumping his soul from his frail little body.

Connie did not know Midge was in the house, else he never would have risked laying the prize on the arm of the least comfortable chair in the room, the better to observe its shining beauty. As Midge entered from the kitchen, the crippled boy covered the coin with his hand, but the movement lacked the speed requisite to escape his brother's quick eye.

"Watcha got there?" demanded Midge.

"Nothin'," said Connie.

"You're a one-legged liar!" said Midge.

He strode over to his brother's chair and grasped the hand that concealed the coin.

"Let loose!" he ordered.

Connie began to cry.

"Let loose and shut up your noise," said the elder, and jerked his brother's hand from the chair arm.

The coin fell onto the bare floor. Midge pounced on it. His weak mouth widened in a triumphant smile.

"Nothin', huh?" he said. "All right, if it's nothin' you don't want it."

"Give that back," sobbed the younger.

"I'll give you a red nose, you little sneak! Where'd you steal it?"

"I didn't steal it. It's mine. A lady give it to me after she pretty near hit me with a car."

"It's a crime she missed you," said Midge.

Midge started for the front door. The cripple picked up his crutch, rose from his chair with difficulty, and, still sobbing, came toward Midge. The latter heard him and stopped.

"You better stay where you're at," he said.

"I want my money," cried the boy.

"I know what you want," said Midge.

Doubling up the fist that held the half dollar, he landed with all his strength on his brother's mouth. Connie fell to the floor with a thud, the crutch tumbling on top of him. Midge stood beside the prostrate form.

"Is that enough?" he said. "Or do you want this, too?"

And he kicked him in the crippled leg.

"I guess that'll hold you," he said.

There was no response from the boy on the floor. Midge looked at him a moment, then at the coin in his hand, and then went out into the street, whistling.

An hour later, when Mrs. Kelly came home from her day's work at Faulkner's Steam Laundry, she found Connie on the floor, moaning. Dropping on her knees beside him, she called him by name a score of times. Then she got up and, pale as a ghost, dashed from the house. Dr. Ryan left the Kelly abode about dusk and walked toward Halsted Street. Mrs. Dorgan spied him as he passed her gate.

"Who's sick, Doctor?" she called.

"Poor little Connie," he replied. "He had a bad fall."

"How did it happen?"

"I can't say for sure, Margaret, but I'd almost bet he was knocked down."

"Knocked down!" exclaimed Mrs. Dorgan. "Why, who—?"

"Have you seen the other one lately?"

"Michael? No, not since mornin'. You can't be thinkin'—"

"I wouldn't put it past him, Margaret," said the doctor gravely.

"The lad's mouth is swollen and cut, and his poor, skinny little leg is bruised. He surely didn't do it to himself and I think Ellen suspects the other one."

"Lord save us!" said Mrs. Dorgan. "I'll run over and see if I can help."

"That's a good woman," said Dr. Ryan, and went on down the street.

Near midnight, when Midge came home, his mother was sitting at Connie's bedside. She did not look up.

"Well," said Midge, "what's the matter?"

She remained silent. Midge repeated his question.

"Michael, you know what's the matter," she said at length.

"I don't know nothin'," said Midge.

"Don't lie to me, Michael. What did you do to your brother?"

"Nothin'."

"You hit him."

"Well, then, I hit him. What of it? It ain't the first time."

Her lips pressed tightly together, her face like chalk, Ellen Kelly rose from her chair and made straight for him. Midge backed against the door.

"Lay off'n me, Ma. I don't want to fight no woman."

Still she came on, breathing heavily.

"Stop where you're at, Ma," he warned.

There was a brief struggle and Midge's mother lay on the floor before him.

"You ain't hurt, Ma. You're lucky I didn't land good. And I told you to lay off'n me."

"God forgive you, Michael!"

Midge found Hap Collins in the showdown game at the Royal.

"Come on out a minute," he said.

Hap followed him out on the walk.

"I'm leavin' town for a w'ile," said Midge.

"What for?"

"Well, we had a little run-in up to the house. The kid stole a half buck off'n me, and when I went after it he cracked me with his crutch. So I nailed him. And the old lady came at me with a chair and I took it off'n her and she fell down."

"How is Connie hurt?"

"Not bad."

"What are you runnin' away for?"

"Who the hell said I was runnin' away? I'm sick and tired o' gettin' picked on; that's all. So I'm leavin' for a w'ile and I want a piece o' money."

"I ain't only got six bits," said Happy.

"You're in bad shape, ain't you? Well, come through with it."

Happy came through.

"You oughtn't to hit the kid," he said.

"I ain't astin' you who can I hit," snarled Midge. "You try to put somethin' over on me and you'll get the same dose. I'm goin' now."

"Go as far as you like," said Happy, but not until he was sure that Kelly was out of hearing.

Early the following morning, Midge boarded a train for Milwaukee. He had no ticket, but no one knew the difference. The conductor remained in the caboose.

On a night six months later, Midge hurried out of the "stage door" of the Star Boxing Club and made for Duane's saloon, two blocks away. In his pocket were twelve dollars, his reward for having battered up one Demon Dempsey through the six rounds of the first preliminary.

It was Midge's first professional engagement in the manly art. Also it was the first time in weeks that he had earned twelve dollars.

On the way to Duane's he had to pass Niemann's. He pulled his cap over his eyes and increased his pace until he had gone by. Inside Niemann's stood a trusting bartender, who for ten days had staked Midge to drinks and allowed him to ravage the lunch on a promise to come in and settle the moment he was paid for the "prelim."

Midge strode into Duane's and aroused the napping bartender by slapping a silver dollar on the festive board.

"Gimme a shot," said Midge.

The shooting continued until the wind-up at the Star was over and part of the fight crowd joined Midge in front of Duane's bar. A youth in the early twenties, standing next to young Kelly, finally summoned sufficient courage to address him.

"Wasn't you in the first bout?" he ventured.

"Yeh," Midge replied.

"My name's Hersch," said the other.

Midge received the startling information in silence.

"I don't want to butt in," continued Mr. Hersch, "but I'd like to buy you a drink."

"All right," said Midge, "but don't overstrain yourself."

Mr. Hersch laughed uproariously and beckoned to the bartender.

"You certainly gave that wop a trimmin' tonight," said the buyer of the drink, when they had been served. "I thought you'd kill him."

"I would if I hadn't let up," Midge replied. "I'll kill 'em all."

"You got the wallop all right," the other said admiringly.

"Have I got the wallop?" said Midge. "Say, I can kick like a mule. Did you notice them muscles in my shoulders?"

"Notice 'em? I couldn't help from noticin' 'em," said Hersch. "I says to the fella sittin' alongside o' me, I says: 'Look at them shoulders! No wonder he can hit,' I says to him."

"Just let me land and it's goodbye, baby," said Midge. "I'll kill 'em all."

The oral manslaughter continued until Duane's closed for the night. At parting, Midge and his new friend shook hands and arranged for a meeting the following evening.

For nearly a week the two were together almost constantly. It was Hersch's pleasant role to listen to Midge's modest revelations concerning himself, and to buy every time Midge's glass was empty. But there came an evening when Hersch regretfully announced that he must go home to supper.

"I got a date for eight bells," he confided. "I could stick till then, only I must clean up and put on the Sunday clo'es, 'cause she's the prettiest little thing in Milwaukee."

"Can't you fix it for two?" asked Midge.

"I don't know who to get," Hersch replied. "Wait, though. I got a sister and if she ain't busy, it'll be O.K. She's no bum for looks herself."

So it came about that Midge and Emma Hersch and Emma's brother and the prettiest little thing in Milwaukee foregathered at Wall's and danced half the night away. And Midge and Emma danced every dance together, for though every little onestep seemed to induce a new thirst of its own, Lou Hersch stayed too sober to dance with his own sister.

The next day, penniless at last in spite of his phenomenal ability to make someone else settle, Midge Kelly sought out Doc Hammond, matchmaker for the Star, and asked to be booked for the next show.

"I could put you on with Tracy for the next bout," said Doc.

"What's they in it?" asked Midge.

"Twenty if you cop," Doc told him.

"Have a heart," protested Midge. "Didn't I look good the other night?"

"You looked all right. But you aren't Freddie Welsh yet by a consid'able margin."

"I ain't scared of Freddie Welsh or none of 'em," said Midge.

"Well, we don't pay our boxers by the size of their chests," Doc said. "I'm offerin' you this Tracy bout. Take it or leave it."

"All right: I'm on," said Midge, and he passed a pleasant afternoon at Duane's on the strength of his booking.

Young Tracy's manager came to see Midge the night before the show.

"How do you feel about this go?" he asked.

"Me?" said Midge. "I feel all right. What do you mean, how do I feel?"

"I mean," said Tracy's manager, "that we're mighty anxious to win, 'cause the boy's got a chanct in Philly if he cops this one."

"What's your proposition?" asked Midge.

"Fifty bucks," said Tracy's manager.

"What do you think I am, a crook? Me lay down for fifty bucks. Not me!"

"Seventy-five, then," said Tracy's manager.

The market closed on eighty and the details were agreed on in short order. And the next night Midge was stopped in the second round by a terrific slap on the forearm.

This time Midge passed up both Niemann's and Duane's, having a sizable account at each place, and sought his refreshment at Stein's farther down the street.

When the profits of his deal with Tracy were gone, he learned, by first-hand information from Doc Hammond and the matchmakers at the other "clubs," that he was no longer desired for even the cheapest of preliminaries. There was no danger of his starving or dying of thirst while Emma and Lou Hersch lived. But he made up his mind, four months after his defeat by Young Tracy, that Milwaukee was not the ideal place for him to live.

"I can lick the best of 'em," he reasoned, "but there ain't no more chanct for me here. I can maybe go east and get on somewheres. And besides—"

But just after Midge had purchased a ticket to Chicago with the money he had "borrowed" from Emma Hersch "to buy shoes," a heavy hand was laid on his shoulder and he turned to face two strangers.

"Where are you goin', Kelly?" inquired the owner of the heavy hand.

"Nowheres," said Midge. "What the hell do you care?"

The other stranger spoke:

"Kelly, I'm employed by Emma Hersch's mother to see that you do right by her. And we want you to stay here till you've done it."

"You won't get nothin' but the worst of it, monkeying with me," said Midge.

Nevertheless, he did not depart for Chicago that night. Two days later, Emma Hersch became Mrs. Kelly, and the gift of the bridegroom, when once they were alone, was a crushing blow on the bride's pale cheek.

Next morning, Midge left Milwaukee as he had entered it—by fast freight.

"They's no use kiddin' ourself any more," said Tommy Haley. "He might get down to thirty-seven in a pinch, but if he done below that a mouse could stop him. He's a welter; that's what he is and he knows it as well as I do. He's growed like a weed in the last six months. I told him, I says, 'If you don't quit growin' they won't be nobody for you to box, only Willard and them.' He says, 'Well, I wouldn't run away from Willard if I weighed twenty pounds more.' "

"He must hate himself," said Tommy's brother.

"I never seen a good one that didn't," said Tommy. "And Midge is a good one; don't make no mistake about that. I wisht we could of got Welsh before the kid growed so big. But it's too late now. I won't make no holler, though, if we can match him up with the Dutchman."

"Who do you mean?"

"Young Goetz, the welter champ. We mightn't not get so much dough for the bout itself, but it'd roll in afterward. What a drawin' card we'd be, 'cause the people pays their money to see the fella with the wallop, and that's Midge. And we'd keep the title just as long as Midge could make the weight."

"Can't you land no match with Goetz?"

"Sure, 'cause he needs the money. But I've went careful with the kid so far and look at the results I got! So what's the use of takin' a chanct? The kid's comin' every minute and Goetz is goin' back faster'n big Johnson did. I think we could lick him now; I'd bet my life on it. But six mont's from now they won't be no risk. He'll of licked hisself before that time. Then all as we'll have to do is sign up with him and wait for the referee to stop it. But Midge is so crazy to get at him now that I can't hardly hold him back."

The brothers Haley were lunching in a Boston hotel. Dan had come down from Holyoke to visit with Tommy and to watch the latter's protégé go twelve rounds, or less, with Bud Cross. The bout promised little in the way of a contest, for Midge had twice stopped the Baltimore youth and Bud's reputation for gameness was all that had earned him the date. The fans were willing to pay the price to see Midge's haymaking left, but they wanted to see it used on an opponent who would not jump out of the ring the first time he felt its crushing force. Bud Cross was such an opponent, and his willingness to stop boxing gloves with his eyes, ears, nose and throat had enabled him to escape the horrors of honest labor. A game boy was Bud, and he showed it in his battered, swollen, discolored face.

"I should think," said Dan Haley, "that the kid'd do whatever you tell him after all you've done for him."

"Well," said Tommy, "he's took my dope pretty straight so far, but he's so sure of hisself that he can't see no reason for waitin'. He'll do what I say, though; he'd be a sucker not to."

"You got a contrac' with him?"

"No, I don't need no contrac'. He knows it was me that drug him out o' the gutter and he ain't goin' to turn me down now when he's got the dough and bound to get more. Where'd he of been at if I hadn't listened to him when he first came to me? That's pretty near two years ago now, but it seems like last week. I was settin' in the s'loon acrost from the Pleasant Club in Philly, waitin' for McCann to count the dough and come over, when this little bum blowed in and tried to stand the house off for a drink. They told him nothin' doin' and to beat it out o' there, and then he seen me and come over to where I was settin' and ast me wasn't I a boxin' man and I told him who I was. Then he ast me for money to buy a shot and I told him to set down and I'd buy it for him.

"Then we got talkin' things over and he told me his name and told me about fight'n' a couple o' prelims out of Milwaukee. So I says, 'Well, boy, I don't know how good or how rotten you are, but you won't never get nowheres trainin' on that stuff.' So he says he'd cut it out if he could get on in a bout and I says I would give him a chanct if he played square with me and didn't touch no more to drink. So we shook hands and I took him up to the hotel with me and give him a bath and the next day I bought him some clo'es. And I staked him to eats and sleeps for over six weeks. He had a hard time breakin' away from the polish, but finally I thought he was fit and I give him his chanct. He went on with Smiley Sayer and stopped him so quick that Smiley thought sure he was poisoned.

"Well, you know what he's did since. The only beatin' in his record was by Tracy in Milwaukee before I got hold of him, and he's licked Tracy three times in the last year.

"I've gave him all the best of it in a money way and he's got seven thousand bucks in cold storage. How's that for a kid that was in the gutter two years ago? And he'd have still more yet if he wasn't so nuts over clo'es and got to stop at the good hotels and so forth."

"Where's his home at?"

"Well, he ain't really got no home. He came from Chicago and his mother canned him out o' the house for bein' no good. She give him a raw deal, I guess, and he says he won't have nothin' to do with her unless she comes to him first. She's got a pile o' money, he says, so he ain't worryin' about her."

The gentleman under discussion entered the café and swaggered to Tommy's table, while the whole room turned to look.

Midge was the picture of health despite a slightly colored eye and an ear that seemed to have no opening. But perhaps it was not his healthiness that drew all eyes. His diamond horseshoe tie pin, his purple cross-striped shirt, his orange shoes and his light-blue suit fairly screamed for attention.

"Where you been?" he asked Tommy. "I been lookin' all over for you."

"Set down," said his manager.

"No time," said Midge. "I'm goin' down to the w'arf and see 'em unload the fish."

"Shake hands with my brother Dan," said Tommy.

Midge shook with Holyoke Haley.

"If you're Tommy's brother, you're O.K. with me," said Midge, and the brothers beamed with pleasure.

Dan moistened his lips and murmured an embarrassed reply, but it was lost on the young gladiator.

"Leave me take twenty," Midge was saying. "I prob'ly won't need it, but I don't like to be caught short."

Tommy parted with a twenty-dollar bill and recorded the transaction in a small book the insurance company had given him for Christmas.

"But," he said, "it won't cost you no twenty to look at them fish. Want me to go along?"

"No," said Midge hastily. "You and your brother here prob'ly got a lot to say to each other."

"Well," said Tommy, "don't take no bad money and don't get lost. And you better be back at four o'clock and lay down a w'ile."

"I don't need no rest to beat this guy," said Midge. "He'll do enough layin' down for the both of us."

And laughing even more than the jest called for, he strode out through the fire of admiring and startled glances.

The corner of Boylston and Tremont was the nearest Midge got to the wharf, but the lady awaiting him was doubtless a more dazzling sight than the catch of the luckiest Massachusetts fisherman. She could talk, too—probably better than the fish.

"O you Kid!" she said, flashing a few silver teeth among the gold. "O you fighting man!"

Midge smiled up at her.

"We'll go somewheres and get a drink," he said. "One won't hurt."

In New Orleans five months after he had rearranged the map of Bud Cross for the third time, Midge finished training for his championship bout with the Dutchman.

Back in his hotel after the final workout, Midge stopped to chat with some of the boys from up north, who had made the long trip to see a champion dethroned, for the result of the bout was so nearly a foregone conclusion that even the experts had guessed it.

Tommy Haley secured the key and the mail and ascended to the Kelly suite. He was bathing when Midge came in, half an hour later.

"Any mail?" asked Midge.

"There on the bed," replied Tommy from the tub.

Midge picked up the stack of letters and postcards and glanced over them. From the pile he sorted out three letters and laid them on the table. The rest he tossed into the wastebasket. Then he picked up the three and sat for a few moments holding them, while his eyes gazed off into space. At length he looked again at the three unopened letters in his hand; then he put one in his pocket and tossed the other two at the basket. They missed their target and fell on the floor.

"Hell," said Midge, and stooping over picked them up.

He opened one postmarked Milwaukee and read:

Dear Husband:

I have wrote to you so many times and got no anser and I dont know if you ever got them, so I am writeing again in the hopes you will get this letter and anser. I dont like to bother you with my trubles and I would not only for the baby and I am not asking you should write to me but only send a little money and I am not asking for myself but the baby has not been well a day sence last Aug. and the dr. told me she cant live much longer unless I give her better food and thats impossible the way things are. Lou has not been working for a year and what I make dont hardley pay for the rent. I am not asking for you to give me any money, but only you should send what I loaned when convenient and I think it amts. to about $36.00. Please try and send that amt. and it will help me, but if you cant send the whole amt. try and send me something.

Your wife,
EMMA

Midge tore the letter into a hundred pieces and scattered them over the floor.

"Money, money, money!" he said. "They must think I'm made o' money. I s'pose the old woman's after it too."

He opened his mother's letter:

dear Michael Connie wonted me to rite and say you must beet the dutchman and he is sur you will and wonted me to say we wont you to rite and tell us about it, but I guess you havent no time to rite or we herd from you long beffore this but I wish you would rite jest a line or 2 boy because it wuld be better for Connie then & barl of medisin. It wuld help me to keep things going if you send me money now and then when you can spair it but if you cant send no money try and fine time to rite a letter onley a few lines and it will please Connie. jest think boy he hasent got out of bed in over 3 yrs. Connie says good luck.

Your Mother,
ELLEN F. KELLY

"I thought so," said Midge. "They're all alike."

The third letter was from New York. It read:

HON:—This is the last letter you will get from me before your champ, but I will send you a telegram Saturday, but I can't say as much in a telegram as in a letter and I am writing this to let you know I am thinking of you and praying for good luck.

Lick him good hon and don't wait no longer than you have to and don't forget to write me as soon as its over. Give him that little old left of yours on the nose hon and don't be afraid of spoiling his good looks because he couldn't be no homlier than he is. But don't let him spoil my baby's pretty face. You won't will you hon.

Well hon I would give anything to be there and see it, but I guess you love Haley better than me or you wouldn't let him keep me away. But when your champ hon we can do as we please and tell Haley to go to the devil.

Well hon I will send you a telegram Saturday and I almost forgot to tell you I will need some more money, a couple hundred say and you will have to wire it to me as soon as you get this. You will won't you hon.

I will send you a telegram Saturday and remember hon I am pulling for you.

Well goodbye sweetheart and good luck.

GRACE

"They're all alike," said Midge. "Money, money, money."

Tommy Haley, shining from his ablutions, came in from the adjoining room.

"Thought you'd be layin' down," he said.

"I'm goin' to," said Midge, unbuttoning his orange shoes.

"I'll call you at six and you can eat up here without no bugs to pester you. I got to go down and give them birds their tickets."

"Did you hear from Goldberg?" asked Midge.

"Didn't I tell you? Sure; fifteen weeks at five hundred, if we win. And we can get a guarantee o' twelve thousand, with privileges either in New York or Milwaukee."

"Who with?"

"Anybody that'll stand up in front of you. You don't care who it is, do you?"

"Not me. I'll make 'em all look like a monkey."

"Well you better lay down aw'ile."

"Oh, say, wire two hundred to Grace for me, will you? Right away; the New York address."

"Two hundred! You just sent her three hundred last Sunday."

"Well, what the hell do you care?"

"All right, all right. Don't get sore about it. Anything else?"

"That's all," said Midge, and dropped onto the bed.

"And I want the deed done before I come back," said Grace as she rose from the table. "You won't fall down on me, will you, hon?"

"Leave it to me," said Midge. "And don't spend no more than you have to."

Grace smiled a farewell and left the café. Midge continued to sip his coffee and read his paper.

They were in Chicago and they were in the middle of Midge's first week in vaudeville. He had come straight north to reap the rewards of his glorious victory over the broken-down Dutchman. A fortnight had been spent in learning his act, which consisted of a gymnastic exhibition and a ten minutes' monologue on the various excellences of Midge Kelly. And now he was twice daily turning 'em away from the Madison Theater.

His breakfast over and his paper read, Midge sauntered into the lobby and asked for his key. He then beckoned to a bellboy, who had been hoping for that very honor.

"Find Haley, Tommy Haley," said Midge. "Tell him to come up to my room."

"Yes, sir, Mr. Kelly," said the boy, and proceeded to break all his former records for diligence.

Midge was looking out of his seventh-story window when Tommy answered the summons.

"What'll it be?" inquired the manager.

There was a pause before Midge replied.

"Haley," he said, "twenty-five per cent's a whole lot o' money."

"I guess I got it comin', ain't I?" said Tommy.

"I don't see how you figger it. I don't see where you're worth it to me."

"Well," said Tommy, "I didn't expect nothin' like this. I thought you was satisfied with the bargain. I don't want to beat nobody out o' nothin', but I don't see where you could have got anybody else that would of did all I done for you."

"Sure, that's all right," said the champion. "You done a lot for me in Philly. And you got good money for it, didn't you?"

"I ain't makin' no holler. Still and all, the big money's still ahead of us yet. And if it hadn't of been for me, you wouldn't of never got within grabbin' distance."

"Oh, I guess I could of went along all right," said Midge. "Who was it hung that left on the Dutchman's jaw, me or you?"

"Yes, but you wouldn't been in the ring with the Dutchman if it wasn't for how I handled you."

"Well, this won't get us nowheres. The idear is that you ain't worth no twenty-five per cent now and it don't make no difference what come off a year or two ago."

"Don't it?" said Tommy. "I'd say it made a whole lot of difference."

"Well, I say it don't and I guess that settles it."

"Look here, Midge," Tommy said, "I thought I was fair with you, but if you don't think so, I'm willin' to hear what you think is fair. I don't want nobody callin' me a Sherlock. Let's go down to business and sign up a contrac'. What's your figger?"

"I ain't namin' no figger," Midge replied. "I'm sayin' that twenty-five's too much. Now what are you willin' to take?"

"How about twenty?"

"Twenty's too much," said Kelly.

"What ain't too much?" asked Tommy.

"Well, Haley, I might as well give it to you straight. They ain't nothin' that ain't too much."

"You mean you don't want me at no figger?"

"That's the idear."

There was a minute's silence. Then Tommy Haley walked toward the door.

"Midge," he said, in a choking voice, "you're makin' a big mistake, boy. You can't throw down your best friends and get away with it. That damn woman will ruin you."

Midge sprang from his seat.

"You shut your mouth!" he stormed. "Get out o' here before they have to carry you out. You been spongin' off o' me long enough. Say one more word about the girl or about anything else and you'll get what the Dutchman got. Now get out!"

And Tommy Haley, having a very vivid memory of the Dutchman's face as he fell, got out.

Grace came in later, dropped her numerous bundles on the lounge and perched herself on the arm of Midge's chair.

"Well?" she said.

"Well," said Midge, "I got rid of him."

"Good boy!" said Grace. "And now I think you might give me that twenty-five per cent."

"Besides the seventy-five you're already gettin'?" said Midge.

"Don't be no grouch, hon. You don't look pretty when you're grouchy."

"It ain't my business to look pretty," Midge replied.

"Wait till you see how I look with the stuff I bought this mornin'!"

Midge glanced at the bundles on the lounge.

"There's Haley's twenty-five per cent," he said, "and then some."

The champion did not remain long without a manager. Haley's successor was none other than Jerome Harris, who saw in Midge a better meal ticket than his popular-priced musical show had been.

The contract, giving Mr. Harris twenty-five per cent of Midge's earnings, was signed in Detroit the week after Tommy Haley had heard his dismissal read. It had taken Midge just six days to learn that a popular actor cannot get on without the ministrations of a man who thinks, talks and means business. At first Grace objected to the new member of the firm, but when Mr. Harris had demanded and secured from the vaudeville people a one-hundred dollar increase in Midge's weekly stipend, she was convinced that the champion had acted for the best.

"You and my missus will have some great old times," Harris told Grace. "I'd of wired her to join us here, only I seen the Kid's bookin' takes us to Milwaukee next week, and that's where she is."

But when they were introduced in the Milwaukee hotel, Grace admitted to herself that her feeling for Mrs. Harris could hardly be called love at first sight. Midge, on the contrary, gave his new manager's wife the many times over and seemed loath to end the feast of his eyes.

"Some doll," he said to Grace when they were alone.

"Doll is right," the lady replied, "and sawdust where her brains ought to be."

"I'm liable to steal that baby," said Midge, and he smiled as he noted the effect of his words on his audience's face.

On Tuesday of the Milwaukee week the champion successfully defended his title in a bout that the newspapers never reported. Midge was alone in his room that morning when a visitor entered without knocking. The visitor was Lou Hersch.

Midge turned white at sight of him.

"What do you want?" he demanded.

"I guess you know," said Lou Hersch. "Your wife's starvin' to death and your baby's starvin' to death and I'm starvin' to death. And you're dirty with money."

"Listen," said Midge, "if it wasn't for you, I wouldn't never saw your sister. And, if you ain't man enough to hold a job, what's that to me? The best thing you can do is keep away from me."

"You give me a piece o' money and I'll go."

Midge's reply to the ultimatum was a straight right to his brother-in-law's narrow chest.

"Take that home to your sister."

And after Lou Hersch had picked himself up and slunk away, Midge thought: "It's lucky I didn't give him my left or I'd of croaked him. And if I'd hit him in the stomach, I'd of broke his spine."

There was a party after each evening performance during the Milwaukee engagement. The wine flowed freely and Midge had more of it than Tommy Haley ever would have permitted him. Mr. Harris offered no objection, which was possibly just as well for his own physical comfort.

In the dancing between drinks, Midge had his new manager's wife for a partner as often as Grace. The latter's face as she floundered round in the arms of the portly Harris belied her frequent protestations that she was having the time of her life.

Several times that week, Midge thought Grace was on the point of starting the quarrel he hoped to have. But it was not until Friday night that she accommodated. He and Mrs. Harris had disappeared after the matinee and when Grace saw him again at the close of the night show, she came to the point at once.

"What are you tryin' to pull off?" she demanded.

"It's none o' your business, is it?" said Midge.

"You bet it's my business; mine and Harris's. You cut it short or you'll find out."

"Listen," said Midge, "have you got a mortgage on me or somethin'? You talk like we was married."

"We're goin' to be, too. And tomorrow's as good a time as any."

"Just about," said Midge. "You got as much chanct o' marryin' me tomorrow as the next day or next year and that ain't no chanct at all."

"We'll find out," said Grace.

"You're the one that's got somethin' to find out."

"What do you mean?"

"I mean I'm married already."

"You lie!"

"You think so, do you? Well, s'pose you go to this here address and get acquainted with my missus."

Midge scrawled a number on a piece of paper and handed it to her. She stared at it unseeingly.

"Well," said Midge, "I ain't kiddin' you. You go there and ask for Mrs. Michael Kelly, and if you don't find her, I'll marry you tomorrow before breakfast."

Still Grace stared at the scrap of paper. To Midge it seemed an age before she spoke again.

"You lied to me all this w'ile."

"You never ast me was I married. What's more, what the hell difference did it make to you? You got a split, didn't you? Better'n fifty-
fifty."

He started away.

"Where you goin?"

"I'm goin' to meet Harris and his wife."

"I'm goin' with you. You're not goin' to shake me now."

"Yes, I am, too," said Midge quietly. "When I leave town tomorrow
night, you're going to stay here. And if I see where you're goin' to make
a fuss, I'll put you in a hospital where they'll keep you quiet. You can
get your stuff tomorrow mornin' and I'll slip you a hundred bucks. And
then I don't want to see no more o' you. And don't try and tag along
now or I'll have to add another K.O. to the old record."

When Grace returned to the hotel that night, she discovered that
Midge and the Harrises had moved to another. And when Midge left
town the following night, he was again without a manager, and Mr. Harris
was without a wife.

Three days prior to Midge Kelly's ten-round bout with Young Milton
in New York City, the sporting editor of the *News* assigned Joe Morgan
to write two or three thousand words about the champion to run with
a picture layout for Sunday.

Joe Morgan dropped in at Midge's training quarters Friday afternoon. Midge, he learned, was doing road work, but Midge's manager,
Wallie Adams, stood ready and willing to supply reams of dope about
the greatest fighter of the age.

"Let's hear what you've got," said Joe, "and then I'll try to fix up
something."

So Wallie stepped on the accelerator of his imagination and shot
away.

"Just a kid; that's all he is; a regular boy. Get what I mean? Don't
know the meanin' o' bad habits. Never tasted liquor in his life and would
prob'bly get sick if he smelled it. Clean livin' put him up where he's at.
Get what I mean? And modest and unassumin' as a schoolgirl. He's so
quiet you wouldn't never know he was round. And he'd go to jail before
he'd talk about himself.

"No job at all to get him in shape, 'cause he's always that way. The
only trouble we have with him is gettin' him to light into these poor
bums they match him up with. He's scared he'll hurt somebody. Get
what I mean? He's tickled to death over this match with Milton, 'cause
everybody says Milton can stand the gaff. Midge'll maybe be able to cut

loose a little this time. But the last two bouts he had, the guys hadn't no business in the ring with him, and he was holdin' back all the w'ile for the fear he'd kill somebody. Get what I mean?"

"Is he married?" inquired Joe.

"Say, you'd think he was married to hear him rave about them kiddies he's got. His fam'ly's up in Canada to their summer home and Midge is wild to get up there with 'em. He thinks more o' that wife and them kiddies than all the money in the world. Get what I mean?"

"How many children has he?"

"I don't know, four or five, I guess. All boys and every one of 'em a dead ringer for their dad."

"Is his father living?"

"No, the old man died when he was a kid. But he's got a grand old mother and a kid brother out in Chi. They're the first ones he thinks about after a match, them and his wife and kiddies. And he don't forget to send the old woman a thousand bucks after every bout. He's goin' to buy her a new home as soon as they pay him off for this match."

"How about his brother? Is he going to tackle the game?"

"Sure, and Midge says he'll be a champion before he's twenty years old. They're a fightin' fam'ly and all of 'em honest and straight as a die. Get what I mean? A fella that I can't tell you his name come to Midge in Milwaukee onct and wanted him to throw a fight and Midge give him such a trimmin' in the street that he couldn't go on that night. That's the kind he is. Get what I mean?"

Joe Morgan hung around the camp until Midge and his trainers returned.

"One o' the boys from the *News*," said Wallie by way of introduction. "I been givin' him your fam'ly hist'ry."

"Did he give you good dope?" he inquired.

"He's some historian," said Joe.

"Don't call me no names," said Wallie smiling. "Call us up if they's anything more you want. And keep your eyes on us Monday night. Get what I mean?"

The story in Sunday's *News* was read by thousands of lovers of the manly art. It was well written and full of human interest. Its slight inaccuracies went unchallenged, though three readers, besides Wallie Adams and Midge Kelly, saw and recognized them. The three were Grace, Tommy Haley and Jerome Harris, and the comments they made were not for publication.

Neither the Mrs. Kelly in Chicago nor the Mrs. Kelly in Milwaukee knew that there was such a paper as the New York *News*. And even if they had known of it and that it contained two columns of reading matter about Midge, neither mother nor wife could have bought it. For the *News* on Sunday is a nickel a copy.

Joe Morgan could have written more accurately, no doubt, if instead of Wallie Adams, he had interviewed Ellen Kelly and Connie Kelly and Emma Kelly and Lou Hersch and Grace and Jerome Harris and Tommy Haley and Hap Collins and two or three Milwaukee bartenders.

But a story built on their evidence would never have passed the sporting editor.

"Suppose you can prove it," that gentleman would have said. "It wouldn't get us anything but abuse to print it. The people don't want to see him knocked. He's champion."

Primo Levi

Decathlon Man

Primo Levi, an Italian Jew, a survivor of Auschwitz, stunned the literary world with his ruminations on the Holocaust. His themes were condemnation, absolution, and salvation. His "lucent and humane restraint," as Cynthia Ozick has written, proved to be in suicidal conflict with his suppressed "rage of resentment." And so he did end his own life, in 1987. This savagely powerful poem may be read as more than the simple ordeal of a marathon man.

Believe me, the marathon is nothing,
So are the hammer and the weights: no single contest
Can compare with our ordeal.
I won, yes: I'm more famous today than yesterday,
But a lot older, and worn out.
I ran the four hundred like a hawk,
Without pity for the runner just behind me.
Who was he? No one in particular, a novice,
Never seen before,
A poor Third World wretch,
But the man running beside you is always a monster.
I broke his back, the way I wanted to;
Relishing his agony, I didn't feel my own.
As for the pole vault, that was less easy,
But luckily for me the judges
Didn't notice my trick
And I did the five metres well.

In the case of the javelin, that's my secret:
You don't have to hurl it against the sky.
The sky is empty: why would you want to run it through?
All you need do is picture, at the far end of the meadow,
The man or woman you want dead,
And the javelin will turn into a weapon.
It will scent blood, and will fly farther.
I wouldn't know what to say about the fifteen hundred;
I ran it in a state of dizziness
And with cramps, determined, desperate,
Terrified by the convulsive drumbeat of my heart.
I won, but it cost me a lot.
Afterward the discus was lead-heavy
And fell out of my hand, slippery
With my broken veteran's sweat.
They booed me from the sidelines;
Don't think I didn't hear it.
But what do you people require of us?
What more can you demand?
To take off into the air?
Compose a poem in Sanskrit?
Arrive at the end of *pi?*
Console the sorrowful?
Operate by compassion's rules?

(Translated from the Italian by Ruth Feldman)

A. J. Liebling

Donnybrook Farr

A. J. Liebling once wrote, "A fighter's hostilities come out naturally with his sweat, and when his job is done he feels good because he has expressed himself." So must Liebling have felt about everything he wrote, from food to war to boxing; he was a Sugar Ray Robinson of his craft, darting and dancing and sniping and, in the end, always hitting home. Liebling claimed to have gotten the fighting call in 1917 at age thirteen, when a bachelor uncle taught the youngster both the rudiments and the legend of the sport. Liebling said he boxed until 1946 when, as he writes, "the fellow I was working with said he could not knock me out unless I consented to rounds longer than nine seconds." He had quit writing about boxing for The New Yorker *earlier, in 1939, when he became a war correspondent. But in 1951 he returned to the "low life," and wrote a series of memorable pieces, including this one. Only Mr. Liebling could make mythic a Welsh newspaperman named Tommy Farr, who in an earlier life survived fifteen rounds with "Joe Louey."*

The Sweet Science, like an old rap or the memory of love, follows its victim everywhere. When Phil Drake, a horse, not a prizefighter, won the Epsom Derby of 1955 at odds of 12 to 1, I had five nickers (Mayfair for pounds) on his nose. After deducting another five I had bet on one of the losers I had a net profit of fifty-five quid, better than one hundred and fifty dollars, which I took with me to the Champagne Bar under the grandstand. After a race won by a 12–1 shot, it is the most accessible section of the buffet. While there, I caught sight of some English boxing writers I know and wanted to see; they were struggling to reach a more animated and less expensive sector of the bar. It was a shame I had to down my champagne so quickly, but there wasn't enough to go around, so I finished it off and then sneaked up behind them, saying something about the smallness of the world.

It was at the bar, with my profits in my pocket and my champagne in me, that I learned there was soon to be a fifteen-round fight in Dublin for the featherweight championship of Europe. The defending champion, a Frenchman named Ray Famechon, had been induced to go there to fight the challenger, a boy from the North of Ireland, but not a Protestant, known as Billy Spider II Kelly. This Kelly, my friends said, was the British and British Empire champion, and a man of promise. One could fly to Dublin in a little more than an hour, and return just as expeditiously the morning after the battle. But what decided me to go was the news that the fight was going to be held in Donnybrook, an outlying part of Dublin that is universally synonymous with an unofficial, free-for-all fight. Professional fights have been less numerous in Dublin, but some of them have been illustrious. Pierce Egan, the Blind Raftery of the London prize ring, was a part-time Dublin man himself, and has re-counted the triumphs of Dan Donnelly, the first great Irish heavyweight, against two Englishmen, whose names escape my memory. They fought on the turf of the Curragh, a racecourse where, I am reliably informed by Tim Costello, a restaurateur of my acquaintance, small boys are still led out to view Donnelly's heelprints. Dan was no tippytoes fighter, and although he fought the Englishmen separately, he could have beaten them both together, make no doubt of it. Within my own lifetime, Battling Siki, the ingenuous Senegalese known to legend as the Ignoble Savage, was lured to Dublin to defend the world's light-heavyweight title, which he had acquired from Georges Carpentier, against Mike McTigue, an Irishman polished by travel. The bout was on March 17, 1923, and McTigue got the decision. McTigue's home-grounds success appeared to be the precedent most plausibly applicable to the proposed match at Donnybrook, for I knew that Famechon, who has boxed in the United States, was hardly likely to fell Kelly like an ox; the biggest piece of an ox Famechon has ever felled, I imagine, is a *tournedos*. The boxing writers told me that the referee was to be a neutral, appointed by the European Boxing Union, but even a neutral might prove suggestible at Donnybrook.

When I got my Aer Lingus ticket and reservation (Aer Lingus is the Irish airline), I found that the line had put on extra flights, rolling out old DC-3s, which take two and a half hours for the trip, to supplement their new English-built Viscounts, which take only an hour and twenty-five minutes. Because I applied late, I was put on a DC-3. When I came aboard, the only vacant seat was next to a large, fair-haired man of resolute and familiar appearance. The seats were narrow, the leg room was limited, and it was easy to see why the place next to the big fellow had been left to the last. To establish relations, I asked him how much he weighed, and he said, as if used to being asked the question, "Fourteen stone eleven and a half," which works out to two hundred and seven and a half pounds. I said, "I weigh sixteen stone, very nearly"—very nearly seventeen, I meant. We scrunched together like bulls in a horse trailer, and he grunted, "I'm only three pound more than when I fought Joe Louey."

"*Did* you?" I asked politely.

"If I didn't, I don't know 'oo put the rooddy loomps on my 'ead," he said pleasantly, and the hand-stitched face, with the high cheekbones, narrow eyes, and Rock of Gibraltar chin, came back to me out of the late thirties. He was Tommy Farr, the old Welsh heavyweight who went fifteen rounds with Joe Louis in 1937. There is a half-established legend in Britain that he was twisted out of the decision, which he wasn't. Farr does nothing actively to favor the myth, but he doesn't discourage it, either. He also fought a series of savage bouts, with varied fortunes, against fellows like Max Baer, and against them, he thinks, he got all the worst of it when he lost. "But I love the States," he said. "I made a lot of money there. That's what I fought for, eh? Money." He rubbed a thumb like a hammer against a rectangular index finger. "Two hundred and ninety-six fights I had. Do you think it was for a rooddy lark?"

I said no, and he said, "It was my profession. I well and truly served my apprenticeship, and then I wanted money. That's why they didn't like me over there at first—the press didn't like me. Because I didn't let them mess me about, that's why. I wanted my rest. Didn't want them banging about downstairs after eleven. My manager had a fridgeful of liquor for them, and 'e'd bring them in all hours. All right for 'im wasn't it? 'E didn't 'ave to fight. They liked 'im fine. Robbed me of fifty or sixty thousand quid, they did."

I asked him how the American press had robbed him of fifty or sixty thousand pounds, and he explained that it was by saying he would have no chance against Louis. "Spoiled the gate, they did," he said.

I tried to console him by recalling how extravagantly they had praised him after the fight, but he grumbled, "That didn't 'elp the gate."

Somehow the money had slipped between the hard knuckles. So now, he said, he was launched on a second career. I asked him what it was. He was looking fit and prosperous, in a smashing dark-gray pin-striped suit, and wearing a good thin watch. In the light of this exterior, I was scarcely prepared for his answer.

"I'm a write-ter," he said. "I love write-ting. I give it to them straight. No split affinitives, you know, or other Oxfer stooff. Oh, of coorse I split an affinitive now and then, to show I know how, but I don't believe in it." He was writing boxing, he told me, for the *Sunday Pictorial,* a once-a-week tabloid, with a circulation of five and a half million, that was creeping up on the eight million circulation of that older-established phenomenon, the *News of the World.* "I thank God I 'ave found a way to make a living for my dear wife and kids," Farr said. "It seems I'm a natural-born write-ter. I've hod five revisions of contract since I came with the *Pictorial.*"

He was going to report the fight, and I asked him for a bit of professional inside on Kelly. "He's a very good methodical boxer," he said, "with a fine sense of anticipation." It was to prove a practically perfect synopsis of Kelly; he might have added only that Kelly too often anticipates the worst. Farr's experience in the United States was much in his mind. "I couldn't be a good-time Charlie," he said. "When I was a kid, I was taught not to talk or joke or laugh at the table. 'You come 'ere to eat,' my old man used to say to me. 'When you eat, go.' A man can't change from what 'e's brought up to be, can he? He wasn't a bad old man. He taught me the importance of a good left. He was very aggressive. When he was fighting, they used to say 'e was a throwback to the cave man. 'When you go into the ring, you're a hoonter,' he'd say. 'Don't hop about like you were fighting in a rooddy balloon on the end of a stick.'"

Farr told me he had written in the *Pictorial* that Don Cockell, the Englishman who recently tried to take Marciano's heavyweight crown in San Francisco, had no sympathy coming. "He had sixteen pound on Marciano," Farr said. "'E should of set about 'im. I got 'oondred and eight letters, all approving. My boss got nineteen letters, all disapproving. He phoned me up. 'That's grand,' he said. 'Keep up the good work. They'll be something extra in the post for you tomorrow.'"

Farr said he was going to spend the night at the Royal Hibernian Hotel, where his paper had reserved a room for him, and it was there that I, too, eventually found a room. I met him again at dinner; he was eating with three businessmen from Derry, young Kelly's home town, whom he had taken into the aura of his greatness. Between courses he autographed cards for the young busboys and the waiters. "Is it true that you fought Joe Louey, Mr. Farr?" they would ask him, and he would reply, with a rugged laugh, "If I didn't, I don't know 'oo put the rooddy loomps on my 'ead." It had happened before the little busboys were born, and they thought of it as something historic.

After dinner—a modest collation of honey dew melon and *darne de saumon au Chablis,* the Irish salmon being exceptional—the five of us drove to Donnybrook in the Derrymen's car. The streets were full of automobiles from the North of Ireland and the three free counties of Ulster; my associates could pick them out by the license plates. One car we came up behind had a hand-lettered sign on its rear window reading "Won't you come into my parlor? said the Spider to the Ray." Farr, who, like most Welshmen, can sing, paid his passage with "The Londonderry Air." "It used to be my speciality," he said, and broke forth:

> *"Oh, Danny Boy—ta loora loo loo loora loo,*
> *Oh, Danny Boy—ta loora loora loo!*
> *Oh, come ye* BACK—"

We were the success of the cavalcade.

The fight, as I knew by that time, having had a chance to read an evening newspaper, was to be held in a monster garage, just built by the municipality to house all the omnibuses of Dublin. Six thousand seven hundred and fifty chairs had been borrowed from caterers and undertakers; the one I got was tagged "O'Connell's," but I don't know which line of work O'Connell is in. The bout was being staged by Jack Solomons, the London promoter, with the cooperation of the officials in charge of An Tóstal, a kind of Gaelic old home week, which included an ecclesiological exhibition at Maynooth, a children's art competition, and an event listed in the papers as "Dun Laoghaire—Blackrock Ceili —an Tóstal, Aras an Baile (8 P.M.)," and evidently reserved for Gaelic speakers. Famechon was to get three thousand pounds, which makes a tidy sum in francs (three million), or even in dollars (eight thousand four hundred). Kelly was to get two thousand pounds and, in the unanimous opinion of the Derrymen, the European featherweight championship as well, after which Solomons had promised him a match with Sandy Saddler for the world's title. Saddler fought Famechon in Paris last year, and knocked him out in six rounds. Now Famechon was thirty years old and Kelly twenty-three, and both had made the featherweight limit of a hundred and twenty-six pounds at two o'clock that afternoon.

Famechon had been around a long time—a very good fighter by European standards but not top-class by ours. I had heard at the Neutral Corner Restaurant, in New York, which is an international exchange for trade information, that he was definitely on the downgrade.

I had expected a delay at the gate, but Mr. Farr swept me in with him—in the double capacity of journalist and celebrity, he had the run of the house—and an usher conducted me to the O'Connell chair, in the second row ringside, where my neighbors regarded me with the respect due my illustrious sponsorship. The low ceiling of the bus garage kept the cigarette smoke down, and, although the soiree had not progressed past the first preliminary, the ring was enveloped in a blue haze, giving the scene the look of a painting of a club fight by Bellows. The strained, awkward boxers in the ring carried out the motif; the salient feature of "Stag at Sharkey's," I have always thought, is that both the central figures are simply pushers. The principals in this bout were a Dublin man and a Belfast man, of whom the former was the more inept. After the fifth round the master of ceremonies announced that the Dublin man had "retired," and a buzz of sympathy ran through the hall. The restraint was studious, as if each member of the audience had come to the hall determined to keep his temper.

The ushers, who wore badges denominating them "stewards," were fanatical about making customers crouch in the aisles while any boxing was going on, and conducted them to their chairs only during the one-minute intervals between rounds. It was like Town Hall during a séance of the New Friends of Music. Since horizontal distances were great in the garage, it took some arrivals from two to four rounds to reach their seats. The round before the Dublin man retired, a small, merry-looking man with a pointy nose and an even more finely pointed waxed mustache passed along the aisle in front of the first ringside row, bent over like a crab. The man next to me pulled my arm. "It's Alfie Byrne, the Lord Mayor," he said. His Lordship was taking no chances of alienating a voter. There was a large Irish harp in electric bulbs on one wall and another, in green paint, on the wall opposite. I saw no tricolors.

The *ambiance* warmed a bit with the next bout—a lightweight match between a heavy-muscled, pyknic Galwayman, not much more than five feet tall, named McCoy, and a more conventionally constructed fellow from Belfast, named Sharpe. (Belfast, like most industrial cities, produces a large crop of boxers.) Galwaymen, in popular myth, are hot-tempered and unpredictable, and transplanted Galwaymen, of whom there were many in the audience, are vociferously loyal. The little fellow started out at a terrific pace, moving his arms as if in a pillow fight. A cry of "Up, Galway! Come on, McEye!" spontaneously dispelled the decorum of the evening. It seemed impossible that McEye could keep on moving his arms at that rate for more than a minute, but he did, and the astonished Belfast man, after waiting for him to run down, joined in the fun. But each time Sharpe administered to the animated half keg a conventional uppercut to the chin—he knew the antidotes academically prescribed for a violent attack by a short opponent—McEye would loose a flurry of blows that reminded me of a passage in "The Song of Roland": "I will strike seven hundred or a thousand good blows." Six hundred and ninety-nine or nine hundred and ninety-eight would miss, but for the Belfast man it was like trying to hit through an electric fan. The fellow sitting next to me jiggled with the effort of maintaining his composure; he seemed to be in the grip of an electric vibrator. After every round, he would grab me and ask, "Would you say the little fellow is ahead now?" I would nod, and he would turn and grab the fellow on the other side, a sporty type who was escorting a platinum blonde. This Blazes Boylan—it is impossible to be in Dublin without Joyce—was a purist. "Sharpe is landing the cleaner punches," he would say. The man between us would wait until Blazes turned back to the blonde, and then pluck my arm again. "Do you know," he would say in a conspiratorial way, "I don't agree with that man at all." Neither did the referee, who gave the decision to McEye and perpetual motion. There are no judges at European professional bouts, and the referee decides. My neighbor and I exchanged friendly glances, secure in our connoisseurship.

The announcer now had his great moment. "My Lord Mayor, ladies and gentlemen!" he called, and began introducing visiting celebrities— Freddie Mills, the Englishman who briefly held the light-heavyweight championship of the world before Joey Maxim won it; my sponsor Farr, who got a great hand; and, climactically, "the original" Spider Kelly, the father of the hero of the evening. (I had heard of at least one earlier Spider Kelly, the man who said to his seconds, "What I need ain't advice—it's strength." But that had been in California, and it would have been a quibble to bring it up at Donnybrook.) The original Irish Spider Kelly was a puckish little man with a red face and heavy black eyebrows. He had held the British and British Empire featherweight championships himself twenty years before, I knew from my newspaper fill-in, and had guided Spider II's instruction from his first tottering essays at footwork. The audience included many fathers, more sons, and quite a number of mothers and sisters. (There was also a good speckling of Roman collars.)

A cheer for old Spider was an endorsement of the principle of the family, and he got it.

A fanfare of hunting horns was sounded at the remote end of the garage, and another cheer began, distant at first, louder as its object approached the ring. It was Spider II, surrounded by his faction. He was a baby-faced boy with a crew cut, who looked more like eighteen than twenty-three. The calves of his legs resembled those of a school quarter-miler—large and rounded—but his torso and arms, white and boyish, were less impressively developed. The Frenchman, whose entry was heralded by another but less enthusiastic fanfare, was sleek, wide-shouldered, long-armed, and spindle-shanked. He looked not much younger than Spider I, but his antiquity inspired no comparable demonstration of respectful affection by the crowd. The master of ceremonies implored the audience to stop smoking during the coming contest, and all the men within my sight extinguished their cigarettes. He next introduced the boxers, giving their weights to the ounce—Kelly had a ten-ounce weight advantage—and, finally, the referee, who received a polite, un-suspicious cheer. I did not hear his name, but the man next to me said, "Some kind of a Dutchman." It appeared likely, for the referee had the buttery tint so common among Hollanders, and walked about the ring with the exaggerated spryness of a Teuton being dashing. He had a snipe nose that pointed at the ceiling, and held himself so straight that his Adam's apple created a noticeable deviation from the vertical, pushing a neat bow tie in front of it.

The gong rang, and the men came timidly from their corners amid thunderous cheers. "Don't let us pretend to be impartial," a fellow wrote in the *Irish Press* the next morning. "We all wanted the best man to win, and Billy Kelly was the best man for us." Confirming Farr's description, Kelly went to work methodically; he landed a light tap on the French-man's nose, parried a return with his right, and then tapped twice more. Famechon floundered at him a bit, like a fellow reaching over a man's shoulder to shake hands with someone behind him, and the round ended with no damage to either. The man next to me turned his face from the carnage and said, "Is he doing all right?" I showed him my program, on which I had marked the round even, and he said, "That other fellow has a very dangerous look."

After the second round, Kelly settled down to work, and a very promising workman he looked, drawing leads, popping the slower Frenchman with fast, precise jabs, and once, in the fourth, even landing a really good right uppercut to the diaphragm in close. When Famechon started a punch, Kelly would be going in another direction. Usually when the Frenchman got close to him, Kelly would cease trying to do harm and concentrate on escape, as if he were fighting a middleweight instead of a gaffer his own size. He was good at ducking and slipping away, but nobody was ever hurt by being ducked away from. Still, he outboxed his man round after round—I gave him four in a row—and the bus garage swelled with the sound of shouting. The jabs had little sting, but since Kelly was younger than Famechon, it appeared reasonable that he would keep on piling up points as the fight went on, and at the end would take the decision. By the seventh, Famechon, having apparently decided that the boy couldn't hurt him at all, was rushing after him, slapping and pushing but unable to accomplish much. And so they went, round after round—Kelly almost never using his right except to block and never following an advantage beyond a second or third light pop when he had his man set up for a real one. At the beginning of every round he crossed himself, and whenever Famechon's slaps strayed low he would look appealingly at the referee. As they came up for the fifteenth, I had them all square on my card—six rounds for each and two even—but I had a feeling that Kelly's margins had been a trifle clearer. I gave him the final round, which was as tantalizingly ineffectual as all the others, and as hard to pick a winner in. Just the same, I was sure that Spider II deserved the decision—and meanly suspected that he would be sure to receive it even if he hadn't done quite so well. It was then that the Dutchman, to quote one Irish writer, "rose" Famechon's hand. I thought I could write a fair account of what followed, but when I saw the story on the first page of the *Irish Press* next morning, I realized that the writer, a Mr. John Healy, had probably had more experience in that kind of going:

> There was a long pause as a stunned audience, who had watched the young Spider swap punches at a terrific pace in the last two rounds, slowly gathered what it meant—Billy Kelly had lost the fight.
> And then, slowly at first, until it gathered momentum and burst like a rumbling volcano, they got to their feet and cut loose with a solid barrage of catcalls, boos, whistles and shouts. Angry spectators swarmed up to and tried clambering over the Press table. A bottle whizzed over my head into the ring. [I missed this, or at any rate it missed me.] A coat, flung in rage, flapped on the ropes. [It did.] Chairs were bumbled. A squad of Gardai and plainclothes

detectives surrounded the ring. ["Gardai" is Gaelic for uniformed police, and monstrous big ones these were.]

They were still booing and cheering Billy when he was escorted from the ring minutes later. All down that long avenue of jam-packed people, they screamed their admiration. "You're the winner, Billy!" or "You're the champ!" Grown men cried their rage in the sea of faces. . . .

That's just about the way it was. Taking a more moderate line, a Mr. Ben Kiely, on the sports page, wrote, "There's no doubt in the world about it—the raising of Ray Famechon's hand was one of the greatest shocks in Franco-Irish history. Because for the crowd in the Donnybrook Garage Billy Kelly was the man for their money."

Famechon, whose hundred-and-third professional fight it was, looked relieved but not astonished. He probably thought he had won, as any fighter does who has made it at all close. Kelly sat in his corner with head almost between his knees, the picture of dejection, like a bright boy who has failed to get 100 in an arithmetic test because the teacher came up with the wrong answer. He had played it safe for fifteen rounds and failed to obtain the reward of thrift and diligence. The most interesting figure in the ring, for many reasons, was the referee; the man about to get lynched is undeniably the center of attention at a lynching. It is unlikely that it had occurred to him when he rose Famechon's hand that he would be immoderately happy to see the Amsterdam airport again. The Kelly rooters were standing in the aisles and on the undertakers' chairs, which assumed a new significance. Devil an usher could make devil a customer sit down. The referee, encouraged by a number of big men in mufti, probably detectives, who had entered the ring, got as far as the ropes, climbed through them to the ring apron, and stood there like a fellow who has never gone off a diving board and wishes he hadn't walked out to the end. He was as pale as the inside of a Gouda cheese. The Gardai marched to the edge of the ring below him and formed a phalanx, into which they lowered him down. They then marched forward, with the Dutchman in the center. A small man in a raincoat tried to cut in from the rear, swinging a punch under a cop's armpit. The Garda turned around, laughing, and slung him about twenty feet, using the man's raincoat as a hammer thrower uses the wire on the hammer. The Lord Mayor slunk out as self-effacingly as he had entered. The wild shouting continued, the ushers were ignored for another five minutes, and then everybody began to laugh and chat and light up cigarettes again, in preparation for the bouts that would wind up the program. (It was apparently permissible to suffocate all boxers except those in the main event.) Since the tag end of the program was of small interest, I soon made my way out into the night and a pouring rain.

By the time I got back to the Royal Hibernian, Mr. Farr was established before a late snack of cold chicken and cold ham, with a few bottles of Guinness. He said he had already filed his story for the *Sunday Pictorial,* and readily recited what he thought the best bits of it for me. Like me, he thought Kelly had deserved to win. "Kelly hos nothing for the seeker of blood and thunder, but those who enjoy the grace of movement and textbook poonching will be fully satisfied by the Derry craftsman," he said, which is the way it appeared in the *Pictorial,* except for the Welsh stresses. He writes a very pretty style. He thought, though, that Kelly had been overcautious—that he had had little to beat. We adjourned to the lounge, in which bona-fide residents are allowed to drink as late as the night porter, a crabbed old humorist, will serve them, and there were joined by a number of gentlemen from Northern Ireland, including the trio who had transported us to the fight. Before bringing us a new round of drinks, the porter would make each of us give his room number, and we would count off, beginning with a Mr. Cassidy from Derry—I think he had No. 58—and going all the way round to a man from Donegal whose name I forget but who weighed eighteen stone seven and collected first editions. It was not so much that the porter expected our bona-fide status to change between rounds, I think, as that he wished to determine our degree of responsibility. A fellow who forgot the number of his room might have been refused the next drink. But nobody did forget.

Mr. Farr, who had switched from Guinness to Cointreau, was naturally the oracle of the occasion, and won the golden opinion of all until he burst out ingenuously, "The truth is that the lod fights like he was in a rooddy balloon at the end of a rooddy stick. Every time t'other lod 'it 'im in the goot, 'e looked ot the referee. Is the referee 'is rooddy grondmother? Was he too prroud to reciprrocate?" He rose, granitic and dignified. "I must take an early plane in the morning," he said. "Bock to my sweet wife and wonderful children. Each Saturday ofternoon I take the kids to the cinema and tea. High tea." He made his way to the lift, the pattern of a literary man who leads a sane family life.

I stayed on until the porter himself decided to go to bed, at dawn. He has insomnia in the dark, he said.

Ed Linn

The Kid's Last Game

When Ed Linn came to Fenway Park to cover Ted Williams's fare-well address in 1951, he managed to get in the Red Sox clubhouse before that last game. Forty-one years later, Linn, working on a biography of Ted Williams, called the great hitter on the telephone and reminded Williams who he was and that he had been in the clubhouse on that historic occasion.

"I know you," Williams said testily, "and I remember what I said to you then—'What are you doing here?'"

Linn replied, "That's not what you said. You said, 'You got a ————ing nerve coming in here.'"

Linn has written numerous books on sports and other subjects, among them (as coauthor) Bill Veeck's autobiography Veeck As in Wreck, *which Red Smith called the best sports book ever written. While you're waiting for the Linn biography of Williams (it's sched-uled for publication in 1993), try this epic closeup on the Splendid Splinter in his memorable last official appearance at the plate.*

Wednesday, September 26 was a cold and dreary day in Boston, a curious bit of staging on the part of those gods who always set the scene most carefully for Ted Williams. It was to be the last game Ted would ever play in Boston. Not until the game was over would Williams let it be known that it was the last game he would play anywhere.

Ted came into the locker room at 10:50, very early for him. He was dressed in dark brown slacks, a yellow sport shirt and a light tan pullover sweater, tastily brocaded in the same color. Ted went immediately to his locker, pulled off the sweater, then strolled into the trainer's room.

Despite all the triumphs and the honors, it had been a difficult year for him. As trainer Jack Fadden put it: "It hasn't been a labor of love for Ted this year; it's just been labor." On two separate occasions, he had come very close to giving it all up.

The spring training torture had been made no easier for Ted by manager Billy Jurges. Jurges believed that the only way for a man Ted's age to stay in condition was to reach a peak at the beginning of the season and hold it by playing just as often as possible. "The most we can expect from Williams," Jurges had said, at the time of Ted's signing, "is 100 games. The least is pinch-hitting." Ted played in 113 games.

Throughout the training season, however, Ted seemed to be having trouble with his timing. Recalling his .254 average of the previous season, the experts wrote him off for perhaps the 15th time in his career. But on his first time at bat in the opening game, Ted hit a 500-foot home run, possibly the longest of his career, off Camilo Pascual, probably the best pitcher in the league. The next day, in the Fenway Park opener, he hit a second homer, this one off Jim Coates. Ted pulled a leg muscle running out that homer, though, and when a man's muscles go while he is doing nothing more than jogging around the bases, the end is clearly in sight.

It took him almost a month to get back in condition, but the mysterious virus infection that hits him annually, a holdover from his service in Korea, laid him low again almost immediately. Since the doctors have never been able to diagnose this chronic illness, the only way they can treat him is to shoot a variety of drugs and antibiotics into him, in the hope that one of them takes hold. Ted, miserable and drugged when he finally got back in uniform, failed in a couple of pinch-hitting attempts and was just about ready to quit. Against the Yankees, Ralph Terry struck him out two straight times. The third time up, the count went to 3–2 when Williams unloaded on a waist-high fastball and sent it into the bullpen in right-center, 400 feet away.

The blast triggered the greatest home-run spurt of Ted's career. Seven days later, he hit his 500th home run. He had started only 15 1960 games and he had hit eight 1960 homers. When he hit his 506th (and 11th of the year), he had homered once in every 6.67 times at bat.

Cold weather always bothered Ted, even in his early years, and so when he strained his shoulder late in August, he was just about ready to announce his retirement again. He had found it difficult to loosen up even in fairly warm weather, and to complicate matters he had found it necessary—back in the middle of 1959—to cut out the calisthenics routine he had always gone through in the clubhouse. The exercising had left him almost too weary to play ball.

Ted started every game so stiff that he was forced to exaggerate an old passion for swinging at balls, only in the strike zone. In his first time at bat, he would look for an inside pitch between the waist and knees, the only pitch he could swing at naturally. In the main, however, Ted was more than willing to take the base on balls his first time up.

He stayed on for two reasons. Mike Higgins, who had replaced Jurges as Sox Manager, told him bluntly. "You're paid to play ball, so go out and play." The strength behind those words rested in the fact that both Williams and Higgins knew very well that owner Tom Yawkey would continue to pay Ted whether he played or not.

In addition, the Red Sox had two series remaining with the Yankees and Orioles, who were still locked together in the pennant race. Ted did not think it fair to eliminate himself as a factor in the two-team battle. He announced his retirement just after the Yankees clinched the pennant.

Four days earlier, Ted had been called to a special meeting with Yawkey, Higgins, Dick O'Connell (who was soon to be named business manager) and publicity director Jack Malaney. This was to offer Ted the job of general manager, a position that had been discussed occasionally in the past.

Ted refused to accept the title until he proved he could do the job. He agreed, however, to work in the front office in 1961, assisting Higgins with player personnel, and O'Connell with business matters.

The coverage of Ted's last game was at a minimum. It was thought for a while that *Life* magazine wanted to send a crew down to cover the game, but it developed that they only wanted to arrange for Ted to represent them at the World Series. Dave Garroway's "Today" program tried to set up a telephone interview the morning of the game, but they couldn't get in touch with Ted. The Red Sox, alone among big-league clubs, have offered little help to anyone on the public relations front— and never any help at all where Ted Williams was concerned. Ted didn't live at the Kenmore Hotel with the rest of the unattached players. He lived about 100 yards down Commonwealth Avenue, at the Somerset. All calls and messages for him were diverted to the manager's office.

The ceremonies that were to mark his departure were rather limited, too. The Boston Chamber of Commerce had arranged to present him with a silver bowl, and the mayor's office and governor's office had quickly muscled into the picture. By Wednesday morning, however, the governor's office—which had apparently anticipated something more spectacular—begged off. The governor's spokesman suggested the presentation of a scroll at Ted's hotel, a suggestion which Ted simply ignored.

The only civilian in the clubhouse when Ted entered was the man from *Sport*, and he was talking to Del Baker, who was about to retire, too, after 50 years in the game. Ted looked over, scowled, seemed about to say something but changed his mind.

Our man was well aware what Ted was about to say. The Red Sox have a long-standing rule—also unique in baseball—that no reporter may enter the dressing room before the game, or the first 15 minutes after the game. It was a point of honor with Ted to pick out any civilian who wasn't specifically with a ballplayer and to tell him, as loudly as possible: "You're not supposed to be in here, you know."

Sure enough, when our man started toward Ted's locker in the far corner of the room, Ted pointed a finger at him and shouted: "You're not supposed to be in here, you know."

"The same warm, glad cry of greeting I always get from you," our man said. "It's your last day. Why don't you live a little?"

Ted started toward the trainer's room again, but wheeled around and came back. "You've got a nerve coming here to interview me after the last one you wrote about me!"

Our man wanted to know what was the matter with the last one.

"You called me 'unbearable,' that's what's the matter."

The full quote, it was pointed out, was that he "was sometimes unbearable but never dull," which holds a different connotation entirely.

"You've been after me for 12 years, that flogging magazine," he said, in his typically well-modulated shout. "Twelve years. I missed an appointment for some kind of luncheon. I forgot what happened . . . it doesn't matter anyway . . . but I forgot some appointment 12 years ago and *Sport* Magazine hasn't let up on me since."

Our man, lamentably eager to disassociate himself from this little magazine, made it clear that while he had done most of *Sport*'s Williams' articles in the past few years, he was not a member of the staff. "And," our man pointed out, "I have been accused of turning you into a combination of Paul Bunyan and Santa Claus."

"Well, when you get back there, tell them what . . . (he searched for the appropriate word, the *mot juste* as they say in the dugouts) . . . what *flog-heads* they are. Tell them that for me."

Our man sought to check the correct spelling of the adjectives with him but got back only a scowl. Ted turned around to fish something out of a cloth bag at the side of his locker. "Why don't you just write your story without me?" he said. "What do you have to talk to me for?" And then, in a suddenly weary voice: "What can I tell you now that I haven't told you before?"

"Why don't you let me tell you what the story is supposed to be?" our man said. "Then you can say yes or no." It was an unfortunate way to put the question since it invited the answer it brought.

"I can tell you before you tell me," Ted shouted. "No! No, no, no."

Our man had the impression Williams was trying to tell him something. He was right. "Look," Williams said. "If I tell you I don't want to talk to you, why don't you just take my word for it?"

The clubhouse boy had come over with a glossy photo to be signed, and Ted sat down on his stool, turned his back and signed it.

Although we are reluctant to bring *Sport* into the context of the story itself, Ted's abiding hatred toward us tells much about him and his even longer feud with Boston sportswriters. Twelve years ago, just as Ted said, an article appeared on these pages to which he took violent exception. (The fact that he is so well aware that it *was* 12 years ago suggests that he still has the magazine around somewhere, so that he can fan the flames whenever he feels them dying.) What Ted objected to in that article was an interview with his mother in San Diego. Ted objects to any peering into his private life. When he holes himself up in his hotel, when he sets a barrier around the clubhouse, when he disappears into the Florida Keys at the end of the season, he is deliberately removing himself from a world he takes to be dangerous and hostile. His constant fighting with the newspapermen who cover him most closely is a part of the same pattern. What do newspapermen represent except the people who are supposed to pierce personal barriers? Who investigate, who pry, *who find out?*

Ted's mother has been a Salvation Army worker in San Diego all her life. She is a local character, known—not without affection—as "Salvation May." Ted himself was dedicated to the Salvation Army when he was a baby. His generosity, his unfailing instinct to come to the aid of any underdog, is in direct line with the teachings of the Army, which is quite probably the purest charitable organization in the world. Even as a boy, Ted regularly gave his 30-cent luncheon allowance to classmates he considered more needy than himself, a considerable sacrifice since the Williams family had to struggle to make ends meet.

When Ted signed with San Diego at the age of 17, he was a tall, skinny kid (6–3, 146 pounds). He gave most of his $150-a-month salary toward keeping up the family house and he tried to build up his weight by gorging himself on the road where the club picked up the check. One day, Ted was coming into the clubhouse when Bill Lane, the owner of the Padres, motioned him over. In his deep, foghorn voice, Lane said: "Well, kid, you're leading the list. You've got the others beat."

Ted, pleased that his ability was being noted so promptly, smiled and asked: "Yeah, what list?"

"The dining room list," Lane said. "Hasn't anyone told you that your meal allowance is supposed to be five dollars a day?"

Nobody had. "Okay, Bill," Ted said, finally. "Take anything over five dollars off my salary."

Bill did, too.

Even before *Sport* went into details about his background, the Boston press had discovered his weak point and hit him hard and—it must be added—most unfairly. During Ted's second season with the Sox, one reporter had the ill grace to comment, in regard to a purely personal dispute: "But what can you expect of a youth so abnormal that he didn't go home in the off-season to see his own mother?"

When Williams' World War II draft status was changed from 1A to 3A after he claimed his mother as a dependent, one Boston paper sent a private investigator to San Diego to check on her standard of living; another paper sent reporters out onto the street to ask casual passers-by to pass judgment on Ted's patriotism.

Reporters were sent galloping out into the street to conduct a public-opinion poll once again when Williams was caught fishing in the Everglades while his wife was giving birth to a premature baby.

A press association later sent a story out of San Diego that Ted had sold the furniture out from under his mother—although a simple phone call could have established that it wasn't true. Ted had bought the house and the furniture for his mother. His brother—who had been in frequent trouble with the law—had sold it. The Boston papers picked up that story and gave it a big play, despite the fact that every sports editor in the city had enough background material on Ted's family to know—even without checking—that it couldn't possibly be true. It was, Ted's friends believed, their way of punishing him for not being "co-operative."

Ted had become so accustomed to looking upon any reference to his family as an unfriendly act that when *Sport* wrote about his mother, he bristled—even though her final quote was: "Don't say anything about Teddy except the highest and the best. He's a wonderful son." And when he searched for some reason why the magazine would do such a thing to him, he pounced upon that broken appointment, which everybody except himself had long forgotten.

After Ted had signed the photograph the day of his last game, he sat on his stool, his right knee jumping nervously, his right hand alternately buttoning and unbuttoning the top button of his sport shirt.

When he stripped down to his shorts, there was no doubt he was 42. The man once called The Splendid Splinter—certainly one of the most atrocious nicknames ever committed upon an immortal—was thick around the middle. A soft roll of loose fat, drooping around the waist, brought on a vivid picture of Archie Moore.

Williams is a tall, handsome man. If they ever make that movie of his life that keeps being rumored around, the guy who plays Bret Maverick would be perfect for the part. But ballplayers age quickly. Twenty years under the sun had baked Ted's face and left it lined and leathery. Sitting there, Ted Williams had the appearance of an old Marine sergeant who had been to the battles and back.

Sal Maglie, who had the end locker on the other side of the shower-room door, suddenly caught Ted's attention. "You're a National Leaguer, Sal," Ted said, projecting his voice to the room at large. "I got a hundred dollars that the Yankees win the World Series. The Yankees will win it in four or five games."

"I'm an American Leaguer now," Sal said, quietly.

"A hundred dollars," Ted said. "A friendly bet."

"You want a friendly bet? I'll bet you a friendly dollar."

"Fifty dollars," Ted said.

"All right," Sal said. "Fifty dollars." And then, projecting his own voice, he said: "I like the Pirates, anyway."

Williams went back to his mail, as the others dressed and went out onto the field.

At length, Ted picked up his spikes, wandered into the trainer's room again, and lifting himself onto the table, carefully began to put a shine on them. A photographer gave him a ball to sign.

Ted gazed at it with distaste, then looked up at the photographer with loathing. "Are you crazy?" he snapped.

The photographer backed away, pocketed the ball and began to adjust his camera sights on Ted. "You don't belong in here," Ted shouted. And turning to the clubhouse boy, he barked: "Get him out of here."

The locker room had emptied before Ted began to dress. For Ted did not go out to take batting practice or fielding practice. He made every entrance onto the field a dramatic event. He did not leave the locker room for the dugout until 12:55, only 35 minutes before the game was scheduled to start. By then, most of the writers had already gone up to Tom Yawkey's office to hear Jackie Jensen announce that he was returning to baseball.

As Ted came quickly up the stairs and into the dugout, he almost bumped into his close friend and fishing companion, Bud Leavitt, sports editor of the Bangor *Daily News.* "Hi, Bud," Ted said, as if he were surprised Leavitt was there. "You drive up?"

A semi-circle of cameramen closed in on Williams, like a bear trap, on the playing field just up above. Ted hurled a few choice oaths at them, and as an oath-hurler Ted never bats below .400. He guided Leavitt against the side of the dugout, just above the steps, so that he could continue the conversation without providing a shooting angle for the photographers. The photographers continued to shoot him in profile, though, until Ted took Leavitt by the elbow and walked him the length of the dugout. "Let's sit down," he said, as he left, "so we won't be bothered by all these blasted cameramen."

If there had been any doubt back in the locker room that Ted had decided to bow out with typical hardness, it had been completely dispelled by those first few minutes in the dugout. On his last day in Fenway Park, Ted Williams seemed resolved to remain true to his own image of himself, to permit no sentimentality or hint of sentimentality to crack that mirror through which he looks at the world and allows the world to look upon him.

And yet, in watching this strange and troubled man—the most remarkable and colorful and full-blooded human being to come upon the athletic scene since Babe Ruth—you had the feeling that he was overplaying his role, that he had struggled through the night against the impulse to make his peace, to express his gratitude, to accept the great affection that the city had been showering upon him for years. In watching him, you had the clear impression that in resisting this desire he was overreacting and becoming more profane, more impossible and— yes—more unbearable than ever.

Inside Ted Williams, there has always been a struggle of two opposing forces, almost two different persons. (We are fighting the use of the word schizophrenia.) The point we are making is best illustrated through Williams's long refusal to tip his hat in acknowledgment of the cheering crowds. It has always been his contention that the people who cheered him when he hit a home run were the same people who booed him when he struck out—which, incidentally, is probably not true at all. More to our point, Ted has always insisted that although he would rather be cheered than booed, he really didn't care what the fans thought of him, one way or the other.

Obviously, though, if he really didn't care he wouldn't have bothered to make such a show of not caring. He simply would have touched his finger to his cap in that automatic, thoughtless gesture of most players and forgot about it. Ted, in short, has always had it both ways. He gets the cheers and he pretends they mean nothing to him. He is like a rich man's nephew who treats his uncle with disrespect to prove he is not interested in his money, while all the time he is secretly dreaming that the uncle will reward such independence by leaving him most of the fortune.

Ted has it even better than that. The fans of Boston have always wooed him ardently. They always cheered him all the louder in the hope that he would reward them, at last, with that essentially meaningless tip of the hat.

This clash within Williams came to the surface as he sat and talked with Leavitt, alone and undisturbed. For, within a matter of minutes, the lack of attention began to oppress him; his voice began to rise, to pull everybody's attention back to him. The cameramen, getting the message, drifted toward him again, not in a tight pack this time but in a loose and straggling line.

With Ted talking so loudly, it was apparent that he and Leavitt were discussing how to get together, after the World Series, for their annual post-season fishing expedition. The assignment to cover the Series for *Life* had apparently upset their schedule.

"After New York," Ted said, "I'll be going right to Pittsburgh." He expressed his hope that the Yankees would wrap it all up in Yankee Stadium, so that he could join Leavitt in Bangor at the beginning of the following week. "But, dammit," he said, "if the Series goes more than five games, I'll have to go back to Pittsburgh again."

Leavitt reminded Ted of an appearance he had apparently agreed to make in Bangor. "All right," Ted said. "But no speeches or anything."

A young, redheaded woman, in her late twenties, leaned over from her box seat alongside the dugout and asked Ted if he would autograph her scorecard.

"I can't sign it, dear," Ted said. "League rules. Where are you going to be after the game?"

"You told me that once before," she said unhappily.

"Well, where are you going to be?" Ted shouted, in the impatient way one would shout at an irritating child.

"Right here," she said.

"All right."

"But I waited before and you never came."

He ignored her.

Joe Cronin, president of the American League, came down the dugout aisle, followed by his assistant, Joe McKenney. Through Cronin's office, the local 9:00 newsfeature program which follows the "Today" program in Boston had scheduled a filmed interview with Ted. The camera had already been set up on the home-plate side of the dugout, just in front of the box seats. Cronin talked to Ted briefly and went back to reassure the announcer that Ted would be right there. McKenney remained behind to make sure Ted didn't forget. At last, Ted jumped up and shouted: "Where is it, Joe, dammit?"

When Ted followed McKenney out, it was the first time he had stuck his head onto the field all day. There were still not too many fans in the stands, although far more than would have been there on any other day to watch a seventh-place team on a cold and threatening Wednesday afternoon. At this first sight of Ted Williams, they let out a mighty roar.

As he waited alongside interviewer Jack Chase, Ted bit his lower lip, and looked blankly into space, both characteristic mannerisms. At a signal from the cameraman, Chase asked Ted how he felt about entering "the last lap."

All at once, Ted was smiling. "I want to tell you, Jack, I honestly feel good about it," he said, speaking in that quick charming way of his. "You can't get blood out of a turnip, you know. I've gone as far as I can and I'm sure I wouldn't want to try it any more."

"Have we gone as far as we can with the Jimmy Fund?" he was asked.

Ted was smiling more broadly. "Oh, no. We could never go far enough with the Jimmy Fund."

Chase reminded Ted that he was scheduled to become a batting coach.

"Can you take a .250 hitter and make a .300 hitter out of him?"

"There has always been a saying in baseball that you can't make a hitter," Ted answered. "But I think you can *improve* a hitter. More than you can improve a fielder. More mistakes are made in hitting than in any other part of the game."

At this point, Williams was literally encircled by photographers, amateur and pro. The pros were taking pictures from the front and from the sides. Behind them, in the stands, dozens of fans had their cameras trained on Ted, too, although they could hardly have been getting anything except the No. 9 on his back.

Ted was asked if he were going to travel around the Red Sox farm system in 1961 to instruct the young hitters.

"All I know is that I'm going to spring training," he said. "Other than that, I don't know anything."

The interview closed with the usual fulsome praise of Williams, the inevitable apotheosis that leaves him with a hangdog, embarrassed look upon his features. "I appreciate the kind words," he said. "It's all been fun. Everything I've done in New England from playing left field and getting booed, to the Jimmy Fund."

The Jimmy Fund is the money-raising arm of the Children's Cancer Hospital in Boston, which has become the world center for research into cancer and for the treatment of its young victims. Ted has been deeply involved with the hospital since its inception in 1947, serving the last four years as general chairman of the fund committee. He is an active chairman, not an honorary one. Scarcely a day goes by, when Ted is in Boston, that he doesn't make one or two stops for the Jimmy Fund somewhere in New England. He went out on the missions even days when he was too sick to play ball. (This is the same man, let us emphasize, who refuses to attend functions at which he himself is to be honored.) He has personally raised something close to $4,000,000 and has helped to build a modern, model hospital not far from Fenway Park.

But he has done far more than that. From the first, Williams took upon himself the agonizing task of trying to bring some cheer into the lives of these dying children and, perhaps even more difficult, of comforting their parents. He has, in those years, permitted himself to become attached to thousands of these children, knowing full well that they were going to die, one by one. He has become so attached to some of them that he has chartered special planes to bring him to their deathbeds.

Whenever one of these children asks to see him, whatever the time, he comes. His only stipulation is that there must be no publicity, no reporters, no cameramen.

We once suggested to Ted that he must get some basic return from all this work he puts into the Jimmy Fund. Ted considered the matter very carefully before he answered: "Look," he said, finally, "it embarrasses me to be praised for anything like this. The embarrassing thing is that I don't feel I've done anything compared to the people at the hospital who are doing the important work. It makes me happy to think I've done a little good; I suppose that's what I get out of it.

"Anyway," he added, thoughtfully, "it's only a freak of fate, isn't it, that one of those kids isn't going to grow up to be an athlete and I wasn't the one who had the cancer."

At the finish of the filmed interview he had to push his way through the cameramen between him and the dugout. "Oh——," he said.

But when one of them asked him to pose with Cronin, Ted switched personalities again and asked, with complete amiability, "Where is he?"

Cronin was in the dugout. Ted met Joe at the bottom of the steps and threw an arm around him. They grinned at each other while the pictures were being taken, talking softly and unintelligibly. After a minute, Ted reached over to the hook just behind him and grabbed his glove. The cameramen were still yelling for another shot as he started up the dugout steps. Joe, grinning broadly, grabbed him by the shoulder and yanked him back down. While Cronin was wrestling Ted around and whacking him on the back, the cameras clicked. "I got to warm up, dammit," Ted was saying. He made a pawing gesture at the cameramen, as if to say, "I'd like to belt you buzzards." This, from all evidence, was the picture that went around the country that night, because strangely enough, it looked as if he were waving a kind of sad goodbye.

When he finally broke away and raced up the field, he called back over his shoulder, "See you later, Joe." The cheers arose from the stands once again.

The Orioles were taking infield practice by then, and the Red Sox were warming up along the sideline. Ted began to play catch with Pumpsie Green. As he did—sure enough—the cameramen lined up just inside the foul line for some more shots, none of which will ever be used. "Why don't you cockroaches get off my back?" Ted said, giving them his No. 1 sneer. "Let me breathe, will you?"

The bell rang before he had a chance to throw two dozen balls. Almost all the players went back to the locker room. Remaining on the bench were only Ted Williams, buttoned up in his jacket, and Vic Wertz. One of the members of the ground crew came with a picture of Williams. He asked Ted if he would autograph it. "Sure," Ted said. "For you guys, anything."

Vic Wertz was having his picture taken with another crew member. Wertz had his arm around the guy and both of them were laughing. "How about you, Ted?" the cameraman asked. "One with the crewmen?"

Ted posed willingly with the man he had just signed for, with the result that the whole herd of cameramen came charging over again. Ted leaped to his feet. "Twenty-two years of this bull——," he cried.

The redhead was leaning over the low barrier again, but now three other young women were alongside her. One of them seemed to be crying, apparently at the prospect of Ted's retirement. An old photographer, in a long, weatherbeaten coat, asked Ted for a special pose. "Get lost," Ted said. "I've seen enough of you, you old goat."

Curt Gowdy, the Red Sox broadcaster, had come into the dugout to pass on some information about the pre-game ceremonies. Ted shouted, "The devil with all you miserable cameramen." The women continued to stare, in fascination, held either by the thrill of having this last long look at Ted Williams or by the opportunity to learn a few new words.

A Baltimore writer came into the dugout, and Ted settled down beside him. He wanted to know whether the writer could check on the "King of Swat" crown that had been presented to him in his last visit to Baltimore. Ted wasn't sure whether he had taken it back to Boston with him or whether the organization still had it.

"You know," he told the writer, "Brown's a better pitcher now than he's ever been. Oh, he's a great pitcher. Never get a fat pitch from him. When he does, it comes in with something extra on it. Every time a little different. He knows what he's doing."

Ted is a student of such things. He is supposed to be a natural hitter, blessed with a superhuman pair of eyes. We are not about to dispute this. What we want to say is that when Ted first came to the majors, the book on him was that he would chase bad balls. "All young sluggers do," according to Del Baker, who was managing Detroit when Ted came up. "Ted developed a strike zone of his own, though, by the second year."

When Ted took his physical for the Naval Reserve in World War II, his eyes tested at 20/10 and were so exceptional in every regard that while he was attending air gunnery school he broke all previous Marine records for hitting the target sleeve. But Ted has a point of his own here: "My eyesight," he says, "is now 20/15. Half the major-leaguers have eyes as good as that. It isn't eyesight that makes a hitter; it's practice. *Con-sci-en-tious* practice. I say that Williams has hit more balls than any guy living, except maybe Ty Cobb. I don't say it to brag; I just state it as a fact. From the time I was 11 years old, I've taken every possible opportunity to swing at a ball. I've swung and I've swung and I've swung."

Ted always studied every little movement a pitcher made. He always remained on the bench before the game to watch them warming up. From his first day to his last, he hustled around to get all possible information on a new pitcher.

It has always been his theory that we are all creatures of habit, himself included. Pitchers, he believes, fall into observable patterns. A certain set of movements foretells a certain pitch. In a particular situation, or on a particular count, they go to a particular pitch. There were certain pitchers, Ted discovered, who would inevitably go to their big pitch, the pitch they wanted him to swing at, on the 2–2 count.

And so Ted would frequently ask a teammate, "What was the pitch he struck you out on?" or "What did he throw you on the 2–2 pitch?"

When a young player confessed he didn't know what the pitch had been, Ted would grow incredulous. "You don't know the pitch he struck you out on? I'm not talking about last week or last month. I'm not even talking about yesterday. Today! Just now! I'm talking about the pitch he struck you out on just now!"

Returning to his seat on the bench, he'd slump back in disgust and mutter: "What a rockhead. The guy's taking the bread and butter out of his mouth and he don't even care how."

In a very short time, the player would have an answer ready for Williams. Ted always got the young hitters thinking about their craft. He always tried to instruct them, to build up their confidence. "When you want to know who the best hitter in the league is," he'd tell the rookies, "just look into the mirror."

Among opposing players, Williams was always immensely popular. Yes, even among opposing pitchers. All pitchers love to say: "Nobody digs in against *me.*" Only Ted Williams was given the right to dig in without getting flipped. Around the American League, there seemed to be a general understanding that Williams had too much class to be knocked down.

Waiting in the dugout for the ceremonies to get underway, Ted picked up a bat and wandered up and down the aisle taking vicious practice swings.

The photographers immediately swooped in on him. One nice guy was taking cameras from the people in the stands and getting shots of Ted for them.

As Ted put the bat down, one of them said: "One more shot, Teddy, as a favor."

"I'm all done doing any favors for you guys," Williams said. "I don't have to put up with you any more, and you don't have to put up with me."

An old woman, leaning over the box seats, was wailing: "Don't leave us, Ted. Don't leave us."

"Oh, hell," Ted said, turning away in disgust.

The redhead asked him plaintively: "Why don't you act nice?"

Ted strolled slowly toward her, grinning broadly. "Come on, dear," he drawled, "with that High Street accent you got there."

Turning back, he stopped in front of the man from *Sport,* pointed over his shoulder at the cameramen and asked: "You getting it all? You getting what you came for?"

"If you can't make it as a batting coach," our man said, "I understand you're going to try it as a cameraman."

"What does *Sport* Magazine think I'm going to do?" Ted asked. "That's what I want to know. What does *Sport* Magazine think I'm going to be?"

Speaking for himself, our man told him, he had not the slightest doubt that Ted was going to be the new general manager.

"*Sport* Magazine," Ted said, making the name sound like an oath. "Always honest. Never prejudiced."

At this point, he was called onto the field. Taking off his jacket, he strode out of the dugout. The cheers that greeted him came from 10,454 throats.

Curt Gowdy, handling the introductions, began: "As we all know, this is the final home game for—in my opinion and most of yours—the greatest hitter who ever lived. Ted Williams.

There was tremendous applause.

"Twenty years ago," Gowdy continued, "a skinny kid from San Diego came to the Red Sox camp . . ."

Ted first came to the Red Sox training camp at Sarasota in the spring of 1938. General manager Eddie Collins, having heard that Ted was a creature of wild and wayward impulse, had instructed second-baseman Bobby Doerr to pick him up and deliver him, shining and undamaged.

It was unthinkable, of course, that Ted Williams would make a routine entrance. Just before Doerr was set to leave home, the worst flood of the decade hit California and washed out all the roads and telephone lines. When Williams and Doerr finally arrived in Sarasota, ten days late, there was a fine, almost imperceptible drizzle. Williams, still practically waterlogged from the California floods, held out a palm, looked skyward, shivered and said in a voice that flushed the flamingoes from their nests: "So this is Florida, is it? Do they always keep this state under a foot of water?"

Williams suited up for a morning workout out in the field, jawed good-naturedly with the fans and got an unexpected chance to hit when a newsreel company moved in to take some batting-cage shots.

The magic of Ted Williams in a batter's box manifested itself that first day in camp. The tall, thin rookie stepped into the box, set himself in his wide stance, let his bat drop across the far corner of the plate, wiggled his hips and shoulders and jiggled up and down as if he were trying to tamp himself into the box. He moved his bat back and forth a few times, then brought it back into position and twisted his hands in opposite directions as if he were wringing the neck of the bat. He was set for the pitch.

And somehow, as if by some common impulse, all sideline activity stopped that day in 1938. Everybody was watching Ted Williams.

"Controversial, sure," Gowdy said, in bringing his remarks about Ted to a close, "but colorful."

The chairman of the Boston Chamber of Commerce presented Ted a shining, silver Paul Revere Bowl "on behalf of the business community of Boston." Ted seemed to force his smile as he accepted it.

A representative of the sports committee of the Chamber of Commerce then presented him with a plaque "on behalf of visits to kids' and veterans' hospitals."

Mayor John Collins, from his wheelchair, announced that "on behalf of all citizens" he was proclaiming this day "Ted Williams Day." The mayor didn't know how right he was.

As Mayor Collins spoke of Ted's virtues ("Nature's best, nature's nobleman."), the muscle of Ted's upper left jaw was jumping, constantly and rhythmically. The mayor's contribution to Ted Williams Day was a $1,000 donation to the Jimmy Fund from some special city fund.

Gowdy brought the proceedings to a close by proclaiming: "Pride is what made him great. He's a champion, a thoroughbred, a champion of sports." Curt then asked for "a round of applause, an ovation for No. 9 on his last game in his Boston." Needless to say, he got it.

Ted waited, pawed at the ground with one foot. Smiling, he thanked the mayor for the money. "Despite the fact of the disagreeable things that have been said of me—and I can't help thinking about it—by the Knights of the Keyboard out there (he jerked his head toward the press box), baseball has been the most wonderful thing in my life. If I were starting over again and someone asked me where is the one place I would like to play, I would want it to be in Boston, with the greatest owner in baseball and the greatest fans in America. Thank you."

He walked across the infield to the dugout, where the players were standing, applauding along with the fans. Ted winked and went on in.

In the press box, some of the writers were upset by his gratuitous rap at them. "I think it was bush," one of them said. "Whatever he thinks, this wasn't the time to say it."

Others made a joke of it. "Now that he's knighted me," one of them was saying, "I wonder if he's going to address me as Sir."

In the last half of the first inning, Williams stepped in against Steve Barber with Tasby on first and one out. When Barber was born—February 22, 1939—Ted had already taken the American Association apart, as it has never been taken apart since, by batting .366, hitting 43 home runs and knocking in 142 runs.

Against a lefthander, Williams was standing almost flush along the inside line of the batter's box, his feet wide, his stance slightly closed. He took a curve inside, then a fastball low. The fans began to boo. The third pitch was also low. With a 3–0 count, Ted jumped in front of the plate with the pitch, like a high-school kid looking for a walk. It was ball four, high.

He got to third the easy way. Jim Pagliaroni was hit by a pitch, and everybody moved up on a wild pitch. When Frank Malzone walked, Jack Fisher came in to replace Barber. Lou Clinton greeted Jack with a rising liner to dead center. Jackie Brandt started in, slipped as he tried to reverse himself, but recovered in time to scramble back and make the catch. His throw to the plate was beautiful to behold, a low one-bouncer that came to Gus Triandos chest high. But Ted, sliding hard, was in under the ball easily.

Leading off the third inning against the righthanded Fisher, Ted moved back just a little in the box. Fisher is even younger than Barber, a week younger. When Fisher was being born—March 4, 1939—Ted was reporting to Sarasota again, widely proclaimed as the super-player of the future, the Red Sox' answer to Joe DiMaggio.

Ted hit Fisher's 1–1 pitch straightaway, high and deep. Brandt had plenty of room to go back and make the catch, but still, as Williams returned to the bench, he got another tremendous hand.

Up in the press box, publicity man Jack Malaney was announcing that uniform No. 9 was being retired "after today's game." This brought on some snide remarks about Ted wearing his undershirt at Yankee Stadium for the final three games of the season. Like Mayor Collins, Malaney was righter than he knew. The uniform was indeed going to be retired after the game.

Williams came to bat again in the fifth inning, with two out and the Sox trailing, 3–2. And this time he unloaded a tremendous drive to right center. As the ball jumped off the bat, the cry, "He did it!" arose from the stands. Right-fielder Al Pilarcik ran back as far as he could, pressed his back against the bullpen fence, well out from the 380-foot sign, and stood there, motionless, his hands at his sides.

Although it was a heavy day, there was absolutely no wind. The flag hung limply from the pole, stirring very occasionally and very faintly.

At the last minute, Pilarcik brought up his hands and caught the ball chest high, close to 400 feet from the plate. A moan of disappointment settled over the field, followed by a rising hum of excited conversation and then, as Ted came back toward the first-base line to get his glove from Pumpsie Green, a standing ovation.

"Damn," Ted said, when he returned to the bench at the end of the inning. "I hit the living hell out of that one. I really stung it. If that one didn't go out, nothing is going out today!"

In the top of the eighth, with the Sox behind 4–2, Mike Fornieles came to the mound for the 70th time of the season, breaking the league record set by another Red Sox relief star, Ellis Kinder. Kinder set his mark in 1953, the year Williams returned from Korea.

As Fornieles was warming up, three teen-agers jumped out of the grandstand and ran toward Ted. They paused only briefly, however, and continued across the field to the waiting arms of the park police.

Ted was scheduled to bat second in the last of the eighth, undoubtedly his last time at bat. The cheering began as soon as Willie Tasby came out of the dugout and strode to the plate, as if he was anxious to get out of there and make way for the main event. Ted, coming out almost directly behind Tasby, went to the on-deck circle. He was down on one knee and just beginning to swing the heavy, lead-filled practice bat as Tasby hit the first pitch to short for an easy out.

The cheering seemed to come to its peak as Ted stepped into the box and took his stance. Everybody in the park had come to his feet to give Ted a standing ovation.

Umpire Eddie Hurley called time. Fisher stepped off the rubber and Triandos stood erect. Ted remained in the box, waiting, as if he were oblivious to it all. The standing ovation lasted at least two minutes, and even then Fisher threw into the continuing applause. Only as the ball approached the plate did the cheering stop. It came in low, ball one. The spectators remained on their feet, but very suddenly the park had gone very quiet.

If there was pressure on Ted, there was pressure on Fisher, too. The Orioles were practically tied for second place, so he couldn't afford to be charitable. He might have been able to get Ted to go after a bad pitch, and yet he hardly wanted to go down in history as the fresh kid who had walked Ted Williams on his last time at bat in Boston.

The second pitch was neck high, a slider with, it seemed, just a little off it. Ted gave it a tremendous swing, but he was just a little out in front of the ball. The swing itself brought a roar from the fans, though, since it was such a clear announcement that Ted was going for the home run or nothing.

With a 1–1 count, Fisher wanted to throw a fastball, low and away. He got it up too much and in too much, a fastball waist high on the outside corner. From the moment Ted swung, there was not the slightest doubt about it. The ball cut through the heavy air, a high line drive heading straightaway to center field toward the corner of the special bullpen the Red Sox built for Williams back in 1941.

Jackie Brandt went back almost to the barrier, then turned and watched the ball bounce off the canopy above the bullpen bench, skip up against the wire fence which rises in front of the bleachers and bounce back into the bullpen.

It did not seem possible that 10,000 people could make that much noise.

Ted raced around the bases at a pretty good clip. Triandos had started toward the mound with the new ball, and Fisher had come down to meet him. As Ted neared home plate, Triandos turned to face him, a big smile on his face. Ted grinned back.

Ted didn't exactly offer his hand to Pagliaroni after he crossed the plate, but the young catcher reached out anyway and made a grab for it. He seemed to catch Ted around the wrist. Williams ran back into the dugout and ducked through the runway door to get himself a drink of water.

The fans were on their feet again, deafening the air with their cheers. A good four or five minutes passed before anybody worried about getting the game underway again.

When Ted ducked back into the dugout, he put on his jacket and sat down at the very edge of the bench, alongside Mike Higgins and Del Baker. The players, still on their feet anyway, crowded around him, urging him to go out and acknowledge the cheers.

The fans were now chanting, "We want Ted . . . we want Ted . . . we want Ted." Umpire Johnny Rice, at first base, motioned for Ted to come out. Manager Mike Higgins urged him to go on out. Ted just sat there, his head down, a smile of happiness on his face.

"We wanted him to go out," Vic Wertz said later, "because we felt so good for him. And we could see he was thrilled, too. For me, I have to say it's my top thrill in baseball."

But another player said: "I had the impression—maybe I shouldn't say this because it's just an impression—that he got just as much a kick out of refusing to go out and tip his hat to the crowd as he did out of the homer. What I mean is he wanted to go out with the home run, all right, but he also wanted the home run so he could sit there while they yelled for him and tell them all where to go."

Mike Higgins had already told Carroll Hardy to replace Ted in left field. As Clinton came to bat, with two men out, Higgins said: "Williams, left field." Ted grabbed his glove angrily and went to the top step. When Clinton struck out, Ted was the first man out of the dugout. He sprinted out to left field, ignoring the cheers of the fans, who had not expected to see him again. But Higgins had sent Hardy right out behind him. Ted saw Carroll, and ran back in, one final time. The entire audience was on its feet once again, in wild applause.

Since it is doubtful that Higgins felt Williams was in any great need of more applause that day, it is perfectly obvious that he was giving Ted one last chance to think about the tip of the hat or the wave of the hand as he covered the distance between left field and the dugout.

Ted made the trip as always, his head down, his stride unbroken. He stepped on first base as he crossed the line, ducked down into the dugout, growled once at Higgins and headed through the alleyway and into the locker room.

He stopped only to tell an usher standing just inside the dugout: "I guess I forgot to tip my hat."

To the end, the mirror remained intact.

After the game, photographers were permitted to go right into the clubhouse, but writers were held to the 15-minute rule. One writer tried to ride in with the photographers, but Williams leveled that finger at him and said: "You're not supposed to be here."

Somehow or other, the news was let out that Ted would not be going to New York, although there seems to be some doubt as to whether it was Williams or Higgins who made the announcement. The official Boston line is that it had been understood all along that Ted would not be going to New York unless the pennant race was still on. The fact of the matter is that Williams made the decision himself, and he did not make it until after he hit the home run. It would have been foolish to have gone to New York or anywhere else, of course. Anything he did after the Boston finale would have been an anticlimax.

One of the waiting newspapermen, a pessimist by nature, expressed the fear that by the time they were let in, Ted would be dressed and gone.

"Are you kidding?" a member of the anti-Williams clique said. "This is what he lives for. If the game had gone 18 innings, he'd be in there waiting for us."

He was indeed waiting at his locker, with a towel wrapped around his middle. The writers approached him, for the most part, in groups. Generally speaking, the writers who could be called friends reached him first, and to these men Ted was not only amiable but gracious and modest.

Was he going for the home run?

"I was gunning for the big one," he grinned. "I let everything I had go. I really wanted that one."

Did he know it was out as soon as it left the bat?

"I knew I had really given it a ride."

What were his immediate plans?

"I've got some business to clean up here," he said. "Then I'll be covering the World Series for *Life*. After that, I'm going back to Florida to see how much damage the hurricane did to my house."

The other players seemed even more affected by the drama of the farewell homer than Ted. Pete Runnels, practically dispossessed from his locker alongside Ted's by the shifts of reporters, wandered around the room shaking his head in disbelief. "How about that?" he kept repeating. "How about that? How about that?"

As for Ted, he seemed to be in something of a daze. After the first wave of writers had left, he wandered back and forth between his locker and the trainer's room. Back and forth, back and forth. Once, he came back with a bottle of beer, turned it up to his lips and downed it with obvious pleasure. For Ted, this is almost unheard of. He has always been a milk and ice-cream man, and he devours them both in huge quantities. His usual order after a ball game is two quarts of milk.

Williams remained in the locker room, making himself available, until there were no more than a half-dozen other players remaining. Many of the writers did not go over to him at all. From them, there were no questions, no congratulations, no good wishes for the future. For all Ted's color, for all the drama and copy he had supplied over 22 years, they were glad to see him finally retire.

When Ted finally began to get dressed, our man went over and said:

"Ted, you must have known when Higgins sent you back out that he was giving you a final chance to think about tipping the hat or making some gesture of farewell. Which meant that Higgins himself would have liked you to have done it. While you were running back, didn't you have any feeling that it might be nice to go out with a show of good feeling?"

"I felt nothing," he said.

"No sentimentality? No gratitude? No sadness?"

"I said *nothing*," Ted said. "Nothing, nothing, nothing!"

As our man was toting up the nothings, Ted snarled, "And when you get back there tell them for me that they're full of . . ." There followed a burst of vituperation which we can not even begin to approximate, and then the old, sad plaint about those 12 years of merciless persecution.

Fenway Park has an enclosed parking area so that the players can get to their cars without beating their way through the autograph hunters. When Ted was dressed, though, the clubhouse boy called to the front office in what was apparently a prearranged plan to bring Williams's car around to a bleacher exit.

At 4:40, 45 minutes after the end of the game and a good hour after Ted had left the dugout, he was ready to leave. "Fitzie," he called out, and the clubhouse boy came around to lead the way. The cameramen came around, too.

The locker-room door opens onto a long corridor, which leads to another door which, in turn, opens onto the backwalks and understructure of the park. It is this outer door which is always guarded.

Waiting in the alleyway, just outside the clubhouse door, however, was a redheaded, beatnik-looking man, complete with the regimental beard and the beachcomber pants. He handed Ted a ball and mentioned a name that apparently meant something to him. Ted took the ball and signed it.

"How come you're not able to get in?" he said. "If they let the damn newspapermen in, they ought to let you in." Walking away, trailed by the platoon of cameramen, he called out to the empty air: "If they let the newspapermen in, they should have let him in. If they let the newspapermen in, they should let everybody in."

He walked on through the backways of the park, past the ramps and pillars, at a brisk clip, with Fitzie bustling along quickly to stay up ahead. Alongside of Williams, the cameramen were scrambling to get their positions and snap their pictures. Williams kept his eyes straight ahead, never pausing for one moment. "Hold it for just a minute, Ted," one of them said.

"I've been here for 22 years," Ted said, walking on. "Plenty of time for you to get your shot."

"This is the last time," the cameraman said. "Co-operate just this one last time."

"I've co-operated with you," Ted said. "I've co-operated too much."

Fitzie had the bleacher entrance open, and as Ted passed quickly through, a powder-blue Cadillac pulled up to the curb. A man in shirt sleeves was behind the wheel. He looked like Dick O'Connell, whose appointment as business manager had been announced the previous night.

Fitzie ran ahead to open the far door of the car for Ted. Three young women had been approaching the exit as Ted darted through, and one of them screamed: "It's him!" One of the others just let out a scream, as if Ted had been somebody of real worth, like Elvis or Fabian. The third woman remained mute. Looking at her, you had to wonder whether she would ever speak again.

Fitzie slammed the door, and the car pulled away. "It was him," the first woman screamed. "Was it *really* him? Was it *him?*"

Her knees seemed to give away. Her girl friends had to support her. "I can't catch my breath," she said. "I can hear my heart pounding." And then, in something like terror: "I CAN'T BREATHE."

Attracted by the screams, or by some invisible, inexplicable grapevine, a horde of boys and men came racing up the street. Ted's car turned the corner just across from the bleacher exit, but it was held up momentarily by a red light and a bus. The front line of pursuers had just come abreast of the car when the driver swung around the bus and pulled away.

There are those, however, who never get the word. Down the street, still surrounding the almost empty parking area, were still perhaps 100 loyal fans waiting to say their last farewell to Ted Williams.

In Boston that night, the talk was all of Williams. Only 10,454 were at the scene, but the word all over the city was: "I knew he'd end it with a home run . . ." and "I was going to go to the game, but—"

In future years, we can be sure, the men who saw Ted hit that mighty shot will number into the hundreds of thousands. The wind will grow strong and mean, and the distance will grow longer. Many of the reports of the game, in fact, had the ball going into center-field bleachers.

The seeds of the legend have already been sown. George Carens, an elderly columnist who is more beloved by Ted than by his colleagues, wrote:

"Ted was calm and gracious as he praised the occupants of the

Fenway press penthouse at home plate before the game began. Afterwards he greeted all writers in a comradely way, down through his most persistent critics. In a word, Ted showed he can take it, and whenever the spirit moves him he will fit beautifully into the Fenway PR setup."

Which shows that people hear what they want to hear and see what they want to see.

In New York the next day, Phil Rizzuto informed his television audience that Ted had finally relented and tipped his hat after the home run.

And the *Sporting News* headline on its Boston story was:

> "SPLINTER TIPS CAP
> TO HUB FANS AFTER
> FAREWELL HOMER"

A New York Sunday paper went so far as to say that Ted had made "a tender and touching farewell speech" from the home plate at the end of the game.

All the reports said that Ted had, in effect, called his shot because it was known that he was shooting for a home run. Who wants to bet that, in future years, there will not be a story or two insisting that he *did* point?

The legend will inevitably grow, and in a way it is a shame. A man should be allowed to die the way he lived. He should be allowed to depart as he came. Ted Williams chose his course early, and his course was to turn his face from the world around him. When he walked out of the park, he kept his eyes to the front and he never looked back.

The epitaph for Ted Williams remains unchanged. He was sometimes unbearable but he was never dull. Baseball will not be the same without him. Boston won't be quite the same either. Old Boston is acrawl with greening statues of old heroes and old patriots, but Ted has left a monument of his own—again on his own terms—in the Children's Cancer Hospital.

He left his own monument in the record books too. For two decades he made the Red Sox exciting in the sheer anticipation of his next time at bat.

He opened his last season with perhaps the longest home run of his career and he closed it with perhaps the most dramatic. It was typical and it was right that the Williams Era in Boston should end not with a whimper. It was entirely proper that it should end with a bang.

So, the old order passeth and an era of austerity has settled upon the Red Sox franchise.

And now Boston knows how England felt when it lost India.

Robert Lipsyte

Is Connors a Killer?

It was a fine day for New York sports fans when Robert Lipsyte returned to The New York Times. *That was in 1991, twenty years after he had left the* Times *("I went out for a cigar and came back") to pursue his own writing. Lipsyte has been a prize-winning magazine writer and a prize-winning television essayist, and in between he has written twelve books. Here he is, in top form as usual, describing the elemental child of tennis—Jimmy Connors.*

Sixteen years ago, in a motel room in Orlando, I tried to watch a telecast of George Foreman fighting five opponents in a row, but I never got to see more than a minute at a time because Angelo Dundee, the great boxing trainer, kept switching the channel. He wanted to watch Jimmy Connors fight John Newcombe.

"Connors is a killer," said Angelo. "He's got timing, guts, he knows just when to come in and dig. Would've made a helluva fighter."

Connors the Killer has been both the beacon and the aberration of the Great Yuppie Carnival at Flushing Meadows these past two weeks. Contemporary tennis players have been built out of junk bonds and downtown art, hyped, inflated, driven, sponsored, and most of them seem whiney (see Aaron Krickstein's blood blister) or silly (Monica Seles complaining about her 17-year-old life's "distractions") or a bit grand (the Croatian patriot Goran Ivanisevic declaring, "My racquet is my gun") compared with someone as elemental as Jimmy Connors. His age is only relevant because so many in the crowd have seen him play for longer than Aaron or Monica or Goran have lived; it is not his longevity but his neediness that sucks the gallery dry, his willingness to give up body and soul for their attention and love. Jimmy is a child; not an adolescent

444

like most athletes, but a child. Say, 2 years old, when everything is gorgeously, hilariously, maddeningly naked.

But after Connors, the emotional pickings have been slim. John McEnroe is not emotional, he is tortured, and the agony of the artist at work is exciting only when it leaks out on the ceiling of the Sistine Chapel. McEnroe has been finger-painting on velvet lately. Martina seems gallant enough, but she has become more interesting as a person than as an athlete. Her description of her bisexuality to Barbara Walters on TV recently was one of the most provocatively intelligent I've heard. Martina said, in effect, that she could go to bed with either sex, but preferred to wake up with a woman. She found women more emotionally satisfying as companions. It was all said so matter-of-factly that it raised the level of that particular dialogue. Then again, when sports figures get serious—Billy Sunday, Muhammad Ali, Bill Bradley—they can be very direct.

While most athletes, particularly pro team sports athletes, follow fashion, tennis players have always been in the avant-garde of popular culture. Perhaps it is because they began as the intimate servants, like hairdressers, of the rich and tanned. No wonder independents like Jack Kramer and Pancho Gonzalez and Billie Jean King preferred to be paid like grownups even if the life was harder.

"We're on the edge of culture shock," Billie Jean King liked to say in the 70's, even as she was experimenting with bicoastal marriage, bisexual relationships and, in what became the feminist equivalent of invading Grenada, the victory over Bobby Riggs.

It was in tennis that we first met Western Euro-trash, beautiful, delightful, cynical, jaded, and it was in tennis we met the first wave of East Europeans yearning for the freedom to buy condos in Marina del Rey. But the Romanians, the Russians and the Czechoslovaks who came to play tennis rather than play art could not coast on the adoration of claques and collectors. They had to win. Even now, when tennis players are ranked, like golfers and stockbrokers, by money earned, they still have to step into cockpits like the stadium at Flushing Meadows and show us what they've really got.

Like art, tennis has the capacity to stop your heart and leave the indelible memory of a moment in which a human flew. And, like the art media, the tennis media is largely scandalous or sycophantic, shoveling out words that have no meaning and that muddy memories. In tennis, such words as "courage," "tragedy" and "heroism" should never be applied to yuppies trying to stick more billboards on their racquets or shoes or shirts. Somewhere under all that gear may be a human being, but it's hard to tell. The healthiest will never let us find out what really makes them tick, because then we will try to take them apart to see for ourselves.

Yet who can deny the pleasure that these children give us, these pampered, hypochondriacal egomaniacs. No wonder David Dinkins, elected to be Mayor Dad, divided his time among Crown Heights, the Union Square Station and Flushing Meadows. People are killed in New York every day; the playpen is Open but once a year.

And Connors reminds us all how much we have given up by growing up. Lucky Jimmy. If only we could once again stop the party in the living room, make all the grownups applaud our naughty words, dance through the hors d'oeuvres, posture and preen and be a Terrible Two, the only time when a human being will be loved for conquering the world while crying.

Jack London

The Waves at Waikiki

This nonfiction piece appeared in a travel book Jack London wrote in 1911 called The Cruise of the Snark. *One of London's stops on the* Snark, *a ketch he built himself, was the Hawaiian Islands. There he was introduced to a new and daring sport called "surf-riding." Watching the "brown, kingly species of man" conquer the foaming surf summoned up London's own macho desires, and within days he too was on top of a heavy board doing battle with another of life's forces of nature. And, like the characters in his fiction, winning that battle.*

That is what it is, a royal sport for the natural kings of earth. The grass grows right down to the water at Waikiki Beach, and within fifty feet of the everlasting sea. The trees also grow down to the salty edge of things, and one sits in their shade and looks seaward at a majestic surf thundering in on the beach to one's very feet. Half a mile out, where is the reef, the white-headed combers thrust suddenly skyward out of the placid turquoise-blue and come rolling in to shore. One after another they come, a mile long, with smoking crests, the white battalions of the infinite army of the sea. And one sits and listens to the perpetual roar, and watches the unending procession, and feels tiny and fragile before this tremendous force expressing itself in fury and foam and sound. Indeed, one feels microscopically small, and the thought that one may wrestle with this sea raises in one's imagination a thrill of apprehension, almost of fear. Why, they are a mile long, these bull-mouthed monsters, and they weigh a thousand tons, and they charge in to shore faster than a man can run. What chance? No chance at all, is the verdict of the shrinking ego; and one sits, and looks, and listens, and thinks the grass and the shade are a pretty good place in which to be.

And suddenly, out there where a big smoker lifts skyward, rising like a sea-god from out of the welter of spume and churning white, on the giddy, toppling, overhanging and down-falling, precarious crest appears the dark head of a man. Swiftly he rises through the rushing white. His black shoulders, his chest, his loins, his limbs—all is abruptly projected on one's vision. Where but the moment before was only the wide desolation and invincible roar, is now a man, erect, full-statured, not struggling frantically in that wild movement, not buried and crushed and buffeted by those mighty monsters, but standing above them all, calm and superb, poised on the giddy summit, his feet buried in the churning foam, the salt smoke rising to his knees, and all the rest of him in the free air and flashing sunlight, and he is flying through the air, flying forward, flying fast as the surge on which he stands. He is a Mercury—a brown Mercury. His heels are winged, and in them is the swiftness of the sea. In truth, from out of the sea he has leaped upon the back of the sea, and he is riding the sea that roars and bellows and cannot shake him from its back. But no frantic outreaching and balancing is his. He is impassive, motionless as a statue carved suddenly by some miracle out of the sea's depth from which he rose. And straight on toward shore he flies on his winged heels and the white crest of the breaker. There is a wild burst of foam, a long tumultuous rushing sound as the breaker falls futile and spent on the beach at your feet; and there, at your feet, steps calmly ashore a Kanaka, burnt golden and brown by the tropic sun. Several minutes ago he was a speck a quarter of a mile away. He has "bitted the bull-mouthed breaker" and ridden it in, and the pride in the feat shows in the carriage of his magnificent body as he glances for a moment carelessly at you who sit in the shade of the shore. He is a Kanaka—and more, he is a man, a member of the kingly species that has mastered matter and the brutes and lorded it over creation.

And one sits and thinks of Tristram's last wrestle with the sea on that fatal morning; and one thinks further, to the fact that that Kanaka has done what Tristram never did, and that he knows a joy of the sea that Tristram never knew. And still further one thinks. It is all very well, sitting here in cool shade of the beach, but you are a man, one of the kingly species, and what that Kanaka can do, you can do yourself. Go to. Strip off your clothes that are a nuisance in this mellow clime. Get in and wrestle with the sea; wing your heels with the skill and power that reside in you; bit the sea's breakers, master them, and ride upon their backs as a king should.

And that is how it came about that I tackled surf-riding. And now that I have tackled it, more than ever do I hold it to be a royal sport. But first let me explain the physics of it. A wave is a communicated agitation. The water that composes the body of a wave does not move. If it did, when a stone is thrown into a pond and the ripples spread away in an ever-widening circle, there would appear at the center an ever-increasing hole. No, the water that composes the body of a wave is stationary. Thus, you may watch a particular portion of the ocean's surface and you will see the same water rise and fall a thousand times to the agitation communicated by a thousand successive waves. Now imagine this communicated agitation moving shoreward. As the bottom shoals, the lower portion of the wave strikes land first and is stopped. But water is fluid, and the upper portion has not struck anything, wherefore it keeps on communicating its agitation, keeps on going. And when the top of the wave keeps on going, while the bottom of it lags behind, something is bound to happen. The bottom of the wave drops out from under and the top of the wave falls over, forward, and down, curling and cresting and roaring as it does so. It is the bottom of a wave striking against the top of the land that is the cause of all surfs.

But the transformation from a smooth undulation to a breaker is not abrupt except where the bottom shoals abruptly. Say the bottom shoals gradually for from quarter of a mile to a mile, then an equal distance will be occupied by the transformation. Such a bottom is that off the beach of Waikiki, and it produces a splendid surf-riding surf. One leaps upon the back of a breaker just as it begins to break, and stays on it as it continues to break all the way in to shore.

And now to the particular physics of surf-riding. Get out on a flat board, six feet long, two feet wide, and roughly oval in shape. Lie down upon it like a small boy on a coaster and paddle with your hands out to deep water, where the waves begin to crest. Lie out there quietly on the board. Sea after sea breaks before, behind, and under and over you, and rushes in to shore, leaving you behind. When a wave crests, it gets steeper. Imagine yourself, on your board, on the face of that steep slope. If it stood still, you would slide down just as a boy slides down a hill on his coaster. "But," you object, "the wave doesn't stand still." Very true, but the water composing the wave stands still, and there you have the secret. If ever you start sliding down the face of that wave, you'll keep on sliding and you'll never reach the bottom. Please don't laugh.

The face of that wave may be only six feet, yet you can slide down it a quarter of a mile, or half a mile, and not reach the bottom. For, see, since a wave is only a communicated agitation or impetus, and since the water that composes a wave is changing every instant, new water is rising into the wave as fast as the wave travels. You slide down this new water, and yet remain in your old position on the wave, sliding down the still newer water that is rising and forming the wave. You slide precisely as fast as the wave travels. If it travels fifteen miles an hour, you slide fifteen miles an hour. Between you and shore stretches a quarter of mile of water. As the wave travels, this water obligingly heaps itself into the wave, gravity does the rest, and down you go, sliding the whole length of it. If you still cherish the notion, while sliding, that the water is moving with you, thrust your arms into it and attempt to paddle; you will find that you have to be remarkably quick to get a stroke, for that water is dropping astern just as fast as you are rushing ahead.

And now for another phase of the physics of surf-riding. All rules have their exceptions. It is true that the water in a wave does not travel forward. But there is what may be called the send of the sea. The water in the overtoppling crest does move forward, as you will speedily realize if you are slapped in the face by it, or if you are caught under it and are pounded by one mighty blow down under the surface panting and gasping for a half a minute. The water in the top of a wave rests upon the water in the bottom of the wave. But when the bottom of the wave strikes the land, it stops, while the top goes on. It no longer has the bottom of the wave to hold it up. Where was solid water beneath it, is now air, and for the first time it feels the grip of gravity, and down it falls, at the same time being torn asunder from the lagging bottom of the wave and flung forward. And it is because of this that riding a surf-board is something more than a mere placid sliding down a hill. In truth, one is caught up and hurled shoreward as by some Titan's hand.

I deserted the cool shade, put on a swimming suit, and got hold of a surf-board. It was too small a board. But I didn't know, and nobody told me. I joined some little Kanaka boys in shallow water, where the breakers were well spent and small—a regular kindergarten school. I watched the little Kanaka boys. When a likely-looking breaker came along, they flopped upon their stomachs on their boards, kicked like mad with their feet, and rode the breaker in to the beach. I tried to emulate them. I watched them, tried to do everything that they did, and failed utterly. The breaker swept past, and I was not on it. I tried again and again. I kicked twice as madly as they did, and failed. Half a dozen would be around. We would all leap on our boards in front of a good breaker. Away our feet would churn like the stern-wheels of river steamboats, and away the little rascals would scoot while I remained in disgrace behind.

I tried for a solid hour, and not one wave could I persuade to boost me shoreward. And then arrived a friend, Alexander Hume Ford, a globe trotter by profession, bent ever on the pursuit of sensation. And he had found it at Waikiki. Heading for Australia, he had stopped off for a week to find out if there were any thrills in surf-riding, and he had become wedded to it. He had been at it every day for a month and could not yet see any symptoms of the fascination lessening on him. He spoke with authority.

"Get off that board," he said. "Chuck it away at once. Look at the way you're trying to ride it. If ever the nose of that board hits bottom, you'll be disemboweled. Here, take my board. It's a man's size."

I am always humble when confronted by knowledge. Ford knew. He showed me how properly to mount his board. Then he waited for a good breaker, gave me a shove at the right moment, and started me in. Ah, delicious moment when I felt that breaker grip and fling me! On I dashed, a hundred and fifty feet, and subsided with the breaker on the sand. From that moment I was lost. I waded back to Ford with his board. It was a large one, several inches thick, and weighed all of seventy-five pounds. He gave me advice, much of it. He had had no one to teach him, and all that he had laboriously learned in several weeks he communicated to me in half an hour. I really learned by proxy. And inside of half an hour I was able to start myself and ride in. I did it time after time, and Ford applauded and advised. For instance, he told me to get just so far forward on the board and no farther. But I must have got some farther, for as I came charging in to land, that miserable board poked its nose down to bottom, stopped abruptly, and turned a somersault, at the same time violently severing our relations. I was tossed through the air like a chip and buried ignominiously under the downfalling breaker. And I realized that if it hadn't been for Ford, I'd have been disemboweled. That particular risk is part of the sport, Ford says. Maybe he'll have it happen to him before he leaves Waikiki, and then, I feel confident, his yearning for sensation will be satisfied for a time.

When all is said and done, it is my steadfast belief that homicide is worse than suicide, especially if, in the former case, it is a woman. Ford saved me from being a homicide. "Imagine your legs are a rudder," he said. "Hold them close together, and steer with them." A few minutes later I came charging in on a comber. As I neared the beach, there, in the water, up to her waist, dead in front of me, appeared a woman. How was I to stop that comber on whose back I was? It looked like a dead woman. The board weighed seventy-five pounds, I weighed a hundred and sixty-five. The added weight had a velocity of fifteen miles per hour. The board and I constituted a projectile. I leave it to the physicists to figure out the force of the impact upon that poor, tender woman. And then I remembered my guardian angel, Ford. "Steer with your legs!" rang through my brain. I steered with my legs, I steered sharply, abruptly, with all my legs and with all my might. The board sheered around broadside on the crest. Many things happened simultaneously. The wave gave me a passing buffet, a light tap as the taps of waves go but a tap sufficient to knock me off the board and smash me down through the rushing water to bottom, with which I came in violent collision and upon which I was rolled over and over. I got my head out for a breath of air and then gained my feet. There stood the woman before me. I felt like a hero. I had saved her life. And she laughed at me. It was not hysteria. She had never dreamed of her danger. Anyway, I solaced myself, it was not I but Ford that saved her, and I didn't have to feel like a hero. And besides, that leg-steering was great. In a few minutes more of practice I was able to thread my way in and out past several bathers and to remain on top of my breaker instead of going under it.

"Tomorrow," Ford said, "I am going to take you out into the blue water."

I looked seaward where he pointed, and saw the great smoking combers that made the breakers I had been riding look like ripples. I don't know what I might have said had I not recollected just then that I was one of a kingly species. So all that I did say was, "All right, I'll tackle them tomorrow."

The water that rolls in on Waikiki Beach is just the same as the water that laves the shores of all the Hawaiian Islands; and in ways, especially from the swimmer's standpoint, it is wonderful water. It is cool enough to be comfortable, while it is warm enough to permit a swimmer to stay in all day without experiencing a chill. Under the sun or the stars, at high noon or at midnight, in midwinter or in midsummer, it does not matter when, it is always the same temperature—not too warm, not too cold, just right. It is wonderful water, salt as old ocean itself, pure and crystal-clear. When the nature of the water is considered, it is not so remarkable after all that the Kanakas are one of the most expert of swimming races.

So it was, next morning, when Ford came along, that I plunged into the wonderful water for a swim of indeterminate length. Astride of our surf-boards, or, rather, flat down upon them on our stomachs, we paddled out through the kindergarten where the little Kanaka boys were at play. Soon we were out in deep water where the big smokers came roaring in. The mere struggle with them, facing them and paddling seaward over them and through them, was sport enough in itself. One had to have his wits about him, for it was a battle in which mighty blows were struck, on one side, and in which cunning was used on the other side—a struggle between insensate force and intelligence. I soon learned a bit. When a breaker curled over my head, for a swift instant I could see the light of day through its emerald body; then down would go my head, and I would clutch the board with all my strength. Then would come the blow, and to the onlooker on shore I would be blotted out. In reality the board and I have passed through the crest and emerged in the respite of the other side. I should not recommend those smashing blows to an invalid or delicate person. There is weight behind them, and the impact of the driven water is like a sand-blast. Sometimes one passes through half a dozen combers in quick succession, and it is just about that time that he is liable to discover new merits in the stable land and new reasons for being on shore.

Out there in the midst of such a succession of big smoky ones, a third man was added to our party, one Freeth. Shaking the water from my eyes as I emerged from one wave and peered ahead to see what the next one looked like, I saw him tearing in on the back of it, standing upright on his board, carelessly poised, a young god bronzed with sunburn. We went through the wave on the back of which he rode. Ford called to him. He turned an air-spring from his wave, rescued his board from its maw, paddled over to us and joined Ford in showing me things. One thing in particular I learned from Freeth, namely, how to encounter the occasional breaker of exceptional size that rolled in. Such breakers were really ferocious, and it was unsafe to meet them on top of the board. But Freeth showed me, so that whenever I saw one of that caliber rolling down on me, I slid off the rear end of the board and dropped down beneath the surface, my arms over my head and holding the board. Thus, if the wave ripped the board out of my hands and tried to strike me with it (a common trick of such waves), there would be a cushion of water a foot or more in depth, between my head and the blow. When the wave passed, I climbed upon the board and paddled on. Many men have been terribly injured, I learn, by being struck by their boards.

The whole method of surf-riding and surf-fighting, I learned, is one of nonresistance. Dodge the blow that is struck at you. Dive through the wave that is trying to slap you in the face. Sink down, feet first, deep under the surface, and let the big smoker that is trying to smash you go by far overhead. Never be rigid. Relax. Yield yourself to the waters that are ripping and tearing at you. When the undertow catches you and drags you seaward along the bottom, don't struggle against it. If you do, you are liable to be drowned, for it is stronger than you. Yield yourself to that undertow. Swim with it, not against it, and you will find the pressure removed. And, swimming with it, fooling it so that it does not hold you, swim upward at the same time. It will be no trouble at all to reach the surface.

The man who wants to learn surf-riding must be a strong swimmer, and he must be used to going under the water. After that, fair strength and common sense are all that is required. The force of the big comber is rather unexpected. There are mix-ups in which board and rider are torn apart and separated by several hundred feet. The surf-rider must take care of himself. No matter how many riders swim out with him, he cannot depend upon any of them for aid. The fancied security I had in the presence of Ford and Freeth made me forget that it was my first swim out in deep water among the big ones. I recollected, however, and rather suddenly, for a big wave came in, and away went the two men on its back all the way to shore. I could have been drowned a dozen different ways before they got back to me.

One slides down the face of a breaker on his surf-board, but he has to get started to sliding. Board and rider must be moving shoreward at a good rate before the wave overtakes them. When you see the wave coming that you want to ride in, you turn tail to it and paddle shoreward with all your strength, using what is called the windmill stroke. This is a sort of spurt performed immediately in front of the wave. If the board is going fast enough, the wave accelerates it, and the board begins its quarter-of-a-mile slide.

I shall never forget the first big wave I caught out there in the deep water. I saw it coming, turned my back on it and paddled for dear life. Faster and faster my board went, till it seemed my arms would drop off. What was happening behind me I could not tell. One cannot look behind and paddle the windmill stroke. I heard the crest of the wave hissing and churning, and then my board was lifted and flung forward. I scarcely knew what happened the first half-minute. Though I kept my eyes open, I could not see anything, for I was buried in the rushing white of the crest. But I did not mind. I was chiefly conscious of ecstatic bliss at having caught the wave. At the end of the half-minute, however, I began to see things, and to breathe. I saw that three feet of the nose of my board was clear out of water and riding on the air. I shifted my weight forward, and made the nose come down. Then I lay, quite at rest in the midst of the wild movement, and watched the shore and the bathers on the beach grow distinct. I didn't cover quite a quarter of a mile on that wave, because, to prevent the board from diving, I shifted my weight back, but shifted it too far and fell down the rear slope of the wave.

It was my second day at surf-riding, and I was quite proud of myself. I stayed out there four hours, and when it was over, I was resolved that on the morrow I'd come in standing up. But that resolution paved a distant place. On the morrow I was in bed. I was not sick, but I was very unhappy, and I was in bed. When describing the wonderful water of Hawaii I forgot to describe the wonderful sun of Hawaii. It is a tropic sun, and, furthermore, in the first part of June, it is an overhead sun. It is also an insidious, deceitful sun. For the first time in my life I was sunburned unawares. My arms, shoulders, and back had been burned many times in the past and were tough; but not so my legs. And for four hours I had exposed the tender backs of my legs, at right-angles, to that perpendicular Hawaiian sun. It was not until after I got ashore that I discovered the sun had touched me. Sunburn at first is merely warm; after that it grows intense and the blisters come out. Also, the joints, where the skin wrinkles, refuse to bend. That is why I spent the next day in bed. I couldn't walk. And that is why, today, I am writing this in bed. It is easier to than not to. But tomorrow, ah, tomorrow, I shall be out in that wonderful water, and I shall come in standing up, even as Ford and Freeth. And if I fail tomorrow, I shall do it the next day, or the next. Upon one thing I am resolved: the *Snark* shall not sail from Honolulu until I, too, wing my heels with the swiftness of the sea, and become a sunburned, skin-peeling Mercury.

Federico García Lorca

Lament for Ignacio Sánchez Mejías

Spain's best-known modern poet was also a playwright, and three of his tragic dramas, Blood Wedding, Yerma, *and* The House of Bernardo Alba, *are performed frequently today. This formal lament for Lorca's friend who was killed at five in the afternoon is considered the greatest elegy in modern Spanish poetry. According to Benét's* Reader's Encyclopedia, *"the figure of one man facing death in the bullring brought to full expressive power Lorca's tragic sense of violent death." Lorca was killed by Falangist soldiers in 1936 in the opening days of the Spanish Civil War. He was thirty-eight years old.*

I. Cogida and Death

At five in the afternoon.
It was exactly five in the afternoon.
A boy brought the white sheet
at five in the afternoon.
A frail of lime ready prepared
at five in the afternoon.
The rest was death, and death alone
at five in the afternoon.

The wind carried away the cottonwool
at five in the afternoon.
And the oxide scattered crystal and nickel
at five in the afternoon.

Now the dove and the leopard wrestle
at five in the afternoon.
And a thigh with a desolate horn
at five in the afternoon.
The bass-string struck up
at five in the afternoon.
Arsenic bells and smoke
at five in the afternoon.
Groups of silence in the corners
at five in the afternoon.
And the bull alone with a high heart!
At five in the afternoon.
When the sweat of snow was coming
at five in the afternoon,
when the bull ring was covered in iodine
at five in the afternoon.
death laid eggs in the wound
at five in the afternoon.
At five in the afternoon.
Exactly at five o'clock in the afternoon.

A coffin on wheels is his bed
at five in the afternoon.
Bones and flutes resound in his ears
at five in the afternoon.
Now the bull was bellowing through his forehead
at five in the afternoon.
The room was iridescent with agony
at five in the afternoon.
In the distance the gangrene now comes
at five in the afternoon.
Horn of the lily through green groins
at five in the afternoon.
The wounds were burning like suns
at five in the afternoon,
and the crowd was breaking the windows
at five in the afternoon.
At five in the afternoon.
Ah, that fatal five in the afternoon!
It was five by all the clocks!
It was five in the shade of the afternoon!

2. The Spilled Blood

I will not see it!

Tell the moon to come
for I do not want to see the blood
of Ignacio on the sand.

I will not see it!

The moon wide open.
Horse of still clouds,
and the grey bull ring of dreams
with willows in the barreras.

I will not see it!

Let my memory kindle!
Warn the jasmines
of such minute whiteness!

I will not see it!

The cow of the ancient world
passed her sad tongue
over a snout of blood
spilled on the sand,
and the bulls of Guisando,
partly death and partly stone,
bellowed like two centuries
sated with treading the earth.
No.
I do not want to see it!
I will not see it!

Ignacio goes up the tiers
with all his death on his shoulders.
He sought for the dawn
but the dawn was no more.
He seeks for his confident profile

and the dream bewilders him.
He sought for his beautiful body
and encountered his opened blood.
I will not see it!
I do not want to hear it spurt
each time with less strength:
that spurt that illuminates
the tiers of seats, and spills
over the corduroy and the leather
of a thirsty multitude.
Who shouts that I should come near!
Do not ask me to see it!

His eyes did not close
when he saw the horns near,
but the terrible mothers
lifted their heads.
And across the ranches,
an air of secret voices rose,
shouting to celestial bulls,
herdsmen of pale mist.
There was no prince in Seville
who could compare with him,
nor sword like his sword
nor heart so true.
Like a river of lions
was his marvellous strength,
and like a marble torso
his firm drawn moderation.
The air of Andalusian Rome
gilded his head
where his smile was a spikenard
of wit and intelligence.
What a great torero in the ring!
What a good peasant in the sierra!
How gentle with the sheaves!
How hard with the spurs!
How tender with the dew!
How dazzling in the fiesta!
How tremendous with the final
banderillas of darkness!

But now he sleeps without end.
Now the moss and the grass
open with sure fingers
the flower of his skull.
And now his blood comes out singing;
singing along marshes and meadows,
sliding on frozen horns,
faltering soulless in the mist,
stumbling over a thousand hoofs
like a long, dark, sad tongue,
to form a pool of agony
close to the starry Guadalquivir.
Oh, white wall of Spain!
Oh, black bull of sorrow!
Oh, hard blood of Ignacio!
Oh, nightingale of his veins!
No.
I will not see it!
No chalice can contain it,
no swallows can drink it,
no frost of light can cool it,
nor song nor deluge of white lilies,
no glass can cover it with silver.
No.
I will not see it!

3. The Laid Out Body

Stone is a forehead where dreams grieve
without curving waters and frozen cypresses.
Stone is a shoulder on which to bear Time
with trees formed of tears and ribbons and planets.

I have seen grey showers move towards the waves
raising their tender riddled arms,
to avoid being caught by the lying stone
which loosens their limbs without soaking the blood.

For stone gathers seed and clouds,
skeleton larks and wolves of penumbra:

but yields not sounds nor crystals nor fire,
only bull rings and bull rings and more bull rings without
   walls.

Now, Ignacio the well born lies on the stone.
All is finished. What is happening? Contemplate his face:
death has covered him with pale sulphur
and has placed on him the head of a dark minotaur.

All is finished. The rain penetrates his mouth.
The air, as if mad, leaves his sunken chest,
and Love, soaked through with tears of snow,
warms itself on the peak of the herd.

What are they saying? A stenching silence settles down.
We are here with a body laid out which fades away,
with a pure shape which had nightingales
and we see it being filled with depthless holes.

Who creases the shroud? What he says is not true!
Nobody sings here, nobody weeps in the corner,
nobody pricks the spurs, nor terrifies the serpent.
Here I want nothing else but the round eyes
to see this body without a chance of rest.

Here I want to see those men of hard voice.
Those that break horses and dominate rivers;
those men of sonorous skeleton who sing
with a mouth full of sun and flint.

Here I want to see them. Before the stone.
Before this body with broken reins.
I want to know from them the way out
for this captain strapped down by death.

I want them to show me a lament like a river
which will have sweet mists and deep shores,
to take the body of Ignacio where it loses itself
without hearing the double panting of the bulls.

Loses itself in the round bull ring of the moon
which feigns in its youth a sad quiet bull:
loses itself in the night without song of fishes
and in the white thicket of frozen smoke.

I don't want them to cover his face with handkerchiefs
that he may get used to the death he carries.
Go, Ignacio; feel not the hot bellowing.
Sleep, fly, rest: even the sea dies!

4. Absent Soul

The bull does not know you, nor the fig tree,
nor the horses, nor the ants in your own house.
The child and the afternoon do not know you
because you have died for ever.

The back of the stone does not know you,
nor the black satin in which you crumble.
Your silent memory does not know you
because you have died for ever.

The autumn will come with small white snails,
misty grapes and with clustered hills,
but no one will look into your eyes
because you have died for ever.

Because you have died for ever,
like all the dead of the Earth,
like all the dead who are forgotten
in a heap of lifeless dogs.

Nobody knows you. No. But I sing of you.
For posterity I sing of your profile and grace.
Of the signal maturity of your understanding.
Of your appetite for death and the taste of its mouth.
Of the sadness of your once valiant gaiety.

It will be a long time, if ever, before there is born
an Andalusian so true, so rich in adventure.
I sing of his elegance with words that groan,
and I remember a sad breeze through the olive trees.

(Translated from the Spanish by Stephen Spender and J. I. Gili)

Norman Mailer

Ego

Although Norman Mailer has taken, late in life, to deriding the art of nonfiction, he has been one of its greatest contemporary practitioners. Sometimes he has disguised that fact. He subtitled Armies of the Night, *which won a Pulitzer Prize for him in 1968,* History as a Novel, the Novel as History. *And* The Executioner's Song, *which won the Pulitzer Prize for* fiction *in 1980, was originally published as nonfiction. Does it matter? Not really with this writer and leading personage of his time. "Ego," for instance, is a sports story ("the finest sports article ever written," said a one-time editor of* Life *magazine, which was where the story was published), but, in his inimitable fashion, Mailer is dealing with a larger theme— "the central phenomenon of the twentieth century." It's that word called* ego.

It is the great word of the twentieth century. If there is a single word our century has added to the potentiality of language, it is ego. Everything we have done in this century, from monumental feats to nightmares of human destruction, has been a function of that extraordinary state of the psyche which gives us authority to declare we are sure of ourselves when we are not.

Muhammad Ali begins with the most unsettling ego of all. Having commanded the stage, he never pretends to step back and relinquish his place to other actors—like a six-foot parrot, he keeps screaming at you that he is the center of the stage. "Come here and get me, fool," he says. "You can't, 'cause you don't know who I am. You don't know *where* I am. I'm human intelligence and you don't even know if I'm good or evil." This has been his essential message to America all these years. It is intolerable to our American mentality that the figure who is probably most prominent to us after the president is simply not comprehensible, for he could be a demon or a saint. Or both! Richard Nixon, at least, appears comprehensible. We can hate him or we can vote for him, but at least we disagree with each other about him. What kills us about a.k.a. Cassius Clay is that the disagreement is inside us. He is *fascinating*—attraction and repulsion must be in the same package. So, he is obsessive. The more we don't want to think about him, the more we are obliged to. There is a reason for it. He is America's Greatest Ego. He is also, as I am going to try to show, the swiftest embodiment of human intelligence we have had yet, he is the very spirit of the twentieth century, he is the prince of mass man and the media. Now, perhaps temporarily, he is the fallen prince. But there still may be one holocaust of an urge to understand him, or try to, for obsession is a disease. Twenty little obsessions are twenty leeches on the mind, and one big obsession can become one big operation if we refuse to live with it. If Muhammad Ali defeats Frazier in the return bout, then he'll become the national obsession and we'll elect him president yet—you may indeed have to vote for any man who could defeat a fighter as great as Joe Frazier and still be Muhammad Ali. That's a great combination!

Yes, ego—that officious and sometimes efficient exercise of ignorance-as-authority—must be the central phenomenon of the twentieth century, even if patriotic Americans like to pretend it does not exist in their heroes. Which, of course, is part of the holy American horseball. The most monstrous exhibition of ego by a brave man in many a year was Alan Shepard's three whacks at a golf ball while standing on the moon. There, in a space suit, hardly able to stand, he put a club head on an omnipurpose tool shaft, and, restricted to swinging his one arm, dibbled his golf ball on the second try. On the third it went maybe half a mile—a nonphenomenal distance in the low gravitational field of the lunar sphere.

"What's so unpleasant about that?" asked a pleasant young jet-setter.

Aquarius, of the old book, loftily replied, "Would you take a golf ball into St. Patrick's and see how far you can hit it?"

The kid nodded his head. "Now that you put it that way, I guess I wouldn't, but I was excited when it happened. I said to my wife, 'Honey, we're playing golf on the moon.'"

Well, to the average fight fan, Cassius Clay has been golf on the moon. Who can comprehend the immensity of ego involved? Every fighter is in a whirligig with his ego. The fight game, for example, is filled with legends of fighters who found a girl in an elevator purposefully stalled between floors for two minutes on the afternoon of a main-event fight. Later, after he blew the fight, his irate manager blew his ears. "Were you crazy?" the manager asked. "Why did you do it?"

"Because," said the fighter, "I get these terrible headaches every afternoon, and only a chick who knows how, can relieve them."

Ego is driving a point through to a conclusion you are obliged to reach without knowing too much about the ground you cross between. You suffer for a larger point. Every good prizefighter must have a large ego, then, because he is trying to demolish a man he doesn't know too much about, he is unfeeling—which is the ground floor of ego; and he is full of techniques—which are the wings of ego. What separates the noble ego of the prizefighters from the lesser ego of authors is that the fighter goes through experiences in the ring which are occasionally immense, incommunicable except to fighters who have been as good, or to women who have gone through every minute of an anguish-filled birth, experiences which are finally mysterious. Like men who climb mountains, it is an exercise of ego which becomes something like soul—just as technology may have begun to have transcended itself when we reached to the moon. So, two great fighters in a great fight travel down subterranean rivers of exhaustion and cross mountain peaks of agony, stare at the light of their own death in the eye of the man they are fighting, travel into the crossroads of the most excruciating choice of karma as they get up from the floor against the appeal of the sweet swooning catacombs of oblivion—it is just that we do not see them this way, because they are not primarily men of words, and this is the century of words, numbers, and symbols. Enough.

We have come to the point. There are languages other than words, languages of symbol and languages of nature. There are languages of the body. And prizefighting is one of them. There is no attempting to comprehend a prizefighter unless we are willing to recognize that he speaks with a command of the body which is as detached, subtle, and comprehensive in its intelligence as any exercise of mind by such social engineers as Herman Kahn or Henry Kissinger. Of course, a man like Herman Kahn is by report gifted with a bulk of three hundred pounds. He does not move around with a light foot. So many a good average prizefighter, just a little punchy, does not speak with any particular éclat. That doesn't mean he is incapable of expressing himself with wit, style, and an esthetic flair for surprise when he boxes with his body, any more than Kahn's obesity would keep us from recognizing that his mind can work with strength. Boxing is a dialogue between bodies. Ignorant men, usually black, and next to illiterate, address one another in a set of *conversational* exchanges which go deep into the heart of each other's matter. It is just that they converse with their physiques. But unless you believe that you cannot receive a mortal wound from an incisive remark, you may be forced to accept the novel idea that men doing friendly boxing have a conversation on which they can often thrive. William Buckley and I in a discussion in a living room for an evening will score points on one another, but enjoy it. On television, where the stakes may be more, we may still both enjoy it. But put us in a debating hall with an argument to go on without cease for twenty-four hours, every encouragement present to humiliate each other, and months of preparation for such a debate hooplas and howlers of publicity, our tongues stuck out at one another on TV, and repercussions in Vietnam depending on which one of us should win, then add the fatigue of harsh lights, and a moderator who keeps interrupting us, and we are at the beginning of a conversation in which at least one of us will be hurt, and maybe both. Even hurt seriously. The example is picayune, however, in relation to the demands of a fifteen-round fight—perhaps we should have to debate nonstop for weeks under those conditions before one of us was carried away comatose. Now the example becomes clearer: Boxing is a rapid debate between two sets of intelligence. It takes place rapidly because it is conducted with the body rather than the mind. If this seems extreme, let us look for a connection. Picasso could never do arithmetic when he was young because the number seven looked to him like a nose upside down. So to learn arithmetic would slow him up. He was a future painter—his intelligence resided somewhere in the coordination of the body and the mind. He was not going to cut off his body from his mind by learning numbers. But most of us do. We have minds which work fairly well and bodies which sometimes don't. But if we are white and want to be comfortable we put our emphasis on learning to talk with the mind. Ghetto cultures, black, Puerto Rican, and Chicano cultures having less expectation of comfort tend to stick with the wit their bodies provide. They speak to each other with their bodies, they signal with their clothes. They talk with many a silent telepathic intelligence. And doubtless feel the frustration of being unable to express the subtleties of their states in words, just as the average middle-class white will feel unable to carry out his dreams of glory by the uses of his body. If black people are also beginning to speak our mixture of formal English and jargon-polluted American with real force, so white corporate America is getting more sexual and more athletic. Yet to begin to talk about Ali and Frazier, their psyches, their styles, their honor, their character, their greatness, and their flaws, we have to recognize that there is no way to comprehend them as men like ourselves—we can only guess at their insides by a real jump of our imagination into the science Ali invented—he was the first psychologist of the body.

Okay. There are fighters who are men's men. Rocky Marciano was one of them. Oscar Bonavena and Jerry Quarry and George Chuvalo and Gene Fullmer and Carmen Basilio, to name a few, have faces which would give a Marine sergeant pause in a bar fight. They look like they could take you out with the knob of bone they have left for a nose. They are all, incidentally, white fighters. They have a code—it is to fight until they are licked, and if they have to take a punch for every punch they give, well, they figure they can win. Their ego and their body intelligence are both connected to the same source of juice—it is male pride. They are substances close to rock. They work on clumsy skills to hone them finer, knowing if they can obtain parity, blow for blow with any opponent, they will win. They have more guts. Up to a far-gone point, pain is their pleasure, for their character in combat is their strength to trade pain for pain, loss of faculty for loss of faculty.

One can cite black fighters like them. Henry Hank and Reuben Carter, Emile Griffith and Benny Paret. Joe Frazier would be the best of them. But black fighters tend to be complex. They have veins of unsuspected strength and streaks when they feel as spooked as wild horses. Any fight promoter in the world knew he had a good fight if Fullmer went against Basilio, it was a proposition as certain as the wages for the week. But black fighters were artists, they were relatively moody, they were full of the surprises of Patterson or Liston, the virtuosities of Archie Moore and Sugar Ray, the speed, savagery, and curious lack of substance in Jimmy Ellis, the vertiginous neuroses of giants like Buster Mathis. Even Joe Louis, recognized by a majority in the years of his own championship as the greatest heavyweight of all time, was surprisingly inconsistent with minor fighters like Buddy Baer. Part of the unpredictability of their performances was due to the fact that all but Moore and Robinson were heavyweights. Indeed, white champions in the top division were equally out of form from fight to fight. It can, in fact, be said that heavyweights are always the most lunatic of prizefighters. The closer a heavyweight comes to the championship, the more natural it is for him to be a little bit insane, secretly insane, for the heavyweight champion of the world is either the toughest man in the world or he is not, but there is a real possibility he is. It is like being the big toe of God. You have nothing to measure yourself by. Lightweights, welterweights, middleweights can all be exceptionally good, fantastically talented— they are still very much in their place. The best lightweight in the world knows that an unranked middleweight can defeat him on most nights, and the best middleweight in the world will kill him every night. He knows that the biggest strongman in a tough bar could handle him by sitting on him, since the power to punch seems to increase quickly with weight. A fighter who weighs two-forty will punch more than twice as hard as a fighter who weighs one-twenty. The figures have no real basis, of course, they are only there to indicate the law of the ring: a good big man beats a good little man. So the notion of prizefighters as hardworking craftsmen is most likely to be true in the light and middle divisions. Since they are fighters who know their limitations, they are likely to strive for excellence in their category. The better they get, the closer they have come to sanity, at least if we are ready to assume that the average fighter is a buried artist, which is to say a *body* artist with an extreme amount of violence in him. Obviously the better and more successful they get, the more they have been able to transmute violence into craft, discipline, even body art. That is human alchemy. We respect them and they deserve to be respected.

But the heavyweights never have such simple sanity. If they become champions they have to have inner lives like Hemingway or Dostoyevsky, Tolstoy or Faulkner, Joyce or Melville or Conrad or Lawrence or Proust. Hemingway is the example above all. Because he wished to be the greatest writer in the history of literature and still be a hero with all the body arts age would yet grant him, he was alone and he knew it. So are heavyweight champions alone. Dempsey was alone and Tunney could never explain himself and Sharkey could never believe himself nor Schmeling nor Braddock, and Carnera was sad and Baer an indecipherable clown; great heavyweights like Louis had the loneliness of the ages in their silence, and men like Marciano were mystified by a power which seemed to have been granted them. With the advent, however, of the great modern black heavyweights, Patterson, Liston, then Clay and Frazier, perhaps the loneliness gave way to what it had been protecting itself against—a surrealistic situation unstable beyond belief. Being a black heavyweight champion in the second half of the twentieth century (with black revolutions opening all over the world) was now not unlike being Jack Johnson, Malcolm X, and Frank Costello all in one. Going down the aisle and into the ring in Chicago was conceivably more frightening for Sonny Liston than facing Patterson that night—he was raw as uncoated wire with his sense of retribution awaiting him for years of prison pleasures and underworld jobs. Pools of paranoia must have reached him like different washes of color from different sides of the arena. He was a man who had barely learned to read and write—he had none of the impacted and mediocre misinformation of all the world of daily dull reading to clot the antenna of his senses—so he was keen to every hatred against him. He knew killers were waiting in that mob, they always were, he had been on speaking terms with just such subjects himself—now he dared to be king—any assassin could strike for his revenge upon acts Liston had long forgot; no wonder Liston was in fear going into the ring, and happier once within it.

And Patterson was exhausted before the fight began. Lonely as a monk for years, his daily gym work the stuff of his meditation, he was the first of the black fighters to be considered, then used, as a political force. He was one of the liberal elite, an Eleanor Roosevelt darling, he was political mileage for the NAACP. Violent, conceivably to the point of murder if he had not been a fighter, he was a gentleman in public, more, he was a man of the nicest, quietest, most private good manners. But monastic by inclination. Now, all but uneducated, he was appealed to by political blacks to win the Liston fight for the image of the Negro. Responsibility sat upon him like a comic cutback in a silent film where we return now and again to one poor man who has been left to hold a beam across his shoulders. There he stands, hardly able to move. At the end of the film he collapses. That was the weight put on Patterson. The responsibility to beat Liston was too great to bear. Patterson, a fighter of incorruptible honesty, was knocked out by punches hardly anybody saw. He fell in open air as if seized by a stroke. The age of surrealistic battles had begun. In the second fight with Liston, Patterson, obviously more afraid of a repetition of the first nightmare than anything else, simply charged his opponent with his hands low and was knocked down three times and out in the first round. The age of body psychology had begun and Clay was there to conceive it.

A kid as wild and dapper and jaybird as the president of a down-home college fraternity, bow tie, brown-and-white shoes, sweet, happy-go-lucky, *raucous,* he descended on Vegas for the second Patterson-Liston fight. He was like a beautiful boy surrounded by doting aunts. The classiest-looking middle-aged Negro ladies were always flanking him in Vegas as if to set up a female field of repulsion against any evil black magnetic forces in the offing. And from the sanctuary of his ability to move around crap tables like a kitten on the frisk, he taunted black majestic king-size Liston before the fight and after the fight. "You're so ugly," he would jeer, crap table safely between them, "that I don't know how you can get any uglier."

"Why don't you sit on my knee and I'll feed you your orange juice," Liston would rumble back.

"Don't insult me, or you'll be sorry. 'Cause you're just an ugly slow bear."

They would pretend to rush at one another. Smaller men would hold them back without effort. They were building the gate for the next fight. And Liston was secretly fond of Clay. He would chuckle when he talked about him. It was years since Liston had failed to knock out his opponent in the first round. His charisma was majestic with menace. One held one's breath when near him. He looked forward with obvious amusement to the happy seconds when he would take Clay apart and see the expression on that silly face. In Miami he trained for a three-round fight. In the famous fifth round when Clay came out with caustic in his eyes and could not see, he waved his gloves at Liston, a look of abject horror on his face, as if to say, "Your younger brother is now an old blind beggar. Do not strike him." And did it with a peculiar authority. For Clay looked like a ghost with his eyes closed, tears streaming, his extended gloves waving in front of him like a widow's entreaties. Liston drew back in doubt, in bewilderment, conceivably in concern for his new great reputation as an ex-bully; yes, Liston reacted like a gentleman, and Clay was home free. His eyes watered out the caustic, his sight came back. He cut Liston up in the sixth. He left him beaten and exhausted. Liston did not stand up for the bell to the seventh. Maybe Clay had even defeated him earlier that day at the weigh-in when he had harangued and screamed and shouted and whistled and stuck his tongue out at Liston. The Champ had been bewildered. No one had been able ever to stare him in the eyes these last four years. Now a boy was screaming at him, a boy reported to belong to Black Muslims, no, stronger than that, a boy favored by Malcolm X who was braver by reputation than the brave, for he could stop a bullet any day. Liston, afraid only, as he put it, of crazy men, was afraid of the Muslims for he could not contend with their allegiance to one another in prison, their puritanism, their discipline, their martial ranks. The combination was too complex, too unfamiliar. Now, their boy, in a pain of terror or in a mania of courage, was screaming at him at the weigh-in. Liston sat down and shook his head, and looked at the press, now become his friend, and wound his fingers in circles around his ears, as if saying, Whitey to Whitey, "That black boy's nuts." So Clay made Liston Tom it, and when Liston missed the first jab he threw in the fight by a foot and a half, one knew the night would not be ordinary in the offing.

For their return bout in Boston, Liston trained as he had never before. Clay got a hernia. Liston trained hard. Hard training as a fighter grows older seems to speak of the dull deaths of the brightest cells in all the favorite organs; old fighters react to training like beautiful women to washing floors. But Liston did it twice, once for Clay's hernia, and again for their actual fight in Maine, and the second time he trained, he aged as a fighter, for he had a sparring partner, Amos Lincoln, who was one of the better heavyweights in the country. They had wars with one another every afternoon in the gym. By the day before the fight, Liston was as relaxed and sleepy and dopey as a man in a steambath. He had fought his heart out in training, had done it under constant pressure from Clay who kept telling the world that Liston was old and slow and could not possibly win. And their fight created a scandal, for Liston ran into a short punch in the first round and was counted out, unable to hear the count. The referee and timekeeper missed signals with one another while Clay stood over fallen Liston screaming, "Get up and fight!" It was no night for the fight game, and a tragedy for Clay since he had trained for a long and arduous fight. He had developed his technique for a major encounter with Liston and was left with a horde of unanswered questions including the one he could never admit—which was whether there had been the magic of a real knockout in his punch or if Liston had made—for what variety of reasons!—a conscious decision to stay on the floor. It did him no good.

He had taken all the lessons of his curious life and the outrageously deep comprehension he had of the motivations of his own people—indeed, one could even approach the beginnings of a Psychology of the Blacks by studying his encounters with fighters who were black—and had elaborated that into a technique for boxing which was almost without compare. A most cultivated technique. For he was no child of the slums. His mother was a gracious pale-skinned lady, his father a bitter wit pride-oriented on the family name of Clay—they were descendants of Henry Clay, the orator, on the white side of the family, nothing less, and Cassius began boxing at twelve in a police gym, and from the beginning was a phenomenon of style and the absence of pain, for he knew how to use his physical endowment. Tall, relatively light, with an exceptionally long reach even for his size, he developed defensive skills which made the best use of his body. Working apparently on the premise that there was something obscene about being hit, he boxed with his head back and drew it further back when attacked, like a kid who is shy of punches in a street fight, but because he had a waist which was more supple than the average fighter's neck, he was able to box with his arms low, surveying the fighter in front of him, avoiding punches by the speed of his feet, the reflexes of his waist, the long spoiling deployment of his arms which were always tipping other fighters off balance. Added to this was his psychological comprehension of the vanity and confusion of other fighters. A man in the ring is a performer as well as a gladiator. Elaborating his technique from the age of twelve, Clay knew how to work on the vanity of other performers, knew how to make them feel ridiculous and so force them into crucial mistakes, knew how to set such a tone from the first round—later he was to know how to begin it a year before he would even meet the man. Clay knew that a fighter who had been put in psychological knots before he got near the ring had already lost half, three quarters, no, all of the fight could be lost before the first punch. That was the psychology of the body.

Now, add his curious ability as a puncher. He knew that the heaviest punches, systematically delivered, meant little. There are club fighters who look like armadillos and alligators—you can bounce punches off them forever and they never go down. You can break them down only if they are in a profound state of confusion, and the bombardment of another fighter's fists is never their confusion but their expectation. So Clay punched with a greater variety of mixed intensities than anyone around, he played with punches, was tender with them, laid them on as delicately as you put a postage stamp on an envelope, then cracked them in like a riding crop across your face, stuck a cruel jab like a baseball bat held head on into your mouth, next waltzed you in a clinch with a tender arm around your neck, winged away out of reach on flying legs, dug a hook with the full swing of a baseball bat hard into your ribs, hard pokes of a jab into the face, a mocking soft flurry of pillows and gloves, a mean forearm cutting you off from coming up on him, a cruel wrestling of your neck in a clinch, then elusive again, gloves snake-licking your face like a whip. By the time Clay had defeated Liston once and was training for the second fight, by the time Clay, now champion and renamed Muhammad Ali, and bigger, grown up quickly and not so mysteriously (after the potent ego soups and marrows of his trip through Muslim Africa) into a Black Prince, Potentate of his people, new Poombah of Polemic, yes, by this time, Clay—we will find it more natural to call him Ali from here on out (for the Prince will behave much like a young god)—yes, Muhammad Ali, Heavyweight Champion of the World, having come back with an amazing commitment to be leader of his people, proceeded to go into training for the second Liston fight with a commitment and then a genius of comprehension for the true intricacies of the Science of Sock. He alternated the best of sparring partners and the most ordinary, worked rounds of dazzling speed with Jimmy Ellis—later, of course, to be champion himself before Frazier knocked him out— rounds which displayed the high esthetic of boxing at its best, then lay against the ropes with other sparring partners, hands at his sides as if it were the eleventh or thirteenth round of an excruciating and exhausting fight with Liston where Ali was now so tired he could not hold his hands up, could just manage to take punches to the stomach, rolling with them, smothering them with his stomach, absorbing them with backward moves, sliding along the ropes, steering his sparring partner with passive but off-setting moves of his limp arms. For a minute, for two minutes, the sparring partner—Shotgun Sheldon was his name— would bomb away on Ali's stomach much as if Liston were tearing him apart in later rounds, and Ali weaving languidly, sliding his neck for the occasional overhead punch to his face, bouncing from the rope into the punches, bouncing back away from the punches, as if his torso had become some huge boxing glove to absorb punishment, had penetrated through into some further conception of pain, as if pain were not pain if you accepted it with a relaxed heart, yes, Ali let himself be bombarded on the ropes by the powerful bull-like swings of Shotgun Sheldon, the expression of his face as remote, and as searching for the last routes into the nerves of each punch going in as a man hanging on a subway strap will search into the meaning of the market quotations he has just read on the activities of a curious stock. So Ali relaxed on the ropes and took punches to the belly with a faint disdain, as if, curious punches they did not go deep enough and after a minute of this, or two minutes, having offered his body like the hide of a drum for a mad drummer's solo, he would snap out of his communion with himself and flash a tattoo of light and slashing punches, mocking as the lights on water, he would dazzle his sparring partner, who, arm-weary and punched out, would look at him with eyes of love, complete was his admiration. And if people were ever going to cry watching a boxer in training, those were the moments, for Ali had the far-off concentration and disdain of an artist who simply cannot find anyone near enough or good enough to keep him and his art engaged, and all the while was perfecting the essence of his art, which was to make the other fighter fall secretly, helplessly, in love with him. Bundini, a special trainer, an alter ego with the same harsh, demoniac, witty, nonstop powers of oration as Ali himself—he even looked a little like Ali—used to weep openly as he watched the workouts.

Training session over, Ali would lecture the press, instruct them—looking beyond his Liston defense to what he would do to Patterson, mocking Patterson, calling him a rabbit, a white man's rabbit, knowing he was putting a new beam on Patterson's shoulders, an outrageously helpless and heavy beam of rage, fear, hopeless anger and secret black admiration for the all-out force of Ali's effrontery. And in the next instant Ali would be charming as a movie star on the make speaking tenderly to a child. If he was Narcissus, so he was as well the play of mood in the water which served as mirror to Narcissus. It was as if he knew he had disposed of Patterson already, that the precise attack of calling him a rabbit would work on the weakest link—wherever it was—in Patterson's tense and tortured psyche and Patterson would crack, as indeed, unendurably for himself, he did, when their fight took place. Patterson's back gave way in the early rounds, and he fought twisted and in pain, half crippled like a man with a sacroiliac, for eleven brave and most miserable rounds before the referee would call it and Ali, breaking up with his first wife then, was unpleasant in the ring that night, his face ugly and contemptuous, himself well on the way to becoming America's most unpopular major American. That, too, was part of the art—to get a public to the point of hating him so much the burden on the other fighter approached the metaphysical—which is where Ali wanted it. White fighters with faces like rock embedded in cement would trade punch for punch. Ali liked to get the boxing where it belonged—he would trade metaphysic for metaphysic with anyone.

So he went on winning his fights and growing forever more unpopular. How he inflamed the temper of boxing's white establishment, for they were for the most part a gaggle of avuncular drunks and hardbitten hacks who were ready to fight over every slime-slicked penny, and squared a few of their slippery crimes by getting fighters to show up semblance-of-sober at any available parish men's rally and charity church breakfast—"Everything I am I owe to boxing," the fighter would mumble through his dentures while elements of gin, garlic, and goddess-of-a-girlie from the night before came off in the bright morning fumes.

Ali had them psyched. He cut through moribund coruscated dirty business corridors, cut through cigar smoke and bushwah, hypocrisy and well-aimed kicks to the back of the neck, cut through crooked politicians and patriotic pus, cut like a laser, point of the point, light and impersonal, cut to the heart of the rottenest meat in boxing, and boxing was always the buried South Vietnam of America, buried for fifty years in our hide before we went there, yes, Ali cut through the flag-dragooned salutes of drunken dawns and said, "I got no fight with those Vietcongs," and they cut him down, thrust him into the three and a half years of his martyrdom. Where he grew. Grew to have a little fat around his middle and a little of the complacement muscle of the clam to his world-ego. And grew sharper in mind as well, and deepened and broadened physically. Looked no longer like a boy, but a sullen man, almost heavy, with the beginnings of a huge expanse across his shoulders. And developed the patience to survive, the wisdom to contemplate future nights in jail, grew to cultivate suspension of belief and the avoidance of disbelief—what a rack for a young man! As the years of hope for reinstatement, or avoidance of prison, came up and waned in him, Ali walked the tightrope between bitterness and apathy, and had enough left to beat Quarry and beat Bonavena, beat Quarry in the flurry of a missed hundred punches, ho! how his timing was off! beat him with a calculated whip, snake-like whip, to the corrugated sponge of dead flesh over Quarry's Irish eyes—they stopped it after the third on cuts—then knocked out Bonavena, the indestructible, never stopped before, by working the art of crazy mixing in the punches he threw at the rugged—some of the punches Ali threw that night would not have hurt a little boy—the punch he let go in the fifteenth came in like a wrecking ball from outer space. Bonavena went sprawling across the ring. He was a house coming down.

Yet it may have been the blow which would defeat him later. For Ali had been tired with Bonavena, lackluster, winded, sluggish, far ahead on points but in need of the most serious work if he were to beat Frazier. The punch in the last round was obliged, therefore, to inflame his belief that the forces of magic were his, there to be called upon when most in need, that the silent leagues of black support for his cause—since their cause was as his own—were like some cloak of midnight velvet, there to protect him by black blood, by black sense of tragedy, by the black consciousness that the guilt of the world had become the hinge of a door that they would open. So they would open the way to Frazier's chin, the blacks would open the aisle for his trip to the gods.

Therefore he did not train for Frazier as perhaps he had to. He worked, he ran three miles a day when he could have run five, he boxed some days and let a day and perhaps another day go, he was relaxed, he was confident, he basked in the undemanding winter sun of Miami, and skipped his rope in a gym crowded with fighters, stuffed now with working fighters looking to be seen, Ali comfortable and relaxed like the greatest of movie stars, he played a young fighter working out in a corner on the heavy bag—for of course every eye was on him—and afterward doing sit-ups in the back room and having his stomach rubbed with liniment, he would talk to reporters. He was filled with confidence there was no black fighter he did not comprehend to the root of the valve in the hard-pumping heart, and yes, Frazier, he assured everybody, would be easier than they realized. Like a little boy who had grown up to take on a mountain of responsibility he spoke in the deep relaxation of the wise, and teased two of the reporters who were present and fat. "You want to drink a lot of water," he said, "good cold water instead of all that liquor rot-your-gut," and gave the smile of a man who had been able to intoxicate himself on water (although he was, by repute, a fiend for soft drinks), "and fruit and good clean vegetables you want to eat and chicken and steak. You lose weight then," he advised out of kind secret smiling thoughts, and went on to talk of the impact of the fight upon the world. "Yes," he said, "you just think of a stadium with a million people, ten million people, you could get them all in to watch they would all pay to see it live, but then you think of the hundreds of millions and the billions who are going to see this fight, and if you could sit them all down in one place, and fly a jet plane over them, why that plane would have to fly for an hour before he would reach the end of all the people who will see this fight. It's the greatest event in the history of the world, and you take a man like Frazier, a good fighter, but a simple hardworking fellow, he's not built for this kind of pressure, the eyes," Ali said softly, "of that many people upon him. There's an experience to pressure which I have had, fighting a man like Liston in Miami the first time, which he has not. He will cave in under the pressure. No, I do not see any way a man like Frazier can whup me, he can't reach me, my arms are too long, and if he does get in and knock me down I'll never make the mistake of Quarry and Foster or Ellis of rushing back at him, I'll stay away until my head clears, then I begin to pop him again, pop! pop!" a few jabs, "no there is no way this man can beat me, this fight will be easier than you think."

There was one way in which boxing was still like a street fight and that was in the need to be confident you would win. A man walking out of a bar to fight with another man is seeking to compose his head into the confidence that he will certainly triumph—it is the most mysterious faculty of the ego. For that confidence is a sedative against the pain of punches and yet is the sanction to punch your own best. The logic of the spirit would suggest that you win only if you deserve to win: the logic of the ego lays down the axiom that if you don't think you will win, you don't deserve to. And, in fact, usually don't; it is as if not believing you will win opens you to the guilt that perhaps you have not the right, you are too guilty.

So training camps are small factories for the production of one rare psychological item—an ego able to bear huge pain and administer drastic punishment. The flow of Ali's ego poured over the rock of every distraction, it was an ego like the flow of a river of constant energy fed by a hundred tributaries of black love and the love of the white left. The construction of the ego of Joe Frazier was of another variety. His manager, Yancey "Yank" Durham, a canny foxy light-skinned Negro with a dignified mien, a gray head of hair, gray mustache and a small but conservative worthy's paunch, plus the quick-witted look of eyes which could spot from a half mile away any man coming toward him with a criminal thought, was indeed the face of a consummate jeweler who had worked for years upon a diamond in the rough until he was now and at last a diamond, hard as the transmutation of black carbon from the black earth into the brilliant sky-blue shadow of the rarest shining rock. What a fighter was Frazier, what a diamond of an ego had he, and what a manager was Durham. Let us look.

Sooner or later, fight metaphors, like fight managers, go sentimental. They go military. But there is no choice here. Frazier was the human equivalent of a war machine. He had tremendous firepower. He had a great left hook, a left hook frightening even to watch when it missed, for it seemed to whistle; he had a powerful right. He could knock a man out with either hand—not all fighters can, not even very good fighters. Usually, however, he clubbed opponents to death, took a punch, gave a punch, took three punches, gave two, took a punch, gave a punch, high speed all the way, always working, pushing his body and arms, short for a heavyweight, up through the middle, bombing through on force, reminiscent of Jimmy Brown knocking down tacklers, Frazier kept on coming, hard and fast, a hang-in, hang-on, go-and-get him, got-him, got-him, slip and punch, take a punch, wing a punch, whap a punch, never was Frazier happier than with his heart up on the line against some other man's heart, let the bullets fly—his heart was there to stand up at the last. Sooner or later, the others almost all fell down. Undefeated like Ali, winner of twenty-three out of twenty-six fights by knockout, he was a human force, certainly the greatest heavyweight force to come along since Rocky Marciano. (If those two men had ever met, it would have been like two Mack trucks hitting each other head-on, then backing up to hit each other again—they would have kept it up until the wheels were off the axles and the engines off the chassis.) But this would be a different kind of fight. Ali would run, Ali would keep hitting Frazier with long jabs, quick hooks and rights while backing up, backing up, staying out of reach unless Frazier could take the punishment and get in. That was where the military problem began. For getting in against the punishment he would take was a question of morale, and there was a unique situation in this fight—Frazier had become the white man's fighter, Mr. Charley was rooting for Frazier, and that meant blacks were boycotting him in their heart. That could be poison to Frazier's morale, for he was twice as black as Clay and half as handsome, he had the rugged decent life-worked face of a man who had labored in the pits all his life, he looked like the deserving modest son of one of those Negro cleaning women of a bygone age who worked from six in the morning to midnight every day, raised a family, endured and occasionally elicited the exasperated admiration of white ladies who would kindly remark, "That woman deserves something better in her life." Frazier had the mien of the son, one of many, of such a woman, and he was the hardest-working fighter in training many a man had ever seen, he was conceivably the hardest-working man alive in the world, and as he went through his regimen, first boxing four rounds with a sparring partner, Kenny Norton, a talented heavyweight from the Coast with an almost unbeaten record, then working on the heavy bag, then the light bag, then skipping rope, ten to twelve rounds of sparring and exercise on a light day, Frazier went on with the doggedness, the concentration, and the pumped-up fury of a man who has had so little in his life that he can endure torments to get everything, he pushed the total of his energy and force into an absolute abstract exercise of will so it did not matter if he fought a sparring partner or the heavy bag, he lunged at each equally as if the exhaustion of his own heart and the clangor of his lungs were his only enemies, and the head of a fighter or the leather of the bag as it rolled against his own head was nothing but some abstract thunk of material, not a thing, not a man, but thunk! thunk! something of an obstacle, thunk! thunk! thunk! to beat into thunk! oblivion. And his breath came in rips and sobs as he smashed into the bag as if it were real, just that heavy big torso-sized bag hanging from its chain but he attacked it as if it were a bear, as if it were a great fighter and they were in the mortal embrace of a killing set of exchanges of punches in the middle of the eighth round, and rounds of exercise later, skipping rope to an inhumanly fast beat for this late round in the training day, sweat pouring like jets of blood from an artery, he kept swinging his rope, muttering, "Two-million-dollars-and-change, two-million-dollars-and-change," railroad train chugging into the terminals of exhaustion. And it was obvious that Durham, jeweler to his diamond, was working to make the fight as abstract as he could for Frazier, to keep Clay out of it—for they would not call him Ali in their camp—yes, Frazier was fortifying his ego by depersonalizing his opponent, Clay was, thunk! the heavy bag, thunk! and thunk!—Frazier was looking to get no messages from that cavern of velvet when black people sent their good wishes to Ali at midnight, no, Frazier would insulate himself with prodigies of work, hardest-working man in the hell-hole of the world, and on and on he drove himself into the depressions each day of killing daily exhaustion.

That was one half of the strategy to isolate Frazier from Ali, hard work and thinking of thunking on inanimate Clay; the other half was up to Durham who was running front relations with the blacks of North Philly who wandered into the gym, paid their dollar, and were ready to heckle on Frazier. In the four rounds he boxed with Norton, Frazier did not look too good for a while. It was ten days before the fight and he was in a bad mood when he came in, for the word was through the gym that they had discovered one of his favorite sparring partners, just fired that morning, was a Black Muslim and had been calling Ali every night with reports, that was the rumor, and Frazier, sullen and cold at the start, was bopped and tapped, then walloped by Norton moving fast with the big training gloves in imitation of Ali, and Frazier looked very easy to hit until the middle of the third round when Norton, proud of his something like twenty wins and one loss, beginning to get some ideas himself about how to fight champions, came driving in to mix it with Frazier, have it out man to man and caught a right which dropped him, left him looking limp with that half-silly smile sparring partners get when they have been hit too hard to justify any experience or any money they are going to take away. Up till then the crowd had been with Norton. There at one end of the Cloverlay gym, a street-level storefront room which could have been used originally by an automobile dealer, there on that empty, immaculate Lysol-soaked floor, designed when Frazier was there for only Frazier and his partners to train (as opposed to Miami where Ali would rub elbows with the people) here the people were at one end, the end off the street, and they jeered whenever Norton hit Frazier, they laughed when Norton made him look silly, they called out, "Drop the mother," until Durham held up a gentlemanly but admonishing finger in request for silence. Afterward, however, training completed, Durham approached them to answer questions, rolled with their sallies, jived the people back, subtly enlisted their sympathy for Frazier by saying, "When I fight Clay, I'm going to get him somewhere in the middle rounds," until the blacks quipping back said angrily, "You ain't fighting him, Frazier is."

"Why you call him Clay?" another asked. "He Ali."

"His name is Cassius Clay to me," said Durham.

"What you say against his religion?"

"I don't say nothing about his religion and he doesn't say anything about mine. I'm a Baptist."

"You going to make money on this?"

"Of course," said Durham, "I got to make money. You don't think I work up this sweat for nothing."

They loved him. He was happy with them. A short fat man in a purple suit wearing his revival of the wide-brim bebop hat said to Durham, "Why don't you get Norton to manage? He was beating up on *your* fighter," and the fat man cackled for he had scored and could elaborate the tale for his ladies later how he had put down Yank, who was working the daily rite on the edge of the black street for his fighter, while upstairs, dressed, and sucking an orange, sweat still pouring, gloom of excessive fatigue upon him, Frazier was sitting through his two-hundredth or two-thousandth interview for this fight, reluctant indeed to give it at all. "Some get it, some don't," he had said for refusal, but relented when a white friend who had done roadwork with him interceded, so he sat there now against a leather sofa, dark blue suit, dark T-shirt, mopping his brow with a pink-red towel, and spoke dispiritedly of being ready too early for the fight. He was waking up an hour too early for roadwork each morning now. "I'd go back to sleep but it doesn't feel good when I do run."

"I guess the air is better that hour of the morning."

He nodded sadly. "There's a limit to how good the air in Philly can get."

"Where'd you begin to sing?" was a question asked.

"I sang in church first," he replied, but it was not the day to talk about singing. The loneliness of hitting the bag still seemed upon him as if in his exhaustion now, and in the thoughts of that small insomnia which woke him an hour too early every day was something of the loneliness of all blacks who work very hard and are isolated from fun and must wonder in the just-awakened night how large and pervasive was the curse of a people. "The countdown's begun," said Frazier, "I get impatient about now."

For the fight, Ali was wearing red velvet trunks, Frazier had green. Before they began, even before they were called together by the referee for instructions, Ali went dancing around the ring and glided past Frazier with a sweet little-boy smile, as if to say, "You're my new playmate. We're going to have fun." Ali was laughing. Frazier was having nothing of this and turned his neck to embargo him away. Ali, having alerted the crowd by this first big move, came prancing in again. When Frazier looked ready to block him, Ali went around, evading a contact, gave another sweet smile, shook his head at the lack of high spirit. "Poor Frazier," he seemed to say.

At the weigh-in early that afternoon Ali looked physically resplendent; the night before in Harlem, crowds had cheered him; he was coming to claim his victory on the confluence of two mighty tides—he was the mightiest victim of injustice in America and he was also—the twentieth century was nothing if not a tangle of opposition—he was also the mightiest narcissist in the land. Every beard, dropout, homosexual, junkie, freak, swinger, and plain simple individualist adored him. Every pedantic liberal soul who had once loved Patterson now paid homage to Ali. The mightiest of the black psyches and the most filigreed of the white psyches were ready to roar him home, as well as every family-loving hardworking square American who genuinely hated the war in Vietnam. What a tangle of ribbons he carried on his lance, enough cross purposes to be the knight-resplendent of television, the fell hero of the medium, and he had a look of unique happiness on television when presenting his program for the course of the fight, and his inevitable victory. He would be as content then as an infant splashing the waters of the bathinette. If he was at once a saint and a monster to any mind which looked for category, any mind unwilling to encounter the thoroughly dread-filled fact that the twentieth century breed of man now in birth might be no longer half good and half evil—generous and greedy by turns—but a mutation with Cassius Muhammad for the first son—then that mind was not ready to think about Twentieth Century Man. (And indeed Muhammad Ali had twin poodles he called Angel and Demon.) So now the ambiguity of his presence filled the Garden before the fight was fairly begun, it was as if he had announced to that plural billion-footed crowd assembled under the shadow of the jet which would fly over them that the first enigma of the fight would be the way he would win it, that he would initiate his triumph by getting the crowd to laugh at Frazier, yes, first premise tonight was that the poor black man in Frazier's soul would go beserk if made a figure of roll-off-your-seat amusement.

The referee gave his instructions. The bell rang. The first fifteen seconds of a fight can be the fight. It is equivalent to the first kiss in a love affair. The fighters each missed the other. Ali blocked Frazier's first punches easily, but Ali then missed Frazier's head. That head was bobbing as fast as a third fist. Frazier would come rushing in, head moving like a fist, fists bobbing too, his head working above and below his forearm, he was trying to get through Ali's jab, get through fast and sear Ali early with the terror of a long fight and punches harder than he had ever taken to the stomach, and Ali in turn, backing up, and throwing fast punches, aimed just a trifle, and was therefore a trifle too slow, but it was obvious. Ali was trying to shiver Frazier's synapses from the start, set waves of depression stirring which would reach his heart in later rounds and make him slow, deaden nerve, deaden nerve went Ali's jab flicking a snake tongue, whoo-eet! whoo-eet! but Frazier's head was bobbing too fast, he was moving faster than he had ever moved before in that bobbing nonstop never-a-backward step of his, slogging and bouncing forward, that huge left hook flaunting the air with the confidence it was enough of a club to split a tree, and Ali, having missed his jabs, stepped nimbly inside the hook and wrestled Frazier in the clinch. Ali looked stronger here. So by the first forty-five seconds of the fight, each had surprised the other profoundly. Frazier was fast enough to slip through Ali's punches, and Ali was strong enough to handle him in the clinches. A pattern had begun. Because Ali was missing often, Frazier was in under his shots like a police dog's muzzle on your arm, Ali could not slide from side to side, he was boxed in, then obliged to go backward, and would end on the ropes again and again with Frazier belaboring him. Yet Frazier could not reach him. Like a prestidigitator Ali would tie the other's punches into odd knots, not even blocking them yet on his elbows or his arms, rather throwing his own punches as defensive moves, for even as they missed, he would brush Frazier to the side with his forearm, or hold him off, or clinch and wrestle a little of the will out of Frazier's neck. Once or twice in the round a long left hook by Frazier just touched the surface of Ali's chin, and Ali waved his head in placid contempt to the billions watching as if to say, "This man has not been able to hurt me at all."

The first round set a pattern for the fight. Ali won it and would win the next. His jab was landing from time to time and rights and lefts of no great consequence. Frazier was hardly reaching him at all. Yet it looked like Frazier had established that he was fast enough to get in on Ali and so drive him to the ropes and to the corners, and that spoke of a fight which would be determined by the man in better condition, in better physical condition rather than in perfect psychic condition, the kind of fight Ali could hardly want for his strength was in his pauses, his nature passed along the curve of every dialectic, he liked, in short, to fight in flurries, and then move out, move away, assess, take his time, fight again. Frazier would not let him. Frazier moved in with the snarl of a wolf, his teeth seemed to show through his mouthpiece, he made Ali work. Ali won the first two rounds but it was obvious he could not continue to win if he had to work all the way. And in the third round Frazier began to get to him, caught Ali with a powerful blow to the face at the bell. That was the first moment where it was clear to all that Frazier had won a round. Then he won the next. Ali looked tired and a little depressed. He was moving less and less and calling upon a skill not seen since the fight with Chuvalo when he had showed his old ability, worked on all those years ago with Shotgun Sheldon, to lie on the ropes and take a beating to the stomach. He had exhausted Chuvalo by welcoming attacks on the stomach but Frazier was too incommensurable a force to allow such total attack. So Ali lay on the ropes and wrestled him off, and moved his arms and waist, blocking punches, slipping punches, countering with punches—it began to look as if the fight would be written on the ropes, but Ali was getting very tired. At the beginning of the fifth round, he got up slowly from his stool, very slowly. Frazier was beginning to feel that the fight was his. He moved in on Ali jeering, his hands at his side in mimicry of Ali, a street fighter mocking his opponent, and Ali tapped him with long light jabs to which Frazier stuck out his mouthpiece, a jeer of derision as if to suggest that the mouthpiece was all Ali would reach all night.

There is an extortion of the will beyond any of our measure in the exhaustion which comes upon a fighter in early rounds when he is already too tired to lift his arms or take advantage of openings there before him, yet the fight is not a third over, there are all those rounds to go, contractions of torture, the lungs screaming into the dungeons of the soul, washing the throat with a hot bile that once belonged to the liver, the legs are going dead, the arms move but their motion is limp, one is straining into another will, breathing into the breath of another will as agonized as one's own. As the fight moved through the fifth, the sixth and the seventh, then into the eighth, it was obvious that Ali was into the longest night of his career, and yet with that skill, that research into the pits of every miserable contingency in boxing, he came up with odd somnambulistic variations, holding Frazier off, riding around Frazier with his arm about his neck, almost entreating Frazier with his arms extended, and Frazier leaning on him, each of them slowed to a pit-a-pat of light punches back and forth until one of them was goaded up from exhaustion to whip and stick, then hook and hammer and into the belly and out, and out of the clinch and both looking exhausted, and then Frazier, mouth bared again like a wolf, going in and Ali waltzing him, tying him, tapping him lightly as if he were a speed bag, just little flicks, until Frazier, like an exhausted horse finally feeling the crop, would push up into a trot and try to run up the hill. It was indeed as if they were both running up a hill. As if Frazier's offensive was so great and so great was Ali's defense that the fight could only be decided by who could take the steepest pitch of the hill. So Frazier, driving, driving, trying to drive the heart out of Ali, put the pitch of that hill up and up until they were ascending an unendurable slope. And moved like somnambulists slowly working and rubbing one another, almost embracing, next to locked in the slow moves of lovers after the act until, reaching into the stores of energy reaching them from cells never before so used, one man or the other would work up a contractive spasm of skills and throw punches at the other in the straining slow-motion hypnosis of a deepening act. And so the first eight rounds went by. The two judges scored six for Frazier, two for Ali. The referee had it even. Some of the press had Ali ahead—it was not easy to score. For if it were an alley fight, Frazier would win. Clay was by now hardly more than the heavy bag to Frazier. Frazier was dealing with a man, not a demon. He was not respectful of that man. But still! It was Ali who was landing the majority of punches. They were light, they were usually weary, but some had snap, some were quick, he was landing two punches to Frazier's one. Yet Frazier's were hardest. And Ali often looked as tender as if he were making love. It was as if he could now feel the whole absence of that real second fight with Liston, that fight for which he had trained so long and so hard, the fight which might have rolled over his laurels from the greatest artist of pugilism to the greatest brawler of them all—maybe he had been prepared on that night to beat Liston at his own, be more of a slugger, more of a man crude to crude than Liston. Yes, Ali had never been a street fighter and never a whorehouse knock-it-down stud, no, it was more as if a man with the exquisite reflexes of Nureyev had learned to throw a knockout punch with either hand and so had become champion of the world without knowing if he was the man of all men or the most delicate with special privilege endowed by God. Now with Frazier, he was in a sweat bath (a mudpile, a knee, elbow, and death-thumping chute of a pit) having in this late year the fight he had sorely needed for his true greatness as a fighter six and seven years ago, and so whether ahead, behind or even, terror sat in the rooting instinct of all those who were for Ali for it was obviously Frazier's fight to win, and what if Ali, weaknesses of character now flickering to the surface in a hundred little moves, should enter the valve of prizefighting's deepest humiliation, should fall out half conscious on the floor and not want to get up. What a death to his followers.

The ninth began. Frazier mounted his largest body attack of the night. It was preparations-for-Liston-with-Shotgun-Sheldon, it was the virtuosity of the gym all over again, and Ali, like a catcher handling a fast-ball pitcher, took Frazier's punches, one steamer, another steamer, wing! went a screamer, a steamer, warded them, blocked them, slithered them, winced from them, absorbed them, took them in and blew them out and came off the ropes and was Ali the Magnificent for the next minute and thirty seconds. The fight turned. The troops of Ali's second corps of energy had arrived, the energy for which he had been waiting long agonizing heartsore vomit-mean rounds. Now he jabbed Frazier, he snake-licked his face with jabs faster than he had thrown before, he anticipated each attempt of Frazier at counterattack and threw it back, he danced on his toes for the first time in rounds, he popped in rights, he hurt him with hooks, it was his biggest round of the night, it was the best round yet of the fight, and Frazier full of energy and hordes of sudden punishment was beginning to move into that odd petulant concentration on other rituals besides the punches, tappings of the gloves, stares of the eye, that species of mouthpiece-chewing which is the prelude to fun-strut in the knees, then Queer Street, then waggle on out, drop like a steer.

It looked like Ali had turned the fight, looked more like the same in the tenth, now reporters were writing another story in their minds where Ali was not the magical untried Prince who had come apart under the first real pressure of his life but was rather the greatest Heavyweight Champion of all time for he had weathered the purgatory of Joe Frazier.

But in the eleventh, that story also broke. Frazier caught him, caught him again and again, and Ali was near to knocked out and swayed and slid on Queer Street himself, then spent the rest of the eleventh and the longest round of the twelfth working another bottom of hell, holding off Frazier who came on and on, sobbing, wild, a wild honor of a beast, man of will reduced to the common denominator of the will of all of us back in that land of the animal where the idea of man as a tool-wielding beast was first conceived. Frazier looked to get Ali forever in the eleventh and the twelfth, and Ali, his legs slapped and slashed on the thighs between each round by Angelo Dundee, came out for the thirteenth and incredibly was dancing. Everybody's story switched again. For if Ali won this round, the fourteenth and the fifteenth, who could know if he could not win the fight? . . . He won the first half of the thirteenth, then spent the second half on the ropes with Frazier. They were now like crazy death-march-maddened mateys coming up the hill and on to home, and yet Ali won the fourteenth, Ali looked good, he came out dancing for the fifteenth, while Frazier, his own armies of energy finally caught up, his courage ready to spit into the eye of any devil black or white who would steal the work of his life, had equal madness to steal the bolt from Ali. So Frazier reached out to snatch the magic punch from the air, the punch with which Ali topped Bonavena, and found it and thunked Ali a hell and hit Ali a heaven of a shot which dumped Muhammad into 50,000 newspaper photographs—Ali on the floor! Great Ali on the floor was out there flat singing to the sirens in the mistiest fogs of Queer Street (same look of death and widowhood on his far-gone face as one had seen in the fifth blind round with Liston) yet Ali got up, Ali came sliding through the last two minutes and thirty-five seconds of this heathen holocaust in some last exercise of the will, some iron fundament of the ego not to be knocked out, and it was then as if the spirit of Harlem finally spoke and came to rescue and the ghosts of the dead in Vietnam, something held him up before arm-weary triumphant near-crazy Frazier who had just hit him the hardest punch ever thrown in his life and they went down to the last few seconds of a great fight, Ali still standing and Frazier had won.

The world was talking instantly of a rematch. For Ali had shown America what we all had hoped was secretly true. He was a man. He could bear moral and physical torture and he could stand. And if he could beat Frazier in the rematch we would have at last a national hero who was hero of the world as well, and who could bear to wait for the next fight? Joe Frazier, still the champion, and a great champion, said to the press, "Fellows, have a heart—I got to live a little. I've been working for ten long years." And Ali, through the agency of alter-ego Bundini, said—for Ali was now in the hospital to check on the possible fracture of a jaw—Ali was reported to have said, "Get the gun ready—we're going to set traps." Oh, wow. Could America wait for something so great as the Second Ali-Frazier?

Jim Murray

Helpful Hints

Jim Murray has entertained readers of the Los Angeles Times, *and those who read his syndicated column elsewhere, for much of the second half of the twentieth century. Joyous entertainment it is, with Murray's irresistible blend of irreverence and outrageous wit. Murray's tendency has always been to mourn over the limitations of his profession. "Our triumphs are small, our canvas limited," he once wrote. "Walter Lippmann would get profoundly depressed. When we talk of 'Birds,' we mean the ones in Baltimore, not in the White House. In our own little world, the Cardinals are largely Protestant." Don't listen to Mr. Murray. Just read this how-to on golf and you'll see how honorable is his profession.*

It was in the middle of the PGA that I caught Arnold Palmer looking at me as if I were a four-foot putt he needed to win the tournament.

"What," he asked menacingly, "do you mean by knocking my golf book?"

"Mr. Palmer," I told him, hoping somebody would mark where I was on the green in case he knocked me into a sand trap, "I didn't knock your golf book, I knocked all golf books." He looked unconvinced.

"See," I told him. "Your book, 'My Game and Yours,' has a lot to do with your game but very little to do with mine."

"What," he asked, hitching up his pants and selecting the right club to split the fairway with me, "would you write?"

It was a good question. And I am herewith offering the Old Pro's handy hints to better golf, to be titled "My Game and the Hell with Palmer's."

In the first place, all the pros can teach you how to hit the "intentional slice." It's the unintentional slice we have to work on. There are several things you have to look for to tell you when you are going to hit the unintentional slice. It is often the result of too much right hand—at the bar before the match.

Other tell-tale signs include sweating in the palms just before the shot and a slight tremor in the knees. If you just bet five dollars on the hole, it is a sure sign the unintentional slice is coming up. You don't have to check the wind condition, the distance to the hole, the curvature of the earth or the time of day. Just stand at right angles to the hole. Pray, if you want. And let fly. With a little luck, the ball will banana right into center fairway and leave you with only seven easy shots to the green.

Now, I am the world's foremost master at the topped shot. Not everyone can learn to play this delicate little line drive around the green with finesse. The important thing to remember on this shot is not to keep your head down. You louse up the shot if you do. The preferred position for the head at the finish of the swing is looking right up into the sun. This way you'll not only not hit the ball square, you'll not even know where it went. The shot calls for you to inquire anxiously, "Did you see it?" the minute the ball leaves the blade. Never have any more conversation with your caddy than that. Never let him tell you anything more than how deep the hole is and what time it is.

The sand trap shot is the easiest shot in golf in my game. Remember, you do not hit the ball, just the sand. Right? Okay, so hit the sand. What's so tough about that?

There is entirely too much emphasis on par in golf. Forget par. I have a friend, Myron Cope, who once took four fans—complete misses—on a par 3 tee. He bogeyed the hole before he left the tee. This is the right mental attitude to have. Having gone one over par before he even struck the ball, he could now settle down and play up to his capabilities—an 11. The secret of golf is relaxation, but does Arnold Palmer's book tell you to relax any better than that?

On the 40-yard chip to the green I can shave five strokes off your game if you will remember one important thing: don't concentrate. Think of the mortgage, the fight you had with your wife last night, the fact the boss thinks you're in the office. Try to remember if you shut off the bathtub water before you left home.

It is imperative you bend your elbow on this shot. And, at impact, look up. The only fun in the game, Jackie Burke says, is watching the ball fly through the air. Yours, of course, will only fly through the grass, but remember, nobody's perfect. Even the pros miss one now and again.

Your shot will come off beautifully if you remember those five checkpoints: no concentration, head up, elbow bent, teeth chattering and tongue out.

The pros tell you to keep your weight on the right foot going back and the left foot coming down. Hogwash. Don't keep your weight on either foot. On the 39-foot topped chip shot, it's even better if you fall down. Miss just one of these handy Murray reminders and the first thing you know you will hit a perfect 9-iron shot and it will fly over the green, over the trees and out into the parking lot and you will have to drop another ball. The beauty of the Murray system is you never have a lost ball. If your glasses are clean and you can see 30 feet in any direction, your ball will never leave your sight.

If your caddy coaches you on the tee, "Hit it down the left side with a little draw," ignore him. All you do on the tee is try not to hit the caddy.

The fairway wood shot is fairly simple. The object here is to move the ball 11 feet, hopefully forward. Again, you begin by collapsing your left arm. If you can't collapse your left arm, you can't play the shot. Just remember, Nicklaus would be sure to louse up this shot. But not you.

Ball-marking for fun and profit would be another important chapter in the Murray book. Say you have a 40-foot putt. You can eliminate at least the first two feet of this by artful ball-marking. The preferred method is to have a pocket full of coins which fall out in a shower as you bend over to mark your spot. Pick all of them up except the one nearest the hole. You can cut off the last six feet of the putt by inquiring innocently after your third putt, "Gimme that?" Argue that it's inside the leather even if it's barely inside the green. You've got to be tough in this game.

If you're three-and-a-half feet from the hole and playing with dopes who don't consider that a tap-in, remember to hit it firm. Never up, never in. You will end up 20 feet from the hole on the other side but it will help to keep you from crying if you yell "Bite!" or "Sit!" or "Hit something!" as it slithers past. On the way back, try to stub the putter in the grass and you can keep your poise by shouting "Legs. Get Legs." Try not to take more than four putts.

There are any number of artificial aids you can buy but remember that liquor is the best. It can't help your game but if you play the way I am telling you, it can't hurt it either. Also you won't give a damn. I would never recommend gloves, unless, of course, it's cold.

Okay. Now that you've read this, go out and get "Your Game and Mine" and ask yourself who's giving the best advice on how to master this stinking game, me or Palmer.

William Nack

A Coming of Age

"Our careers started at the same time," said William Nack, referring to himself and a racehorse named Secretariat. In 1972, Nack was given the opportunity to work as Newsday's *horse-racing writer. He went on to win four Eclipse awards (the Oscars for horse-racing journalism). Secretariat went on to win the Triple Crown in 1973 and establish himself as one of the most fabled racehorses of all time. From Nack's book,* Secretariat: The Making of a Champion, *here is the story of the birth and grooming of a special athlete.*

This is a story about a horse, but it is also about the people around him, and the land, and the people who came to the land who built the barns and grew the grass and bought the feed, who searched the world for the finest blooded horses and bought them when they found them, who chose the mares and bred the studs and raised the horses and flipped the coins and crossed their fingers—always hoping for the best, the fastest animal on earth. There is much room for outrageous luck in the breeding of racehorses, but there is also some crawl space for shrewdness and work, and sometimes, with enough of that, things come together in the end. As they did that night.

It was almost midnight in Virginia, late for the farmlands north of Richmond, when the hour came—when the phone rang in Howard Gentry's home and two men were out the front door, hastily crossing the lawn to the car. They climbed in, forcing the doors to against the cold, and swung out the driveway onto the deserted road. They took off north. It was one of those hours when time is measured not by clocks but by uterine contractions, and the intervals between were getting shorter. Not far away, in a small wooden barn, beneath a solitary light, a mare was about to give birth. The men were rushing toward the barn to help her.

Howard Gentry had been manager of the Meadow Stud in Doswell for 20 years. Beside him was Raymond White Wood, a longtime friend and neighbor, for years Gentry's companion at straight pool, a railroad conductor by occupation and himself a modest breeder of thoroughbred horses. It was the night of March 29, 1970, not the kind of night to leave the velvet green of a pool table, with its friendly click and spin of conversation, to rush outdoors, but Gentry was anxious. Down in Barn 17A, the two-stall foaling barn near the western border of the farm, an aging broodmare named Somethingroyal was going into labor for the 14th time in her 18 years. And she was carrying a foal by Bold Ruler, the preeminent sire in America.

While Bold Ruler had become a champion progenitor of the species, probably the greatest in American history, Somethingroyal had made a mark as one of its most important mares. She was the kind of mare that breeders seek to found families and raise dynasties. She was already the dam of Sir Gaylord, a most gifted racehorse, the colt favored to win the 1962 Kentucky Derby until he broke down the day before the race.

So Howard Gentry would remember that he felt anxious, more so than usual, to be done with it, to get the foal delivered. He thought about the equipment and wondered if it was all there—the enema, the cup, the iodine and the antibiotics. He had told Bob Southworth to look in on the mare, but Southworth was not the regular night watchman and Gentry hoped he had called in time.

Gentry stopped the car about 100 feet from the barn and he and Wood cut across the wet grass. Gentry looked into the stall and walked quietly inside. Somethingroyal was breathing quickly, her nostrils flared. She was walking the stall. She seemed on edge, nervous. Gentry felt her neck and shoulder. She was warm and sweating slightly.

He left the stall, checking for the iodine, the enema, the cup for the iodine and the bowl for the water to wash the nipples for the suckling foal. The three men waited at the door, watching the old mare pace, circling as if caged, and spoke idly in unremembered conversations.

At midnight Somethingroyal stopped pacing and lay down, collapsing on the bed of straw. Gentry slipped on his rubber gloves and dropped to his knees beside her. Her water bag broke, spilling fluid. Any moment now, the foal.

The tip of the left foot appeared first, and Gentry waited for the other. In a normal birth, the front feet come out together, the head between the legs, so Gentry watched for the other foot. And then he decided to wait no longer. He feared the leg might be folded under, or twisted, positions that could cause injury to the shoulder under the extreme pressures of birth, so he reached his arm inside the vagina and felt the head, which was in a good position. He dropped his hand down to the right leg and felt for the hoof. He found it curled under, as he had thought, so he uncurled it gently, bringing the leg out. "Won't be long now," he said to Wood.

Somethingroyal pushed, paused, panted, and pushed again, and Gentry guided but did not pull the legs, not yet. He always waits for the shoulder to emerge before pulling. The legs came out together, then the head, with a splash of white down the face. Finally the shoulders emerged. The mare paused and Gentry took the front legs and waited for her to rest, always letting her lead the dance, push and relax, push and relax.

It was a good-sized foal. Gentry called Wood to his side. They pulled together for several moments. As the foal came out and Gentry saw the size of the shoulders and the size of the bones, he feared that it might have hips so wide they would have trouble clearing the opening. When the rib cage cleared, Gentry guided the hips, the mare needing help.

Then he was out, lying on the bed of straw, and the mare was panting and sweating and Gentry was asking Southworth for the cup of iodine. Southworth broke the umbilical by pulling the foal around to the mare's head so she could lick him, and Gentry cauterized the wound with iodine. He then gave the foal four ccs. of the antibiotics as a precautionary measure. Southworth rubbed him down with a dry towel to stimulate circulation of the blood. The colt was chestnut, with three white feet.

The Virginia of Caroline County, of Meadow Stud, does not recall the Old South of cotton plantations and magnolias under moonlight and willowy, straight-backed women drifting about the lawns and gardens of the Tidewater. Caroline County seems closer in spirit to Stephen Crane than Stephen Foster, a starker and less storybook Virginia than the mountains and the valleys, a place where old times are often just as well forgotten. It is tomato and melon country now, watermelons and muskmelons, and fields for grazing horses and cattle and cultivated stretches for corn and soybeans. It was not always so prosperous or so peaceful.

Set in a line between Washington and Richmond, The Meadow was once part of a neck of land that joined a nation with two heads. In consequence, the land and whatever civilization had been built on it came out of the Civil War years badly gored. The fighting began just 70 miles to the north, at Bull Run, and it ended not far to the southwest, at Appomattox Court House. The Morris family, living on The Meadow at the time, hid the family silver in the well.

The Chenerys and their relatives were the residents of The Meadow by the end of the century, leading a hardscrabble existence. There was little money in the family until Christopher Tompkins Chenery became what he set out to be—a man of substance and horses and part of the landed gentry. As a young man he switched from engineering to finance and by the late 1920s had begun to climb to the presidency of a string of utility companies. He became wealthy quickly and moved to Pelham Manor, N.Y. Up North he founded the Boulder Brook Club, a riding club in Scarsdale. He played some polo. He hunted with the Goldens Bridge Hounds. He had an office in Manhattan. And he sent his children to good schools. He was enough of a sentimentalist, though, to want to return to The Meadow someday, and in 1935 he did, on a trip to see a prospective boarding school for his daughter. Penny Chenery Tweedy would recall the day many years later. "I guess I expected a plantation with white pillars, but it was an unpainted, three-story, gaunt, old, stark wooden house," she said. "A mongrel dog lay under the porch, and chickens pecked around the steps."

Chris Chenery's car nosed into the yard. There was a silence, and Penny Tweedy recalls her father looking perplexed, then angry. He told his wife and daughter to remain in the car, that the house might be ridden with lice. He went inside, but did not stay long, and he said nothing when he came back to the car, started it up and drove to a house across the road.

There the Chenerys called on Hardenia Hunter Ferguson, a cousin. She had managed to hold on to her land even through the Depression, and she talked as if all the surrounding places would somehow come back to the family. Penny remembered, "She cocked her head almost coquettishly and said, 'Chris, don't those lovely elm trees arch prettily over the old house there? Such a pity it had to pass from family hands! That did it. To my mother's despair he bought The Meadow a year later."

The foal subsisted on Somethingroyal's milk for the first 35 days of his life. Then the youngster's regimen was supplemented with grain, preparing him for weaning; the mare was tied in the stall and the colt given small portions of crushed oats and sweet feed. He grew quickly as the summer passed, grew to the day when Christopher Chenery's executive secretary for 33 years, Elizabeth Ham, visited the farm and looked at the foals. Miss Ham noted in her log on July 28, 1970:

"Ch. c Bold Ruler—Somethingroyal

Three white stockings—well-made Colt—Might be a little light under the knees—Stands well on pasterns—Good straight hind leg—Good shoulders and hindquarters—You would have to like him."

Summer cooled into October. The daily rations of the Bold Ruler colt were boosted periodically, up to five and finally to six quarts of grain a day by the time he was separated from Somethingroyal.

With autumn, too, came the time to name the weanlings. In this matter The Jockey Club rules are stringent. For example, a name cannot be that of a famous horse, the trademark of a product, the name of an illustrious or infamous person, alive or dead—and it cannot contain more than 18 characters, including punctuation. One name after another was submitted and rejected by The Jockey Club stewards—The Meadow sent in a total of six, two sets of three names each, for the colt.

The first choice in the first set was Scepter, a name that Penny Tweedy liked. The second, suggested by Miss Ham, was Royal Line. The third was Mrs. Tweedy's Something Special. All three were quickly rejected. The first name of the second set was Game of Chance, which Mrs. Tweedy suggested, as she did the second, Deo Volente, a name for which she had been trying to gain acceptance: her maternal grandfather used to say, whenever he was planning to do something, that he would do it, *"Deo volente,"* Latin for "God willing." (The stewards were not willing, no doubt because it used the name of an Illustrious Being.)

Miss Ham suggested the third name on that list. She had once been the secretary of Norman Hezekiah Davis, a banker and diplomat who served in a number of ambassadorial posts for the United States, including that of chairman of the American delegation to the disarmament conference in Geneva, the home of the League of Nations' Secretariat.

Secretariat, Miss Ham thought, had a nice ring to it, and the name was submitted as the last on the second list. The following January the stewards advised The Meadow that the colt by Bold Ruler—Somethingroyal, by Princequillo, with the white star and stripe and the three white stockings, born on March 30, 1970, had been registered under the name of Secretariat.

Secretariat grew out above the match-stick legs, his ration of grain increasing from six quarts to seven, on to eight as he lengthened, height-ened and widened through his yearling year of 1971.

That September a 2-year-old Meadow Stud colt named Riva Ridge raced to a handy victory in the $75,000-added Futurity Stakes, and two days afterward the chief delegates from the stable victory party arrived at The Meadow. There were Penny Tweedy, Elizabeth Ham and a volatile little French Canadian, Lucien Laurin, Meadow stable's new trainer.

Three decades had passed since Laurin was ruled off the racetrack for alleged possession of an illegal battery in Rhode Island; since he galloped horses for Alfred Vanderbilt at Sagamore Farm; since Vander-bilt, believing in his innocence, had moved to have the ruling lifted. Laurin remembered that mediocre early career, with its painful moments and long winter and summer days under sheds from West Virginia through New England and Canada. It was a difficult circuit; low purses, sore and crippled horses banished from Long Island, small tracks, living from day to day.

Laurin was born about 50 miles north of Montreal, in St. Paul, Quebec, a town in which he did not stay long. He left school early to work at Delorimier Park, a half-mile oval in Montreal where he first exercised horses and finally, in 1929, he became a jockey. He was mod-erately successful, reaching his professional zenith when he rode Sir Michael to victory in the King's Plate in 1935. His career as a rider finally took him to that summer morning in 1938 when he walked into the jockeys' room at Narragansett Park, took off his jacket, hung it behind him and sat down to play a game of cards.

"The next thing I know, they said, 'The steward wants to see you downstairs,' " Laurin remembers. "And I said, 'For what?' " He got to his feet and went downstairs, into the office of one of the stewards. The steward put the battery device on the table in front of him and said, "What are you doing with this in your pocket?"

It was hopeless. Laurin would later insist that he was framed, that the battery was planted in his jacket, that he had an idea who did him in but would not say who. His voice still carries an exasperated edge when he talks of it. "I was playing cards and somebody put it in my pocket. That's the truth," he says.

Now he was 60 years old, with silver hair and elfish grin and traces of his heritage in his voice. He had come a long way from that black day in 1938, building steadily, if unspectacularly, a reputation as a shrewd conditioner of the thoroughbred horse. From Delorimier Park in Canada he had found his way to Aqueduct, Belmont Park and Saratoga and ended up making a substantial living on that most competitive racing circuit in America. And here he was at Chris Chenery's farm in northern Virginia, with Riva Ridge, a potential champion, in his barn back at Belmont Park. In all the years Laurin trained, he had never had a champion 2-year-old colt with a shot at the Derby, the ability to win the Triple Crown—the big horse. Now, at the twilight of his training career, he had Riva Ridge, and he was standing with Mrs. Tweedy and Miss Ham looking at next year's Meadow 2-year-olds when Secretariat was led toward the gathering. In the notes she took that day Penny Tweedy wrote under Secretariat's name, "Big (turns out left front—LL), good bone, a bit swaybacked—very nice—lovely smooth gait." LL meant Lucien Laurin, but if the colt's left fore did turn out slightly and he was a trifle swaybacked (he quickly grew out of both conditions), Secretariat raised Laurin's eyebrows.

"Mr. Laurin," the man at the colt's head said. "This is the horse that will make you forget Riva Ridge."

All Secretariat had in the beginning was the look of an athlete, and Lucien was wary of appearances. In his years on the racetrack he had seen too many equine jocks come and go; to Laurin, Secretariat at this stage was just another untried thoroughbred.

As a youngster Secretariat did not awe the clockers at Hialeah, either. There were no quarter-mile workouts in :22 seconds, no leveling off into a flat run, all business, from the quarter pole at the top of the stretch to the wire—no such heady flights.

Ron Turcotte was with Lucien Laurin one morning at Hialeah, just outside the shed, when four 2-year-olds were led from the barn and began circling them, grooms holding the bridles. It was just a passing comment in a passing moment, as Turcotte would recall it later.

"Want to get on him?" said Lucien, as Secretariat walked past.

"Sure, love to."

Turcotte jumped aboard Secretariat that morning for the first time, guiding him out to the racetrack with the others, in Indian file, turning right, counterclockwise, on the dirt track. Laurin told them to let the youngsters gallop easily, side by side, in a schooling exercise designed to accustom them to other horses running next to them. The four colts took off at a slow gallop around the mile-and-an-eighth oval, galloping abreast. The riders stood high in the saddles, going easily. Secretariat seemed almost lackadaisical. The red horse plopped along in casual indifference, his head down, a big, awkward, clumsy colt, Turcotte remembers. Galloping past the palm trees and the infield lake, Jockey Miles Neff, riding Twice Bold, reached his stick over and slapped Turcotte on the rump. "Whee-ew!" yelled Turcotte. Laughter on the backstretch. Charlie Davis was riding inside on All or None, and Turcotte leaned over and jabbed Davis in the rear with his stick and Davis almost went over All or None, screaming. This was not all intended for fun. Exercise boys do it to get young horses accustomed to quick movement, to shouts and to noise. A horse race is not a quiet affair.

The colt next to Secretariat drifted out and banged against him, and the red horse countered with a grunt.

"Ummpphhhh. . . ."

He didn't alter course, just drifted back and took up the same path he'd been on before the bumping. "He was just a big likable fellow," Turcotte said. Then the colt came out again, sideswiping him a second time—"Ummpphhhh. . . ."

Confidence did not come easily to this young red horse. There was the morning in late February when Laurin boosted Turcotte up on Secretariat for a quarter-mile workout, not an easy gallop but a speed drill, with three other young colts—Gold Bag, Twice Bold and Young Hitter. It was time to teach them how to run, how to level out and reach for ground, something all horses have to learn.

"No race riding, boys!" Lucien called to the four as they walked their horses to the racetrack that morning, through Sunny Fitzsimmons Lane and out the quarter-mile bend under the spanking brightness of the morning. "No race riding! We're schooling them today. Stay head and head." The riders reached the track and circled it, around the turn at a gallop abreast. They headed for the three-eighths pole, then pulled to a stop, lining up still abreast, and walked several yards together. They wanted to start all at once. They clucked to their horses and went into a jog, picking up speed slowly, slowly, slowly. . . .

Nearing the quarter pole, the four riders chirped again, and the horses started leveling and reaching out, bodies lower to the ground. Twice Bold, Gold Bag and Young Hitter accelerated rapidly, gathering up the pace from an easy gallop to a run as they raced past the quarter pole and entered the straight.

Turcotte picked up Secretariat's reins and clucked at him, not yelling, trying to give the horse a feel for the game. He sensed a bewilderment in the colt. He gathered Secretariat together, gave him time to steady himself and get his legs under him. They finally somehow synchronized, but the other three colts had already blown away from him. Turcotte saw the more precocious horses far up the track as Secretariat battled along and started to find himself.

They dusted Secretariat easily that morning, beating him by about 15 lengths and racing the quarter mile down the lane in 23 seconds. Secretariat finished in about 26 seconds. He was no Bold Ruler, and Turcotte recalls the feeling of awkwardness: "He just didn't know what it was all about. I asked him and he was plain confused. Didn't know which leg to put down first."

Periodically, as Secretariat worked out in Florida, Penny Tweedy asked Lucien about the red horse, and he hardly reflected buoyant hope.

"He hasn't shown me much," Lucien would say.

Or, "He's not ready. I have to get the fat off him first."

Or, "I have to teach him to run. He's big, awkward and doesn't know what to do with himself."

Secretariat was beaten more than once in training sessions that winter at Hialeah. Gold Bag beat him again. So did Twice Bold and the filly, All or None. So did a colt named Angle Light. He wasn't beaten by 15 lengths again, but he did keep on losing. Laurin avoided telling Penny Tweedy that other horses were trouncing Secretariat in the mornings.

The accident happened in mid-April, on a gray, wet morning when the track was mire. It occurred shortly after Apprentice Jockey Paul Feliciano, under contract to Lucien, hopped aboard Secretariat for a routine gallop. Feliciano had his feet out of the stirrups, dangling them at Secretariat's side, when Laurin spotted him. Lucien raised his voice in warning.

"Put your feet in the irons!" he yelled. "Be careful with that horse! Don't take no chances . . . he plays, and he'll drop you, I swear to God."

Feliciano's feet rose into the stirrups, which he was wearing too short, and someone dimly recalls Laurin calling, "Drop your irons!" What Laurin wanted Feliciano to do was lengthen his stirrups for greater balance.

The horses moved from the stable area toward the training track, and Laurin followed in his station wagon. Secretariat and the other horses walked onto the muddy surface and began, one by one, to take off at a slow gallop. Feliciano, his reins loose, guided Secretariat near the outside rail and stood up in the saddle as the colt cantered through the long stretch toward the clocker's shed, passed it and began heading into the first bend. It happened fast, but Feliciano spoke almost in stop action about it later. He heard a horse working to his left, on the rail, his hooves splashing and slapping at the mud as he drilled past.

"I heard the noise. It was a split-second thing. He stopped, propped, wheeled and turned left, and I knew what was going to happen . . . I think he knew I was going off, too, was already slipping, because he turned around from under me. I landed on my face."

Secretariat, riderless, head and tail up, reins flapping, took off clockwise around the racetrack, racing the wrong way back toward the gap from which he had come. Laurin saw him and in an instant was speeding back. Asked if they shouldn't pick up Paul, who was lying in the mud, Lucien snapped, "*Let* him lie in the mud!"

The car zipped into the stable area. Laurin saw Secretariat standing there, as calm as if he were waiting for a taxicab. Lucien's companion climbed from the car and walked carefully toward Secretariat, who stood looking at him curiously. The man reached out and grabbed the reins, and Laurin immediately took off for the barn, leaving him to walk Secretariat home.

Meanwhile, Paul Feliciano, 20, born and raised on Union Street in the Park Slope section of Brooklyn, lifted his face from the mud at the seven-eighths pole of the training track and started walking around the oval toward the barn area. He did not want to return to Barn Five and the morning bustle of stablehands, with Secretariat arriving riderless at the shed, with Lucien Laurin waiting for him there. He feared Laurin. Other things had happened since he had come to work for Lucien that year at Hialeah. The headstrong Gold Bag had run off with him, as he had with other riders, and Laurin had ranted at him. Paul had not forgotten the incident. And had no illusions as to what Lucien would say this time. "I knew what was going to happen when I got back to the barn," he said. "I was thinking I didn't want to go back. But I knew I had to."

It was a 10-minute walk. By then Secretariat was standing in his stall, with blankets stacked up on his back, the back wrenched and his muscles tied up so badly that he couldn't move. Secretariat would not leave the barn for almost two weeks.

"That son of a gun ain't worth a quarter!" Laurin raved to one stablehand. Paul arrived shortly after Laurin's comment about him.

He would remember only bits and pieces of the ensuing tirade. "You better listen to me, young man!" Lucien told him. "You better pay attention when you're on those horses! Wake up!"

Turning away, Laurin said to him, "I want to see you in my office."

On the screened-in porch at the top of the staircase by the office, Feliciano stood and listened for five minutes as Laurin reproached and reproved him. Finally he said, "You come by in the morning and pick up your contract and your check."

"What could I do?" Paul pleaded. "He stopped when that other horse came by and I lost my balance."

It was no use. Feliciano was fired, and that was that.

Of course, Laurin had told him the same thing after Gold Bag had run away with him and the next day acted as if nothing had happened. But this time, Feliciano thought, he had raised such hell, seemed so angry, that he must be dead serious. Despondent and confused, Feliciano took that home with him. He believed that Laurin had given him a good chance to ride all but his best horses, had been generous and given him live mounts, not bums. Now that was finished, and with it a good chance to make it as a jockey.

The following morning Feliciano walked under the shed of Barn Five, coming early to pick up his contract. Lucien, arriving about seven, came into the shed telling his assistant trainer which exercise boy to put on what horse. He looked at Paul standing there waiting for his contract. "Put Paul on that one to gallop," Lucien said matter-of-factly.

And that was the last Feliciano heard of it.

Jim Gaffney, an exercise boy for more than two decades and an employee in mutuels for 12 years, went to work for The Meadow stable while Secretariat was getting over the cramped muscles suffered the day he backed out from under Feliciano. It was Gaffney who rode Secretariat his first day back on the track. He had been warned of the colt's trick of ducking to the left after pulling up from a gallop, the curtsy he had executed so beautifully with Paul two weeks before.

Secretariat walked to the training track that morning and stood for several seconds, looking to the left and right. Gaffney did not hurry him. He let him stand there and watch the morning bustle.

Walking off toward the clocker's shed, Secretariat ducked left, but Gaffney, riding with long stirrups, stuck with him. The colt had been confined for a few weeks and he was feeling his unburned oats; he galloped off strongly, pulling hard on the bit. Every day Gaffney gave him more rein. After several days the colt relaxed and, as he had done at Hialeah, he started plopping along easily.

Secretariat soon stopped ducking to the left. Gaffney had put a special bit with a prong on its left side in the colt's mouth, and had worked for days on the problem, exerting pressure on the right line every time the colt started to dip.

Gaffney grew to believe, weeks before the horse ever took a competitive step on a racetrack, that he was special. His whole morning at the racetrack began to revolve around Secretariat. He rode the red horse steadily, building the animal up in his own mind, telling stablehands of the youngster's extraordinary future, boasting about him to grooms and hotwalkers and even to his wife Mary over breakfast. "He was like a third child to Jimmy," said Mary Gaffney.

Gaffney told his mother about the colt, too, detailing for her all his manifold gifts. She responded by knitting a pommel pad (inserted as protection under the front of the saddle) with Secretariat's name knitted in blue across a white background. And Gaffney purchased two white saddle cloths and took them to a woman who did needlework. He paid her $24 to stitch SECRETARIAT into the section that is visible below the rear of the saddle. Finally, he took one of Lucien's exercise saddles home, the saddle he always used when he rode the colt, and hammered SECRETARIAT into it, giving the letters a scriptural flourish.

The red horse returned to serious work on May 18, when he went three-eighths of a mile in :37 seconds, yet no one but a few clockers, Meadow stablehands and avid horseplayers paid any attention to it. Laurin had his mind on Riva Ridge and the Preakness Stakes, the second race in the Triple Crown series. (Riva Ridge had won the Derby, but the colt, with Turcotte up, finished fourth in the Preakness on a muddy track. On June 10 Riva Ridge would cruise to the front at the beginning of the mile-and-a-half Belmont Stakes and win by seven lengths. But the Triple Crown would have to wait for Secretariat.)

The red horse grew in strength through May and June and was beginning to learn how to run. On June 6, three days before Riva Ridge's Belmont Stakes, Secretariat wore blinkers for the first time and went half a mile in :47⅗ seconds, the fastest half-mile work in his life.

On June 15, with the blinkers, Secretariat worked from the starting gate and dashed five-eighths of a mile in 1:00⅕ seconds. On June 24, on a sloppy track, the official clockers for the *Daily Racing Form* noted that Secretariat's 1:12⅘ seconds for six furlongs was the fastest workout at the distance that morning. (The clockers themselves had come a long way since the horse's first appearance in Florida, when they spelled his name "Secretarial.")

That day Lucien called Penny Tweedy and asked her if she would come to Aqueduct, saying that he wanted her to see Secretariat run his first race.

"I think he's finally coming around," he said. They decided to enter the colt in a race on July 4, an $8,000 maiden event for colts and geldings at 5½ furlongs, with the start on the backstretch near the far turn.

The red horse's ability was no secret now. Sweep, the nom de plume for *Daily Racing Form* handicapper Jules Schanzer, advised his readers on July 4, "Secretariat, a half-brother to Sir Gaylord, appears greatly advanced in his training. The newcomer by Bold Ruler stepped 6 furlongs in 1:12⅘ over a sloppy Belmont course June 24 and such outstanding speed entitles him to top billing."

Feliciano was to be up, and since he was still an apprentice, Secretariat was allowed to carry 113 pounds, five pounds less than the other maidens in the race. That weight allowance was the only break he had all day.

Members of The Meadow stable bet with both hands, most of it on the red horse's nose, but not Gaffney. He did not think Feliciano liked the colt or had enough confidence in him.

Lucien was sitting in a box seat with Penny Tweedy when the horses, in single file, walked past the grandstand in the post parade and then turned and broke into warmup gallops. It was nearing two o'clock. There was a wind blowing south out of Queens, south against the horses walking to the starting gate up the backstretch, south toward Kennedy International Airport across the highway, south toward Jamaica Bay. Bettors, some already moving toward the rail on the homestretch, were busy making Secretariat the tepid $3.10-to-$1 favorite.

Big Burn, Jockey Braulio Baeza on him, stepped into post position one. An assistant starter took hold of Secretariat—the colt was wearing his blue-and-white checkered blinkers—and led him into post two. The door slammed shut behind him. Feliciano patted the youngster on the neck and waited. It was 2:02. Strike the Line stood in gate three next to Secretariat. Jacinto Vasquez sat on Quebec in post four. It was nearing 30 seconds after 2:02.

Dave Johnson, the track announcer, looked through his binoculars toward the starting gate and clicked on the lever of the loudspeaker system. "It is now post time," said Johnson.

It came all at once—the break, the sounds and the collision. The gates crashed open and the bell screamed and the horses vaulted upward and came down in a bound, Secretariat breaking sharply through in one, two, three strides. Quebec sliced across Strike the Line, and Vasquez hollered, but there was nothing that anyone could do; Quebec had slammed into Secretariat, not sideways in a grazing blow but almost perpendicularly, plowing into his right shoulder. Like a fullback struck on his blind side as he drives up the middle, Secretariat staggered and veered to the left, crashing into Big Burn. For several moments it appeared as if the red horse had two tacklers hanging on him, as if he were trying to grind out yardage with Quebec and Big Burn leaning on him and trying to bring him down. Secretariat's legs were chopping savagely, and Feliciano heard him groaning as he worked to regain his balance. He straightened out, but he was in 11th place, next to Strike the Line. Then Secretariat began digging, trying to pick up speed as they headed for the turn, 300 yards ahead. He was not getting with it as fast as the others.

The horses were strung out as they approached the turn, and Secretariat started drifting. Moving to the bend, he seemed confused, and he wavered momentarily to the right, bumping a roan called Rove. Feliciano took back on the left rein, leaving the right line flapping, and the red horse leaned left to make the bend. There was nothing else Feliciano could do. Everything was going wrong.

There was no place to run on the inside, with Jacques Who lapped on him there, and the rail clogged up in front. Horses were pounding on his right, leaving no room for Feliciano to swing Secretariat out and get him rolling in the clear. A wall of four horses was shifting around in front of him. He had only two horses beaten as he raced for the ⅜th pole midway around the turn for home, and he had nowhere to go. The colt started to run up a hole opening in front of him, but that squeezed shut, too. He was working to get with it, as if looking for the holes himself.

Secretariat was a Cadillac in a traffic jam of Chevrolets and Datsuns. But Lucien Laurin, watching the break from the side, had missed the crunch at the start. He was astounded. The red horse had always broken well in his morning trials, not slowly, like this, and then foundering. As the field made the bend for the straight, passing the ⁵⁄₁₆th pole, Count Successor was in the lead, Knightly Dawn beside him, Master Achiever third, and Herbull on the outside fourth. The pace was brisk for 2-year-olds, and Secretariat was about 10 lengths behind. As they came into the stretch, it appeared for a moment as though Feliciano were going to swing the colt to the outside. But, almost running up on other horses' heels, the jockey had to check him abruptly. Nearing the ³⁄₁₆th pole, Secretariat suddenly veered on a sharp diagonal to the left, lunging for space as it opened on the rail, and took off. He was a youngster looking for spots, looking and moving for running room. Daylight in front of him, horses on the outside of the rail, Feliciano drove Secretariat down the lane. He was not riding a quitter. Secretariat, gaining, passed a tiring Knightly Dawn, and then Jacques Who. He was gathering momentum, picking up speed, cutting into Master Achiever's lead in bounds—eight lengths, to seven and then to six as Master Achiever raced for the wire. He cut the lead to five lengths, then to 4½, then to four as he passed the 16th pole. He was in the hunt and Feliciano was asking him for more steam, reaching back and strapping him once right-handed.

A small hole opened between Master Achiever and the rail, and Feliciano drove the colt toward it. With ground running out, Secretariat was now running faster than all the others, cutting the lead to three lengths, to two lengths as the wire loomed, then to a length and a half. Suddenly the hole on the rail closed as Master Achiever came over, and as the wire swept overhead Feliciano had to stand up and take Secretariat back to prevent him from running up Master Achiever's heels. He had closed about eight lengths on the leaders in a powerful run through the stretch, but he finished fourth, a length and a quarter behind Herbull, to earn $480, his first purse. "He gave me three runs that day! Three!" Feliciano said later. But as he crossed the finish line the first thought that came to Paul's mind was, "Boy, I'm going to catch hell."

Down in the box seats, Penny Tweedy smiled as she saw the colt race under the wire—she, too, was unaware of the collision—and turned and told Lucien, "Gee, that's pretty good for a first start."

Laurin jumped from his chair in the box, kicked it and growled, "He should *never* have been beaten!" His reaction startled Penny. Lucien had told her only that he thought she ought to be there for the colt's first start, not that he was so certain the colt would win. There had been nothing of the sort, only that his workouts had impressed the trainer and that he appeared to be coming along.

Feliciano pulled the colt to a halt at the bend, turned him around, clucked to him and galloped slowly back to the unsaddling area by the paddock scale, where jockeys weigh in after a race. As he returned he looked over his left shoulder toward the paddock and saw precisely what he expected to see: Lucien standing there waiting for him.

Paul climbed down from Secretariat, thinking what he would say to Lucien, preparing himself. All he could do, he thought, was tell the truth.

Feliciano weighed in, handed the saddle and pads to a valet and went to Lucien, who waved a scolding finger in Paul's face. "You sure as hell messed that one up!" he said. Feliciano would recall later that Laurin was yelling loudly and that it was embarrassing, with all those people standing around. He said, "I'm sorry, Mr. Laurin . . . I had all sorts of trouble."

Later that day, when Feliciano walked into the paddock to ride another horse for Laurin, he saw the trainer smiling at him. Quietly, Lucien apologized, saying he had seen the films. He hadn't known about the battering Feliciano and Secretariat had taken at the start, he said.

Even so, it surprised Paul when he picked up a list of entries days later and saw, for the fourth race on July 15, a three-quarter-mile sprint for colts and geldings: "Secretariat . . . Feliciano, P."

Handicapper Jules Schanzer said of Secretariat on July 15 in the *Daily Racing Form,* "Secretariat turned in a remarkable performance after being badly sloughed at the start of his rough recent preview. The half-brother to Sir Gaylord turned on full steam after settling into his best stride and was devouring ground rapidly through the stretch run. Today's added distance is a plus factor that can help him leave the maiden ranks." Nor did the bettors abandon Secretariat, sending him off as the $1.30-to-$1 favorite over Master Achiever.

When Feliciano met with Lucien in the paddock before the race, they spoke only briefly. "Don't do like you did last time," Laurin said. "Just stay out of trouble and let him run. He shouldn't get beat." So Feliciano was rehearsing what he would do to keep Secretariat in the clear. He decided he wouldn't rush him, even if he broke slowly, but rather let him settle into stride and move when he pulled it all together.

At 3:09, into stall No. 1 moved Fleet 'n Royal, the colt who had finished third, a nose in front of Secretariat on July 4. An assistant starter took Secretariat's rein on the left side and led him into stall No. 8, to the outside of Jacques Who and to the inside of Bet On It, a gelding with a quick turn of foot. The instant before the red horse stepped into the starting gate Feliciano reached to his forehead and pulled a pair of plastic goggles over his eyes. Secretariat gave no signs of nervousness at the post. He stood relaxed inside the gate, looking casually ahead.

Starter George Cassidy, standing atop a platform about 10 yards in front of the gate, watched for the moment when the heads stopped turning, when the legs stopped dancing and the horses waited as one in the gate. At 3:09½ he pressed the button, the gates popped open and the 11 horses bounded forth.

Secretariat broke alertly, but almost immediately fell back to last, half a length behind Jacques Who. As others barreled for the lead, beginning to string out, he trailed the field. (This dilatory start, like others to come, gave rise to the false notion that the battering he took in his first race had made Secretariat timid at the break.)

Now he was pumping and driving, trying to move with the field, digging and pushing and reaching for whatever ground he could grab, but he was not getting there as fast as the others.

Feliciano sensed the colt was having no easy time, so he sat tight as they raced for the bend, not reaching back and strapping him, not hollering. Instead, he pumped with his arms, in rhythm with the stride, asking for whatever the colt could give.

Through that first quarter mile Feliciano was wondering whether Secretariat would ever find his stride, and all he could do was keep him to the outside, clear of traffic, and wait. He began to worry after the first furlong, with only five furlongs to go and still no horse running beneath him.

Then as the field raced for the turn Paul began to feel it happening. A coming together of stride and movement, a kind of leveling out and "smoothening," which retired exercise boy Jimmy Weininger once described, in tones of reverence, as ". . . the oddest thing . . . a horse, he's in first gear and then he's in fourth gear, and it's sort of like flying, taking off. It's the oddest thing."

Feliciano remembers clearly that sudden sense of Secretariat running easily, the feeling of power being generated beneath him. Heading for the quarter pole, Paul felt the momentum, the thrust into another gear. "He was running faster and faster and faster." Sitting still, Feliciano rode the surge.

Secretariat was on the outside, moving past Perilous Serenade and Monetary Crisis and Scantling and Fleet 'n Royal. He was still almost seven lengths behind, but by the time the field was midway around the turn Secretariat had bounded past Irish Flavor and was moving six horses wide, choo-chooing toward home. He was a running horse with nothing in front of him now but running room, moving on his left lead as he swung around horses. Paul was like a fighter swarming in.

"I knew I was a winner. I knew it then," he said.

Nearing the stretch Secretariat passed Impromptu, and entering the straight he had Jacques Who measured, coming to him at the ³⁄₁₆ths pole. He drove past Master Achiever and went after Bet On It as the leader neared the eighth pole. He was half a length behind, then head and head, and then he had the lead.

The crowd was shouting. Feliciano reached back and hit Secretariat once as he got to the front, and then hand-rode him as he led Bet On It half a length with a furlong to go, as he increased his lead to two and three lengths passing the 16th pole, and finally to four and to five and to six lengths as he raced under the wire.

Feliciano stood up in the stirrups and felt the sweet elation flowing as he galloped toward the clubhouse turn, eased back on his reins and brought the red horse to a stop.

Secretariat's winning purse was only $4,800, but it was the promise of what was to come. This was a son of Bold Ruler from a Princequillo mare, and he had run as though he knew he had a future. Up in the press box a Baltimore turf writer named Clem Florio jumped to his feet as Secretariat crossed the line. Turning to a colleague, Florio said loudly, "That's my Derby horse for next year!"

Everyone heard him.

Jay Neugeboren

Fixer's Home

Jay Neugeboren's first novel, Big Man, *received critical acclaim for the author's searing portrait of a basketball star caught up in the point-fixing basketball scandals of the early 1950s. Neugeboren has written a number of fine short stories and novels since, including* Listen, Reuben Fontañez, *and* Corky's Brother. *In 1981, fifteen years after the publication of* Big Man, *the editor of* Inside Sports *magazine asked Neugeboren to have Mack Davis, the fictional hero of* Big Man, *look back at those scandals. Here is the return of the one-time big man.*

Trouble is, I still keep thinking too much about what was. You ever pick a dime off the top of a backboard? You do that, you got it made, man. In the pros, there's some guys can do it now—Dr. J, he's the best—but back then, only a few could get up there, most of them 6-10 or over. In the schoolyard—I wasn't even out of high school yet, still had all these scouts and coaches buggin' me—I did it the first time. They boosted Big Ed up on someone's shoulders to put it there, then all the guys cheered me on. Took me three shots, but I made it. I was king then. I mean, you make it big time—high school, college, pro, I don't care where, it never compares with being king of your own schoolyard. You can take all the fame and shove it.

I walk through the gates and the guys sitting along the fence, younger guys, they looking at me the way I look at Big Ed when I was their age, and they say, "Hi, Mack!" or "Hey, Mack, babe—you want nexts with me?" and I see this look in their eyes like they'd give their right arm to be me—man, that was all I needed then. I was home free. Big Ed, he was the one who got me into the fixes, first time. He once got a ladder before we played Duke, in the old Garden on 50th Street, he put a dime up and in the stands, thousands of them, they went out of their boxes when I aced up and snatched the mother. But it still didn't compare with being king of your own schoolyard.

I figured that out a long time ago. You get out there when you're young, on a sunny day, and you listen to the older guys gas with each other about who's got what shots and what moves and who can fake who out of whose jock, and you just ache to have them talk to you. Hell, you get brought up in a white boy's schoolyard, hear them argue for years about every ballplayer ever was—I mean, they could quote you figures—you can't help let it get to you. You play out there, you're real loose. When I sail up there and snatch that dime that first time—man, that was the high spot. If I died right then, I die happy. I think about that lots.

Still go down to the schoolyard on weekends, my age, find we got some other dumb old men like to drag their asses around the court. Mostly we sit along the fence, between games, watching the new kids play. No white boys here anymore. A few years back, they said this was a neighborhood in transition. I liked that. Only what I say now to the guys, I tell them I call it a neighborhood that already transished, and they all laugh, tell me I got a way with words. The white boys, they all gone to live on Long Island and New Jersey, they all doctors and lawyers and teachers. The kids I play with now, I was playing high school and college, most of them weren't born.

Oh yeah, one of them says to me once, he hears us talking about how things were back then. How much you make then?

I too embarrassed to tell him, the pennies I sold out for. So I just look at him hard, say he better mind his own business. Back then, though, anybody mention the fixes, it was like somebody's mother got cancer, things got so quiet. All these white guys always kissing my ass cause I had such a great jump shot, cause I come from their neighborhood, none of them ever man enough to come up to me and ask me to my face why I did it. Or how I felt after. Except this one time, some little kid named Izzie, about 12 years old, he picked me for nexts like he always did. He says to me if you're so good, what college you play for?

So I say back I don't play for no college.

How come? he asks me.

Cause I was in the fixes, I say.

Everything goes quiet then, and I look around and ask the guys on the court how come they stop playing. They start right back in. Nobody like to mess with me in those days. Oh yeah. I'm the big man, real mean.

You mean to be mean, Mack, the guys used to say. But this kid Izzie, he asks me what I do if I don't play ball and I tell him I work at the Minit-Wash, washing down cars, you know? That's how come I got such clean hands. Yeah, me, I got the cleanest hands of any fixer around. After that, nobody ever asks me anything about the fixes.

In the papers, though, these reporters, they get all preachy about us guys who shave points, want to know why we did it. Most of the players, they go to court with me, they get the same Holy Joe voices and tell the Judge they're real sorry they let everybody down and fixed games, but when it comes my turn, I'm the only guy who don't say he's sorry. The only thing I'm sorry about, I say, is when they turn the money off.

All these guys always wanting to know why I did it. I tell this one reporter, Gross, from the old *New York Post*, they give me a pain. I did it for money, what they think? The college paid me, I did what they wanted. Gamblers paid, I work for them. Bookies paid more than gamblers, I signed up with them. Nobody giving me an education cause they like my looks. . . .

Sometimes, sitting out there on a nice warm day, my ass on concrete, my back up against the wire fence, drinking a cold Coke and letting the sweat dry under my T-shirt, I can't figure how all that happened 30 years ago. Where you been since then, I want to ask. Where you *been?* Sometimes when I chug through a bunch of bodies and feel my feet lift off the ground without weights in them, feel myself move like somebody I used to know real well—sometimes when that ball moves off my fingertips and hits that metal backboard in just the right spot and goes through that net *swish* like you know what, it all seems gone, like nothing bad ever happened. All those years, like nothing ever changed.

But it ain't so, and when I get down to the schoolyard this last time, and I'm warming up between games, pumping in some jumpers from around the circle, listening to the guys tease me about my pot belly and my bald dome, I hear them saying there's this new set of fixes. Oh yeah? I ask. Who they say done it?

Some Catholic kids, one of the guys says, and I got to laugh, them getting only guys from a Catholic school this time. My day, this real powerhouse, he got the Catholic boys off free. Oh yeah, everybody in the schoolyard knew that. Those Catholic players, they shaving points and rigging games along with the rest of us, but when the D. A. Hogan, he gets his lists ready and calls us all in, all you got in that room with

Hogan mostly were Jews and blacks. You don't take my word for it, you go look at the names some time. Me, I got their names down in my head like the lineup from the '51 Dodgers, like all those other fixers were brothers who lost the same stuff I did. Oh yeah, Herb Cohen and Fats Roth and Irwin Dambrot and Connie Schaff and Eddie Roman and Leroy Smith and Floyd Layne and Sherm White and Ed Warner, they all still there in my head, floating around our own schoolyard. White and Warner, they the best—I had to go some to keep up with them.

They got some boys from the Midwest, too, and some Catholic kids, too. That Cardinal Spellman, he live in the powerhouse, corner of Madison and 50th, next to St. Patrick's, and every time I go by, I still spit. Divine intervention, that's what Big Ed calls it when we talk, but I don't laugh. Still, I got to smile now, to see the way things change. That cardinal gone now and he can't help these Catholic boys even if he wanted to.

They gas on about the new fixes, how this one player, he's a real altar boy, and how the big man this time, he was only doing it for a hobby, cause his main job was running the $5 million Lufthansa gig. Oh yeah, I think, there's still guys dumber than me. Now that this guy puts the finger on guys in the mob, we don't take bets on him getting social security.

The kids on the court, they all in high school, when they sit down between games and hear us talking about the fixes, they don't even blink. They talk to each other about how many tape decks they got and which truck they got it off of and they don't pay these new fixes no mind at all.

I close my eyes and think about the names of the new boys, and I lean back against the fence, try to see what they look like. I got no photos, though. I listen to how they set this new fix up and I hear the guys talk about how great Connie Hawkins and Roger Brown and Doug Moe would of been, they'd got their chance in the NBA when they were in their prime, and I even hear one of the guys tell me how I was robbed, I got blacklisted. I open my eyes a minute, tell him what I said back then, about what kind of list they got for the white boys. He laughs and when he does I got to close my eyes real quick. All that stuff about clean hands and blacklists and why I did it—who you fooling back then, Mack? I got this pain down low in my gut, and I'm trying to knock their words out of the way so I can see things clear, try to feel what these new boys must be feeling now.

Oh yeah, that pain tell you something, Mack. You never even been inside that new Madison Square Garden they got, it gonna hurt so much. You never even gone to see Hawkins play, when he got in the pros. Sure. Who you fooling? They take away the only thing you love, and how you ever gonna tell anybody that? How you gonna live the rest of your life, you can't do the only thing you good at, the only thing you been taught to do?

These questions come shooting in my head and I don't like it. I try to knock them out of the way, too, and when I do, I get this real strange picture there instead. There's this long hallway and I'm walking down the middle and I got to stop every few feet to shake hands with these guys I used to know, and they're all sitting in wheelchairs. There's Roy Campanella and Maurice Stokes and Ernie Davis and Junius Kellogg and Brian Piccolo and Big Daddy Lipscomb and Tom Stith and Darryl Stingley and even this guy named Pete Gray, who played baseball with one arm, and Monty Stratton, who played with a wooden leg, and at the end of the tunnel, there's old Jackie Robinson, the greatest player who ever lived, you ask me, and he's got his son sitting next to him. I bend over to shake their hands and I can't figure out why they're in wheelchairs if they're both dead so many years now—Jackie Jr. strung out good on drugs, then clean just in time to get wiped off the highway in a sports car—and Jackie, all white-haired and fuzzy and smiling real broad, dead when he was about the age I'm at now. He reaches up to me with his hand and wishes me good luck with that soft, high-pitched voice, and I tell him I'm real sorry that his son died first, before he did.

I open my eyes and see that one of the guys been trying to get me to move and now he's razzing me about my fat ass and how I don't play no different asleep or awake. This kid named Jim, about my height, 6-6, only he weighs about 80 pounds less, he points to my belly and laughs. Why he got to worry? The ball comes to him first thing, down low, he gives me a head fake and he's slamming the ball through and his men slapping his hands and he's grinning real big. One of my guys says to show him how the old fixers used to do it. Jim, he asks me how come the other guy calls me a fixer—cause of the way I let him get around me? I tell him to shut his ass and give his mouth a chance, and he laughs some more.

Oh yeah, I think. They take away my life cause I shave a few points, but that ain't nothing to what athletes been doing since, sniffing and shooting up and buggering each other and all the rest, only these days they get to write books about it after. Under the basket, back up against the fence, the guys still talking about how these new fixes got rigged, remembering the time, back in our day, when two teams played each other, both teams supposed to go down at the same time for different gamblers, and all I want to do is go over and tell them to shut their big mouths, too. The ball comes into my man and he gives me a head fake. This time, I don't go for it, then he tries to go under me with his dipsy-doodle crap, I get my leg out quick and let him have it where he lives. Then I got the ball from him, he's all bent over, and I roll over this other kid who ain't nearly as big and I'm going up real high, as high as an old man can go, and drop that ball in without touching the rim. Two points for our side.

The other two guys on my team, they try to rank me out about taking it easy cause I old enough to be my man Jim's grandfather, but I don't say anything. The only thing I wait for is the feel of that ball in my hands, dumb me. What else I gonna do?

Joyce Carol Oates

Rape and the Boxing Ring

Ever since Joyce Carol Oates's father took her to Golden Gloves matches in Buffalo, New York, and justified the legalized violence he was exposing his young daughter to by saying, "Boxers don't feel pain quite the same way we do," Oates has been fascinated with the sport. Oates's fascination resulted in an acclaimed 1987 collection of essays titled On Boxing. *In one of the essays, a young heavyweight champion named Mike Tyson explained his brutal ring strategy: "I try to catch my opponent on the tip of his nose because I want to punch the bone into his brain." Tyson's "strategy" was an effective one and earned him millions of dollars. But what happens when that blood lust, that physical aggression, is not confined to the ring? In this 1992* Newsweek *essay, Oates sees the paradox of boxing in the rape conviction of Mike Tyson.*

Mike Tyson's conviction on rape charges in Indianapolis is a minor tragedy for the beleaguered sport of boxing, but a considerable triumph for women's rights. For once, though bookmakers were giving 5–1 odds that Tyson would be acquitted, and the mood of the country seems distinctly conservative, a jury resisted the outrageous defense that a rape victim is to be blamed for her own predicament. For once, a celebrity with enormous financial resources did not escape trial and a criminal conviction by settling with his accuser out of court.

That boxing and "women's rights" should be perceived as opposed is symbolically appropriate, since of all sports, boxing is the most aggressively masculine, the very soul of war in microcosm. Elemental and dramatically concise, it raises to an art the passions underlying direct human aggression; its fundamentally murderous intent is not obscured by the pursuit of balls or pucks, nor can the participants expect help from teammates. In a civilized, humanitarian society, one would expect such a blood sport to have died out, yet boxing, sponsored by gambling casinos in Las Vegas and Atlantic City, and broadcast by cable television, flourishes: had the current heavyweight champion, Evander Holyfield, fought Mike Tyson in a title defense, Holyfield would have earned no less than $30 million. If Tyson were still champion, and still fighting, he would be earning more.

The paradox of boxing is that it so excessively rewards men for inflicting injury upon one another that, outside the ring, with less "art," would be punishable as aggravated assault, or manslaughter. Boxing belongs to that species of mysterious masculine activity for which anthropologists use such terms as "deep play": activity that is wholly without utilitarian value, in fact contrary to utilitarian value, so dangerous that no amount of money can justify it. Sports-car racing, stunt flying, mountain climbing, bullfighting, dueling—these activities, through history, have provided ways in which the individual can dramatically, if sometimes fatally, distinguish himself from the crowd, usually with the adulation and envy of the crowd, and traditionally, the love of women. Women—in essence, Woman—is the prize, usually self-proffered. To look upon organized sports as a continuum of Darwinian theory—in which the sports-star hero flaunts the superiority of his genes—is to see how displays of masculine aggression have their sexual component, as ingrained in human beings as any instinct for self-preservation and reproduction. In a capitalist society, the secret is to capitalize upon instinct.

Yet even within the very special world of sports, boxing is distinct. Is there any athlete, however celebrated in his own sport, who would not rather reign as the heavyweight champion of the world? If, in fantasy at least, he could be another Muhammad Ali, or Joe Louis, or indeed, Mike Tyson in his prime? Boxing celebrates the individual man in his maleness, not merely in his skill as an athlete—though boxing demands enormous skill, and its training is far more arduous than most men could endure for more than a day or two. All athletes can become addicted to their own adrenaline, but none more obviously than the boxer, who, like Sugar Ray Leonard, already a multimillionaire with numerous occupations outside the ring, will risk serious injury by coming back out of retirement; as Mike Tyson has said, "Outside of boxing, everything is so boring." What makes boxing repulsive to many observers is precisely what makes boxing so fascinating to participants.

This is because it is a highly organized ritual that violates taboo. It flouts such moral prescriptions as "Thou shalt not kill." It celebrates, not meekness, but flamboyant aggression. No one who has not seen live boxing matches (in contrast to the sanitized matches broadcast over television) can quite grasp its eerie fascination—the spectator's sense that he or she is a witness to madness, yet a madness sanctioned by tradition and custom, as finely honed by certain celebrated practitioners as an artist's performance at the highest level of genius, and, yet more disturbing, immensely gratifying to the audience. Boxing mimics our early ancestors' rite of bloody sacrifice and redemption; it excites desires most civilized men and women find abhorrent. For some observers, it is frankly obscene, like pornography; yet, unlike pornography, it is not fantasy but real, thus far more subversive.

The paradox for the boxer is that, in the ring, he experiences himself as a living conduit for the inchoate, demonic will of the crowd: the expression of their collective desire, which is to pound another human being into absolute submission. The more vicious the boxer, the greater the acclaim. And the financial reward—Tyson is reported to have earned $100 million. (He who at the age of 13 was plucked from a boys' school for juvenile delinquents in upstate New York.) Like the champion gladiators of Roman decadence, he will be both honored and despised, for, no matter his celebrity, and the gift of his talent, his energies spring from the violation of taboo and he himself is tainted by it.

Mike Tyson has said that he does not think of boxing as a sport. He sees himself as a fantasy gladiator who, by "destructing" opponents, enacts others' fantasies in his own being. That the majority of these others are well-to-do whites who would themselves crumple at a first blow, and would surely claim a pious humanitarianism, would not go unnoted by so wary and watchful a man. Cynicism is not an inevitable consequence of success, but it is difficult to retain one's boyish naiveté in the company of the sort of people, among them the notorious Don King, who have surrounded Tyson since 1988, when his comanager, Jim Jacobs, died. As Floyd Patterson, an ex-heavyweight champion who has led an exemplary life, has said, "When you have millions of dollars, you have millions of friends."

It should not be charged against boxing that Mike Tyson *is* boxing in any way. Boxers tend to be fiercely individualistic, and Tyson is, at the least, an enigma. He began his career, under the tutelage of the legendary trainer Cus D'Amato, as a strategist, in the mode of such brilliant technicians as Henry Armstrong and Sugar Ray Robinson. He was always aware of a lineage with Jack Dempsey, arguably the most electrifying of all heavyweight champions, whose nonstop aggression revolutionized the sport and whose shaved haircut and malevolent scowl, and, indeed, penchant for dirty fighting, made a tremendous impression upon the young Tyson.

In recent years, however, Tyson seems to have styled himself at least partly on the model of Charles (Sonny) Liston, the "baddest of the bad" black heavyweights. Liston had numerous arrests to his credit and served time in prison (for assaulting a policeman); he had the air, not entirely contrived, of a sociopath; he was always friendly with racketeers, and died of a drug overdose that may in fact have been murder. (It is not coincidental that Don King, whom Tyson has much admired, and who Tyson has empowered to ruin his career, was convicted of manslaughter and served time in an Ohio prison.) Like Liston, Tyson has grown to take a cynical pleasure in publicly condoned sadism (his "revenge" bout with Tyrell Biggs, whom he carried for seven long rounds in order to inflict maximum damage) and in playing the outlaw; his contempt for women, escalating in recent years, is a part of that guise. The witty obscenity of a prefight taunt of Tyson's—"I'll make you into my girlfriend"—is the boast of the rapist.

Perhaps rape itself is a gesture, a violent repudiation of the female, in the assertion of maleness that would seem to require nothing beyond physical gratification of the crudest kind. The supreme macho gesture —like knocking out an opponent and standing over his fallen body, gloves raised in triumph.

In boxing circles it is said—this, with an affectionate sort of humor—that the heavyweight champion is the 300-pound gorilla who sits anywhere in the room he wants; and, presumably, takes any female he wants. Such a grandiose sense of entitlement, fueled by the insecurities and emotions of adolescence, can have disastrous consequences. Where once it was believed that Mike Tyson might mature into the greatest heavyweight of all time, breaking Rocky Marciano's record of 49 victories and no defeats, it was generally acknowledged that, since his defeat of Michael Spinks in 1988, he had allowed his boxing skills to deteriorate. Not simply his ignominious loss of his title to the mediocre James (Buster) Douglas in 1990, but subsequent lackluster victories against mediocre opponents made it clear that Tyson was no longer a serious, nor even very interesting, boxer.

The dazzling reflexes were dulled, the shrewd defensive skills drilled into him by D'Amato were largely abandoned: Tyson emerged suddenly as a conventional heavyweight like Gerry Cooney, who advances upon his opponent with the hope of knocking him out with a single punch—and does not always succeed. By 25, Tyson seemed already middle aged, burnt out. He would have no great fights after all. So, strangely, he seemed to invite his fate outside the ring, with sadomasochistic persistence, testing the limits of his celebrity's license to offend by ever-escalating acts of aggression and sexual effrontery.

The familiar sports adage is surely true, one's ultimate opponent is oneself.

It may be objected that these remarks center upon the rapist, and not his victim; that sympathy, pity, even in some quarters moral outrage flow to the criminal and not the person he has violated. In this case, ironically, the victim, Desiree Washington, though she will surely bear psychic scars through her life, has emerged as a victor, a heroine: a young woman whose traumatic experience has been, as so few traumas can be, the vehicle for a courageous and selfless stand against the sexual abuse of women and children in America. She seems to know that herself, telling *People* magazine, "It was the right thing to do." She was fortunate in drawing a jury who rejected classic defense ploys by blaming the victim and/or arguing consent. Our criminal-justice system being what it is, she was lucky. Tyson, who might have been acquitted elsewhere in the country, was unlucky.

Whom to blame for this most recent of sports disgraces in America? The culture that flings young athletes like Tyson up out of obscurity, makes millionaires of them and watches them self-destruct? Promoters like Don King and Bob Arum? Celebrity hunters like Robin Givens, Tyson's ex-wife, who seemed to have exploited him for his money and as a means of promoting her own acting career? The indulgence generally granted star athletes when they behave recklessly? When they abuse drugs and alcohol, and mistreat women?

I suggest that no one is to blame, finally, except the perpetrator himself. In Montieth Illingworth's cogently argued biography of Tyson, *Mike Tyson: Money, Myth and Betrayal*, Tyson is quoted, after one or another public debacle: "People say 'Poor guy.' That insults me. I despise sympathy. So I screwed up. I made some mistakes. 'Poor guy,' like I'm some victim. There's nothing poor about me."

Sadaharu Oh and David Falkner

Sadaharu Oh's Final Bow

"Oh's story reads like Bernard Malamud's The Natural, *edited by Ernest Hemingway, with research by James Michener," said* The New York Times's *George Vecsey of Sadaharu Oh's autobiography,* A Zen Way of Baseball. *Here, in his last game as a player, Oh, the man who hit more home runs (868) than anyone else in professional baseball, reflects on his legendary career.*

O
utside, the warm autumn sun shone on the grass. The grass had yellowed during the summer and was dying now. White clouds floated in the clear sky above. The light of the sun, so particular now, carried a hint of winter. The sounds of the crowd filling the stands came to me like the low rumbling of an island surf. The game would be starting soon. Everything was as usual, except . . .

> The sound of the crowd.
> The clear colors of the sky.
> The warmth of the sun.
> The light of winter coming.

My last game, my very last game. Twenty-two years leading to this moment—a whole lifetime. I realized that I was standing alone in this locker room. I had not meant to linger behind, but I had—and now I was by myself in an empty room that seemed more like a warehouse: row on row of lockers, empty trunks of equipment, signs of life everywhere but no one to be seen. I felt enclosed in this space, as though in a dream just before waking, unable to stir myself past those final restraints of sleep. Why was I standing here? I wanted to follow my team-mates, but I didn't. I became conscious of how foolish I felt just standing there alone. I moved to a bench and sat down. I was thinking about my uniform number.

My uniform number was One—all the years I was in high school and all the years I was a major league ballplayer. Number One. People made something of that. BIG ONE the press blurbs read. Big One! What is a "big one"? I don't put that down. I enjoyed it too much. But I know who I am—or who I have been. I am ordinary. No larger, no smaller than life-size. But my number matters to me. In my mind's eye, I see my number on my uniform jersey in the only way that it has ever been important—showing toward the pitcher as I assume my batting stance. When I was at my best, I turned my back almost ninety degrees toward the pitcher. I felt like a rough Japanese sea. My number suddenly rose toward the pitcher like a dark wave just before I struck.

I blinked. I looked down and saw that I had been gripping my cap so tightly in both hands that I was in danger of tearing it. I wiped my face. I had been crying. So strange. Why was I behaving like this? Get up, go out there, join your teammates! But I was not ready.

I am a professional ballplayer, I told myself. A professional. The word has meaning for me as few others in my vocabulary do. There is a standard of performance you must maintain. It is the best you are able to give and then more—and to maintain that at a level of consistency. No excuses for the demands of your ego or the extremes of your emotions. It is an inner thing. I held myself to that standard for twenty-two years. It is my proudest achievement.

I saw my face in a locker-room mirror used for shadow batting. A kind of mirror I had stood before for perhaps thousands of hours in my pro career. My face looked odd to me, eyes a little swollen, the expression open and easy, almost as if I were a child again rather than a man of forty.

"Get yourself together, Number One!"

"Easy, give the man time. He has it coming."

My voices. For me, the tough one, the hard one nearly always wins out:

"It is November 16, 1980. You are in Fujisakidai Stadium in Ku-mamoto, Kyushu. The opponents are the Hanshin Tigers. Your team-mates and the fans are waiting. . . ."

The other:

"This is your very last game, last time you will swing the bat. This game is for you, just you. There is something in it for you. Take your time. Be kind to yourself. . . ."

I have been a pro baseball player for so long. More than half my time on earth. I barely had the time of my boyhood just to myself. I hit 868 home runs. More than Babe Ruth or Hank Aaron, more than any man on either side of the Pacific. I was a home-run champion for fifteen years, thirteen of them in a row. I hit thirty or more home runs for nineteen consecutive seasons. I led the league in RBIs thirteen times, in batting five times. I won the Triple Crown back to back in 1973 and 1974 and was the league's MVP nine times. I walked more than 2,500 times, leading the league in walks for eighteen straight seasons. In 1972, Japanese professional baseball introduced fielding awards—the Diamond Glove—equivalent of the Golden Glove awards in America. I won a Diamond Glove thereafter for nine consecutive seasons till I retired.

But I am not Babe Ruth or Hank Aaron. I cannot compare myself with them any more than they might have compared themselves with me. I am the Japanese Oh Sadaharu. And I should probably qualify that, too. I am only half-Japanese! I take my records seriously, of course. Athletes are very fond of saying that they look forward to having successors come along to break their records. There is always the figure of the former record holder trotting out on the field to embrace the new record holder. It is part of the show. But if it happens to me, I'll be sad. I'll be photographed smiling and shaking hands and embracing like all the other old-timers, but I'll be very sad. I want my records to stand. And yet, while I am proud of my records, I am prouder still of this matter of duration. It represents something different, harder to explain. . . .

There are two figures who have been a constant inspiration for me throughout my career. Lou Gehrig and Miyamoto Musashi. Gehrig was a home-run hitter, but his greatest achievement was as "the Iron Man," playing 2,130 consecutive games. That is not just an athletic record (which it is and will be most likely forever), it is more an event of the spirit. It is impossible to play through fourteen straight seasons simply as a body showing up. You must be filled with something in your soul that enables you to withstand bruises and injuries and pressures of boredom and fatigue. The stretch of so many years and so many games leaves you with that one game, that one day where you simply sit down. But Gehrig never did. There was something in him—not necessarily physical strength—that enabled him to endure. The Japanese word for spirit-power is *ki*. It is both spiritual and physical. They are not to be separated. Thus the *quality* of Lou Gehrig's play during that incredible stretch was as much determined by his spirit as by the "iron" in his body. He was a man whose great talents were enhanced by spirit-discipline. He wanted to retire later than he did. His physical body betrayed him. His spirit never did. On Independence Day, 1939, knowing that he was dying, he told fans in Yankee Stadium not only about how lucky he was but also that he was truly happy. It was his Independence Day.

Musashi, the legendary Japanese samurai, beat his archrival Kojiro with more than strength and technique—it was also spirit-discipline. Musashi began as a young, headstrong boy and learned through years of daily practice that he was the possessor of something far more important than his sword. Kojiro was probably the better technician, but Musashi, in the end, beat him. And then gave up fighting.

The sound of a wave is an ordinary happening in this world . . .
But who can sound the wave a hundred feet below?

The mirror across the way did not show me what was in my own body now. Beyond the doorway was the warm sun of Kyushu, a crowd of people, my teammates, another baseball game. I was not retiring just because my body would no longer permit me to play; nor was I, like Musashi, retiring to seek out solitude in the mountains. I was leaving because in this, my final year, I had also discovered that I no longer had the desire to play. My heart was no longer on fire. I could no longer play up to my own standards.

Records come and go. So does celebrity. Because my profession took place in the public eye, people have attached more importance to my comings and goings than they might have otherwise. I have been asked all kinds of questions in my career—questions about war and peace, art, politics, religion—and I've always had this odd feeling of being both flattered and embarrassed. The opinions of someone who has spent his life chasing a little white ball around a field really ought not be offered as oracles from the Buddha. I was a home-run hitter (as I later became an assistant manager). But I found in the world of baseball something I might never have found if I had done something else. It was surprising and unexpected. Baseball was for me, too, a form of spirit-discipline, a way to make myself a better person—although I surely never sought discipline for such a reason. It became my Way, as the tea ceremony or flower arranging or the making of poems were the Ways of others.

"Mr. Oh, it is time!"

"Yes. I'll be there."

The crowd in Kyushu, like the weather, was warm and encouraging. A good day in a good atmosphere to end it.

"Batting fourth, Number One, Oh. Number One, Oh!"

Last time as cleanup hitter, last time to swing the special Ishii bat, last time to try for one more, just one more. . . . Yes, of course I wanted to go out that way. In the last game of the official season I had gone hitless. I wished God had let it be otherwise. But there had been only this gift of an extension of the regular season, so peculiar to Japanese baseball. In America the season ends with the World Series. Here, after the Japan Series, some of our teams regularly make trips to remote areas of the country that normally don't see live major league baseball during the season. It is done as a tribute to the fans, and the games, though considered exhibitions, are well attended and hard fought.

Our opponent that afternoon was our traditional rival, the Hanshin Tigers. It was the bottom of the fifth inning. The newspapers, the day following, said it was exactly 1:56 in the afternoon. The Tigers' pitcher —Norikazu Miyata—was young and inexperienced, and he threw me a ball I saw well. I hit it into the bleachers in right-center field. I circled the bases for the last time. (By coincidence, my first hit as a major leaguer had also been a home run.) Yes, this was the way I wanted to end it. But, then, a curious thing happened. As I crossed second base, heading toward third, I saw the players on the Hanshin bench leave the dugout and come toward the third baseline. By the time I reached the bag, they were lined up from third base to home plate. Some of the players in the field had also joined them. Even though they stood formally, at attention, there were expressions of genuine affection on their faces. I was very moved. I slowed my trot so I could shake hands with each of them in thanks. As I approached each player, he took off his cap, bowed to me, and shook my hand. At home plate, the manager of the Tigers presented me with a large bouquet of yellow autumn flowers. The crowd cheered. I waved to them, and bowed to the stands and the other players, then I went out to the mound to encourage the Tiger pitcher and to wish him well in the future.

My opponents lifted my spirits and, in doing so, reminded me of something that I had spent twenty-two years learning. That opponents and I were really one. My strength and skills were only one half of the equation. The other half was theirs. And standing there that day in Kyushu as my past became the future in a single moment, the years dropped away and I was a young boy again, coming out of high school to this strange, exciting world of professional baseball. How full of hope and strength and eagerness I was! I saw in the faces of the young players near me on the field the same look of expectation. In their eyes was the same will to combat, the same dream of creating records; and to me, because I was a celebrated old-timer now, they were kind enough to pay respect for a job well done.

But my job is not done, it is only beginning—and where the future will take me I do not know. I learned as a boy, because fate put me in the way of a master teacher, that practical training in skills, if done in a certain way, was also a method of spirit-discipline. And in combat, I learned to give up combat. I learned in fact, there were no enemies. An opponent was someone whose strength joined to yours created a certain result. Let someone call you enemy and attack you, and in that moment they lost the contest. It was hard to learn this—perhaps I am only just beginning to follow its lead—but my baseball career was a long, long initiation into a single secret: that at the heart of all things is love. We are, each of us, one with the universe that surrounds us—in harmony with it, not in conspiracy against it. To live by being in harmony with what surrounds you is to be reminded that every end is followed by a new beginning—and that the humblest of life's offerings is as treasured as the greatest in the eyes of the Creator.

George Orwell

The Sporting Spirit

In his review of Michael Shelden's biography of George Orwell published in 1991, Samuel Hynes wrote that, among other things, Orwell cared about good writing. And then Hynes said: "But his writing also has another quality that is crucial to the life of language now: its fierce intemperateness." You will find a prime example of the distinctive Orwell intemperateness in this essay on British football, football crowds, the Olympic Games, and other matters relating to the dark side of sports. It is perhaps the least sentimental piece in this entire volume, by a man who was never given to sentimentality, and comes from his landmark work—his four-volume Collected Essays, Journals, and Letters.*

Now that the brief visit of the Dynamo football team* has come to an end, it is possible to say publicly what many thinking people were saying privately before the Dynamos ever arrived. That is, that sport is an unfailing cause of ill-will, and that if such a visit as this had any effect at all on Anglo-Soviet relations, it could only be to make them slightly worse than before.

Even the newspapers have been unable to conceal the fact that at least two of the four matches played led to much bad feeling. At the Arsenal match, I am told by someone who was there, a British and a Russian player came to blows and the crowd booed the referee. The Glasgow match, someone else informs me, was simply a free-for-all from the start. And then there was the controversy, typical of our nationalistic

---

* The Moscow Dynamos, a Russian football team, toured Britain in the autumn of 1945 playing against leading British clubs.

age, about the composition of the Arsenal team. Was it really an all-England team, as claimed by the Russians, or merely a league team, as claimed by the British? And did the Dynamos end their tour abruptly in order to avoid playing an all-England team? As usual, everyone answers these questions according to his political predilections. Not quite everyone, however. I noted with interest, as an instance of the vicious passions that football provokes, that the sporting correspondent of the russophile *News Chronicle* took the anti-Russian line and maintained that Arsenal was not an all-England team. No doubt the controversy will continue to echo for years in the footnotes of history books. Meanwhile the result of the Dynamos' tour, in so far as it has had any result, will have been to create fresh animosity on both sides.

And how could it be otherwise? I am always amazed when I hear people saying that sport creates goodwill between the nations, and that if only the common peoples of the world could meet one another at football or cricket, they would have no inclination to meet on the battlefield. Even if one didn't know from concrete examples (the 1936 Olympic Games, for instance) that international sporting contests lead to orgies of hatred, one could deduce it from general principles.

Nearly all the sports practised nowadays are competitive. You play to win, and the game has little meaning unless you do your utmost to win. On the village green, where you pick up sides and no feeling of local patriotism is involved, it is possible to play simply for the fun and exercise: but as soon as the question of prestige arises, as soon as you feel that you and some larger unit will be disgraced if you lose, the most savage combative instincts are aroused. Anyone who has played even in a school football match knows this. At the international level sport is frankly mimic warfare. But the significant thing is not the behaviour of the players but the attitude of the spectators: and, behind the spectators, of the nations who work themselves into furies over these absurd contests, and seriously believe—at any rate for short periods—that running, jumping and kicking a ball are tests of national virtue.

Even a leisurely game like cricket, demanding grace rather than strength, can cause much ill-will, as we saw in the controversy over body-line bowling and over the rough tactics of the Australian team that visited England in 1921. Football, a game in which everyone gets hurt and every nation has its own style of play which seems unfair to foreigners, is far worse. Worst of all is boxing. One of the most horrible sights in the world is a fight between white and coloured boxers before a mixed audience. But a boxing audience is always disgusting, and the behaviour of the women, in particular, is such that the army, I believe, does not allow them to attend its contests. At any rate, two or three years ago, when Home Guards and regular troops were holding a boxing tournament, I was placed on guard at the door of the hall, with orders to keep the women out.

In England, the obsession with sport is bad enough, but even fiercer passions are aroused in young countries where games playing and nationalism are both recent developments. In countries like India or Burma, it is necessary at football matches to have strong cordons of police to keep the crowd from invading the field. In Burma, I have seen the supporters of one side break through the police and disable the goalkeeper of the opposing side at a critical moment. The first big football match that was played in Spain about fifteen years ago led to an uncontrollable riot. As soon as strong feelings of rivalry are aroused, the notion of playing the game according to the rules always vanishes. People want to see one side on top and the other side humiliated, and they forget that victory gained through cheating or through the intervention of the crowd is meaningless. Even when the spectators don't intervene physically they try to influence the game by cheering their own side and "rattling" opposing players with boos and insults. Serious sport has nothing to do with fair play. It is bound up with hatred, jealousy, boastfulness, disregard of all rules and sadistic pleasure in witnessing violence: in other words it is war minus the shooting.

Instead of blah-blahing about the clean, healthy rivalry of the football field and the great part played by the Olympic Games in bringing the nations together, it is more useful to inquire how and why this modern cult of sport arose. Most of the games we now play are of ancient origin, but sport does not seem to have been taken very seriously between Roman times and the nineteenth century. Even in the English public schools the games cult did not start till the later part of the last century. Dr Arnold, generally regarded as the founder of the modern public school, looked on games as simply a waste of time. Then, chiefly in England and the United States, games were built up into a heavily-financed activity, capable of attracting vast crowds and rousing savage passions, and the infection spread from country to country. It is the most violently combative sports, football and boxing, that have spread the widest. There cannot be much doubt that the whole thing is bound up with the rise of nationalism—that is, with the lunatic modern habit of identifying oneself with large power units and seeing everything in terms of competitive prestige. Also, organised games are more likely to flourish in urban communities where the average human being lives a sedentary or at least a confined life, and does not get much opportunity for creative labour. In a rustic community a boy or young man works off a good deal of his surplus energy by walking, swimming, snowballing, climbing trees, riding horses, and by various sports involving cruelty to animals, such as fishing, cock-fighting and ferreting for rats. In a big town one must indulge in group activities if one wants an outlet for one's physical strength or for one's sadistic impulses. Games are taken seriously in London and New York, and they were taken seriously in Rome and Byzantium: in the Middle Ages they were played, and probably played with much physical brutality, but they were not mixed up with politics nor a cause of group hatreds.

If you wanted to add to the vast fund of ill-will existing in the world at this moment, you could hardly do it better than by a series of football matches between Jews and Arabs, Germans and Czechs, Indians and British, Russians and Poles, and Italians and Jugoslavs, each match to be watched by a mixed audience of 100,000 spectators. I do not, of course, suggest that sport is one of the main causes of international rivalry; big-scale sport is itself, I think, merely another effect of the causes that have produced nationalism. Still, you do make things worse by sending forth a team of eleven men, labelled as national champions, to do battle against some rival team, and allowing it to be felt on all sides that whichever nation is defeated will "lose face".

I hope, therefore, that we shan't follow up the visit of the Dynamos by sending a British team to the USSR. If we must do so, then let us send a second-rate team which is sure to be beaten and cannot be claimed to represent Britain as a whole. There are quite enough real causes of trouble already, and we need not add to them by encouraging young men to kick each other on the shins amid the roars of infuriated spectators.

Richard Price

Bear Bryant's Miracles

In this piece, published by Playboy *in 1979, the author of such street-sharp novels as* The Wanderers, Blood Brothers, *and* Clockers *detours from the city to the unfamiliar terrain of Alabama where he is to meet with a Southern deity named Paul "Bear" Bryant. The imposing stature of one of college football's most fabled coaches has Price contemplating a haircut and a quick perusal of the scriptures before his scheduled audience with the man in the houndstooth hat.*

Because I grew up in a multiethnic environment in New York City, the South has always conjured up some bad news reactions on word-association tests for me: Klan, lynch, redneck, moonshine, speedtrap towns and death . . . lots of death.

As the years have passed, I've started hearing some flip sides. There's the "New South," with Atlanta as cosmopolitan as New York. I've heard that, despite the headline horrors, Southerners get along racially better than Northerners. And that foreign blacks prefer the upfrontness of the South to the hypocritical liberal bullshit of the North.

But despite all my revisionist thoughts, the only good images that have held up in my head are Southern novelists and the University of Alabama football team. The novelists because they are good or great and the Crimson Tide because, like Notre Dame, they are the New York Yankees of college football. I don't give a rat's ass about football, college or otherwise, and I'm not crazy about regimentation or bullet-head activities. But I do admire winners.

And as ignorant as I am of the "real" South and football in general, even *I* know that the man behind the winning tradition at Alabama is a magnetic, scary John Wayne type named Paul "Bear" Bryant. I would see him every few years on a televised bowl game, standing on the side lines, craggy-faced, in that houndstooth hat. I figured he was some kind of coaching genius. I also got the notion that he was somebody I was very glad not to have as a teacher in any course I was flunking.

On the plane headed for Birmingham, I am armed with two documents: *Bear,* coach Bryant's autobiography; and the 1978 *Alabama Football Crimson Tide Press Guide. Bear* doesn't do much for me—it's a little too cagily humble. The *Press Guide,* on the other hand, has me freaking out six ways to Sunday. These guys are *monsters.* Even the handsome fraternity types have that combat-veteran look about them.

The other things that are dizzying in the press book are the win-loss stats. They're almost pornographic. Since Bryant went to Alabama in 1958, the Tide's record has been 193–38–8. In the past eight years, try 85–11—that's almost 11 wins per season. They were in 20 bowl games in a row, won all but one Southeastern Conference title since 1971 ('76 went to Georgia), won five national championships since 1961 and have a home record of 60–1, with 45 straight victories.

Bryant is the winningest active coach, with 284 victories in 34 years at four schools, and is third in total wins only to Amos Alonzo Stagg and Pop Warner as far as the history of the game goes.

At the Birmingham airport, I start wondering why the hell I am keying in so much on the hairdos I see all around me. The Dolly Parton pompadours, the rock-a-billy duck asses, the military knuckleheads. Then I look in a mirror. With the possible exception of a photo of Duane Allman, I have the longest hair of anybody I've seen all day. I start getting visions of rusty scissors in a sheriff's office. Ah, that's all Hollywood horseshit, I tell myself. But I do go into a men's room and remove my earring.

Bryant Hall is where all the players have to live for the four or five years they're at Alabama. It was among the first sports dorms in the country and it received a lot of flak for special treatment, pampering, athletic elitism. Since then, sports dorms have popped up all over, but the controversy still goes on.

In any event, as I go there for lunch with Kirk McNair, Alabama's sports information director, I expect to see something between a palace and a beachfront condominium. What I see is more like a cross between a dorm and a housing project. The place looks like shit. Off the lobby is a TV room and the dining room. Players walk by. Some are mammoth, with roast-beef shoulders and hamhock thighs, and they shuffle sway-backed into the dining room; others aren't much bigger than I am. Alabama opts for quickness over bulk; consequently, it's not that big a team.

I eat with McNair and a Birmingham sportswriter, plus a short, heavy Italian guy who runs a restaurant in town, is a freak for the team and supplies everybody with food. He just likes to hang around with the boys.

From where we sit, I can see the guys taking the empty trays to the disposal area. They all seem to shuffle, drag their feet like they're saving it up for practice—or else they have that sprightly pigeon-toed jock walk, as if they're about to sprint across a room keeping a soccer ball afloat with their toes and knees.

I don't hear anybody mention Bear Bryant. In fact, he doesn't have that much personal contact with his players. He's got a huge staff of coaching assistants who get down in the dirt with them.

But he's there. He's in that room. He *is* the team and everybody knows it.

A football is laid out with a white pen by the tray-disposal area, and the players sign the ball after they get rid of their trays. Some kid is going to get the best birthday present in the entire state. Or maybe it's for his old man.

Later that afternoon, I'm taken to the grass practice field. The sports offices are in the coliseum and there's a long underground walkway that connects with the closed-to-the-public Astroturf practice field. The first thing I notice as I come up to ground level, slightly drunk on the waft of freshly cut grass, is a tower. A huge 50-foot-high observation post.

And up there is my first shot of Bear, slouched against the railing, wearing a beat-up varsity jacket, a baseball cap, a megaphone hanging from one wrist. He doesn't move, just leans back like he's lost in thought. Below him, there are maybe 100 guys running plays, mashing into one another in the dirt, attacking dummies. A massive division of labor of violence, speed and strength. Assistant coaches are all over, screaming, barking, shoving, soothing (though not too much), encouraging. A sound track of grunts, growls, roars and commands floats in the spring air. And above it all, Bear doesn't move, he doesn't even seem to be inter-ested. It's as though he's a stranded lifeguard, six months off season, wondering how the hell he got up there and how the hell he's gonna get down.

The most terrifying workout I see that day is called the gauntlet drill. You take three linemen, line them up one behind the other about ten feet apart. Then a relatively small running back is placed about five feet in front of the first lineman, and at the sound of a whistle, he tries to get past the first lineman. If he does, the lineman gets the shit chewed out of him by the defensive coach. If he doesn't, the running back gets dumped on his ass by an enormous amount of meat and gear. Either way, he has to set to, go around the second lineman, then the third. Somehow, with that coach bawling and shoving the lineman who fucked up, I feel more anxiety for the lineman than I do for the halfback.

On the Astroturf field, there are two practice scrimmages with referees. I sit on the side-line bench with a number of pro scouts, a few privileged civilians and a bunch of shaggy-haired 12-year-olds who walk up and down the side line imitating that pigeon-toed jock walk, chewing gum and trying to look like future prospects. Like me, every few minutes they sneak a glance at the tower to check out the big man.

The players are wearing jerseys of one of five colors. Red jersey—first-string offense. White—first-string defense. Blue—second-string defense. Green—second-string offense. And gold. Gold signifies "Don't tackle this man," which means the guy is either a quarterback (quarterbacks never get tackled in practice) or nursing an injury.

I look up at the tower. Bear is gone.

The bench we're sitting on divides the pits and the Astroturf from a long, flat grassy field with just a few goal posts at one distant end. Bear makes it down to earth and, head still down, slowly ambles over to the grassy field. Some of the 12-year-olds notice and nudge one another. He's walking away. Going home. Hands in pockets. The bench divides the two shows: the number-one college team working out to the west and the coach slowly walking alone to the east.

I turn my back on the players and watch Bear walk. He gets out about 50 yards toward the walkway back to the coliseum when a player on crutches, hobbling toward the Astroturf, meets him at mid-field. They stop, exchange a few words (the crutches do *not* fall away as I would prefer) and the wounded player swings along toward the crowd.

Bear stands there, staring at his shoes, scratching his nose. Then, without looking up, he puts a whistle in his mouth, shoots a couple of weak toots I think only I can hear, and suddenly the earth is shaking and I'm caught in a buffalo stampede. Every player has immediately dropped everything and is tearing ass over to Bear.

They say no one *ever* walks for a second from the beginning to the end of an Alabama practice. Within 20 seconds of his whistle, Bear is surrounded in a square by four perfect lines. Blue jersey, south; white, north; red, east; green, west. Bear squints into the distance. A player leaps forward out of the tense and taut blue south—they're all in a slight crouch, eyes on the blue leader, who jerks his hands toward his helmet and, in a twinkling, they follow suit; he jerks his hands down to his flexed thighs, halfway up to his chest, a half jerk up, down, a feint, finger tips to the helmet. The entire blue squad is frozen except for its arms. Back and knees bent, eyes and neck straight ahead, they play flawless follow-the-leader for 15 seconds, then stand up straight, arching their backs, and clap and cheer for themselves.

As soon as they applaud, the leader of the green west leaps out and leads his squad through a perfect 15-second drill. The green applaud themselves. Bear stands alone in the center of all this, a deity, a religious rock being rapidly salaamed by an army of jocks. The green cheer is immediately followed by the white north, then applause, then red east. Fifteen flawless seconds each of heartstopping precision—Bear Bryant the centerpiece, looking nowhere, everywhere, watching or lost in thought.

Then every one of them is running back to where he came from. Back to the dirt, the Astroturf, the tackling sled. Back over my head and shoulders. And once again, Bear is alone on the field, hands in pockets just like 120 seconds before. He has not said a thing, seemingly never looked at anyone. Behind me, the practices are in full swing. I watch coach Bryant amble over to his tower and slowly ascend the 50 feet to his platform, resume his slouch against the railing and check out whatever those flinty eyes deem in need of checking out. Holy shit and kiss my ass. That was known as a quickness drill.

In terms of glory, there are no individual stars at Alabama. It really is a team team. It has had plenty of All-Americans, plenty of pro stars such as Lee Roy Jordan, Joe Namath, Ken Stabler, but by and large, you don't hear that much about individuals besides the coach.

How does he do it? The team is composed predominantly of home boys, who must have grown up worshiping Bear Bryant. I think of those 12-year-olds cock-walking the side lines, one-eying the tower. Every year, the coach gets a batch of players who have been spoon-fed Bear stories and glories all their lives. So for an adolescent athlete from Birmingham, Florence, Demopolis, Bessemer to hear "Bear wants you"—it would turn him into a raving kamikaze, or at least a stout and loyal fellow. I don't think Bear has to try very hard anymore to get players with the right "attitude."

My first interview the following morning is with Steadman Shealy. We meet under the chandelier in the football dorm. Shealy isn't much bigger than I am, but he's a lot blonder and tanner. He also has a firmer handshake, better manners and a neater appearance. Shealy's the first-string quarterback.

We go up to his room and I get my first gander at the living arrangements. The dorm rooms are tiny, with two beds, cinder-block walls and the usual campus-bookstore assortment of banal posters. Shealy, at least, is average-human-being-sized. I try to imagine two nose guards sharing a room this narrow.

Shealy sits on his bed, confident, serene, courteous, helpful and cheerful. And he's not putting me on. I ask him why he chose to go to Alabama, assuming he could have played anywhere in the South. I expect him to rave about Bear, but instead he says, "I really thought this is where God wanted me to come."

I sit up a little straighter. At first I don't know if he's talking about the Lord or Bear, but then he says the second reason was the opportunity to play for coach Bryant—that Alabama has "something extra" in its winning tradition. And then he says something I will hear in the next several interviews: "And I want to be a winner."

On the cover of *Bear* is the quote "I ain't nothing but a winner."

Shealy talks of Bear's father image, of how the coach applies football to life (another thing I'll hear again), of what it takes to win. All hokey stuff in the abstract—but not to Shealy or the others. The guys talk about these bland notions as though they were tenets of radical politics.

Shealy's religiosity, as exotic to me as Bora-Bora, seems a natural extension of the team spirit. He is a Christian soldier, a leader and a follower. Not many of the guys say they're religious, but—at least in interviews—there are no wise guys, no cynics. Frankly, all this clear-eyed devotion makes me extremely uncomfortable, but maybe that's *my* problem.

And where does Shealy see himself five years from now? "Coachin' or Christian ministry . . . it all depends on what doors God opens up." None of what he says about the coach, about winning and life is all that insightful, but his eyes and chin tell the story. He has no room in his face for sarcasm, despair or doubt. He loves the coach, he loves the team, he loves Christ: a clean-cut, all-American, God, Bear and 'Bama man if ever there were one.

Attitude. I know Bryant doesn't tolerate any guff from anybody. He suspended two of his most famous players, Namath and Stabler, for infractions. No matter who you are, if you don't toe the line, the man will personally clean out your locker for you. Bear says in his book that he works best with the kid who doesn't know he's not terribly talented but plays his heart out. He's more attuned to that kind of athlete than to the hot-dog natural. Sort of like making the New York Yankees out of a bunch of Rocky types. The great American combo: underdog, superstar.

My next interview is with Don Jacobs, the second- or possibly third-string quarterback. He picked Alabama because, growing up in north Alabama, that's all you hear: "Alabama this, Alabama that." He says in the southern part of the state, boys are partial to Auburn, but Alabama is the "number-one university in your mind."

"The first time I talked with coach Bryant," says Jacobs, "I was scared to death. I was afraid to say anything at all. But he was real nice. He talked about Pat Trammel [a star on the 1961 championship team], 'cause Trammel was from Scottsboro, my home town. Said he hoped I was good as Trammel."

Bear, I'm thinking, is a frightening man, but from what I gather of the impressions and memories of players, he's not a screamer, puncher, growler. He's a man of few words, not even one for pep talks. Jacobs has never seen him get really angry, never lose his cool, never jump on anybody's case.

I ask Jacobs how I should conduct myself when I meet Bear. "Be real courteous," he says. "Say 'Yes, sir, no, sir.' Just be yourself."

"Should I get a haircut?"

"I dunno. *I* wouldn't go in there like that. When you go see him, you always shave, look real nice, don't wear sloppy clothes. Lots of players tell you there's a lot of things you don't do when you see coach Bryant. It's been passed down through history. You always take your hat off in the house, stuff like that."

Awe and respect. Dedication and honor. And, oh, yes, talent.

In the early afternoon, I see a few players hanging out with some girls in front of Bryant Hall. A big dude comes walking in with his dad, mom, sis and his pretty gal. The father looks like a big baggy version of his son. Maybe the present son will come to this dorm 20 years later with *his* son. Football is a family sport. Everybody is proud of everybody. Bryant pushes that a lot in his talks to his players.

This is from a midweek, midseason talk to his 1964 national champs:

> After the game, there are three types of people. One comes
> in and he ain't played worth killing, and he's lost. And he gets
> dressed and out of there as quick as he can. He meets his girl and

his momma, and they ain't too damn glad to see him. And he goes off somewhere and says how "the coach shoulda done this or that," and "the coach don't like me," and "I didn't play enough." And everybody just nods.

And the second type will sit there awhile, thinking what he could have done to make his team a winner. And he'll shed some tears. He'll finally get dressed, but he doesn't want to see anybody. His momma's out there. She puts on a big act and tells him what a great game he played, and he tells her if he had done this or that, he'd be a winner, and that he will be a winner—next week.

And then there's the third guy. The winner. He'll be in there hugging everybody in the dressing room. It'll take him an hour to dress. And when he goes out, it's a little something extra in it when his daddy squeezes his hand. His momma hugs and kisses him, and that little old ugly girl snuggles up, proud to be next to him. And he *knows* they're proud. And why.

That afternoon, I have an interview with one of the black players, a nose guard named Byron Braggs. I have seen only a small photo of him in the press book and know that on the first day of practice his freshman year, he almost died of heatstroke but came back to be a top lineman.

I'm checking out my biceps in the empty lounge of Bryant Hall when I look up and jump 90 feet—there's Braggs, 6'6", 260 pounds, wearing a Cat-tractor hat. We go up to his room, which consists of a large roommate, a TV, a stereo and a full-size refrigerator. They must sleep standing up.

Braggs is a little different from the others I've talked with—a little less awestruck, more blasé. He came to Alabama because his "folks picked it for me. It's near home."

What does he think about Bryant? "A lot of guys are scared of him," says Braggs. "They're in awe of his presence. But I just look at him like anybody else. I'm just happy he can remember my name. He mixes up a lot of names and faces, but two minutes later, he'll remember and apologize."

Ten years ago, Alabama was segregated. When I ask Braggs if prejudice lingers, he just shrugs. "It doesn't bother me," he says. "There were times when things looked shaky, but there are no major problems."

And is state-wide football fever a white fever, or does it affect black Alabamans, too? "Up until about eight to ten years ago," says Braggs, "it was mainly white. I didn't even *know* about Alabama. I would watch Notre Dame, USC with O. J. Simpson. I didn't really notice Alabama until they beat USC out there. That was the first time I knew they had a team. And since they had black players, a lot more people became fans of the team. My folks and others follow the team now. In my home town, people have become real fans."

How about those things Bryant teaches—about character and football and life? "It's life and death out there on the field sometimes. It all ties in. Some coaches like Bryant, John McKay, Ara Parseghian tend to have a definite pull on which way you're looking after you graduate. They're sort of like the last shaping process that someone is going to do to you. From then on, you do it from within."

Bragg's advice on how to relate to the coach? "Talk to him straight. Don't beat around the bush. He's not impressed with slickness or guys trying to fool him."

Taking a breather between interviews, I walk around campus a bit, grooving on the coeds in their summer dresses, the chirping of the birds, the flora of the South. Old brick and columns. There's not one physically ugly person on the campus.

Back on campus that afternoon, I interview defensive end Gary DeNiro. The reason I pick him is that he's from Youngstown, Ohio, which is definitely Ohio State turf.

He went to Alabama, he says, because he "didn't like Woody Hayes's coaching that much" and was "always an Alabama fan.

"I like that the coach plays a lot of guys who are small [DeNiro is six feet, 210 pounds]. Up North, they play bigger people. Coach Bryant plays the people who want to play."

"How about your Ohio State buddies? What was the reaction when they found out you were going to play for Alabama?"

"They thought I made a big mistake. That I'd come down here and they'd still be fighting the Civil War. They were wrong."

DeNiro's first impression of Bryant?

"He's a legend. Like meeting someone you always wanted to meet. Once Alabama wanted me, I didn't have no trouble makin' up my mind. I remember one time I was loafin' when I was red-shirted, which is a hard time, 'cause you practice like everyone else, but come Friday night, when the team goes, you stay home. Anyway, I was 'puttin' in a day,' as coach calls it, and he caught me and yelled, 'DeNiro, who you think you're tryin' to fool?' And from then on, I never loafed. There's really no place for it on the field."

"How about contact with the coach?"

"Maybe two or three times a year. He says his door is always open, but I'll go in just maybe to say goodbye before I go home or something—nothing more. He has coaching meetings every day. He tells the coaches what he thinks, then we'll have meetings with the coaches in the afternoon and they'll tell us what we're doing wrong. And then about three, four times a week, we'll have a meeting with coach Bryant. We'll all go in as a group. He'll tell us what he sees overall. I imagine he gets more contact with the upperclassmen, because they're the leaders and they'll get it across to the team."

"Where do you see yourself five years from now?"

"Hopefully, with a lot of money. Maybe pro ball if I'm not too small—coach Bryant proved the little man can work out. Or maybe I'll coach. Coach Bryant is the legend of all coaches. If he is behind you, no telling how many doors can open for you."

No telling is right. There's a club based in Birmingham consisting of all Bear Bryant alumni now in the business world. They meet with graduating senior team members and help them find both summer and career jobs. Many kids want, if not to play pro, which most of them *do* want, to take a crack at coaching. There's also a big business school down there and a strong education program. But whatever they *do* choose, if they stay in Alabama, playing for Bear and then going into anything in athletics or business is like graduating *summa cum laude.* Even outside Alabama, the alumni network is nationwide. I hear that one of the biggest diamond dealers in New York's 47th Street district is an Alabama grad.

These interviews are frustratingly inconclusive. All this nonsense concerning life, character, winners' attitudes—of course it's going to come across bland and boringly obvious on a tape recorder. But it's really a combat camaraderie, a brotherhood of suffering and surviving, a growing together in a violent, competitive world. And being rewarded by being called best. Call it character, call it chicken soup, but it's really love. Love of the boss man. Love of one another and love of victory. All this hoopla about football applied to life comes down to this: *I was the best in the world once. I know what that tastes like. I want more.* Roll, Tide!

In areas of rural poverty, football is the American passion play, the emotional outlet for all the rage, boredom and bad breaks—just as basketball is in urban areas.

In *The Last Picture Show,* an entire Texas town lived for high school football; and that's a common phenomenon. In our dissociated culture—despite whatever grace, glory and beauty they evoke in the best teams and players—contact sports serve two functions: They allay boredom, divert people from thinking about the dreariness of their lives; and they help people channel their rage.

You can go to a revival in Selma on Friday or you can scream your lungs out in Bryant-Denny Stadium in Tuscaloosa on Saturday. The bottom line at both is transference of a lot of anger into a socially acceptable outlet.

Like in football, there's a lot of beatific beauty in Gospel, but it's a bit beside the point. As coach Karl Marx once said, football is the opiate of the people. And not just here: There are soccer riots in the Third World stadiums. Christs for a day bloodying themselves in Latin-American pageants. Millions marching to Mecca. A lady in Selma once told me, "People leave Bryant stadium like they're in a religious trance."

It's my day to interview Bear, and, to be honest, I'm scared. I consider giving myself a haircut with nail clippers. My heart is calling Kong to the gates.

McNair takes me up to the offices on the top floor of the coliseum, where I sit in the spacious waiting room. The walls are covered with floor-to-ceiling black-and-white blowups of every major bowl stadium —Rose, Orange, Sugar, Bluebonnet, Gator, Tangerine, you name it.

Everybody walking around is named Coach. It's like sitting in a room with all the tall, stately, aging cowboys of Hollywood. A room full of Gary Cooper–Ben Johnson look-alikes, all nodding to one another. "Mornin', coach." "Hey, coach." "Nice day, coach." If I were to scream out "Coach!" there would be a ten-way collision. And everybody looks like Bear Bryant.

Several times I see someone walk in and hear someone say, "Hey, coach," and I jump up, drop my tape recorder and extend my hand. After the fifth false alarm, I ignore the next look-alike. Too bad. That one is the mold.

I walk into his office, a large wood-paneled room with a color TV, a massive cluttered desk and a view of the practice field. Coach Bryant is cordial—patient but distant. He has been interviewed perhaps six times a week since coming to Alabama.

He looks all of his 66 years—his face is like an aerial shot of a drought area. His eyes are glittering hard. His hands are huge and gnarled. He needs a haircut himself.

As I fumble around with the tape recorder, explaining that I'm not a sportswriter, he opens a pack of unfiltered Chesterfields. He's dressed like a retired millionaire entertainer—casual natty. A pale-blue golf sweater, checked blue slacks and spiffy black loafers. When he laughs, all the creases in his face head toward his temples and he lets out a deep, gravelly "Heh-heh." When he's annoyed, his eyebrows meet over his nose and I feel like jogging back to New York. His movements are slow; he seems almost phlegmatically preoccupied.

All in all, I like the guy, though I couldn't see being in a sensory-awareness class together.

The interview is a bit of a bust. I'm glad I have the tape recorder, because I can't understand a damn thing he says. He sort of mutters from his diaphragm in his artesian-well-deep Arkansas drawl and it's like listening to a language you studied for only a year in high school.

Bear sits sideways in his chair, legs crossed, elbow on the back rest, absently rubbing his forehead and smoking those Chesterfields. I sit a few feet away in a pulled-up chair, a spiral notebook in my lap open to my questions. I tentatively slide my tape recorder toward him from the corner of his desk.

"Coach, you're pretty much an American hero these days. I was wondering who *your* heroes are." (Please don't kill me.)

He pouts, shrugs. "Well, my heroes are John Wayne, Bob Hope, General Patton . . . J. Edgar Hoover, although he ain't too popular, I guess. . . ." He mentions various sports stars through the ages—from Babe Ruth to contemporary players—then he nods toward the tape recorder and says, "I suppose you'd like me to say Einstein."

"Nah, nah, nah. Einstein, no . . . no, not at all."

"Of course, with my heroes, as I get older, *they* get older."

"Yeah, ha, ha."

I ask a few boring questions about defining character, defining motivation, defining a winning attitude, none of which he can define but all of which he can sure talk about.

"I cain't define character," he says, "but it's important, especially to those who don't have that much natural ability—on the football field or elsewhere."

Next comes my New York hotsy-totsy question.

"In *Bear,* I read about how you motivate players, psych them up. I also read that you understand people better than any other coach. Comprehension like that seems to be one of the attributes of a good psychiatrist. What do you feel about the field of psychiatry?"

He gives a chuckle. "Well, I don't know nothing about psychiatrists. I prob'ly need one, but I don't know the secret of motivatin' people— an' if I did, I wouldn't tell anyone."

Then he goes on about motivation. At one point, he says, "I remember one time. . . ." And about five minutes later, he says, "That was the damnedest . . . heh-heh," in that noble garble of his.

Then his face darkens and he says, "I guess that ain't funny to you."

I almost shit. A joke! He told me a joke! Laugh, you asshole! Fake it!

I haven't heard a word he's said. I give a sick grin, say, "Naw, that's funny, that's funny!" and give my own "Heh-heh." My armpits feel flooded.

For a while, I go sociological and nonsports, thinking maybe I can get him to admire my sensitive and probing mind—or at least throw him some questions that are a little more interesting than the traditional Southern sports groupie journalist fare.

"Are your players . . . uh . . . afraid of you?" ('Cause I'm about to do a swan dive out this window, coach.)

He sits up a little.

"Afraid of me? Shit, heh-heh. I'm the best friend they got. Some haven't been around here much. They might be a little reluctant. I dunno. But if somebody's doin' poorly, I'll come after him. But I dunno what they'd be afraid of me about."

One period in college history that has always fascinated me is the late Sixties—mainly because it was a transcendent radical bubble between the Fifties and the Seventies, but also because that's when I was an undergraduate. I wonder what it was like to be a football player then, when regimentation was so reactionary—when long hair and a taste for dope were *de rigueur.* I know that Bryant's worst years since coming to Alabama were 1969 and 1970. Is there any connection?

"I did a real poor job of recruiting and coaching," he says. "Every youngster in America was goin' through a rebellious period. Nobody wanted anybody to tell 'im anything. I remember a boy sittin' right there an' tellin' me, 'I just wanna be like any other student.' Well, shit. He can't *be* like any other student. The players have to take pride in the fact that football means that much to 'em. That's where the sacrificin' comes in. That they *are* willin' to do without doin' some things. Without havin' some things other students have, to be playin' football, to win a championship."

"What was the campus attitude toward football at that time?"

"I really don't know that much about what goes on over there [*nodding toward the window*]. I always tell 'em they're the best in the world, at pep rallies and all. Whether they said anything about me I don't know. I was just doin' a lousy job then."

"As an Alabaman, how do you feel about the image that your state has in the national eye, which is mainly a negative or fearful one?"

He doesn't like that question. His eyebrows start knitting a sweater.

"I dunno if that's true or not. I traveled all over the country. A large percentage of Alabamans consider the Yankees their baseball team, or the Red Sox. The only difference I see is that it ain't as crowded down here, people aren't in such a hurry. I'm afraid of New York City. It ain't just what I heard, it's what I seen. I dunno if we got as many thieves, crooks and murderers down here percentagewise, but, hell, it's so many of them in New York. I don't care to leave the hotel—alone or with money in my pocket."

"How about the football-dorm system? Is it still under fire for separatism?"

"Naw. About ten years ago, we were the first school to build one. They called it Alabama Hilton, Bryant Hilton. But everyone's built one since then."

"Is there any criticism because the players are segregated from the rest of the campus?"

"Well, a lot of coaches don't do that, but I was brought up on it and we're gonna do it. If anyone rules against it, we won't, but I know that's one of the ways that help us win. You live under the same roof together, fightin' for the same thing. If you don't see one another but occasionally, you have other interests, you don't know what's goin' on. And I can see 'em over there, too. I like to see 'em. If one of them lives in an apartment and's sick for a week, his mother's not even there. I want 'em where I can find 'em, look at 'em."

That's it. Bear doesn't move, just gazes out the window. I don't move. I feel stuck. I don't know how to say goodbye. I ask about Astroturf. About the coming A Day game. Bear says that he'd rather not even have it, but the alumni have things planned around it.

Outside the office, he signs my copy of *Bear.* I say "Howdy-do" and split.

Later in the week, I get a note from Bear via McNair that he wants to add Oral Roberts, Billy Graham, Arnold Palmer and Jack Nicklaus to his list of heroes—all American fat cats who made it through personal enterprise and charisma.

McNair says he's never heard Bear mention Patton before and makes the analogy that in World War Two, to die for Patton was an honor and that the coach is the only other person he knows of whom people feel that way about.

Days later, I'm still smarting about that missed joke. I feel I understand something then about why this man is successful. There is something about him—about *me* in that moment when I blew being an appreciative audience—that goes past embarrassment. I feel like I let him down. I feel like I could have pleased him by laughing, made him like me for a moment, could have broken through the interviewer-interviewee roles for a few seconds in a way that would have made me feel like a million bucks *because it would have given him pleasure.* There is something in Bear's subdued dignity, his cordial distance that got to me. He is a man of *character.* I could see myself having done Mexican tail spins during that interview to get his admiration or just his acknowledgment. And this was just a magazine assignment. If I were one of his five-year players, I could see myself doing 90 mph through a goal post to get a pat on the back. And, frankly, I can't define motivation, either, but whatever it is that he lays on his boys, I got a tiny ray of it myself. The man could literally crush you by letting you know you were a disappointment to him. Shit, maybe I've just seen too many John Wayne movies.

I did go down to McNair's office, though, with the queasy feeling that I've blown it. Not the interview so much, but I'm left with the feeling that if Bryant had to go over Pork Chop Hill, I wouldn't be his first choice in the assault squadron.

"I didn't understand a damn thing he said!" I half complain to McNair.

"Listen to this!" I play back Bear's joke-anecdote for him and two other guys in the office. Instead of commiserating, they are all on the floor, howling with laughter.

"I never heard that one before!" says a trainer, wiping tears from his eyes.

"That's the funniest thing I ever heard!" says McNair.

"Yeah, well, I think you guys are a little funny, too," I mutter.

McNair translates the joke for me. Bear was recalling an old Kentucky-Tennessee game, a real "bloodletter." During the half, a guy named Doc Rhodes (I can't figure out what his relation to the team was) went into the Kentucky locker room and delivered "the damnedest talk I evah heard." He had one big old boy just slobbering at the bit. The only problem was that big old boy wasn't playing.

In the last quarter of the game, Tennessee was down on the Kentucky 15 and the coach finally sent the big old boy in. He ran halfway onto the field; then he went running back to the side lines and said, "Coach, can Doc Rhodes talk at me again?"

I guess you had to be there.

Linda Robertson

Pride and Poison

*"Behind all the years of practice and all the hours of glory waits
that inexorable terror of living without the game," wrote Bill Bradley (see page 81). Ted Hendricks, the former linebacker for the
Baltimore Colts and Oakland Raiders, and the subject of this profile,
has been living that terror since his retirement in 1984. "I've been
stagnant," said Hendricks. "I'm still looking for something that
would excite me." But Hendricks's search for thrills to replace the
ones he experienced on so many Sunday afternoons has been futile
and frustrating. Life after the applause for Hendricks, as for so
many other ex-athletes, has been a "perpetual anticlimax." This
1990 piece, written by Linda Robertson, first appeared in* The Miami
Herald *and was also included in Houghton Mifflin's* Best Sports
Writing of 1991.

T he January day Ted Hendricks was elected to the Pro Football Hall
of Fame, he visited his favorite hometown haunts.

He heard the announcement on TV at the Interliner Lounge,
a cave of a bar with Eastern Airlines strike posters on the walls. Cheers
rose from the smoky darkness. Everybody there knows Ted. Drinks on
the house.

Hendricks called his mother, who lives nearby. He called Wisconsin
to tell Audrey Matuszak, mother of the late John Matuszak, Hendricks's
best friend on the Oakland and Los Angeles Raiders. "I made it, Mom
Tooz!"

Then a limousine pulled up at the Interliner. Hendricks and his
friends piled in, picked up some gyros, and drove around Miami Springs,
celebrating.

It was one of the best days of Hendricks's life, and one of the worst.

The greatest football player to come out of Dade County had reached the pinnacle of his career. And after weeks of being sober, he had started drinking again.

First stop on the limo tour January 27 was the Hurricane Bar and Grill, where there's a painting of All-American Hendricks in his University of Miami uniform, emerging from the surf like some amphibious warrior. Drinks on the house.

Next, Mike's Lounge on Northwest 36th Street. Punches to the shoulder of the linebacker who won fans with his antics. Remember the time he rode into training camp on a horse with an orange traffic cone as his lance? Remember the Halloween he came to practice wearing a pumpkin carved in the shape of a helmet? Drinks on the house.

The limo went to Art Bruns's Executive Club. Hendricks's gruff voice took on a stentorian tone. He loosened molars with slaps on the back, repeated the same double-entendre jokes. Drinks on the house.

Hendricks was headed for another bar when his neighbor, Margie Palmer, decided to go home. She was so happy for him, but she saw the toasts as poison.

"He fell off the wagon that night," Palmer said. "He started doing beers, got into Manhattans, and then, what was it? Blackberry brandy. That was his favorite. I told myself, 'He'll straighten out tomorrow.' But it was one big party all week."

In Miami Springs, Ted Hendricks will always be the favorite son. But he has not made a smooth transition from hero to citizen. For Hendricks, star of Hialeah High, the University of Miami, and the NFL, the laurel has withered. He is living a perpetual anticlimax.

He does not have a job. When asked his occupation, he says "retired." He is divorced. His three children live out west. He lives alone in a small house with sparse furniture.

A recent day was typical. He cleaned the pool, played golf, answered fan mail, programmed the big-screen TV, then went out. He knows he is being pulled by the warm current that winds through his hometown. Does he fight the current or ride with it?

"I've been stagnant," said Hendricks, forty-two. "I'm having trouble with the crossword in the morning. My brain's not deteriorating, it's just been nonfunctional for so long."

Most of his old teammates have weaned themselves off adrenaline. He has not. "I'm still looking for something that would excite me. Sometimes, I drink out of boredom."

Hendricks will be inducted into the Hall of Fame August 4, the six foot seven linebacker with skinny legs nicknamed the Mad Stork. He revolutionized his position by roaming the field—blocking kicks, sacking quarterbacks, intercepting passes.

He was the leader of the Raiders, ferocious, fun-loving misfits who won Super Bowl titles in 1977, 1981, and 1984. He was the personification of the pirate logo on his helmet.

Today, everyone wants to share a moment with the great Ted Hendricks. He just can't say no:

"Hi, Ted, can I have an autograph?"

"Ted, buddy, can you play in a golf tournament for charity?"

"Teddy, have I got a deal for you!"

"Ted, can I buy you a drink?"

They don't see his quiet side, only the gregarious man who always has time for his friends, so many friends.

"When you stop loaning money and buying drinks for your so-called friends, they'll disappear," said Fred Wilcox, who runs a golf-cart business at Ted's defunct Crooked Creek Country Club. "But Ted can't resist. He likes to b.s. with people."

After he had Thanksgiving dinner with his mother and brother last year, an old friend called with an invitation to go out. Hendricks had been in a sober period, but he succumbed that night. He hated himself for it, and dialed his own number. "Hey, asshole, I'm checking on you," he thundered into his answering machine. The message was there when he got home the next morning.

When Margie Palmer's mother, Meta Klein, was alive, she scolded Hendricks about his drinking.

He often went over to play cards with Mrs. Klein, who had lost a foot to diabetes. When she fell out of bed or had trouble moving, Palmer called, "Hey, Crane, I need help." He would come and lift Mrs. Klein back into bed, or onto the toilet.

She died last year at age eighty-three. "Went out on Ted's number," Palmer said.

Hendricks is hard to fathom—scary when he's drunk, humble when he's not, witty almost all the time. He can be kind and generous.

"He is such a gentle giant," Palmer said. "I've had fights with people who have seen Ted out drunk and unpleasant. I tell them they have no idea what he's really like."

The traits that made Hendricks a great player—stubbornness, pride, supreme control of the body, a certain reckless abandon—now make it difficult for him to seek help. He once went through rehabilitation but says he won't do it again.

"The problem is," Hendricks said, "I play as hard off the field as I did on it. I try to reach as far as I can, but I can't reach that high anymore."

Hendricks played in 215 straight NFL games over fifteen seasons. In 1983, his last season, he had abdominal muscle pulls so severe he had to roll out of bed and pull his pants on sideways as he lay on the floor.

"What do you think is the best painkiller in the world?" Hendricks asked. He turned down the shots of cortisone, but not of Jack Daniel's.

Raiders trainer George Anderson said it was "amazing he could play so well despite the liquor and wear and tear. His last season, at age thirty-six, it caught up to him."

Drinking was a staple of NFL life. After a road game, players were handed beers and an ice pack as they got on the plane. After a home game, there were cocktail parties.

Hendricks spent five years in Baltimore and one year in Green Bay, then moved to Oakland, where his drinking accelerated with "the hard-living, hard-drinking Raiders," said his ex-wife, Jane Hartman-Tew.

Training camp was in the Napa Valley, and Hendricks and Matuszak led expeditions to the wineries. "Ted would come in the huddle with purple teeth and tongue from the red wine," said ex-linebacker Phil Villapiano, now New York manager for a shipping company. "His drinking was a joke. Then we tried to talk to him about it. [Owner] Al Davis finally said, 'Teddy, you got to get help or you got to go.' "

He decided to go. Hendricks retired after the 1984 Super Bowl and moved back to Miami Springs.

Audrey Matuszak wants him out of there. "I've offered him my house as sanctuary," she said. Hendricks calls her frequently since John Matuszak died of an accidental overdose of prescription painkillers last June.

"I would like to hide him away here in Wisconsin, where he could walk around and clear his head."

Once Hendricks had the athlete's infrastructure: curfews, rubdowns, playbooks, adoring fans. He had everything done for him. Agents negotiated his contracts.

Inevitably, the cheering stopped. Most pro athletes "have to grind through a tough transition," said ex-kicker Errol Mann, now a stockbroker in South Dakota. "Show me something with the same type of return, emotionally and financially."

Other Raiders found a niche: Art Shell coaches the team, Gene Upshaw heads the players' union. Hendricks still drifts, burdened by a series of bad business deals. His biggest investment, Crooked Creek golf course, has been overgrown and idle since 1983.

There have been other dubious ventures: a limo service, a three-hundred-acre ranch in Florida ("the environmentalists got me"), a gold-mining claim on the Yuba River in California, the former O.J.'s Lounge in West Dade, and a quarter horse whose best finish was tenth. Hendricks traded him in for the feed bill.

He estimates he has lost close to one million dollars in all.

"I figured the world was like a football team," Hendricks said. "You trust the people you play with. I depended on people who just wanted to play with my money. I guess I listen to everybody without doing things on my own."

Hendricks lives day to day. He put off a hernia operation until recently. "I can't plan a vacation. Something better might come along."

His income is from "bits and pieces" of investments. County records paint a bleak picture: about $114,000 in taxes are overdue on the golf course, his house, and a Springs condo he rents out.

Hendricks muses about what to do. He considered becoming an engineer, or working for NASA. He was interested in dentistry, "but would you want these big hands trying to fit into your mouth?"

"I could be a pilot, or a CIA agent," he said. "I had a new one today, going through the list of possibilities—counseling. But I have enough problems of my own."

Wilcox said he has "tried to get Ted interested in different jobs, teach him the golf-cart business. But he's got too much pride to ask for a job, not in a hundred years."

Hendricks has no endorsements, either: "I thought about the Lite Beer commercials," he said, "but I hate to influence kids that way. They might grow up to be like me."

Hendricks's favorite poet is William Blake. He quotes Blake as affirmation of his own philosophy that "excess is best": "The cistern contains; the fountain overflows. Sooner murder an infant in its cradle than nurse unacted desires." Hendricks introduced Blake's work to Matuszak.

"There are no in betweens," he said. "Just like with Tooz and I. When you're up, you're way up. When you get depressed, you go way down. We aren't Keats people."

That must have been a sight, a six-seven linebacker and a six-eight defensive end poring over poems. But Theodore Paul Hendricks has never been your typical jock.

He was born in Guatemala. His parents, Angela Bonatti and the late Maurice (Sonny) Hendricks, a native Texan, met there while working for Pan Am.

Hendricks speaks Spanish fluently. He has read books on Mayan culture. He graduated 72nd of 1,400 in his 1965 Hialeah High class.

At UM, he majored in physics and took electromagnetic theory and differential equations, but he never went back to finish twelve hours for his degree.

"He could be anything he wants to be, that's the kind of potential he has," Hendricks's UM coach, Charlie Tate, said once. "Why, he could even be governor."

Hendricks has a copy of Blake's "The Tyger" pasted to the first page of his football scrapbook:

> When the stars threw down their spears,
> And water'd heaven with their tears
> Did he smile his work to see?
> Did he who made the Lamb make thee?
> Tyger! Tyger! burning bright
> In the forests of the night,
> What immortal hand or eye
> Dare frame thy fearful symmetry?

The Lamb in Ted made him the last one out of stadiums because he signed so many autographs. He visits children's hospitals around the country and stops by Miami's Veterans Administration Hospital. He plays an endless string of fund-raising sports events. He has coached Special Olympians.

"He uses his body like a big Jerry Lewis," said Tom Romanik of Cloverleaf Lanes.

Hendricks let Eddie Barwick, who lived in the garage apartment behind his house, skip rent payments when Barwick, an Eastern Airlines mechanic, went on strike. "He has a heart as big as he is," Barwick said.

Ted the Lamb will pick up your tab, open the door for you, kiss the back of your hand, present you with a yellow hibiscus flower from his backyard.

It is 11:45 A.M. on a fall weekday at Mike's Lounge in Miami Springs. Hendricks has agreed to a luncheon interview. The Tiger in Ted is throwing down peppermint schnapps. His breath is like a blowtorch. He mumbles the answer to a question, and is asked to repeat it.

"What, CAN'T YOU HEAR ME?" he roars. "AM I NOT E-NUNCIATING CLEARLY?"

Everyone is staring. "Teddy, people are trying to eat," says a waitress wearily.

"OH, EXCUUUUSE ME."

Another question. He responds with an off-color joke and a spine-jarring pat on the back.

"Let's get OUT OF HERE." Hendricks has decided to continue the interview at his house.

He leads the way, driving his 1972 Mercedes rapidly down a back street, but under control. There are two old newspapers on his front steps. Inside the Florida room, he pops in a Who tape. He turns up the volume until conversation is reduced to shouting. He's singing along, imitating the guitar licks.

The visitor slips out the back door to the patio and walks, at first casually, then quickly, to the car. He's six-seven, the visitor is five-seven. End of interview. He doesn't seem to notice.

Suddenly, Hendricks comes through his front door. The visitor rolls down the window to say goodbye and he reaches in, trying to grab the keys in the ignition.

"DON'T LIKE MY MUSIC?" He is not smiling.

"Ted, please call when you want to talk."

He hesitates, withdraws. He stands in the driveway, with the front door open and the Who playing, shrinking in the rear-view mirror like the fade-out of a movie.

Hendricks has an idea of his behavior when he's drunk. "My mind is still working, but I'm a monster on the outside," he said. "I've got to learn to tone myself down. I wish I could keep that control and still have a good time."

Hendricks's ex-wife, Hartman-Tew, said there were times she and their two sons were afraid of him when he arrived at their Orinda, California, home after an evening out.

The boys—now seventeen and twenty years old—say they are still concerned about their father's "phases." But when he is inducted into the Hall of Fame in Canton, Ohio, they will be there. So will an eight-year-old half-sister they have never seen; Hendricks had his daughter with another woman after he and his wife split up.

"When he's got his head screwed on, he's a great father and a loving, kind, sensitive man," Hartman-Tew said. "When he drank, I couldn't get in there to touch the person I knew. He'd say, 'It's my life. I'm having a good time.' He didn't recognize what was crumbling around him."

Nothing captures Hendricks's frustration more than his golf course.

At the corner of Southwest 104th Street and 97th Avenue a low brick wall advertises "Open to the public." Below that are chips off letters that once spelled Crooked Creek Country Club. In fact, it hasn't been open since 1983, when Hendricks shut it down for lack of business.

He is here on his tractor to mow fairway 5. The neighbors have complained again about the snake-infested overgrowth. "It's a jungle out there. I call this my estate, all one hundred ten acres of it."

Hendricks estimates he has plowed $600,000 into the golf course.

His makeshift office is the former pro shop. The bar is covered with dust. Next to the unused cash register, a spider web undulates. There are holes in the ceiling, golfing cartoons on the walls. A sign says, "Sorry, no rain checks."

Heavy rains in 1983 finally forced Hendricks to close the course, which had deteriorated under his former business partners while he was in Oakland. He came home one time to find "all the employees out by the pool looking at girls in swimming suits. There was forty-five thousand dollars' worth of carts that turned to junk."

He decided to build houses, but Crooked Creek's neighbors stood behind a deed that requires the land to remain a golf course through 2066. "They didn't want to listen to a solution," he said. "So let them look at my eyesore."

Neighbors filed an injunction when Hendricks started hauling away topsoil to sell it. He says they use it as a dump, and when he finds clippings and old tires, he throws them back into their yards. Said neighbor Gloria Kreider, "A lot of people won't cut one blade of grass if it belongs to Hendricks."

He often says that selling the course will remove a weight holding him down. After many attempts to sell, he hopes to close on a joint venture with a Chicago company. "I just want to finish this deal so I don't have to spend my days in a bar."

Last summer, Hendricks was the life of the party during a charity golf event at ex-Dolphin Earl Morrall's Arrowhead course in Davie.

He was performing a slapstick routine, pretending to whiff his shots, stomping his opponents' balls into the ground, cracking jokes. He and the rest of his foursome had a full stock of beer.

Hendricks took a swig and laughed, and the wet spot on the front of his shorts grew into a patch.

He looked down. "Don't make me laugh," he said. "It'll only get worse."

"Ted is in fine form today," one man said, chuckling.

And so it went, Hendricks in his long-brimmed "Mad Stork" hat and stained shorts, hitting an occasional brilliant shot, his partners lucky to be paired with such an entertaining celebrity.

The charity event represented one of the setbacks since Hendricks got out of rehab.

One morning in spring 1989, after five drinks, he began shaking uncontrollably. He asked his neighbors to take him to South Miami Hospital.

"When he was in the hospital," Raiders trainer Anderson said, "I asked Ted, 'Is *this* enough to scare you?' He said he'd wait and see when he got out."

"I figured they'd give me an injection and I'd calm down," Hendricks said. On the third day, he wanted to leave. Doctors said no.

"I threatened to call the Miami Springs police, which was insane," Hendricks said. "Then they brought in fifteen or twenty interns. I looked at the odds and went back to bed."

His mother called that night. "She said, 'I want you to stay in there—for me—for twenty-eight days,'" Hendricks said. "I did her a favor. But I'll never do it again."

The Interliner is the meeting place for a recent weekday interview. Hendricks is, as usual, fidgety—constantly tugging at his mustache, tapping his fingers together.

He and his golfing partner play joker poker. BIG TED is recognized on the video screen for his high score. "Jokers are wild," he said, "just like the characters in here."

Hendricks orders a Budweiser. Then a Bud Dry. Then three Bud Lights. When he finishes, the bartender taps the empty can on the bar. He nods. In two hours, he drinks nine beers.

He is reminded that at a previous interview here, after a round of golf last fall, he was chugging club sodas.

"That must have been when I was on the wagon, when my tolerance was low. Now, I'm sticking with beer. I can control it.

"I don't want to be some bombed-out guy. My mom asked me, 'Do you crave alcohol?' I said no. It's just fun. To stop, all I have to do is look in the mirror and *think*. Can't brainwash this brain."

Miami Springs Police Lieutenant Robert Miller said that "Ted has made a change for the better—if he makes mistakes, he'll 'fess up." Hendricks has not been arrested by Springs cops, but they have shown him the door.

"It's always tough to live down a negative reputation," Miller said. "Recognizing you have a problem is half the solution."

Before he died last June, John Matuszak recognized his problem, and was trying to get Hendricks to confront his own. "The last time I saw Tooz, he said, 'I hope you make it,' " Hendricks said.

Hendricks was a pallbearer for Matuszak. He resented the obituaries depicting his friend as a drug- and alcohol-addicted wild man. He remembered him as the six-eight Santa Claus who visited hospitals.

He saw himself in Matuszak, another football player fighting to reconcile the tiger and the lamb.

Audrey Matuszak sees the resemblance, too. "These boys have been idolized since high school. What happens after that?" she said. "They're like children—they need lots of love, real love."

Philip Roth

Oh, to Be a Center Fielder

Baseball has always been one of Philip Roth's preoccupations as a writer (as part of his search for contemporary Jewish identity; many Jewish-American writers use baseball similarly). His 1991 prize-winning memoir of his father's life, Patrimony, *found father and son sharing a passion for baseball, and particularly for the New York Mets. His 1973 novel,* The Great American Novel, *examined the mixture of baseball and the American dream. And his 1969 novel,* Portnoy's Complaint, *which secured his fame as a leading novelist of his generation, possibly for his wide-open stance to sex, also contains this plaintive love song to a variation of the game: softball.*

Center field is the position I play for a softball team that wears silky blue-and-gold jackets with the name of the club scrawled in big white felt letters from one shoulder to the other: S E A B E E S, A.C. Thank God for the Seabees A.C.! Thank God for center field! Doctor, you can't imagine how truly glorious it is out there, so alone in all that space . . . Do you know baseball at all? Because center field is like some observation post, a kind of control tower, where you are able to see everything and everyone, to understand what's happening the instant it happens, not only by the sound of the struck bat, but by the spark of movement that goes through the infielders in the first second that the ball comes flying at them; and once it gets beyond them, "It's mine," you call, "it's mine," and then after it you go. For in center field, if you can get to it, it *is* yours. Oh, how unlike my home it is to be in center field, where no one will appropriate unto himself anything that I say is *mine!*

Unfortunately, I was too anxious a hitter to make the high school team—I swung and missed at bad pitches so often during the tryouts for the freshman squad that eventually the ironical coach took me aside and said, "Sonny, are you sure you don't wear glasses?" and then sent me on my way. But did I have form! did I have style! And in my playground softball league, where the ball came in just a little slower and a little bigger, I am the star I dreamed I might become for the whole school. Of course, still in my ardent desire to excel I too frequently swing and miss, but when I connect, it goes great distances, Doctor, it flies over fences and is called a home run. Oh, and there is really nothing in life, nothing at all, that quite compares with that pleasure of rounding second base at a nice slow clip, because there's just no hurry anymore, because that ball you've hit has just gone sailing out of sight . . . And I could field, too, and the farther I had to run, the better. "I got it! I got it! I got it!" and tear in toward second, to trap in the webbing of my glove— and barely an inch off the ground—a ball driven hard and low and right down the middle, a base hit, someone thought . . . Or back I go, "*I got it, I got it*—" back easily and gracefully toward that wire fence, moving practically in slow motion, and then that delicious Di Maggio sensation of grabbing it like something heaven-sent over one shoulder . . . Or running! turning! leaping! like little Al Gionfriddo—a baseball player, Doctor, who once did a very great thing . . . Or just standing nice and calm—nothing trembling, everything serene—standing there in the sunshine (as though in the middle of an empty field, or passing the time on the street corner), standing without a care in the world in the sunshine, like my king of kings, the Lord my God, The Duke Himself (Snider, Doctor, the name may come up again), standing there as loose and as easy, as happy as I will ever be, just waiting by myself under a high fly ball (*a towering fly ball*, I hear Red Barber say, as he watches from behind his microphone—hit out toward Portnoy; *Alex under it, under it*), just waiting there for the ball to fall into the glove I raise to it, and yup, there it is, *plock*, the third out of the inning (*and Alex gathers it in for out number three, and, folks, here's old C.D. for P. Lorillard and Company*), and then in one motion, while old Connie brings us a message from Old Golds, I start in toward the bench, holding the ball now with the five fingers of my bare left hand, and when I get to the infield— having come down hard with one foot on the bag at second base—I shoot it gently, with just a flick of the wrist, at the opposing team's shortstop as he comes trotting out onto the field, and still without breaking stride, go loping in all the way, shoulders shifting, head banging, a touch pigeon-toed, my knees coming slowly up and down in an altogether brilliant imitation of The Duke. Oh, the unruffled nonchalance of that game! There's not a movement that I don't know still down in the tissue of my muscles and the joints between my bones. How to bend over to pick up my glove and how to toss it away, how to test the weight of the bat, how to hold it and carry it and swing it around in the on-deck circle, how to raise that bat above my head and flex and loosen my shoulders and my neck before stepping in and planting my two feet exactly where my two feet belong in the batter's box—and how, when I take a called strike (which I have a tendency to do, it balances off nicely swinging at bad pitches), to step out and express, if only through a slight poking with the bat at the ground, just the right amount of exasperation with the powers that be . . . yes, every little detail so thoroughly studied and mastered, that it is simply beyond the realm of possibility for any situation to arise in which I do not know how to move, or where to move, or what to say or leave unsaid . . . And it's true, is it not?—incredible, but apparently true—there are people who feel in life the ease, the self-assurance, the going on, that I used to feel as the center fielder for the Seabees? Because it wasn't, you see, that one was the best center fielder imaginable, only that one knew exactly, and down to the smallest particular, how a center fielder should conduct himself. And there are people like that walking the streets of the U.S. of A.? I ask you, why can't I be one! Why can't I exist now as I existed for the Seabees out there in center field! Oh, to be a center fielder, a center fielder—and nothing more!

Damon Runyon

Bred for Battle

Damon Runyon, Jimmy Breslin wrote in his engaging 1991 biography of the man who invented the "Roaring Twenties," did something practically nobody else could do—"put a smile into a newspaper, which usually has as much humor as a bus accident." Runyon, Breslin also claimed, invented a street that never really existed, Broadway. Out of this Broadway came a stream of "Runyonesque" guys and dolls who loomed larger than life on the page and in the theater and movies and made a world smile. This story is full of such characters—Spider McCoy; Harry the Horse; heavyweight Shamus Mulrooney, "The Fighting Harp"; and Shamus's son, Thunderbolt Mulrooney, a heavyweight seemingly bred for battle except for that faraway look in his eyes—and the fact that his musical instrument of choice was the zither.

One night a guy by the name of Bill Corum, who is one of these sport scribes, gives me a Chinee for a fight at Madison Square Garden, a Chinee being a ducket with holes punched in it like old-fashioned Chink money, to show that it is a free ducket, and the reason I am explaining to you how I get this ducket is because I do not wish anybody to think I am ever simple enough to pay out my own potatoes for a ducket to a fight, even if I have any potatoes. Personally, I will not give you a bad two-bit piece to see a fight anywhere, because the way I look at it, half the time the guys who are supposed to do the fighting go in there and put on the old do-se-do, and I consider this a great fraud upon the public, and I do not believe in encouraging dishonesty.

But of course I never refuse a Chinee to such events, because the

way I figure it, what can I lose except my time, and my time is not worth
more than a bob a week the way things are. So on the night in question
I am standing in the lobby of the Garden with many other citizens, and
I am trying to find out if there is any skullduggery doing in connection
with the fight, because any time there is any skullduggery doing I love
to know it, as it is something worth knowing in case a guy wishes to
get a small wager down. Well, while I am standing there, somebody
comes up behind me and hits me an awful belt on the back, knocking
my wind plumb out of me, and making me very indignant indeed. As
soon as I get a little of my wind back again, I turn around figuring to
put a large blast on the guy who slaps me, but who is it but a guy by
the name of Spider McCoy, who is known far and wide as a manager of
fighters.

Well, of course I do not put the blast on Spider McCoy, because he
is an old friend of mine, and furthermore, Spider McCoy is such a guy
as is apt to let a left hook go at anybody who puts the blast on him,
and I do not believe in getting in trouble, especially with good left-
hookers.

So I say hello to Spider, and am willing to let it go at that, but Spider
seems glad to see me, and says to me like this: "Well, well, well, well,
well!" Spider says.

"Well," I say to Spider McCoy, "how many wells does it take to
make a river?"

"One, if it is big enough," Spider says, so I can see he knows the
answer all right. "Listen," he says, "I just think up the greatest proposition I ever think of in my whole life, and who knows but what I can
interest you in same."

"Well, Spider," I say, "I do not care to hear any propositions at this
time, because it may be a long story, and I wish to step inside and see
the impending battle. Anyway," I say, "if it is a proposition involving
financial support, I wish to state that I do not have any resources whatever at this time."

"Never mind the battle inside," Spider says. "It is nothing but a tank
job, anyway. And as for financial support," Spider says, "this does not
require more than a pound note, tops, and I know you have a pound
note because I know you put the bite on Overcoat Obie for this amount
not an hour ago. Listen," Spider McCoy says, "I know where I can place
my hands on the greatest heavyweight prospect in the world to-day,
and all I need is the price of car-fare to where he is."

Well, off and on, I know Spider McCoy twenty years, and in all this time I never know him when he is not looking for the greatest heavy-weight prospect in the world. And as long as Spider knows I have the pound note, I know there is no use trying to play the duck for him, so I stand there wondering who the stool pigeon can be who informs him of my financial status.

"Listen," Spider says, "I just discover that I am all out of line in the way I am looking for heavyweight prospects in the past. I am always looking for nothing but plenty of size," he says. "Where I make my mistake is not looking for blood lines. Professor D just smartens me up," Spider says. Well, when he mentions the name of Professor D, I commence taking a little interest, because it is well known to one and all that Professor D is one of the smartest old guys in the world. He is once a professor in a college out in Ohio, but quits this dodge to handicap the horses, and he is a first-rate handicapper, at that. But besides knowing how to handicap the horses, Professor D knows many other things, and is highly respected in all walks of life, especially on Broadway.

"Now then," Spider says, "Professor D calls my attention this after-noon to the fact that when a guy is looking for a race horse, he does not take just any horse that comes along, but he finds out if the horse's papa is able to run in his day, and if the horse's mamma can get out of her own way when she is young. Professor D shows me how a guy looks for speed in a horse's breeding away back to its great-great-great-great-grandpa and grandmamma," Spider McCoy says.

"Well," I say, "anybody knows this without asking Professor D. In fact," I say, "you can look up a horse's parents to see if they can mud before betting on a plug to win in heavy going."

"All right," Spider says, "I know all this myself, but I never think much about it before Professor D mentions it. Professor D says if a guy is looking for a hunting dog he does not pick a Pekingese pooch, but he gets a dog that is bred to hunt from away back yonder, and if he is after a game chicken he does not take a Plymouth Rock out of the back yard. So then," Spider says, "Professor D wishes to know why, when I am looking for a fighter, I do not look for one who comes of fighting stock. Professor D wishes to know," Spider says, "why I do not look for some guy who is bred to fight, and when I think this over, I can see the professor is right.

"And then all of a sudden," Spider says, "I get the largest idea I ever have in all my life. Do you remember a guy I have about twenty years back by the name of Shamus Mulrooney, the Fighting Harp?" Spider says. "A big, rough, tough heavyweight out of Newark?"

"Yes," I say, "I remember Shamus very well indeed. The last time I see him is the night Pounder Pat O'Shea almost murders him in the old Garden," I say. "I never see a guy with more ticker than Shamus, unless maybe it is Pat."

"Yes," Spider says, "Shamus has plenty of ticker. He is about through the night of the fight you speak of, otherwise Pat will never lay a glove on him. It is not long after this fight that Shamus packs in and goes back to bricklaying in Newark, and it is also about this same time," Spider says, "that he marries Pat O'Shea's sister, Bridget.

"Well, now," Spider says, "I remember they have a boy who must be around nineteen years old now, and if ever a guy is bred to fight it is a boy by Shamus Mulrooney out of Bridget O'Shea, because," Spider says, "Bridget herself can lick half the heavyweights I see around nowadays if she is half as good as she is the last time I see her. So now you have my wonderful idea. We will go to Newark and get this boy and make him heavyweight champion of the world."

"What you state is very interesting indeed, Spider," I say. "But," I say, "how do you know this boy is a heavyweight?"

"Why," Spider says, "how can he be anything else but a heavyweight, what with his papa as big as a house, and his mamma weighing maybe a hundred and seventy pounds in her step-ins? Although of course," Spider says, "I never see Bridget weigh in in such manner.

"But," Spider says, "even if she does carry more weight than I will personally care to spot a doll, Bridget is by no means a pelican when she marries Shamus. In fact," he says, "she is pretty good-looking. I remember their wedding well, because it comes out that Bridget is in love with some other guy at the time, and this guy comes to see the nuptials, and Shamus runs him all the way from Newark to Elizabeth, figuring to break a couple of legs for the guy if he catches him. But," Spider says, "the guy is too speedy for Shamus, who never has much foot anyway."

Well, all that Spider says appeals to me as a very sound business proposition, so the upshot of it is, I give him my pound note to finance his trip to Newark.

Then I do not see Spider McCoy again for a week, but one day he calls me up and tells me to hurry over to the Pioneer gymnasium to see the next heavyweight champion of the world, Thunderbolt Mulrooney.

I am personally somewhat disappointed when I see Thunderbolt Mulrooney, and especially when I find out his first name is Raymond and not Thunderbolt at all, because I am expecting to see a big, fierce guy with red hair and a chest like a barrel, such as Shamus Mulrooney has when he is in his prime. But who do I see but a tall, pale looking young guy with blond hair and thin legs.

Furthermore, he has pale blue eyes, and a far-away look in them, and he speaks in a low voice, which is nothing like the voice of Shamus Mulrooney. But Spider seems satisfied with Thunderbolt, and when I tell him Thunderbolt does not look to me like the next heavyweight champion of the world, Spider says like this: "Why," he says, "the guy is nothing but a baby, and you must give him time to fill out. He may grow to be bigger than his papa. But you know," Spider says, getting indignant as he thinks about it, "Bridget Mulrooney does not wish to let this guy be the next heavyweight champion of the world. In fact," Spider says, "she kicks up an awful row when I go to get him, and Shamus finally has to speak to her severely. Shamus says he does not know if I can ever make a fighter of this guy because Bridget coddles him until he is nothing but a mush-head, and Shamus says he is sick and tired of seeing the guy sitting around the house doing nothing but reading and playing the zither."

"Does he play the zither yet?" I ask Spider McCoy.

"No," Spider says, "I do not allow my fighters to play zithers. I figure it softens them up. This guy does not play anything at present. He seems to be in a daze most of the time, but of course everything is new to him. He is bound to come out okay, because," Spider says, "he is certainly bred right. I find out from Shamus that all the Mulrooneys are great fighters back in the old country," Spider says, "and furthermore he tells me Bridget's mother once licks four Newark cops who try to stop her from pasting her old man, so," Spider says, "this lad is just naturally steaming with fighting blood."

Well, I drop around to the Pioneer once or twice a week after this, and Spider McCoy is certainly working hard with Thunderbolt Mulrooney. Furthermore, the guy seems to be improving right along and gets so he can box fairly well and punch the bag, and all this and that, but he always has that far-away look in his eyes, and personally I do not care for fighters with far-away looks.

Finally one day Spider calls me up and tells me he has Thunderbolt Mulrooney matched in a four-round preliminary bout at the St. Nick with a guy by the name of Bubbles Browning, who is fighting almost as far back as the first battle of Bull Run, so I can see Spider is being very careful in matching Thunderbolt. In fact, I congratulate Spider on his carefulness. "Well," Spider says, "I am taking this match just to give

Thunderbolt the feel of the ring. I am taking Bubbles because he is an old friend of mine, and very deserving, and furthermore," Spider says, "he gives me his word he will not hit Thunderbolt very hard and will become unconscious the instant Thunderbolt hits him. You know," Spider says, "you must encourage a young heavyweight, and there is nothing that encourages one so much as knocking somebody unconscious."

Now of course it is nothing for Bubbles to promise not to hit anybody very hard because even when he is a young guy, Bubbles cannot punch his way out of a paper bag, but I am glad to learn that he also promises to become unconscious very soon, as naturally I am greatly interested in Thunderbolt's career, what with owning a piece of him, and having an investment of one pound in him already.

So the night of the fight, I am at the St. Nick very early, and many other citizens are there ahead of me, because by this time Spider McCoy gets plenty of publicity for Thunderbolt by telling the boxing scribes about his wonderful fighting blood lines, and everybody wishes to see a guy who is bred for battle, like Thunderbolt.

I take a guest with me to the fight by the name of Harry the Horse, who comes from Brooklyn, and as I am anxious to help Spider McCoy all I can, as well as to protect my investment in Thunderbolt, I request Harry to call on Bubbles Browning in his dressing room and remind him of his promise about hitting Thunderbolt. Harry the Horse does this for me, and furthermore he shows Bubbles a large revolver and tells Bubbles that he will be compelled to shoot his ears off if Bubbles forgets his promise, but Bubbles says all this is most unnecessary, as his eyesight is so bad he cannot see to hit anybody, anyway.

Well, I know a party who is a friend of the guy who is going to referee the preliminary bouts, and I am looking for this party to get him to tell the referee to disqualify Bubbles in case it looks as if he is forgetting his promise and is liable to hit Thunderbolt, but before I can locate the party, they are announcing the opening bout, and there is Thunderbolt in the ring looking very far away indeed, with Spider McCoy behind him.

It seems to me I never see a guy who is so pale all over as Thunderbolt Mulrooney, but Spider looks down at me and tips me a large wink, so I can see that everything is as right as rain, especially when Harry the Horse makes motions at Bubbles Browning like a guy firing a large revolver at somebody, and Bubbles smiles, and also winks.

Well, when the bell rings, Spider gives Thunderbolt a shove toward the center, and Thunderbolt comes out with his hands up, but looking more far away than somewhat, and something tells me that Thunderbolt by no means feels the killer instinct such as I love to see in fighters. In fact, something tells me that Thunderbolt is not feeling enthusiastic about this proposition in any way, shape, manner, or form. Old Bubbles almost falls over his own feet coming out of his corner, and he starts bouncing around making passes at Thunderbolt, and waiting for Thunderbolt to hit him so he can become unconscious. Naturally, Bubbles does not wish to become unconscious without getting hit, as this may look suspicious to the public.

Well, instead of hitting Bubbles, what does Thunderbolt Mulrooney do but turn around and walk over to a neutral corner, and lean over the ropes with his face in his gloves, and bust out crying. Naturally, this is a most surprising incident to one and all, especially to Bubbles Browning.

The referee walks over to Thunderbolt Mulrooney and tries to turn him around, but Thunderbolt keeps his face in his gloves and sobs so loud that the referee is deeply touched and starts sobbing with him. Between sobs he asks Thunderbolt if he wishes to continue the fight, and Thunderbolt shakes his head, although as a matter of fact no fight whatever starts so far, so the referee declares Bubbles Browning the winner, which is a terrible surprise to Bubbles. Then the referee puts his arm around Thunderbolt and leads him over to Spider McCoy, who is standing in his corner with a very strange expression on his face. Personally, I consider the entire spectacle so revolting that I go out into the air, and stand around awhile expecting to hear any minute that Spider McCoy is in the hands of the gendarmes on a charge of mayhem.

But it seems that nothing happens, and when Spider finally comes out of the St. Nicks, he is only looking sorrowful because he just hears that the promoter declines to pay him the fifty bobs he is supposed to receive for Thunderbolt's services, the promoter claiming that Thunderbolt renders no service.

"Well," Spider says, "I fear this is not the next heavyweight champion of the world after all. There is nothing in Professor D's idea about blood lines as far as fighters are concerned, although," he says, "it may work out all right with horses and dogs, and one thing and another. I am greatly disappointed," Spider says, "but then I am always being disappointed in heavyweights. There is nothing we can do but take this guy back home, because," Spider says, "the last thing I promised Bridget Mulrooney is that I will personally return him to her in case I am not able to make him heavyweight champion, as she is afraid he will get lost if he tries to find his way home alone."

So the next day, Spider McCoy and I take Thunderbolt Mulrooney over to Newark and to his home, which turns out to be a nice litte house in a side street with a yard all around and about, and Spider and I are just as well pleased that old Shamus Mulrooney is absent when we arrive, because Spider says that Shamus is just such a guy as will be asking a lot of questions about the fifty bobbos that Thunderbolt does not get.

Well, when we reach the front door of the house, out comes a big fine-looking doll with red cheeks, all excited, and she takes Thunderbolt in her arms and kisses him, so I know this is Bridget Mulrooney, and I can see she knows what happens, and in fact I afterwards learn that Thunderbolt telephones her the night before.

After a while she pushes Thunderbolt into the house and stands at the door as if she is guarding it against us entering to get him again, which of course is very unnecessary. And all this time Thunderbolt is sobbing no little, although by and by the sobs die away, and from somewhere in the house comes the sound of music I seem to recognize as the music of a zither.

Well, Bridget Mulrooney never says a word to us as she stands in the door, and Spider McCoy keeps staring at her in a way that I consider very rude indeed. I am wondering if he is waiting for a receipt for Thunderbolt, but finally he speaks as follows: "Bridget," Spider says, "I hope and trust that you will not consider me too fresh, but I wish to learn the name of the guy you are going around with just before you marry Shamus. I remember him well," Spider says, "but I cannot think of his name, and it bothers me not being able to think of names. He is a tall, skinny, stoop-shouldered guy," Spider says, "with a hollow chest and a soft voice, and he loves music."

Well, Bridget Mulrooney stands there in the doorway, staring back at Spider, and it seems to me that the red suddenly fades out of her cheeks, and just then we hear a lot of yelling, and around the corner of the house comes a bunch of five or six kids, who seem to be running from another kid. This kid is not very big, and is maybe fifteen or sixteen years old, and he has red hair and many freckles, and he seems very mad at the other kids. In fact, when he catches up with them, he starts belting away at them with his fists, and before anybody can as much as say boo, he has three of them on the ground as flat as pancakes, while the others are yelling bloody murder.

Personally, I never see such wonderful punching by a kid, especially with his left hand, and Spider McCoy is also much impressed, and is watching the kid with great interest. Then Bridget Mulrooney runs out and grabs the frecklefaced kid with one hand and smacks him with the other hand and hauls him, squirming and kicking, over to Spider McCoy and says to Spider like this:

"Mr. McCoy," Bridget says, "this is my youngest son Terence, and though he is not a heavyweight, and will never be a heavyweight, perhaps he will answer your purpose. Suppose you see his father about him sometime," she says, "and hoping you will learn to mind your own business, I wish you a very good day."

Then she takes the kid into the house under her arms and slams the door in our kissers, and there is nothing for us to do but walk away. And as we are walking away, all of a sudden Spider McCoy snaps his fingers as guys will do when they get an unexpected thought, and says like this: "I remember the guy's name," he says. "It is Cedric Tilbury, and he is a floorwalker in Hamburgher's department store, and," Spider says, "how he can play the zither!"

I see in the papers the other day where Jimmy Johnston, the match maker at the Garden, matches Tearing Terry Mulrooney, the new sensation in the lightweight division, to fight for the championship, but it seems from what Spider McCoy tells me that my investment with him does not cover any fighters in his stable except maybe heavyweights. And it also seems that Spider McCoy is not monkeying with heavyweights since he gets Tearing Terry.

Bill Russell

Champions

The Memoirs of an Opinionated Man *is the appropriate subtitle of* Bill Russell's autobiography Second Wind, *written with Taylor Branch. Russell has never been shy about expressing his opinions no matter what the consequences. In this selection from the book, Russell tells what it takes to become a champion. From a man who played on a gold-medal-winning Olympic basketball team, and whose teams copped two NCAA championships and eleven NBA crowns, his opinion on the subject can be considered authoritative.*

O ver the years Red worked me over regularly. He'd make a casual remark to me about how well someone on an opposing team was playing. I wouldn't say anything, but the remark would fester in my mind because I didn't think the guy was playing *that* well, so I'd work extra hard the next time we faced that player's team. Only later would it hit me that Red's remark hadn't been casual after all. Everything he did was calculated. As I got to know him better I'd laugh whenever he started telling me that Bill Bradley was the greatest college basketball player who'd ever played. This meant we had a big game coming up with the Knicks and Red wanted me to help Satch guard Bradley. We'd both know what was going on, but it didn't matter.

Red didn't have to work hard to appeal to my pride because I was basically self-motivated. I showed up ready for (almost) every game, and all I needed were occasional boosts. An unusually high percentage of the Celtics were the same, driven by something inside them that didn't need much outside fuel. Cousy was that way, and so were Sharman, K.C., Ramsey and Havlicek. Sam Jones was a special case, but his motivation also depended largely on himself. There is no question in my mind that we won championships because so many of us had so much confidence that the air was thick with it.

But contrary to what people think, a self-motivated athlete is rarely one who "eats, sleeps and drinks" his sport to the point that all his self-worth, and even his self-respect, depend on his performance. The all-consuming players value themselves as people only because they play ball. Now if that's the case, you'd expect them to play their hearts out, right? Wrong. They don't, because such players usually don't like themselves. They choke or complain or have strange things going on inside their heads that injure their performance. In a kind of self-fulfilling prophecy, such athletes prepare an excuse for themselves against the time when they don't play well—or don't play at all.

Some top athletes *are* one-dimensional, I believe—that is, they have no belief in themselves outside of sports—and I don't think any champion completely escapes the feeling that his drive depends on a fear of being diminished elsewhere as a person. The long-distance runner is likely to worry that only perversity is making him run the tenth mile of his daily workout, and there are equivalent worries in all other sports. Every now and then, either you or your sport is going to seem worthless, and you have to deal with those feelings.

"You're a bum," is a phrase you hear constantly in sports from fans and writers, and players even say it to themselves. They take it personally and get all shook up about it. They'll grit their teeth, make a stupendous play at a crucial moment, and then say to everyone, including themselves, "See? I'm not a bum." Every aspect of Reggie Jackson's character and talent came under attack in New York in 1977 until he hit three home runs in the seventh game of the World Series and silenced all his critics. There was a lot of pressure in his head, but Reggie could still see the ball. You don't just go into a trance and wake up when the ball goes over the fence. Despite the pressure, Reggie's mind worked well enough to guess what the pitcher would throw, his eyes worked well enough to see it, and his body worked well enough to smack it out of the park. Those are the marks of a champion, but neither Reggie nor the fans nor the writers should fool themselves that his bat speaks for his character.

Any athlete will identify with his score, statistics or reputation, and it's a struggle to keep a sense of your self-worth that's independent of those elements. Many of the Celtics succeeded; we had an extra feeling of confidence beyond the game itself, because we knew we'd be all right no matter how the game came out. Ironically, this feeling of independence makes you play better, and also helps you assume what I call the star's responsibility.

I never ran out of the huddle to the jump circle when I played. Other players would be slapping each other and pumping themselves up, but I'd always take my time and walk out slowly, my arms folded in front of me. I'd look at everybody disdainfully, like a sleepy dragon who can't be bothered to scare off another would-be hero. I wanted my look to say, "Hey, the King's here tonight!" It was an act I developed over my first two or three seasons, and almost always somebody fell for it. When I sensed anybody on the other team thinking, "I'm gonna show that son of a bitch!" I knew I had him. My little show was aimed at the guards and forwards on the other team; I wanted them to drive on me and try to beat me all night, even if it meant they made me look bad, because then they wouldn't be playing their game. They couldn't guard one of my teammates as well if they were thinking about humiliating me. Part of my responsibility to the team, as I saw it, was to divert an extra portion of the opponent's attack on myself. My teammates would know that they could take risks on defense because I was ready to pick up their men if they slipped by and came to the bucket. Some nights I'd point to a guy on the other team and call, "Send him in here! Let him come!" I wanted the Celtics to let the player drive on through if he wanted to, because I thought I could block his shot. Even if I didn't, I might mess up his head a little.

Sometimes I'd make a speech out in the jump circle. "All right, guys," I'd say to the other team, "Ain't no lay-ups out here tonight. I ain't gonna bother you with them fifteen footers 'cause I don't feel like it tonight, but I ain't gonna have no lay-ups!" Or I'd lean over to one of the forwards and say, "If you come in to shoot a lay-up off me you'd better bring your salt and pepper because you'll be eating basketballs." Of course I wouldn't say anything like that to Oscar Robertson or Jerry West; there are some guys you don't do that to. But many players would psyche themselves out if you gave them half a chance.

Star players have an enormous responsibility beyond their statistics—the responsibility to pick their team up and carry it. You have to do this to win championships—and to be ready to do it when you'd rather be a thousand other places. You have to say and do the things that will make your opponents play worse and your teammates play better. I always thought that the most important measure of how good a game I'd played was how much better I'd made my teammates play. In order to do this I would have to play well myself, to get the rebounds to start the breaks, to set the picks to get the shots and to score the points off their passes. But I could do these things and still neglect that extra load, which was what helped us win.

Some of my contemporaries in the NBA carried their teams in different ways. Oscar Robertson was like an assistant coach on the court. At a certain point in the third or fourth quarter he'd take over the game; you could see fire coming out of his nose, and he'd start yelling at his teammates. Getting them ready to make a run, Oscar would sit outside dribbling for a few seconds, and every time the ball hit the floor you'd hear his fierce chant: "Hey! Shit! Come on! Play! Goddam! Play!" Then he'd take off with his teammates all fired up, and you knew you'd have to hang on. Oscar literally *made* Wayne Embry into a good player. Wayne was a mild-mannered man before Oscar got hold of him and showed him what a monster he could be with all his size and strength.

After a few seasons with the Celtics, I noticed that Sam Jones could take over a game too. He wouldn't do it the way Oscar did, or nearly as often, but sometimes he gave off a feeling that he simply would not let us lose this game. He'd shoot, steal and score lay-ups, and when the other team tried to gang up on him, he'd feed the rest of us for easy baskets. Sam took on a glow that said, "This game's over."

But it only happened about one game in twenty, and I puzzled over it for a long time. I couldn't figure it out, so one day I asked, "Sam, why don't you play like that all the time?"

"No, I don't want to do that," he said without the slightest hesitation. He knew exactly what I meant, and he'd already thought about it. "I don't want the responsibility of having to play like that every night."

I was floored. "It would mean a lot of money," I said.

"I know," Sam replied, "but I don't want to do it."

Sam knew how good he was, but he made a choice and lived with it. Many players since him have refused to make that choice; they want the star's money without the responsibility. While I believe that players should be paid as much as the market thinks them worth, I also think the star's money carries the extra load.

I respected Sam's choice, but I didn't understand it. There were a lot of things about Sam I didn't understand. One night when we were playing in St. Louis he got the ball wide open at the foul line; nobody was near him, which is like giving the Celtics two points. But he just stood there two or three seconds and let the defense recover. None of us could believe what he'd seen.

"Sam, *why* didn't you shoot?" I asked, as if I was about to cry.

" 'Cause I couldn't see the bucket."

"You *what?*"

"I couldn't see the bucket," he repeated seriously, as though the statement made sense.

"What do you mean you couldn't see the bucket!" I screamed.

"I couldn't see it," he said. "The light was shining in my eyes, and I didn't like the way it looked."

I kept waiting for him to laugh, but he was serious, so there was nothing to do but shrug my shoulders.

When I first started coaching I called Sam over one day and said, "I want you to call the plays when you come up the court." It was a routine assignment.

"I can't call the plays," he said.

Something was wrong. "What do you mean?"

"I don't have the authority to call the plays," said Sam.

I tried to control myself. "Sam," I said. "I'm the coach, and I just *gave* you the authority!"

"Oh, no," he said, as if he'd caught me trying to pull a fast one. "You're the coach, but I still don't have the authority, so I can't call the plays."

He looked at me as if he knew he was in the right. I don't know exactly how I looked back at him, but I couldn't think of any response that seemed right, so I sighed. "You're right, Sam," I said quietly. "You can't call the plays."

I never could guess what Sam was going to do or say, with one major exception: I knew exactly how he would react in our huddle during the final seconds of a crucial game. I'm talking about a situation when we'd be one point behind, with five seconds to go in a game that meant not just first place or pride but a whole season, when *everything* was on the line. You're standing there feeling weak. The pressure weighs down on you so brutally that it crushes your heart as flat as a pizza, and you feel it thudding down around your stomach. During that time-out the question will be who'll take the shot that means the season, and Red would be looking around at faces, trying to decide what play to call. It's a moment when even the better players in the NBA will start coughing, tying their shoelaces and looking the other way. At such moments I knew what Sam would do as well as I know my own name. "Gimme the ball," he'd say. "I'll make it." And all of us would look at him, and we'd know by looking that he meant what he said. Not only that, you knew that he'd make it. Sam would be all business, but there'd be a trace of a smile on his face, like a guy who was meeting a supreme test and was certain he'd pass it. "You guys get out of the way," he'd say.

For many years I tried to figure out where this quality came from inside him. I never could, but I did know I could rely on his word whenever he got that look. Occasionally he'd even have it in advance. In 1966, Red's last year of coaching, we fell behind the Cincinnati Royals two games to one in the semi-finals of the play-offs. We'd promised the championship to Red as a farewell present, and to do so we had to beat Cincinnati two games straight. With Robertson playing like a demon and the first of these games on their court, things were looking grim. Sam drew me aside before that first game. "You get this one, Russ," he said, "and you won't have to worry about the one back in Boston. I'll take care of that myself."

I looked at Sam and saw he had that look, and I knew he meant what he said. He wasn't telling me that he was going to lay down on me in Cincinnati; he was just saying that he felt the moment coming back in Boston, and that game was salted away. I trusted him, and what he said uplifted me in both games. I had felt I was supposed to carry the team all the time, but here was Sam telling me he'd carry us half way. He was speaking in his championship voice.

Whenever the pressure was the greatest, Sam was eager for the ball. To me, that's one sign of a champion. Even with all the talent, the mental sharpness, the fun, the confidence and your focus honed down to winning, there'll be a level of competition where all that evens out. Then the pressure builds, and for the champion it is a test of heart. Heart in champions is a funny thing. People mistake it for courage, though there's no moral element to it. To me, you display courage when you take a stand for something you believe to be morally right, and do so in the face of adversity or danger. That's not what sports is about. Heart in champions has to do with the depth of your motivation, and how well your mind and body react to pressure. It's concentration— that is, being able to do what you do best under maximum pain and stress.

Sam Jones has a champion's heart. On the court he always had something in reserve. You could think he'd been squeezed of his last drop of strength and cunning, but if you looked closely, you'd see him coming up with something else he'd tucked away out of sight. Though sometimes he'd do things that made me want to break him in two, his presence gave me great comfort in key games. Under pressure, we had hidden on our team a class superstar of the highest caliber. In Los Angeles, Jerry West was called "Mr. Clutch," and he was, but in the seventh game of a championship series I'll take Sam over any player who's ever walked on a court.

Consistency under pressure is a certain kind of psychological steadiness that I first noticed at the 1956 Olympic Games in Melbourne. The U.S. track team had a sprinter named Bobby Morrow. Most people didn't think he was the best in the world because others had beaten his best time. But there was one thing everybody knew: Morrow would always run his best race in the championship heat. If the best he could do was 10.2 seconds in the 100-meter dash, you had to run a 10.1 in order to beat him; you'd never win running a 10.25. You couldn't go out there hoping he'd be upset or nervous or hung over or unprepared in any way. You might be faster than Bobby Morrow and completely convinced that you were, but you still had to go out there and prove it. Morrow matched his best time in heat after heat at the games, and wound up with two gold medals.

An athlete gains a special confidence when he thinks and performs like Bobby Morrow did, because he knows that win or lose, he'll give a champion's performance. The Celtics were that way, and so I never thought we'd lose a single play-off series—except in 1967, when I knew Wilt's Philadelphia 76ers were a superior team. Actually, I even believed we might win that one if we hung in there; there was no assurance that the 76ers would play their best under pressure, but they did.

Once you're ready to play like a champion in every game, you're entitled to hope for a performance that surpasses your own expectations. Every champion athlete has a moment when everything goes so perfectly for him that he slips into a gear that he didn't even know was there. It's easy to spot that perfect moment in a sport like track. I remember watching the 1968 Olympics in Mexico City, when the world record in the long jump was just under 27 feet. Then Bob Beamon flew down the chute and leaped out over the pit in a majestic jump that I have seen replayed many times. There was an awed silence when the announcer said that Beamon's jump measured 29 feet 2¼ inches. Generally world records are broken by fractions of inches, but Beamon had exceeded the existing record by more than two feet. On learning what he had done, Beamon slumped down on the ground and cried. To all those who saw it, this was an unforgettable moment in sport. Most viewers' image of Beamon ends with the picture of him weeping on the ground, but in fact he got up and took some more jumps that day. I like to think that he did so because he had jumped for so long at his best that *even then* he didn't know what might come out of him. At the end of the day he wanted to be absolutely sure that he'd had his perfect day. That's a champion.

All the years I played basketball I looked for that perfect game. I knew that it wouldn't come unless I was ready to play for every second the same way Bobby Morrow ran those sprints. I never had that perfect day, and I graded myself after every game to see how far in my own mind I fell short. The best score I ever gave myself was 65 on a scale of 100. It was a game in Boston in 1964, which I consider my best year. I got between thirty and thirty-five rebounds, made a high percentage of my shots, blocked a dozen shots, started a lot of fast breaks, intimidated my opponents and made them lose their concentration, and said the right things to my teammates to keep us playing confidently as a team. Above all, I felt inspired because my intuitions were right on target, running ahead of the game, and I felt in harmony with the sport. Despite all this, the game was not perfect. Errors stuck in my mind. I'd embarrassed myself missing free throws, looking like a shot putter; I'd missed five or six passes I'd seen but failed to make; and I didn't set five or six screens. Also, I'd failed to control certain impulses that can plague your game. On several occasions, for instance, I'd crashed the boards for a rebound that I *knew,* from both the angle and the shooter's habits, would bounce long to the side. I should have gotten those rebounds. All in all, I couldn't give myself a grade higher than 65.

This grading process never took me long. I could do it in less than a minute in front of my locker, in the shower or in the car driving home. Although I usually forgot the score of a game before I'd even left the locker room, the plays themselves would stay in my mind until I made a conscious effort to forget them. I could grade myself by watching the game again in my head, using that mental camera I'd discovered back in high school on my trip to the Northwest. This never changed, and neither did my conviction, once the Celtics became champions, that no one—whether Red, a teammate, an opponent, a fan or a reporter—could grade my performance as well as I could.

Basketball is not like Beamon's long jumping. A basketball player thinks and makes thousands of moves in every game that he falls short on by his own standards, however vague they are. Also, there are, by anyone's standards, clear-cut signs of failure; how can you play the "perfect game" if you miss a free throw or a field goal? But in addition, basketball is a team game, and this more than anything else changes the way performances should be measured. I never quite expected to have a day like Beamon's. Those scores gave me a way to push myself, to remind me of how much the game demands of any player. But it was not my motivation for playing the game, nor did it give me the greatest pleasure from it.

Irwin Shaw

The Eighty-Yard Run

Washington Post *book critic Jonathan Yardley once said of Irwin Shaw, "He sees clearly, he understands what he sees, and he describes it pointedly." For five decades Shaw wrote compelling and poignant short stories for publications such as* The New Yorker, Harper's Bazaar, Esquire, *and* The Saturday Evening Post. *"The Eighty-Yard Run," about a frustrated ex-jock whose one moment of glory was performed during a college football practice, exemplifies all of what made Shaw a master at his craft.*

The pass was high and wide and he jumped for it, feeling it slap flatly against his hands, as he shook his hips to throw off the halfback who was diving at him. The center floated by, his hands desperately brushing Darling's knee as Darling picked his feet up high and delicately ran over a blocker and an opposing linesman in a jumble on the ground near the scrimmage line. He had ten yards in the clear and picked up speed, breathing easily, feeling his thigh pads rising and falling against his legs, listening to the sound of cleats behind him, pulling away from them, watching the other backs heading him off toward the sideline, the whole picture, the men closing in on him, the blockers fighting for position, the ground he had to cross, all suddenly clear in his head, for the first time in his life not a meaningless confusion of men, sounds, speed. He smiled a little to himself as he ran, holding the ball lightly in front of him with his two hands, his knees pumping high, his hips twisting in the almost girlish run of a back in a broken field. The first halfback came at him and he fed him his leg, then swung at the last moment, took the shock of the man's shoulder without breaking stride, ran right through him, his cleats biting securely into the turf. There was only the safety man now, coming warily at him, his arms crooked, hands spread. Darling tucked the ball in, spurted at him, driving hard, hurling himself along, his legs pounding, knees high, all two hundred pounds bunched into controlled attack. He was sure he was going to get past the safety man. Without thought, his arms and legs working beautifully together, he headed right for the safety man, stiff-armed him, feeling blood spurt instantaneously from the man's nose onto his hand, seeing his face go awry, head turned, mouth pulled to one side. He pivoted away, keeping the arm locked, dropping the safety man as he ran easily toward the goal line, with the drumming of cleats diminishing behind him.

How long ago? It was autumn then, and the ground was getting hard because the nights were cold and leaves from the maples around the stadium blew across the practice fields in gusts of wind, and the girls were beginning to put polo coats over their sweaters when they came to watch practice in the afternoons. . . . Fifteen years. Darling walked slowly over the same ground in the spring twilight, in his neat shoes, a man of thirty-five dressed in a double-breasted suit, ten pounds heavier in the fifteen years, but not fat, with the years between 1925 and 1940 showing in his face.

The coach was smiling quietly to himself and the assistant coaches were looking at each other with pleasure the way they always did when one of the second stringers suddenly did something fine, bringing credit to them, making their $2,000 a year a tiny bit more secure.

Darling trotted back, smiling, breathing deeply but easily, feeling wonderful, not tired, though this was the tail end of practice and he'd run eighty yards. The sweat poured off his face and soaked his jersey and he liked the feeling, the warm moistness lubricating his skin like oil. Off in a corner of the field some players were punting and the smack of leather against the ball came pleasantly through the afternoon air. The freshmen were running signals on the next field and the quarter-back's sharp voice, the pound of the eleven pairs of cleats, the "Dig, now *dig!*" of the coaches, the laughter of the players all somehow made him feel happy as he trotted back to midfield, listening to the applause and shouts of the students along the sidelines, knowing that after that run the coach would have to start him Saturday against Illinois.

Fifteen years, Darling thought, remembering the shower after the workout, the hot water steaming off his skin and the deep soapsuds and all the young voices singing with the water streaming down and towels going and managers running in and out and the sharp sweet smell of oil of wintergreen and everybody clapping him on the back as he dressed and Packard, the captain, who took being captain very seriously, coming over to him and shaking his hand and saying, "Darling, you're going to go places in the next two years."

The assistant manager fussed over him, wiping a cut on his leg with alcohol and iodine, the little sting making him realize suddenly how fresh and whole and solid his body felt. The manager slapped a piece of adhesive tape over the cut, and Darling noticed the sharp clean white of the tape against the ruddiness of the skin, fresh from the shower.

He dressed slowly, the softness of his shirt and the soft warmth of his wool socks and his flannel trousers a reward against his skin after the harsh pressure of the shoulder harness and thigh and hip pads. He drank three glasses of cold water, the liquid reaching down coldly inside of him, soothing the harsh dry places in his throat and belly left by the sweat and running and shouting of practice.

Fifteen years.

The sun had gone down and the sky was green behind the stadium and he laughed quietly to himself as he looked at the stadium, rearing above the trees, and knew that on Saturday when the 70,000 voices roared as the team came running out onto the field, part of that enormous salute would be for him. He walked slowly, listening to the gravel crunch satisfactorily under his shoes in the still twilight, feeling his clothes swing lightly against his skin, breathing the thin evening air, feeling the wind move softly in his damp hair, wonderfully cool behind his ears and at the nape of his neck.

Louise was waiting for him at the road, in her car. The top was down and he noticed all over again, as he always did when he saw her, how pretty she was, the rough blond hair and the large, inquiring eyes and the bright mouth, smiling now.

She threw the door open. "Were you good today?" she asked.

"Pretty good," he said. He climbed in, sank luxuriously into the soft leather, stretched his legs far out. He smiled, thinking of the eighty yards. "Pretty damn good."

She looked at him seriously for a moment, then scrambled around, like a little girl, kneeling on the seat next to him, grabbed him, her hands along his ears, and kissed him as he sprawled, head back, on the seat cushion. She let go of him, but kept her head close to his, over his. Darling reached up slowly and rubbed the back of his hand against her cheek, lit softly by a street lamp a hundred feet away. They looked at each other, smiling.

Louise drove down to the lake and they sat there silently, watching the moon rise behind the hills on the other side. Finally he reached over, pulled her gently to him, kissed her. Her lips grew soft, her body sank into his, tears formed slowly in her eyes. He knew, for the first time, that he could do whatever he wanted with her.

"Tonight," he said. "I'll call for you at seven-thirty. Can you get out?"

She looked at him. She was smiling, but the tears were still full in her eyes. "All right," she said. "I'll get out. How about you? Won't the coach raise hell?"

Darling grinned. "I got the coach in the palm of my hand," he said. "Can you wait till seven-thirty?"

She grinned back at him. "No," she said.

They kissed and she started the car and they went back to town for dinner. He sang on the way home.

Christian Darling, thirty-five years old, sat on the frail spring grass, greener now than it ever would be again on the practice field, looked thoughtfully up at the stadium, a deserted ruin in the twilight. He had started on the first team that Saturday and every Saturday after that for the next two years, but it had never been as satisfactory as it should have been. He never had broken away, the longest run he'd ever made was thirty-five yards, and that in a game that was already won, and then that kid had come up from the third team, Diederich, a blank-faced German kid from Wisconsin, who ran like a bull, ripping lines to pieces Saturday after Saturday, plowing through, never getting hurt, never changing his expression, scoring more points, gaining more ground than all the rest of the team put together, making everybody's All-American, carrying the ball three times out of four, keeping everybody else out of the headlines. Darling was a good blocker and he spent his Saturday afternoons working on the big Swedes and Polacks who played tackle and end for Michigan, Illinois, Purdue, hurling into huge pile-ups, bobbing his head wildly to elude the great raw hands swinging like meat-cleavers at him as he went charging in to open up holes for Diederich coming through like a locomotive behind him. Still, it wasn't so bad. Everybody liked him and he did his job and he was pointed out on the campus and boys always felt important when they introduced their girls to him at their proms, and Louise loved him and watched him faithfully in the games, even in the mud, when your own mother wouldn't know you, and drove him around in her car keeping the top down because she was proud of him and wanted to show everybody that she was Christian Darling's girl. She bought him crazy presents because her father was rich, watches, pipes, humidors, an icebox for beer for his room, curtains, wallets, a fifty-dollar dictionary.

"You'll spend every cent your old man owns," Darling protested once when she showed up at his rooms with seven different packages in her arms and tossed them onto the couch.

"Kiss me," Louise said, "and shut up."

"Do you want to break your poor old man?"

"I don't mind. I want to buy you presents."

"Why?"

"It makes me feel good. Kiss me. I don't know why. Did you know that you're an important figure?"

"Yes," Darling said gravely.

"When I was waiting for you at the library yesterday two girls saw you coming and one of them said to the other, 'That's Christian Darling. He's an important figure.'"

"You're a liar."

"I'm in love with an important figure."

"Still, why the hell did you have to give me a forty-pound dictionary?"

"I wanted to make sure," Louise said, "that you had a token of my esteem. I want to smother you in tokens of my esteem."

Fifteen years ago.

They'd married when they got out of college. There'd been other women for him, but all casual and secret, more for curiosity's sake, and vanity, women who'd thrown themselves at him and flattered him, a pretty mother at a summer camp for boys, an old girl from his home town who'd suddenly blossomed into a coquette, a friend of Louise's who had dogged him grimly for six months and had taken advantage of the two weeks that Louise went home when her mother died. Perhaps Louise had known, but she'd kept quiet, loving him completely, filling his rooms with presents, religiously watching him battling with the big Swedes and Polacks on the line of scrimmage on Saturday afternoons, making plans for marrying him and living with him in New York and going with him there to the night clubs, the theaters, the good restaurants, being proud of him in advance, tall, white-teethed, smiling, large, yet moving lightly, with an athlete's grace, dressed in evening clothes, approvingly eyed by magnificently dressed and famous women in theater lobbies, with Louise adoringly at his side.

Her father, who manufactured inks, set up a New York office for Darling to manage and presented him with three hundred accounts, and they lived on Beekman Place with a view of the river with fifteen thousand dollars a year between them, because everybody was buying everything in those days, including ink. They saw all the shows and went to all the speak-easies and spent their fifteen thousand dollars a year and in the afternoons Louise went to the art galleries and the matinees of the more serious plays that Darling didn't like to sit through and Darling slept with a girl who danced in the chorus of *Rosalie* and with the wife of a man who owned three copper mines. Darling played squash three times a week and remained as solid as a stone barn and Louise never took her eyes off him when they were in the same room together, watching him with a secret, miser's smile, with a trick of coming over to him in the middle of a crowded room and saying gravely, in a low voice, "You're the handsomest man I've ever seen in my whole life. Want a drink?"

Nineteen twenty-nine came to Darling and to his wife and father-in-law, the maker of inks, just as it came to everyone else. The father-in-law waited until 1933 and then blew his brains out and when Darling went to Chicago to see what the books of the firm looked like he found out all that was left were debts and three or four gallons of unbought ink.

"Please, Christian," Louise said, sitting in their neat Beekman Place apartment, with a view of the river and prints of paintings by Dufy and Braque and Picasso on the wall, "please, why do you want to start drinking at two o'clock in the afternoon?"

"I have nothing else to do," Darling said, putting down his glass, emptied of its fourth drink. "Please pass the whisky."

Louise filled his glass. "Come take a walk with me," she said. "We'll walk along the river."

"I don't want to walk along the river," Darling said, squinting intensely at the prints of paintings by Dufy, Braque and Picasso.

"We'll walk along Fifth Avenue."

"I don't want to walk along Fifth Avenue."

"Maybe," Louise said gently, "you'd like to come with me to some art galleries. There's an exhibition by a man named Klee. . . ."

"I don't want to go to any art galleries. I want to sit here and drink

Scotch whisky," Darling said. "Who the hell hung those goddam pictures up on the wall?"

"I did," Louise said.

"I hate them."

"I'll take them down," Louise said.

"Leave them there. It gives me something to do in the afternoon. I can hate them." Darling took a long swallow. "Is that the way people paint these days?"

"Yes, Christian. Please don't drink any more."

"Do you like painting like that?"

"Yes, dear."

"Really?"

"Really."

Darling looked carefully at the prints once more. "Little Louise Tucker. The middle-western beauty. I like pictures with horses in them. Why should you like pictures like that?"

"I just happen to have gone to a lot of galleries in the last few years . . ."

"Is that what you do in the afternoon?"

"That's what I do in the afternoon," Louise said.

"I drink in the afternoon."

Louise kissed him lightly on the top of his head as he sat there squinting at the pictures on the wall, the glass of whisky held firmly in his hand. She put on her coat and went out without saying another word. When she came back in the early evening, she had a job on a woman's fashion magazine.

They moved downtown and Louise went out to work every morning and Darling sat home and drank and Louise paid the bills as they came up. She made believe she was going to quit work as soon as Darling found a job, even though she was taking over more responsibility day by day at the magazine, interviewing authors, picking painters for the illustrations and covers, getting actresses to pose for pictures, going out for drinks with the right people, making a thousand new friends whom she loyally introduced to Darling.

"I don't like your hat," Darling said, once, when she came in in the evening and kissed him, her breath rich with Martinis.

"What's the matter with my hat, Baby?" she asked, running her fingers through his hair. "Everybody says it's very smart."

"It's too damned smart," he said. "It's not for you. It's for a rich, sophisticated woman of thirty-five with admirers."

Louise laughed. "I'm practicing to be a rich, sophisticated woman of thirty-five with admirers," she said. He stared soberly at her. "Now, don't look so grim, Baby. It's still the same simple little wife under the hat." She took the hat off, threw it into a corner, sat on his lap. "See? Homebody Number One."

"Your breath could run a train," Darling said, not wanting to be mean, but talking out of boredom, and sudden shock at seeing his wife curiously a stranger in a new hat, with a new expression in her eyes under the little brim, secret, confident, knowing.

Louise tucked her head under his chin so he couldn't smell her breath. "I had to take an author out for cocktails," she said. "He's a boy from the Ozark Mountains and he drinks like a fish. He's a Communist."

"What the hell is a Communist from the Ozarks doing writing for a woman's fashion magazine?"

Louise chuckled. "The magazine business is getting all mixed up these days. The publishers want to have a foot in every camp. And anyway, you can't find an author under seventy these days who isn't a Communist."

"I don't think I like you to associate with all those people, Louise," Darling said. "Drinking with them."

"He's a very nice, gentle boy," Louise said. "He reads Ernest Dowson."

"Who's Ernest Dowson?"

Louise patted his arm, stood up, fixed her hair. "He's an English poet."

Darling felt that somehow he had disappointed her. "Am I supposed to know who Ernest Dowson is?"

"No, dear. I'd better go in and take a bath."

After she had gone, Darling went over to the corner where the hat was lying and picked it up. It was nothing, a scrap of straw, a red flower, a veil, meaningless on his big hand, but on his wife's head a signal of something . . . big city, smart and knowing women drinking and dining with men other than their husbands, conversation about things a normal man wouldn't know much about, Frenchmen who painted as though they used their elbows instead of brushes, composers who wrote whole symphonies without a single melody in them, writers who knew all about politics and women who knew all about writers, the movement of the proletariat, Marx, somehow mixed up with five-dollar dinners and the best-looking women in America and fairies who made them laugh and half-sentences immediately understood and secretly hilarious and wives who called their husbands "Baby." He put the hat down, a scrap of straw and a red flower, and a little veil. He drank some whisky straight and went into the bathroom where his wife was lying deep in her bath, singing to herself and smiling from time to time like a little girl, paddling the water gently with her hands, sending up a slight spicy fragrance from the bath salts she used.

He stood over her, looking down at her. She smiled up at him, her eyes half closed, her body pink and shimmering in the warm, scented water. All over again, with all the old suddenness, he was hit deep inside him with the knowledge of how beautiful she was, how much he needed her.

"I came in here," he said, "to tell you I wish you wouldn't call me 'Baby.' "

She looked up at him from the bath, her eyes quickly full of sorrow, half-understanding what he meant. He knelt and put his arms around her, his sleeves plunged heedlessly in the water, his shirt and jacket soaking wet as he clutched her wordlessly, holding her crazily tight, crushing her breath from her, kissing her desperately, searchingly, regretfully.

He got jobs after that, selling real estate and automobiles, but somehow, although he had a desk with his name on a wooden wedge on it, and he went to the office religiously at nine each morning, he never managed to sell anything and he never made any money.

Louise was made assistant editor, and the house was always full of strange men and women who talked fast and got angry on abstract subjects like mural painting, novelists, labor unions. Negro short-story writers drank Louise's liquor, and a lot of Jews, and big solemn men with scarred faces and knotted hands who talked slowly but clearly about picket lines and battles with guns and leadpipe at mine-shaft-heads and in front of factory gates. And Louise moved among them all, confidently, knowing what they were talking about, with opinions that they listened to and argued about just as though she were a man. She knew everybody, condescended to no one, devoured books that Darling had never heard of, walked along the streets of the city, excited, at home, soaking in all the million tides of New York without fear, with constant wonder.

Her friends liked Darling and sometimes he found a man who wanted to get off in the corner and talk about the new boy who played fullback for Princeton, and the decline of the double wingback, or even the state of the stock market, but for the most part he sat on the edge of things, solid and quiet in the high storm of words. "The dialectics of the situation . . . The theater has been given over to expert jugglers . . . Picasso? What man has a right to paint old bones and collect ten thousand dollars for them? . . . I stand firmly behind Trotsky . . . Poe was the last American critic. When he died they put lilies on the grave of American criticism. I don't say this because they panned my last book, but . . ."

Once in a while he caught Louise looking soberly and consideringly at him through the cigarette smoke and the noise and he avoided her eyes and found an excuse to get up and go into the kitchen for more ice or to open another bottle.

"Come on," Cathal Flaherty was saying, standing at the door with a girl, "you've got to come down and see this. It's down on Fourteenth Street, in the old Civic Repertory, and you can only see it on Sunday nights and I guarantee you'll come out of the theater singing." Flaherty was a big young Irishman with a broken nose who was the lawyer for a longshoreman's union, and he had been hanging around the house for six months on and off, roaring and shutting everybody else up when he got in an argument. "It's a new play, *Waiting for Lefty;* it's about taxi-drivers."

"Odets," the girl with Flaherty said. "It's by a guy named Odets."

"I never heard of him," Darling said.

"He's a new one," the girl said.

"It's like watching a bombardment," Flaherty said. "I saw it last Sunday night. You've got to see it."

"Come on, Baby," Louise said to Darling, excitement in her eyes already. "We've been sitting in the Sunday *Times* all day, this'll be a great change."

"I see enough taxi-drivers every day," Darling said, not because he meant that, but because he didn't like to be around Flaherty, who said things that made Louise laugh a lot and whose judgment she accepted on almost every subject. "Let's go to the movies."

"You've never seen anything like this before," Flaherty said. "He wrote this play with a baseball bat."

"Come on," Louise coaxed, "I bet it's wonderful."

"He has long hair," the girl with Flaherty said. "Odets. I met him at a party. He's an actor. He didn't say a goddam thing all night."

"I don't feel like going down to Fourteenth Street," Darling said, wishing Flaherty and his girl would get out. "It's gloomy."

"Oh, hell!" Louise said loudly. She looked coolly at Darling, as though she'd just been introduced to him and was making up her mind about him, and not very favorably. He saw her looking at him, knowing there was something new and dangerous in her face and he wanted to say something, but Flaherty was there and his damned girl, and anyway, he didn't know what to say.

"I'm going," Louise said, getting her coat. "I don't think Fourteenth Street is gloomy."

"I'm telling you," Flaherty was saying, helping her on with her coat, "it's the Battle of Gettysburg, in Brooklynese."

"Nobody could get a word out of him," Flaherty's girl was saying as they went through the door. "He just sat there all night."

The door closed. Louise hadn't said good night to him. Darling walked around the room four times, then sprawled out on the sofa, on top of the Sunday *Times*. He lay there for five minutes looking at the ceiling, thinking of Flaherty walking down the street talking in that booming voice, between the girls, holding their arms.

Louise had looked wonderful. She'd washed her hair in the afternoon and it had been very soft and light and clung close to her head as she stood there angrily putting her coat on. Louise was getting prettier every year, partly because she knew by now how pretty she was, and made the most of it.

"Nuts," Darling said, standing up. "Oh, nuts."

He put on his coat and went down to the nearest bar and had five drinks off by himself in a corner before his money ran out.

The years since then had been foggy and downhill. Louise had been nice to him, and in a way, loving and kind, and they'd fought only once, when he said he was going to vote for Landon. ("Oh, Christ," she'd said, "doesn't *anything* happen inside your head? Don't you read the papers? The penniless Republican!") She'd been sorry later and apologized for hurting him, but apologized as she might to a child. He'd tried hard, had gone grimly to the art galleries, the concert halls, the bookshops, trying to gain on the trail of his wife, but it was no use. He was bored, and none of what he saw or heard or dutifully read made much sense to him and finally he gave it up. He had thought, many nights as he ate dinner alone, knowing that Louise would come home late and drop silently into bed without explanation, of getting a divorce, but he knew the loneliness, the hopelessness, of not seeing her again would be too much to take. So he was good, completely devoted, ready at all times to go any place with her, do anything she wanted. He even got a small job, in a broker's office and paid his own way, bought his own liquor.

Then he'd been offered the job of going from college to college as a tailor's representative. "We want a man," Mr. Rosenberg had said, "who as soon as you look at him, you say, 'There's a university man.' " Rosenberg had looked approvingly at Darling's broad shoulders and well-kept waist, at his carefully brushed hair and his honest, wrinkleless face. "Frankly, Mr. Darling, I am willing to make you a proposition. I have inquired about you, you are favorably known on your old campus, I understand you were in the backfield with Alfred Diederich."

Darling nodded. "Whatever happened to him?"

"He is walking around in a cast for seven years now. An iron brace. He played professional football and they broke his neck for him."

Darling smiled. That, at least, had turned out well.

"Our suits are an easy product to sell, Mr. Darling," Rosenberg said. "We have a handsome, custom-made garment. What has Brooks Brothers got that we haven't got? A name. No more."

"I can make fifty, sixty dollars a week," Darling said to Louise that night. "And expenses. I can save some money and then come back to New York and really get started here."

"Yes, Baby," Louise said.

"As it is," Darling said carefully, "I can make it back here once a month, and holidays and the summer. We can see each other often."

"Yes, Baby." He looked at her face, lovelier now at thirty-five than it had ever been before, but fogged over now as it had been for five years with a kind of patient, kindly, remote boredom.

"What do you say?" he asked. "Should I take it?" Deep within him he hoped fiercely, longingly, for her to say, "No, Baby, you stay right here," but she said, as he knew she'd say, "I think you'd better take it."

He nodded. He had to get up and stand with his back to her, looking out the window, because there were things plain on his face that she had never seen in the fifteen years she'd known him. "Fifty dollars is a lot of money," he said. "I never thought I'd ever see fifty dollars again." He laughed. Louise laughed, too.

Christian Darling sat on the frail green grass of the practice field. The shadow of the stadium had reached out and covered him. In the distance the lights of the university shone a little mistily in the light haze of evening. Fifteen years. Flaherty even now was calling for his wife, buying her a drink, filling whatever bar they were in with that voice of his and that easy laugh. Darling half-closed his eyes, almost saw the boy fifteen years ago reach for the pass, slip the halfback, go skittering lightly down the field, his knees high and fast and graceful, smiling to himself because he knew he was going to get past the safety man. That was the high point, Darling thought, fifteen years ago, on an autumn afternoon, twenty years old and far from death, with the air coming easily into his lungs, and a deep feeling inside him that he could do anything, knock over anybody, outrun whatever had to be outrun. And the shower after and the three glasses of water and the cool night air on his damp head and Louise sitting hatless in the open car with a smile and the first kiss she ever really meant. The high point, an eighty-yard run in the practice, and a girl's kiss and everything after that a decline. Darling laughed. He had practiced the wrong thing, perhaps. He hadn't practiced for 1929 and New York City and a girl who would turn into a woman. Somewhere, he thought, there must have been a point where she moved up to me, was even with me for a moment, when I could have held her hand, if I'd known, held tight, gone with her. Well, he'd never known. Here he was on a playing field that was fifteen years away and his wife was in another city having dinner with another and better man, speaking with him a different, new language, a language nobody had ever taught him.

Darling stood up, smiled a little, because if he didn't smile he knew the tears would come. He looked around him. This was the spot. O'Connor's pass had come sliding out just to here . . . the high point. Darling put up his hands, felt all over again the flat slap of the ball. He shook his hips to throw off the halfback, cut back inside the center, picked his knees high as he ran gracefully over two men jumbled on the ground at the line of scrimmage, ran easily, gaining speed, for ten yards, holding the ball lightly in his two hands, swung away from the halfback diving at him, ran, swinging his hips in the almost girlish manner of a back in a broken field, tore into the safety man, his shoes drumming heavily on the turf, stiff-armed, elbow locked, pivoted, raced lightly and exultantly for the goal line.

It was only after he had sped over the goal line and slowed to a trot that he saw the boy and girl sitting together on the turf, looking at him wonderingly.

He stopped short, dropping his arms. "I . . ." he said, gasping a little, though his condition was fine and the run hadn't winded him. "I—once I played here."

The boy and the girl said nothing. Darling laughed embarrassedly, looked hard at them sitting there, close to each other, shrugged, turned and went toward his hotel, the sweat breaking out on his face and running down into his collar.

Red Smith

Miracle of Coogan's Bluff

There is only one saint among American sportswriters, and his name is Red Smith. No other newspaper journalist could match Smith in the elegance and grace and precision of his daily five-hundred-word column, each a gem of language fused to whatever subject he chose, that set unwavering standards for his thirty-seven-year career in New York. The novelist William Kennedy once said, "I tried to learn from the great journalists I grew up reading like Red Smith, who made literature every day." Smith was modest about his professional gifts, and giving to young writers who flocked around him, wanting to learn from him, wanting to receive the Smith touch. How to pick one column out of the peerless thousands to show you that touch? Well, here is a pretty good matchup, the invocation of a sports miracle by the saint himself.

Now it is done. Now the story ends. And there is no way to tell it. The art of fiction is dead. Reality has strangled invention. Only the utterly impossible, the inexpressibly fantastic, can ever be plausible again.

Down on the green and white and earth-brown geometry of the playing field, a drunk tries to break through the ranks of ushers marshaled along the foul lines to keep profane feet off the diamond. The ushers thrust him back and he lunges at them, struggling in the clutch of two or three men. He breaks free, and four or five tackle him. He shakes them off, bursts through the line, runs head-on into a special park cop, who brings him down with a flying tackle.

Here comes a whole platoon of ushers. They lift the man and haul him, twisting and kicking, back across the first-base line. Again he shakes loose and crashes the line. He is through. He is away, weaving out toward center field, where cheering thousands are jammed beneath the windows of the Giants' clubhouse.

At heart, our man is a Giant, too. He never gave up.

From center field comes burst upon burst of cheering, Pennants are waving, uplifted fists are brandished, hats are flying. Again and again the dark clubhouse windows blaze with the light of photographers' flash bulbs. Here comes that same drunk out of the mob, back across the green turf to the infield. Coattails flying, he runs the bases, slides into third. Nobody bothers him now.

And the story remains to be told, the story of how the Giants won the 1951 pennant in the National League. The tale of their barreling run through August and September and into October. . . . Of the final day of the season, when they won the championship and started home with it from Boston, to hear on the train how the dead, defeated Dodgers had risen from the ashes in the Philadelphia twilight. . . . Of the three-game playoff in which they won, and lost, and were losing again with one out in the ninth inning yesterday when—Oh, why bother?

Maybe this is the way to tell it: Bobby Thomson, a young Scot from Staten Island, delivered a timely hit yesterday in the ninth inning of an enjoyable game of baseball before 34,320 witnesses in the Polo Grounds. . . . Or perhaps this is better:

"Well!" said Whitey Lockman, standing on second base in the second inning of yesterday's playoff game between the Giants and Dodgers.

"Ah, there," said Bobby Thomson, pulling into the same station after hitting a ball to left field. "How've you been?"

"Fancy," Lockman said, "meeting you here!"

"Ooops!" Thomson said. "Sorry."

And the Giants' first chance for a big inning against Don Newcombe disappeared as they tagged Thomson out. Up in the press section, the voice of Willie Goodrich came over the amplifiers announcing a macabre statistic: "Thomson has now hit safely in fifteen consecutive games." Just then the floodlights were turned on, enabling the Giants to see and count their runners on each base.

It wasn't funny, though, because it seemed for so long that the Giants weren't going to get another chance like the one Thomson squandered by trying to take second base with a playmate already there. They couldn't hit Newcombe, and the Dodgers couldn't do anything wrong. Sal Maglie's most splendrous pitching would avail nothing unless New York could match the run Brooklyn had scored in the first inning.

The story was winding up, and it wasn't the happy ending that such a tale demands. Poetic justice was a phrase without meaning.

Now it was the seventh inning and Thomson was up, with runners on first and third base, none out. Pitching a shutout in Philadelphia last Saturday night, pitching again in Philadelphia on Sunday, holding the Giants scoreless this far, Newcombe had now gone twenty-one innings without allowing a run.

He threw four strikes to Thomson. Two were fouled off out of play. Then he threw a fifth. Thomson's fly scored Monte Irvin. The score was tied. It was a new ball game.

Wait a moment, though. Here's Pee Wee Reese hitting safely in the eighth. Here's Duke Snider singling Reese to third. Here's Maglie wild-pitching a run home. Here's Andy Pafko slashing a hit through Thomson for another score. Here's Billy Cox batting still another home. Where does his hit go? Where else? Through Thomson at third.

So it was the Dodgers' ball game, 4 to 1, and the Dodgers' pennant. So all right. Better get started and beat the crowd home. That stuff in the ninth inning? That didn't mean anything.

A single by Al Dark. A single by Don Mueller. Irvin's pop-up, Lockman's one-run double. Now the corniest possible sort of Hollywood schmaltz—stretcher-bearers plodding away with an injured Mueller between them, symbolic of the Giants themselves.

There went Newcombe and here came Ralph Branca. Who's at bat? Thomson again? He beat Branca with a home run the other day. Would Charley Dressen order him walked, putting the winning run on base, to pitch to the dead-end kids at the bottom of the batting order? No, Branca's first pitch was a called strike.

The second pitch—well, when Thomson reached first base he turned and looked toward the left-field stands. Then he started jumping straight up in the air, again and again. Then he trotted around the bases, taking his time.

Ralph Branca turned and started for the clubhouse. The number on his uniform looked huge. Thirteen.

Al Stump

Fight to Live

When West Coast magazine writer Al Stump was assigned to col-
laborate with Ty Cobb on Cobb's autobiography, My Life in Baseball, *it was a dubious honor. For Cobb treated his ghost writer the*
same malicious way he treated opposing players. But Stump sur-
vived the ordeal and, after the great but savage ballplayer's death,
wrote his own story for True *magazine in 1961 on what it was like*
working with the irascible Cobb in the last painful years of his life.
"Fight to Live" is the harrowing, brutally graphic tale of a man
possessed by demons he cannot control.

Ever since sundown the Nevada intermountain radio had been
crackling warnings: "Route 50 now highly dangerous. Motorists
stay off. Repeat: AVOID ROUTE 50."

By 1 in the morning the 21-mile, steep-pitched passage from Lake
Tahoe's 7,000 feet into Carson City, a snaky grade most of the way, was
snow-struck, ice-sheeted, thick with rock slides and declared unfit for
all transport vehicles by the State Highway Patrol.

Such news was right down Ty Cobb's alley. Anything that smacked
of the impossible brought an unholy gleam to his eye. The gleam had
been there in 1959 when a series of lawyers advised Cobb that he stood
no chance against the Sovereign State of California in a dispute over
income taxes, whereupon he bellowed defiance and sued the commonwealth for $60,000 and damages. It had been there more recently when
doctors warned that liquor will kill him. From a pint of whisky per day
he upped his consumption to a quart and more.

Sticking out his chin, he told me, "I think we'll take a little run into town tonight."

A blizzard rattled the windows of Cobb's luxurious hunting lodge on the crest of Lake Tahoe, but to forbid him anything—even at the age of 73—was to tell an ancient tiger not to snarl. Cobb was both the greatest of all ballplayers and a multimillionaire whose monthly income from stock dividends, rents and interests ran to $12,000. And he was a man contemptuous, all his life, of any law other than his own.

"We'll drive in," he announced, "and shoot some craps, see a show and say hello to Joe DiMaggio—he's in Reno at the Riverside Hotel."

I looked at him and felt a chill. Cobb, sitting there haggard and unshaven in his pajamas and a fuzzy old green bathrobe at 1 o'clock in the morning, wasn't fooling.

"Let's not," I said. "You shouldn't be anywhere tonight but in bed."

"Don't argue with me!" he barked. "There are fee-simple sonsofbitches all over the country who've tried it and wish they hadn't." He glared at me, flaring the whites of his eyes the way he'd done for 24 years to quaking pitchers, basemen, umpires and fans.

"If you and I are going to get along," he went on ominously, *"don't increase my tension."*

We were alone in his isolated 10-room $75,000 lodge, having arrived six days earlier, loaded with a large smoked ham, a 20-pound turkey, a case of Scotch and another of champagne, for purposes of collaborating on Ty's book-length autobiography—a book which he'd refused to write for 30 years, but then suddenly decided to place on record before he died. In almost a week's time we hadn't accomplished 30 minutes of work.

The reason: Cobb didn't need a risky auto trip into Reno, but immediate hospitalization, and by the emergency-door entrance. He was desperately ill and had been even before we'd left California.

We had traveled 250 miles to Tahoe in Cobb's black Imperial limousine, carrying with us a virtual drugstore of medicines. These included Digoxin (for his leaky heart), Darvon (for his aching back), Tace (for a recently-operated-upon malignancy for the pelvic area), Fleet's compound (for his infected bowels), Librium (for his "tension"—that is, his violent rages), codeine (for his pain) and an insulin needle-and-syringe kit (for his diabetes), among a dozen other panaceas which he'd substituted for doctors. Cobb despised the medical profession.

At the same time, his sense of balance was almost gone. He tottered about the lodge, moving from place to place by grasping the furniture.

On any public street, he couldn't navigate 20 feet without clutching my shoulder, leaning most of his 208 pounds upon me and shuffling along at a spraddle-legged gait. His bowels wouldn't work: they impacted, repeatedly, an almost total stoppage which brought moans of agony from Cobb when he sought relief. He was feverish, with no one at his Tahoe hideaway but the two of us to treat this dangerous condition.

Everything that hurts had caught up with his big, gaunt body at once and he stuffed himself with pink, green, orange, yellow and purple pills—guessing at the amounts, often, since labels had peeled off many of the bottles. But he wouldn't hear of hospitalizing himself.

"The hacksaw artists have taken $50,000 from me," he said, "and they'll get no more." He spoke of "a quack" who'd treated him a few years earlier. "The joker got funny and said he found urine in my whisky. I fired him."

His diabetes required a precise food-insulin balance. Cobb's needle wouldn't work. He'd misplaced the directions for the needed daily insulin dosage and his hands shook uncontrollably when he went to plunge the needle into a stomach vein. He spilled more of the stuff than he injected.

He'd been warned by experts from Johns Hopkins to California's Scripps Clinic—that liquor was deadly. Tyrus snorted and began each day with several gin-and-orange-juices, then switched to Old Rarity Scotch, which held him until night hours, when sleep was impossible, and he tossed down cognac, champagne or "Cobb Cocktails"—Southern Comfort stirred into hot water and honey.

A careful diet was essential. Cobb wouldn't eat. The lodge was without a cook or manservant—since, in the previous six months, he had fired two cooks, a male nurse and a handyman in fits of anger— and any food I prepared for him he pushed away. As of the night of the blizzard, the failing, splenetic old king of ballplayers hadn't touched food in three days, existing solely on quarts of booze and booze mixtures.

My reluctance to prepare the car for the Reno trip burned him up. He beat his fists on the arms of his easy chair. "I'll go alone!" he threatened.

It was certain he'd try it. The storm had worsened, but once Cobb set his mind on an idea, nothing could change it. Beyond that I'd already found that to oppose or annoy him was to risk a violent explosion. An event of a week earlier had proved *that* point. It was then I discovered that he carried a loaded Luger wherever he went and looked for opportunities to use it.

En route to Lake Tahoe, we'd stopped overnight at a motel near

Hangtown, California. During the night a party of drunks made a loud commotion in the parking lot. In my room next to Cobb's, I heard him cursing and then his voice, booming out the window.

"Get out of here, you ——————heads!"

The drunks replied in kind. Then everyone in the motel had his teeth jolted.

Groping his way to the door, Tyrus the Terrible fired three shots into the dark that resounded like cannon claps. There were screams and yells. Reaching my door, I saw the drunks climbing each other's backs in their rush to flee. The frightened motel manager, and others, arrived. Before anyone could think of calling the police, the manager was cut down by the most caustic tongue ever heard in a baseball clubhouse.

"What kind of a pest house is this?" roared Cobb. "Who gave you a license, you mugwump? Get the hell out of here and see that I'm not disturbed! I'm a sick man and I want it quiet!"

"B-b-beg your pardon, Mr. Cobb," the manager said feebly. He apparently felt so honored to have baseball's greatest figure as a customer that no police were called. When we drove away the next morning, a crowd gathered and stood gawking with open mouths.

Down the highway, with me driving, Cobb checked the Luger and reloaded its nine-shell clip. "Two of those shots were in the air," he remarked. "The *third* kicked up gravel. I've got permits for this gun from governors of three states. I'm an honorary deputy sheriff of California and a Texas Ranger. So we won't be getting any complaints."

He saw nothing strange in his behavior. Ty Cobb's rest had been disturbed—therefore he had every right to shoot up the neighborhood.

About then I began to develop a twitch of the nerves, which grew worse with time. In past years, I'd heard reports of Cobb's weird and violent ways, without giving them much credence. But until early 1960 my own experience with the legendary Georgian had been slight, amounting only to meetings in Scottsdale, Arizona, and New York to discuss book-writing arrangements and to sign the contract.

Locker-room stories of Ty's eccentricities, wild temper, ego and miserliness sounded like the usual scandalmongering you get in sports. I'd heard that Cobb had flattened a heckler in San Francisco's Domino Club with one punch; had been sued by Elbie Felts, an ex–Coast League player, after assaulting Felts; that he booby-trapped his Spanish villa at Atherton, California, with high-voltage wires; that he'd walloped one of his ex-wives; that he'd been jailed in Placerville, California, at the age of 68 for speeding, abusing a traffic cop and then inviting the judge to return to law school at his, Cobb's, expense.

I passed these things off. The one and only Ty Cobb was to write his memoirs and I felt highly honored to be named his collaborator.

As the poet Cowper reflected, "The innocents are gay." I was eager to start. Then—a few weeks before book work began—I was taken aside and tipped off by an in-law of Cobb's and one of Cobb's former teammates with the Detroit Tigers that I hadn't heard the half of it. "Back out of this book deal," they urged. "You'll never finish it and you might get hurt."

They went on: "Nobody can live with Ty. Nobody ever has. That includes two wives who left him, butlers, housekeepers, chauffeurs, nurses and a few mistresses. He drove off all his friends long ago. Max Fleischmann, the yeast-cake heir, was a pal of Ty's until the night a houseguest of Fleischmann's made a remark about Cobb spiking other players when he ran the bases. The man only asked if it was true. Cobb knocked the guy into a fish pond and after that Max never spoke to him again. Another time, a member of Cobb's family crossed him—a woman, mind you. He broke her nose with a ball bat.

"Do you know about the butcher? Ty didn't like some meat he bought. In the fight, he broke up the butcher shop. Had to settle $1,500 on the butcher out of court."

"But I'm dealing with him strictly on business," I said.

"So was the butcher," replied my informants. "In baseball, a few of us who really knew him well realized that he was wrong in the head—unbalanced. He played like a demon and had everybody hating him because he *was* a demon. That's how he set all those records that nobody has come close to since 1928. It's why he was always in a brawl, on the field, in the clubhouse, behind the stands and in the stands. The public's never known it, but Cobb's always been off the beam where other people are concerned. Sure, he made millions in the stock market—but that's only cold business. He carried a gun in the big league and scared hell out of us. He's mean, tricky and dangerous. Look out that he doesn't blow up some night and clip you with a bottle. He specializes in throwing bottles.

"Now that he's sick he's worse than ever. And you've signed up to stay with him for months. You poor sap."

Taken aback, but still skeptical, I launched the job—with my first task to drive Cobb to his Lake Tahoe retreat, where, he declared, we could work uninterrupted.

As indicated, nothing went right from the start. The Hangtown gun-play incident was an eye-opener. Next came a series of events, such as Cobb's determination to set forth in a blizzard to Reno, which were too strange to explain away. Everything had to suit his pleasure or he had a tantrum. He prowled about the lodge at night, suspecting trespassers, with the Luger in hand. I slept with one eye open, ready to move fast if necessary.

At 1 o'clock of the morning of the storm, full of pain and 90-proof, he took out the Luger, letting it casually rest between his knees. I had continued to object to a Reno excursion in such weather.

He looked at me with tight fury and said, biting out the words:

"In 1912—and you can write this down—I killed a man in Detroit. He and two other hoodlums jumped me on the street early one morning with a knife. I was carrying something that came in handy in my early days—a Belgian-made pistol with a heavy raised sight at the barrel end.

"Well, the damned gun wouldn't fire and they cut me up the back."

Making notes as fast as he talked, I asked, "Where in the back?"

"WELL, DAMMIT ALL TO HELL, IF YOU DON'T BELIEVE ME, COME AND LOOK!" Cobb flared, jerking up his shirt. When I protested that I believed him implicitly, only wanted a story detail, he picked up a half-full whisky glass and smashed it against the brick fireplace. So I gingerly took a look. A faint whitish scar ran about five inches up the lower left back.

"Satisfied?" jeered Cobb.

He described how after a battle, the men fled before his fists.

"What with you wounded and the odds 3–1," I said, "that must have been a relief."

"Relief? Do you think they could pull that on *me?* I WENT AFTER THEM!"

Where anyone else would have felt lucky to be out of it, Cobb chased one of the mugs into a dead-end alley. "I used that gunsight to rip and slash and tear him for about 10 minutes until he had no face left," related Ty, with relish. "Left him there, not breathing, in his own rotten blood."

"What was the situation—where were you going when it happened?"

"To catch a train to a ball game."

"You saw a doctor, instead?"

"I DID NOTHING OF THE SORT, DAMMIT! I PLAYED THE NEXT DAY AND GOT TWO HITS IN THREE TIMES UP!"

Records I later inspected bore out every word of it: on June 3, 1912, in a bloodsoaked, makeshift bandage, Ty Cobb hit a double and triple for Detroit, and only then was treated for the knife wound. He was that kind of ballplayer through a record 3,033 games. No other player burned with Cobb's flame. Boze Bulger, a great oldtime baseball critic, said, "He was possessed by the Furies."

Finishing his tale, Cobb looked me straight in the eye.

"You're driving me into Reno tonight," he said softly. The Luger was in his hand.

Even before I opened my mouth, Cobb knew he'd won. He had a sixth sense about the emotions he produced in others: in this case, fear. As far as I could see (lacking expert diagnosis and as a layman understands the symptoms), he wasn't merely erratic and trigger-tempered, but suffering from megalomania, or acute self-worship; delusions of persecution; and more than a touch of dipsomania.

Although I'm not proud of it, he scared hell out of me most of the time I was around him.

And now he gave me the first smile of our association. "As long as you don't aggravate my tension," he said, "we'll get along."

Before describing the Reno expedition, I would like to say in this frank view of a mighty man that the greatest, and strangest, of all American sport figures had his good side, which he tried to conceal. During the final ten months of his life I was his one constant companion. Eventually, I put him to bed, prepared his insulin, picked him up when he fell down, warded off irate taxi drivers, bartenders, waiters, clerks and private citizens whom Cobb was inclined to punch, cooked what food he could digest, drew his bath, got drunk with him and knelt with him in prayer on black nights when he knew death was near. I ducked a few bottles he threw, too.

I think, because he forced upon me a confession of his most private thoughts, that I know the answer to the central, overriding secret of his life: was Ty Cobb psychotic throughout his baseball career?

Kids, dogs and sick people flocked to him and he returned their instinctive liking. Money was his idol, but from his $4 million fortune he assigned large sums to create the Cobb Educational Foundation, which financed hundreds of needy youngsters through college. He built and endowed a first-class hospital for the poor of his backwater home town, Royston, Georgia. When Ty's spinster sister, Florence, was crippled, he tenderly cared for her until her last days. The widow of a onetime American League batting champion would have lived in want but for Ty's steady money support. A Hall of Fame member, beaned by a pitched ball and enfeebled, came under Cobb's wing for years. Regularly he mailed dozens of anonymous checks to indigent old ballplayers (relayed by a third party)—a rare act among retired tycoons in other lines of business.

If you believe such acts didn't come hard for Cobb, guess again: he was the world's champion pinchpenny.

Some 150 fan letters reached him each month, requesting his autograph. Many letters enclosed return-mail stamps. Cobb used the stamps for his own outgoing mail. The fan letters he burned.

"Saves on firewood," he'd mutter.

In December of 1960, Ty hired a one-armed "gentleman's gentleman" named Brownie. Although constantly criticized, poor Brownie worked hard as cook and butler. But when he mixed up the grocery order one day, he was fired with a check for a week's pay—$45—and sent packing.

Came the middle of that night and Cobb awakened me.

"We're driving into town *right now*," he stated, "to stop payment on Brownie's check. The bastard talked back to me when I discharged him. He'll get no more of my money."

All remonstrations were futile. There was no phone, so we had to drive the 20 miles from Cobb's Tahoe lodge into Carson City, where he woke up the president of the First National Bank of Nevada and arranged for a stop-pay on the piddling check. The president tried to conceal his anger—Cobb was a big depositor in his bank.

"Yes, sir, Ty," he said. "I'll take care of it first thing in the morning."

"You goddamn well better," snorted Cobb. And then we drove through the 3 a.m. darkness back to the lake.

But this trip was a light workout compared to that Reno trip.

Two cars were available at the lodge. Cobb's 1956 Imperial had no tire chains, but the other car did.

"We'll need both for this operation," he ordered. "One car might get stuck or break down. I'll drive mine and you take the one with chains. You go first. I'll follow your chain marks."

For Cobb to tackle precipitous Route 50 was unthinkable in every way. The Tahoe road, with 200 foot drop-offs, has killed a recorded 80 motorists. Along with his illness, his drunkenness, and no chains, he had bad eyes and was without a driver's license. California had turned him down at his last test; he hadn't bothered to apply in Nevada.

Urging him to ride with me was a waste of breath.

A howling wind hit my car a solid blow as we shoved off. Sleet stuck to the windshield faster than the wipers could work. For the first three miles, snowplows had been active and at 15 mph, in second gear, I managed to hold the road. But then came Spooner's Summit, 7,000 feet high, and then a steep descent of nine miles. Behind me, headlamps blinking, Cobb honked his horn, demanding more speed. Chainless, he wasn't getting traction. *The hell with him,* I thought. Slowing to third gear, fighting to hold a roadbed I couldn't see even with my head stuck out the window, I skidded along. No other traffic moved as we did our crazy tandem around icy curves, at times brushing the guard rails. Cobb was blaring his horn steadily now.

And then here came Cobb.

Tiring of my creeping pace, he gunned the Imperial around me in one big skid. I caught a glimpse of an angry face under a big Stetson hat and a waving fist. He was doing a good 30 mph when he'd gained 25 yards on me, fishtailing right and left, but straightening as he slid out of sight in the thick sleet.

I let him go. Suicide wasn't in my contract.

The next six miles was a matter of feeling my way and praying. Near a curve, I saw tail lights to the left. Pulling up, I found Ty swung sideways and buried, nosedown, in a snow bank, his hind wheels two feet in the air. Twenty yards away was a sheer drop-off into a canyon.

"You hurt?" I asked.

"Bumped my ———— head," he muttered. He lit a cigar and gave four-letter regards to the Highway Department for not illuminating the "danger" spot. His forehead was bruised and he'd broken his glasses.

In my car, we groped our way down-mountain, a nightmare ride, with Cobb alternately taking in Scotch from a thermos jug and telling me to step on it. At 3 a.m. in Carson City, an all-night garageman used a broom to clean the car of snow and agreed to pick up the Imperial—"when the road's passable." With dawn breaking, we reached Reno. All I wanted was a bed and all Cobb wanted was a craps table.

He was rolling now, pretending he wasn't ill, and with the Scotch bracing him. Ty was able to walk into the Riverside Hotel casino with a hand on my shoulder and without staggering so obviously as usual. Everybody present wanted to meet him. Starlets from a film unit on location in Reno flocked around and comedian Joe E. Lewis had the band play *Sweet Georgia Brown*—Ty's favorite tune.

"Hope your dice are still honest," he told Riverside co-owner Bill Miller. "Last time I was here I won $12,000 in three hours."

"How I remember, Ty," said Miller. "How I remember."

A scientific craps player who'd won and lost huge sums in Nevada in the past, Cobb bet $100 chips, his eyes alert, not missing a play around the board. He soon decided that the table was "cold" and we moved to another casino, then a third. At this last stop, Cobb's legs began to grow shaky. Holding himself up by leaning on the table edge with his forearms, he dropped $300, then had a hot streak in which he won over $800. His voice was a croak as he told the other players, "Watch 'em and weep."

But then suddenly his voice came back. When the stickman raked the dice his way, Cobb loudly said, "You touched the dice with your hand."

"No, sir," said the stickman. "I did *not.*"

"I don't lie!" snarled Cobb.

"I don't lie either," insisted the stickman.

"Nobody touches my dice!" Cobb, swaying on his feet, eyes blazing, worked his way around the table toward the croupier. It was a weird tableau. In his crumpled Stetson and expensive camel's-hair coat, stained and charred with cigarette burns, a three-day beard grizzling his face, the gaunt old giant of baseball towered over the dapper gambler.

"You fouled the dice. I saw you," growled Cobb, and then he swung.

The blow missed, as the stickman dodged, but, cursing and almost falling, Cobb seized the wooden rake and smashed it over the table. I jumped in and caught him under the arms as he sagged.

And then, as quickly as possible, we were put into the street by two large uniformed guards. "Sorry, Mr. Cobb," they said, unhappily, "but we can't have this."

A crowd had gathered and as we started down the street, Cobb swearing and stumbling and clinging to me, I couldn't have felt more conspicuous if I'd been strung naked from the neon arch across Reno's main drag, Virginia Street. At the streetcorner, Ty was struck by an attack of breathlessness. "Got to stop," he gasped. Feeling him going limp on me, I turned his six-foot body against a lamppost, braced my legs and with an underarm grip held him there until he caught his breath. He panted and gulped for air.

His face gray, he murmured, "Reach into my left-hand coat pocket." Thinking he wanted his bottle of heart pills, I did. But instead pulled out a six-inch-thick wad of currency, secured by a rubber band. "Couple of thousand there," he said weakly. "Don't let it out of sight."

At the nearest motel, where I hired a single, twin-bed room, he collapsed on the bed in his coat and hat and slept. After finding myself some breakfast, I turned in. Hours later I heard him stirring. "What's this place?" he muttered.

I told him the name of the motel—Travelodge.

"Where's the bankroll?"

"In your coat. You're wearing it."

Then he was quiet.

After a night's sleep, Cobb felt well enough to resume his gambling. In the next few days, he won more than $3,000 at the tables, and then we went sightseeing in historic Virginia City. There, as in all places, he stopped traffic. And had the usual altercation. This one was at the Bucket of Blood, where Cobb accused the bartender of serving watered Scotch. The bartender denied it. Crash! Another drink went flying.

Back at the lodge a week later, looking like the wrath of John Barleycorn and having refused medical aid in Reno, he began to suffer new and excruciating pains—in his hips and lower back. But between groans he forced himself to work an hour a day on his autobiography. He told inside baseball tales never published:

". . . Frank Navin, who owned the Detroit club for years, faked his turnstile count to cheat the visiting team and Uncle Sam. So did Big Bill Devery and Frank Farrell, who owned the New York Highlanders—later called the Yankees."

". . . Walter Johnson, the Big Train, tried to kill himself when his wife died."

". . . Grover Cleveland Alexander wasn't drunk out there on the mound, the way people thought—he was an epileptic. Old Pete would fall down with a seizure between innings, then go back and pitch another shutout."

". . . John McGraw hated me because I tweaked his nose in broad daylight in the lobby of the Oriental Hotel, in Dallas, after earlier beating the hell out of his second baseman, Buck Herzog, upstairs in my room."

But before we were well started, Cobb suddenly announced we'd go riding in his 23-foot Chris-Craft speedboat, tied up in a boathouse below the lodge. When I went down to warm it up, I found the boat sunk to the bottom of Lake Tahoe in 15 feet of water.

My host broke all records for blowing his stack when he heard the news. He saw in this a sinister plot. "I told you I've got enemies all around here! It's sabotage as sure as I'm alive!"

A sheriff's investigation turned up no clues. Cobb sat up all night for three nights with his Luger. "I'll salivate the first dirty skunk who steps foot around here after dark," he swore.

Parenthetically, Cobb had a vocabulary all his own. To "salivate" something meant to destroy it. Anything easy was "soft-boiled," to outsmart someone was to "slip him the oskafagus," and all doctors were "truss-fixers." People who displeased him—and this included almost everyone he met—were "fee-simple sonsofbitches," "mugwumps" or (if female) "lousy slits."

Lake Tahoe friends of Cobb's had stopped visiting him long before, but one morning an attractive blonde of about 50 came calling. She was an old chum—in a romantic way, I was given to understand, of bygone years—but Ty greeted her coldly. "Lost my sexual powers when I was 69," he said, when she was out of the room. "What the hell use to me is a woman?"

The lady had brought along a three-section electric vibrator bed, which she claimed would relieve Ty's back pains. We helped him mount it. He took a 20-minute treatment. Attempting to dismount, he lost balance, fell backward, the contraption jackknifed and Cobb was pinned, yelling and swearing, under a pile of machinery.

When I freed him and helped him to a chair, he told the lady—in the choicest gutter language—where she could put her bed. She left, sobbing.

"That's no way to talk to an old friend, Ty," I said. "She was trying to do you a favor."

"And you're a hell of a poor guest around here, too!" he thundered. "You can leave any old time!" He quickly grabbed a bottle and heaved it in my direction.

"Thought you could throw straighter than that!" I yelled back.

Fed up with him, I started to pack my bags. Before I'd finished, Cobb broke out a bottle of vintage Scotch, said I was "damned sensitive," half-apologized, and the matter was forgotten.

While working one morning on an outside observation deck, I heard a thud inside. On his bedroom floor, sprawled on his back, lay Ty. He was unconscious, his eyes rolled back, breathing shallowly. I thought he was dying.

There was no telephone. "Eavesdropping on the line," Cobb had told me. "I had it cut off." I ran down the road to a neighboring lodge and phoned a Carson City doctor, who promised to come immediately.

Back at the lodge, Ty remained stiff and stark on the floor, little bubbles escaping his lips. His face was bluish-white. With much straining,

I lifted him halfway to the bed and by shifting holds finally rolled him onto it, and covered him with a blanket. Twenty minutes passed. No doctor.

Ten minutes later, I was at the front door, watching for the doctor's car, when I heard a sound. There stood Ty, swaying on his feet. "You want to do some work on the book?" he said.

His recovery didn't seem possible. "But you were out cold a minute ago," I said.

"Just a dizzy spell. Have 'em all the time. Must have hit my head on the bedpost when I fell."

The doctor, arriving, found Cobb's blood pressure standing at a grim 210 on the gauge. His temperature was 101 degrees and, from gross neglect of his diabetes, he was in a state of insulin shock, often fatal if not quickly treated. "I'll have to hospitalize you, Mr. Cobb," said the doctor.

Weaving his way to a chair, Cobb angrily waved him away. "Just send me your bill," he grunted. "I'm going home."

"Home" was the multimillionaire's main residence at Atherton, California, on the San Francisco Peninsula, 250 miles away, and it was there he headed later that night. With some hot soup and insulin in him, Cobb recovered with the same unbelievable speed he'd shown in baseball. In his heyday, trainers often sewed up deep spike cuts in his knees, shins and thighs, on a clubhouse bench, without anesthetic, and he didn't lose an inning. Grantland Rice one 1920 day sat beside a bedridden, feverish Cobb, whose thighs, from sliding, were a mass of raw flesh. Sixteen hours later, he hit a triple, double, three singles and stole two bases to beat the Yankees. On the Atherton ride, he yelled insults at several motorists who moved too slowly to suit him. Reaching Atherton, Ty said he felt ready for another drink.

My latest surprise was Cobb's 18-room, two-story, richly landscaped Spanish-California villa at 48 Spencer Lane, an exclusive neighborhood. You could have held a ball game on the grounds.

But the $90,000 mansion had no lights, no heat, no hot water.

"I'm suing the Pacific Gas & Electric Company," he explained, "for overcharging me on the service. Those rinky-dinks tacked an extra $16 on my bill. Bunch of crooks. When I wouldn't pay, they cut off my utilities. Okay—I'll see them in court."

For months previously, Ty Cobb had lived in a totally dark house. The only illumination was candlelight. The only cooking facility was a portable Coleman stove, such as campers use. Bathing was impossible, unless you could take it cold. The electric refrigerator, stove, deep-freeze, radio and television, of course, didn't work. Cobb had vowed to "hold the fort" until his trial of the P.G.&E. was settled. Simultaneously, he had filed a $60,000 suit in San Francisco Superior Court against the State of California to recover state income taxes already collected—on the argument that he wasn't a permanent resident of California, but of Nevada, Georgia, Arizona and other waypoints. State's attorneys claimed he spent at least six months per year in Atherton, thus had no case.

"I'm gone so much from here," he claimed, "that I'll win hands down." All legal opinion, I later learned, held just the opposite view, but Cobb ignored their advice.

Next morning, I arranged with Ty's gardener, Hank, to turn on the lawn sprinklers. In the outdoor sunshine, a cold-water shower was easier to take. From then on, the back yard became my regular washroom.

The problem of lighting a desk so that we could work on the book was solved by stringing 200 feet of cord, plugged into an outlet of a neighboring house, through hedges and flower gardens and into the window of Cobb's study, where a single naked bulb, hung over the chandelier, provided illumination.

The flickering shadows cast by the single light made the vast old house seem haunted. No "ghost" writer ever had more ironical surroundings.

At various points around the premises, Ty showed me where he'd once installed high-voltage wires to stop trespassers. "Curiosity-seekers?" I asked. "Hell, no," he said. "Detectives broke in here once looking for evidence against me in a divorce suit. After a couple of them got burned, they stopped coming."

To reach our bedrooms, Cobb and I groped our way down long, black corridors. Twice he fell in the dark. And then, collapsing completely, he became so ill that he was forced to check in at Stanford Hospital in nearby Palo Alto. Here another shock was in store.

One of the physicians treating Ty's case, a Dr. E. R. Brown, said, "Do you mean to say that this man has traveled 700 miles in the last month without medical care?"

"Doctor," I said, "I've hauled him in and out of saloons, motels, gambling joints, steam baths and snowbanks. There's no holding him."

"It's a miracle he's alive. He has almost every major ailment I know about."

Dr. Brown didn't reveal to me Ty's main ailment, which news Cobb, himself, broke late one night from his hospital bed. "It's cancer," he said, bluntly. "About a year ago I had most of my prostate gland removed when they found it was malignant. Now it's spread up into the back bones. These pill-peddlers here won't admit it, but I haven't got a chance."

Cobb made me swear I'd never divulge the fact before he died. "If it gets in the papers, the sob sisters will have a field day. I don't want sympathy from anybody."

At Stanford, where he absorbed seven massive doses of cobalt radiation, the ultimate cancer treatment, he didn't act like a man on his last legs. Even before his strength returned, he was in the usual form.

"They won't let me have a drink," he said, indignantly. "I want you to get me a bottle. Smuggle it in in your tape-recorder case."

I tried, telling myself that no man with terminal cancer deserves to be dried up, but sharp-eyed nurses and orderlies were watching. They searched Ty's closet, found the bottle and over his roars of protest appropriated it.

"We'll have to slip them the oskefagus," said Ty.

Thereafter, a drink of Scotch-and-water sat in plain view in his room, on his bedside table, under the very noses of his physicians—and nobody suspected a thing. The whisky was in an ordinary water glass, and in the liquid reposed Ty's false teeth.

There were no dull moments while Cobb was at the hospital. He was critical of everything. He told one doctor that he was not even qualified to be an interne, and told the hospital dietician—at the top of his voice—that she and the kitchen workers were in a conspiracy to poison him with their "foul" dishes. To a nurse he snapped, "If Florence Nightingale knew about you, she'd spin in her grave."

(Stanford Hospital, incidentally, is one of the largest and top-rated medical plants in the United States.)

But between blasts he did manage to buckle down to work on the book, dictating long into the night into a microphone suspended over his bed. Slowly the stormy details of his professional life came out. He spoke often of having "forgiven" his many baseball enemies, then lashed out at them with such passionate phrases that it was clear he'd done no such thing. High on his "hate" list were McGraw; New York sportswriters; Hub Leonard, a pitcher who in 1926 accused Cobb and Tris Speaker of "fixing" a Detroit-Cleveland game; American League President Ban Johnson; onetime Detroit owner Frank Navin; former Baseball Commissioner Kenesaw Mountain Landis; and all those who intimated that Cobb ever used his spikes on another player without justification.

After a night when he slipped out of the hospital, against all orders, and we drove to a San Francisco Giants-Cincinnati Reds game at Candlestick Park, 30 miles away, Stanford Hospital decided it couldn't help Tyrus R. Cobb, and he was discharged. For extensive treatment his bill ran to more than $1,200.

"That's a nice racket you boys have here," he told the discharging doctors. "You clip the customers and then every time you pass an undertaker, you wink at him."

"Goodbye, Mr. Cobb," snapped the medical men.

Soon after this Ty caught a plane to his native Georgia and I went along. "I want to see some of the old places again before I die," he said.

It now was Christmas eve of 1960 and I'd been with him for three months and completed but four chapters. The project had begun to look hopeless. In Royston, a village of 1,200, Cobb headed for the town cemetery. I drove him there, we parked, and I helped him climb a windswept hill through the growing dusk. Light snow fell. Faintly, yule chimes could be heard.

Amongst the many headstones, Ty looked for the plot he'd reserved for himself while in California and couldn't locate it. His temper began to boil. "Dammit, I ordered the biggest damn mausoleum in the graveyard! I know it's around here somewhere." On the next hill, we found it: a large, marble, walk-in-size structure with "Cobb" engraved over the entrance.

"You want to pray with me?" he said, gruffly. We knelt and tears came to his eyes.

Within the tomb, he pointed to crypts occupied by the bodies of his father, Prof. William Herschel Cobb, his mother, Amanda (Chitwood) Cobb, and his sister, Florence, whom he'd had disinterred and placed here. "My father," he said reverently, "was the greatest man I ever knew. He was a scholar, state senator, editor and philosopher. I worshipped him. So did all the people around here. He was the only man who ever made me do his bidding."

Arising painfully, Ty braced himself against the marble crypt that soon would hold his body. There was an eerie silence in the tomb. He said deliberately:

"My father had his head blown off with a shotgun when I was 18 years old—*by a member of my own family.* I didn't get over that. I've never gotten over it."

We went back down the hill to the car. I asked no questions that day.

Later, from family sources and old Georgia friends of the baseball idol, I learned about the killing. One night in August of 1905, they related, Professor Cobb announced that he was driving from Royston to a neighboring village and left home by buggy. But, later that night, he doubled back and crept into his wife's bedroom by way of the window. "He suspected her of being unfaithful to him," said these sources. "He thought he'd catch her in the act. But Amanda Cobb was a good woman. She was all alone when she saw a menacing figure climb through her window and approach her bed. In the dark, she assumed it to be a robber. She kept a shotgun handy by her bed and she used it. Everybody around here knew the story, but it was hushed up when Ty became famous."

News of the killing reached Ty in Augusta, where he was playing minor league ball, on August 9. A few days later he was told that he'd been purchased by the Detroit Tigers, and was to report immediately. "In my grief," Cobb says in the book, "it didn't matter much. . . ."

Came March of 1961 and I remained stuck to the Georgia Peach like court plaster. He'd decided that we were born pals, meant for each other, that we'd complete a baseball book beating anything ever published. He had astonished doctors by rallying from the spreading cancer and, between bouts of transmitting his life and times to a tape-recorder, was raising more whoopee than he had at Lake Tahoe and Reno.

Spring-training time for the big leagues had arrived and we were ensconced in a $30-a-day suite at the Ramada Inn at Scottsdale, Arizona, close by the practice parks of the Red Sox, Indians, Giants and Cubs. Here, each year, Cobb held court. He didn't go to see anybody; Ford Frick, Joe Cronin, Ted Williams, and other diamond notables came to him. While explaining to sportswriters why modern stars couldn't compare to the Wagners, Lajoies, Speakers, Jacksons, Mathewsons and Planks of his day, Ty did other things.

For one, he commissioned a noted Arizona artist to paint him in oils. He was emaciated, having dropped from 208 pounds to 176. The preliminary sketches showed up his sagging cheeks and thin neck.

"I wouldn't let you kalsomine my toilet," ripped out Ty, and fired the artist.

But at analyzing the Dow-Jones averages and playing the stock market, he was anything but eccentric. Twice a week he phoned experts around the country, determined good buys and bought in blocks of 500 to 1,500 shares. He made money consistently, even when bedridden, with a mind that read behind the fluctuations of a dozen different issues.

"The State of Georgia," Ty remarked, "will realize about one million dollars from inheritance taxes when I'm dead. But there isn't a man alive who knows what I'm worth." According to the *Sporting News,* there was evidence upon Cobb's death that his worth approximated $12 million. Whatever the true figure, he did not confide the amount to me—or, most probably, to anyone except attorneys who drafted his last will and testament. And Cobb fought off making his will until the last moment.

His fortune began in 1908, when he bought into United (later General) Motors; as of 1961, he was "Mr. Coca Cola," holding more than 20,000 shares of that stock, valued at $85 per share. Wherever we traveled, he carried with him, stuffed into an old brown bag, more than $1 million in stock certificates and negotiable government bonds. The bag never was locked up. Cobb assumed nobody would dare rob him. He tossed the bag into any handy corner of a room, inviting theft. And in Scottsdale it turned up missing.

Playing Sherlock, he narrowed the suspects to a room maid and a man he'd hired to cook meals. When questioned, the maid broke into tears and the cook quit (fired, said Cobb). Hours later, I discovered the bag under a pile of dirty laundry.

Major league owners and league officials hated to see him coming, for he thought their product was putrid and said so, incessantly. "Today they hit for ridiculous averages, can't bunt, can't steal, can't hit-and-run, can't place-hit to the opposite field and you can't call them ballplayers." He told sportswriters, "I blame Frick, Cronin, Bill Harridge, Horace Stoneham, Dan Topping and others for wrecking baseball's traditional league lines. These days, any tax-dodging mugwump with a bankroll can buy a franchise, field some semi-pros and get away with it. Where's our integrity? Where's *baseball?*"

No one could quiet Cobb. Who else had a lifetime average of .367, made 4,191 hits, scored 2,244 runs, won 12 batting titles, stole 892 bases, repeatedly beat whole teams single-handedly? Who was first into the Hall of Fame? Not Babe Ruth—but Cobb, by a landslide vote.

By early April, he could barely make it up the ramp of the Scottsdale Stadium, even hanging onto me. He had to stop, gasping for breath, every few steps. But he kept coming to games—loving the sounds of the ball park. His courage was tremendous. "Always be ready to catch me if I start to fall," he said. "I'd hate to go down in front of the fans."

People of all ages were overcome with emotion upon meeting him; no sports figure I've known produced such an effect upon the public.

We went to buy a cane. At a surgical supply house, Cobb inspected a dozen $25 malacca sticks, bought the cheapest, $4, white-ash cane they had. "I'm a plain man," he informed the clerk, the $7,500 diamond ring on his finger glittering.

But pride kept the old tiger from ever using the cane, any more than he'd wear the $600 hearing aid built into the bow of his glasses.

One day a Mexican taxi-driver aggravated Cobb with his driving. Throwing the fare on the ground, he waited until the cabbie had bent to retrieve it, then tried to punt him like a football.

"What's your sideline," he inquired, "selling opium?"

It was all I could do to keep the driver from swinging on him. Later, a lawyer called on Cobb, threatening a damage suit. "Get in line, there's 500 ahead of you," said Tyrus, waving him away.

Every day was a new adventure. He was fighting back against the pain that engulfed him again—cobalt treatments no longer helped— and I could count on trouble anywhere we went. He threw a salt-shaker at a Phoenix waiter, narrowly missing. One of his most treasured friendships—with Ted Williams—came to an end.

From the early 1940's, Williams had sat at Ty Cobb's feet. They often met, exchanged long letters on the art of batting. At Scottsdale one day, Williams dropped by Ty's rooms. He hugged Ty, fondly rumpled his hair and accepted a drink. Presently the two greatest hitters of past and present fell into an argument over what players should comprise the all-time, all-star team. Williams declared, "I want DiMaggio and Hornsby on my team over anybody you can mention."

Cobb's face grew dark. "Don't give me that! Hornsby couldn't go back for a pop fly and he lacked smartness. DiMaggio couldn't hit with Speaker or Joe Jackson."

"The hell you say!" came back Williams, jauntily. "Hornsby out-hit *you* a couple of years."

Almost leaping from his chair, Cobb shook a fist. He'd been given the insult supreme—for Cobb always resented, and finally hated, Rogers Hornsby. Not until Cobb was in his 16th season did Hornsby top him in the batting averages. "Get . . . away from me!" choked Cobb. "Don't come back!"

Williams left with a quizzical expression, not sure how much Cobb meant it. The old man meant it all the way. He never invited Williams back, nor talked to him, nor spoke his name again. "I cross him off," he told me.

We left Arizona shortly thereafter for my home in Santa Barbara, California. Now failing fast, Tyrus had accepted my invitation to be my guest. Two doctors inspected him at my beach house by the Pacific and gave their opinions: he had a few months of life left, no more. The cancer had invaded the bones of his skull. His pain was intense, unrelenting—requiring heavy sedation—yet with teeth bared and sweat pouring down his face, he fought off medical science. "They'll never get me on their damned hypnotics," he swore. "I'll never die an addict . . . an idiot. . . ."

He shouted, "Where's anybody who cares about me? Where are they? The world's lousy . . . no good."

One night later, on May 1, Cobb sat propped up in bed, overlooking a starlit ocean. He had a habit, each night, of rolling up his trousers and placing them under his pillows—an early-century ballplayer's trick, dating from the time when Ty slept in strange places and might be robbed. I knew that his ever-present Luger was tucked into that pants-roll.

I'd never seen him so sunk in despair. At last the fire was going out. "Do we die a little at a time, or all at once?" he wondered aloud. "I think Max had the right idea."

The reference was to his onetime friend, multimillionaire Max Fleischmann, who'd cheated lingering death by cancer some years earlier by putting a bullet through his brain. Ty spoke of Babe Ruth, another cancer victim. "If Babe had been told what he had in time, he could've got it over with."

Had I left Ty that night, I believe he would have pulled the trigger. His three living children (two were dead) had withdrawn from him. In the wide world that had sung his fame, he had not one intimate friend remaining.

But we talked, and prayed, until dawn, and then sleep came; in the morning, aided by friends, I put him into a car and drove him home, to the big, gloomy house in Atherton. He spoke only twice during the six-hour drive.

"Have you got enough to finish the book?" he asked.

"More than enough."

"Give 'em the word then. I had to fight all my life to survive. They all were against me . . . tried every dirty trick to cut me down. But I beat the bastards and left them in the ditch. Make sure the book says that. . . ."

I was leaving him now, permanently, and I had to ask one question I'd never put to him before.

"Why did you fight so hard in baseball, Ty?"

He'd never looked fiercer than then, when he answered. "I did it for my father, who was an exalted man. They killed him when he was still young. They blew his head off the same week I became a major leaguer. He never got to see me play. But I knew he was watching me and I never let him down."

You can make what you want of that. Keep in mind what Casey Stengel said, later: "I never saw anyone like Cobb. No one even close to him. When he wiggled those wild eyes at a pitcher, you knew you were looking at the one bird nobody could beat. It was like he was superhuman."

To me it seems that the violent death of a father whom a sensitive, highly-talented boy loved deeply, and feared, engendered, through some strangely supreme desire to vindicate that father, the most violent, successful, thoroughly maladjusted personality ever to pass across American sports. The shock tipped the 18-year-old mind, making him capable of incredible feats.

Off the field, he was still at war with the world. For the emotionally disturbed individual, in most cases, does not change his pattern. To reinforce that pattern, he was viciously hazed by Detroit Tiger veterans when he was a rookie. He was bullied, ostracized and beaten up—in one instance, a 210-pound catcher named Charlie Schmidt broke the 165-pound Ty Cobb's nose. It was persecution immediately heaped upon the deepest desolation a young man can experience.

Yes, Ty Cobb was a badly disturbed personality. It is not hard to understand why he spent his entire life in deep conflict. Nor why a member of his family, in the winter of 1960, told me, "I've spent a lot of time terrified of him . . . I think he was psychotic from the time that he left Georgia to play in the big league."

"Psychotic" is not a word I'd care to use. I believe that he was far more than the fiercest of all competitors. He was a vindicator who believed that "father was watching" and who could not put that father's terrible fate out of his mind. The memory of it threatened his sanity.

The fact that he recognized and feared this is revealed in a tape-recording he made, in which he describes his own view of himself: "I was like a steel spring with a growing and dangerous flaw in it. If it is wound too tight or has the slightest weak point, the spring will fly apart and then it is done for. . . ."

The last time I saw him, he was sitting in his armchair in the Atherton mansion. The place still was without lights or heat. I shook his hand in farewell, and he held it a moment longer.

"What about it? Do you think they'll remember me?" He tried to say it as if it didn't matter.

"They'll always remember you," I said.

On July 8, I received in the mail a photograph of Ty's mausoleum on the hillside in the Royston cemetery with the words scribbled on the back: *"Any time now."* Nine days later he died in an Atlanta hospital. Before going, he opened the brown bag, piled $1 million in negotiable securities beside his bed and placed the Luger atop them.

From all of major league baseball, three men and three only appeared for his funeral.

E. M. Swift

Hockey Miracle

*A goalie for a 1–22 Princeton hockey team, E. M. Swift tried out
for the United States Olympic team in 1976. He didn't make the
cut, but four years later, on assignment for* Sports Illustrated, *Swift
was in Lake Placid to cover the U.S. hockey team as they dramatically captured both a gold medal and the attention of the
world. Seven months later, with time to absorb the stunning victory,
Swift wrote this "Sportsmen of the Year" piece for* Sports Illustrated
*about a collection of scrappy athletes pushed to accomplish the
improbable by a hard-driving, masterfully manipulative coach.*

The impact was the thing. One morning they were 19 fuzzy-cheeked
college kids and a tall guy with a beard, and the next. . . . WE BEAT
THE RUSSIANS! In Babbitt, Minn., hometown of Forward Buzzie
Schneider, guys went into their backyards and began firing shotguns
toward the heavens. Kaboom! Kaboom! WE BEAT THE RUSSIANS! In
Santa Monica a photographer heard the outcome of the game and went
into his local grocery store, a mom-and-pop operation run by an elderly
immigrant couple. "Guess what," he said. "Our boys beat the Russians."
The old grocer looked at him. "No kidding?" Then he started to cry. *"No
kidding?"*

In Winthrop, Mass., 70 people gathered outside the home of Mike
Eruzione, who had scored the winning goal, and croaked out the national
anthem. Not *God Bless America,* which is what the players were singing
in Lake Placid. *The Star-Spangled Banner.*

One man was listening to the game in his car, driving through a
thunderstorm, with the U.S. clinging to a 4–3 lead. He kept pounding his

617

hands on the steering wheel in excitement. Finally he pulled off the highway and listened as the countdown started . . . 5 . . . 4 . . . 3 . . . 2 . . . 1 . . . WE BEAT THE RUSSIANS! He started to honk his horn. He yelled inside his car. It felt absolutely wonderful. He got out and started to scream in the rain. There were 10 other cars pulled off to the side of the road, 10 other drivers yelling their fool heads off in the rain. They made a huddle, and then they hollered together—WE BEAT THE RUS-SIANS! Perfect strangers dancing beside the highway with 18-wheelers zooming by and spraying them with grime.

We. The U.S. Olympic hockey team wasn't a bunch of weird, freaky commando types. They were our boys. Clean-cut kids from small towns, well-groomed and good-looking, who loved their folks and liked to drink a little beer. Our boys. Young men molded by a coach who wasn't afraid to preach the values of the good old Protestant work ethic, while ever prepared to stuff a hockey stick down an offending opponent's throat. And don't think that didn't matter, given the political climate at the time—the hostages, Afghanistan, the pending Olympic boycott of the Moscow Games.

But there was more to the story than the moment of victory.

The members of the 1980 U.S. Olympic hockey team weren't named Sportsmen of the Year because of the 60 minutes they played one Friday afternoon in February. The game with the Soviet Union meant nothing to the players politically. Even its impact was largely lost on them until much later, confined as they were to the Olympic Village in Lake Placid, listening to one dinky local radio station and reading no newspapers. "If people want to think that performance was for our country, that's fine," says Mark Pavelich, the small, quiet forward who set up Eruzione's winning goal. "But the truth of the matter is, it was just a hockey game. There was enough to worry about without worrying about Afghanistan or winning it for the pride and glory of the United States. We wanted to win it for ourselves."

Not ourselves as in I, me, mine. Ourselves the team. Individually, they were fine, dedicated sportsmen. Some will have excellent pro hockey careers. Others will bust. But collectively, they were a tran-scendant lot. For seven months they pushed each other on and pulled each other along, from rung to rung, until for two weeks in February they—a bunch of unheralded amateurs—became the best hockey team in the world. The best *team.* The whole was greater than the sum of its parts by a mile. And they were not just a team, they were innovative and exuberant and absolutely unafraid to succeed. They were a perfect reflection of how Americans wanted to perceive themselves. By gum, it's still in us! It was certainly still in *them.*

So for reminding us of some things, and for briefly brightening the days of 220 million people, we doff our caps to them, *in toto.* Sportsmen of the Year.

Leadership, of course, was the key. These guys didn't descend on their skates from a mountaintop preaching teamwork and brotherhood. Are you kidding? They were allstars, *la crème de la crème.* Many had egos yay big and heads the size of pumpkins. Fifteen of the 20 had been drafted by NHL clubs and considered the Games a stepping-stone to the big time. They could showcase their individual talents, prove they could handle a grueling schedule, and, thank-you-bub, where do I sign? Herb Brooks, the coach, made it the most painful stepping-stone of their lives.

"He treated us all the same," says every last member of the team. "Rotten."

Karl Malden, the actor who plays Brooks in the forthcoming ABC-TV movie on the team, *Miracle on Ice,* which will be aired in March, has never met Brooks, but he has studied him on videotape, especially his eyes. "I'd hate to meet him in a dark alley," Malden says. "I think he's a little on the neurotic side. Maybe more than a little. Any moment you think he's going to jump out of his skin."

That's one man's opinion. Malden, that hard-boiled scowler who has no pity in his heart for anyone leaving home without American Express traveler's checks, was brought to tears not once but twice by the sight of Goaltender Jim Craig asking "Where's my father?" after the team had beaten Finland to win the gold medal, first on television, then months later on videotape. Truly, this team plucked many different heartstrings.

Brooks was as sentimental as a stone throughout. After the victory over Finland, he shook hands with two or three people behind the bench, then disappeared into the dressing room. Says Malden, "He could have smiled just once, during the game with Norway, or Romania. But he didn't. Then after working seven months for something, the moment he gets it he walks away from it. You tell me, is that a normal man?"

All right. No. But Malden is wrong about one thing. If you were to meet Brooks in a dark alley, you wouldn't be frightened. He would barely notice you. His mind would be a million miles away. You'd wonder where. He's a driven perfectionist. His wife, Patty, an attractive, bubbly woman, recalls seeing their daughter, Kelly, crawling around and straightening rugs when she was 10 months old. Patty groaned, "Oh, my God, I've got another one!" Brooks is also a brilliant motivator and, like all great coaches, an innovator. He motivates largely through fear. Schneider, who also played under Brooks for three years at the University of Minnesota, says, "He pats you on the back but always lets you know he has the knife in the other hand."

Significantly, the pat is on the back, the knife is front and center. Brooks isn't one to sneak around confrontation. "I gave our guys every opportunity to call me an honest son of a bitch," he says now. "Hockey players are going to call you a son of a bitch at times anyway, in emotion. But they could call me an honest one because everything was up front."

They do, and it requires very little emotion. But most—if not all— of the players realize that if Brooks had been any different, they couldn't possibly have accomplished what they did. "It was a lonely year for me," says Brooks. "Very lonely. But it was by design. I never was close to my university players because they were so young. But this team had everything I wanted to be close to, everything I admired: the talent, the psychological makeup, the personality. But I had to stay away. If I couldn't know all, I didn't want to know one, because there wasn't going to be any favoritism."

Players like Phil Verchota, who played for Brooks for four years at Minnesota and then all of last year, have still never heard so much as a "Nice day today, eh, Phil?" out of Brooks. "Say hi, and you'll get hi back," Verchota says. "Not even that sometimes." The man scared the daylights out of them. Gave them the willies. He wasn't human. But he could coach, and they never questioned that for a second.

Which isn't to say they never questioned his methods. (His obsession, of course, was a given.) One of the devices Brooks used to select his final team was a psychological test of more than 300 questions that he had specially prepared. He was looking for a certain type of player, and the test was designed to show how certain people would react under stress. He thought he'd try it. There would be 68 players at the August tryout camp in Colorado Springs, and he had to cut them down to 26 in a matter of days. He would leave no stone unturned.

One player—an eventual Olympic hero—said, "Herb, I'm not taking this. I don't believe in that stuff."

"Why's that?" Brooks asked.

"Oh, it's a lot of bull, psychology."

"Well, wait a minute. Here's what it might show. It's not as important as what goes on out on the ice, but it's something we can use. I don't want to miss anything."

"I don't want to take it," the player said.

Brooks nodded. "O.K. Fine. You just took it. You told me everything I wanted to know." He was steaming.

"How'd I do?"

"You flunked."

The next day the player took the test.

What kind of competitor was Brooks looking for? Big strong kids who could *skate through a wall?* Guys who could *fly?* Who could *pay the price?* Who could make the puck *tap dance?* Good Lord, spare us. Brooks wanted young, educated kids who were willing to break down stereotypes, were willing to throw old wives' tales about conditioning and tactics out the window. He wanted open-minded people who could skate. "The ignorant people, the self-centered people, the people who don't want to expand their thoughts, they're not going to be the real good athletes," Brooks says. "They're not going to be able to keep that particular moment, that game, that season in the proper perspective. I believe it. Understand this world around you."

When Brooks talks about "ignorant, self-centered people who don't want to expand their thoughts," he's describing 90% of the National Hockey League. For better or worse, most of the players trying out for the Olympic team were hoping to jump from there to the pros. So they wanted to show the NHL scouts that they could do it the NHL way— ugh, me fight, me chop, me muck. That doesn't work in international hockey, and Brooks would have none of it. The players had to learn a new style of play in seven months. In simplest terms, they had to learn what any touch-football player knows by the fifth grade—that crisscross patterns and laterals are more effective than the plunge. They had to learn not to retaliate, which is almost un-American.

All that was easy, because weaving, passing, holding onto the puck is simply a more enjoyable way to play the game. Smashing that stereotype was a cinch. But conditioning? There is no mind in the world that is open enough to enjoy the tortures of Herbies.

Herbies are a relatively common form of windsprint that all hockey players do, but only the Olympians call them by that name. End line to blue line and back, to red line and back, to far blue line and back, all the way down and back. Rest. Two or three sets of Herbies at the end of practice is about as much punishment as most coaches are willing to dish out. The day before a game, it's a rare coach indeed who'll submit his players to even one Herbie, and by the time you reach the NHL, your Herbie days are pretty much over. Hey, we're in the bigs now. We play ourselves into shape.

Bull. In the 1979 Challenge Cup the Soviets skated rings around the NHL All-Stars late in the games. The Russians can do Herbies till the cows come home. They skate as hard in the last shift of a game as they do in the first, and it has nothing to do with emotion or adrenaline. They have always been the best-conditioned hockey players in the world.

Peter Stastny, the Czechoslovakian Olympic star who defected last summer to the NHL's Quebec Nordiques, says the one thing that most shocked the international hockey community about the performance of the young Americans (average age: 22) was their conditioning. The Soviets had always been at one level, with everybody else at a level below. Suddenly here are a bunch of *Americans,* for heaven's sake, whom the Russians are huffing and puffing to keep up with in the third period. Who *are* those guys? In the seven games played in the Olympics, the U.S. team was outscored nine goals to six in the first period, but outscored its opponents *16–3* in the third. What got into them? Steroids?

Herbies.

"It's a selling job," says Brooks. "When you want to push people who are living a good life in an affluent society, you have to do a selling job." The sales pitch went like this: Skate or you're off the team. You're gone. No pro contract. No big money. Gone.

In his own words, Brooks was "smart enough to know I was dumb." How do you get a hockey player in shape the way the Russians were in shape? Nobody knew, not in the hockey world. So Brooks went to coaches of track and swimming—areas in which American athletes have been trained to compete successfully on the international level—and found out about anaerobics, flexibility exercises, underloading, overloading, pulse rates, the works. Then he transferred this information to his players, who, because they were educated, because they were open-minded, were willing to listen. Willing to give it a try. Sure, we'll run up and down that hill to the Holiday Inn after practices. Sure, we'll do another Herbie. Twenty-five minutes of sprints today without pucks? Sure, we'll do it. And for six months they hated Brooks's guts.

There was a moment of truth for this team. A moment when they became one. It was back in September of 1979 when they were playing a game in Norway. It ended in a 4–4 tie, and Brooks, to say the least, was dissatisfied. "We're going to skate some time today," he told them afterward. Then he sent them back onto the ice.

Forward Dave Silk recalls it this way: "There were 30 or 40 people still in the stands. First they thought we were putting on a skating exhibition, and they cheered. After a while they realized the coach was mad at us for not playing hard, and they booed. Then they got bored and left. Then the workers got bored, and they turned off the lights."

Doing Herbies in the dark . . . it's terrifying. But they did them. Schneider happened to have been thrown out of the game, and he had already changed into his street clothes. He was watching in horror as his teammates went up and back, up and back. Again and again and again. But instead of feeling reprieved, he felt guilty. "Should I get my skates on, Patty?" he asked Assistant Coach Craig Patrick. "Cool it, Buzz," Patrick replied.

It ended at last, and Brooks had the players coast slowly around the rink so that the lactic acid could work itself out of their muscles. And that was when Forward Mark Johnson broke his stick over the boards. Mark Johnson, who made the team go. Mark Johnson, who was its hardest worker, its smartest player. Mark Johnson, whom Brooks never, *ever* had to yell at. And you know what Brooks said— *screamed*—after skating those kids within an inch of their lives? "If I ever see a kid hit a stick on the boards again, I'll skate you till you *die!*" They believed him. And they *would have died,* just to spite him. Says Silk, "I can remember times when I was so mad at him I tried to skate so hard I'd collapse, so I could say to him, '*See what you did?*' " But they weren't an all-star team anymore. They were together in this, all for one. And Brooks was the enemy. And don't think he didn't know it. It was a lonely year by design, all right.

"He knew exactly where to quit," says John Harrington, a forward whose place on the team was never secure. "He'd push you right to the limit where you were ready to say, 'I've had it, I'm throwing it in'—and then he'd back off."

For Brooks, the trick was knowing where that limit was for every player. They may have been a team, but they were still 20 different personalities. The first time Brooks saw Silk skate at the Colorado Springs training camp, he took him aside and said, "I don't know if you *can't* skate or you *won't* skate, but I intend to find out." Silk had been an All-America at Boston University and had the reputation of playing his best in the biggest games. Brooks wanted him on the Olympic team, but he knew that Silk needed more speed. So he promised to ride him, to embarrass him, to rant and rave at him all season long. And even *then,* Brooks implied, he'd probably be too slow. For three months Brooks gave Silk not one single word of encouragement. *Silk, you're too damn slow!* Then one day in practice the team was warming up, skating around the rink, when Silk heard, "Keep at it, your skating's getting better." He looked around and saw Brooks. "He never even looked at me," Silk says. "He kind of whispered it on the way by. It made me feel so good I wanted to skate around and holler."

When Brooks was at Minnesota, he had an unofficial rule against facial hair. He would have liked a clean-shaven Olympic team, too. Trouble was, Ken Morrow, the team's steadiest defenseman, a gentle giant who minded his own business, happened to have a beard already. He'd had one in college, and he rather liked it. And the New York Islanders rather liked Morrow. So rather than risk pushing Morrow too far, rather than risk having the little matter of a beard be the straw that sent Morrow to the big money six months ahead of his teammates, Brooks came up with a rule custom-made to keep Morrow around. Anyone who had had a beard before training camp could keep it. It was new growth that was a no-no.

Brooks treated Johnson differently, too. Johnson is a competitor, one of those rare players who find the puck on their stick all night long. He is absolutely dedicated to hockey, and was dedicated to the team— a leader by example. Yet, until September, Johnson had no idea where he stood. No one did—Brooks had an ax over everyone's head. But Brooks took Johnson aside shortly after the Skate Till You Die episode and told him, "You're the guy who's going to make or break us. When you're really playing, our whole team gets better."

"It was a real shocker," Johnson recalls. "I was just worried about making the club, and he throws a curve like that at you. What can you say? You take a big gulp and swallow it down."

Craig knew he was the man who would be in goal. He had played brilliantly in the 1979 World Cup championship tournament for Brooks, and by waiting a year to turn professional, he had been all but assured of being the starting goalie for the Olympics. But while the personalities of the rest of the team fit together like a jigsaw puzzle, Craig's cockiness and penchant for yapping kept him apart. He wore on people. For Christmas his teammates gave him a giant jawbreaker, hoping to shut him up. But what the heck, he was the *goalie,* and goalies are kind of ding-y anyway, right? But the psyche of a team is a fragile thing, and when Brooks saw he had a goaltender who wasn't going to fit in, he made sure that he wasn't going to start *messing things up.* So he told Craig to keep his trap shut about whose fault the goals were, shoulder the blame himself, and buy the beer after the game. Don't muddy the waters. It was funny; Craig and Brooks struck up a friendship during the year. They were voluntary outcasts who worked, played and thought very much as one.

There was a player on the team who had Brooks's ear—the captain, Eruzione. Brooks had wanted him to be captain practically from the start. He was a leader; he was sensitive; he was a catalyst. But the captain had to be elected by the team. So Brooks campaigned. He confided in Eruzione in front of the other players, assigned him responsibilities, showed him respect. He was even prepared to miscount the ballots, but he didn't have to. The players liked Mike, too. But even Eruzione wasn't spared Brooks's menacing knife. With three games remaining in their exhibition schedule and the first Olympic game less than two weeks away, Brooks called Eruzione aside and told him he wasn't playing well. *Uh-huh.* Mike, you're a great captain and a great guy, but you've got to start pulling your oar. *Uh-huh.* Or else I'll have to tell the press you've hurt your back and are coming to Lake Placid as an assistant coach. *SAY WHAT?*

He was going to cut his own captain! After 57 games he was going to say, "Come along and be my assistant—you aren't good enough!" Well, the hell with you. And Eruzione went out and scored five goals in those last three games. Not only that, when word got out that the coach was prepared to cut the *captain*—holy cow, I'd better work my little behind off. And Brooks did the same thing to Craig, telling him it was too bad, but obviously he had worked him too hard, played him in too many games, and now the goalie was fighting the puck and the only thing to do was to get Steve Janaszak, his backup, ready. . . . *SAY WHAT?* You're not giving my job away *now,* not *now,* not after six months of this crud. . . . But you're fighting the puck, Jimmy. . . . I'll fight you, you cur. . . . I'll show you who's ready and who's not.

So they went to Lake Placid united as ever against their coach. *They would show him!* Twenty players, the ones who had survived all the cuts, still hungry to prove themselves. Six who had traveled with the team all year were dropped just before Lake Placid. The last forward to go was a young man named Ralph Cox. Brooks himself had been the last forward cut from the gold-medal-winning 1960 U.S. hockey team, and the one time all year that his callous front came down was when he cut Cox. "He was such a gentleman that I cried on it," says Brooks. "I had a little flashback of myself at the time. And you know what he told me? True story. He said, 'That's all right, coach, I understand. You guys are going to win the gold medal.' *Ralph Cox* said that. And when we won it, that's who I thought of. Ralph Cox."

At the time, though, Brooks was thinking, "What have you been smoking, Coxy?" The U.S. team was seeded No. 7 in the eight-team field and had the toughest draw in the tournament, facing Sweden and Czechoslovakia—the second and third seeds—in the first two games. Further, in the final exhibition game, the Soviets—almost exactly the same team that had whipped the NHL All-Stars a year earlier—had routed the U.S. 10–3. Welcome to the big time, Yanks. The Americans were hoping for a bronze.

They hoped to get two points in those first two games, one win or two ties. If they didn't, they could pack it in, because there'd be no chance for a medal. The scouting report on Sweden said that technically the Swedes were as good as any team in the world at skating, passing and shooting, but in tough games their spirit could be broken. But you couldn't let them get a lead on you. Stay close.

In the first period the young, nervous U.S. team stayed close. The Swedes led 1–0, and they had outshot the Americans 16–7, but Craig had kept the U.S. hopes alive with outstanding work in goal. And the Americans had some chances of their own—both Rob McClanahan and Eric Strobel missed breakaways in the first four minutes. So now it was behind them, those first-period jitters.

But in the dressing room Brooks was furious. *Insane.* McClanahan had suffered a severe charley horse—McClanahan, who played on the first line with Johnson, who was left wing on the power play, who could *fly*—and one of the trainers told him to get his equipment off and put ice on the bruise, that's all for tonight. A *trainer,* for heaven's sake. And McClanahan *did* it. He was sitting in there in his underwear, an ice pack on his thigh, and the door flew open and there came Brooks, and *was he mad!* "You gutless son of a bitch! Nobody's going belly-up now!"

"Instead of coming in and yelling at us as a team, he picked on Robbie," Johnson recalls. "It was the craziest locker room I've ever been in. He's swearing. Everyone else is swearing. Robbie's swearing and crying. Then Robbie follows him out into the hall and is screaming at him, 'I'll show you!' And in a minute here's the door flying open again and Herbie's coming back yelling, 'It's about time you grew up, you baby. . . .' "

At that point Johnson yelled at Eruzione to get Brooks out of there. Can you beat that? *The star player was yelling at the captain to get the coach out of the locker room.* Finally, Jack O'Callahan, a defenseman who wasn't dressed for the game because of an injury, grabbed Brooks from behind; Brooks and McClanahan were jawbone to jawbone and O'Callahan was afraid they'd start swinging. Meanwhile, the rest of the team was sitting there thinking, *"We're one period into the Olympics, down one lousy goal, and the coach loses his marbles."*

But had he? McClanahan put his stuff back on, and the U.S. team went onto the ice, outshot the Swedes in the second period and tied the game 1–1. McClanahan couldn't even sit down between shifts; his leg was too sore to bend. He'd stand there at the end of the bench, as far away from Brooks as he could get, then hop out when it came time to play. *I'll show you!* And he finished the tournament with five goals, tying Johnson and Schneider for tops on the team. Sweden scored early in the third period to take a 2–1 lead, but in the final minute the U.S. pulled Craig from the net and Bill Baker boomed home the tying goal off a centering pass from Mark Pavelich with 27 seconds left. The U.S. had pulled out one of the two points it needed and, what's more, everybody got to know each other a little better. "It was mayhem in here," Schneider said afterward. "But that's what's going to win it for us, emotion and talent put together."

Said Brooks, "Maybe I've been a little too nice to some of these guys." Honestly.

The fanfare didn't really start to build until after the U.S. beat Czechoslovakia 7–3 two nights later. That was the game in which, with little time remaining and the game well in hand, Johnson was injured by a dirty check (no pun) and on TV the nation heard the wrath of Herb Brooks firsthand. His proposal to wed a Koho hockey stick with a certain Czechoslovakian gullet provoked 500 irate letters, but it also piqued the curiosity of the non-hockey-minded public. Hey, this guy's *all right!* And those players. They're so *young.* Let's keep an eye on these guys—but what's icing?

Norway . . . Romania . . . West Germany, down they went, each game a struggle in the early going, pulled out in the third period when those nameless kids who looked about 15 simply blew the opposition away. And afterward the players would line up at center ice and smile those great big wonderful smiles, many of which actually displayed teeth, and *salute the fans.* They'd hoist their sticks to the fans on one side of the rink; then they'd turn around and hoist them to the other side. It was a terrific routine.

One of the reasons they still *were* nameless was that Brooks had forbidden them to attend the post-game press conferences, enraging both the U.S. Olympic Committee brass and the players' agents. The players themselves were none too keen on the idea, either, though they understood the reasoning. This team wasn't built around stars, and the press conferences were set up to handle only three players. You couldn't have three players getting all the publicity and not believing they were the stars. So no players attended them. Only Brooks. Then when the press accused Brooks of hogging the limelight, *he* refused to attend anymore and sent Craig Patrick in his place. Now everyone was mad at *him.* But without the pressure of the spotlight, the team stayed just as loosey-goosey as a colt on a romp. Hey, this was *fun!* But the Russians were coming.

The day before the U.S.-Soviet game, Brooks held a meeting after practice and told his players that the Russians were ripe; they were lethargic changing lines, their passes had lost their crispness. All season long he had told them that Boris Mikhailov, 13 years the Soviet captain, looked like Stan Laurel. You can't skate against Stan Laurel? The players would roll their eyes: *Here goes Herbie. . . .* But now, 24 hours before the game, they could see it. The Russians *were* ripe. The timing was right. Forget that 10–3 pre-Olympic defeat. That was a lifetime ago. It was, too.

"The Russians were ready to cut their own throats," says Brooks. "But we had to get to the point to be ready to pick up the knife and hand it to them. So the morning of the game I called the team together and told them, 'It's *meant to be.* This is your moment and it's going to happen.' It's kind of corny and I could see them thinking, 'Here goes Herb again. . . .' But I *believed* it."

The idea was to stay close. "It was in the backs of our minds that we might win," recalls Schneider, "but nobody would say it. They'd think you were off your rocker." Craig made some big saves early, but the Russians scored first. Five minutes later Schneider tied it on a 50-foot shot from the left boards. The Soviets took the lead again, but with one second left in the first period Johnson scored to make it 2–2. That was a big goal. When the Russians came out for the second period, Vladislav Tretiak no longer was in goal; he'd been yanked. Vladimir Myshkin was in the nets, the same Myshkin who had shut out the NHL All-Stars in the '79 Challenge Cup. The Soviets got the only goal of the second period and outshot the Americans 12–2.

Brooks told his players to divide the third period into four five-minute segments. They didn't have to tie the game in the first segment, or even the second. There was lots of time. Stay with them. Make them skate. The first five minutes of the third period were scoreless. Then at 8:39 Mark Johnson tied the game 3–3 on a power play. Bedlam. Go, clock, go! "I remember thinking we might actually have a chance to tie," says Pavelich. But the U.S. team had barely had a chance to think of that improbability when Eruzione scored what Harrington calls "one of the great slop goals of all time." The puck was behind the Soviet net and Harrington and a Soviet defenseman were battling for it. Somehow the puck squirted along the boards to Pavelich, who hammered at it and was promptly smashed face-first into the glass. He never saw the end result. The puck caromed off the boards and slid into the slot, directly to Eruzione, whom Pavelich hadn't seen. Eruzione snapped a wrist shot past Myshkin. There were exactly 10 minutes to go. U.S. 4, U.S.S.R. 3.

That's how it ended. No one remembers much about those final 10 minutes except that they took forever. No one breathed. The shifts were insanely short because, by the players' admission, no one wanted to be on the ice when the Great Red Bear awoke and there was hell to pay. Craig, who had been tying up the puck at every opportunity during the tournament, slowing down the play, now wouldn't touch it. *I don't want it, man, you take it!* He was afraid, and rightly so, that if his teammates lined up for a face-off in their own zone and had time to think about the absurdity of leading the Russians, had time to peer up at the clock and brood about the time remaining, their knees would turn to goo.

But they never panicked. Shoot, this was a ball compared with doing Herbies in the dark. Indeed, if anyone panicked it was the Russians, who started to throw in the puck and chase it—NHL hockey, by gosh—who misfired shots, and who, at the end, never pulled their goalie, never gave it that last desperate try that the U.S. had made work against Sweden.

And then it was over. The horn sounded and there was that unforgettable scene of triumph, the rolling and hugging and flinging of sticks. The flags. My God, what a sight. There was the shaking of hands, the staggered, reluctant exit from the ice. But it wasn't until the U.S. players were back in the locker room that the enormity of what they had done hit them. "It was absolutely quiet," recalls Janaszak. "Some guys were crying a little. You got the impression that the game wasn't over, because no one is ever up a goal on the Russians when a game is over. No one believed it."

It was then that somebody started a chorus of "God Bless America," 20 sweaty guys in hockey uniforms chanting, ". . . from the mountains, to the valleys, na-na-na-na-na, na-na-na . . . !" Nobody knew the words. And where was Brooks? Holed up in the men's room, afraid to come out and ruin their celebration. "I almost started to cry," he says. "It was probably the most emotional moment I'd ever seen. Finally I snuck out into the hall, and the state troopers were all standing there crying. Now where do you go?"

Of course, the tournament wasn't over yet. If the U.S. had lost to the Finns on Sunday, it would have finished in *fourth place*. No medal. Brooks came into the locker room Saturday, took one look at guys signing sticks and pictures, and began throwing things around and telling them, *"You aren't good enough for all this attention! You're too damn young! You don't have the talent!"* So the eyes rolled and the lips buttoned—but they listened, because what he was saying was obvious to all of them by now. They had come too far to blow it. And on Sunday they won the gold medal by beating an excellent Finnish team 4–2, but they needed three goals in the third period to do it. Really, they weren't even worried. They *knew* they would do it, because if you can outscore the Russians in the third period, two goals to none, you can sure as heck outscore the Finns. They believed absolutely in themselves. And Verchota, McClanahan and Johnson went out and scored—bing, bing, bing.

They counted down the seconds, slapping their sticks on the boards, screaming to each other, to the refs, to the crowd. Again pandemonium, slightly less frenzied than two days before, the handshakes and the gradual retreat from the scene of their triumph. And then a bit of irony. The cameras captured the goalie, Craig, searching the crowd for his father. It brought tears; it made him a hero in the eyes of the country. But, in truth, he was searching for someone to share this moment with. Like Brooks, he was separate, apart from this team. He had no close friendships, and now he needed one.

The final, uplifting moment they gave us was at the gold-medal ceremony, when Eruzione called his teammates up on the platform with him. After that they marched around the rink as if they owned the place, singing and carrying on. They were definitely not cooling it; they were happy young men. And they *did* own the place. They owned the whole country for a while. It just made you want to pick up your television set and take it to bed with you. It really made you feel good.

It is over now. Unlike other clubs, Olympic teams self-destruct into 20 different directions and careers afterward—at least in this country. There is never a next year for them. They write their story once. Sportsmen of the Year.

Gay Talese

The Silent Season of a Hero

Gay Talese's astonishingly versatile writing career—books on the Mafia, The New York Times *(where he worked for twelve years), American sex lives, his own family, plus his magazine profiles on public figures—set new standards for nonfiction. This profile of Joe DiMaggio appeared in* Esquire *in 1966 and became a classic of its kind.*

"I would like to take the great DiMaggio fishing," the old man said. "They say his father was a fisherman. Maybe he was as poor as we are and would understand."

—Ernest Hemingway, *The Old Man and the Sea*

I t was not quite spring, the silent season before the search for salmon, and the old fishermen of San Francisco were either painting their boats or repairing their nets along the pier or sitting in the sun talking quietly among themselves, watching the tourists come and go, and smiling, now, as a pretty girl paused to take their picture. She was about twenty-five, healthy and blue-eyed and wearing a red turtleneck sweater, and she had long, flowing blond hair that she brushed back a few times before clicking her camera. The fishermen, looking at her, made admiring comments but she did not understand because they spoke a Sicilian dialect; nor did she notice the tall gray-haired man in a dark suit who stood watching her from behind a big bay window on the second floor of DiMaggio's Restaurant that overlooks the pier.

He watched until she left, lost in the crowd of newly arrived tourists that had just come down the hill by cable car. Then he sat down again at the table in the restaurant, finishing his tea and lighting another cigarette, his fifth in the last half hour. It was eleven-thirty in the morning. None of the other tables was occupied, and the only sounds came from the bar, where a liquor salesman was laughing at something the head-waiter had said. But then the salesman, his briefcase under his arm, headed for the door, stopping briefly to peek into the dining room and call out, "See you later, Joe." Joe DiMaggio turned and waved at the salesman. Then the room was quiet again.

At fifty-one, DiMaggio was a most distinguished-looking man, aging as gracefully as he had played on the ballfield, impeccable in his tailoring, his nails manicured, his 6-foot 2-inch body seeming as lean and capable as when he posed for the portrait that hangs in the restaurant and shows him in Yankee Stadium swinging from the heels at a pitch thrown twenty years ago. His gray hair was thinning at the crown, but just barely, and his face was lined in the right places, and his expression, once as sad and haunted as a matador's, was more in repose these days, though, as now, tension had returned and he chainsmoked and occasionally paced the floor and looked out the window at the people below. In the crowd was a man he did not wish to see.

The man had met DiMaggio in New York. This week he had come to San Francisco and had telephoned several times but none of the calls had been returned because DiMaggio suspected that the man, who had said he was doing research on some vague sociological project, really wanted to delve into DiMaggio's private life and that of DiMaggio's former wife, Marilyn Monroe. DiMaggio would never tolerate this. The memory of her death is still very painful to him, and yet, because he keeps it to himself, some people are not sensitive to it. One night in a supper club a woman who had been drinking approached his table, and when he did not ask her to join him, she snapped:

"All right, I guess I'm *not* Marilyn Monroe."

He ignored her remark, but when she repeated it, he replied, barely controlling his anger, "No—I wish you were, but you're not."

The tone of his voice softened her, and she asked, "Am I saying something wrong?"

"You already have," he said. "Now will you please leave me alone?"

His friends on the wharf, understanding him as they do, are very careful when discussing him with strangers, knowing that should they inadvertently betray a confidence he will not denounce them but rather will never speak to them again; this comes from a sense of propriety not inconsistent in the man who also, after Marilyn Monroe's death, directed that fresh flowers be placed on her grave "forever."

Some of the old fishermen who have known DiMaggio all his life remember him as a small boy who helped clean his father's boat, and as a young man who sneaked away and used a broken oar as a bat on the sandlots nearby. His father, a small mustachioed man known as Zio Pepe, would become infuriated and call him *lagnuso* (lazy) *meschino* (good-for-nothing) but in 1936 Zio Pepe was among those who cheered when Joe DiMaggio returned to San Francisco after his first season with the New York Yankees and was carried along the wharf on the shoulders of the fishermen.

The fishermen also remember how, after his retirement in 1951, DiMaggio brought his second wife, Marilyn, to live near the wharf, and sometimes they would be seen early in the morning fishing off DiMaggio's boat, the *Yankee Clipper,* now docked quietly in the marina, and in the evening they would be sitting and talking on the pier. They had arguments, too, the fishermen knew, and one night Marilyn was seen running hysterically, crying as she ran, along the road away from the pier, with Joe following. But the fishermen pretended they did not see this; it was none of their affair. They knew that Joe wanted her to stay in San Francisco and avoid the sharks in Hollywood, but she was confused and torn then—"She was a child," they said—and even today DiMaggio loathes Los Angeles and many of the people in it. He no longer speaks to his onetime friend, Frank Sinatra, who had befriended Marilyn in her final years, and he also is cool to Dean Martin and Peter Lawford and Lawford's former wife, Pat, who once gave a party at which she introduced Marilyn Monroe to Robert Kennedy, and the two of them danced often that night, Joe heard, and he did not take it well. He was very possessive of her that year, his close friends say, because Marilyn and he had planned to remarry; but before they could she was dead, and DiMaggio banned the Lawfords and Sinatra and many Hollywood people from her funeral. When Marilyn Monroe's attorney complained that DiMaggio was keeping her friends away, DiMaggio answered coldly, "If it weren't for those friends persuading her to stay in Hollywood she would still be alive."

Joe DiMaggio now spends most of the year in San Francisco, and each day tourists, noticing the name on the restaurant, ask the men on the wharf if they ever see him. Oh yes, the men say, they see him nearly every day, they have not seen him yet this morning, they add, but he should be arriving shortly. So the tourists continue to walk along the piers past the crab vendors, under the circling sea gulls, past the fish 'n' chip stands, sometimes stopping to watch a large vessel steaming toward the Golden Gate Bridge which, to their dismay, is painted red. Then they visit the Wax Museum, where there is a life-size figure of DiMaggio in uniform, and walk across the street and spend a quarter to peer through the silver telescopes focused on the island of Alcatraz, which is no longer a Federal prison. Then they return to ask the men if DiMaggio has been seen. Not yet, the men say, although they notice his blue Impala parked in the lot next to the restaurant. Sometimes tourists will walk into the restaurant and have lunch and will see him sitting calmly in a corner signing autographs and being extremely gracious with everyone. At other times, as on this particular morning when the man from New York chose to visit, DiMaggio was tense and suspicious.

When the man entered the restaurant from the side steps leading to the dining room, he saw DiMaggio standing near the window, talking with an elderly maître d' named Charles Friscia. Not wanting to walk in and risk intrusion, the man asked one of DiMaggio's nephews to inform Joe of his presence. When DiMaggio got the message he quickly turned and left Friscia and disappeared through an exit leading down to the kitchen.

Astonished and confused, the visitor stood in the hall. A moment later Friscia appeared and the man asked, "Did Joe leave?"

"Joe who?" Friscia replied.

"Joe DiMaggio!"

"Haven't seen him," Friscia said.

"You haven't *seen* him! He was standing right next to you a second ago!"

"It wasn't me," Friscia said.

"You were standing next to him. I saw you. In the dining room."

"You must be mistaken," Friscia said, softly, seriously. "It wasn't me."

"You *must* be kidding," the man said, angrily, turning and leaving the restaurant. Before he could get to his car, however, DiMaggio's nephew came running after him and said, "Joe wants to see you."

He returned expecting to see DiMaggio waiting for him. Instead he was handed a telephone. The voice was powerful and deep and so tense that the quick sentences ran together.

"You are invading my rights, I did not ask you to come, I assume you have a lawyer, you must have a lawyer, get your lawyer!"

"I came as a friend," the man interrupted.

"That's beside the point," DiMaggio said. "I have my privacy. I do not want it violated, you'd better get a lawyer. . . ." Then, pausing, DiMaggio asked, "Is my nephew there?"

He was not.

"Then wait where you are."

A moment later DiMaggio appeared, tall and red-faced, erect and beautifully dressed in his dark suit and white shirt with the gray silk tie and the gleaming silver cuff links. He moved with big steps toward the man and handed him an airmail envelope, unopened, that the man had written from New York.

"Here," DiMaggio said. "This is yours."

Then DiMaggio sat down at a small table. He said nothing, just lit a cigarette and waited, legs crossed, his head held high and back so as to reveal the intricate construction of his nose, a fine sharp tip above the big nostrils and tiny bones built out from the bridge, a great nose.

"Look," DiMaggio said, more calmly. "I do not interfere with other people's lives. And I do not expect them to interfere with mine. There are things about my life, personal things, that I refuse to talk about. And even if you asked my brothers they would be unable to tell you about them because they do not know. There are things about me, so many things, that they simply do not know. . . ."

"I don't want to cause trouble," the man said. "I think you're a great man, and. . . ."

"I'm not great," DiMaggio cut in. "I'm not great," he repeated, softly. "I'm just a man trying to get along."

Then DiMaggio, as if realizing that he was intruding upon his own privacy, abruptly stood up. He looked at his watch.

"I'm late," he said, very formal again. "I'm ten minutes late. *You're* making me late."

The man left the restaurant. He crossed the street and wandered over to the pier, briefly watching the fishermen hauling their nets and talking in the sun, seeming very calm and contented. Then, after he had turned and was headed back toward the parking lot, a blue Impala stopped in front of him and Joe DiMaggio leaned out the window and asked, "Do you have a car?" His voice was very gentle.

"Yes," the man said.

"Oh," DiMaggio said. "I would have given you a ride."

———

Joe DiMaggio was not born in San Francisco but in Martinez, a small fishing village twenty-five miles northeast of the Golden Gate. Zio Pepe had settled there after leaving Isola delle Femmine, an islet off Palermo where the DiMaggios had been fishermen for generations. But in 1915, hearing of the luckier waters off San Francisco's wharf, Zio Pepe left Martinez, packing his boat with furniture and family, including Joe who was one year old.

San Francisco was placid and picturesque when the DiMaggios arrived, but there was a competitive undercurrent and struggle for power along the pier. At dawn the boats would sail out to where the bay meets the ocean and the sea is rough, and later the men would race back with their hauls, hoping to beat their fellow fishermen to shore and sell it while they could. Twenty or thirty boats would sometimes be trying to gain the channel shoreward at the same time, and a fisherman had to know every rock in the water, and later know every bargaining trick along the shore, because the dealers and restaurateurs would play one fisherman off against the other, keeping the prices down. Later the fishermen became wiser and organized, predetermining the maximum amount each fisherman would catch, but there were always some men who, like the fish, never learned, and so heads would sometimes be broken, nets slashed, gasoline poured onto their fish, flowers of warning placed outside their doors.

But these days were ending when Zio Pepe arrived, and he expected his five sons to succeed him as fishermen, and the first two, Tom and Michael, did; but a third, Vincent, wanted to sing. He sang with such magnificent power as a young man that he came to the attention of the great banker, A. P. Giannini, and there were plans to send him to Italy for tutoring and the opera. But there was hesitation around the DiMaggio household and Vince never went; instead he played ball with the San Francisco Seals and sportswriters misspelled his name.

It was DeMaggio until Joe, at Vince's recommendation, joined the team and became a sensation, being followed later by the youngest brother, Dominic, who was also outstanding. All three later played in the big leagues and some writers like to say that Joe was the best hitter, Dom the best fielder, Vince the best singer, and Casey Stengel once said: "Vince is the only player I ever saw who could strike out three times in one game and not be embarrassed. He'd walk into the clubhouse whistling. Everybody would be feeling sorry for him, but Vince always thought he was doing good."

After he retired from baseball Vince became a bartender, then a milkman, now a carpenter. He lives forty miles north of San Francisco in a house he partly built, has been happily married for thirty-four years, has four grandchildren, has in the closet one of Joe's tailor-made suits that he has never had altered to fit, and when people ask if he envies Joe he always says, "No, maybe Joe would like to have what I have. He won't admit it, but he just might like to have what I have." The brother Vince most admired was Michael, "a big earthy man, a dreamer, a fisherman who wanted things but didn't want to take from Joe, or to work in the restaurant. He wanted a bigger boat, but wanted to earn it on his own. He never got it." In 1953, at the age of forty-four, Michael fell from his boat and drowned.

Since Zio Pepe's death at seventy-seven in 1949, Tom, at sixty-two the oldest brother—two of his four sisters are older—has become nominal head of the family and manages the restaurant that was opened in 1937 as Joe DiMaggio's Grotto. Later, Joe sold out his share, and now Tom is the co-owner of it with Dominic. Of all the brothers, Dominic, who was known as the "Little Professor" when he played with the Boston Red Sox, is the most successful in business. He lives in a fashionable Boston suburb with his wife and three children and is president of a firm that manufactures fiber-cushion materials and grossed more than $3,500,000 last year.

Joe DiMaggio lives with his widowed sister, Marie, in a tan stone house on a quiet residential street not far from Fisherman's Wharf. He bought the house almost thirty years ago for his parents, and after their death he lived there with Marilyn Monroe; now it is cared for by Marie, a slim and handsome dark-eyed woman who has an apartment on the second floor, Joe on the third. There are some baseball trophies and plaques in the small room off DiMaggio's bedroom, and on his dresser are photographs of Marilyn Monroe, and in the living room downstairs is a small painting of her that DiMaggio likes very much: it reveals only her face and shoulders and she is wearing a very wide-brimmed sun hat, and there is a soft sweet smile on her lips, an innocent curiosity about her that is the way he saw her and the way he wanted her to be seen by others—a simple girl, "a warm big-hearted girl," he once described her, "that everybody took advantage of."

The publicity photographs emphasizing her sex appeal often offended him, and a memorable moment for Billy Wilder, who directed her in *The Seven Year Itch*, occurred when he spotted DiMaggio in a large crowd of people gathered on Lexington Avenue in New York to watch a scene in which Marilyn, standing over a subway grating to cool herself, had her skirts blown high by a sudden wind below. "What the hell is going on here?" DiMaggio was overheard to have said in the crowd, and Wilder recalled, "I shall never forget the look of death on Joe's face."

He was then thirty-nine, she was twenty-seven. They had been married in January of that year, 1954, despite disharmony in temperament and time: he was tired of publicity, she was thriving on it; he was intolerant of tardiness, she was always late. During their honeymoon in Tokyo, an American general had introduced himself and asked if, as a patriotic gesture, she would visit the troops in Korea. She looked at Joe. "It's your honeymoon," he said, shrugging, "go ahead if you want to."

She appeared on ten occasions before 100,000 servicemen, and when she returned she said, "It was so wonderful, Joe. You never heard such cheering."

"Yes, I have," he said.

Across from her portrait in the living room, on a coffee table in front of a sofa, is a sterling-silver humidor that was presented to him by his Yankee teammates at a time when he was the most talked-about man in America, and when Les Brown's band had recorded a hit that was heard day and night on the radio:

> . . . From Coast to Coast, that's all you hear
> Of Joe the One-Man Show
> He's glorified the horsehide sphere,
> Jolting Joe DiMaggio . . .
> Joe . . . Joe . . . DiMaggio . . . we want you on our side. . . .

The year was 1941, and it began for DiMaggio in the middle of May after the Yankees had lost four games in a row, seven of their last nine, and were in fourth place, five-and-a-half games behind the leading Cleveland Indians. On May 15th, DiMaggio hit only a first-inning single in a game that New York lost to Chicago, 13–1; he was barely hitting .300, and had greatly disappointed the crowds that had seen him finish with a .352 average the year before and .381 in 1939.

He got a hit in the next game, and the next, and the next. On May 24th, with the Yankees losing 6–5 to Boston, DiMaggio came up with runners on second and third and singled them home, winning the game, extending his streak to ten games. But it went largely unnoticed. Even DiMaggio was not conscious of it until it had reached twenty-nine games in mid-June. Then the newspapers began to dramatize it, the public became aroused, they sent him good-luck charms of every description, and DiMaggio kept hitting, and radio announcers would interrupt programs to announce the news, and then the song again: "Joe . . . Joe . . . DiMaggio . . . we want you on our side. . . ."

Sometimes DiMaggio would be hitless his first three times up, the tension would build, it would appear that the game would end without his getting another chance—but he always would, and then he would hit the ball against the left-field wall, or through the pitcher's legs, or between two leaping infielders. In the forty-first game, the first of a doubleheader in Washington, DiMaggio tied an American League record that George Sisler had set in 1922. But before the second game began a spectator sneaked onto the field and into the Yankees' dugout and stole DiMaggio's favorite bat. In the second game, using another of his bats, DiMaggio lined out twice and flied out. But in the seventh inning, borrowing one of his old bats that a teammate was using, he singled and broke Sisler's record, and he was only three games away from surpassing the major-league record of forty-four set in 1897 by Willie Keeler while playing for Baltimore when it was a National League franchise.

An appeal for the missing bat was made through the newspapers. A man from Newark admitted the crime and returned it with regrets. And on July 2, at Yankee Stadium, DiMaggio hit a home run into the left-field stands. The record was broken.

He also got hits in the next eleven games, but on July 17th in Cleveland, at a night game attended by 67,468, he failed against two pitchers, Al Smith and Jim Bagby, Jr., although Cleveland's hero was really its third baseman, Ken Keltner, who in the first inning lunged to his right to make a spectacular backhanded stop of a drive and, from the foul line behind third base, he threw DiMaggio out. DiMaggio received a walk in the fourth inning. But in the seventh he again hit a hard shot at Keltner, who again stopped it and threw him out. DiMaggio hit sharply toward the shortstop in the eighth inning, the ball taking a bad hop, but Lou Boudreau speared it off his shoulder and threw to the second baseman to start a double play and DiMaggio's streak was stopped at fifty-six games. But the New York Yankees were on their way to winning the pennant by seventeen games, and the World Series too, and so in August, in a hotel suite in Washington, the players threw a surprise party for DiMaggio and toasted him with champagne and presented him with this Tiffany silver humidor that is now in San Francisco in his living room. . . .

Marie was in the kitchen making toast and tea when DiMaggio came down for breakfast; his gray hair was uncombed but, since he wears it short, it was not untidy. He said good morning to Marie, sat down and yawned. He lit a cigarette. He wore a blue wool bathrobe over his pajamas. It was eight A.M. He had many things to do today and he seemed cheerful. He had a conference with the president of Continental Television, Inc., a large retail chain in California of which he is a partner and vice-president; later he had a golf date, and then a big banquet to attend, and, if that did not go on too long and he were not too tired afterward, he might have a date.

Picking up the morning paper, not rushing to the sports page, DiMaggio read the front-page news, the people-problems of '66: Kwame Nkrumah was overthrown in Ghana, students were burning their draft cards (DiMaggio shook his head), the flu epidemic was spreading through the whole state of California. Then he flipped inside through the gossip columns, thankful they did not have him in there today—they had printed an item about his dating "an electrifying airline hostess" not long ago, and they also spotted him at dinner with Dori Lane, "the frantic frugger" in Whiskey à Go Go's glass cage—and then he turned to the sports page and read a story about how the injured Mickey Mantle may never regain his form.

It had all happened so quickly, the passing of Mantle, or so it seemed; he had succeeded DiMaggio as DiMaggio had succeeded Ruth, but now there was no great young power hitter coming up and the Yankee management, almost desperate, had talked Mantle out of retirement; and on September 18, 1965, they gave him a "day" in New York during which he received several thousand dollars' worth of gifts—an automobile, two quarter horses, free vacation trips to Rome, Nassau, Puerto Rico —and DiMaggio had flown to New York to make the introduction before 50,000: it had been a dramatic day, an almost holy day for the believers who had jammed the grandstands early to witness the canonization of a new stadium saint. Cardinal Spellman was on the committee, President Johnson sent a telegram, the day was officially proclaimed by the Mayor of New York, an orchestra assembled in center field in front of the trinity of monuments to Ruth, Gehrig, Huggins; and high in the grandstands, billowing in the breeze of early autumn, were white banners that read: "Don't Quit Mick," "We Love the Mick."

The banners had been held by hundreds of young boys whose dreams had been fulfilled so often by Mantle, but also seated in the grandstands were older men, paunchy and balding, in whose middle-aged minds DiMaggio was still vivid and invincible, and some of them remembered how one month before, during a pre-game exhibition of Old-timers' Day in Yankee Stadium, DiMaggio had hit a pitch into the left-field seats, and suddenly thousands of people had jumped wildly to their feet, joyously screaming—the great DiMaggio had returned, they were young again, it was yesterday.

But on this sunny September day at the Stadium, the feast day of Mickey Mantle, DiMaggio was not wearing No. 5 on his back nor a black cap to cover his graying hair; he was wearing a black suit and white shirt and blue tie, and he stood in one corner of the Yankees' dugout waiting to be introduced by Red Barber, who was standing near home plate behind a silver microphone. In the outfield Guy Lombardo's Royal Canadians were playing soothing soft music; and moving slowly back and forth over the sprawling green grass between the left-field bullpen and the infield were two carts driven by grounds keepers and containing dozens and dozens of large gifts for Mantle—a 6-foot, 100-pound Hebrew National salami, a Winchester rifle, a mink coat for Mrs. Mantle, a set of Wilson golf clubs, a Mercury 95-horse power outboard motor, a Necchi portable, a year's supply of Chunky Candy. DiMaggio smoked a cigarette, but cupped it in his hands as if not wanting to be caught in the act by teen-aged boys near enough to peek down into the dugout. Then, edging forward a step, DiMaggio poked his head out and looked up. He could see nothing above except the packed towering green grandstands that seemed a mile high and moving, and he could see no clouds or blue sky, only a sky of faces. Then the announcer called out his name—*"Joe DiMaggio!"*—and suddenly there was a blast of cheering that grew louder and louder, echoing and reechoing within the big steel canyon, and DiMaggio stomped out his cigarette and climbed up the dugout steps and onto the soft green grass, the noise resounding in his ears, he could almost feel the breeze, the breath of 50,000 lungs upon him, 100,000 eyes watching his every move and for the briefest instant as he walked he closed his eyes.

Then in his path he saw Mickey Mantle's mother, a smiling elderly woman wearing an orchid, and he gently reached out for her elbow, holding it as he led her toward the microphone next to the other dignitaries lined up on the infield. Then he stood, very erect and without expression, as the cheers softened and the Stadium settled down.

Mantle was still in the dugout, in uniform, standing with one leg on the top step, and lined on both sides of him were the other Yankees who, when the ceremony was over, would play the Detroit Tigers. Then into the dugout, smiling, came Senator Robert Kennedy, accompanied by two tall curly-haired young assistants with blue eyes, Fordham freckles. Jim Farley was the first on the field to notice the Senator, and Farley muttered, loud enough for others to hear, "Who the hell invited *him?*"

Toots Shor and some of the other committeemen standing near Farley looked into the dugout, and so did DiMaggio, his glance seeming cold, but he remaining silent. Kennedy walked up and down within the dugout shaking hands with the Yankees, but he did not walk onto the field.

"Senator," said the Yankees' manager, Johnny Keane, "why don't you sit down?" Kennedy quickly shook his head, smiled. He remained standing, and then one Yankee came over and asked about getting relatives out of Cuba, and Kennedy called over one of his aides to take down the details in a notebook.

On the infield the ceremony went on, Mantle's gifts continued to pile up—a Mobilette motor bike, a Sooner Schooner wagon barbecue, a year's supply of Chock Full O'Nuts coffee, a year's supply of Topps Chewing Gum—and the Yankee players watched, and Maris seemed glum.

"Hey, Rog," yelled a man with a tape recorder, Murray Olderman, "I want to do a thirty-second tape with you."

Maris swore angrily, shook his head.

"It'll only take a second," Olderman said.

"Why don't you ask Richardson? He's a better talker than me."

"Yes, but the fact that it comes from you . . ."

Maris swore again. But finally he went over and said in an interview that Mantle was the finest player of his era, a great competitor, a great hitter.

Fifteen minutes later, standing behind the microphone at home plate, DiMaggio was telling the crowd, "I'm proud to introduce the man who succeeded me in center field in 1951," and from every corner of the Stadium the cheering, whistling, clapping came down. Mantle stepped forward. He stood with his wife and children, posed for the photographers kneeling in front. Then he thanked the crowd in a short speech, and turning, shook hands with the dignitaries standing nearby. Among them now was Senator Kennedy, who had been spotted in the dugout five minutes before by Red Barber, and been called out and introduced. Kennedy posed with Mantle for a photographer, then shook hands with the Mantle children, and with Toots Shor and James Farley and others. DiMaggio saw him coming down the line and at the last second he backed away, casually, hardly anybody noticing it, and Kennedy seemed not to notice it either, just swept past shaking more hands. . . .

Finishing his tea, putting aside the newspaper, DiMaggio went upstairs to dress, and soon he was waving good-bye to Marie and driving toward his business appointment in downtown San Francisco with his partners in the retail television business. DiMaggio, while not a millionaire, has invested wisely and has always had, since his retirement from baseball, executive positions with big companies that have paid him well. He also was among the organizers of the Fisherman's National Bank of San Francisco last year, and, though it never came about, he demonstrated an acuteness that impressed those businessmen who had thought of him only in terms of baseball. He has had offers to manage big-league baseball teams but always has rejected them, saying, "I have enough trouble taking care of my own problems without taking on the responsibilities of twenty-five ballplayers."

So his only contact with baseball these days, excluding public appearances, is his unsalaried job as a batting coach each spring in Florida with the New York Yankees, a trip he would make once again on the following Sunday, three days away, if he could accomplish what for him is always the dreaded responsibility of packing, a task made no easier by the fact that he lately has fallen into the habit of keeping his clothes in two places—some hang in his closet at home, some hang in the back room of a saloon called Reno's.

Reno's is a dimly lit bar in the center of San Francisco. A portrait of DiMaggio swinging a bat hangs on the wall, in addition to portraits of other star athletes, and the clientele consists mainly of the sporting crowd and newspapermen, people who know DiMaggio quite well and around whom he speaks freely on a number of subjects and relaxes as he can in few other places. The owner of the bar is Reno Barsocchini, a broad-shouldered and handsome man of fifty-one with graying wavy hair who began as a fiddler in Dago Mary's tavern thirty-five years ago. He later became a bartender there and elsewhere, including DiMaggio's Restaurant, and now he is probably DiMaggio's closest friend. He was the best man at the DiMaggio-Monroe wedding in 1954, and when they separated nine months later in Los Angeles, Reno rushed down to help DiMaggio with the packing and drive him back to San Francisco. Reno will never forget the day.

Hundreds of people were gathered around the Beverly Hills home that DiMaggio and Marilyn had rented, and photographers were perched in the trees watching the windows, and others stood on the lawn and behind the rose bushes waiting to snap pictures of anybody who walked out of the house. The newspapers that day played all the puns—"Joe Fanned on Jealousy"; "Marilyn and Joe—Out at Home"—and the Hollywood columnists, to whom DiMaggio was never an idol, never a gracious host, recounted instances of incompatibility, and Oscar Levant said it all proved that no man could be a success in two national pastimes. When Reno Barsocchini arrived he had to push his way through the mob, then bang on the door for several minutes before being admitted. Marilyn Monroe was upstairs in bed, Joe DiMaggio was downstairs with his suitcases, tense and pale, his eyes bloodshot.

Reno took the suitcases and golf clubs out to DiMaggio's car, and then DiMaggio came out of the house, the reporters moving toward him, the lights flashing.

"Where are you going?" they yelled.

"I'm driving to San Francisco," he said, walking quickly.

"Is that going to be your home?"

"That *is* my home and always has been."

"Are you coming back?"

DiMaggio turned for a moment, looking up at the house.

"No," he said, "I'll never be back."

Reno Barsocchini, except for a brief falling out over something he will not discuss, has been DiMaggio's trusted companion ever since, joining him whenever he can on the golf course or on the town, otherwise waiting for him in the bar with other middle-aged men. They may wait for hours sometimes, waiting and knowing that when he arrives he may wish to be alone; but it does not seem to matter, they are endlessly awed by him, moved by the mystique, he is a kind of male Garbo. They know that he can be warm and loyal if they are sensitive to his wishes, but they must never be late for an appointment to meet him. One man, unable to find a parking place, arrived a half-hour late once and DiMaggio did not talk to him again for three months. They know, too, when dining at night with DiMaggio, that he generally prefers male companions and occasionally one or two young women, but never wives; wives gossip, wives complain, wives are trouble, and men wishing to remain close to DiMaggio must keep their wives at home.

When DiMaggio strolls into Reno's bar the men wave and call out his name, and Reno Barsocchini smiles and announces, "Here's the Clipper!", the "Yankee Clipper" being a nickname from his baseball days.

"Hey, Clipper, Clipper," Reno had said two nights before, "where you been, Clipper? . . . Clipper, how 'bout a belt?"

DiMaggio refused the offer of a drink, ordering instead a pot of tea, which he prefers to all other beverages except before a date, when he will switch to vodka.

"Hey, Joe," a sportswriter asked, a man researching a magazine piece on golf, "why is it that a golfer, when he starts getting older, loses his putting touch first? Like Snead and Hogan, they can still hit a ball well off the tee, but on the greens they lose the strokes. . . ."

"It's the pressure of age," DiMaggio said, turning around on his bar stool. "With age you get jittery. It's true of golfers, it's true of any man when he gets into his fifties. He doesn't take chances like he used to. The younger golfer, on the greens, he'll stroke his putts better. The old man, he becomes hesitant. A little uncertain. Shaky. When it comes to taking chances the younger man, even when driving a car, will take chances that the older man won't."

"Speaking of chances," another man said, one of the group that had gathered around DiMaggio, "did you see that guy on crutches in here last night?"

"Yeah, had his leg in a cast," a third said. "Skiing."

"I would never ski," DiMaggio said. "Men who ski must be doing it to impress a broad. You see these men, some of them forty, fifty, getting onto skis. And later you see them all bandaged up, broken legs. . . ."

"But skiing's a very sexy sport, Joe. All the clothes, the tight pants, the fireplace in the ski lodge, the bear rug—Christ, nobody goes to ski. They just go out there to get it cold so they can warm it up. . . ."

"Maybe you're right," DiMaggio said. "I might be persuaded."

"Want a belt, Clipper?" Reno asked.

DiMaggio thought for a second, then said, "All right—first belt tonight."

Now it was noon, a warm sunny day. DiMaggio's business meeting with the television retailers had gone well; he had made a strong appeal to George Shahood, president of Continental Television, Inc., which has eight retail outlets in Northern California, to cut prices on color television sets and increase the sales volume, and Shahood had conceded it was worth a try. Then DiMaggio called Reno's bar to see if there were any messages, and now he was in Lefty O'Doul's car being driven along Fisherman's Wharf toward the Golden Gate Bridge en route to a golf course thirty miles upstate. Lefty O'Doul was one of the great hitters in the National League in the early thirties, and later he managed the San Francisco Seals when DiMaggio was the shining star. Though O'Doul is now sixty-nine, eighteen years older than DiMaggio, he nevertheless possesses great energy and spirit, is a hard-drinking, boisterous man with a big belly and roving eye; and when DiMaggio, as they drove along the highway toward the golf club, noticed a lovely blond at the wheel of a car nearby and exclaimed, "Look at *that* tomato!" O'Doul's head suddenly spun around, he took his eyes off the road, and yelled, "Where, *where?*" O'Doul's golf game is less than what it was—he used to have a two-handicap—but he still shoots in the 80s, as does DiMaggio.

DiMaggio's drives range between 250 and 280 yards when he doesn't sky them, and his putting is good, but he is distracted by a bad back that both pains him and hinders the fullness of his swing. On the first hole, waiting to tee off, DiMaggio sat back watching a foursome of college boys ahead swinging with such freedom. "Oh," he said with a sigh, "to have *their* backs."

DiMaggio and O'Doul were accompanied around the golf course by Ernie Nevers, the former football star, and two brothers who are in the hotel and movie-distribution business. They moved quickly up and down the green hills in electric golf carts, and DiMaggio's game was exceptionally good for the first nine holes. But then he seemed distracted, perhaps tired, perhaps even reacting to a conversation of a few minutes before. One of the movie men was praising the film *Boeing, Boeing*, starring Tony Curtis and Jerry Lewis, and the man asked DiMaggio if he had seen it.

"No," DiMaggio said. Then he added, swiftly, "I haven't seem a film in eight years."

DiMaggio hooked a few shots, was in the woods. He took a No. 9 iron and tried to chip out. But O'Doul interrupted DiMaggio's concentration to remind him to keep the face of the club closed. DiMaggio hit the ball. It caromed off the side of his club, went skipping like a rabbit through the high grass down toward a pond. DiMaggio rarely displays any emotion on a golf course, but now, without saying a word, he took his No. 9 iron and flung it into the air. The club landed in a tree and stayed up there.

"Well," O'Doul said, casually, "there goes *that* set of clubs."

DiMaggio walked to the tree. Fortunately the club had slipped to the lower branch and DiMaggio could stretch up on the cart and get it back.

"Every time I get advice," DiMaggio muttered to himself, shaking his head slowly and walking toward the pond, "I shank it."

Later, showered and dressed, DiMaggio and the others drove to a banquet about ten miles from the golf course. Somebody had said it was going to be an elegant dinner, but when they arrived they could see it was more like a county fair; farmers were gathered outside a big barnlike building, a candidate for sheriff was distributing leaflets at the front door, and a chorus of homely ladies were inside singing "You Are My Sunshine."

"How did we get sucked into this?" DiMaggio asked, talking out of the side of his mouth, as they approached the building.

"O'Doul," one of the men said. "It's his fault. Damned O'Doul can't turn *anything* down."

"Go to hell," O'Doul said.

Soon DiMaggio and O'Doul and Ernie Nevers were surrounded by the crowd, and the woman who had been leading the chorus came rushing over and said, "Oh, Mr. DiMaggio, it certainly is a pleasure having you."

"It's a pleasure being here, ma'am," he said, forcing a smile.

"It's too bad you didn't arrive a moment sooner, you'd have heard our singing."

"Oh, I heard it," he said, "and I enjoyed it very much."

"Good, good," she said. "And how are your brothers Dom and Vic?"

"Fine. Dom lives near Boston. Vince is in Pittsburgh."

"Why, *hello* there, Joe," interrupted a man with wine on his breath, patting DiMaggio on the back, feeling his arm. "Who's gonna take it this year, Joe?"

"Well, I have no idea," DiMaggio said.

"What about the Giants?"

"Your guess is as good as mine."

"Well, you can't count the Dodgers out," the man said.

"You sure can't," DiMaggio said.

"Not with all that pitching."

"Pitching is certainly important," DiMaggio said.

Everywhere he goes the questions seem the same, as if he has some special vision into the future of new heroes, and everywhere he goes, too, older men grab his hand and feel his arm and predict that he could still go out there and hit one, and the smile on DiMaggio's face is genuine. He tries hard to remain as he was—he diets, he takes steam baths, he is careful; and flabby men in the locker rooms of golf clubs sometimes steal peeks at him when he steps out of the shower, observing the tight muscles across his chest, the flat stomach, the long sinewy legs. He has a young man's body, very pale and little hair; his face is dark and lined, however, parched by the sun of several seasons. Still he is always an impressive figure at banquets such as this—an *immortal*, sportswriters called him, and that is how they have written about him and others like him, rarely suggesting that such heroes might ever be prone to the ills of mortal men, carousing, drinking, scheming; to suggest this would destroy the myth, would disillusion small boys, would infuriate rich men who own ballclubs and to whom baseball is a business dedicated to profit and in pursuit of which they trade mediocre players' flesh as casually as boys trade players' pictures on bubble-gum cards. And so the baseball hero must always act the part, must preserve the myth, and none does it better than DiMaggio, none is more patient when drunken old men grab an arm and ask, "Who's gonna take it this year, Joe?"

Two hours later, dinner and the speeches over, DiMaggio is slumped in O'Doul's car headed back to San Francisco. He edged himself up, however, when O'Doul pulled into a gas station in which a pretty red-haired girl sat on a stool, legs crossed, filing her fingernails. She was about twenty-two, wore a tight black skirt and tighter white blouse.

"Look at *that*," DiMaggio said.

"Yeah," O'Doul said.

O'Doul turned away when a young man approached, opened the gas tank, began wiping the windshield. The young man wore a greasy white uniform on the front of which was printed the name "Burt." DiMaggio kept looking at the girl, but she was not distracted from her fingernails. Then he looked at Burt, who did not recognize him. When the tank was full, O'Doul paid and drove off. Burt returned to his girl; DiMaggio slumped down in the front seat and did not open his eyes again until they'd arrived in San Francisco.

"Let's go see Reno," DiMaggio said.

"No, I gotta go see my old lady," O'Doul said. So he dropped DiMaggio off in front of the bar, and a moment later Reno's voice was announcing in the smoky room, "Hey, here's the Clipper!" The men waved and offered to buy him a drink. DiMaggio ordered a vodka and sat for an hour at the bar talking to a half dozen men around him. Then a blond girl who had been with friends at the other end of the bar came over, and somebody introduced her to DiMaggio. He bought her a drink, offered her a cigarette. Then he struck a match and held it. His hand was unsteady.

"Is that me that's shaking?" he asked.

"It must be," said the blond. "I'm calm."

Two nights later, having collected his clothes out of Reno's back room, DiMaggio boarded a jet; he slept crossways on three seats, then came down the steps as the sun began to rise in Miami. He claimed his luggage and golf clubs, put them into the trunk of a waiting automobile, and less than an hour later he was being driven into Fort Lauderdale, past palm-lined streets, toward the Yankee Clipper Hotel.

"All my life it seems I've been on the road traveling," he said, squinting through the windshield into the sun. "I never get a sense of being in any one place."

Arriving at the Yankee Clipper Hotel, DiMaggio checked into the largest suite. People rushed through the lobby to shake hands with him, to ask for his autograph, to say, "Joe, you look great." And early the next morning, and for the next thirty mornings, DiMaggio arrived punctually at the baseball park and wore his uniform with the famous No. 5, and the tourists seated in the sunny grandstands clapped when he first appeared on the field each time, and then they watched with nostalgia as he picked up a bat and played "pepper" with the younger Yankees, some of whom were not even born when, twenty-five years ago this summer, he hit in fifty-six straight games and became the most celebrated man in America.

But the younger spectators in the Fort Lauderdale park, and the sportswriters, too, were more interested in Mantle and Maris, and nearly every day there were news dispatches reporting how Mantle and Maris felt, what they did, what they said, even though they said and did very little except walk around the field frowning when photographers asked for another picture and when sportswriters asked how they felt.

After seven days of this, the big day arrived—Mantle and Maris would swing a bat—and a dozen sportswriters were gathered around the big batting cage that was situated beyond the left-field fence; it was completely enclosed in wire, meaning that no baseball could travel more than thirty or forty feet before being trapped in rope; still Mantle and Maris would be swinging, and this, in spring, makes news.

Mantle stepped in first. He wore black gloves to help prevent blisters. He hit right-handed against the pitching of a coach named Vern Benson, and soon Mantle was swinging hard, smashing line drives against the nets, going *ahhh ahhh* as he followed through with his mouth open.

Then Mantle, not wanting to overdo it on his first day, dropped his bat in the dirt and walked out of the batting cage. Roger Maris stepped in. He picked up Mantle's bat.

"This damn thing must be thirty-eight ounces," Maris said. He threw the bat down into the dirt, left the cage and walked toward the dugout on the other side of the field to get a lighter bat.

DiMaggio stood among the sportswriters behind the cage, then turned when Vern Benson, inside the cage, yelled, "Joe, wanna hit some?"

"No chance," DiMaggio said.

"Com'on, Joe," Benson said.

The reporters waited silently. Then DiMaggio walked slowly into the cage and picked up Mantle's bat. He took his position at the plate but obviously it was not the classic DiMaggio stance; he was holding the bat about two inches from the knob, his feet were not so far apart, and, when DiMaggio took a cut at Benson's first pitch, fouling it, there was none of that ferocious follow-through, the blurred bat did not come whipping all the way around, the No. 5 was not stretched full across his broad back.

DiMaggio fouled Benson's second pitch, then he connected solidly with the third, the fourth, the fifth. He was just meeting the ball easily, however, not smashing it, and Benson called out, "I didn't know you were a choke hitter, Joe."

"I am now," DiMaggio said, getting ready for another pitch.

He hit three more squarely enough, and then he swung again and there was a hollow sound.

"Ohhh," DiMaggio yelled, dropping his bat, his fingers stung, "I was waiting for that one." He left the batting cage rubbing his hands together. The reporters watched him. Nobody said anything. Then DiMaggio said to one of them, not in anger nor in sadness, but merely as a simply stated fact, "There was a time when you couldn't get me out of there."

Rick Telander

Foster Park

In 1974, Rick Telander, a recent graduate of Northwestern University, left Chicago to live for a summer in Brooklyn's Flatbush section. Telander, writer of numerous Sports Illustrated *articles and the author of an indictment of college sports,* The 100-Yard Lie, *spent that summer "hanging out" at a playground known as Foster Park, where the central focus, as it is at so many inner-city playgrounds, is the basketball action. Telander turned the experience into a book,* Heaven Is a Playground, *published in 1976. Meet the inhabitants of that little bit of Brooklyn heaven.*

Coming around the corner of Foster and Nostrand at dusk, I see a ten-foot fence and the vague movements of people. Men sit on car hoods and trunks, gesturing, passing brown paper bags, laughing. Stains on the sidewalk sparkle dully like tiny oil slicks in a gray ocean. Garbage clogs the gutters. At the main entrance to Foster Park, I step quickly to the side to dodge a pack of young boys doing wheelies through the gate. When I came out of the subway, I had asked directions from an elderly woman with a massive bosom like a bushel of leaves, and while she spoke I had involuntarily calculated the racial mix around me—ten percent white, ten percent Latin, eighty percent black. Now, as I walk into the park I am greeted by a lull in the noise, pulling back like musicians fading out to display the rhythm section at work: a million basketballs whack-whacking on pavement.

Rodney Parker is there on the first court, standing still thirty feet from the basket, slowly cocking the ball. He is wearing red sneakers, sweat pants, and a sun visor that splits his Afro like a line between two cumulus clouds. His tongue is pointed out the side of his mouth, and as he shoots, he tilts his entire body sideways like a golfer coaxing home a putt.

The ball arcs up and through the iron hoop and Rodney bursts into laughter. "Oh my God, what a shot! Pay up, Clarence. Who's next, who's got money!"

In 1966, Rodney, his wife, and two children moved from the East New York district of Brooklyn to the Vanderveer Homes, the housing project that cups Foster Park like a palm on the north and east sides. At that time the area was a predominantly Jewish, Irish, and Italian neighborhood of tidy shops, taverns, and flower beds. The Parkers were among the very first blacks to move into the Vanderveer and Rodney, a basketball fanatic since childhood, became one of the first blacks to hang out at Foster Park.

Never one to maintain a low profile, Rodney was soon organizing games between the white neighborhood players and his black friends from East New York and Bedford-Stuyvesant. On weekends he would preside over these frequently wild contests, usually from his vantage point as fifth man on a team that might include several college stars and pros. He would be everywhere, screaming, refereeing, betting money on his thirty-foot shots, with two hundred, three hundred or more people whooping it up on the sidelines. For identification purposes some people began referring to the playground as "Rodney's Park."

Then as now, Rodney's occupation was that of ticket scalper, a free-lance bit of wheeling-dealing that took him to all the big sporting events in the New York area, and put him in contact with most of the sporting stars. He already knew several basketball heroes from his neighborhood, among them, pros Lenny Wilkens and Connie Hawkins, and with the connections he made through scalping, it wasn't long before Rodney was giving reports on Brooklyn players to coaches and scouts and any-one else who might be interested.

Rodney, whose education ended in ninth grade and whose basket-ball abilities were never better than average, derived a deep sense of personal worth from his hobby. "I can do things that nobody can," he liked to say. He helped boys get scholarships to college, he pushed them into prep schools, he got them reduced rates to basketball camps, he even arranged for two of the local white baseball players to get tryouts with the New York Mets. He became known around the park as somebody who could help out if you played ball and weren't getting anywhere on your own. Kids said that Rodney knew everybody in the world.

Now, seeing me by the fence, he comes over and demands that I play in a game immediately to help me get acquainted with "the guys." He charges into the middle of the players and throws commands left and right. This is the rabble—the young men who populate every New York City playground all summer long. Faceless, earnest, apathetic, talented, hoping, hopeless, these are the minor characters in every ghetto drama. They move, drifting in and out in response to Rodney's orders.

The ball bounces away from one of the players and is picked up by a small boy on the sidelines. He dribbles it with joy.

"Gimme that ball 'fore I inject this shoe five feet up your black ass and out your brain," hollers a somber-looking player named Calvin Franks.

The boy dribbles, wriggling his hips and taunting. Franks lunges at the youth who drops the ball and sprints through a hole in the fence into the street.

Franks retrieves the ball and begins talking to himself. "Calvin Franks has the ball, oh shit, is he bad. He takes the man to the base. . . . No, no, he shakes one! . . . two! . . . he's on wheels . . . the crowd stands to watch the All American . . ." Franks shoots and the ball rolls up and around the rim like a globe on its axis, then falls out. "He's fouled! Butchered! They gots to send him to the line . . ."

The sun is gone now, passed behind the buildings in a false, city sunset. Old women with stockings rolled to their ankles doze near the slides.

A boy locates his younger brother who had errands to do at home and pulls him from a card game. "I'll kick yo' ass!" he shouts, slapping his brother in the face. The youth runs out of the park, blood flowing from his nose. The friends at the game laugh and pick up the cards. Crashes of glass rise above the voices, forming a jagged tapestry interwoven with soul music and sirens.

I am placed on a team with four locals and the game begins. Rodney walks to the sidelines and starts coaching. He hollers at the players to pass the ball, not to be such stupid fools. Do they want to spend their whole useless lives as nobodies in the ghetto? Pass, defense. "You're hopeless! Fourteen-year-old Albert King could kill you all," he shouts.

"Rodney, my man, my man! This is pro material," screams Calvin Franks. "Kareem Jabbar come to Foster Park."

There are no lights in the park and vision is rapidly disappearing. The lights, I learned last summer, were removed several years ago to keep boys from playing basketball all night long.

"What? What's happenin' here?" says a young, stocky player named Pablo Billy, his eyes wide in mock surprise as he dribbles between his legs and passes behind his back.

"Boom! She go boom!" yells Franks.

"You done now, Skunk," answers Lloyd Hill, a skinny 6'3" forward with arms like vines and large yellowish eyes.

"Here come the street five! Jive alive. Loosey goosey."

"Look at him!" shrieks a player named Clarence, apparently referring to himself, as he spins out of a crowd. "His body just come like this."

The fouls become more violent now, with drive-in lay-ups being invitations for blood. I don't consider myself a bad basketball player, a short forward who at twenty-five could probably play on a few mediocre high school teams, but out here I pass the ball each time I get it, not wanting to make a fool of myself. Players are jumping over my head.

"Gonna shake it, bake it, and take it to the . . ." A youth named Eddie has his shot batted angrily out to half court. "Nullify that shit," says someone called "Muse" or "Music," I can't tell which.

The Vanderveer project rises on our left like a dark red embattlement against the sky, TV's flickering deep within like synchronized candles. The complex covers parts of four city blocks and houses nearly ten thousand people, a small American town. At one time—no more than ten years ago—the Vanderveer was totally white. Flatbush itself (a name coming from *Vlacke Bos* which is Dutch for wooded plain) was a haven for the working and middle-class whites who had fled Manhattan and inner Brooklyn, believing no city problems could reach this far.

By settling in the neighborhood, Rodney and the other first blacks started the chain reaction again. Within days, white residents began leaving. Apartment for Rent signs went up as fast as the rented vans carried families and belongings out further to Canarsie, Sheepshead Bay, or Long Island. The exodus continued in an unbroken stream until by 1970 the Vanderveer and surrounding area was less than half white. By 1974, whites had become a small minority and the Vanderveer Homes had turned entirely black, the number being split fairly evenly between West Indian immigrants and "native born." Soon, the real signs of decay began to appear—the broken glass, graffiti, garbage, and battered buildings that had been predicted by the doomsayers all along.

If, indeed, there was any plus side to the degeneration, it showed itself on the Foster Park courts where a new grade and style of basketball was developing. Premier leapers and ballhandlers appeared almost overnight. Patterned play and set shots dissolved to twisting dunks and flashy moves. Black players seemed to bring more of themselves to the playground—rather than follow proven structures they experimented and "did things" on court. Soon they controlled the tempo on the half-block of asphalt between Foster and Farragut, and the whites, who came as visitors the way the blacks once had, seemed ponderous and mechanical in comparison.

To Rodney it was simple justice. "Blacks own the city," he said. "They should own the game, too."

But as the talent escalated, so did the problems. Almost every boy now came from a broken home and was, or had been, in some kind of trouble. The athletic potential had multiplied but the risk had doubled.

I think about this as I attempt to guard my man, wondering if he's had it bad, if he has dreams. He blocks me and I push off, feeling his heart through his jersey, pounding hard.

There is almost total darkness now. Yellowish speckles from a street light fan through a tree at the other end but do not come this far. Teammates and opponents have merged and the only thing I can do is hold on to my man and not let him disappear. Rodney is still hollering. "Pass, dammit. Pass like Danny Odums. Hit the boards! Looking for another Fly! Who's gonna fly out of the ghetto?"

Passes have become dangerous, starting off as dark orbs which do not move but simply grow larger and blacker until at the last second hands must be thrown up in protection. The first ball that smacks dead into a player's face is greeted with hoots.

Lloyd Hill unleashes his "standing jump shot" and the ball disappears into the night. It reenters, followed by a sharp pop as it whacks straight down on someone's finger.

"Oooh, god day-yam! Pull this shit out, Leon. Thing's all crunched up." The damaged joint is grabbed and yanked. There is a similar pop. "Eeeeee! Lorda . . . ahh . . . there, now she walking around a little . . ."

"Where's Franks?" shouts Lloyd Hill. "Where'd he went just when I'm shooting the rock in his eyeball."

Franks reappears from the side.

"It's gone."

"What's gone," Lloyd asks.

"The bike."

"What bike?"

"My bike."

"You ain't got a bike, fool."

"Friend gave it to me. Had it right over there."

The ball is punched out of Rodney's arm as little kids appear like phantoms out of the darkness to shoot and dribble during the break.

"Shit, Franks, that ain't funny."

"It's terrible."

"Can't laugh. Heh, he, he."

"Five seconds, gone. Man walks in and rides out."

"Hee ga-heeee."

"It's terrible and I ain't laughing."

"Hooo hoo ooooohhhh . . . they steal things in the ghetto."

"Niggers . . . hoo hoooo . . . they take your shit."

"Some little spook halfway to Fulton Street . . ."

"Hoo ha hoo haaa . . . peddlin' his ass off in the mother-fuckin' ghetto . . ."

"In the for real Ghet-toe . . ." Franks is now laughing hysterically, doubled up and slapping palms.

The darkness is complete. The old people have gone home. Slow-moving orange dots point out groups of boys smoking reefers under the trees. Two other basketball games are going on, but the farthest can only be heard. I start to wonder what I'm doing here, in this game, under these conditions. Playing basketball in total darkness is an act of devotion similar to fishing on land. Soon, I know, someone will rifle a pass and shatter my nose.

"Come on now, let's be serious," says Eddie. "We down, twenty-four, twenty-one."

The ball is returned and the contest starts again. Laughter fades and the bicycle is forgotten. Everything is in earnest and yet I am blind; I cannot follow the game with my ears. Rodney shouts but does not exist. Quietly, on an inbounds play, I walk off the court.

"Hey, hold it," says Lloyd. "Where's that white dude we had?"

"Yeh, we only got four men." Someone counts. "Where'd he go, Rod?" The players look around.

"He went to get some water, I think. He's not used to this shit, he's quitting. Just get another man."

"Come on, little brother," says the tall player called "Muse" or "Music" to one of the hangers-on. "Put the weight to this dude and keep him outta the sky."

From thirty feet away on the bench, I can barely see the occasional sparkle of medallions as they catch the street lights along Foster Avenue. I'm exhausted and relish the chance to wipe my face with my shirt and rub my sore knees. I can hear the players' voices, and it sounds to me like they'll go all night.

Rose Tremain

England!—England!

Rose Tremain is a British writer whose poise and power grow with each succeeding novel. Here, from her newest novel, Sacred Country, *a group of patients at a mental institution are watching the 1960 soccer World Cup matches. Among them is Estelle, the mother in the novel, who suddenly finds herself "at the pinnacle of the world."*

Sonny gave me a dog. He couldn't give me the baby I'd longed for, so he thought I would be capable of loving a dog instead. It was an Alsatian puppy. Sonny put it into my arms and said: "It's called Wolf." I suppose he expected me to swoon with happiness and cradle the dog's head against my breast. But I felt nothing for it, zero, as they say on "Top of the Pops." I let it drop out of my arms. Sonny swore. He's forgotten he ever had any manners and once held his cap in his hands and stood with his head bowed. I walked away. Then I turned and watched him. He picked up Wolf and sat down and put him on his knee. *He* is the one capable of loving a dog, not I.

I came to Mountview because I was about to commit a crime. Mountview is an institution that used to be a stately home. I planned my crime. In my dreams and out. I was going to take the train to Lowestoft and take a suitcase full of the things I'd need. . . . But I see the magnitude of it now. I see the terror and pain I was going to cause. I saw all of this just in time.

And I have been rewarded. I am in love. My love is far away and never speaks to me but this is the way of the world. He is Bobby Moore, the captain of England. His hair, on the TV screen, is white. He has a dimpled smile. All that I care about now is his destiny and the destiny of what he calls the "squad." And that is all any of us at Mountview cares about. We have forgotten our lives and what was in them. They are filled up with dreams of England's glory. We sit in the dark and chant with the crowd: "England!—England! England!—England!" And we have new enemies: their names are Pelé and Jairzinho and Eusebio and de Michele and Weber and Beckenbauer. It is summer outside but we hardly notice it. And even the nurses, with nothing to be cured of and with nothing to try to forget, you see them sidling into the room and standing still and watching and you know their heads are emptying themselves of everything but football. They forget time. They forget to remind you to go to Ops Wing for your treatments. They're sliding away. We're all sliding away fast. And we don't want it to end.

England are in Group One. We drew nil-nil with Uruguay. We beat Mexico two-nil and France two-nil. My love and my hero, Moore, is a visionary captain, so the commentators say. He knows how to read the game, how to turn defense into attack. Only his head is suspect, so they say. *He is suspect in the air*. So I want to write a girlish letter: "Dear Bobby, We have this one and only thing in common: our heads are not to be relied upon . . ."

My head took me to a caravan site. I could see it clearly: old caravans with peeling paint waiting in the hot sun. I could see the families occupying their little bits of ground and all the things they left lying about, tricycles, blankets and anoraks. And prams. Sometimes the prams were empty and sometimes they were not. Sometimes they were parked in the square of caravan shade, with a stretched white net over them, and under the net there was a baby, sleeping.

I know that if I had gone there, this place would have been exactly as I'd seen it in my mind. My head is not suspect in this way; I can see things in advance of seeing them and know precisely how they are going to be. I was going to steal a child. I was going to buy tins of milk for it and nappies and castor oil cream. I was going to take it to Scotland, to a wilderness where I would not be found. I knew this was a criminal act, but I also knew that I was going to do it. I didn't think about what would come after.

The quarter-finals are coming. Oh God. If Bobby and the squad lose, there is going to be weeping here. Even among the nurses. So I say to Sister Matthews: "Have ready all the medication. Have stuff that will send us to sleep for four years until the next World Cup. And in this way, you will save on time and on tea and on the cost of laundry." I laugh and Sister Matthews laughs. She looks at me approvingly. The staff at Mountview think if you can make a joke, you are almost well again, almost ready to be sent back to wherever you came from.

The place I came from has changed, changed. Even our neighbor, Grace Loomis, has started to complain that the weeds on our land seed themselves in her fields. It is harvest time and Sonny and Tim and the combine and the dog, Wolf, are alone with it and it is beyond what they can manage. I said to Sonny, on the morning he drove me here, "Sell the land. That's the best hope. Sell to the Loomises and then we can all rest." He drove and said nothing. He's fifty, but he looks like an old man. At the gates of Mountview, he said, "Never." Then we stopped and he got out and handed me my suitcase and he said it again: "Never, Estelle."

We are playing Argentina. They have beaten Spain, West Germany and Switzerland. We are told they are football-mad. In all the slums and back alleys of their cities, day and night, winter and summer, their lunacy goes on. When they line up on the Wembley turf and their national anthem is played, they cross themselves. Like Timmy, they believe in a Creator. But their creator doesn't save them from a header by Hurst. Their goalkeeper kneels on the ground. He wishes he was not here but far away in his own country, in some hot street hung with familiar washing.

On the day of the final, England v. West Germany, I was due for one of my treatments, but I didn't want to go. Because after a treatment, you wake and you feel nothing, no anger, no joy, no longing, no sadness, nothing. All the love you had for anything has gone. You are still and empty and white. You have no desire. You cannot believe you ever stood up in the TV room and shouted "England!—England!"

I went into one of the greenhouses and hid. Tomatoes were being grown in it and they scented the moist air. I sat in a sliver of shade by the water tank. I felt afraid for England and for Bobby Moore and his smile. My mother was a person who dreamed of glory and she passed those dreams to me. And now I was waiting in a greenhouse for the hour of England's trial to arrive. I thought, the worst thing to happen would be a power cut. Not to see this, not to suffer it, would be worse than seeing it and seeing it lost. For it is only infrequently that I am able to care, one way or another, about something in my life.

I had cared about the child. I had the room waiting—Mary's old room—painted blue and hung with mobiles made out of balsa wood and glass. For two years, I endured Sonny's attempts at impregnation, until I saw they were futile. Then I planned my crime. The only thing that stopped me from committing it was a memory. It concerned Mary. It was a memory so distant, it seemed to belong in another life, not mine. It was a memory of losing Mary in a field, in darkness. She was lost for three hours—one hour for every year of her life—and Sonny and I were in despair.

So I remembered how it was going to be for the mother of the stolen baby. I saw her come to the pram and find it empty. I saw her snatch up the little pram quilt and hold it to her mouth. I saw the ugliness of it all and the terror. I sat down and picked up our black telephone. I dialed the doctor's number. I said: "I want to go to Mountview. I want to have my old room, please, with its view of the garden."

They came and found me in the greenhouse. They were understanding. They said I could have my treatment another day. They asked me kindly whether I had eaten many tomatoes. I replied that I'd eaten none because I was so sick with fear for the squad. And they said: "Well, come along, Estelle. It's nearly time."

Now, we're into "extra time." The score is two-all. "Extra time" is a different quality of time, hung with doom, as if the whole world were about to end. There is suffering in the room. There are no more cries of "England!—England!" There is a smell of urine and sorrow. An old man who used to be a postman says: "They're finished. Look at them."

But I can see that Bobby is still urging them on. He shouts at them. His face is streaming with sweat, his socks are down, but he still wants them to attack. And they haven't given up: Jackie Charlton, Bobby Charlton, Nobby Stiles, Martin Peters, Ray Wilson . . . I turn round to say to the man from the GPO, "They're not finished. Not yet." And in that second, while I have turned away, Geoff Hurst scores. His shot has hit the bar and dropped behind the line. A cheer goes up, around Wembley and around the room. A cheer and then a hush. The goal is disputed. The Germans appeal against it. On the faces of Haller and Webber and Beckenbauer there is a petrified look. The goal is allowed. Another, mightier cheer goes up. In the room, Sister Matthews is weeping. The postman has climbed onto his chair and is waving his arms in the air. And we see it come toward us again: glory.

We are at the end of what we can endure. "Extra time" passes more slowly than ordinary time. Extra is short for extra-ordinary. I say aloud: "They should resume normal time." Someone screams at me not to speak. I put my fingers over my eyes exactly as I remember doing when I was told that Livia had died in the sky.

Then it's over. In the dying seconds of it Hurst scores again. It is won. It is safe. My love, Bobby, and his England are at the pinnacle of the world and all the mad of the shires and the counties and the cities are shouting and weeping their hearts dry.

I want to hurl myself, like Livia, into the clouds. I want to dissolve and become suspect in the air.

Quincy Troupe

Poem for My Father

We first heard the poem one morning on National Public Radio being read by the author. It stunned the senses. Quincy Troupe has written ten books, poetry, and other works, including, with Miles Davis, Miles: The Autobiography. *He was about eight years old when he first started watching his father play baseball. How good a catcher was he, we asked the son. "Second-greatest catcher of all time," was his reply, "behind Josh Gibson."*

Father, it was an honor to be there, in the dugout
with you, the glory of great black men swinging their lives
as bats, at tiny white balls
burning in at unbelievable speeds, riding up & in & out
a curve breaking down wicked, like a ball falling off a table
moving away, snaking down, screwing its stitched magic
into chitlin circuit air, its comma seams spinning
again toward breakdown, dipping, like a hipster
bebopping a knee-dip stride in the charlie parker forties
wrist curling like a swan's neck
behind a "slick" black back
cupping an invisible ball of dreams

& you there father, regal as an african obeah man
sculpted out of wood from a sacred tree of no name no place origin
thick branches branching down into cherokee & someplace else lost
way back in africa, the sap running dry
crossing from north carolina into georgia, inside grandmother mary's
womb, where your mother had you in the violence of that red soil

ink blotter news gone now into blood graves
of american blues sponging rococo
truth long gone as dinosaurs
the agent-oranged landscape of former names
absent of african polysyllables, dry husk consonants there
now in their place, names flat as polluted rivers
& that guitar string smile always snaking across
some virulent american redneck faces
scorching, like atomic heat mushrooming over nagasaki
& hiroshima, the fever blistered shadows of it all
inked as etchings into sizzling concrete

but you there father through it all, a yardbird solo
riffin on bat & ball glory, breaking down the fabricated myths
of white major league legends, of who was better than who
beating them at their own crap
game with killer bats, as bud powell swung his silence into beauty
of a josh gibson home run skittering across piano keys of bleachers
shattering all manufactured legends up there in lights
struck out white knights on the risky edge of amazement
awe, the miraculous truth sluicing through
steeped & disguised in the blues
confluencing, like the point at the cross
when a fastball hides itself in a curve breaking
down & away in a wicked sly grin posed as an ass
scratching uncle tom, who like satchel paige
delivering his famed hesitation pitch before coming
back with a hard high fast one, is slicker, sliding
quicker than a professional hitman—
the deadliness of it all, the sudden strike
like that of the "brown bomber's" crossing right
or sugar ray robinson's lightning, cobra bite

& you there father through it all catching rhythms
of chono pozo balls drumming like conga beats into your catcher's mitt
hard & fast as "cool papa" bell jumping into bed
before the lights went out

of the old negro baseball league, a promise
you were, father, a harbinger, of shock waves, soon come

John R. Tunis

The Mother of a Champion

In an interview with sportswriter Jerome Holtzman, John R. Tunis remembered a dinner he had with fellow Harvard graduate Joseph Kennedy and his family on Cape Cod. "Young Johnny (the future president) had been naughty and his father was angry," recalled Tunis. "He said, 'You do that again, Johnny, and I won't allow you to read any more of Mr. Tunis's books.' Johnny ran upstairs crying." For children like young Johnny Kennedy, baseball stories such as The Kid from Tompkinsville, The Keystone Kids, *and* The Kid Comes Back *were infectious. But Tunis never considered his writing "juvenile," and his prose, which wasn't confined only to baseball, appeared regularly in the* New York Post *and* The New Yorker *among other "adult" journals. Tunis, who once played a doubles tennis match with Suzanne Lenglen, often wrote about tennis and, in particular, tennis as played by women. This 1929 story concerns a young female tennis star hard driven to excel both on and off the court by her overly protective mother. Yes, they could be overly protective in 1929 just as they are today.*

She sat before a most inadequate mirror in the dressing room, an unsophisticated girl of twenty-one preparing to take her part in the great drama that was soon to begin outside. In the corner of the room sat her mother buried in a wicker armchair covered with faded cretonne, murmuring nothings—affectionate and anxious nothings; but nothings, nevertheless—to which her daughter paid no attention. The business of appearing before the public as a world-famous athlete is a serious business, not to be undertaken lightly or indiscreetly.

From the array of bottles, tubes, and glass jars with glass stoppers on the narrow table she took cold cream out of a square receptacle marked "Cleansing" and spread it carefully over her face. With the aid of a towel she rubbed it off with careful, adept movements. Then she took another kind of cream from another jar labeled "Tissue," massaging it in with practiced fingers. Next she seized a bottle bearing the magic word "Astringent" on a paper label and dashed the pinkish fluid all over her countenance. Finally came the really important part of her make-up. For just a second she glanced bewilderingly over the regiment of bottles and jars which lined the table and with a quick gesture selected one bearing the entrancing name, "Florentine Lemon Skin Food." The skin food made from the lemons of Florence she delicately smoothed in a thin layer about her cheeks and chin; next from a square box of "Florentine Flower Powder, Spanish Rachel Shade," she suffused her tortured face in flesh-colored chalk. A careful and scientific application of lipstick, a longish session with a pencil along the eyebrows; at last she was ready. No more, it is true, so unsophisticated-looking at close view. But after all, what of that?

Her mother, meanwhile, had been growing impatient.

"They're waiting for you out there, Florence . . . hadn't you better hurry? . . . Goodness sakes, you didn't used to take so much trouble with all these powders and things when you first started. . . . I remember back in twenty-two . . ."

"Oh, cut that Civil War stuff, Mother. You make me tired with your everlasting . . ."

A knock at the door interrupted the conversation. "Are you ready, Miss Farley? Your opponent's waiting for you."

"All ready," sang out the Champion in the tone which made the newspapers describe her as "Happy Florence Farley, the Girl with the Laughing Voice."

"Com*ming,* com*ming.* Come along, Mother dear." And she emerged from the dressing room with her arm about her mother's waist. Inseparable, those two!

In the narrow hallway outside they were soon parted by the crowd that pressed and eddied about them. Schoolgirl autograph collectors demanded the Champion's signature, not realizing that the Champion never signed albums before a match. After a match, yes, before a match, never! More than one title had been lost through writer's cramp. It was just this attention to detail which had brought Florence Farley to the position she now occupied.

Someone seized her arm; an invitation for the weekend was bellowed through the din and confusion.

"To Southampton? Oooohh, how lovely. I'd just adore to come. But really, I hardly know. You'll have to ask Mother; you see she just won't let me go anywhere without her."

A burst of applause rippled through the crowd as she stepped outside the door of the clubhouse. The photographers hurried to their points of vantage, the officials came eagerly forward to greet her, the crowd indicated its approval. The Champion was going into action to defend her title.

2.

Throughout Florence Farley's career her mother has consistently remained in the background; the general public who follow sports is as a rule unaware of her existence. But if any one person can be said to be responsible for the astounding success of Florence Farley in the world of amateur games, certainly Mrs. Farley should have most of the credit.

Plainville, New York, is an hour and six minutes from the Grand Central Station. It has two banks, three drugstores, a weekly newspaper, a country club, and a population of commuters who take the eight-one to town every morning and return by the five-ten every evening. They are met at the station by their wives, plump ladies dressed in unbecoming but fashionable hats who drive three-thousand-dollar sedans on which the husbands spend their lives trying to earn the monthly installments. When Jim Farley moved out to Plainville in order that six-year-old Florence could have a yard to run in and air to breathe, he was lucky to have enough money left, after paying the first installment on the purchase price and the interest six months in advance on the first and second mortgages, to be able to buy a secondhand Ford. If you knew Plainville you would realize that people who drive secondhand Fords are hardly likely to be adopted by the social leaders of the town.

Not that Jim Farley cared. But his wife cared very much indeed. It hurt her that Jim was in the cotton-goods business and prospering indifferently, while the husbands of the ladies who drove the three-thousand-dollar sedans were in radio or real estate or stocks and bonds or something that was prospering. It hurt most of all that she and Jim were never asked to join the Country Club. To be sure they had no money to join the Country Club, they did not desire to join the Country Club; yet the fact that they were unasked was difficult to swallow. In Plainville either you belonged to the Country Club or you did not. The Farleys did not.

Curiously enough it was Florence who was to solve this problem for her worried mother; it was Florence who was the first of the Farleys to establish herself at the Club. At the age of eleven this long-legged child was such a capable little sportswoman that she was continually being asked to go up on the hill to play with the Patterson children or the Davis girls, all older but by no means her equal. From taking on and defeating the Pattersons and the Davises, it was but a step to being asked to engage some older players. At last one sunny afternoon in midsummer Mrs. Farley was officially invited up to see Florence play with Mrs. Jenkins, a player at one time of national repute. Knowing nothing at all of games or sport, Mrs. Farley sat upon the porch of the clubhouse a silent and aloof figure, until the moment when her off-spring came up the path to the steps, her face red but her manner triumphant, her pigtails damp with perspiration, but her bearing that of a conqueror. Behind her labored the clumsy Mrs. Jenkins, tired, panting, exhausted; Mrs. Jenkins who never knew Mrs. Farley when the latter's Ford was parked behind her new magnificent limousine each night for the five-ten. That particular afternoon, however, she was unusually cordial.

"Give that child of yours time, Mrs. Farley, and she'll be a great player some day. I know what I'm telling you, too."

Mrs. Farley smiled serenely and put her arm around Florence's moist back. In her victorious daughter she was beginning to see an opening to the Country Club and to Plainville society.

3.

The Farleys joined the Country Club the next spring. Their open Ford was even seen once or twice at the Saturday night dances, parked each evening near the gorgeous new limousine of Mrs. Jenkins. More often than not, however, it was left at home, and they went in someone else's car. For as seasons merged into one another and Jim Farley's infant grew older and bolder, it became apparent to everyone with eyes to see that she was a player of real promise, a player who could defeat many of the men about the Club. At the end of several years Florence Farley was a name to conjure with in Plainville; if you could defeat the Farley child your ability needed no further discussion. You were immediately put down as a very useful player. In fact, so well known did Florence become about town that it was practically necessary, as Mrs. Farley explained to Jim one night, for them to have a new car, and a closed one at that. When Jim mumbled that he couldn't afford to while cotton was selling so low that it wasn't worth picking off the bushes, his wife reminded him that for Florence's sake they couldn't afford not to. This settled the argument.

It was fortunate that they did have that closed car when the Pattersons suggested that they all go over to Jamestown where Lucile Patterson and Florence could play in the junior tournament being held for the first time at the Jamestown Country Club. After much planning and consulting, the eight-mile trip across country was undertaken. Lucile was put out of the play by eleven o'clock in the morning. Mrs. Patterson remembered a luncheon engagement and hurried away shortly afterward, leaving her daughter to return with Mrs. Farley and Florence and the Cup at seven-ten. By the time they got home the news had spread all about Plainville; Jim Farley, who had to walk home from the station, heard it the moment he stepped off the train. Three people called out to him the good news as he walked up Pleasant Street; in fact, the whole town was aware of the feat of his child. He had supper waiting for them when they returned, tired but happy.

"A damned good performance for the kid," he said, as he kissed her with delight. "Good child."

Nor was Mrs. Farley any less pleased than her husband. But had they known that their troubles were starting, they might have been more sober in their happiness. Two weeks later Mr. George P. Clements, the president of the Club, called upon the Farleys one evening to extend his congratulations. In the course of the conversation he also exposed plans under way for adventures in more distant fields.

"We were thinking, that is, a number of us were thinking, of sending Florence down to compete in the National Junior Championships at Hot Springs next summer."

"Ooohh," interjaculated Florence impulsively. "Ooohh, Mother, wouldn't that be wonderful?" To her Hot Springs was as far away as Russia. Or Fairyland. But she stopped short when she observed the distress upon her parent's usually placid countenance.

"I'm sorry, Mr. Clements, but who could go down with her? Of course, the trip would be dandy, and I'd just love for her to go, but I couldn't think of letting her go that far with just a lot of girls."

"Certainly not, Mrs. Farley, certainly not. We intend to have you both go."

Then Mrs. Farley *was* shocked. "Why, Mr. Clements! Both of us! It would last a week. That would cost, that would cost . . . why . . . a hundred dollars!"

The President of the Country Club was unmoved. Quietly he agreed that it would.

"Yes, yes, p'raps. But you see it's this way, Mrs. Farley. They's a number of us prominent men about town been watching your little girl now for some time. We've all of us noticed the progress she's made and we're anxious to encourage it. Wanna encourage sport among the youngsters. Fine thing, athletics. Teaches 'em to be, you know, manly, fair play, all that sort of thing. And then besides"—here he leaned slightly toward Jim Farley as though a mere woman could hardly understand the details of business—"And then, besides, it's mighty good properganda for the town, mighty good properganda to have a little girl like Florence get her name in the papers occasionally. Why, they's any number of folks never heard of Plainville until she won that title the other day over to Jamestown. I understand the week after that we got a lot of inquiries for the new real-estate development back of Johnson's woods; hadn't had any prospects for that property for two years. Now Mr. Simmonds, the president of the Trust Company, you know he's influential in the Chamber of Commerce too, well, he thinks he, that is we, I mean they could find ways and means to get you and Florence down there to Hot Springs without it costing you or Mr. Farley one red cent. Not one cent. Do you see?" And he paused for a moment to allow the combined munificence of the Chamber of Commerce and the President of the Trust Company to take effect. It took effect immediately.

Mrs. Farley saw. She saw for the moment even more than Mr. Clements did. And the sight dazzled her somewhat. Mr. Clements, thinking that she was dazzled only by the prospect of a trip to Hot Springs, pressed home the argument.

"And a first-rate vacation, too, Mrs. Farley. Not but what I'm sure our little girl here wouldn't bring us back some more glory, heh, heh, heh . . ."

The little girl was not as sure as he was. But a trip to Hot Springs! . . . They went next summer as planned.

It was at Hot Springs during the Junior Championships that they first met Duncan Fletcher, the Vice-President of the Eastern Association, and a power in the sport. Duncan Fletcher was a suave young mucker with a million dollars from his father, and clothes and manners from a New York tailor. His one ambition in school and college had been to become a champion; early in his career it became evident that he had neither the persistence nor the patience; accordingly he gave up this desire and decided that, if he could not be a champion, at least he could be the friend of champions. His eye was fixed ultimately upon the presidency of the National Association; little by little he had climbed up from being a mere delegate from his own club to being a sectional delegate, a councilman, then a director, and finally one of the two vice-presidents of the Eastern Association. His next step was a minor office in the National Association; he was a hand-shaker par excellence, knew everyone, made himself known to everyone; and under the circumstances it was not surprising that he happened to bump into Florence and her mother the morning after they arrived. What surprised them, and also flattered them slightly, was the fact that he knew all their history.

Ten minutes of conversation with Mrs. Farley convinced Duncan Fletcher that he was in luck. They had arrived in the rain the previous night without hotel accommodations, their reservations having been carelessly made in the name of Mrs. Hurley. Players were all accommodated ("special rate to players and their families at the Alhambra during the tournament," page 8, circular of the championships) in the Annex. The Annex was directly over the kitchen; sleep was impossible there after five A.M. No one had spoken to them, practice was difficult to obtain, a cold west wind was blowing and, in short, Mrs. Farley was ready to return home. In fact, a timetable with trains marked was in her hand when Duncan Fletcher addressed them. During those next few moments of crisis the Vice-President of the Eastern Association was at his best; he displayed that marvelous executive ability which was to win him such a prominent place in the world of sport. A quarter of an hour later he had secured a suite for them in the main building at no extra cost, obtained tape and bound up Florence's blistered hand with care and skill, seen that they had a good table in the dining room, and installed a dozen roses in their sitting room. Naturally, mother and daughter were charmed by his attention and a flattery not too obtuse.

"Just the nicest man," as Mrs. Farley wrote home that night to Mr. Farley on the monogrammed paper of the hotel.

And so he was. Possibly, however, Duncan Fletcher's niceness would have been more to his credit had he not noticed Florence work out that morning from a vantage spot on the clubhouse porch. That was before he had tried to make himself useful, before he made inquiries at the desk about the little girl in the lemon-colored sweater and the insignificant woman sitting watching her in a rocking chair on the veranda. Mr. Fletcher was a gentleman with a distinct eye to the future.

The championships lasted six days, during which Duncan Fletcher was an ever-present help in time of trouble. On the last afternoon, the afternoon of the finals, when Florence returned to the clubhouse with her National Junior Championship, flushed, happy, triumphant, she was presented with a bouquet of roses tied in satin ribbon, more roses than she could carry. The runner-up, who was badly beaten, was also presented with an enormous bunch which she laid aside, remarking, "I'd have preferred a better score and fewer flowers."

Luckily the Vice-President of the Eastern Association did not hear this catty remark. He was at the moment telling Florence's mother that he knew from the start that the child had it in her. This was the exact truth. Nor was his delight in her victory in the least disingenuous, his enthusiasm one bit forced. Mr. Duncan Fletcher knew a good thing when he saw it.

4.

Some eight months later Plainville was honored by a visit from the Vice-President of the Eastern Association. This visit, which took place in the living room of the Farley home, was attended by Mr. Farley (reduced to silence and marveling at his wife's wonderful ability to get things for Florence without paying for them), that good lady, and Florence herself, just a bit dazed at the prospect unfolding itself before her. Naturally Mr. Clements as the President of Florence's home club was also present, rubbing his hands in delight and importance. Ever since her picture had appeared in the Sunday Rotogravure Section as "Suburban Miss Who Wins Title, Happy Florence Farley of Plainville, N.Y., at Hot Springs," Mr. Clements had had the Chamber of Commerce behind him to a man.

Mr. Fletcher, however, saw visions of the future in fresh woods and pastures new. He imagined himself, without too much effort, described as the "man who discovered Florence Farley." In fact, immediately after her victory in the Junior Championships Mr. Fletcher explained to all the newspapermen who came to his dinner—"just a small, informal affair, boys"—that he had found her in a little country town outside New York and, recognizing her ability at once with his keen tactical eye, had sent her down to Hot Springs on his own initiative. He has told this story so often now and it has been printed so much that he believes it himself. So does everyone else, including Mrs. Farley and Florence.

"Well, Mrs. Farley, of course you know best; but it seems to me that in a way you really owe it to Florence to give up this next summer to her and let her play in the National Championships. Frankly, I don't think I've ever seen such a promising youngster, not since Miss Benton at any rate. And next season, next season, you know, are the Olympics in Berlin. A great chance for her to have a trip abroad, and you too; it's a fine education. If she does well this summer I'm almost sure, in fact, I can almost guarantee that she will be sent over by the Association."

Mrs. Farley's mind was dancing, dancing, but her face was calm and undisturbed. "Well, I hardly know whether we could arrange to devote a whole summer to it, practicing and so forth. And then there's Florence's singing. She has made so much progress in the past six months I sort of hate to interrupt all that. And Mr. Farley's vacation, he likes to have us go to the camp with him; don't you, Jim?"

Mr. Farley gulped, swallowed hard as the eyes of the room were upon him, some almost resentfully it seemed, and nodded. He could not speak.

"Why, Jim Farley would be the proudest man in this whole county if his little girl was to win the national title, wouldn't you, Jim?" interposed Mr. Clements in an overpowering voice.

The truth was that, thanks to Mr. Clements' aid and assistance, Jim Farley was now a member of the club car which always was attached to the eight-one and the five-ten. It was also true that since his introduction into this society he had lost about a hundred and fourteen dollars at bridge, most of it to Mr. Clements, who held more than one bad debt, a subject on which Mr. Farley had neglected to inform his family. In a feeble voice he supported the arguments adduced by Mr. Fletcher for his daughter's career.

"As for the singing, she can study while she's abroad next summer at the Olympics. Certainly, study mornings, y'know. A few weeks under Lebaudy or Obendorfer is worth ten years from some hack over this side." Mr. Fletcher voiced his opinions about musical education with conviction. "Honestly, Mrs. Farley, if you don't take advantage of this opportunity you'll regret it all your life."

Mrs. Farley was impressed; but she was not a lady to take steps without being sure of things. Accordingly she remarked tentatively, "But so much money, Mr. Fletcher, all this time practicing, and then going way out there to Omaha for the National Championships—"

"Not a word about money," said Mr. Fletcher with the air of a person who is waving aside a subject slightly obscene. "Not a word. You see, the Eastern Association has a special fund for just such purposes. We send you and Florence west about a month before the tournament begins, to get acclimated, and then on the way you'll stop off at one or two invitation affairs, select affairs in the bigger places. You'll meet some mighty nice people, Mrs. Farley, just the best kind of people in Chicago and St. Louis."

If Mrs. Farley had had any doubts from the start, which she had not, this last sentence would have definitely erased them. For some years she had been hoping in a vague way to be able to develop Florence's voice; but as she told Jim Farley that evening in bed, Florence was growing up, and it was a chance for her to meet some really well-bred people. He agreed, suggested that he take his vacation when they return, and remarked that business was none too good at the moment anyhow.

So Mrs. Farley and Florence went west. Of all their campaigns they still look on this as the happiest; for the little girl in pigtails found everything so new and strange, found everyone so cordial and hospitable, found conditions for playing so perfect that she enjoyed herself enormously, more in fact than she was ever to enjoy herself in the future when the duties and responsibilities of being a champion were always with her. Her game also progressed; she suffered one or two defeats at the hands of local players in minor tournaments, just enough to make her work hard at strengthening her weak points. She practiced assiduously, asked advice from older players, and by the time the Championships rolled round was playing better than she had ever played in all her life.

Now her mother had a task to restrain that eager, impetuous child. Her duty it was to see that Florence played enough and not too much, that she ate the proper food, that she went to bed early and got up early, that she took every morning the exercises the doctor had prescribed for those recalcitrant muscles, in short, that she lived the life which would mean victory. Each day for weeks before the tournament Mrs. Farley walked over to the club with Florence, sat there when she was practicing, took her back to the hotel, first making sure that she was well wrapped up against a possible cold. And gradually, little though she knew about sports, Mrs. Farley began to note the improvement in her daughter's game. Little by little it was borne in upon her that this child of hers had the makings of a champion. Perhaps, after all, Florence had best give up the idea of a singing career. Was she not destined for greater things?

Meanwhile Mr. Duncan Fletcher had not neglected to keep the press informed of the progress of "My little protégée," as he used to call Florence on every possible occasion. But even the newspapermen were unprepared for her successes in that tournament. She went through the first three days with ease, defeated her opponents without difficulty, and on the next-to-last day put out a former national titleholder. Mrs. Wing, it was true, was no longer in the top class; she was still good enough to make trouble for most players. That afternoon lived long in Mrs. Farley's memory; the crowd deserting the other contestants to watch her picturesque child in pigtails, the murmurs and rumors and reports flying about the clubhouse, the whisper from someone behind her that Mrs. Wing had just been badly beaten by "that infant from New York." And the afternoon lived with her for another reason.

He caught her while she was waiting for Florence to dress after the match. Yes, she was Mrs. Farley. His card said he was Mr. Raymond K. Noble, Western Manager for the *Daily Mail* Syndicate. He had been ordered by his New York office to see Mrs. Farley because the manager in the main office saw in Florence a future national champion. Would she care to write for the *Daily Mail* Syndicate?

Mrs. Farley was shocked. Florence write? She couldn't spell c-a-t; composition was her weakest subject. And her writing was terrible, just simply terrible. Now if Mr. Noble had asked her to sing. . . . That gentleman smiled ever so slightly and explained that his company was not interested in singers. He also explained that in most editorial offices there were trained reporters who did much of the actual writing and could send proofs to Florence "for correction." He also explained that he did not himself believe that Florence was well known enough to the sporting public to begin writing immediately; but that next year if she won the title it was possible that the *Daily Mail* might find room for her in its pages. With great delicacy he offered Mrs. Farley a check for five hundred dollars and explained that to save her trouble personally he had drawn up a contract which she need merely sign as Florence's guardian. Mrs. Farley took the contract and looked at it a minute. Two years before she would have signed anything on Florence's behalf for fifty dollars. As it was, she replied that she would be glad to take the contract back to her hotel, study it, and let him know her wishes in the matter. For in the background she had a vision of the astute Mr. Fletcher coming to her aid.

Inside of the hour Mr. Fletcher was actually reading the contract in her bedroom in the hotel. With a superb gesture he read it, tore it in two, and tossed it to the floor. Mrs. Farley was impressed, as he intended, and thanked herself more than ever that she had been cautious. Could Florence write and still maintain her amateur standing? Oh, yes, yes indeed. But that contract? Never! Sign no contract which tied one up at a salary of only three thousand a year for five years. That was Mr. Fletcher's advice. He explained that the manager was correct in asserting that most athletic stars had help and assistance in their literary endeavors. He departed, assuring Mrs. Farley that other contracts would not be long in presenting themselves. Mrs. Farley was learning rapidly. When Florence the next afternoon went brilliantly down to defeat before the best woman player in the country, she learned more things.

Three gentlemen from other syndicates were waiting for her at her hotel when she returned, while Mr. Noble was there with yet another and a more generous contract. Mrs. Farley took them all, as well as the cards of their representatives, and retired to her room, saying nothing. On her table was a wire from her husband:

COMPANY IN FINANCIAL DIFFICULTIES LOST JOB BETTER RETURN
IMMEDIATELY JIM.

Mrs. Farley sat looking out the window while Florence dressed for her first dance, the championship ball at the clubhouse for which as a special favor she was to be allowed to wear her hair up. Carefully the mother spread those four contracts out on the table, carefully she studied them, a look in her eyes that the wives of the commuters in Plainville would never have recognized. Then she slowly took the receiver off the hook. From the bathroom Florence heard her mother's voice, vaguely realizing that it was not the voice of her mother at all.

"Central, 8900. . . . Mr. Townsend, please. . . . Mr. Townsend? This is Mrs. Farley; yes, Florence Farley's mother. Mr. Townsend, we expect to leave for home tomorrow at noon. I wonder if you could come round to the hotel for a few minutes before we leave and see me? At ten? That's fine. Ten o'clock. Good-by, Mr. Townsend."

5.

Florence Farley's hair was up on her head when they went south for the National Championships that next summer; but her mother was still the person to be consulted whenever a decision was required.

"My pictures for your magazine? Oooohh, I don't know; you'll have to ask Mother. A dance at the club next week? I'd just adore to go; but I'd better speak about it to Mother first, she rarely lets me go out when I'm in training, you know. The contract for next season? Oooohh, Mr. Townsend, that's entirely up to Mother." Where she played before the Championships, what homes they would or would not live at (for wherever the Farleys went now they were honored and welcome guests)— everything was for her mother to decide. Incidentally, it was Mrs. Farley's idea, when she read about the benefit concert to be given, that Florence should put on her best hat and interview the manager. Florence was surprised at the warmth of the reception she received. Mrs. Farley was not surprised.

It was her first appearance in public. Florence's voice was young, fresh, powerful, if unequal and untrained. But the songs she sang were wisely chosen; they were not beyond her range, and she had the natural self-possession of one who has long appeared as a performer before crowds. Moreover, she was young, pretty, attractive. For weeks before the concert she was advertised and billboarded; the concert hall was jammed with an audience that came out of curiosity. Of ten newspapers which commented upon the concert the next morning, nine spoke of Miss Florence Farley, and all used the word "versatile" at least once.

Mrs. Farley had by this time acquired no small share of business acumen. It was necessary inasmuch as her husband possessed none whatsoever. Jim Farley was looking for his third job while his wife and daughter were visiting in Newport or Palm Beach, meeting titled Europeans and the stock-market nobility of the United States with poise and discrimination. This sort of thing was all very well; but Mrs. James Farley had her eye on a greater goal. When Florence went to college that fall she took singing lessons four days a week with the best instructor the neighboring city provided.

All this was a drain on the Farley family resources. Perhaps one should say upon the family's resources upon the female side. But the Dean was so helpful; having in some strange manner heard of Florence's athletic and artistic record, he succeeded in procuring for her a four-year scholarship devoted to "needy and deserving students of the Baptist faith." Mrs. Farley herself was a Methodist, but luckily she had no religious intolerance whatsoever. And it was nice to have Florence in a college where she could get singing lessons all winter; the way in which that girl neglected her voice culture in summer was really awful!

It was during her freshman year that the question of the Olympics arose. Mr. Fletcher, now the President of the National Association, telephoned Mrs. Farley that Florence was expected to sail with the rest of the team in June, a week before her final examinations. This meant losing the credit for her whole year's work. Even Mrs. Farley, who could hardly be said to be indifferent to the many advantages, educational and otherwise, promised by a trip to Europe, was aghast at the thought of a season in school gone for nothing. Accordingly she took the next train to consult the Dean. Once again she found him more than kind—such a nice man, a real nice man, as she told Jim on her return. Jim, who was now looking for his fifth job and was getting to be known as "Florence Farley's father," grunted when he heard that familiar phrase.

"H'm, why yes, Mrs. Farley," said the Dean in his private office, "yes, I think we can arrange that difficulty. Here in the University we have what are called travel credits, credits granted when a student wishes to spend time doing research work at the Sorbonne and Oxford or Cambridge. Now of course, this isn't exactly what Miss Farley is going over for; but I have no doubt in view of the favorable publicity that will accrue, and considering the help her name will be to our new Endowment Drive for the University, that it can be arranged satisfactorily."

And so it was. The day before they sailed Mrs. Farley interviewed Mr. Townsend. Plans had already been made for the Berlin correspondent of the *Mail* syndicate to "assist" Florence while she was in Europe; every day during the two-month period a story was to be wired back to New York. For this work Mrs. Farley naturally felt that her daughter should have more than the original contract specified. Mr. Townsend, however, was not impressed with the argument that a trip to the Olympics had not been foreseen at the time the papers had been signed.

"Well, you know best," sighed Mrs. Farley. She had progressed a long, long way from the astonished mother who imagined that it would cost a hundred dollars to keep herself and Florence for a week at Hot Springs! At the back of her mind was Jim Farley, at that moment tramping the streets of the city for still another job; before her eyes was the picture of the little white house on that back road in Plainville which needed a coat of paint, a new shingled roof, a decent furnace. . . . "Well, of course you must decide, Mr. Townsend. I was only thinking that the MacIntyre Syndicate has been anxious to secure Florence's services for some time, and as her contract with you expires this coming fall—"

"Wait a minute, Mrs. Farley, just wait a minute, please. Now let's talk this over quietly. I didn't say your terms weren't reasonable; I think they are. It's the boss I have to convince, you know. We never paid such a big sum to anyone in sport before. Don't know what he'd say about it. I mean he likes Miss Farley's stuff, and all that, but—well, I'll tell you what to do. You're sailing on the *Luxuria* at midnight? Suite B, A deck. Fine. Now I tell you what. I'll come down to the boat by ten, at the latest, with his answer. And don't you do anything about next year until you hear from me. Understand? Those MacIntyre people—I'd hate to see Miss Farley tied up with a gang of pirates like that, honest I would."

The *Luxuria* sailed at midnight with the Farley family, or at least the female portion of it. The next morning the *Daily Mail* in a large half-page advertisement announced that Miss Florence Farley would write every day for the next two months "a complete, accurate, and lively description of the Olympics from the viewpoint of the competitor."

In Mr. Townsend's safe was a new contract running for another two years. It carried a figure in ink, written over a typewritten figure, and was for exactly three times as much as Miss Florence Farley had been receiving previously.

At the moment that the *Luxuria* was being warped out of her pier, the Berlin correspondent of the *Daily Mail* was sitting in a small office in the Friedrichstrasse, waving a long telegram at his assistant.

"Gotta write all the stuff for this girl champion, Farley. What the hell do they think I am, besides all my regular work to shove this on me? I'll send 'em what I please, that's what I'll do, and if they don't like it they can fire me. Sick of this job; the more work you do the more they give you. Can you imagine that, Jake, writing stuff for a schoolgirl?"

6.

Neither Florence nor her mother to this day can tell you how they happened to meet Cynthia Gladesborough in Berlin, who introduced them, or where they were presented. Somebody at a tea, a dinner dance, somebody after or during the Games brought them together; the meeting proved mutually beneficial. Lady Gladesborough, who it appeared had no home, was at home quite as much in Berlin and Rome as in London. She had a bigger, a broader conception of sport and the function of sport than even Mrs. Farley; she could look ahead and visualize the future in a manner that was impossible for the little lady from Plainville, New York.

Cynthia, Lady Gladesborough, was the sort of woman it did not help to be seen with in public in London. Long before Mrs. Farley discovered this, the Englishwoman had proved her indispensability in many ways. Left without money after the War, with nothing but a title and her wits to keep her from starvation, the only remaining member of the Gladesborough family had done rather well by herself in the years since the Armistice. Did you wish to be presented at Court? See Cynthia Gladesborough. Did you wish a shooting place for August where you would be in and not out of society? Cynthia Gladesborough would procure it for you. Was it your wish to be distinguished during the London season? Anything could be managed provided you knew Cynthia Gladesborough . . . and had money.

Berlin was a field less fertile to her endeavors than London, which was perhaps the reason why she happened to fasten on Florence and her mother. For several days she studied them, wondering how they could be made profitable, until she heard from the parent of the daughter's remarkable versatility. A singer? Just the thing. That next afternoon she was back with a proposition so delicately veiled, so gently insinuated, that one felt it would be cruel to refuse. In fact, she always made you feel you were doing her a favor. It appeared that Lady Mountaspen, the wife of the British Ambassador, had seen Florence at the Games and had been so struck with her charm. Would dear Mrs. Farley bring her daughter to a small dinner at the Embassy, and perhaps she could induce Florence to sing one or two of those topping Negro spirituals afterward? Just one or two. Needless to say, dear Mrs. Farley would not refuse, would understand how the Ambassadress felt, and could accept this small check. For some pet charity, you know. Once the thing was done the second time was easier by far.

It was at the Embassy party that they met Mary Garden. The great singer listened with interest and attention to the fresh-faced girl who had that afternoon jumped from being a Champion to becoming a World's Champion, and said conventionally nice things to the mother afterward. From this the story spread that Florence had "studied under Mary Garden," as the billboards put it later on at home. What with the singing and writing, their stay in Berlin was not unprofitable, and on the whole enjoyable. But the best part of their trip was the visit to London, where they planned to spend a week and actually remained, thanks to the indefatigable Cynthia Gladesborough, until just before college opened in the fall.

"Have you heard Florence Farley sing?" "Have you seen Florence Farley play yet?" These were the questions London society asked itself continually during their visit. She gave a few exhibitions, more than living up to her reputation as a World's Champion, mercilessly beating the Englishwomen pitted against her. Unlike those toughened, tanned, weather-beaten specimens of British womanhood who opposed her on the fields of sport, she was still an eager, happy, attractive schoolgirl, smiling, frowning, anxious, impetuous, joyous, and dismayed in turn. She was a girl, not a human machine. London, and particularly London society and that part of London society eager for lions, had almost forgotten that a female champion in sport could flatter the lust of the eye. In ten days Florence Farley had captured the city. Her name was in every newspaper, her picture in every magazine, her songs upon every lip.

She and her mother were feted and entertained wherever they went. Her fees rose with her popularity. To dine with Florence Farley and her mother was an expensive undertaking; to be asked to dinner when they were present was indeed a testimony to your importance in the great world. Several weeks before they left, a concert manager called upon Mrs. Farley with suggestions for one afternoon appearance. He was sent packing by Cynthia Gladesborough, who returned late in the day with a manager willing to put Florence on for five matinees in succession.

THE ONLY CHANCE TO SEE AND HEAR THE VERSATILE WORLD'S CHAMPION.

HEAR FLORENCE FARLEY SING HER FAMOUS AMERICAN NEGRO SPIRITUALS.

The performance was adequately advertised, and before daybreak of the first afternoon a queue was waiting in a chilling drizzle for the doors to open ten hours later. Seats were obtainable only from Keith, Prowse and Co., at an amazing premium; hundreds were turned away at each matinee.

Meanwhile back in Plainville, Jim Farley was parking his new straight eight in the garage which had just been built under his careful supervision. He had ceased looking for a job.

7.

By the end of Florence's second year as Champion of the World, her relationship to her mother had undergone a subtle change. The change was more real than apparent. Externally they were just the same "good pals" as ever. Outwardly Florence and her mother were inseparable; whatever they did, her mother's opinion was requested, wherever they went, her mother was consulted. At any rate in public. But in private, in their twin beds in the hotel room, in the privacy of their suite on A deck of the *Luxuria* (the one occupied by the Prince when he crossed in '22) an astonished world would have learned that the mother of Happy Florence Farley, the Girl with the Laughing Voice, simply did not count in the general scheme of things. Florence was her own manager now.

Nor could one deny that the Champion was able to take care of herself in a broken field, either. The years of exacting discipline to master a sport in many ways as complicated as an art or a profession, the constant subjugation of herself to her work, the encounters with the keenest minds in championship matches, minds which had to be mastered and subdued before their possessors were worsted physically—all this had taught her many a stern lesson from which she did not fail to draw profit. Her relations with the press, with the officials of the Association upon whose favors so much depended, with her various business associates, were all nicely adjusted and attuned. She knew the men and policies as well as the politics of the National Association as her mother could never know or hope to know them; she kept a control of affairs that her mother could never keep and, using that lady as a shield, she ran her life upon the narrow ridge between amateurism and professionalism with a skill and hardihood that even her parent, who was frequently exasperated and always uneasy about her, was forced to admire.

Thus the telephone rang in their private suite. The secretary—Florence's first big dispute with her mother was over the secretary, it was also her first big victory—answered.

"Mr. Fletcher, Miss Farley."

"Oh—I'm too busy. Tell him to call later—no, give me the phone, I suppose I'd better talk now. . . . Hello, Duncan. What's that? Not today, my dear. I don't think I can. No, I'm all tied up today, Duncan. Well, let me see. Come up at one and take me to lunch. No, I'll meet you, meet you at the Ritz. Yes, at one. Good-by."

"Florence!" her mother expostulated. "How rude you're getting to be. Asking Mr. Fletcher to take you to lunch at the Ritz. And besides, he is such a prominent man in the Association, you'll get into trouble—"

"Well, if Dunc Fletcher wants to see me he'll have to buy me a meal, that's all. Besides, he isn't prominent any more. Or he won't be after next winter. Mr. Baker's going in. Yes, they're getting Fletcher out; he's much too old-fashioned for this crowd. They need some new blood, wake 'em up a little."

Her mother gasped at the news. Mr. Fletcher out of the Association? It was as if the President of the United States had suddenly died. As if the country had gone mad. Mr. Fletcher out. She could not foresee their future without his help and assistance, so closely had he been bound up in their lives for years past. Again the telephone tinkled.

"Mr. Baker," droned the secretary. "Oh, just a minute please, Mr. Baker." And she handed the instrument to Florence, who indeed had reached for it as his name was spoken.

The voice of the Champion was as different when she answered from the casual tone she used with Mr. Fletcher as her game was different against different kinds of players. "Ooohh, Mr. Baker, it's so good of you to bother to call me up. . . . Yes, I want to see you, too. . . . There are just hundreds of things I must ask your advice about. . . . Baltimore? Well, I don't know about Baltimore; but perhaps you—that's one of the things I'm anxious to discuss with you. . . . You don't? . . . Oh, he's a friend of yours. Of course, if he's a friend of yours that makes all the difference in the world. I'd love to play Baltimore. But when can I see you, Mr. Baker? Today. . . . That'll be delightful. . . . Could you come up and have some tea with me here at five? Yes, at five. . . . Don't send up your name, just come up, 1486. At five. I'll be looking forward to seeing you. Good-by."

The doorbell jingled. On tiptoe the secretary left the room. She returned a minute later. "The young lady from the *Times-Dispatch,* Miss Farley. That interview, you know. Mr. Smith arranged for it last week."

"A girl? But I thought—I imagined they were sending a man. I just hate girl reporters. Horrid things. Well, I suppose I'll have to see her. Take her into the parlor. And then get that interview out of the file and read it to me while I'm doing my hair."

Ten minutes later the girl reporter, notebook in hand, was getting from the lips of Miss Farley, the World's Champion, an interview which would please any managing editor.

"Yes, I take my sport, you know, just as a game. My music is the principal thing in my life. Of course, I believe a champion has a duty, a great duty to the public who support games. . . . A duty to play fair, to win or lose with a smile. Yes, that's the chief thing about sport, isn't it? A message to the girls of America? Tell them not to take any game too seriously. That's what I always say to my Mumsy. Remember it's just a game, win or lose. Now music, that's a thing you can devote your life to, can't you? With me, my sport has always been secondary to my music, even when I was a teeny, weeny child. I remember Mary Garden—oh, yes, I know her very well; you see she gave me the benefit of her great knowledge when I was in Berlin two years ago—well, I remember Mary saying to me once that whatever one loves one should make the really big thing in one's life. And I really love my music. Sport—oh, I've played off and on since I was ten, I think. Yes, but I always play in moderation.

"Engaged? To Lindbergh? Oh, dear, no. I just adore him; don't you? But we're simply friends, that's all. He likes to come out to the house when he's tired after a trip and have me sing, you know—sing something simple to him. My new songs? Some new spirituals. Negro spirituals, you know. I just think they're dandy, don't you? This one is new, 'Corn Chowder In De Cabin,' and so is this, 'Scrubbin' On De Ol' Washboard.' I got those from the dearest old mammy when I was playing in the Southern Championships in Tallahassee this spring. Mother thinks they're the best. You see I always talk all my songs over with Mumsy first. In fact I tell her everything—all my problems. She's the darlingest mother.

"The new President of the Association. Mr. Baker? Oooohh, are you sure? You heard . . . you did? I just adore Mr. Baker. But you mustn't put that in the paper, will you? Mr. Fletcher was a lovely man, too. But Mr. Baker is—well, he's more dignified, isn't he? I mean he's more conservative. In a way. Not that I don't get along with Mr. Fletcher, oh, perfectly. We're old friends, very old friends. But I admire conservative people, don't you? I like all the officials, though; we never have the slightest difficulty. The amateur rule? Oh, no, there's never any trouble. I lean backward to observe all the rules of the Association—set an example; a champion should. Don't you think? Yes. Is that all? So good of you to take the trouble to come way up here on a hot day like this. Don't forget my message to the American girls, will you? Play fair. Don't take games too seriously. Lose or win with a smile. That's the one great lesson sport teaches us. Thank you so much. Good-by. Good-by. . . .

"God, what a woman! Miss Jackson! *Miss Jackson!* Get hold of Mr. Baker. How do I know where he is? Tell him to come round at four instead of five. And ask him to bring his car."

8.

No girl ever won the championship of the United States eight times in succession. Miss Florence Farley was getting ready to do so, and what she set her mind upon doing she seldom failed in. At the moment she was seated in front of the same dressing table she had been seated before as a child with pigtails down her back when she went out for her first championship. Eight years later she was Champion of the World, devoting more attention to her countenance than she did when she appeared upon the concert stage, an event which happened with greater frequency as the years rolled by. The only difference in the room was that her mother, who had occupied the wicker armchair in previous years, was no longer present. Today it held precariously Miss Farley's secretary, notebook in hand. Upon the floor was a pile of opened letters.

From an array of bottles, tubes, and glass jars with glass stoppers on the narrow table, she took cold cream out of a square white receptacle marked "Cleansing," spreading it carefully over her face. This, by the way, is the cream you have seen advertised as assisting Miss Florence Farley, Champion of the World, to keep freckles off her face under the hottest sun.

"From Nelson's Stores," droned the secretary. "A concert, on the twenty-ninth, with two stars from the Metropolitan."

"Price?" said the Champion, briskly, between rubs.

"No mention."

"Write 'em and tell 'em our price. No, hold on . . . they've got lots of money. Write and ask their terms."

Meanwhile she took another kind of cream from another bottle marked "Tissue," then with the aid of a towel wiped them both off with careful, adept movements. This, by the way, is the cream you may have noticed advertised on the billboards as used by Florence Farley, the World's Champion, to preserve a perfect complexion.

"Gunmetal Soap, testimonial. Five hundred, name, thousand for picture, advertising display, and interview why Gunmetal benefits face pores."

The World's Champion was in the act of grabbing a bottle bearing the magic word "Astringent." A paper label pasted on the bottle bore the words, "As used by Florence Farley." She paused a moment, the container suspended in the air, and dictated a reply.

"Miss Farley directs me to say she would be happy to see you Tuesday at four-thirty at the Ritz to discuss the matter contained in yours of the whatever it is. Next."

"Indianapolis, Lincoln, Nebraska, and Los Angeles want you the same week next month. You have that held open for the Newport party with Mr. Duggan and his family . . ."

"Never mind that bird. What's the best of the three? Los Angeles? Yes, they know how to spend money out there. All right. Wire them to send reservations on the Sunset Limited from New Orleans the week before the tournament. And we go to New Orleans, tell them, on that fast train of the Pennsy. Next."

With a deft hand she touched the tops of the bottles and boxes on the table and picked out a square cardboard container bearing the entrancing name, "Farley Flower Powder, Spanish Rachel Shade." The white chalk suffused her tortured face. There was a knock at the door.

"Yes." Her voice had the timbre and the sweetness that had made her name famous to music lovers the world over, that had thrilled audiences (and managers) from San Diego to Albany.

"It's me, Florence."

The voice of the Champion dulled perceptibly. "Oh. Come in."

Her mother entered. "I just wanted to know, dear . . . I just wondered where we were going next month. Your father telephoned this morning and thought maybe when you were through with the Championships we might all be able to spend a week at the old camp. You know we haven't been there for years."

"Can't, Mumsy. Los Angeles." And she continued with earnestness and diligence the application of the lipstick.

"Across the continent in mid-July? Why, Florence! I thought it was all fixed up . . . I thought you were going to Newport with those Providence people."

"Uhuh. I had it down for Newport, but the Los Angeles crowd have the dough. They put up a proposition that's too good to refuse."

"Florence," said her mother, reprovingly but also a little timidly. "Florence, you oughtn't to talk that way. It's disgraceful."

"There you go again, Mumsy. Cut the Civil War stuff, will you? I'm not in this for my health exclusively, understand? And what's more, I haven't got much more time left as champion, either."

A knock at the door. "Miss Farley. Are you ready? They're waiting outside."

"Com*ming,* com*ming.* All ready," sang out the Champion in the voice that made the newspapers call her Happy Florence Farley, the Girl with the Laughing Voice.

"Come along, Mother, dear." And the Champion emerged from the dressing room with her arm about her mother's waist. Inseparable, those two!

Gene Tunney

My Fights with Jack Dempsey

In 1926, 120,000 people were on hand in Philadelphia to witness the first Gene Tunney–Jack Dempsey fight. The rematch a year later in Chicago's Soldier Field drew almost the same number. The Tunney-Dempsey fights were two of the most memorable events during sports' first golden age. They were memorable not only because of the pairing of two great fighters, but also because of the distinctions in their styles both in and out of the ring. Dempsey was the Manassa Mauler, a sometime copper miner and sometime hobo who articulated best with his fists. Tunney was the student of the sport, a learned boxer who relaxed by reading Shakespeare. Each fighter had his backers: Tunney, the intellectual crowd, Dempsey, the working class. Some twenty years after the events, Tunney, the most erudite of heavyweight champions, recalls with remarkable clarity the two historic fights.

The laugh of the twenties was my confident insistence that I would defeat Jack Dempsey for the heavyweight championship of the world. To the boxing public, this optimistic belief was the funniest of jokes. To me, it was a reasonable statement of calculated probability, an opinion based on prize-ring logic.

The logic went back to a day in 1919, to a boat trip down the Rhine River. The First World War having ended in victory, the Army was sending a group of A.E.F. athletes to give exhibitions for doughboys in the occupation of the German Rhineland. I was light heavyweight champion of the A.E.F. Sailing past castles on the Rhine, I was talking with the Corporal in charge of the party. Corporal McReynolds was a peacetime sportswriter at Joplin, Missouri, one of those Midwestern newspapermen who combined talent with a copious assortment of knowledge. He had a consummate understanding of boxing, and I was asking him a question of wide interest in the A.E.F. of those days.

We had been hearing about a new prizefight phenomenon in the United States, a battler burning up the ring back home. He was to meet Jess Willard for the heavyweight championship. His name was Jack Dempsey. None of us knew anything about him, his rise to the challenging position for the title had been so swift. What about him? What was he like? American soldiers were interested in prizefighting. I was more than most—an A.E.F. boxer with some idea of continuing with a ring career in civilian life.

The Corporal said yes, he knew Jack Dempsey. He had seen Dempsey box a number of times, had covered the bouts for his Midwestern newspaper. Dempsey's career had been largely in the West.

"Is he good?" I inquired.

"He's tops," responded Corporal McReynolds. "He'll murder Willard."

"What's he like?" I asked.

The Corporal's reply was vividly descriptive. It won't mean anything to most people nowadays, but at that time it was completely revealing to anyone who read the sports pages. McReynolds said: "He's a big Jack Dillon."

I knew about Jack Dillon, as who didn't thirty years ago? He was a middleweight whose tactics in the ring were destructive assault—fast, shifty, hard-hitting, weaving in with short, savage punches, a knocker-out, a killer. Dillon even looked like Dempsey, swarthy, beetlebrowed, and grim—a formidable pair of Jacks.

I thought the revelation over for a moment, and recalled: "Jack Dillon was beaten by Mike Gibbons, wasn't he?"

"Yes," replied the Corporal. "I saw that bout. Gibbons was too good a boxer. He was too fast. His defense was too good. Dillon couldn't lay a glove on him."

Mike Gibbons was the master boxer of his time, the height of defensive skill, a perfectionist in the art of sparring.

I said to the Corporal: "Well, maybe Jack Dempsey can be beaten by clever boxing."

His reply was reflective, thought out. "Yes," he said, "when Dempsey is beaten, a fast boxer with a good defense will do it."

This, coming from a brainy sportswriter, who knew so much about the technique of the ring and who had studied the style of the new champion, aroused a breathless idea in me. My own ambition in the ring had always been skillful boxing, speed and defense—on the order of Mike Gibbons.

As a West Side kid fooling around with boxing gloves, I had been, for some reason of temperament, more interested in dodging a blow than in striking one. Fighting in preliminary bouts around New York, I had learned the value of skill in sparring. In A.E.F. boxing I had emphasized skill and defense—the more so as during this time I had hurt my hands. Previously I had been a hard hitter. Now, with damaged fists, I had more reason than ever to cultivate defensive sparring.

Sailing down the Rhine, I thought maybe I might be a big Mike Gibbons for the big Jack Dillon. It was my first inkling that someday I might defeat Jack Dempsey for the Heavyweight Championship of the World, which all assumed Jack was about to acquire.

This stuck in mind, and presently the time came when I was able to make some observation firsthand. I was one of the boxers on the card of that first Battle of the Century, the Dempsey-Carpentier fight. I was in the semifinal bout. This place of honor and profit was given to me strictly because of my service title. The ex-doughboys were the heroes of that postwar period, and the light heavyweight championship of the A.E.F. was great for publicity. I was ballyhooed as the "Fighting Marine."

Actually, I had no business in the bout of second importance on that occasion of the first Million Dollar Gate. I was an A.E.F. champ, but we service boxers knew well enough that our style of pugilism was a feeble amateur thing compared with professional prizefighting in the United States. The best of us were mere former prelim fighters, as I was. There were mighty few prominent boxers in Pershing's A.E.F. In World War II you saw champs and near-champs in uniform, but the draft was not so stern in such matters during the war against the Kaiser's Germany.

In the semifinal bout of the Dempsey-Carpentier extravaganza, I, with my bad hands, fought poorly. Nobody there could have dreamed of me as a possible future conqueror of the devastating champ—least of all Jack himself, if he had taken any notice of the semifinal battlers. I won on a technical K.O. from my opponent, but that was only because he was so bad—Soldier Jones of Canada, who, like myself, was in the big show only because he too had an army title—the war covering a multitude of sins.

After the bout, clad in a bathrobe, I crouched at one corner of the ring, and watched the Manassa Mauler exchange blows with the Orchid Man of France. As prize-ring history records, the bout was utterly one-sided; the frail Carpentier was hopelessly overmatched. But it afforded a good look at the Dempsey style.

The Corporal on the boat sailing down the Rhine had been exact in his description of Dempsey. The Champ was, in every respect, a big Jack Dillon—with all the fury and destruction implied by that. No wonder they called him the Man Killer. But, studying intently, I saw enough to confirm the Corporal's estimate that when Dempsey was defeated it would be by a skillful defensive boxer, a big Mike Gibbons. Correct defense would foil the shattering Dempsey attack.

This estimate was confirmed again and again during subsequent opportunities. I attended Dempsey fights, and studied motion pictures of them. More and more I saw how accurate defense could baffle the Man Killer's assault. The culmination was the Shelby, Montana, meeting of Dempsey and Tom Gibbons, the heavyweight younger brother of Mike. Tom, like Mike, was a consummate boxer, and Dempsey couldn't knock him out. For the first time in his championship and near-championship career, the Man Killer failed to flatten an opponent. The public, which had considered Tom Gibbons an easy mark, was incredulous and thought there must have been something peculiar about it. For me there was nothing peculiar, just final proof that good boxing could thwart the murder in the Dempsey fists. There was a dramatic twist in the fact that the final proof was given by a brother of Mike Gibbons.

At the Dempsey-Carpentier fight, I had seen one other thing. Another angle flashed, as at a corner of the ring I watched and studied. Famous in those days was the single dramatic moment, the only moment when the Orchid Man seemed to have a chance. That was when, in the second round, Carpentier lashed out with a right-hand punch. He was renowned for his right, had knocked out English champions with it. He hit Dempsey high on the jaw with all his power.

I was in a position to see the punch clearly and note how Carpentier threw it. He drew back his right like a pitcher with a baseball. The punch was telegraphed all over the place. Yet it landed on a vulnerable spot. How anybody could be hit with a right launched like that was mystifying to one who understood boxing. Dempsey went back on his heels, jarred. Carpentier couldn't follow up, and in a moment Jack was again on the relentless job of wrecking the Orchid Man with body blows. But it was a vivid demonstration that the champion could be hit with a right.

Dempsey was no protective boxer. He couldn't do defensive sparring. He relied on a shifty style, his own kind of defense, and couldn't be hit just any way. His weakness was that he could be nailed with a straight right. Later on, I saw this confirmed in other Dempsey battles. It was dramatized sensationally at the Polo Grounds when the powerful but clumsy Firpo smashed him with a right at the very beginning of the first round, and later blasted Dempsey out of the ring with right-hand punches—the Wild Bull of the Pampas almost winning the championship.

To me it signified that the strategy of defensive boxing might be supplemented by a right-hand punch—everything thrown into a right. It would never do for me to start mixing with the Champ in any knock-down, drag-out exchange of haymakers. He'd knock me out. It would have to be a surprise blow, and it could easily be that. Both Carpentier and Firpo, who had nailed the Champ, were noted for their right—all they had. But Jack would never suspect a Sunday punch from me, stepping in and trying to knock him out with a right.

I was catalogued not only as a defensive boxer but also as a light hitter, no punch. I might wear an opponent down and cut him to pieces, but I couldn't put him to sleep with a knockout slam. That had been true—previously. I had been going along with the handicap of bad hands. I could hit hard enough, but didn't dare for fear of breaking my hands. So I was a comparatively light hitter—and typed as one.

Finally, in desperation, I had to do something about my fragile hands. I went to a lumber camp in Canada for one winter and worked as a woodsman, chopping down trees. The grip of the ax was exercise for my damaged mitts. Months of lumber camp wood chopping and other hand exercises worked a cure. My hands grew strong and hard, my fists rugged enough to take the impact of as powerful a blow as I could land. In subsequent bouts I had little trouble with my hands. This I knew, and others might have been aware of the change, but I was tagged as a feather duster puncher—and that was that. The old philosophy of giving a dog a bad name.

Prizefight publicity often resorts to the ballyhoo of a secret punch, a surprise blow, nearly always a fraud—but I really had the chance. At the beginning of the first round I would step in and put everything I had in a right-hand punch, every ounce of strength. I might score a knockout, or the blow would daze the champion sufficiently to make it easier to outbox him the rest of the way.

I was, meanwhile, fighting my way to the position of challenger. I won the light heavyweight championship from Battling Levinsky and subsequently fought Carpentier, the Orchid Man, and went through a series of savage bouts with Harry Greb, one of the greatest of pugilists. In our first bout, Greb gave me a murderous mauling. In our last, I beat him almost as badly. After a long series of matches with sundry light heavies and heavies I went on to establish myself as heavyweight contender by defeating Tom Gibbons. It was dramatic irony that I earned my shot at the title at the expense of Tom, brother of my model, Mike.

Public opinion of my prospects with Dempsey was loud and summary. The champion is always the favorite, and Dempsey was one of the greatest champions, as destructive a hitter as the prize ring has ever known. He was considered unbeatable, and I was rated as a victim peculiarly doomed to obliteration, pathetic, absurd.

It was argued that I was a synthetic fighter. That was true. As a kid prelim battler, my interest had been in romantic competition and love of boxing, while holding a job as a shipping clerk with a steamship company. As a marine in France, my love of boxing and a distaste for irksome military duties after the armistice brought me back as a competitor in A.E.F. boxing tournaments. We gave our best to entertain our buddies and, incidentally, to avoid guard duty. After the war, when I had grown up, my purpose simply was to develop the sparring ability I had as a means of making money—seeing in the heavyweight championship a proud and profitable eminence.

They said I lacked the killer instinct—which was also true. I found no joy in knocking people unconscious or battering their faces. The lust for battle and massacre was missing. I had a notion that the killer instinct was really founded in fear, that the killer of the ring raged with ruthless brutality because deep down he was afraid.

Synthetic fighter, not a killer! There was a kind of angry resentment in the accusation. People might have reasoned that, to have arrived at the position of challenger, I must have won some fights. They might have noted that, while the champion had failed to flatten Tom Gibbons, I had knocked him out. But then the Dempsey-Gibbons bout was ignored as rather mystifying, one of "those things."

The prizefight "experts" were almost unanimous in not giving me a chance. The sportswriters ground out endless descriptions of the doleful things that would happen to me in the ring with Dempsey. There were, so far as I know, only a few persons prominent in sports who thought I might win, and said so. One was Bernard Gimbel, of the famous mercantile family, a formidable amateur boxer and a student of ring strategy. The others included that prince of sportswriters, the late

W. O. McGeehan, and a few lesser lights in the sportswriting profession. They picked me to win, and were ridiculed. The consensus of the experts was echoed by the public, though with genuine sadness on the part of some.

Suspicion of a hoax started following a visit by a newspaperman to my training camp at Speculator, New York. Associated Press reporter Brian Bell came for an interview. He noticed a book lying on the table next to my bed. Books were unexpected equipment in a prizefight training camp. He was curious and took a look at the volume—*The Way of All Flesh*. That surprised him. The Samuel Butler opus was, at that time, new in its belated fame, having been hugely praised by George Bernard Shaw as a neglected masterpiece. It was hardly the thing you'd expect a prizefighter to be reading, especially while training for a bout with Jack Dempsey.

Brian Bell knew a story when he saw one. He later became one of the chief editors of the Associated Press. Instead of talking fight, he queried me about books. I told him I liked to read Shakespeare. That was the gag. That was the pay-off. The A.P. flashed the story far and wide—the challenger, training for Jack Dempsey, read books, literature—Shakespeare. It was a sensation. The Shakespeare-Tunney legend was born.

When we finally got into the ring at Philadelphia things went so much according to plan that they were almost unexciting to me. During the first minute of sparring, I feinted Dempsey a couple of times, and then lashed out with the right-hand punch, the hardest blow I ever deliberately struck. It failed to knock him out. Jack was tough, a hard man to flatten. His fighting style was such that it was difficult to tag him on the jaw. He fought in a crouch, with his chin tucked down behind his left shoulder. I hit him high, on the cheek. He was shaken, dazed. His strength, speed, and accuracy were reduced. Thereafter it was a methodical matter of outboxing him, foiling his rushes, piling up points, clipping him with repeated, damaging blows, correct sparring.

There was an element of the unexpected—rain. It drizzled and showered intermittently throughout the fight. The ring was wet and slippery, the footing insecure. That was bad for a boxer like me, who depended on speed and sureness of foot for maneuvering. One false step with Jack Dempsey might bring oblivion. On the other hand, the slippery ring also worked to the disadvantage of the champion. A hitter needs secure footing from which to drive his punches, and any small uncertainty underfoot may rob him of his power. So the rain was an even thing except that it might have had the therapeutic value of a shower for a dazed man, and Dempsey was somewhat dazed during the ten rounds. Jack was battered and worn out at the end, and I might have knocked him out if the bout had gone a few rounds more. The decision was automatic, and I was heavyweight champion of the world.

The real argument of the decade grew out of my second bout with Dempsey, at Chicago, the following year—the "long count" controversy. It produced endless talk, sense and nonsense, logic and illogic. To this day in any barroom you can work up a wrangle on the subject of the long count. How long was Tunney on the floor after Dempsey knocked him down? Could he have gotten up if the count had been normal?

To me the mystery has always been how Dempsey contrived to hit me as he did. In a swirl of action, a wild mix-up with things happening fast, Jack might have nailed the most perfect boxer that ever blocked or side-stepped a punch, he was that swift and accurate a hitter. But what happened to me did not occur in any dizzy confusion of flying fists. In an ordinary exchange Dempsey simply stepped in and hit me with a left hook.

It was in the seventh round. I had been outboxing Jack all the way. He hadn't hurt me, hadn't hit me with any effect. I wasn't dazed or tired. I was sparring in my best form, when he lashed out.

For a boxer of any skill to be hit with a left swing in a commonplace maneuver of sparring is sheer disgrace. It was Dempsey's most effective blow, the one thing you'd watch for—you'd better, for the Dempsey left, as prize-ring history relates, was murder. I knew how to evade it, side-step or jab him with a left and beat him to the punch. I had been doing that all along.

I didn't see the left coming. So far as I was concerned, it came out of nowhere. That embarrassed me more than anything else—not to mention the damage done. It was a blow to pride as well as to the jaw. I was vain of my eyesight. My vision in the ring was always excellent. I used to think I could see a punch coming almost before it started. If there was anything I could rely on, it was my sharpness of eye—and I utterly failed to see that left swing.

The only explanation I have ever been able to think of is that in a training bout I had sustained an injury to my right eye. A sparring partner had poked me in the eye with thumb extended. I was rendered completely blind for an instant, and after some medical treatment was left with astigmatism which could easily have caused a blind spot, creating an area in which there was no vision. Our relative positions, when Dempsey hit me, must have been such that the left swing came up into the blind spot, and I never saw it.

With all his accuracy and power Dempsey hit me flush on the jaw, the button. I was knocked dizzy. Whereupon he closed for the kill, and that meant fighting fury at its most destructive. When Dempsey came in for a knockout he came with all his speed and power. I didn't know then how many times he slugged me. I had to look at the motion pictures the next day to find out. There were seven crashing blows, Dempsey battering me with left and right as I fell against the ropes, collapsing to a sitting position on the canvas.

Of what ensued during the next few seconds, I knew nothing. I was oblivious of the most debated incident of the long count and had to be told later on what happened.

The story went back to the Dempsey-Firpo fight, to that wild first round during which Firpo hit the floor in one knock-down after another. This was in New York, where the rule was that a boxer scoring a knock-down must go to a neutral corner and remain there until the referee had completed the count. In the ring with the Wild Bull of the Pampas, Dempsey undoubtedly through excitement of battle violated that rule, as the motion pictures showed clearly afterward.

Jack confesses he remembers nothing that took place during that entire fight. Firpo landed a terrific first blow. Dempsey, after suffering a first-blow knock-down, apparently jumped up to the fray by sheer professional instinct—the fighting heart of a true champion. Instead of going to a corner, Jack would stand over Firpo and slug him as he got up. After one knock-down, Jack stepped over his prostrate opponent to the other side, to get a better shot at him—the referee was in the way. After another knock-down, Dempsey slugged Firpo before the South American had got his hands off the floor, when he was still technically down. The Champ might well have been disqualified for that—not to mention the fact that he was pushed back into the ring when Firpo battered him out. The referee, however, in his confusion permitted all the violations.

The Dempsey-Firpo brawl aroused a storm of protest and brought about a determination that in the future Dempsey should be kept strictly to the rules. In our Chicago bout the regulation applied—go to a neutral corner upon scoring a knock-down. The referee had been especially instructed to enforce this. He was told that, in case of a knock-down, he was not to begin a count until the boxer who had scored the knock-down had gone to a neutral corner.

This was the reason for the long count. Dempsey, having battered me to the canvas, stood over me to hit me the moment I got up—if I did get up. The referee ordered him to a neutral corner. He didn't go. The referee, in accordance with instructions, refrained from giving count until he did go. That imposed on Jack a penalty of four seconds. It was that long before he went to the corner and the referee began the count.

When I regained full consciousness, the count was at two. I knew nothing of what had gone on, was only aware that the referee was counting two over me. What a surprise! I had eight seconds in which to get up. My head was clear. I had trained hard and well, as I always did, and had that invaluable asset—condition. In the proverbial pink, I recovered quickly from the shock of the battering I had taken. I thought—what now? I'd take the full count, of course. Nobody but a fool fails to do that. I felt all right, and had no doubt about being able to get up. The question was what to do when I was back on my feet.

I never had been knocked down before. In all the ring battles and training bouts I had engaged in, I had never previously been on the canvas. But I had always thought about the possibility, and had always planned before each bout what to do if I were knocked down, what strategy to use upon getting up. That depended on the kind of opponent.

I had thought the question out carefully in the case of Jack Dempsey. If he were to knock me down, he would, when I got up, rush me to apply the finisher. He would be swift and headlong about it. Should I try to clinch and thus gain some seconds of breathing space? That's familiar strategy for a boxer after a knock-down. Often it's the correct strategy —but not against Dempsey, I figured. He hit too hard and fast with short punches for it to be at all safe to close for a clinch. He might knock me out.

Another possibility was to get set and hit him as he rushed. That can be effective against a fighter who, having scored a knock-down, comes tearing in wide open, a mark for a heavy blow. If you are strong upon getting to your feet, you can sometimes turn the tables by throwing everything into a punch. Bob Fitzsimmons often did it. But that wouldn't do against Dempsey, I reckoned. He was too tough and hit too hard. He would welcome a slugging match. After having been knocked down, I might not be in any shape to take the risk of stepping in and hitting him.

For my second bout with Dempsey the plan that I decided upon, in case I was knocked down, was based on the thing I had learned about Jack. Word from his training camp had indicated that his legs were none too good. I had learned that his trainers had been giving him special exercises for footwork, because he had slowed down in the legs. That was the cue—match my legs against his, keep away from him, depend on speed of foot, let him chase me until I was sure I had recovered completely from the knock-down.

The plan would work if my own legs were in good shape, after the battering I had taken. That was what I had to think about on the floor in Chicago. My legs felt all right. At the count of nine I got up. My legs felt strong and springy.

Jack came tearing in for the kill. I stepped away from him, moving to my left—circling away from his left hook. As I side-stepped swiftly, my legs had never been better. What I had heard about Dempsey's legs was true. As I circled away from him, he tried doggedly, desperately, to keep up with me—but he was slow. The strategy was okay—keep away from him until I was certain that all the effects of the knock-down had worn off. Once, in sheer desperation, Jack stopped in his tracks and growled at me to stand and fight.

I did—but later, when I knew that my strength, speed, and reflexes were completely normal. I started to close with him and hit him with the encyclopedia of boxing. Presently Dempsey's legs were so heavy that he couldn't move with any agility at all, and I was able to hit him virtually at will. He was almost helpless when the final bell rang—sticking it out with stubborn courage.

I have often been asked—could I have gotten up and carried on as I did without those extra four seconds of the long count? I don't know. I can only say that at the count of two I came to, and felt in good shape. I had eight seconds to go. Without the long count, I would have had four seconds to go. Could I, in that space of time, have gotten up? I'm quite sure that I could have. When I regained consciousness after the brief period of blackout, I felt that I could have jumped up immediately and matched my legs against Jack's, just as I did.

The long count controversy, with all the heated debate, produced a huge public demand for another Dempsey-Tunney fight, number three. Tex Rickard was eager to stage it. He knew, as everybody else did, that it would draw the biggest gate ever. The first Dempsey-Tunney fight grossed over a million seven hundred thousand; the second, over two million and a half. Rickard was sure a third would draw three million. I was willing, eager. I planned to retire after another championship bout, wanted to get all that I could out of it.

But Jack refused. He was afraid of going blind. The battering he had taken around the eyes in his two fights with me alarmed him. The very thing that kept him from being hit on the jaw, his style of holding his chin down behind his shoulder, caused punches to land high. He dreaded the horror that has befallen so many ring fighters and is the terror of them all—the damage that comes from too many punches around the eyes, blindness.

Jack Dempsey was a great fighter—possibly the greatest that ever entered a ring. Looking back objectively, one has to conclude that he was more valuable to the sport or "The Game" than any prizefighter of his time. Whether you consider it from his worth as a gladiator or from the point of view of the box office, he was tops. His name in his most glorious days was magic among his people, and today, twenty years after, the name Jack Dempsey is still magic. This tells a volume in itself. As one who has always had pride in his profession as well as his professional theories, and possessing a fair share of Celtic romanticism, I wish that we could have met when we were both at our unquestionable best. We could have decided many questions, to me the most important of which is whether "a good boxer can always lick a good fighter."

I still say yes.

Anne Tyler

How Clear a Green the Grass Was

Reviewing Anne Tyler's Dinner at the Homesick Restaurant, *John Updike wrote, "Now, in her ninth novel, she has arrived, I think, at a new level of power, and gives us a lucid and delightful yet complex and somber improvisation on her favorite theme, family life." From that novel, here is a sample of Tyler's art—Ezra Tull takes his mother, Pearl, to watch the Baltimore Orioles, her favorite team, play.*

He took her to an afternoon ball game. In her old age, she had become a great Orioles fan. She would listen on the radio if she couldn't attend in person, even staying up past her bedtime if the game went into extra innings. Baseball was the only sport that made sense, she said: clear as Parcheesi, clever as chess. She looked pleased with herself for thinking of this, but Ezra suspected that it had something in common too with those soap operas she enjoyed. Certainly she viewed each game as a drama, and fretted over the gossip that Ezra culled for her from the sports pages—players' injuries, rivalries, slumps, mournful tales of young rookies so nervous they flubbed their only chances. She liked to think of the Orioles as poverty-stricken and virtuous, unable to simply *buy* their talent as richer teams did. Players' looks mattered to her as deeply as if they were movie stars: Ken Singleton's high, shining cheekbones, as described by one of her granddaughters, sent her into a little trance of admiration. She liked to hear how Al Bumbry wiggled his bat so jauntily before a hit; how Stanhouse drove people crazy delaying on the mound. She wished Doug DeCinces would shave off his mustache and Kiko Garcia would get himself a haircut. She thought Earl

Weaver was not fatherly enough to be a proper manager and often, when he replaced some poor sad pitcher who'd barely had a chance, she would speak severely into the radio, calling him "Merle Beaver" for spite and spitting out her words. "Just because he grows his own tomatoes," she said, "doesn't necessarily mean a person has a heart."

Sometimes Ezra would quote her to his friends at the restaurant, and halfway through a sentence he would think, Why, I'm making her out to be a . . . character; and all he'd said would feel like a lie, although of course it had happened. The fact was that she was a very strong woman (even a frightening one, in his childhood), and she may have shrunk and aged but her true, interior self was still enormous, larger than life, powerful. Overwhelming.

They got to the stadium early so his mother could walk at her own pace, which was so slow and halting that by the time they were settled, the lineup was already being announced. Their seats were good ones, close to home plate. His mother sank down gratefully but then had to stand, almost at once, for the national anthem. For *two* national anthems; the other team was Toronto. Halfway through the second song, Ezra noticed that his mother's knees were trembling. "Do you want to sit down?" he asked her. She shook her head. It was a very hot day but her arm, when he took hold of it, was cool and almost unnaturally dry, as if filmed with powder.

How clear a green the grass was! He could see his mother's point: precise and level and brightly colored, the playing field did have the look of a board game. Players stood about idly swinging their arms. Toronto's batter hit a high fly ball and the center fielder plucked it from the sky with ease, almost absentmindedly. "Well!" said Ezra. "That was quick. First out in no time."

There was a knack to his commentary. He informed her without appearing to, as if he were making small talk. "Gosh. Look at that change-up." And "Call that a ball? Skimmed right past his knees. Call that a ball?" His mother listened, face uplifted and receptive, like someone at a concert.

What did she get out of this? She'd have followed more closely, he thought, if she had stayed at home beside her radio. (And she'd never *bring* a radio; she worried people might think it was a hearing aid.) He supposed she liked the atmosphere, the cheering and excitement and the smell of popcorn. She even let him buy her a Styrofoam cup of beer, which was allowed to grow warm after one sip; and when the bugle sounded she called, "Charge," very softly, with an embarrassed little half-smile curling her lips. Three men were getting drunk behind her—booing and whistling and shouting insults to passing girls—but Ezra's mother stayed untroubled, facing forward. "When you come in person," she told Ezra, "you direct your own focus, you know? The TV or the radio men, they might focus on the pitcher when you want to see what first base is doing; and you don't have any choice but to accept it."

A batter swung at a low ball and connected, and Ezra (eyes in every direction) saw how the field came instantaneously alive, with each man following his appointed course. The shortstop, as if strung on rubber bands, sprang upward without a second's preparation and caught the ball; the outfield closed in like a kaleidoscope; the second-base runner pivoted and the shortstop tagged him out. "Yo, Garcia!" a drunk yelled behind them, in that gravelly, raucous voice that some men adopt in ball parks; and he sloshed cold beer down the back of Ezra's neck. "Well . . ." Ezra said to his mother. But he couldn't think how to encompass all that had happened, so finally he said, "We're up, it looks like."

She didn't answer. He turned to her and found her caving in on herself, her head falling forward, the Styrofoam cup slipping from her fingers. "Mother? Mother!" Everyone around him rose and milled and fussed. "Give her air," they told him, and then somehow they had her stretched out on her back, lying where their feet had been. Her face was paper white, immobile, like a crumpled rock. One of the drunks stepped forward to smooth her skirt decorously over her knees, and another stroked her hair off her forehead. "She'll be all right," he told Ezra. "Don't worry. It's only the heat. Folks, make room! Let her breathe!"

Ezra's mother opened her eyes. The air was bright as knife blades, shimmering with a brassy, hard light, but she didn't even squint; and for the first time Ezra fully understood that she was blind. It seemed that before, he hadn't taken it in. He reeled back, squatting at the feet of strangers, and imagined having to stay here forever: the two of them, helpless, flattened beneath the glaring summer sky.

John Updike

Farrell's Caddie

Nothing eludes John Updike's gaze and, unlike that of ordinary mortals, the scrutiny, be it glancing or piercing, is almost instantly transcribed on paper and magically transformed. When dissecting the sometime fairy-tale world of sports, he is often at his keenest. Consider his essay "Hub Fans Bid Kid Adieu," about Ted Williams's last game, or his witty poem, "Tao in the Yankee Stadium Bleachers." And especially this 1991 story published in The New Yorker, *with its mystical overtones and certain conclusion: "Ye can tell a' aboot a man, frae th' way he gowfs."*

When Farrell signed up, with seven other aging members of his local Long Island club, for a week of golf at the Royal Caledonian Links, in Scotland, he didn't foresee the relationship with the caddies. Hunched little men in billed tweed caps and rubberized rain suits, they huddled in the misty gloom as the morning foursomes got organized, and reclustered after lunch, muttering as unintelligibly as sparrows, for the day's second eighteen.

Farrell would never have played thirty-six holes a day in America, let alone walked the distance, but here in Scotland golf was not an accessory to life, drawing upon one's marginal energy; it *was* life, played out of the center of one's being. At first, stepping forth on legs one of which had been broken in a college football game forty years before, and which damp weather or a night of twisted sleep still provoked to a reminiscent twinge, he missed the silky glide and swerve of the accustomed electric cart, its magic-carpet suspension above the whispering fairway; he missed the rattle of spare balls in the retaining shelf, and the round plastic holes to hold drinks, alcoholic or carbonated, and the

704

friendly presence on the seat beside him of another gray-haired sports-man, another warty pickle blanching in the brine of time, exuding for-bearance and the expectation of forbearance, and resigned, like Farrell, to a golfing mediocrity that would gradually make its way down the sloping dogleg of decrepitude to the level green of death.

Here, however, on the heather-rimmed fairways, cut as close as putting surfaces back home, yet with no trace of mower tracks, and cheerfully marred by the scratchings and burrows of the nocturnal rab-bits that lived and bred beneath the impenetrably thorny, waist-high gorse, energy came up through the turf, as if Farrell's cleats were making contact with primal spirits beneath the soil, and he felt he could walk forever. The rolling and treeless terrain, the proximity of the wind-whipped sea, the rain that came and went with the suddenness of thought composed the ancient matrix of the game, and the darkly muttering caddies were also part of this matrix.

That first morning, in the drizzly shuffle around the golf bags, his bag was hoisted up by a hunched shadow who, as they walked together in pursuit of Farrell's first drive (good contact, but pulled to the left, toward some shaggy mounds), muttered half to himself, with those hiccups or glottal stops the Scots accent inserts, "Sandy's wha' they call me."

Farrell hesitated, then confessed, "Gus." His given name, Augustus, had always embarrassed him, but its shortened version seemed a little short on dignity, and at the office, as he had ascended in rank, his colleagues had settled on his initials, "A.D."

"Here, ye want tae geh oover the second boosh fra' th' laift," Sandy said, handing Farrell a 7-iron. The green was out of sight behind the shaggy mounds, which were covered with long tan grass that whitened in waves as gusts flattened it.

"What's the distance?" Farrell was accustomed to yardage mark-ers—yellow stakes, or sprinkler heads.

The caddie looked reflectively at a sand bunker not far off, and then at the winking red signal light on the train tracks beyond, and finally at a large bird, a gull or a crow, winging against the wind beneath the low, tattered, blue-black clouds. "Ah hunnert thirty-eight tae the edge of the green, near a hunnert fifty tae the pin, where they ha' 't."

"I can't hit a 7-iron a hundred fifty. I can't hit it even one forty, against this wind."

Yet the caddie's fist, in a fingerless wool glove, did not withdraw the offered club. "Seven's what ye need."

As Farrell bent his face to the ball, the wet wind cut across his eyes and made him cry. His tears turned the ball into two; he supposed the brighter one was real. He concentrated on taking the club head away slowly and low, initiating his downswing with a twitch of the left hip, and suppressing his tendency to dip the right shoulder. The shot seemed sweet, soaring with a gentle draw up precisely over the second bush. He looked toward the caddie, expecting congratulations or at least some small sign of shared pleasure. But the man, his creased face weathered the strangely even brown of a white actor playing Othello, followed the flight of the ball as he had that of the crow, reflectively. "Yer right hand's a wee bit froward," he observed, and the ball—they saw as they climbed to the green—was indeed pulled to the left, in a deep pot bunker. Furthermore, it was fifteen yards short. The caddie had underclubbed him, but showed no sign of remorse as he handed Farrell the sand wedge. In Sandy's dyed-looking face, pallid gray eyes showed like touches of morning light; it shocked Farrell to realize that the other man, weathered though he was, and bent beneath the weight of a perpetual golf bag, was younger than himself—a prematurely wizened Celt, or Pict, serving one of Northeast America's tall, bloated Anglo-Saxons.

The side of the bunker toward the hole was as tall as Farrell and sheer, built up of bricks of sod in a way never seen at Long Island courses. Rattled, irritated at having been unrepentantly underclubbed, Farrell swung five times into the damp, brown sand, darker than any sand on Long Island. With each swing, the ball thudded beneath the trap's high lip and dribbled back at his feet. "Hit at it well beheend," the caddie advised, "and dinna stop the cloob." Farrell's sixth swing brought the ball bobbling up onto the green, within six feet of the hole.

His fellow Americans lavished ironical praise on the shot, but the caddie, with deadpan solemnity, handed him his putter. "Ae ball tae th' laift," he advised, and Farrell was so interested in this peculiar phrase —the ball as a unit of measure—that his putt stopped short. "Ye forgot tae hit it, Gus," Sandy told him. Farrell tersely nodded. Tingling with nervousness, he felt onstage and obliged to keep up a show of the stoic virtues. Asked for his score, he said loudly, in a theatrical voice, "That was an honest ten."

"We'll call it a six," said the player keeping score, in the forgiving American way.

As the round progressed, through a rapid alternation of brisk showers and silvery sunshine, with rainbows springing up around them and tiny white daisies gleaming underfoot, Farrell and his caddie began to grow into each other, as a foot in damp weather grows into a shoe.

Sandy consistently handed Farrell a club too short to make the green, but Farrell came to accept the failure as his; his caddie was handing the club to the stronger golfer latent in Farrell, and it was Farrell's job to let this superior performer out, to release him from his stiff, soft, more than middle-aged body. On the twelfth hole, called "Dunrobin"—a seemingly endless par 5 with a broad stretch of fairway, bleak and vaguely restless like the surface of the moon, receding over a distant edge marked by two small pot bunkers and a pale-green arm of gorse that extended from the rabbit-undermined thickets on the left—his drive clicked. Something about the ghostly emptiness of this particular hole's terrain, the featurelessness of it, removed Farrell's physical inhibitions; he felt the steel shaft of the driver bend in an elastic curve at his back, and a corresponding springiness awaken in his knees, and knew, as his weight smoothly moved from the right foot to the left, that he would bring the club face squarely into the ball, and indeed did, so that the ball—the last of his new Titleists, the others having disappeared in gorse and heather and cliffside scree—was melting into the drizzle straight ahead almost before he looked up, his head held sideways, as if pillowed on his right ear, just like the heads of the pros on television. "O.K.?" he asked Sandy, mock-modest but also genuinely fearful of some hazard, some trick of the layout, that he had missed taking into account.

"Bonnie shot, sir," the caddie said, and his face, as if touched by a magic wand, crumpled into a smile full of crooked gray teeth, his constantly relit cigarette adhering to one corner. Small matter that Farrell, striving for a repetition of this scarcely precedented distance, topped the following 3-wood, hit a 5-iron fat, and skulled his wedge shot clear across the elevated green. He had for a second awakened the golf giant sleeping among his muscles, and imagined himself vindicated in the other man's not quite colorless, not quite indifferent eyes.

Dinner, for this week of excursion, was a repeating male event, the same eight Long Island males, their hair growing curly and their faces ruddy away from the dry Manhattan canyons and air-conditioned compartments where they had accumulated their little fortunes. They discussed their caddies as men, extremely unbuttoned, might discuss their mistresses. "Come on, Freddie, hit it fer once!" the very distinguished banker Frederic R. Panoply boasted his had cried out to him in frustration as, on the third day of his cautious, down-the-middle banker's game, he painstakingly addressed his ball.

Another man's caddie, when asked what he thought of Mrs. Thatcher, had responded with a twinkle, "She'd be a good hump."

Farrell, prim and reserved by nature, had relatively little to offer of his caddie. He worried about the man's incessant smoking, and whether at the end of a round he tipped him too much less than what a Japanese golfer would have given. As the week went by, their relationship had become more intuitive. "A 6-iron?" Farrell would now say, and without a word would be handed the club. Once, he had dared decline an offered 6, asked for the 5, and sailed his unusually well-struck shot into the sedge beyond the green. On the greens, where he at first had been bothered by the caddie's explicit directives, so that he forgot to stroke the ball firmly, he had come to depend upon Sandy's advice, and would expertly tilt his ear close to the caddie's mouth and try to envision the curve of the ball into the center of the hole from "an inch an' a fingernail tae th' laift." Farrell began to sink putts. He began to get pars, as the whitecaps flashed on one side of the links and on the other the wine-red electric commuter trains swiftly glided up to Glasgow and back. This was happiness, on this wasteland between the tracks and the beach, and freedom, of a wild and windy sort. On the morning of his last day, having sliced his first drive into the edge of the rough, between a thistle and what appeared to be a child's weathered tombstone, Farrell bent his ear close to the caddie's mouth for advice, and heard, "Ye'd be better leavin' 'er."

"Beg pardon?" Farrell said, as he had all week, when the glottal, hiccupping accent had become opaque. Today the acoustics were especially bad; a near-gale off the sea was making his rain pants rattle like machine guns, and deformed his eyeballs with air pressure as he tried to squint down. When he could stop seeing double, his lie looked fair—semi-embedded.

"Yer missus," Sandy clarified, passing over the 8-iron. "Ere it's tae late, mon. She was never yer type. Tae proper."

"Shouldn't this be a wedge?" Farrell asked uncertainly.

"Nay, it's sittin' up guid enough," the caddie said, pressing his foot into the heather behind the ball, so it rose up like ooze out of mud. "Ye kin reach with th' 8," he said. "Go fer yer par. Yer fauts er a' in yer mind; ye tend t' play defensive."

Farrell would have dismissed his previous remarks as a verbal mirage amid the clicks and skips of windblown Scots had they not seemed so uncannily true. "Too proper" was exactly what his college friends had said of Sylvia, but he had imagined that her physical beauty had been the real thing, and her propriety a pose she would outgrow, whereas thirty-five married years had revealed the propriety as enduring and the beauty as transient. As to leaving her, this thought would never have entered his head until recently; the mergers-and-acquisitions branch had recently taken on a certain Irma Finegold, with heavy-lidded eyes, full lips painted sharply red, and a curious presumptuous way of teasing Farrell in the eddies of chitchat before and after a conference. She had recently been divorced, and when she talked to Farrell she tapped her lower lip with a pencil eraser and shimmied her shoulders beneath their pads. On nights when the office worked late—he liked occasionally to demonstrate that, far along though he was, he could still pull an all-nighter with the young bucks—there had been between him and Irma shared Chinese meals from greasy take-out cartons, and a shared limo home in the dawn light. On one undreamed-of occasion, there had even been an invitation, which he did not refuse, to interrupt his return to Long Island with an hour at her apartment in Brooklyn.

The 8-iron pinched the ball clean, and the Atlantic gale brought the soaring shot left-to-right toward the pin. "Laift edge, but dinna gi' the hole away," Sandy advised of the putt, and Farrell sank it, for the first birdie of his week of golf.

Now, suddenly, out of the silvery torn sky, sleet and sunshine descended simultaneously, and as the two men walked at the same tilt to the next tee, Sandy's voice came out of the wind, "An' steer clear o' the MiniCorp deal. They've leveraged th' company tae death."

Farrell studied Sandy's face. Rain and sleet bounced off the brown skin as if from a waxy preservative coating. Metallic gleams showed as the man surveyed, through narrowed eyelids, the watery horizon. Farrell pretended he hadn't heard. On the tee he was handed a 3-wood, with the advice, "Ye want tae stay short o' th' wee burn. The wind's come aroond behind, bringin' the sun with it."

As the round wore on, the sun did struggle through, and a thick rainbow planted itself over the profile of the drab town beyond the tracks, with its soot-black steeples and distillery chimneys. By the time of the afternoon's eighteen, there was actually blue sky, and oblique solar rays. Pockets of lengthening shadows showed the old course to be everywhere curvacious, crest and swale, like the body of a woman. Forty feet off the green on the fourteenth ("Whinny Brae"), Farrell docilely accepted the caddie's offer of a putter, and rolled it up and over the close-mowed irregularities to within a gimme of the hole. His old self would have skulled or fluffed a chip. "Great advice," he said, and in his flush of triumph challenged the caddie: "But Irma *loves* the MiniCorp deal."

"Aye, 't keeps the twa o' you togither. She's fairful ye'll wander off, i' th' halls o' corporate power."

"But whatever does she see in me?"

"Lookin' fer a faither, the case may be. Thet first husband o' hers was meikle immature. And also far from yer own income bracket."

Farrell felt his heart sink at the deflating shrewdness of the analysis. His mind elsewhere, absented by bittersweet sorrow, he hit one pure shot after another. Looking to the caddie for praise, however, he met the same impassive, dour, young-old visage, opaque beneath the billed tweed cap. Tomorrow, the man would caddie for someone else, and Farrell would be belted into a business-class seat within a 747. On the home stretch of holes—one after the other strung out along the tracks, as the Victorian brick clubhouse, with its turrets and neo-Gothic arches, drew closer and closer—Farrell begged for advice. "The 5-wood, or the 3-iron? The three keeps it down out of the wind, but I feel more confident with the wood, the way you've got me swinging."

"The five'll be ower and gone, ye're a' pumped up. Take the 4-iron. Smooth it on, laddie. Aim fer th' little broch."

"Broch?"

"Wee stone fortress, frae th' days we had our own braw king." He added, "An' ye might be thinkin', Gus, aboot takin' early retirement. The severance deals won't be so sweet aye. Ye kin free yerself up, an' take on some consults, fer th' spare change."

"Just what I was thinking, if Irma's a will-o'-the-wisp."

"Will-o'-the-wisp, do ye say? Ye're a speedy lairner."

Farrell felt flattered and wind-scoured, here in this surging universe of green and gray. "You think so, Sandy?"

"I ken sae. Ye can tell a' aboot a man, frae th' way he gowfs."

Mark Winegardner

October in Miami, Ohio

The magazine Entertainment Weekly *called* Prophet of the Sand-lots *"the real cloth of which* Field of Dreams *is just a polyester version." The author, Mark Winegardner, follows a major-league scout, Tony Lucadello, on an epic journey through the heartland to watch players in high school, college, and American Legion games. In his lifetime, Lucadello had logged over two million miles and signed up forty-nine major-league players, two of the most notable being Mike Schmidt and Ferguson Jenkins. Here he is, caught by his talented Boswell, in Miami, Ohio, as an era of the game nears its end, as a scout decides his own fate, too. Shortly after Winegardner left him, Lucadello killed himself.*

Fall baseball is more than just the World Series, although not much more. While Reggie Jackson gives himself the nickname "Mr. October," while Carlton Fisk waves his extra-inning homer fair and a journeyman pitcher named Don Larsen pitches a perfect game, pro prospects work out in what's called the Florida Instructional League, dreaming of spring training. But about the only people playing baseball in October not receiving paychecks for their time are college kids.

With the school year barely underway, college coaches convene their teams, the returning lettermen, the new hotshots on scholarship and the walk-ons. For the upperclassmen, it's a time to get reacquainted, to find out how their friends did in the summer leagues and to see if any of the newcomers are going to be worth knowing. For the new recruits, it's a time to make first impressions on new teammates, to wonder how much playing time they'll get this coming April and to imagine how their varsity status will impress the Tri-Delts. For the walk-ons, it's a time to glance for acceptance on the face of the coaches, after every catch, every throw, every swing of the bat. For the coaches, it's a time to think about lineup cards yet to be, about teaching that tall lefty how to throw a decent change-up, about making that new shortstop into a center fielder, and sadly, about how to tell some of the new freshmen their extracurricular time might be better spent in the glee club.

For Tony Lucadello, it's a time to get the last look of the season at the players in his "follow" file and to see if any of the new kids ought to join that file. At colleges all over the Midwest, many of those freshman, though new to other scouts, aren't new to Tony; when he finds a high schooler he likes but who isn't developed enough to risk money on, Tony calls up the coaches of the programs he admires, and tells them, Hey, son, there's a catcher up north of Ft. Wayne who might fit into your program.

We got to the ballpark early. Miami had an intrasquad doubleheader planned on this October Sunday, when most of the student body was in the dorms watching the Cincinnati Bengals on black-and-white TVs, having a few bagels delivered, drinking Hudepohl beer, and worrying about that Western Civ test tomorrow. Tony and I were the first people there, even before the team. The sun glinted off the aluminum bleachers at Stanley G. McKie Field, and we sat down behind home plate, chatting about the weather, taking in deep breaths of fall air and reveling in the joy of a green ball field encased by a preposterously beautiful university.

Miami University looks like a seventh-grader's idea of college. A land-grant institution established in 1809, Miami is a campus of wooded commons, ivy-covered walls, redbrick Georgian buildings and fifteen thousand scrubbed, toothy undergraduates who wear bright clothes adorned with Greek letters and hate people who call their school "Miami of Ohio." "Miami was a university before Florida was a state," we'll tell you, adding that our average SAT score towers over that of those tanned boneheads at the other Miami. One of the bookstore's best-selling T-shirts reads, "Miami Is in Ohio, Damn It!"

Tony began walking around the perimeter of the field, scouring the ground with his eyes, like a man who's lost his car keys. "I do this before every game."

"Do what?"

"Look for money. I'm known for it. The other scouts, when they see me at a game, they'll ask, 'Hey, Tony, you find any money?' "

"My dad used to have one of those metal detector things. He used to go out in public parks and dig up bottle caps and rusty spoons."

"I just got into the habit of it. I can't even remember how. At first

I guess it was just something to pass the time. Scouts are alone quite a bit, you see, and since I don't drink or chase the women, this is what I use to pass the time. Now, it's a little more than that. When I can't find any more pennies, that's when I'll know I don't have the eyes to be a scout. That's when I'll hang it up."

Tony and I had covered the third-base side of the ballpark, and we wound our way around the backstop and up the firstbase line. Tony said he usually had the most success under the bleachers.

I'm terrible at stuff like this. When I was a kid, I got involved with this outdoorsy group in my high school, at my grandfather's urging. On field trips it was always other people who'd say, Hey, look at that elk, and I'd always be the guy going, Where, where, show me. "How much money do you find?"

"Depends," Tony said. "My best year was 1972. I got almost twenty-seven bucks then." He walked to the end of the bleachers, then shook his head. "Don't look like there's much here." He pulled up the furry collar of his overcoat and thrust his hands into his pockets. "What do you think I do with all this money? Come on, guess."

"Buy your wife a present?"

He smiled. "No. I keep it all in a jar and then, on September fifteenth of every year I give it to the first church I happen to see."

"Oh."

He shrugged. "I'm not a religious man. I don't know why I do that. I just have, for years and years. The first church I see, no matter where I am that day, no matter what denomination. Makes me feel good, that's the only explanation I got."

Tony slapped me on the back, and we took a seat in the bleachers. "You didn't know what you were getting yourself into, did you, traveling with a crazy old man like me?"

The first batter for the White team was a tall, thin, left-handed sophomore center fielder named Fred VanderPeet. "He's been lifting weights and eating good," Tony said. "Look at him. How much would you say he weighs?"

"One seventy."

"About right. He's six three, so he could gain a little more. Last year he played at one sixty. I see him filling out to about one eighty-five."

The pitcher for the Gray team, a stocky junior with a herky-jerky motion, was behind VanderPeet, 2 and 0.

"Now, look at the good live body that batter has," Tony said, as

VanderPeet took a ball. "Eighty-seven percent of the game of baseball is played below the waist. Just look at the way that lead knee of his twitches back and then steps into the pitch. But not so soon he commits himself. He's tall and skinny, but his body position is good and his center of gravity is about right."

VanderPeet walked.

"Good," Tony said. "Now we can see him run the bases."

Next up, the second baseman looked like a good batter—at a glance. But everything VanderPeet had below the waist, this kid lacked. Both legs were stiff and locked into position, and when each pitch came, he stepped into it, committing himself before he had any idea where the ball would be. He checked his swing even on a wild pitch. VanderPeet advanced to second on the pitch and then, trying to stretch it to third, was caught in a rundown and tagged out by the shortstop.

Tony just nodded.

"Good runner?" I asked.

Tony nodded. "I scout by looking for pluses. This boy has an awful lot of pluses, and speed may be the biggest."

"Yeah, but he was tagged out because he was greedy."

"That's a minus. On the other hand, it shows good competitiveness, trying to take an extra base in a meaningless game like this. Look, you can talk yourself out of any player. But what I do is add up the pluses and see if that's enough for me."

The batter lined out, and the next guy up was the White team's shortstop, Tim Naehring. Even I knew that the best athletes, the best prospects, are likely to be those playing the most demanding positions: catcher, pitcher, shortstop, and center fielder. Most big-league second and third basemen are converted shortstops; most right and left fielders are converted center fielders. The media guide said that Naehring had been all-conference last season. "How about this guy, Tony? Is he on your follow list?"

"*Oh*, yes." Tony watched Naehring more carefully than he had the first two batters, talking less, studying more. Naehring swung and missed.

"Good hard swing, though?" I said, looking for acceptance.

"Oh, yeah," Tony said. "This is the place to study right-handed hitters, about a third of the way up the first-base line. Here, you can see their face and six of their eight sides."

Naehring struck out swinging to end the inning. If I hadn't seen Tony study Naehring so intently, I might have dismissed him. The pitcher had nothing: no speed, no control, no technique, yet here he struck out an all-conference shortstop with ease.

"We'll never get him," Tony said. "He's going to go in the first three rounds next year, but I'm afraid he'll be gone by the time we pick. He may have struck out, but this game means nothing. He showed me good body control. Let's move."

Tony walked up the line, almost even with first base, and sat down. We were probably the only people there not related to or dating one of the players.

"What'd you mean," I asked, "about the player's eight sides?"

"That's how I analyze their body, by looking individually at the top front, back, right and left sides and the bottom front, back, right and left sides. That makes eight."

The Gray team had a little rally going, but Tony wasn't really paying attention to that. His eyes were on Naehring. When the cleanup hitter smashed a grounder deep into the hole—a ball I'd thought was a base hit—Naehring knocked it down and fired it to first, beating the runner by a full step. Tony whispered, "Third base."

"Excuse me?"

"That was a good play—for this level. But he don't have soft hands. What he does have is quick reactions and a strong arm. Hits for power, too. I'm projecting him as a third baseman."

Tony jockeyed himself all over the field, even under the bleachers, and I made a mental note to ask later what his method was. I didn't want to distract him any more than I already had, so for the rest of the game I kept quiet and tagged along.

In the third inning VanderPeet hit a triple, but Tony talked more about his good running form than the hit itself. The next inning he began to study the White team's left fielder, a kid named Tim Carter, who had made two good catches already and whose batting stance raised the old scout's eyebrow.

"I don't know him," Tony said. "In between games of this double-header, I'll go ask the coach."

For the rest of the game, Tony studied the every move of VanderPeet, Naehring, and Carter. Two other players hit home runs without getting Tony the least bit interested in them, yet Carter drew a walk that made Tony sure he'd discovered a prospect.

I flipped through the media guide and read that Mike Mungovan, a big first baseman, had led the team in hitting last year. VanderPeet and Carter had hardly even played. In between the fifth and sixth, I asked

Tony about that. He didn't even know who Mungovan was. I pointed him out, and Tony nodded. "He doesn't do anything for me. His body isn't live, he can't throw. He can hit with a little power, *at this level,* but that's the only plus I see."

VanderPeet homered in the seventh.

"I've seen all I need to see for today," Tony said. "That wind's blowing through me now. Let's go say hello to Jon Pavlisko, and then we'll go home."

Pavlisko, Miami's coach, a stocky forty-four-year-old who had played a few years in the Red Sox system, met us at the fence. He tried to get Tony to accept a dinner invitation, but Tony said he didn't want to intrude. "A young man like you, Jon, should have dinner with his family. We'll have dinner in the spring."

Pavlisko figured Tony was there to see Naehring, and he talked the shortstop up, extolling his virtues as a player, a student and a human being. VanderPeet, apparently, is something of a flake, though Pavlisko didn't come out and say so. When Tony asked about Carter, Pavlisko was clearly surprised. I don't think he wanted Tony to see that surprise. Pavlisko stammered some, said, "Yes, he's got some potential."

The coach again offered to buy the scout dinner, but Tony said he had a place to stay in Richmond. He shook hands, waved good-bye and headed toward his white Chevy.

I asked Jon Pavlisko and, yes, Tony Lucadello was the first major league scout to see something in Tim Carter. Jon smiled. "I'll tell you what: he's not ever the last."

W. B. Yeats

At Galway Races

One of the three or four masters of the literature of the twentieth century, William Butler Yeats was born in Ireland, and many of his poetic works concentrated on the tragic violence of Irish history. But the immense strength of his poetry, exemplified by the poem that justly closes this volume, was his power of symbolic expression. In a summary of his life and work from the book 20th Century Culture, *this was said about Yeats: "He seized upon myths, and invented his own, in pursuit of a view of man's nature and of human history."*

There where the course is,
Delight makes all of the one mind,
The riders upon the galloping horses,
The crowd that closes in behind:
We, too, had good attendance once,
Hearers and hearteners of the work;
Aye, horsemen for companions,
Before the merchant and the clerk
Breathed on the world with timid breath.
Sing on: somewhere at some new moon,
We'll learn that sleeping is not death,
Hearing the whole earth change its tune,
Its flesh being wild, and it again
Crying aloud as the racecourse is,
And we find hearteners among men
That ride upon horses.